PRAISE FOR HELLOWEEN

“*Helloween* proves once again Ralston is more than the writer of *Woom*... he’s one of the best paranormal horror writers currently. Just phenomenal."

— STEVE STRED, AUTHOR OF *MASTODON* AND *CHURN THE SOIL*

“*Helloween* is like *Ghostland* on Red Bull. One of my top 5 horror reads of 2024."

— RJ CLARK, AUTHOR OF THE *STAYCATION* SERIES

“*Helloween* proves there’s no subgenre of horror Duncan can’t write. If you haven’t considered Ralston the king of indie horror, this small town epic will prove it to you.”

— GAGE GREENWOOD, AUTHOR OF *BUNKER DOGS* AND *ON A CLEAR DAY, YOU CAN SEE BLOCK ISLAND*

HELLOWEEN

Duncan Ralston

SHADOW WORK PUBLISHING

This story is a work of fiction. Names, characters, places and incidents are either the product of the author's imagination or are used fictitiously. Any resemblance to actual persons, living or dead, is entirely coincidental.

ALSO BY DUNCAN RALSTON

Gristle & Bone (collection)

Salvage (novella)

Wildfire (novella)

Woom (novella)

The Method (novel)

Video Nasties (collection)

Ebenezer (novella)

Ghostland (novel)

In Every Dark Corner (collection)

Afterlife: Ghostland 2.0 (novel)

The Midwives (novel)

Ghostland: Infinite (novel)

Gross Out (novel)

Ghostland: Ghost Hunter Edition (omnibus)

Try Not to Die: At Ghostland w/ Mark Tullius (gameboook)

Puzzle House (novel)

Pedo Island Bloodbath (novel)

Contents

For Dad,
Who nurtured my love of Halloween.

PART ONE

GATE NIGHT

Chapter 1

1

October 31st, 2001
Film Set / Downtown Crooks Corner

Darla Knight did not want to be here. This town, this shoot, it was all her agent's bright idea to get her faded star shining again, and she was only marginally interested in any of it. The script was fine for low-budget horror, but the director was unseasoned and the weather in Crooks Corner was crummy this time of year. It might be fine for tourists in search of autumn foliage, but the rain and cold was taxing, especially since Darla was used to the near-constant sunshine of Southern California.

The day before Halloween was another miserable day, and the last she would spend above ground. The sky had been overcast and threatening to rain or snow all afternoon, the chill in the air bone-deep. To keep the film equipment from getting too cold, the crew had set up heaters inside the old farmhouse where they were shooting, but Darla still had to don gloves between shots just to keep her fingers from freezing.

Part of her missed Los Angeles, more for its warmth and endless sun than the people. She was still a smalltown girl at heart, and this small town, with its fresh air and crowdless streets, reminded her of the one in which she'd grown up, bringing back memories both good and bad. When she'd left Clavell, Wyoming at seventeen her opinion on small towns was that their citizens led small lives with even smaller minds. Having spent the last two decades in sunny California, she'd concluded small minds could be found everywhere, and some of the smallest lived very large lives in the city she'd called home for almost twenty-five years.

"Thirty-six roles, Jean-Claude," Darla said on the phone in her trailer outside the farmhouse set during an afternoon five. "Thirty-six roles and not a single one worth a damn."

"What about *Psycho Kitties*?" her agent asked. "That film put you on the map."

"If this is 'on the map,' where's my star on Hollywood Boulevard? I'd be lucky to get a star on MapQuest. *You are here*, you know? And where *is* here, exactly, J.C.? I'm shooting a nothing horror movie with no-name talent for a hack director in the middle of New England. I could be painting. I *should* be painting."

She heard Jean-Claude fiddling with his lighter, firing up one of his horrendous rum-dipped cigarillos with the plastic tips that gave him a moment to decide how to answer. She imagined him puffing away at it, wafting the cloud of smoke out of his squinted eyes before calmly replying: "You know I love your paintings, Darla. The galleries I've gotten you into, they love your paintings. But paintings just don't pay the bills, snookum. Do you know what does? Hmm?"

"Movies," she muttered.

"Beg pardon?"

"*Movies*," she said louder, annoyed.

"Movies," Jean-Claude agreed smarmily. "The business of *show*. So unless you want to lose that pretty little condo in Venice Beach, you need to keep taking the roles that are offered. You should feel *lucky*, snookum! You're no spring chicken. Women your age? In this town?" He huffed dramatically.

"I'm not old, Jean-Claude."

"Of course, you're not old! Not for *out there*," he was quick to add. "But for Los Angeles"—he always pronounced it with a hard G and long E: *Los Ang-galeez*—"you're too old to play the ingenue and not old enough yet for those scenery-chewing *grande dame* roles. If you were Julianne Moore or, I don't know, Emma Thompson, you'd have far better offers to field. But you're not, so you don't. When life hands you lemons, snookum, you squeeze those little yellow bastards and make yourself a White Lady!"

"I am a white lady," Darla said, aggravated. "Although I wouldn't consider myself a *lady*."

"It's a *cocktail*. From the '20s? It's gin o'clock in Los Angaleez, Darla, and I've been dry all morning. This time again tomorrow?"

Darla didn't feel like they'd hammered anything out, but Jean-Claude wouldn't hang on the phone much longer once he'd cued his exit, whether she pleaded with him or not. Her fingers were still sore from the cold, even though she'd been soaking them in warm water that had turned cool since she'd been on the phone, which was why she'd called in the first place, to get Jean-Claude to step in on her behalf like the bulldog he was. "Fine. But I'm sending for my painting supplies."

"You do that, snookum," he said dismissively, the cigarillo audibly clenched between his teeth. "*Ta*."

The line clicked. Darla dried her hands on the towel the production assistant had provided for her and hung up the portable phone. There was one more scene on today's shooting schedule —one that contained a somewhat complicated Steadicam shot— and they'd be losing light in a few hours. She put her gloves back on and looked at herself in the mirror. Hair and make-up had "aged her up" to play an old woman and several times on set she'd gotten a glimpse of herself in a mirror or window pane and thought for a fleeting moment that she really was as old as living in Hollywood made her feel. She left the trailer, relieved by the fact that she wasn't over the hill, not really, and there was more to life than living role to role. There was painting, which she loved even if it didn't pay the bills. And soon she would have her oils and frames and paint-splashed overalls, singing and dancing to '80s pop music while creating art dictated by no one but herself.

The set of this peculiar little horror-thriller called *House of Doors* was an old farmhouse, which their art department had covered in doors gathered from garage sales, flea markets, estate liquidations and antique stores from California all the way to New Hampshire. Over seventy doors had been screwed into the walls of the old house: various shapes, sizes and colors, some with glass panels, others with wrought iron, stable doors, shuttered doors and barn doors. They covered the old structure from the foundation to the apex of the roof, each one on hinges so they could open and shut as required.

The premise was that each door led the protagonists of the film to different outcomes, sort of a riff on the butterfly effect from Ray Bradbury's "A Sound of Thunder," with multiple reset points for the main characters. Darla starred as the sadistic old woman who owned the house, even though she was only maybe fifteen years older than the twenty-somethings who played the criminal couple on the run. It was an original screenplay, which was nice, considering all of the remakes recently released and in production, both of foreign horror films and old American movies. And it actually allowed her a bit of scenery chewing, despite Jean-Claude's assertion, though most of the heavy lifting, acting-wise, fell on the shoulders of the slightly younger leads.

The rest of that day's shoot went fine, though the old farmhouse never got as warm as she wanted it to be, particularly considering the thin, grimy dressing gown they had her wearing, which was thankfully opaque enough she could wear thermal underwear beneath. After they wrapped for the evening, Darla took a cab to the hotel she'd been staying at on the main drag, which was only a block's walk from the Grand Theater. She thought she'd grab dinner at one of the nearby restaurants, get a bit of what Jean-Claude disdainfully called "local color," then get to sleep early, as tomorrow would be an especially long day of shooting followed by an appearance at the theater.

A towel wrapped around her after a long, hot shower that never quite removed the chill from her bones, she called ahead to the restaurant to be certain they'd have a table. Judging by how the girl on the phone acted, it might have been the first time she'd ever been asked for a reservation. Most of the cast and crew were likely eating in their rooms at the hotel or had driven to Wolfeboro, the "Oldest Summer Resort in America," according to the area brochure Jean-Claude had given her. Crooks Corner had a lower population than the resort town, and lacked in amenities comparatively. The diner she'd picked tonight was the closest to a proper sit-down meal she could find within walking distance to her hotel.

The first snow of the year had dusted the street, big flakes falling languidly from the sky as she left the hotel. She pulled her hood up over her head and paused in the middle of the wet, empty street to let a snowflake land on her tongue. It was magic hour, and despite the cloud cover a warm golden glow dappled the admittedly picturesque downtown buildings. With the light dusting of snow, it looked like a Norman Rockwell painting. Nights like this made her appreciate the opportunities to shoot in these small towns, where she wouldn't typically travel under ordinary circumstances. She hadn't even been back home to visit her mother in... *God*, she thought, *could it be ten years already? Just the calls at Christmas and Mother's Day and her birthday, as if that's enough. I'm a bad daughter. Not like she was a good mother, but still. It was always Dad who called, always Dad who loved me more. Forty-two years old and I'm still trying to make peace with my childhood. How sad is that?*

The roar of an engine caught her attention as she crossed to the diner side of the street, and she leaped up onto the sidewalk, narrowly avoiding the black van that screeched to a halt behind her.

Darla looked around, somewhat frantically. Not a single soul was on the street aside from her and the van. She sighed, realizing it must be one of the production vehicles, and took a step toward it, aggravated that they would trouble her during her off time. The side door swung open and two people in ski masks dressed in black from head to toe leaped out. Realizing her error, she shot a hand into her purse, reaching for her can of mace, but the smaller of the ski-masked assailants wrenched the hand out of her purse and twisted it up behind her back.

"Ow, relax, asshole!" Darla said. "Look, if you want money—"

The larger one grabbed her mouth, shutting her up. She would've bit him if he hadn't been wearing leather gloves. Instead, she did what her personal trainer had showed her and kicked at his groin. The brute stepped back out of the way, her heel grazing the crotch of his pants. She screamed behind his hand as they hauled her into the van, hoping someone—*anyone*—would hear her pleas.

The masked maniacs threw her roughly in the van, tossing her purse on the sidewalk. The door slammed behind them.

As the van sped off, Darla looked into the eyes of her captors. The two who'd grabbed her sat with her. The big guy held her arms behind her back. The smaller one—a woman, judging by what Darla could see of her: slight build, dazzling green eyes and pouty red lips—sat on a bench. The man in the front passenger seat, who was currently pointing a home video camera at her, wore all black and a ski mask like the others.

"Darla Knight!" the cameraman said excitedly. "Darla fucking Knight! I told you, guys. Didn't I fucking *tell you*?"

Psycho fans, Darla thought. *Just my luck.*

"What do you want with me?" she said, desperately trying not to sound as frightened as she was, and failing miserably.

Some actor I am, she thought.

The guy behind the camera tsked. "Ah, ah, not just yet, Miss Knight. It's Devil's Night, we're making a movie... and *you're* gonna be the star. Tie her up!"

Darla cried for help as they passed the brightly lit diner. There were ten or twelve customers along with the staff inside, but nobody appeared to notice the black van roar by.

The big man slapped a gloved hand over her mouth, silencing her cries. The slender woman grabbed her hands, preventing her from pounding on the glass.

Within moments they had tied her up and gagged her, and by then the lights of downtown had already dwindled behind them, dimmed through the tinted glass. The laughter and excitement of the crew of thugs was punctuated by the thrum of her heart in her ears and the steady squeak and buzz of the windshield wipers.

What now? If this was a movie, what would my character do?

She didn't know. And she was afraid the movie these people intended to make wouldn't end with her still living.

2

WILL CRAMPTON, who ran the Crooks Corner Eateria, heard the sound of tires screeching outside and glanced through the front windows in time to see a dark van peeling through the intersection. Its back doors bore the silly smiley face insignia he'd noticed popping up in graffiti all over town. It looked to have been drawn there with soap.

His concern was only momentary—shenanigans on the night before Halloween were to be expected—before returning his attention to his work. It was a slow night at the diner, which was not much of a surprise for a Tuesday, especially when that Tuesday was also the night before Halloween. He expected to see a crowd after the first movie let out across the street, which would mainly be orders of fries and plenty of sodas. Only a few customers sat in the booths and at the counter, mostly regulars and a handful of out-of-towners who were likely just passing through, since he didn't recognize any faces from the movie people. Sheriff Nance sat in a booth talking with a European-looking guy with a spiky blond mullet, a duster jacket and fingerless cycling gloves. The sheriff chortled at something the man said and leaned back in his bench seat, tossing a napkin down onto his plate.

"It was a controlled demolition," Trudy Bell said as Will returned to the counter to top up coffees. This was what she'd been going on about since late September with Randy Jacobs, another Eateria regular. The two of them were as much friends as enemies, and had been for as long as Will had known them, which was at least since his folks had owned the place and he'd worked here as a kid, bussing tables and mopping floors. The regulars had been handed down to him along with the diner when they passed away eight years back. *Cheers* this was not.

"Horseshit," Randy said with a derisive sneer. He was skinny as a beanpole, dressed in his greasy coveralls, a red-checked trapper hat and a green military parka. His cheap cologne and cigarette smoke did nothing to hide the constant stench of automotive grease from his day job running the auto wrecker yard on the western edge of town, another guy who'd inherited his lot in life from his folks just like Will had. "You saw them planes hit the tower just like we all did."

"I *seen* it, but a skyscraper can't just *collapse* from the top down. The weight's the same."

"What the hell are you goin on about?"

Trudy got angry. She'd clearly been chewing on this for some time. "Why would one floor fallin on another make it fall down? There's no weight difference."

"Weight difference? The supports busted, ya dimwit! They're like snowshoes for skyscrapers. They *distribute* the weight."

Trudy shook her head and poured a little more whiskey from her flask into her coffee. She was a large woman in her grimy orange public works vest with graying brown hair that looked like it had the texture of straw. "Naw," she said. "Naw, that don't make no damn sense."

Will shook his head at the both of them as he wiped down the counter. Darla Knight was expected to arrive in a few minutes, and tensions would likely mellow then. Aside from the upcoming mayoral race and the daily horror show on the news with its endless updates and 9/11 footage on repeat, Darla Knight and that movie were all anyone could talk about. It was a good enough distraction, Will figured, and he talked about it often, especially when trying to diffuse conversations about terrorism and the conflict overseas. Besides that, the regulars would want to be on their best behavior, considering how much money the film was bringing to town.

The bell rang above the door and Will looked up expecting to see Ms. Knight. Instead, he saw the mullet-wearing European guy in the trench coat head out into the growing dark. Sheriff Nance got up from his booth then and moseyed his way over to the counter.

"Care for a piece of maple pumpkin pie, Sheriff?" Will asked as Sheriff Nance took an empty stool at the counter, rapping his ring finger on the Formica. "Lydia Townsend made it fresh this morning."

"Satanic cults," Nance said to himself, rather than answer. Bert Nance had always reminded Will of the actor Powers Boothe, with his gravelly voice and expressionless face. The dictionary definition of "straight shooter" could have a picture of him beside it.

Will refilled his coffee. "What's that, Sheriff?"

"Satanic cults, right here in Crooks Corner. You believe that?"

"Not especially, Sheriff."

"Well, that's what buster there just claimed."

"The German guy?" Trudy asked.

Nance's already furrowed brow furrowed slightly more. "Didn't think he was a Kraut. Didn't have a funny accent as far as I noticed, anyhow."

"He *looked* German," Trudy muttered.

Will agreed but remained noncommittal, replacing the empty carafe in the machine and starting another pot.

"Be that as it may, our friend in the long coat assured me we have cultists in our sleepy little town. A *death* cult, specifically."

"He said *Satanists*?" Randy Jacobs raised a single bushy eyebrow quizzically.

"He didn't come right out and say that, not per se. But it seemed to be implied."

Randy shook his head, chopping up his roast beef on toast absently with his fork. "Them doomsday cults, though... it's just they ain't usually Satan worshippers."

Now Sheriff Nance raised an eyebrow, turning slightly to the older man. "That so?"

"No, sir. I mean yes. Waco, them Nike folks, Jim Jones, the Solar Temple," he counted the names off on his nicotine-stained fingers. "They're usually Christian or some kinda wacko religion nobody ever heard of. Can't name a single *Satanic* cult, though there's been satanic *murders*—Ricky Kasso back in '84 comes to mind—just not of the *cult* variety."

"Randy here is our resident Robert Stack," Will joked to the sheriff, who winked in response.

"I prefer Raymond Burr," Randy said, "but thanks all the same."

Trudy slurped her coffee. "What about them Columbine kids?" she asked.

"They wasn't Satanists, they was just a coupla mentally disturbed teenagers."

"You can just say *teenagers*, the rest is a given."

The two friends laughed at that, reminding Will of those two old-timers sitting up in the balcony on *The Muppet Show*.

"Maybe so," Sheriff Nance said, staring out the windows at the growing dark. "Maybe so."

"Alls I know is," Trudy said, leaning over the counter and raising her steaming cup of joe for emphasis, "people out there oughta be a lot more worried 'bout what's in their kids' Halloween candy this year. Friend of mine down in Hackensack said some Middle Eastern fellas bought up all the candy at the Costco, then a whole lot more done the same in Wayne County. Could be another terrorist plot."

Her peace spoken, Trudy took a sip of her Irished coffee and sat back, waiting for Randy to respond. Sometimes Will wondered if she actually believed any of the crap she spouted or if she just liked to stir the pot, winding up her old friend like a top to watch him go off. The little grin Trudy couldn't fully hide behind her coffee cup when Randy finally did respond told Will it might be the latter.

"Now that's a load of bullshit and you know it," Randy said, slapping both palms down on the counter.

Nance chuckled and raised his eyebrows at Will while the two old farts argued. Will grinned and shook his head.

"You have yourself a nice night there, Will," Nance said.

"You too, Sheriff. Hope Gate Night doesn't give you guys too much hassle this year."

"Nothing Crooks Corner's finest can't handle," Nance said with a chuckle, before sauntering off toward the front door. Will wiped down the counter for the twentieth time that night, listening to his regulars prattle on while he waited for the actress to show up. She was already five minutes late by the clock as the chime jingled above the door when Nance stepped out into the night.

3

SHERIFF BERT NANCE left the diner and headed for his cruiser parked around the corner. He moved at a leisurely pace, pulling up the collar of his shearling coat against the chill in the air. Though the street was empty of pedestrians, aside from a lone figure smoking under the theater marquee, plenty of cars were parked on Main Street, including one in front of a hydrant he'd mention to Deputy Sikes. He expected a fair amount of trouble tonight, being the night before Halloween and all, which most folks around here called Gate Night like Will Crampton had, though Nance had also heard it referred to as Cabbage Night or Devil's Night once in a while. Things had gotten pretty bad last year, with two groups of kids in the drunk tank, several kept overnight to "teach them a lesson," as their folks said, which had suited Nance just fine, as well as calls for cow tipping and all manner of mischief, including but not limited to shattered school windows, TP'd houses and punctured tires on vehicles up and down Main Street. There'd been a brawl at the Town Pump after which three of the guys involved had to be sent to Lakes

Region General ER, and a drunk driving accident that had ended with the driver being decapitated by his own windshield.

This year, things had gotten strange earlier than normal: at just past six A.M. Rowena and Chet Thompson called in about a dead lamb left at their farm. Odd thing was, the Thompsons didn't farm lambs. Point of fact, Nance didn't know of anyone in the region who did. In light of his conversation with the fellow in the trench coat just now, it got his detective's mind wandering.

According to Deputy Sikes, the thing looked like it'd been placed there as a warning. Nance wouldn't have been surprised if it had been. Even after almost twenty years of operating their "Halloween Village" haunt at the farm after fall harvest, there were still plenty of busybodies who made it their business to tell people it was "satanic," and for as long as Nance had been sheriff in this town, parishioners from the Catholic church had been putting up flyers weeks ahead of it urging folks to boycott. Nance couldn't legally prevent them from posting what they wanted to so long as they weren't filled with profanity—which was unlikely for church folk—or inciting violence—slightly more likely, it had to be said, since 9/11—but he'd had to resist telling his deputies to go around town and tear them off the bulletin boards in the grocery store, library, post office and legion hall, and from telephone poles all across town.

Nance had his own issues with Reverend Earl. The man was more fire and brimstone than a Baptist tent revival, and it'd been said that he'd been whipping up his parishioners into a frenzy since the terror attacks. Nance pitied any Middle-Easterner who might happen to pass through town, though it wasn't likely, fortunately for them. He wouldn't put it past Earl to chase the poor folks out of town or worse. Nance figured he'd likely stop short of violence, but only reluctantly, turning the other cheek as it said in his Good Book. Instead of expending his energy physically assaulting people, he used it to thump the Bible, and quite aggressively at that.

Reverend Earl had his meddling fingers in just about every aspect of town business, and it irked Nance to no end. But what could he do? He was a peace officer in a sleepy little town, which seemed to be getting bigger every day, despite the town council's arguments and efforts against expansion. It was a nice place for the most part, but it had its ugly side like most towns did. Bar fights, drugs, drunk and disorderly conduct, teenage pregnancies, domestic violence and the like. Of course, there was that murder made to look like a suicide of a former teacher from the high school, but it turned out he'd been hording photos of nude and semi-nude children, and the Staties had taken over the case, thank Christ. Nance didn't suspect he'd have been able to get his deputies to work too hard to find whoever had put that old dog out of his misery. Crooks Corner wasn't some Garrison Keillor small-town fantasy, like folks just passing through might imagine it. And it was a hell of a lot closer to Mellencamp's "Paper in Fire" than either "Small Town" or "Pink Houses."

Now up comes this buster from Miami saying there's a satanic cult in the woods out by the Thompson farm.

Nance huffed out a misty chuckle. He'd have to pay a visit to the Thompsons tonight himself, after that thing with the lamb. Just to say he'd done his due diligence. Might just head out now, before circling back to the station.

"Sheriff Nance! Sheriff Nance!"

Philbert Piper, Jody Piper's boy, came hustling up the sidewalk toward him. He was a gentle giant, a thirty-something man with the IQ of a not too bright six-year-old. His head always leaned forward with his shoulders hunched, and he just about always had a big goofy grin plastered on his moon-shaped face. Whenever Nance saw them together, Jody was straightening the big guy's hair, but it always ended up a haystack like it was now.

"Oh, hey, Philbert. Whatcha got there?"

"Found it on the sidewalk," Philbert Piper said proudly, holding out a purse that looked designer. "Looks like a lady's purse!"

"I see that." Nance took it from the manchild's meaty fist and began rifling through it, looking for ID. It was designer, all right. Had two mirrored and intertwined Cs made of brass on one side. He found the wallet and opened it. "Where's your momma at, Philbert?"

Philbert glanced back over his shoulder. "Cookin supper. Mom says for me to get a can o' mushrooms from the store. We're havin beef pie, that's my favorite."

"Lucky you," Nance said, and meant it. Jody Piper's beef pie was genuinely something to be savored. He fished out the ID with two fingers. The shaggy-blonde woman in the photo was immediately recognizable, but the name was different. The face belonged to Darla Knight, the actress. The name was Kim Jankowski. Nance supposed she must've changed it for her film work. Couldn't say he blamed her, with a name like Jankowski. Not many Polacks in Hollywood, at least by name, aside from that pervert who directed *Chinatown*. He slipped the ID back in the wallet pocket and tucked it into the purse.

"Where'd you find this?"

Philbert was looking past him, frowning toward the diner and the corner store on the other side of the street. Nance snapped his fingers in Philbert's face. The boy had the attention span of a gnat. It was just lucky Philbert had managed to flag Nance down when he did, otherwise he might've just kept the purse thinking he'd had it with him all along, like that memory-loss guy in the movie that ran backwards he'd seen at the drive-in with Madge Collins last summer.

Philbert lost the frown, which Nance might have suspected for concentration in anyone else. "Hey, Sheriff Nance. Guess I already gave you that purse, huh?"

"That you did. Where'd you find it, d'you remember?"

His brown eyes brightened. "Sure do!" He turned and pointed. "Just back there across from the hotel."

"Thank you, Philbert. You go on and get them mushrooms for your momma now."

"Yup! We're havin beef pie. That's my favorite."

"It's real tasty, that it is."

"If you find who dropped that purse you'll tell em Philbert Piper found it, huh? Maybe I could get an award."

"I sure will, Philbert. Tell your momma hello from me, if you remember."

Philbert waved, already lumbering off. "Hello from Sheriff Nance. I'll remember. Bye, Sheriff Nance!"

"You take care, Philbert." Nance chuckled and shook his head as he made his way to where Philbert had found the purse, following alongside the boy's large, wide-gaited footsteps in the skim-coat of snow. Jody Piper had to have the patience of a saint, Nance figured. Philbert was a good kid, never caused any trouble despite being bigger than the entire last three years of Woodchucks linebackers. But having a normal kid was tough enough, and at least that only lasted into their twenties, at the latest.

Nance suspected Philbert didn't have much of a life expectancy beyond his mid- to late-fifties, particularly if his momma went first, but that was fifty or more years living under the same roof. *There but for the grace of God*, Nance thought. His own girls, barely out of their twenties, had already left the nest, both of them living in Portsmouth.

The large wide-spread footprints met what appeared to be a crowd of tracks in the sidewalk. Nance could see where Philbert had picked up the purse, an indent in the snow that was just about the same size. Had Darla Knight been mobbed by fans or even paparazzi? What happened to her then? Aside from Philbert's size elevens, there were no other footprints on the sidewalk leading to or from the hotel, just the ones gathered in this spot. Granted, the asphalt was too wet to see prints in the street.

What he did see were tire treads, leading up to and away from the apparent scuffle. If not for the dropped purse, he could have assumed Darla Knight had been picked up by some folks in the cast and crew, maybe driven off for a surprise celebration. But the dropped purse and the do-si-do of scuffed footprints in the snow seemed to indicate foul play. Possibly even kidnapping.

"Well, this night sure got interesting."

Nance grabbed his radio and almost missed it as he was about to walk away, but he stopped as he caught something apparently drawn into the snow. It was one of those symbols he'd been seeing all over town the past few months: the smiley face with Xs for eyes and a crooked, stitched smile.

Sheriff Nance radioed Madge in dispatch. Suddenly it seemed this sleepy little town of his might be waking up again.

CHAPTER 2

1

Earlier that day
Crooks Corner Secondary School

"*C**ome on**.* Everyone knows that's an urban legend."

Renny Hildebrand sat on the desk's edge in the communications lab, allowing his students a chance to "rap," as he liked to call it. The space was large, about the same size as the shop class next door, though it lacked the power tools, vehicle pit and stench of grease and sawdust. Instead, the comm lab held twenty school desks, where fifteen students in the 11th grade class sat in various states of discomfort. The predominant smells were a miasma of CK One cologne, body odor and Stacy Keats's patchouli deodorant.

A couple of edit suites stood near the door, with a top-of-the-line Amiga 4000T computer and iMac G3 Renny was able to petition the school board to purchase despite budget constraints, each connected to its own MiniDV video cassette recorder. The computers were equipped with Adobe Premiere and Final Cut Pro 2, on which to edit their work.

In the opposing corner, the wall and floor were painted green, and a few studio lights were set up on a ceiling grid for students to do the school news and weather. To the left of the greenscreen, a set of high-up windows looked down from the control room onto a small news set with a desk built by the wood shop students a few years ago. Behind it were two chairs for whomever was unlucky enough to fill the roles of anchor, a roster that rotated every week. Renny's years 11 and 12 classes produced a weekly news broadcast rehearsed and shot during the Wednesday and Thursday classes, to be shown Friday mornings throughout Crooks High. There'd been only two weeks in his time teaching here where a broadcast had been missed, aside from the summer months and both Christmas and spring breaks. The first was following the massacre at Columbine in the spring two years back. The second was the week of the 9/11 attacks less than two months ago, during which the principal, teachers and school board decided it would be too difficult for his classes to report on the tragedy, allowing them time instead to "process their feelings." It was a sentiment Renny agreed with, despite desperately wanting to throw himself into work. He'd had friends in New York City. None of them had been at the Twin Towers, but it had been terrifying for a while there, never knowing when and where another attack might occur.

"We live in a small town," Cody Brockmeyer replied from his desk in the back row. "It's not exactly *urban*."

"Good point, Cody," Renny said. "But Brittany's got a point, too. Crooks Corner may not technically be *urban*, but do we need to live in a city to have our share of urban legends? What's a better name for them, if not? 'Rural legends' makes you think UFOs and the Mothman. Why can't Crooks Corner have our own urban legends, despite, as Cody said, our little town not being particularly 'urban'?"

Cody shrugged and crossed his muscular arms over the CCSS patch on his varsity jacket. Brittany Garner turned slightly from the front row with her tongue stuck out, and Cody crumpled a wad of paper and lobbed it in her direction.

"I don't think it's an urban legend," Walden LaSabre said (his family pronounced their name Le-*Saub*, like the car brand, and it often seemed like people deliberately mispronounced it). He was seventeen and already showing signs of male-pattern baldness beneath his trucker cap, although he was also the only kid in their grade able to grow a thick State Trooper mustache, which he stroked thoughtfully with thumb and forefinger whenever an opportunity presented itself. "I mean, not that we can't have urban legends, just that... I know people who saw that stuff out there in the woods behind the Thompson farm. The weird sticks and all that."

"*Sticks*," Cassandra Flynn sputtered, her dark hair hanging over her face like a mourning veil.

Everyone knew someone who'd seen the "weird symbols" in the woods, or had seen them themselves. They looked like dreamcatchers, only instead of woven patterns of string and feathers, within the circle of twigs was a stitched mouth and Xs for eyes. And graffiti of the image had been showing all over town, spraypainted in alleyways, on the backs of various buildings and under the Geromero Street bridge. The myth of a cult in Crooks Corner had grown over time as more and more of these tags were found.

"The *Blair Witch* guys should sue whoever's putting up all those things for copyright infringement."

"But that's probably what it is, right?" Brittany said. "A what's-it-called? A virus hoax."

"*Viral*," Walden corrected her. "What are you, new?"

Brittany merely scowled and continued scribbling the ever-present spirals that adorned the pages of her notebook. Renny often wondered if she was mildly autistic. Smart as anything, and talented to boot.

"Yeah," Cody agreed. "Couple weeks from now it'll turn out it's just an ad for that horror movie they're shooting on the Hamburg farm."

"It's called *House of Doors*," Cassandra said. "My friend's dad saw Darla Knight at the diner last week. So tragic. He doesn't even *like* her movies."

"How could he not like her movies?" Cody said, clearly offended. "She's like, a legend."

"I know, right?"

"Wait, you have *friends*?" Walden added belatedly. When he got nothing but a snicker from a few other kids he slunk behind his desk and stroked his mustache.

Renny grinned. This was as close to camaraderie as his class had come in the past two months, even in the midst of shooting the weekly news. "So," he said, "we can all agree to disagree whether or not the supposed 'death cult' in the woods is an urban legend—*or rural*," he added swiftly, to quell any potential rebuttal. "But if there *does* happen to be a real cult, which I doubt, I don't want any of you using your mid-term project as an excuse to get into trouble out there in the woods. I won't accept any assignments about it, whether or not it exists. *Are we clear?*" He surveyed the class full of mostly bored-looking students. "Your film is supposed to be *fictional.* That includes mockumentaries like *The Blair Witch Project.*"

"What about *Book of Shadows?*" Cassandra asked.

"*Or* it's unfairly maligned sequel," he emphasized. "All right, one more word about movies before we break off into groups. Movies, or stories in general, carry on the oral tradition"—the kids snickered at this, as every class did, and Renny had learned to carry on without pause—"that we humans have relied upon for millennia to share morals and values and information with one another, through tales of heroism and misfortune. Movies and TV shows are the modern equivalent of our ancient ancestors painting on the walls of their caves. Stories are more important, in my humble opinion, than politics, even science."

Jay Nielson scoffed at this, but again Renny continued unabated.

"*Stories make us who we are.* Without stories—the ones we tell each other and those we tell *ourselves*—we wouldn't be able to form deep emotional bonds with other people. We wouldn't have *society.* We wouldn't have science or religion or art. We never would've made it out of those ancient caves. We'd just be empty sacks of meat bumping into each other as we mindlessly go about our days."

Walden shot up a hand. "I can't speak for everyone else, but I'm an empty meat sack."

Some of the class laughed, and Renny smirked patiently. "Very good, Walden. All right, let's get you all into groups. One, two, three, one, two—" he said, counting as he pointed at students throughout the class. He deliberately made it so Walden LeSabre, Brittany Garner, Cody Brockmeyer, Cassandra Flynn and Jay Nielson—the quiet, moody kid with an aptitude for computers, who'd scoffed at Renny's mention of stories besting science—would all have to work together, despite not seeming to get along. Part of team building, and of growing up in general, was having to work with people you didn't necessarily like or agree with. It was something he dealt with himself on a daily basis, working here. Renny was friendly and outgoing, but he was also considered From Away, meaning he hadn't grown up in Crooks Corner. A few of the teachers were still somewhat guarded around him, as if he couldn't be trusted with town secrets, even though this was his fifth year of living here since he'd started teaching at CCSS.

It made things tough with Elana Stabler, who taught grades nine through twelve Math, since she was friends with just about everyone on staff. No matter how much of a "good word" she'd put in with people, Renny still felt like an outsider. And he supposed he always would, even if they ever worked up the courage to go public with their relationship.

2

ONCE THE TEAMS WERE ASSIGNED, everyone pulled their desks over and began brainstorming, gossiping, sitting silently while tapping their pens and pencils, pretending to be thinking of ideas, or just generally goofing off.

"I think we should make a horror movie," Brittany said, taking the lead in her group, as expected for the honors student. "Mr. Ducharme says it's easier to scare people than make them laugh. And it's easier to make them laugh than it is to make them cry."

"I don't know..." Cody said, sliding down to a slouch in his chair. "If the effects are cheap, people are gonna think it's dumb."

"Cheap effects aren't gonna kill anyone," Walden said. He worked at the theater downtown, and knew more about movies than probably anyone in the class. "Actually, a lot of people love cheap effects. They've got charm. You should see the reactions we get at the Grand when we show *Plan 9* or some of the Troma stuff. Bigger laughs than *Meet the Parents*, and bigger cheers than *Gladiator.*"

Jay put up his hand. He didn't need to put up his hand to talk, but Brittany pointed to him anyhow. "Yes, Jason?"

"What if I don't like horror movies?"

"*What?*" Cody said. "You're joking, right? *Everybody* likes horror movies."

"Actually, that's not true," Jay said. "If you go by box office numbers, horror makes less than comedies, kids movies *and*

Martin Lawrence. The only horror movie that made anything this year was *Scary Movie 2*."

"That was good, though." Cody pulled out the sleeve of his jacket so that only a few fingers were sticking out, which he used to mime pinching toward Cassandra. "'Take my strong hand, child,'" he said, in a passable impression Brittany recognized as the butler from the movie.

Cassandra cringed away from him. "Get *lost*, doofus!"

"So offensive," Brittany said, shaking her head in disdain.

Cody rolled his eyes, removing his hand from his sleeve.

"Wait a second. *Hannibal* did pretty good," Walden said. "That's a horror movie."

Jay pinched his nose in irritation. He'd been voted next to "go Columbine" by several students in the social studies class he and Brittany shared this semester. Not that he'd ever expressed any violent thoughts, just that he was always sighing deeply in class and correcting people in an exasperated tone, like he might snap at any second. Brittany hadn't approved of the poll but she had to admit, he was easily irritated. "*Hannibal* is a psychological thriller with horror elements," he said, practically groaning.

"Same diff."

"*Same diff*," Jay mimicked with a sneer.

"Listen, pipsqueak—"

"*Chillax*, bro," Cody said, grabbing Walden's shoulder.

Walden scowled at Cody until he withdrew the hand, raising them both in peace. Cody was stronger physically, but last year Brittany had personally witnessed Walden stand up to notorious bully Adam Brunt. He'd taken the beating on his feet until Mr. Hildebrand had stepped in and sent both boys to the principal's office. Walden must've known he was outmatched, if not in physical strength certainly in stamina, but he'd still stood between Brunt and whoever Brunt's prey had been that day. He was a smartass and sometimes a bit of a dick, but fearless.

"Guys, let's stay focused," Brittany said. "I don't wanna be stuck doing all the work *again*."

Cody shrugged and nodded. "Brit's right."

"*Brittany*," she said. Only her father called her Brit, and she preferred it that way.

"Hold up," Walden cut in. "*The Mummy Returns* is a horror movie. That movie made bank."

"*Ooh*, burn," Cody said, addressing Jay.

Jay opened his mouth to reply, then shut it again, clearly defeated. Brittany didn't bother to mention it was more of an adventure movie like *Indiana Jones* than a horror movie, since it would weaken her case.

"So," she said, "all those in favor of making a horror movie, say aye."

Four hands shot up quickly. Looking at his opposition, Jay finally raised his hand reluctantly.

"Okay, the ayes have it," Brittany said, and wrote *Student Horror Film* at the top of a new page in her notebook, one free of her doodled spirals. "Let's brainstorm."

3

IT DIDN'T TAKE VERY LONG for the group to arrive at a pretty solid idea. Cassandra's love of *The Blair Witch Project*—and its "unfairly maligned" sequel, as Mr. Hildebrand said—got them thinking about concepts for a "found footage" film in the same vein.

The best thing about the idea was that they could shoot and star in the movie themselves. They'd each had practice on the news set, so none of them had too much anxiety about getting in front of the camera. They weren't sure they could *act*—except for Brittany, who'd taken drama for as long as it had been offered and starred in each school play and musical for as long as any of them could remember—but they all agreed it would be fun to try. Even Jay, clearly the shyest of them, seemed vaguely enthused.

It was Walden who suggested they shoot at Halloween Village, the local haunted attraction. "It's the perfect set," he explained. "It's already got all the horror shit and background actors we'll need."

"Yeah, but you think they'd let us just like, go in there and shoot it?" Cassandra asked.

"We can tell them we're making a documentary for class," Cody said. "I used to pick corn for the Thompsons every year. I bet they'd be happy for the haunt to get more exposure."

"I don't know, guys," Brittany said, absently starting a fresh spiral at the top of the page opposite her notes. "You really think that's a good idea?"

"You're the one that wanted to do a horror movie," Walden said. "Now all of the sudden it's *Sophie's Choice*?"

Cassandra gave him a confused look. "Who's Sophie?"

"It's a movie," Walden said. "With Meryl Streep."

Cassandra sighed. "I feel like you guys know a lot more about pop culture than me and I'm getting a little insecure about it."

Cody chuckled. "To be fair, you probably know more about having sex with dead bodies than the rest of us—"

Mortified, Cassandra smacked him repeatedly in the arm. "Shut up, *scrub*!"

Cody shied away from her slaps, giggling. "Hey, we all have our strengths"—she gave him another good smack—"and weaknesses," he finished with a laugh.

"Hang on," Jay said. "Mr. Hildebrand specifically said we can't do a mockumentary."

Brittany shot up a hand. When Mr. Hildebrand failed to look up from the book he was reading (something called *Which Lie Did I Tell?* by William Goldman), she called his name. He looked up reluctantly, as if whatever was happening in the story was too interesting to just pop in and out of easily.

"Yes, Brittany?"

"You said we couldn't do a mockumentary, right?"

"Oh! Uh, you can do a mockumentary if you want, just not about the cult. I don't want you going out into those woods at night with the school cameras. Got it?"

"Got it," Brittany said, very obviously attempting to conceal her disappointment.

"Sweet. So now we just gotta come up with a name, huh?" Walden said to the group.

"I've got one!" Cody grinned proudly. As he spoke the title, he mimed it appearing across a marquee with his right hand. "*Helloween*," he said dramatically.

The others looked at him, awaiting brilliance. When he added nothing more, Cassandra snorted laughter.

"More like *Smelloween*," Walden said.

"C'mon, guys! That title's *money*. Halloween. Hell." Again, he mimed the marquee: "*Helloween*."

"Yeah, we got it the first time, slugger," Jay said timidly.

Brittany and the others laughed. Even Jay actually cracked a smile for once. Meanwhile, Cody slumped down in his chair with his arms crossed, clearly dispirited.

"Well, let's just put that as a working title for now," Brittany said, and jotted it down.

"Ooh, wouldn't it be cool if we could convince Darla Knight to be in it?" Cassandra asked excitedly.

"That'd be *killer*," Cody agreed. "Hey, isn't she supposed to be signing autographs there tomorrow night?"

"That's why I said it, *scrub*."

"Stop calling me scrub, *pigeon*."

While Cassandra curled her tongue and began to coo like a pigeon, Brittany turned to Walden with a roll of her eyes. "I can already tell how this movie's gonna end," she said.

Walden grinned. "Oh yeah, how's that?"

"We're gonna end up killing each other."

Walden considered it a moment, then nodded. "I could see that, yeah," he said.

CHAPTER 3

1

J ay Nielson heard old-timey music coming from Mr.
Combs's garage as he approached the bungalow on
Browning Street, kicking through the recent fall of sweet-
smelling dry leaves from the sugar maple in his science teacher's
front yard. He'd been working for Combs most days after school
since sometime last spring, helping with easier tasks like welding
and holding things in place while Mr. Combs tinkered, as well as
picking up items needed from the hardware and electronics
stores, from garage sales or left out on front lawns. Computer
parts were especially easy to come by these days, as it seemed like
people were constantly upgrading to the latest model, tossing
out graphics cards, motherboards, RAM and all kinds of electronic parts for their neighbors to pick through, or the garbage
truck to collect. For his duties, he was given fifty dollars a week
and any of the computer parts that Combs didn't require to use
for his own PC at home. It had kept him well-stocked in Rockstar Energy drinks and he never had to scrounge to buy anything
else he might need for gaming.

Mr. Combs was what Jay's mom had called an "eccentric"
after the last parent-teacher conference. Eccentric was a pretty
good way to describe him. *Scatterbrained* was better. He shared
the same somewhat manic attention span as Doc Brown from
Back to the Future, always jumping from one thought to the next,
seemingly without any connection. To school he wore neatly
pressed suits Jay's mother called "loud," with round glasses, and

kept his wavy graying hair long on the sides and back, even though he was balding on top. While in the "lab," which was just his garage, he usually wore a grimy white lab coat.

Jay rapped on the garage door. It was open about a foot, enough for him to see Mr. Combs's shadow slinking across the concrete floor beneath it.

"I don't want to set the world on fire," sang an ethereal voice from a beat-up old Discman, hooked up to a set of wooden case speakers inside the garage. It was playing at such a loud volume Jay doubted his former teacher would be able to hear him knocking.

"Mr. Combs!" he called, beating again on the metal door.

The music shut off abruptly and Mr. Combs's shiny brown leather shoes shuffled toward the door. "James? Is that you?"

"Yeah," Jay said, not bothering to correct him, since Combs called him James all the time, and reminding the man didn't seem to help. Jay's mom had suggested he get a nametag to passive-aggressively help it sink in, but Jay honestly thought even that wouldn't prevent him from doing it. "I got that stuff you wanted."

The garage door made a racket as the motor kicked in. Mr. Combs was bent over, peering out from beneath it when the door rolled up enough for Jay to see him. The bottom of the rubber apron he wore when he was soldering or doing electrical work hung from his waist. He wore his silly brass cinder goggles with the red-tinted lenses that made him look like some kooky steampunk villain.

Finally, the door raised enough for Jay to step under and swing his backpack off his shoulder onto one of the cluttered worktables. Mr. Combs's eyes widened behind the goggles as Jay unzipped the bag and began unloading the items he'd acquired: a 3-1/2-inch floppy disc drive, a hatched Tamagotchi (Jay wasn't sure why it had to be hatched, but Mr. Combs's requests were usually odd like that), a Motorola LX2 beeper, five cordless phone NiCad battery packs (he'd had to really hunt for those through the junk shop, and ended up just stealing a fifth from his kitchen phone which he hoped to buy a replacement for later), the CCD sensors and stepper motor from a photo scanner, and a Reuben sandwich from Tasty's Deli on Dargento Street. The Furby he'd brought here last Thursday stood on the cluttered workbench, its stuffing and plush exterior cast aside, and it stared at him now with its creepy robot owl eyes. Mr. Combs had required it for its infrared sensor and circuit board.

The science teacher turned off the music, rubbing his palms together at the sight of his late lunch—or was it early dinner? Whatever meal it was, he opened the bag and tucked into it immediately, his lips smacking loudly as he spoke. "Hand me the socket wrench, will you?"

Jay looked over the cluttered heap of tools on the side table. He grabbed the socket wrench and handed it to Combs, who wiped his hand on the apron before taking it. He'd already scarfed down the first half, and was breathing heavily through his nose as he chewed, cranking the wrench on a bolt to open the front panel on what he called, simply, "The Machine."

Even after having worked with Mr. Combs since last year, Jay still didn't know what The Machine was supposed to do. Mr. Combs would just tell him it was "extraordinarily important work," and stress how it would "blow the doors" off of "conventional thinking" about the universe. Once, late at night, after having eaten an entire bag of malted milk balls, he'd said that this machine would dwarf the findings of Einstein and Newton. From the look of the thing, with its rectangular metal casing from an old furnace unit, a circular hole where the Lanzar subwoofer from a "tricked out" car stereo had been jerry-rigged, and several blacklights on top, it seemed to be a cross between a giant computer server and some kind of futuristic DJing system. Today's new addition included a video camera on a tripod, pointed at a cleared space on the concrete floor he'd marked with an X of green painter's tape.

Combs removed the front panel on The Machine, revealing the flickering array of lights and diodes, a rugged terrain of capacitors and interconnected circuit boards, and a single green monochrome screen he'd often seen Combs typing on, seemingly responding to messages from elsewhere, like his own little instant messenger program. A computer keyboard and mouse were attached to it from a port on the side, resting on a folding tray table like the ones Jay and his mom ate dinner on while watching reruns of *Friends* followed by *Wheel of Fortune*, both of which he didn't like but watched for his mom's benefit.

Combs snatched the Tamagotchi off the worktable, snapped

it open and with nimble fingers began fiddling to remove some small part from the purple and pink ice cream cone casing. "There," he said, as he stuck whatever he'd plucked out of the toy onto the face of one of the circuit boards.

Then he began typing on the keyboard with one hand, eating the other half of his Reuben with the other. Thousand Island dressing and sauerkraut oozed out from the side and splattered onto the smooth cement floor. Mr. Combs didn't seem to notice. He pressed Enter, and immediately the subwoofer on the front of The Machine began to vibrate, the blacklights strobing disorientingly, making Combs look like he was in a badly animated cartoon as he stepped into the light to turn on the video camera.

Jay couldn't hear anything from the speaker, but the thing was clearly putting out *some sort* of sound. He felt his chest tighten, and his ears felt as though he'd just gone up in an elevator really fast. He stuck a finger in the right one and wiggled it around. There was always too much wax in them to hear anything with great detail but he suspected that wasn't what was preventing him from hearing what was being output from The Machine. It was likely infrasound or ultrasound he'd be unable to hear regardless of the quantity of earwax.

"What's going on?" he shouted. Though he didn't need to raise his voice, Combs had put on a pair of large red protective earmuffs, which made Jay anxious.

"Beg pardon?" Combs shouted back.

Jay clamped his hands over his ears. The pressure in them settled but the queasy dizziness didn't go away. *"I said, what's that sound?"*

"You may feel your eyes begin to oscillate at an abnormal rate! Nothing to be concerned about!"

Jay didn't know what a normal rate for his eyes to oscillate would feel like, but as he scanned the garage for a second pair of earmuffs, he realized his vision *was* jittering. In addition to the other symptoms, it made him both dizzy and queasy, almost like seasickness.

"Almost there!" Combs shouted excitedly, the progression of green lines of text scrolling up the small screen reflecting off the copper goggles he'd put on, the strobing blacklights flashing on their lenses.

Movement caught Jay's eye in the space above the X on the floor, about waist-high. He stared at it, but couldn't make out any shape to it, just an indistinct eddying of black smoke, like car exhaust that had somehow amassed there without an engine in sight.

Something about it seemed otherworldly, alien, and Jay felt the sudden urge to flee from the garage, dash down the driveway and never look back. But the exterior door was rolled down, making a quick exit impossible, and since he'd never once been invited to enter the house from the door by the old refrigerator, he didn't think he could bring himself to do it now, even as scared as the alien cloud made him. Come to think of it, he'd never seen the inside of Mr. Combs house at all. The only thing he knew about Combs's personal life was that he wasn't married, and though he'd seen signs of a cat—kitty litter bags by the fridge and cat food tins in the recycle bin—and Combs had spoken of something called "Hegel," Jay had never seen the cat itself.

Maybe that's what it is, he thought. *The Machine's a super powerful vacuum and it's sucked up a giant hairball.*

The thought might've made him snicker if he wasn't so anxious, if The Machine's low humming and strobing hadn't put him on the verge of passing out, shitting himself or both. *"Mr. Combs, what's happening?"*

"Just one more mo—"

A miniature explosion on one of the circuit boards caused the subwoofer and Jay's vision to instantly stop vibrating. The strobing blacklights flicked off and didn't come back on, and whatever he'd seen in the air—an alien cloud or the world's biggest hairball—vanished immediately. With nothing of it remaining in the air or on the floor, Jay wondered if he'd even seen it at all, or if it was just a hallucination caused by whatever The Machine had done to him. Sighing with relief, he leaned against the table as another wave of nausea came over him.

Combs removed his goggles. "Did you see anything?"

"Did I *what*?" Jay asked, his ears ringing.

"Pardon?"

Jay repeated himself, and Combs frowned. Then he reached up and touched the protective earmuffs, as if he'd forgotten he was wearing them, and peeled them off.

"Did you *see* anything, James?"

Jay was less concerned about Combs screwing up his name than his nausea, and he certainly didn't want to admit to his hallucination, not without knowing exactly what the man was expecting him to see. An alien exhaust cloud? A giant hairball that vanished into thin air? No way, José. Not considering everyone knew why his dad no longer lived with them, and likely expected Jay to join him there someday. "No, I didn't see anything," he lied. "What was I *supposed* to see?"

Mr. Combs struck the air in front of himself with a fist. "Damn! It must've been that Tamagotchi." He fixed Jay with a narrow-eyed gaze. "Are you *certain* it was hatched?"

"Yeah. I mean, I don't know a ton about Tamagotchis.... But it *looked* hatched."

Combs nodded, stroking his chin, as if what he was thinking of made the least bit of sense. In the silence, Jay's stomach rumbled uncomfortably. He usually would've eaten at least a bag of corn nuts by now but he'd been in a rush to get here, since he'd wanted to play around with something on his computer before a *Diablo II* or *Starcraft* session and dinner, and hadn't had time to stop by the Cumby's on his way from school.

"Can I use your bathroom, Mr. Combs?"

"Yes, I suspect the urge to void your bowels will be quite pressing. Go inside. Second door on the left."

Jay wasn't sure if he had to go but he hurried regardless to avoid potential embarrassment. Ordinarily he'd never poop at someone else's house, but it was far better than going at school, and much preferable to shitting his pants.

He opened the door and entered the back hall, leaving Combs behind to figure out what had happened with his beloved Machine. The house smelled like cats and the dim hallway led to a bright living room with a multitiered, carpeted cat tree, upon which a tuxedo cat slept at the very top in a bar of sunlight.

Jay passed the first door on the left and entered the second, closing the door behind himself. The small bathroom was surprisingly pristine aside from the litterbox in the corner directly across from the toilet, from which the smell of urine arose, and the dusting of little gray pebbles on the tiles near it.

With another ripple of nausea, Jay moaned in displeasure. He unzipped, yanked down his pants and underwear, and sat on the cold seat. He urinated immediately, letting out a few relieving farts. Before he could attempt to void his bowels, a cat flap he hadn't noticed in the bottom of the door opened, and the cat slipped through, slinking over to the litter box. It kicked around in the litter with the bell on its collar tinkling, then turned and stared directly at him with its yellow-green eyes as it pooped, making it look easy.

"Aw, come on. I can't go with you watching, dude."

The telephone rang elsewhere in the house. Jay heard the garage door open and a moment later Combs's footsteps as the man trudged past the bathroom. He heard the rattle of the phone being plucked off the cradle, then Combs spoke.

"Hello? Yes, he brought it. No, it didn't work. Did you—?" He paused. "Oh, you *saw* something, did you? For how long? Well, that's certainly promising. What about the subjects, did they—? Yes, well, certainly you should inquire. I don't care what it takes, *get them talking*. Fine. Call me back with any news. *Goodbye.*"

Even without hearing the other side, Jay didn't like the sound of the conversation. Combs's voice sounded harsh, very much unlike him, and he slammed the receiver down, cursing under his breath.

Whatever was going on with Jay's bowels, the emergency seemed to have passed. He wiped even though he'd done nothing but piss, then pulled up his pants and flushed while the cat kicked litter over its turds. Jay hadn't thought the bathroom could possibly smell worse than it had, but he'd been wrong. Cat piss definitely smelled worse with the addition of cat shit. The cat itself eyed him as it stepped out of the litterbox and padded across the floor to the door. Jay kicked at it and it uttered an annoyed yowl, scurrying out of the way of his foot. The flap swung back and forth after its hasty escape.

"Stupid cat."

Jay washed his hands, dried them on a fresh towel and left the bathroom.

"Oh!" Combs said, startled as they almost walked into each other. "I forgot you were here, James."

"Jay. Mr. Combs, what happened in there? What was I supposed to see?"

The science teacher seemed to consider the question, then

looked down at Jay and squeezed his shoulder. Jay winced but otherwise tried not to acknowledge the pain. He just hoped it wasn't a Vulcan clutch, that he wouldn't pass out and wake up on Mr. Combs's couch with that stupid cat staring down at him from its perch. "Jay," the man said, in a rare instance of getting his name right, "you've worked with me for quite some time, correct?"

"Yeeeahhh..." Jay replied, stretching out the word in his slight confusion.

"If I told you something, could you keep it in complete confidence and not tell a single soul?"

Jay winced as Combs's fingers dug deeper into the meat above his collar bone. "Sure. Of course, Mr. Combs."

"Good." Combs let him go finally, with a smile that didn't reach his eyes. Jay resisted the urge to sigh in relief. "The Machine I've been working on, I call it the DEC, or Dark Energy Convertor. You see, James, there exists a theoretical particle called 'dark matter,' which I believe composes the vast majority of the universe. Matter, you see, what you and me and everything around us is made of, absorbs, reflects or emits light. That is how we can see it. What my Machine does—or rather, what it will do once I get it *right*—is make dark energy or dark *matter*, which does not interact with electromagnetic force in its natural state, *visible* to the naked eye. That is why I asked if you saw anything out of the ordinary while The Machine was running."

Jay wasn't sure he understood or believed what his teacher was telling him, but he had heard of dark matter before. The internet called it pseudoscience. "Was that what I supposed to see? Dark matter?"

Mr. Combs stared off at the blank eggshell-white wall, deep in thought. "Of that I'm not quite certain," he said finally. "It could look like anything at all, James. Perhaps even the *absence* of something."

The absence of something, Jay thought, and couldn't help but shudder. Combs's explanation of The Machine made him certain he'd seen *something* hovering in the air above the green X— but having possibly seen a physical *nothing* was even more disturbing.

Whatever it was, he was sure of one thing: he never wanted to see it again.

2

. . .

BRITTANY GARNER HAD FOUND herself caught in a trap she'd inadvertently created for herself.

Shooting a found footage movie for their mid-term project was obviously the wisest choice, having a very low budget, not much time to work on a script, and the extremely amateur actors she'd been stuck with in her group. But shooting it at Halloween Village, despite it being the perfect place as Walden had said, was the worst choice for Brittany. She'd gotten a job there this year, and sheer embarrassment prevented her from telling them, even though it would become very clear to them soon enough, whether she liked it or not. Everyone knew her family was well off and she didn't *need* the job, but her parents thought it would give her some "real-world experience" to have a part-time job "like other kids," so they'd insisted she find something herself, before they used their own influence and connections in town to find something for her, which would no doubt cause even further shame.

When her drama teacher, Mr. Ducharme, put out a call to his students looking for "haunt actors" at the beginning of October, Brittany had jumped at the chance, thinking it would be smart to get experience in an area of the dramatic arts she hadn't yet explored: *fear*. What better place to hone her skills at terrifying people than at the local Halloween attraction, among actors and other kids and adults from the community who clearly reveled in it?

At least no one in her parents' social circles was likely to see her at the haunt, and other kids in school likely wouldn't recognize her under all the makeup—or so she'd thought, until Walden suggested they shoot their project there.

Denise Garner picked her up in the Lexus after drama practice—this semester they were performing *Les Mis*—and drove her back home. They lived in a three-story colonial on a ten-acre property on the outskirts of Crooks Corner, with their own horse stable—Brittany had learned to ride by the age of five, and her all-white Sabino, Midnight, was one of her best friends—an in-ground swimming pool and a large pool house where her older brother Bradley lived like Will in *The Fresh Prince of Bel-Air*. The Garner property backed onto the same woods as the Thompsons' farm five minutes further north, a hundred-acre stretch of Douglas fir, sugar maples, and tall, spindly white pines. Some nights before bed, Brittany stared into the dark woods from her bedroom window, certain she'd spotted movement among the trees while brushing her hair in the mirror. But when she'd look closer, there would be nothing moving out there but the swaying pine boughs. If there had really been anything, the super bright motion-sensor lights would've gone off, waking the horses and probably everyone in the house except Brad. They sometimes winked on for something as small as a raccoon, so she was pretty certain if a person or *something else* was standing out there, they would trigger it.

After what she'd been through out there three years back, she felt like she had every right to be nervous, even scared, but the rumors of a death cult living in the woods made her laugh. She'd lived on the border of those woods all her life. Her dad and older brother hunted out there in the fall. They rode the horses through the miles of trails they'd cut. If a cult had moved onto the land, *someone*—even if not one of the Garners—would've noticed them and called Sheriff Nance to get them kicked out, even though it was technically unowned federal land. You could camp out there, according to her dad, but you couldn't make a mass campsite, and you definitely couldn't build a church or whatever it was this cult was alleged to worship in. Even her dad's deer hunting blind and the trails they'd cut for the horses were technically prohibited.

What wasn't a rumor were the weird totems made out of sticks like Walden had said: the face with a stitched smile and Xs for eyes. Her brother had found one when he and his buddies were out hunting in September, and he'd brought it home for her to see. Considering the same image had popped up in graffiti all over town over the past year, it had given her the creeps, and the voice in her head insisted Brad get rid of it before Dad and Denise got home. If he refused, she'd have told them about the parties he'd been having while they'd been cottaging on Lake Winnipesaukee with their Wolfeboro friends over the summer. Fortunately, he'd very eagerly thrown it out the back door, almost as though it made him just as anxious as it had Brittany, and when she'd looked the next morning, it was gone.

Denise turned the Lexus onto their long brick drive and drove cautiously until they reached the three-car garage. As she pressed the button on the remote and the door began to rise, Brittany leaped out. "Thanks, Denise," she said.

"*Mom,*" Denise called after her, but Brittany had already slammed her door.

Reruns of *Family Matters* and *Full House* played in the background while Brittany did her math homework, sitting cross-legged in front of the TV with their toy poodle Bella sleeping on the floor beside her. There wasn't a lot to do and she finished it well before Renata, their housekeeper, served dinner. Whatever she was cooking smelled amazing, but then everything she cooked tasted good, even if Brittany couldn't always eat as much as she wanted to lest she have to get her costumes retailored.

After supper, Dad drove her in the Range Rover to the Thompson farm. She was already done up in her costume and makeup for what Mr. Thompson called a "psycho clown," but looked more like a serial-killing jester. When he'd first seen the costume, her dad had said, *Whatever you're supposed to be, I'm just glad my clients won't be able to recognize you under all that makeup.*

"How's the musical coming along?" he said now.

Brittany shrugged, watching the dark trees as they passed. "Pretty good, I guess. The kid playing Javert can't sing for crap, though."

"That's too bad."

Again, she shrugged. "What are ya gonna do. At least I get to 'accidentally' smack him around a bit."

Gary Garner laughed as they drove up the gravel road to the farm. "That's my girl."

"Hey, did you feel that earthquake earlier, Dad?" she asked. "A little after school let out? Probably around four?"

Her father frowned. "Earthquake? We haven't had a good one in fifteen years or so, that I recall. You felt an earthquake?"

She nodded, still kind of spooked out about it. "Yeah. The whole gym started shaking right in the middle of my solo. One of the lights, like, crashed down on the stage, just barely missed me." In truth, the light had fallen at least ten feet away, but for the desired effect it helped to embellish.

"Oh, jeez," Dad said, and patted her knee. "Glad you didn't get hurt, pumpkin."

"Me too."

They drove the last few minutes in silence, passing dark, flat farmland on the left and deep black forest on the right. The sky in the west was the same as the dark purple from the bruise wheel in her FX makeup kit.

"Thanks, Dad," she said as she climbed out of the brand-new SUV once they'd reached the farm. The spooky lights were already turned on, the music and horror sound effects blaring. Shouts and cackles could be heard from various places as people practiced, as well as the high buzz of a chainsaw. Customers would start to arrive in a half an hour, but most of the actors liked to get into character well before the public arrived.

"Hey, Brit."

"Yeah?"

"Give your mother a break, huh? She loves you, but it's just... it's difficult for her to understand right now. You know? She'll come around."

Brittany opened her mouth to respond. Someone calling her name from the house prevented her from saying what she wanted to, and she nodded instead. "Okay, Dad."

"Pick you up just after ten."

"Love you," she said.

"Love you back."

She closed the passenger door and headed up to the house, preparing her eyes to spend the next several hours in the dark.

3

CASSANDRA FLYNN HEADED HOME IMMEDIATELY after the school bell rang. She lived in one of the low-income townhouses on Cunningham Road, off the back of the football field. If the jocks weren't busy pummeling each other, trying to determine who'd be the one to eat the soggy bread, she could've easily crossed in a diagonal to her place. Since they were—*oof*ing and grunting like that old song about the men on working on the chain gang her grandma sometimes played on her old record player—Cassandra instead walked along the side of the fence, hoping none of them would notice her.

She was fortunate today. Last week Adam Brunt, linebacker for the CCSS Woodchucks and the town's worst bully—though Cassandra knew of at least three girls who could do more damage with words than any of Brunt's punches ever would—had caught sight of her and wolf whistled. She'd hurried onward, head down, while the other brutes joined him, making lewd gestures and kissy faces until the coach told them to shut up and get their heads back in the game. Now that she thought of it, only Cody had stayed out of it, standing there watching her with his helmet in his hands while the other guys chanted.

She spotted him doing jumping jacks outside the scrimmage line or whatever they called it, and before she could look away, he caught her eye and gave her a small wave. Brunt noticed him waving and turned in her direction with a vicious grin. Cassandra hurried onward, bowing her head, as Brunt and a few others began to laugh.

One benefit of wearing Manic Panic Goth White foundation was that no one could see her cheeks turn red when she was embarrassed. She hustled around to the back alley as she always did when the guys were out on the field so they wouldn't know which house was hers, and entered through the backdoor.

Her eleven-year-old sister Taylor was watching *Powerpuff Girls* in the living room with the volume up high. She turned as Cassandra entered through the kitchen and greeted her with a blinding flash of her Polaroid camera. Aside from Taylor's affinity for photography, she was about as "normie" as they came. She typically wore her hair in pigtails, she did gymnastics some days after school, and listened to the Spice Girls and Destiny's Child like just about every other girl her age. Whereas Cassandra reveled in rebellion: she dressed in all black and kept her dark hair abnormally long, the only afterschool activity she participated in was smoking and doing Wiccan rituals with her few friends in St. Anthony's Cemetery or under the Geromero Street bridge, and the ghetto blaster in her bedroom pounded out Nine Inch Nails, The Cure, Garbage, Hole and The Smiths on a regular rotation.

"Turn that volume down," she said to her sister. "You'll wake up Grammy."

"Grammy's already awake," Taylor replied, flapping the photo that had spit out of the camera's mouth, despite Cassandra having told her multiple times that shaking it could cause the dyes to bleed and the image to bubble, something she'd just learned this semester in comm class. "She's watching her stories."

Opening the fridge, Cassandra called out, "You want a snack?"

"Grammy made me cimannon toast when I got home," Taylor said, mispronouncing it, a childish idiosyncrasy that had lost most of its cuteness the older she'd gotten. Cassandra just shook her head. If Taylor didn't drop the baby words once she hit her tweens, she would definitely make a point of correcting her.

The fridge hummed. Despite how good *cinnamon* toast sounded, Cassandra chose Cheese Whiz on celery with a bottle of Sierra Mist. Another benefit of her white foundation was it made the spray of pimples just below her hairline less visible, an affliction she attributed to her affinity for soda, though it didn't cause her to stop drinking it. She sat down on the sofa behind where Taylor sat cross-legged on the floor, twisted the top off the bottle and guzzled it down, then took a big crunchy bite out of her snack.

Taylor displayed her braces with a wide grin as she showed the photo to Cassandra, who sneered at her own bright white face and look of surprise. "Gawd, I look like a total doofus."

"This one's going on the fridge," Taylor said, snatching it away before Cassandra could take it from her.

"*It better not....*"

"Just kidding!" Taylor said, which seemed to be her favorite phrase these days.

They sat and watched the show in silence for a while. Cassandra wasn't super interested but she didn't want to go up to her room before finishing her snack. "Hey, you haven't done anything today, have you, shrimp?" she asked during a commercial break.

"Played Humphrey?" Taylor said, looking back innocently. "No, not yet. I was waiting for you."

"Good. Come up while I say hi to Grammy."

Taylor got up from her spot on the floor, leaving her camera and a small pile of photos behind. Cassandra trudged up the stairs and Taylor followed behind her.

They'd been playing innocent tricks on their grandmother for a few years now, ever since Cassandra discovered what Taylor could do. The three of them lived alone in the two-story townhouse, giving them plenty of opportunity to mess around. As soon as Cassandra found out about Taylor's "gift," she just had to exploit it, and even though they both loved their grandmother dearly it was still funny to watch her freak out, taking their cue from *The Tom Green Show*, and the pranks Bam played on his dad in *Jackass*.

"Hey, Grammy," Cassandra said, leaning in the doorway to the old woman's room. Grammy Lauren sat up in her Craftmatic adjustable bed watching *Passions*. In today's episode, the witch Tabitha and her doll-turned-real-boy Timmy appeared to be trapped in an attic by a talking tree. *Friggin weird show*, Cassandra thought for probably the hundredth time.

"Oh, hi, Cassandra, dear," Grammy said, not looking away from the small TV on her dresser. "Give Grammy a minute, it's almost commercials."

Cassandra gave Taylor a nod. Her little sister squeezed her eyes shut and television turned off.

"What the hey?" Grammy picked up the remote from her lap and flicked the TV back on. Taylor immediately turned it right off again. "Darn remote," Grammy said, giving it a little smack before pressing the power button again. It came on and turned right off. "Sugar!" She turned to the girls with a resigned expression. "Well, I guess our friend thinks I should pay attention to my dear, sweet granddaughters. How was school, Cassandra?"

"School was okay, Grammy. Has our friend been acting up a lot today?" she asked innocently.

"Not until just now. Funny how that works. Minds his own business 'til the two of you get home." She clucked her tongue disapprovingly. "You know how needy boys can be."

"Weird," Cassandra said.

"Yeah, that's really weird, Grammy," Taylor agreed, almost blowing the whole trick with a sly grin.

"Well, I suppose if I can't watch my stories I may as well come down and put on supper."

Cassandra helped her grandmother out of bed. It had just

been the three of them since their parents died in a car crash when Taylor was five and Cassandra was nine. Grammy Lauren had moved in as soon as she was able to, and they'd managed to keep the house with her social security and the insurance money.

One of Grammy's Hummels on the side table began to shake, right beside them. Grammy yelped and looked at it in terror. "You leave my tchotchkes alone!" she said sternly.

The pumpkin girl Hummel rattled a moment longer, then fell on its side.

"Wow, he must be pretty angry," Cassandra said.

Taylor hid a grin behind her hand.

"Boys will be boys," Grammy said, as if that explained everything. Grammy Flynn thought the ghost haunting their house—which wasn't really a ghost at all—was a young boy she'd named Humphrey, because "he just seems like a Humphrey." Cassandra had asked why and Grammy had said, "You can just tell," which made both sisters laugh, considering it was just the two of them playing the prank. Grammy probably still thought all little girls were made of sugar and spice and everything nice. And if that was ever true, times sure had changed.

Cassandra helped Grammy down the stairs—she was too stubborn to put in one of those chair lifts, even though it would probably be mostly covered by her Medicare—and led her into the kitchen. A repeat of the old *Scooby-Doo* cartoon from back in the day was on the TV. Scoob and Shaggy were once again running away from the freak of the week, this time a giant glowing owl which would probably turn out to be just some janitor playing pranks, kind of like what Cassandra and Taylor were doing to Grammy.

And we would've gotten away with it if it wasn't for those damn kids, she thought with an inward chuckle.

Taylor settled back in front of the TV, while Cassandra helped Grammy get what she needed for supper out of the fridge. She was handing over the ketchup for Grammy's special sloppy joes when the contents of the fridge began to shake and rattle. The pots and pans hanging above the counter shook, and several cupboard doors swung open.

Cassandra turned to her sister with a look of terror. She had no idea Taylor possessed so much power.

"*NO, NO, NO, NO!*" Grammy shouted over the racket, as

items in the fridge toppled, and a couple of Sierra Mist bottles fell out onto the floor, causing twin fountains of soda to spray at Grammy. "Humphrey, you stop this right this instant!"

"Stop it, Taylor!" Cassandra cried. "*Stop!*"

"I'm not doing it!" Taylor called back, looking as frightened as Cassandra felt herself.

Then, as quickly as it started, the shaking stopped. The soda spray fizzled out and the swaying of the pots and pans slowed.

"Woof," Grammy said, shuffling over to the stove to grab a rag. "He's mighty ornery today, isn't he?" She handed the rag to Cassandra. "Blot up that mess, would you, dear?"

Annoyed, Cassandra got down on the floor and started cleaning up the mess, staring daggers at her little sister. Taylor gave her an innocent pout, but Cassandra could just imagine her little sister showing her braces in a big grin and saying, "Just kidding," like she always did.

Guess the joke's on me this time, she thought, wiping up the spill.

4

AFTER PRACTICE, Cody Brockmeyer walked home and made a huge bowl of microwaved mac and cheese to load up on carbs. He ate it sitting in front of the TV, watching *Austin Powers* on DVD for probably the twentieth time. It was his favorite movie ever. *The Spy Who Shagged Me* was good, but the first movie, he could quote just about every line. He did so now, his mouth full as he ate his piping hot bowl of pasta.

The guys wanted to go out tonight and play pranks on some of the teachers, and his mom and dad wouldn't be home from work for a while, since they both commuted over an hour to Seabrook for their jobs at the nuclear power plant. Jenna Brockmeyer was a nuclear engineer and Chuck Brockmeyer was a power reactor operator. They'd met at the plant fresh out of university, married within a few years, and soon after had Cody.

Cody was something of an anomaly in the Brockmeyer family tree. He'd outgrown both of his parents by a full foot by the time he hit fourteen, and was the only one of them with any interest in physical activity outside of walking and the occasional game of badminton or bowling. Their friends liked to joke that it was because they worked at Seabrook Station that Cody had grown up as big and strong as he did, through some sort of gamma radiation like *The Incredible Hulk*. Rather than point out the statistical improbabilities of such a thing and risk losing the few friends they had in the neighborhood, Jenna would mention that her grandfather Lucas, who'd been an Army corporal during the Great War, had towered over just about everyone he'd commanded. Cody preferred the Hulk theory.

Whatever the reason for his large build, he was already being courted by local colleges to play for them. He was a decent student, not stupid by any means, but a sports scholarship would be choice. He played football because Coach Adams had noticed his large physique, and once he'd started playing, he seemed to have a natural aptitude for it. He didn't love the game, but he also didn't hate it, like some athletes hated their chosen sports. It was just something to do after school, a time filler that had fortunately paid off. He wasn't any good at instruments, he couldn't act like Brittany, he was too clumsy to dance, and he didn't like sitting around doing nothing, complaining about being bored. Football was available, so he embraced it.

The portable phone rang on the table by his feet. He cradled the hot bowl of pasta in his lap and bent over to grab it, scrunching up his nose as he got a whiff of his tube socks. "Woof," he said. Then he pressed Talk and answered, "Brockmeyer residence, Cody speaking."

"*Whassup?*" Chimney said on the other end of the line.

"*Whassuuuuuuup?*" Cody replied. It hadn't been funny for at least a year but Mike Stuckey, a defensive lineman who'd received the name "Chimney" when his pants caught fire while lighting a fart in the sixth grade, held on to jokes as long as kids held on to his nickname, which even Mike himself still thought was hilarious.

"You get the eggs?"

"I got eggs. You got T.P.?"

"Yup, me and Fitz got two whole packs of asswipes. Got milk?"

"Ha-ha," Cody said.

Chimney made farting sounds with his armpit. Cody had to

admire the dexterity it would take to do it while cradling the phone against his ear. "Don't light a match," he joked.

"You wish." Chimney munched on something from a crinkly plastic bag, probably those Hot Cheetos he liked. "Aw, dude, are you watching *Austin Powers* again? That movie is *played out*."

"You're played out. I'm psyched for *Goldmember*."

"And you never wanna see *my* gold member," Chimney said with an audible pout.

"Whip it out then!" They both laughed. "Good times," Cody said. "When are we meeting tonight?"

"After dark, under the Geromero Street bridge."

Cody didn't really want to spend his night playing pranks on teachers when he should be studying for Friday's social studies exam, but it was Gate Night, and harmless teen mischief was to be expected. The guys would rag on him if he backed out, anyway, especially since he was the one who'd gotten the crate of eggs from the Thompsons' farm. One hundred eggs could make one hell of a mess tonight. He figured Brunt and the others guys would probably end up chucking whatever was leftover at trick-or-treaters while hanging out the windows of Brunt's Mustang tomorrow night. Exactly the sort of shit Cody had hated when the older kids had done it to him. *Pranks beget pranks*, he thought. *Gotta keep the youth of today on their toes. Besides, it's better than dicking around with Pokémon or prancing around on a broom like Harry freaking Potter*. He likely would've been cajoled into joining them himself if not for the comm project.

"Yo, what was up with that goth chick at practice? You got a thing for her, or what?"

"What?" Cody nearly choked on his pasta. "Nah, dude. She's just in this group with me for comm class."

"Don't lie, dude. You'd hit that."

Cody blushed. "Whatever. I gotta go study for that test."

He agreed to meet the guys under the bridge at seven, and hung up before Chimney could rip on him again about Cassandra. She was cute for a living dead girl, but he could date practically anyone in school. Just because he was between girlfriends at the moment—Melanie MacNamara had broken up with him two weeks ago when she found out he'd made out with her best friend Kelsey—it didn't mean he could just go ahead and date someone outside of his social standing. Still, the whole clique thing annoyed him. Sure, there were *obvious* tragic cases, like Stacy Keats for one, who'd never rise above her druggie skater friend group. But most kids were more than the labels people put on them. If anyone understood that at Crooks High, it was the star quarterback son of two brainiac nuclear scientists.

It was all very *Breakfast Club*, but it was true.

Then there were guys like Adam Brunt who fit nice and neatly into their boxes and never wanted to step outside of them. He fit the school bully mold to a tee, almost as if he was deliberately trying to play up to the stereotype. Cody mostly liked the other guys he hung out with, but only tolerated Brunt because they had the same friends and was on the same team. It was painful to watch him flirt with girls who only liked him because of his car and his status on the team, and it was excruciating having to tolerate his sadistic games just to stay in good with the other guys.

In some ways he wished he was a reject like Walden or Cassandra or Jay Nielson, just so he didn't have to pretend to be friends with assholes like Adam Brunt.

But life wasn't that simple. Cody's dad sometimes said, usually when they had relatives over during the holidays, *You can pick your nose but you can't pick your family*. Cody often felt you couldn't pick your friends, either.

CHAPTER 4

1

Walden LeSabre drove directly to work after school in his beat-up green Chevy Nova. He was one of a handful of staff at the local theater, the Grand. It was mainly a repertory theater these days, but they also ran newer movies a month or so after their release for a week or two, in addition to the oldies they showed, often as a double bill. Mr. Stafford had run the theater for almost fifty years. He'd been what he called an "apprentice" to the man who'd opened the place in 1919, and had taken it over when the old man died. Now Mr. Stafford was the old man. He'd been grooming Walden to take over for him when he retired, and though Walden had his eyes set on getting out of Crooks Corner the moment he graduated, he'd let Mr. Stafford consider him his apprentice as long as it provided him the cash he'd need to move out.

The job itself was fine, with okay pay and decent benefits for part-time, but Walden had his sights set on Hollywood. One of the good things about running the projector, aside from being able to watch movies at work, was that it gave him plenty of free time to jot down ideas or sometimes write full scenes in his screenplay in the projection booth while the movies played. If he'd been working the concessions stand or in the box office, as he had when he'd started there a couple of years ago, he'd be required to clean and sweep during his down time. "If you have time to lean, you have time to clean," was one of Mr. Stafford's favorite phrases. Whereas in the booth, which was actually pretty large and decently lit compared to what he'd expected, he just had to sit there most of the time to make sure nothing happened with the reels or the projector. He'd need to load up the next movie on the second projector to get it ready for the nine o'clock screening, but other than that it was just sitting around and waiting for something bad to happen, which rarely occurred.

He'd been loading up the night's first screening—the first in Italian splatter director Nicolo Funelli's *Ragers* trilogy, starring the legendary Darla Knight herself—when the floor in the projection booth started to shake and the equipment began to rattle. The tremor lasted less than a minute, but when Mr. Stafford came careening into the room, the old man looked terrified as a few heavy film reel cannisters dislodged from their stacks and rolled out onto the red carpeting.

"What in the name of Heaven!" Mr. Stafford cried over the racket, and in the next moment the trembling stopped. He was wearing his magician's cape, top hat and gloves.

"Was that an earthquake?" Having never experienced one before, Walden had to ask.

"That or our old girl is finally giving up the ghost," Mr. Stafford said, his arthritic hands still trembling. He often called the Grand "old girl," which had always made Walden wonder if Stafford had never married because he was already married to the theater. "Her foundation isn't quite what it used to be, but I hope she's got at least a few more decades left in her."

"At least," Walden agreed, hurrying over to gather up the heavy cannisters and put them back in their places. "Hey, Mr. Stafford...?"

"Yes, Walden?"

"I was wondering if I could take tomorrow night off?"

"Tomorrow?" The old man frowned and blinked rapidly. "Why, that's our big Halloween extravaganza!"

"Yeah, I thought about that. But Patrice said she could handle the projection duties for me. She knows how to do it, and you know she's been itching to run it on her own."

"Yes, but *you* are my apprentice projectionist."

Walden bit his lip. He thought about telling Mr. Stafford right then and there he had no intention of taking over the "old girl" once Mr. Stafford retired, and that he wasn't planning to stick around Crooks Corner much longer after he graduated.

Instead, he said, "I have to do this assignment tomorrow. My group voted to do it at Halloween Village, and you know they stop running it after Halloween. It wasn't *my* choice, Mr. Stafford, believe me," he said, even though it had one-hundred percent been his idea. He'd wanted to shoot something at the Thompson farm for years but never had the opportunity. He was even more eager to meet Darla Knight in the hope of getting her to read the treatment for his low-budget horror movie script, to see if she'd have any interest in playing the lead's mother, or at least pass it off to someone who could potentially get it made.

He knew it was unlikely, but Wayne Gretzky once said, "You miss one-hundred percent of the shots you don't take," and even though Walden didn't like hockey as much as the rest of the LeSabre family, he had to agree with The Great One in this case. If Ms. Knight was there tomorrow night, he'd ask her. If she said no, he wouldn't push it or try to sneak it into her bag when she wasn't looking, as much as he wanted to. He'd learned from research it was good protocol to respect professional boundaries. Burning bridges before getting a foot in the door was the worst possible way to make a name for himself in the movie business.

"*Where* is your costume?" Mr. Stafford said.

After all the commotion, Walden didn't know what the old man was talking about for a second. Then he remembered the matching outfit Stafford had brought for him to wear tonight and tomorrow. He'd taken off the white gloves for the somewhat intricate process of loading the film and left them on the cutting desk. The cape and top hat he'd tossed over his backpack on the floor. "Oh. It's pretty hot up here, Mr. Stafford. Nobody sees me so I figured I didn't need to wear it."

"Professionalism is key, my young apprentice," Mr. Stafford said, wagging a bony finger. It remined Walden of the Emperor from *Return of the Jedi*, and the black cape didn't help, although Mr. Stafford was usually pretty nice, aside from running a tight ship. Watching the Special Editions of the original *Star Wars* trilogy at the Grand when he was thirteen or fourteen made Walden instantly fall in love with the theater and want to get a job here. Losing himself in those movies on the big screen was what started him on the path of screenwriting, as he pictured sitting in this same darkened theater watching something he'd written on the big screen.

The reality was less glamorous than his fantasy had been, but he still mostly enjoyed working at the Grand, aside from the occasional lecture from Mr. Stafford. He liked his coworkers, even Jeb who got high in the back alley during shows and always wanted Walden to come to his apartment and see his bearded dragons. He liked being able to spend most of his time writing, and he liked that he got two free tickets every week to any movie, including "premieres," and all the popcorn and soda he wanted.

Overall, it was a pretty good after-school job and a decent way to spend his free time, so he put on his cape and top hat and gloves, even though the getup was slightly embarrassing, especially since it made him twins with the boss. Mr. Stafford watched him as if to make sure he followed through.

"There now," the old man said once Walden was done. "Doesn't that feel more festive?"

"It sure does, Mr. Stafford."

"Now, about tomorrow—"

"Look, it's okay if you—"

"Ah, ah, ah." Mr. Stafford wagged his pointing finger. "Patience is a virtue, Walden. I was about to say, if you need Halloween off to work on a school project, far be it from me to stand in your way. This is an *after-school* job, after all. Your parents certainly wouldn't approve of it getting in the way of your education, would they?"

"I guess not, Mr. Stafford. Thank you."

"And Jebediah will run the projector in your stead. I suppose I can run the box office and take tickets myself. I'll need Patrice to help out at concessions, of course. I suspect it will be a very busy, very exciting night." A twinkle emerged in Mr. Stafford's eyes. "We have a special guest, you know."

"Special guest? Who?"

The old man leaned toward him as if he was about to reveal a secret, though they were the only two in the booth. "Darla Knight will be here, signing autographs."

"Darla Knight?" Walden said, surprised. "*Here?*"

"Why, yes. She is the *lead* female thespian in the film, after all. The Scream Queen *extraordinaire.*"

Walden's shoulders slumped. Ms. Knight couldn't be both here and at the Halloween Village at once, could she? Maybe Cassandra and Cody had gotten it wrong. He had to fight the urge to take back what he'd asked so he could stick around here tomorrow night and get his treatment into her hands. Screw the comm project.

"Thanks again, Mr. Stafford," he said glumly. "Mind if I take five before the show starts?"

"Ah, I'd forgotten the reason I came up here! Have your popcorn and a Coke, Walden. I'll hold down the fort until you return. Pray we don't suffer another tremor in the interim, yes?"

"Absolutely. Thank you, Mr. Stafford."

The old man sat in Walden's chair with a hefty sigh and waved him away.

Walden went downstairs, got a Coke mixed with Sprite from the fountain, and a small bag of popcorn with extra butter and dill pickle seasoning, salty and tangy the way he liked it. He finished the bag before he got outside, where he blended in with the decent-sized crowd, sipping the soda while he fished out his smokes. He felt like an idiot in his top hat and cape, but there were a few others in the line wearing costumes, so he wasn't entirely out of place. When he was a kid, Halloween was the one night of the year when he didn't feel like he stuck out like a sore thumb. He was still somewhat of a social pariah, but he didn't care as much now. He knew his destiny lay elsewhere, and the kids who thought he was weird or a loser or disliked him because of who his mother was would soon be in his rearview mirror.

Darla friggin Knight, he thought, shaking his head as he lit one of his menthol cigarettes. His mom smoked menthol 120s, so they were the first cigarettes he'd tried, and after the initial choking fit, they'd hooked him right away. He'd tried others, like Marlboros and filterless Pall Malls, but menthol Kools were smoother. They tasted like breathing in refreshing, minty air, and he was certain the nicotine rush helped fuel his creativity.

The rumble of a revved engine drew his attention to a familiar muscle car at the stoplights. The big guy riding shotgun turned away as Walden looked, but he was pretty certain it was Cody Brockmeyer. A moment later, Brunt's Mustang peeled away through the intersection.

The whole thing with Brunt still irked him. Brunt had been picking on some pathetic dweeb, this real punching-bag type of kid, a minor niner, and Walden had instinctually stepped in to break it up. He'd even warned the dumbass that Hildebrand was watching and he should cool it. Then Brunt had punched him right between the eyes. He'd seen stars for a few seconds, and the volley of punches that came after that was swift and brutal. It was like Brunt had been waiting to beat on Walden his entire life, just been waiting on any excuse, and once he'd finally gotten it he'd let out all of that pent-up rage in a matter of seconds.

Walden had been in plenty of fights in the past, and he'd taken the beating on his feet. This was nothing new. Brunt had no finesse and no form and merely threw punch after punch at Walden's face and arms and chest. Hildebrand broke it up before Brunt could land a hard enough blow to knock him out, and he'd sent Brunt to the principal's office, then helped Walden to the school nurse, who'd been just packing up. When Walden's dad got home, he'd said it was "just like this town" and "people get older and wiser but some things never change."

After that day, to Walden's surprise, Brunt had left him alone. He'd expected to get regular beatings, but Brunt wouldn't even look at him. Other people sure looked at Walden differently from then on, though, especially fellow outcasts and kids in the lower grades. They looked *up* to him, like by taking Brunt's ass-whupping he'd been crowned King of the Losers.

Even today, when Cody, who was one of Brunt's best buds, told him to "chillax" and put a hand on Walden's shoulder, Walden had shaken it off angrily. He'd expected Cody to get pissed, but he'd let it slide. And Walden was certain it was Cody just now in the passenger seat of Brunt's Mustang. The five of them could've easily rolled up and laid a beating on him in the alley. Instead, Cody had turned away quickly, pretending not to see him.

Maybe he really didn't see me, he thought.

He knew better, though. He'd always been somewhat invisible in town, so he could tell when he was being deliberately avoided. The question was whether Cody was trying to protect him, or if he just didn't like Brunt very much, either.

2

THE NIGHT WAS PRETTY uneventful at Halloween Village, aside from a few groups of guys playing pranks, and one of the "roamers," a psycho clown who stalked around outside the barn scaring customers—Jared Mason was actually a Juggalo in real life and didn't require much extra makeup—had gotten punched in the nose by one terrified girl. He'd had to rush to the farmhouse with real blood pouring down his face. Being the night before Halloween, Chet and Rowena Thompson expected a little mischief. They'd kicked the rowdy boys out on their asses and stuffed Jared's nose full of cotton batting, sending him right back out into the haunt, where he chased and shouted at kids with a nasally voice.

Brittany had screamed herself hoarse by the end of the night, but that was true of most nights since she'd started working here. She'd found early on that she actually *enjoyed* scaring people. The ones who screamed were fun to mess with, but sometimes she chose the quiet ones to follow and stare at until they became so uncomfortable they just scurried away in terror, grabbing for their friends' hands and calling for them to hurry. Her favorites, though, were the guys who acted tough for their buddies or their girlfriend. She'd follow them around with jittery, birdlike movements and stare without saying a word, until the guys got hit by the air blasters she'd been herding them toward and couldn't help but shout or cry out in genuine terror.

Once the front gate closed for the night, a bunch of older actors planned to head out to one of the local bars and most of the kids either had their own rides or waited to get picked up. While Brittany hung around with a few of the other girls waiting for her dad to show up—he was usually early—she spotted an older guy watching them from the parking lot. He wore a long, dark coat and black gloves like a German spy in an old movie, and his blond mullet shimmered as he leaned against the hood of an old beige K-car. The floodlights from the farm, shining through strategically placed segments of cast-iron fence, draped his face and the remaining cars in sinister shadow.

"Guys, don't look," she said. "There's a perv getting an eyeful at eleven o'clock."

"Where?" Cindy Jansen said, looking up from her cigarette to scan the parking lot. As one of the zombie girls in the dungeon, her face and hands were painted gray and covered in oozing sores.

"I said *don't look*."

Heather Platz, who played the daughter in the cannibal family, had her hair sprayed gray and frizzed, and wore her winter jacket over a grimy nightgown. While Cindy searched for the perv, Heather snatched Cindy's smoke and took a drag. "Ew, why is he staring at us?" she muttered.

"Take a picture, creep!" Cindy shouted, standing up from the hay bail she'd been sitting on and cupping her boobs, shoving them upwards in his direction.

Heather snorted out a lungful of smoke. *"Jesus, Cindy.* You're so dramatic."

The guy took the hint and stood up from the hood of his car. He gave them one last look—although Brittany had the feeling he was looking directly at *her* for some reason—before climbing into the driver's seat and leaving the lot.

"That guy was so sketch," Heather said.

"I dunno," Cindy said, snatching back her smoke and taking a quick drag. "I'd probably give him a sympathy handy."

Heather laughed. "You're so gross, Cin!"

Brittany paid no attention as the two girls devolved into a fit of giggles. She watched the K-car's taillights until they disappeared over the horizon to be sure the guy was gone. The creep had really unnerved her for some reason. Also, there was something strangely familiar about his gaunt face and dark eyes that troubled her. Like she'd seen him before, possibly recently.

You have seen him before, said the susurrant, Appalachian male voice that often spoke in her head, causing her to picture the same dark spirals she drew in her notebook, coiling and uncoiling in her mind's eye. The owner of the voice had insisted she call him The Snake. *But where?* he wondered.

In her imagination she drew spirals in the gravel at their feet, a remedy for the urge to draw them in reality, as she considered the question. Had this man been watching her before tonight? Had she spotted him at the mall or outside school or elsewhere and just made the connection? Had he come to one of her shows? Had he been to the haunt on another night? Brittany couldn't recall. Wherever she'd seen him, she hoped she wouldn't see him again any time soon.

Does he know about Bennington? The Snake asked. But of course, she didn't know the answer any more than he did, because if *she* knew, The Snake would know, too. They shared the same body and mind, after all.

Heather got picked up by her brother a few minutes later, leaving Brittany alone with Cindy. She didn't mind Cindy but she wasn't the type of girl she'd hang out with normally at school. She was one of the *grungers*, still listening to Pearl Jam and Alice In Chains and other bands like that. She normally wore Doc Martins and plaid and tatty jeans with a wallet chain, hanging out with skater kids or metalheads mostly.

"What are you gonna do after the haunt?" Cindy asked, sounding like she was just trying to fill the silence.

"You mean for work?"

"Yeah. I was thinking about doing part time at the Burger Palace."

"I'll probably just concentrate on school and drama class."

"Yeah, I guess your 'rents probably got the bills covered, huh? Didn't you used to drive like a Lexus or something?"

"My *mother* took it away."

"Aw, poor thing," Cindy said, exhaling the smoke from yet another cigarette.

Brittiny gritted her teeth. Someone like Cindy Jansen wouldn't know how it felt to be given a luxury car for her Sweet Sixteen only to have it snatched away from her barely a year later. Especially for such a stupid reason.

After a few more minutes of agonizingly dull small talk, Cindy got picked up by her boyfriend, and Mrs. Thompson wandered out to ask if Brittany wanted a ride from her husband. Brittany told her no, that her dad was probably just running late. She'd already asked the Thompsons if she and her group could shoot at the farm tomorrow, and they'd said yes, as long as it didn't affect her performance in the haunt. She'd told them she would only go outside of her regular haunt duties to help out on her breaks.

It was five full minutes before another vehicle came rolling up the drive, gravel crunching under its tires. For a moment Brittany worried it was that creep again, but when the floodlights picked out the silver vehicle as it pulled into the lot, she was struck with a different anxiety.

Her mother sat behind the wheel.

3

BRUNT and the guys arrived under the Geromero Street bridge ten minutes late. They whooped and hollered while Brunt pulled multiple donuts around the old mill parking lot in his shitty 1990 blue Mustang GT, before screeching to a halt under the bridge, near where Cody waited. Brunt sat behind the wheel wearing his red lumberjack jacket with a hoodie and a pair of black Kappa tearaway pants he said he liked to wear for "easier access," which he seemed to think made him sound like he got laid a lot, rather than beating off. Creed's new single Cody had heard a couple of times on MTV2 blasted from the tape deck.

He hefted up the crate of eggs from the ground and got in the front passenger seat, holding the crate on his knees. Chimney, riding bitch in the back, patted him amiably on the shoulder. His short hair, styled and bleached like Eminem's, shone under the dome light until it winked off. Crammed in and hunched over in the back with Chimney was Sean "Fitz" Fitzgerald and Dave MacNamara, the older brother of Cody's most recent ex-girl-friend, Mel, a fact Mac hadn't liked but had finally gotten over. All five played for the Woodchucks. Mac and Fitz were linemen, Fitz, tall and broad, Mac, tall and what he liked to call *big-boned* or *husky*, but Brunt just called *fat*. Chimney was squeezed in be-tween them like a Mac and Fitz sandwich.

"Buckle up, bitch," Brunt said with a sneer. His fluffy teenage mustache and acne-studded cheeks curved upward in a grin as he floored the gas, peeling out from under the bridge. Fitz passed Cody a half-drunk bottle of Avalanche, the electric blue liqueur that tasted like heavily sweetened peppermint mouthwash. Cody shook his head—he rarely drank—and Fitz shrugged, took a swig and passed it to Brunt, who swigged and handed it back.

Cody reached into his left pocket for his gum and popped a piece into his mouth. The cool mint immediately refreshed and rejuvenated him, like a hot cup of coffee in the morning. He held the package of Dentyne Ice Arctic Chill up, offering some to the others as they headed toward downtown. "Gum?"

Fitz and Chimney each took a piece.

"I'm a chaw man," MacNamara said, spitting brown sludge into a hopefully empty Surge can.

"You pass up on peppermint schnapps but you'll chew that shit?" Brunt remarked, glancing sidelong at Cody. "What's with you and gum, anyways?"

Cody shrugged. "I like to have fresh breath."

"Dicks don't care how fresh your breath is when you suck em, Cockmeyer."

Cody made to respond but Fitz interjected with an annoyed moan.

"Dude, this song *sucks*!"

Brunt scowled at him in the rearview. "Fuck you, bud. Scott Stapp is a fuckin legend. We can listen to your rock-rap bullshit the next time *you* drive, like fuckin *never*."

"So whose place are we egging?" Cody asked, eager to change the subject. He didn't mind Creed but was more of an Our Lady Peace and Vertical Horizon guy, despite Brunt insisting they were "pussy bands."

"Figured we hit Miss Stabler's house first," Brunt said.

"Why her?"

"Brunt's still pissed she failed him last year," Chimney said.

"Plus, she won't bang her students," Fitz said.

Cody rolled his eyes, while Mac laughed and gave Fitz a high five scant inches from Chimney's face.

"C'mon, guys," Chimney moaned. "If you wanted to play footsies, one of you shoulda sat in the bitch seat."

Both Mac and Fitz started rubbing Chimney's calves with the soles of their shoes—Mac's grimy white Nikes, Fitz's pristine Airwalks—until Chimney laughed and pushed them away. "Fuck off!"

"Fuck *on*, you get better results," Mac quipped, and Fitz ruffled Chimney's haystack hair.

"Don't act like you don't like it," Fitz said.

Chimney made a fist. "You guys're *this close*, man."

"Hey, shut the fuck up back there," Brunt said, turning up the volume as "You Get What You Give" came on. Cody didn't know how Brunt could call OLP pussies while proudly listening to New Radicals, but when the big fuck-you chant at the end of the song began as they ripped down the main drag, the other guys joyfully shouted along, and Cody eventually joined them, belting the lyrics at the handful of confused and annoyed people on the sidewalk: "*Come around, we'll kick your asses!*"

The song ended before they reached the lights on the corner of Main and Hooper, where a crowd had gathered outside the theater, a mix of teens and adults from their twenties to Mr. Hildebrand's age. According to the marquee, they were showing *Psycho* at seven, and something called *Ragers* at nine-twenty. Cody hadn't heard of the latter, but he'd seen the Hitchcock movie a couple of times on Turner Classics.

How cool would it be to see Helloween on that sign? he thought, imagining it up there the way he'd thought it up during class. *How cool would it be to see our movie in the theater?* Having to work on the project tomorrow was another reason he didn't want to chug Avalanche with the other guys. He didn't want to go to school and practice and then have to spend another several hours at Halloween Village all while dealing with a hangover.

His gaze fell from the marquee to Walden LeSabre, who stood a few feet away from the crowd, dressed in a Dracula cape and top hat, smoking a cigarette. Cody looked away quickly so as not to repeat the incident with Cassandra during today's practice. The last thing he needed was these guys razzing him about being best buds with the one guy brave enough to stand up to Brunt. Or worse, that he was *gay* for him.

Fortunately, Walden didn't look their way until Brunt revved the engine obnoxiously, but the light turned green as Walden and just about everyone else turned to see who the big man with the tiny dick was, and Brunt floored the gas, peeling rubber through the intersection.

Crisis averted, Cody thought.

They arrived at the top off Miss Stabler's street a few minutes later. Brunt cut the lights and idled under a giant red maple, its branches barren, leaves littering the sidewalks, gutters and nearby lawns. "Okay, bitches," Brunt said, leaning on an elbow over his seat to address the guys in the back. "In and out clean, right? Two rolls of asswipe each and one flat of eggs for all of us. We don't wanna shoot our whole wad on one house."

"I'd shoot my wad on Miss Stabler," Mac said.

"You got that right," Fitz agreed.

Brunt laughed sarcastically and smacked Fitz on the forehead. "Keep your dick in your pants and your eyes on the prize, *Shitzgerald*. In and out clean. No fuckin around, got it?"

"Yeah, yeah..." Fitz said miserably, rubbing his head.

"All right, hard count us, Cockmeyer."

Cody had placed the crate of eggs between his legs and taken out a flat, holding them precariously. "Hut one," he counted. "Hut two... hut three... hut hut *hut!*"

Both of the Mustang's doors opened at once and the boys piled out. They crouch-ran down the street, crunching leaves, arms loaded with rolls of toilet paper. Cody ran a little slower, worried about dropping the eggs. He supposed he should've brought the whole crate but thought it would have been harder to access them from the box and a lot heavier to carry. His arms were still sore from practice and hauling the box all the way to the bridge from home.

"Hey, is that—?" he said, stopping for a moment to look. When he realized the guys had run on ahead of him, he hurried to catch up. No one else seemed to care that Mr. Hildebrand's red Ford F-1 pickup was parked three doors down the road from Miss Stabler's house, where Brunt stood dumping his stash of toilet paper onto the lawn.

Her bungalow was indistinguishable from the others around it, neat and tidy with a garage on the side and a well-trimmed lawn. Brunt unraveled the first few loops from a roll, giving it a nice long tail before pitching it at the tree in the front yard. Fitz and MacNamara did the same, dropping their extra ammunition on the grass at their feet, while Cody and Chimney grabbed a couple of eggs each.

Chimney's first shot hit the leaf-carpeted roof and rolled down, cracking on the porch. Cody hesitated a moment before launching one square in the middle of the front door with a heavy splat.

Three more rolls went sailing over the tree and the birdbath and the roof, while Chimney and Cody opened fire on the windows and shutters and porch. They'd just about run out of eggs when the lights flicked on behind the front hall, shining through the stained glass in the door.

"Shit, let's bail," MacNamara whispered harshly, grabbing Fitz's arm as Fitz lobbed his last roll at the TV antenna.

Chimney threw one last egg that went wild and hit the rose trellis at the side of the house, while Brunt threw another roll of toilet paper over the tree. "Come on, dude, let's go," Cody said to Brunt, who bent down for another roll.

The front door swung open suddenly. Mr. Hildebrand stood in the doorway with his shirt unbuttoned. "Hey!" the comm teacher shouted. "Cut it out, you goddamn punks!"

"Come on!" Cody urged, tugging on Brunt's jacket.

"Nah, man—he got it comin," Brunt said through gritted teeth, then chucked the roll directly at Mr. Hildebrand.

In that exact moment Mr. Hildebrand's eyes seemed to adjust to the dark enough to spot Cody, and the teacher's eyes widened in what Cody assumed was recognition. The roll of toilet paper struck the porch at the man's feet and bounced down the steps, leaving a long white tail behind it.

As Brunt finally decided to beat his retreat, Mr. Hildebrand began rolling the toilet paper back up with a sigh of exasperation. Cody considered hanging back to help him out of guilt, but the last thing he wanted was his parents finding out about it and grounding him.

He turned and high-tailed it to catch up with the guys.

4

THEY BROUGHT Darla Knight to the cave as the sun began to sink and the forest grew dark. They only ever entered the woods in the evening, and only from the north side, where their black van was less likely to be spotted with no neighbors on this road at all. The cave was cool and damp and their footfalls echoed, their flashlights and the light from the camera illuminating the rough cavern walls in erratic swaths like prison searchlights during a jailbreak. It was creepy in here after nightfall, though the cave's interior was no more nor less dark than ever. The knowledge that leaving wouldn't bring an end to the darkness, just a different kind of dark, made it worse. But of course, that was the point.

Horror was at least fifty percent atmosphere.

Back in April—or maybe it was May, the days all kind of blended together lately—Darryl Knell discovered the cave in the woods beyond Mr. Ellison's weed farm, and everything had tumbled into place for him, like solving a jigsaw puzzle with no box. He'd been doing shrooms, *finding himself* as they sometimes called it, or at least seeking inspiration. At thirty-three years old, he'd still had no idea what he wanted to do with the rest of his life. All he'd known for sure was that he couldn't sell weed to burnouts for small bills and whatever change they could scrounge from their couches forever. He also didn't want to get into the grow-op side of the business the way Mr. Ellison seemed to want for him.

This revelation had come slowly, as most did within the constant haze of marijuana smoke and psychedelics. He'd fallen into dealing in the tenth grade, and kept at it after dropping out of school the following year, because it gave him spending money and he had no idea what else to do with his life. Besides, all of his friends—or so-called friends—were burnouts, aside from Dino Cafaro, four years his senior, who'd worked at the auto yard after dropping out of school himself, and only drank 40-oz. bottles of Schlitz malt liquor out of paper bags like some wannabe gangsta.

Sometime last spring, Hot Box, another of Darryl's so-called friends, had brought this new guy with him: a cat named Max Strick. Max Strick had gotten into some hot water down in Florida and was staying at Hot Box's shithole on the other side of town while The Heat died down. (Darryl later found out the "hot water" was that he'd been messing around with one too many teenage girls and one of their fathers had threatened to kill him or go to the cops, he didn't care which. By the time Darryl learned this little tidbit of important info, Max Strick was already one of his "regulars," and too deeply rooted within their social group to kick him the fuck out without causing all kinds of bullshit Darryl didn't have the mental energy to deal with.) Max Strick had brought a gym bag full of videotapes with him, including an old Darla Knight movie from the '80s, which they'd watched while sucking huge bong hits of some high-grade shit and eating Frosted Flakes straight from the box. Max Strick— that was how he always referred to himself, never just Max, always Max Strick, so that anyone who referred to him ended up using both names (and considering what Darryl discovered later about his sexual proclivities, he'd wondered if it might be an alias)—with his blond mullet, brown duster jacket, bicycle gloves and mirrored sunglasses, had said Darla was supposed to be coming to Crooks Corner to film a movie in the fall.

This had instantly intrigued Darryl, who'd never met a genuine movie star before, especially not one he'd seen naked, and Darla Knight had shown her tits in several of the tapes Max

Strick had in his gym bag, and full frontal—she had perfect perky tits and a light blonde bush that shimmered like gold in a particular light—in *Psycho Kitties from Hell*. He figured she must've put on some weight or gotten saggy tits in the years since the movie came out, but when he went to the library to use the internet a couple of days later, he'd seen pictures of her and found she was still as hot as she'd been back then. Maybe even hotter, in that school teacher/librarian way.

"What's your deal with her?" Darryl's fuck-buddy-slash-roomie Willa Rafferty asked him irritably a few weeks later. In the interim, he'd rented every movie Darla Knight had ever been in, jerking off to her to the point of chaffing while Willa was at work and the half dozen or so burnouts who'd always seemed to hang around had left. He'd even made a binder with photos of her and started jotting down ideas in it, springboarding from scenes in her other movies that he'd rented at the same corner store Max Strick had stolen *Psycho Kitties* from.

"Darla Knight's gonna be in my movie," he'd told Willa, looking up from the binder wearing a grin that would put Anthony Perkins to shame. Willa insisted it looked more like a serial killer's diary than any movie script she'd ever seen, as if she'd ever seen a real screenplay. As if she was Stanley fucking Kubrick's niece or David Mamet's secretary.

Last summer he'd watched *The Blair Witch Project* at the Grand, and since he already had a video camera from shooting skate shit back in high school, he'd wondered how difficult it would be to shoot a *real* movie. This was his chance to finally put that idea into action. To shit or get off the pot, as his dead-beat dad used to say, and he'd told Willa so. He didn't know how he'd do it, but he'd use every bit of cash he had, if it came down to it. He'd quit smoking weed if that was what it took. He *had* to make this movie. And he had to have Darla Knight in the star-ring role.

"Sure thing, *Stan*," Willa replied, and comparing him to the crazed fan from that Eminem video had pissed Darryl off enough to give Willa a black eye. He'd apologized afterwards, over and over again, but he'd had to sleep in his own ratty mattress on the floor for a week until she finally let him back in her comfortable bed, which was about the time the shiner started to fade, maybe not coincidentally. Willa didn't have a long memory, not like other chicks Darryl had screwed, another perk in addition to taking care of the rent and all of the bills. Even though he made a fair amount of bread selling dope, he tended to spend it all on what she called "stupid shit" when she was feeling sassy, like the Nintendo GameCube he intended to get when it came out in November. And too often he ended up getting high on his own supply, which of course wasn't free. Willa worked tables five days a week at the Eateria, picking up overtime when she could. She was good with her money, which worked out well, more often than not, for Darryl.

The day in April when he'd found the shed in the woods, or the Stones in the cave that finding the shed eventually led him to discover, all of his dreams finally came together into something that felt like a plan.

That first day he'd been tripping on shrooms, wandering through the woods touching all of the nice new buds on the trees, and the shed had seemed to have appeared in front of him like the big black rectangle in Kubrick's *2001*. And like some kind of blast from the past hallucination, this chick from high school came out of the heavy-looking door in the shed, looking agitated. He couldn't imagine what the hell she'd be doing out in the woods behind Mr. Ellison's weed farm. Not that he was worried for the crops or anything. Just curious, since he never usually saw anybody else out in this particular area of the woods. Even hunters seemed to steer clear of it. Darryl had figured being out here where those kids were killed by that escaped convict back in the Sixties or whenever it was would give him inspiration for the movie he'd been planning.

He followed her for ten, maybe fifteen minutes. Time stretched out on shrooms sometimes. Then she'd vanished behind a copse of trees. He looked around and around the area where she'd disappeared... and nothing. No Elana Stabler.

He'd gone back home, but wasn't able to convince himself he'd hallucinated her. It just didn't make *sense*. She was a cute chick, sure. But not enough to hallucinate her in the woods, especially since he hadn't thought of her in ages. She was a math teacher now, which made sense. He remembered her being pretty smart. Stuck-up, too.

The next day he returned at the same time, only this time Elana had a guy and a girl with her that Darryl remembered being browners in their same grade. Real teacher's pet types. Darryl couldn't remember their names, only that they used to call the guy Pukus because it sounded like his last name. He'd heard somewhere a while back that Pukus had gotten married right after high school and had a kid around ten or twelve years old now. The three of them—not the kid, but Elana and the Pukuses, or whatever their name was—had been about half a mile southeast of the shed when Darryl spotted them, and just like Elana the day before, all three of them disappeared. This time, Darryl was sober as a born-again Christian. There was no possible way he could've hallucinated all three of them, not even in an acid flashback. So he'd hung around for about half an hour, until Elana finally reappeared, crawling out of a hole in a small outcropping of rocks Darryl hadn't noticed before and probably wouldn't have at all if he hadn't seen her climbing up out from them. It looked like any other pile of rocks elsewhere in the woods, except that this one apparently had a cave in it.

Elana went back to the shed and stayed in there for a few hours, then went back to collect the two down in the cave. Once they were gone, Darryl crept up to the cave and peered down, using his butane lighter to see. The chasm dropped about ten feet into the earth but someone had set up an aluminum ladder, which if you were able to squeeze through the opening looked easy enough to climb down. From there it appeared to open to a decent sized tunnel which went on much further than the lighter allowed him to see.

For the next couple of weeks, caving became Darryl's new hobby, nearly overshadowing his obsession with Darla Knight—although he'd still rub one out to her nude scenes in *Psycho Kitties* before heading out each morning. He'd figured out Elana's schedule by then—about an hour after school until just before sundown—and made sure to get there early enough to explore before she and the other two arrived to do whatever they were doing.

There were two unfortunate issues to overcome before he could go further: the first was his fear of tight spaces. The second —and Dino and Hot Box would call him a pussy if they'd known—was his fear of the dark.

It took some hemming and hawing and a joint and a half to work up the courage to squeeze himself into the crevasse, feet-first, and then a bit longer to psych himself up enough to leave the outside world behind and actually start climbing down the ladder. Mostly it was the thought that something—some sightless, subterranean creature—could easily grab him by the legs and pull him down while he was standing there with his arms and head sticking up above ground. Once he'd finally gotten fully inside the tunnel, with his feet on solid ground, carrying the two flashlights he'd brought just in case one of them ran out of batteries or the bulb burned out, he started to feel a little less nervous. The cave was wide enough for him to move around freely, even if he still worried it might collapse on him at any time. It was actually even kind of nice down there. Cool and peaceful.

The only time he got this kind of peace normally was on the shitter after Willa went to work. Even jerking off he'd worry some asshole would come banging on the door to ask if he could front them a dimebag, or Willa would come home early and catch him in the act and he'd have to come clean, so to speak, about Darla. This sort of peace was rare indeed.

The darkness was a little more difficult to get over, and in truth he would never truly get over it, even when the whole gang came down here with him. The flashlights helped, but he kept thinking about that woman who got lost in the canyon at Carlsbad Caverns just a week or two before then and didn't get found until the next day. His weed-paranoid mind kept spiraling: *What if the batteries all ran out at the same time and I'm trapped down here in the dark until Elana gets here? What if they decide not to come today and I'm stuck down here overnight? Are there vampire bats in New Hampshire? Do they really suck blood, or is it just a stupid name? Can you drink cave water? Would I have to drink my own* piss?

Eventually he got over this fear enough to get started. The cave itself had actually been lit by small strips of glow-in-the-dark tape, making the path Elana and her cronies used easy enough to follow even if he'd dared to turn off the flashlight. There were a few tight squeezes, but nothing compared to getting through the opening, and after about an hour—he was slow-going, walking cautiously and peering back into the darkness behind him, shining the light back there every time he heard a drop or the echo of his own footfalls—he reached the end of the tunnel system, which opened on a large chamber, about ten to fifteen feet wide and maybe a little taller in height.

In the center of the chamber were two stone pillars that reminded him of the former Twin Towers, like a memorial made of stone, except instead of windows each one had these weird carved symbols he thought might make sense if he'd dropped acid that day instead of smoking weed. Or maybe they weren't the type of words you could *read*. Maybe they weren't any kind of language at all.

Standing there in the chamber in front of those strange pillars, the idea for the movie he'd been banging his head against the wall trying to come up with finally came to him, all at once, like a revelation.

It would be about a group of burnouts who kidnap an actor to make a snuff film in a sacrificial chamber, in the same cave where the murder of two young children had been committed years before by an escaped convict. And not just any actor: Darla fucking Knight. Even the title came to him like a vision from God, the lights on the marquee popping on all at once, illuminating it his head: *Darla's Knightmare*.

One night, while she was filming her movie in town, they would kidnap her, psychologically torture her, and get the performance of a lifetime out of her when it came time for the final "sacrifice" scene. All of this would be caught on camera, and everyone involved would have to pretend they were *actual* psycho kidnappers. They could never drop character, *not once*, but it would all be fake (aside from the kidnapping and psychological torture, he supposed), and in the final scene they'd swap out the real knife for one of those retractable knives and use fake blood, and she'd scream better than she did in *Psycho Kitties* or *Mall of the Dead* or the *Ragers* flicks or any of the other B-horror movies she'd been in.

Because it would be *real*, at least to her.

Then they'd let her go, drop her back where they'd picked her up. They'd get all the free press they could dream of when Darla went to the police. They'd probably even be on the evening news. *You have the right to remain silent*, the cops would say, *anything you say can be used against you in a court of law*. But Darryl would squeal. He'd tell them everything about their movie and how he'd come up with it, and they'd have to repeat all that on the news, and in the courtroom. Then, when Darla and everyone else saw how awesome the footage turned out, when they showed it in front of the people in the courtroom, she'd realize how stupid she'd been and drop the charges. She'd *thank* them for letting her be in their movie. It would finally make her the legend she'd always wanted to be, judging by the interviews he'd read.

And as the mastermind behind it all, Darryl Knell would become a household name, like Tarantino, like the Wachowski Brothers, like Alfred fucking Hitchcock. He would finally get the fame and fortune he'd always deserved, ever since his asshole of a father had walked out on them when Darryl was ten.

The funnest part, the part that would really get the others involved and enjoying themselves, was the symbol, just like in the *Blair Witch* movie. They had to make sure they didn't ever get caught doing it, but it was the *symbol* that would get people talking about the movie even before they knew there was a movie to talk *about*. This was what the Stones told him, what they'd shown him in his mind as he'd studied those weird ancient symbols harder than he'd studied anything in his life other than Darla's tits, trying to decipher their meaning.

True to their word, once Darryl and the others had spray-painted the symbol the Stones had shown him all over town, drawn it in colored chalk on sidewalks near hopscotch squares, scratched it into brick and cement and playground plastic, once they'd left all the little stick smiley faces out in the woods, never seen, never caught, once they'd started planting rumors in people's heads about the Cult of the Smiling Face, the *right kind of people,* people in positions of power like the reverend Charlie Earl and Sheriff Nancy Pants—Max Strick's acting background had come into play here, talking to Sheriff Nancy Pants at the diner tonight, pretending to be a "Satanic cult expert"—and paranoid people who maybe smoked a little too much weed for their own good, like Darryl's so-called friends, or dove headfirst into all of the conspiracy theories, like Hot Box's coworker Trudy on the public works crew, sure enough other people in town started to talk. They talked about a death cult out there in the woods, just like the Stones had whispered to him.

They talked about *rituals.* They talked about *murder.*

The Cult of the Smiling Face had made themselves urban legends, and they weren't even a real cult.

Granted, it had taken a few weeks to convince Willa to at least *consider* the possibility of playing a part in all of this, but only a few days after that to get Hot Box, Max Strick and Dino Cafaro interested. Getting them to agree on the kidnapping took a little more convincing. (Willa had initially suggested all the shrooms he'd been taking had made him "literally a schizo," but he hadn't done any at all since he'd found the Stones—the Stones themselves had gotten him high enough, on visions of fame and fortune.) But the moment they'd all stood quietly in front of the Stones beside him, hearing its language, they'd all understood. It had to be this way. And the weird thing was, he'd known exactly when and where to find Darla Knight when the time came to get her, even though when he'd received that information, like a signal from outer space, the date and time had still been months away.

Willa was sure it couldn't possibly happen the way he'd said, but Darla Knight had come strolling across Main Street from the hotel at exactly seven-twenty-one P.M. on Gate Night just like he'd been told by the Stones, and he'd glanced back at Willa with an *I-told-you-so* look and gunned the engine, peeling out from the snowy patch where they'd parked and slamming on the brakes beside Darla herself.

A small part of him still hadn't believed they would find her at that time at all, that the time would pass and it would all turn out to have been just something he'd made up in his head—the schizophrenic, auditory hallucinations Willa had suggested. When Darla stepped out of the hotel, he'd almost considered she might be a hallucination herself. She was certainly a *vision*: as sexy as she'd ever been in her movies and in any of the dirty films that played in Darryl's mind when he fantasized about her.

Snatching her up had been far easier than any of them anticipated, even though the Stones had assured Darryl it would be. She'd put up a bit of a struggle, but once they'd gotten her in the van it was easy enough to subdue her. Everyone played their parts just like they'd all practiced in the weeks leading up to it, even Willa, who'd been worried about grabbing her right in front of the diner, as if Will Crampton or one of her coworkers might walk by and somehow recognize her even with the ski mask on.

But no one had, and finally the moment had arrived that

Darryl had been seeing visions of ever since he'd first discovered the Stones. He'd known Elana and the two keeners would leave before nightfall tonight just like they had every night, and he knew they wouldn't return tomorrow because he'd heard both Elana and the dweebs saying they had Halloween plans. Even if he hadn't overheard them, the Stones had promised it.

And so, at just past nine o'clock on the night before Halloween, he and the others stood in a semicircle in front of the Stones, in front of *Darla fucking Knight*, each of them wearing the black cloaks they'd gotten for the "ritual" from the Dollar-Save Pharmacy. Darryl and Max Strick held video cameras just like they had in his visions. The cave was pure dark aside from the beams of their flashlights and the lights on the cameras, but Darryl had never felt less afraid in his life.

This was his Big Moment. This was his time to *shine*.

"Now," Darryl said, thumbing the Record button and bringing the viewfinder up to his right eye. "Let's find out just how loud our li'l Scream Queen can get."

CHAPTER 5

1

10:40 A.M., October 31st, 2001
Crooks Corner Secondary School

Cody rushed out of English early and got to comm class while Mr. Hildebrand was still cleaning up from the previous lessons, a few minor niners straggling in the hall by the door. He'd fretted all morning about what Hildebrand might say after catching him and the guys egging and TPing Miss Stabler's house the night before. Would he tell Coach? Would he send him to the principal's office? Get him kicked out of school?

He wished he'd never let Brunt and the guys convince him to do Gate Night with them, but the truth was he hadn't needed convincing. He'd been needing to unwind for a while, with his folks pressuring him about getting into college and worries about scholarships and "giving one-hundred and ten percent this year" as Coach would say, in class and on the field. It was just bad luck Brunt had chosen to prank Miss Stabler, and that Mr. Hildebrand had been there. Cody liked Miss Stabler just fine. He'd felt bad enough messing up her house before he'd discovered Hildebrand had been there with her.

"Oh, hey, Cody," Hildebrand said as he turned from wiping down the blackboard.

"Hey, Mr. Hildebrand."

"Call me Renny."

"Okay," Cody said, though he knew he'd likely still call him Mr. Hildebrand. "Listen, about last night—"

Hildebrand sat on the edge of his desk the way he liked to, which had always struck Cody as trying too hard to be cool. "About that," he said with a heavy sigh. "What you saw..."

"Oh," Cody said, surprised. He'd expected to be reprimanded but now it looked like Hildebrand was more uncomfortable than him. "You mean..."

"Yes. We can keep that between the two of us, right? You won't tell any of your friends or anything?"

"Of course, Mr. Hildebrand. Only..."

Hildebrand's shoulders sagged. "Adam Brunt."

"Yeah. He's got a big mouth. I can try to convince him to keep quiet, but he probably won't."

"Even if you tell him Miss Stabler and I were considering telling Principal Elder?"

"Yeah, then he'd prob'ly just do it out of spite."

"Right," Hildebrand said. "Well, hopefully—"

Brittany entered the room, hugging her bookbag. She looked at the two of them and narrowed her eyes, stopping just inside the door. "Wait... were you just talking about me?"

"We weren't talking about you, Brittany. We were just discussing something personal between Mr. Brockmeyer and myself."

"Oooookay." She hustled between them to her desk at the front and sat down, then began taking out her notebook and pens and methodically laying them down on the desk.

"Go ahead and take your seat, Cody."

"Thanks, Mr. Hildebrand. We're good, right?"

Mr. Hildebrand nodded. "We're good."

While Cody sat at his desk in the back, the others showed up and went to theirs. After a while Mr. Hildebrand told everyone to get into their groups, and the screech of desk footings and chairs filled the room.

Jay seemed excited. "I made a title sequence for the movie last night. It's not one-hundred precent there but I think it looks pretty neat."

Brittany jotted something down on a fresh sheet of paper not covered in the weird spirals she constantly drew.

"*Neat*," Walden repeated snarkily.

"Oh, I called Mr. Thompson about shooting at the farm tonight, but he said you already asked him last night, Brit."

Brittany stopped writing. She didn't correct him for calling her Brit like she had yesterday, and for a long moment she didn't say anything while the others looked at her, awaiting her response.

"Oh, yeah. I called the Thompsons last night," she said, with a distracted tone as she began drawing a spiral in the corner of the page. *Scribble, scribble, scribble* as the circles grew smaller and smaller and smaller. Cody watched the pen swirl, almost as if he was hypnotized. Then he blinked rapidly and looked up to the front of the class, catching Mr. Hildebrand watching him over the top of his book.

"Hey, did you guys feel that earthquake yesterday?" Walden asked during the silence.

"I did," Brittany said eagerly, seemingly just glad to have the subject changed.

Cody frowned. "Earthquake? In Crooks Corner?"

"Yeah. Musta been just after four o'clock."

"I was on the field," Cody said. The only things he might have noticed tremoring were the bleachers, the chain-link fence and goal posts, and those were so rooted in the ground they probably wouldn't have moved short of a bulldozer.

"I felt it, too," Cassandra said with a relieved sigh.

The others turned to Jay, who sank behind his desk with his arms across his chest. "What? I didn't feel anything."

"He was probably beating off and thought the world moved," Cassandra said.

Brittany snorted laughter, then covered her mouth with a hand.

"So funny I forgot to laugh," Jay said, his cheeks turning red. "You guys wanna see this title sequence, or what?"

2

IT TOOK A BIT OF WRANGLING, but Jay finally managed to get everyone gathered around the Edit 1 computer to show them the title sequence he'd brought in on a Zip drive. He was pretty proud of the work he'd put in, using a pirated version of Adobe After Effects from Limewire to superimpose the credits over some sinister-looking footage of the town he'd borrowed from their news intros. He slowed and inversed the colors to make it look creepy, with a horror theme that sounded like jack-in-the-box music he'd gotten from the Killer Tracks music library, and ghostly moans beneath it.

When he'd finished it all this morning before the school bus picked him up, he was sure they'd love it. They'd all want to be friends with him and maybe even hang out after school, playing videogames, or whatever normies did.

Wish in one hand, shit in the other, kid. His dad used to say this to him when he was in one of his down periods, before they'd hauled Rider Nielson off to the looney bin. *Wish in one hand, shit in the other.* Jay had never really understood the phrase back then, but he did now, with both hands full of shit.

The title of the movie zoomed toward the screen over a static shot of the Thompson farm, burning flames flicking off the text, and Cody actually said, "*Whoa...*" For the *O* in *HellOween*, Jay had used the symbol they'd been talking about, the one he'd seen spraypainted all over town. It had looked dumb without it, like saying *Hello* to someone named Ween, and hyphens bracketing the *O* made it feel too much like a cereal brand or something. The effect seemed to impress Cody, and since he was the one who'd come up with the title, Jay felt a swell of pride. He'd guzzled two cans of Rockstar and put in two or three hours of work after dinner making it look just right, so it was good to see that work pay off.

"That actually does look wicked," Cassandra said.

"*Seriously,*" Walden agreed. "I take back what I said about the title, Cody. That's rad as hell."

"'Rad,'" Cody said with a smirk.

"Thanks, you guys."

"Wait, can you go back?" Brittany said sharply, holding her pen and notebook to her chest. "It says 'Directed by Jay Nielson.'"

"We can change whatever," Jay said, though he thought he was probably the only one capable of directing it, aside from maybe Brittany. "It's just a template. Anyway, I put you as the producer, which is even better than director."

"How is producer better than director?" Walden said skeptically. "Scorsese, Kubrick, Lynch, Tarantino..."

Jay waited patiently while Walden listed off a few more famous directors. Then he asked, "Who accepts the Best Picture award at the Oscars?"

The group looked at each other, unsure.

"The producers," Jay answered. "Not the director. They have their own award, but the award for the *overall movie* goes to the producer. Get it?"

Brittany tapped the notebook with her pen. "That's a good point."

Walden shook his head. "But nobody *knows* any producers."

"The Weinsteins. Sam Goldwyn. Jerry Bruckheimer. Joel Silver. Rob Reiner. Don Simpson."

"Nobody who's not a *huge nerd*," Walden clarified, though Jay knew for a fact that Walden knew more about it than he did.

"Whatever. It doesn't matter. If we can't decide who does what we can put the roles into a hat and pick that way."

"Or we could all direct," Cody said.

"We can't *all* direct," he said. "Too many chiefs, not enough Indians."

Brittany tsked, glancing at Walden for some reason. "That's not very P.C., Jason."

"Too many cooks in the kitchen then. *Jeez*. Like I said, it's just a template. Whoever ends up doing what, I'll change it."

"You guys okay over there?" Mr. Hildebrand called, a look of concern furrowing his brow as he wrote names on the chalkboard for the news rotation.

"We're good, Mr. H," Cody said. "We are good, right?"

Walden nodded. "Yeah. It's cool. Right, Jay?"

"Sure," Jay said bitterly, just glad they weren't still talking about the earthquake. The fact that what he'd seen at Mr. Combs's house had coincided timewise with what the rest of the group was calling an "earthquake" made him worry what Mr. Combs had invented was even more dangerous and possibly sinister than he'd thought. He'd barely been able to sleep last night because of what he'd seen, so he'd stayed up drinking Rockstar energy drinks while working on the credits. He was zonked today, but he aimed to catch a nap after school since Mr. Combs didn't need him today, and meet up with everyone at the haunt.

"Okay, guys," Mr. Hildebrand said. "Let's set up for the news run-through. Your positions are listed on the board."

While everyone headed over to the board, Jay popped out his Zip drive and followed reluctantly.

3

WHAT THEY DISCOVERED during the news run-through was enough to take Brittany's mind off what would inevitably happen tonight, and what had happened in the car last night with her mom.

The drive had been silent until Denise had prodded her to hash it out, and Brittany had exploded, bringing up all of her mother's past transgressions and mistakes. Denise had sat there and taken it, at least until they pulled into the garage. At which point she'd put the car in park, turned off the engine and quietly turned to her daughter of seventeen years.

"Brittany, I know you're mad at me for taking the car away but what you did..." She closed her eyes and pinched the bridge of her nose, the way she did when she was irrationally upset. Exactly the way she had the night she'd confronted Brittany with her concerns about what she'd done. "You can't just *do* something like that and expect not to face any consequences."

"You said I could be *anything* I wanted to be when I grow up. Were you just *lying* to me?"

"No, of course not, sweetie. Your father and I... we just didn't expect *that* to be what you'd choose. Although, I suppose we should've seen the signs..."

"So you *were* lying."

"We weren't *lying*, honey. Your father and I will try to understand and support you no matter what you do, but you have to understand, we can't just let things like that go on *under our own roof* with no consequences."

"Dad *does* support me. And it wasn't under your roof."

"Your father has his reasons for being more forgiving than I am. It's just... after what you did, it's going to take some time, Brittany. And until then, we'll drive you wherever you need to go."

"But *why*—?"

"*You took the car.* Do you have any idea what could happen to you—to *us*—if someone found out where you went?"

"I was *careful*."

"All it takes is *one* person seeing you to tear down *everything* your father and I have worked so hard to build. The house, the business, the horses, your brother's education—everything, gone." She snapped her fingers. "Just like that."

The words had hit Brittany pretty hard. Of course, she'd known the potential consequences when she'd done it, but she'd researched and planned so thoroughly she'd thought herself untouchable. Denise was right, though. Even on the backroads with only a few houses dotting the landscape every mile or so, anyone could've been looking out their window and happened to see her shiny silver car pass by. She'd been sloppy, and she needed to be more cautious in the future.

Is that who that creep in the K-car was last night? she thought, sitting behind the news desk writing her script for the news. She was co-anchoring with Cody this week, which meant she had to write her own teleprompter script, but she lacked the focus.

Did someone see you? Is he a detective?

Cool it with that nonsense, honeypie. You were smart. You did good. Just 'cause Denise don't see it, don't make it not so. You can sign that on the dotted line.

Even with his reassurance, Brittany began to sweat under the studio lights. "Do the lights *need* to be on right now, Josh?" she called out to this week's floor director, shading her eyes.

"Sorry!"

The lights flicked off, and Brittany let out a relieved sigh before looking at the page before her. Everyone had either experienced or heard about the earthquake from a friend or family member, so of course it had to be the top story. But the page she'd written on was so thoroughly covered in spirals she could barely read anything she'd written. She must've been drawing them the entire time she'd been thinking about the conversation with her mother last night.

The pencil snapped in her hand. She'd been pressing it so tightly against the page and hadn't even noticed it.

"You all right, Brit?" Cody said, glancing at her warily from the co-anchor seat.

"I'm fine," she said calmly, tearing the page out of her notebook and slipping it into her bookbag.

But Brittany wasn't fine. With her fellow students about to

discover her shameful secret—that she worked at Halloween Village, a *part-time job* just like these plebs—and her parents knowing her *other* dark secret, she was anything but fine.

Turn that frown upside-down, she told herself for the hundredth time that day. And if anyone happened to be looking at her in that exact moment they would've seen the portrait of happiness, even though inside there was nothing but terror and simmering rage.

4

RENNY HILDEBRAND PLOPPED down with his Michelina's Fettucine Alfredo across from Ernie Combs and Elana in the teacher's lounge. He tore off the lid the rest of the way, spiked a forkful and blew on it before wolfing it down. "Did, um, either of you feel that earthquake yesterday? It was all my kids could talk about in class today."

Elana and Combs exchanged a brief look. Combs choked on his food, then cleared his throat and wiped the corners of his lips with a napkin. "Earthquake?" he asked finally, putting the napkin down beside his microwaveable bowl.

"Yeah. I forgot about it, actually. I was grading assignments and my whole apartment just started shaking. I thought it was just a big truck driving past but there was nothing when I went to look."

Elana brought her tomato sandwich to her lips and took a small bite. She ate like a rabbit, which Renny found insanely adorable. "About what time was that?" she said in a casual tone.

"I just got home so probably just before four? Maybe right after? Do you get quakes here often?"

Again, Elana and Combs shared a look, though it didn't appear to be anxious this time. "We have small tremors," Combs said. "Being so close to the White Mountains it's inevitable. Though historically, I don't believe many are high enough on the Richter magnitude scale to be felt, per se."

"I can't remember the last one," Elana said. "Mathematically speaking, I'd say it's improbable that anyone would have felt it. That said, if you and your students say you all felt one..."

Again, she looked at Combs. Renny was getting a strange

vibe from the two of them and if he didn't know better—if Combs was actually interested in anything but science—he might've suspected something was going on between them. Maybe it was a private joke. Or maybe, and this was more likely, it was something an out-of-towner like himself wasn't likely to get.

Whatever it was, he didn't dwell on it for long. He and Elana had planned a night at the movies and a bottle of wine at her house after.

Elana caught his eye across the table and gave him a slight smile. Renny waited for Combs to look away before he returned it.

We need to stop slinking around behind everyone's backs and just tell people about us already, he thought. Elana wasn't ready for that, which made him wonder if she was ashamed of him for some reason or another. Sometimes he felt like this whole town was a cult, one he'd never be allowed to join—not until Elana vouched for him by going public with their love.

Either way, now that Adam Brunt knew, the decision to tell their colleagues and Principal Elder might be made for them. It was unlikely that shit-disturber would keep his mouth shut for long, then the rumor mill would start, and before long Elder would be calling them into her office to confirm whether or not they were true.

Maybe it was for the best. If they made it official, they wouldn't have to sneak around anymore. They'd already planned to go to the Grand tonight for the big event, but now they could go together instead of arriving separately and meeting in their seats. He could put his arm around her instead of slyly holding her hand or touching her knee like some pimple-faced kid with a fluffy teen mustache. They could actually *be seen* together after the movies, could even go across the street to the Eateria for a Coke and some fries and act like a real couple in public.

Elana would never go for it. Not now. There was more at stake for her being a woman, and separated but still not divorced from her ex. Male students would probably high-five Renny, and even some of their colleagues might congratulate him. But the whisper network would be unbearable for Elana. She'd freaked out when he'd come back to bed last night just hearing that Brunt and Cody had spotted him at her door.

In a way, he envied his students. Living on the edge of seventeen as the song went, cares like these weren't a part of their vocabulary. They had different troubles, of course, ones he didn't envy, but for most of them those difficulties would feel pretty silly looking back on them in ten or fifteen years.

No, he and Elana would have to keep their secret a little longer. At least until his late mother's engagement ring had been resized and he found the right opportunity to get down on one knee.

"What?" Elana said, self-consciously wiping her lips with a paper napkin. "Have I got something on my face?"

Renny realized he must've been staring and shook his head vigorously. Combs—who usually seemed to be oblivious to normal human interactions—seemed to notice and glanced between the two of them, then shrugged and resumed eating.

"Nope," Renny replied, faking indifference by returning to his own lunch, hoping to deflect the suspicion.

Maybe it's nothing to do with me, he thought. *Maybe it's this "top-secret" project they've been working on together after school.*

Renny ate his lunch in silence, comforted in the thought that everything between himself and Elana was fine.

Whatever the reason she and Combs were acting weird, Renny thought it was about time Elana told him more about what they'd been doing in Ernie Combs's garage.

Chapter 6

1

Cody and Jay got a ride to the Thompson farm in Walden's beat-up Chevy Nova, and the girls had promised to meet up with them at the haunt a bit later. Neither had said why they didn't want to tag along, but there wasn't enough room for five of them in the car anyhow with all the gear, so it suited the boys fine. Brittany was cute and all, but Cody didn't really want her sitting on his lap, since she'd probably complain the whole time. And Cassandra would probably rather ride in the trunk, or claim if she didn't get the front seat it was because of religious persecution, like the Salem Witch Trials all over again.

"What's shakin, Kevin Bacon?" Walden asked Cody when they picked him up from school after practice.

"Kevin Bacon?" Cody said with a bemused grin as he slipped into the front passenger seat. The car smelled like cigarettes and Walden's cologne: Preferred Stock, if Cody's nose was right. Jay sat in the back with some of the equipment heaped beside him like Walden was his personal chauffer.

"He asked me, 'What up, Billy Crudup?' I don't even know who that is."

Walden looked genuinely disturbed. "You haven't seen *Sleepers? Almost Famous?*"

Jay rolled his eyes. "Those are movie titles, I'm guessing?"

While Walden launched into a tirade about the "new classics" of modern cinema, Cody reached into the front pocket of his jeans for the half-empty pack of Arctic Chill. He popped a piece into his mouth and held up the pack for the others. "Hey, you guys want gum?" They both said no. He shoved it back in his pocket.

"Hey, Walden," Jay said in the back, seemingly done with their little spat. "What's all this?"

Walden glanced in the rearview. "All what?"

"In the box. Looks like those monster puppet things from the '80s."

"Oh! I was supposed to drop those off at the theater."

Cody's ears had perked up at Jay's comment. *You have Boglins?*"

"Sort of," Walden said. "It's promotional stuff for that late showing of *Ragers in Space* tonight. Hopefully we'll get this shit done early and I can drive em over."

"Lemme see one?"

Jay picked one out of the box and handed it to Cody. They looked almost exactly like the single-color Mini Boglins from the early '90s that Chimney'd had a bunch of back in the day, except that they were squishable and more like those Madball toys Chimney's older brother had. Cody squeezed it a few times, considered stuffing it into his pocket, then decided against it and tossed it back into the box.

When they arrived at the farm, it was just after four and still quite bright out, which worked well as they needed to do a lot of coverage shots and some interviews with the Thompsons and their crew before dark. The plan was to make it look like a real documentary until a little after sunset, when the haunt opened. Then they would pretend an actual serial killer was out to get them, using the haunt as a cover for his murders. They would take turns playing the killer with a couple of hooded black cloaks and a prop knife Brittany had borrowed from the drama closet. It was getting brisk out so Cody looked forward to playing the killer for an added layer of clothing, but also because it would be more fun than playing the victim, since he wasn't all that great at acting and could hide his facial expressions behind the cloak.

The haunt actors and tech crew were standing out front in full costume while Mrs. Thompson chatted with them. Most hadn't had their makeup done, or held their masks at their side. One—a spooky-looking female clown—caught Cody's eye for a moment before quickly looking away. Even under the makeup, he was pretty sure he recognized her. Since he'd practically seen everyone in town at one or another of his games, it didn't narrow it down much.

"I saw you last night outside the theater," Cody said to Walden as they began unloading the gear.

Walden lugged the big camera bag out of the back and handed it to Cody. "Boss made us wear costumes. Pretty lame."

"I forgot you worked there." Cody laid the bag at his feet and unzipped it. "Must be a pretty cool job."

Walden shrugged a single shoulder. "It's not bad. We get two free movie passes every week and free soda and popcorn on shift."

"That's phat," Cody said, and immediately felt like a doofus for saying it. Walden glanced at him with a smirk but said nothing.

"We'll take turns shooting once we start making the actual movie," Jay interrupted, pushing past Cody to grab the tripod. "I'll shoot the interviews. Cody, you can do audio."

"You mean I get to hold the boom mic."

"You've got more arm strength, it's only logical."

Walden nodded. "He's got a point, man."

"Fine," Cody said. He just wanted to be helpful, and Jay was better at camera than him anyhow. Cody usually got easily distracted and forgot when to zoom in and out and when to pan, simple things that were important for a camera operator. "What about the girls?"

"Well, when they *get* here, one of them can ask questions and the other can write up the shot-list."

Cody wasn't sure he liked Jay taking charge, but at least he seemed to be on the ball. He figured Brittany would take over once she got here, regardless. But having worked with her before, he wasn't sure who he'd rather take directions from. Jay was a jerk, but Brittany could be pretty strict.

Walden popped a battery on the Panasonic Broadcast AG DVC10 and hoisted it onto his shoulder. It was a pretty decent semi-pro camera, and they'd all made silly short films with them earlier in the semester, so they were pretty familiar with how they worked. At the very least they all knew how to point and shoot.

Cody carried the lights and light gear, Walden the camera, tapes and extra batteries, along with his own handheld in a camera bag slung over his shoulder, and Jay followed behind them with the tripod and cables. As they approached the crowd of teenagers, twenty-somethings and some older veteran actors from the outdoor theater company, the group grew quiet. A few were smoking cigarettes. Cody noticed the girl he'd spotted earlier appeared to be hiding behind some of the taller people, possibly deliberately.

"Holy shit, that's Brittany!" Walden said, just as Cody realized it himself.

Jay hurried a few steps to catch up to them. "Where?"

"The clown in the back," Cody said. "I can't believe she's working here."

Jay huffed. "I can't believe she's got a job."

"No wonder she got all weird about this place," Walden said. "She probably didn't want us to know."

"Why not?"

"Because her dad owns the three biggest car dealerships in the area. She's a spoiled rich kid who doesn't need to work like the rest of us. Probably thinks it's degrading."

"Maybe she's trying to beef up her resumé for college," Cody suggested.

"What college would get hyped seeing 'Halloween haunt actor' on an application? Besides, she's basically Tracy Flick."

"Who's Tracy Flick?" Jay asked.

Walden shook his head in contempt.

"Hey, Mrs. Thompson," Cody said as they reached the group. "These are my friends, Walden and Jay."

"Hey there, Cody. How ya doin?" Mrs. Thompson was a heavyset woman with typically rosy cheeks like Cody's own, though hers were currently covered in gray makeup, prosthetics and gore. She turned to her actors: a mass of creepy clowns, a few skeletons in raggedy clothes, a hillbilly cannibal family (of which Mrs. Thompson seemed to be the matriarch), a couple of psycho nurses whose uniforms were splashed with fake blood, a handful of ghosts without their masks, a few scarecrows, some men and women in forest camo, who looked more like they were supposed to be Army than hunters, and others. All in all, there were about twenty or more. "These are the documentary boys I told you all about," Mrs. Thompson said. "They'll be askin if ya'll want to do interviews but feel free to say no, if you're not comfortable in front of the camera."

"Oh yeah, we're all real camera-shy, Mrs. T.," one of the older guys said. This got a big laugh from the actors.

Mrs. Thompson tsked. "Figured as much. All right, supper's in an hour, go on and get your makeup done and we'll meet up then."

As most of the actors began to saunter off toward the house, Cody and the other two followed them. The Thompson farm had two large barns, two stables and a grain silo. The new barn and stable were further back and held the livestock. The old barn, stable and silo were kept specifically for the haunt and were where some of the best scares could be found. The silo was supposedly especially terrifying, though it didn't seem like much when it was explained as just a pitch-black space with what Mrs. Thompson had called an "overload for the other senses."

The house quickly became a hub of activity. In the living and dining rooms, the furniture had been removed to make space. Several cast members sat in folding chairs getting makeup sprayed on and prosthetics applied by students from the beauty school downtown. The ones who weren't stood by waiting, chatting, laughing, and what Cody could only describe as practicing their scare faces.

"Let's get a few shots of this," Jay said, setting up the tripod in an out of the way corner with a view of both rooms. Walden screwed the camera onto the mount, and Cody plugged the microphone into the audio jack, then stuck the mic into the grip at the end of the telescoping boom pole. They were practically experts already, having set up for hockey and baseball games as well as local and school news stories multiple times. Whether or not they were actually decent at performing the tasks once they got everything set up was another thing.

While Jay took some pans and zooms of the bustle, Walden got out his home MiniDV camera and started filming Cody and Jay. After a bit, Jay noticed and shot him an irritated look.

"What are you doing?" he snapped.

"Shooting the doc about the documentary," Walden replied. "We can splice my footage into the movie, or we can just use it as behind-the-scenes stuff for the DVD."

"*DVD*," Jay said skeptically. "Okay, Tarantino."

"Guys," Cody jumped in. "We should probably get some interviews, huh?"

"We should interview Brittany first," Walden suggested.

Cody spotted her sitting alone in a corner of the dining room, writing something in her notebook, or maybe doodling those spirals like she did in class. "Don't be a dick," he said, then he grinned. "She can do the interviews for us."

"Good idea." Walden grinned slyly and left them without another word, weaving through the crowd to get her.

"It's not fair she's working while we do the project," Jay said as he panned the camera across the room for the tenth time, zooming in on something of interest. "And where's Cassandra?"

"I dunno, maybe we should call her house. Oh hey, Mr. Thompson."

The big man lumbered over, dressed as the patriarch of the cannibal family, with round glasses and a corncob pipe. He clapped Cody on the shoulder with his grimy fingers. "How many times I hafta tell ya, Cody? Call me Chet. Who's your friends?"

"That's Jay, and over there is Walden. You already met Brit, I guess."

"Brittany's been a treat. Real fine gal. A *spark plug*, my pops woulda called her—rest his soul."

Walden said something to Brittany that made her frown. She closed her book angrily, then composed herself, putting on a fake-looking smile.

"You boys got the run of the farm," Mr. Thompson said. "Shoot wherever you like, just not the upstairs here. We don't let anyone go upstairs, 'cept to the toilet."

Cody remembered from when he'd pick corn in June and July, they were very informal and allowed the boys "the run of the farm," as Mr. Thompson had said, but they were particular about not letting anyone upstairs. Made the other boys wonder if they had a sex dungeon or a weird shrine to Britney Spears or something up there. Cody just figured they were private about their actual living space, which seemed pretty reasonable.

One of the makeup artists called Mr. Thompson over and he left them with a friendly, "See you boys around."

After a bit, Walden returned with a reluctant Brittany in tow. "Hey, guys," she said cheerily, but her expression was joyless, unless it was the scary clown makeup making it seem that way. "Chet said I could show you around the haunt and help with the interviews."

"Cool," Cody said. "It must be cool working here."

She shrugged. "Not really. It's just something to put on my admission resumé."

Cody gave Walden a *told-you-so* look. Walden just shrugged.

"Let's get started interviewing," she said. "I know exactly who to talk to first." She turned and waved in the direction of the makeup artists. "Hi, Layla! Hi, Jerry! Could we do an interview with you two for our class project?"

The makeup artist and the scarecrow she was painting both agreed, and the boys picked up the camera gear to shoot it.

2

BRITTANY HAD SEETHED SILENTLY as Walden called her out, required to grin and bear it or risk looking like a psycho in front of all her colleagues and new friends. She knew she should've just pulled off the Band-Aid, that attempting to hide would just make it worse. Instead, she assured herself they wouldn't recognize her, and when they saw her in class tomorrow and asked where she'd been, she'd tell them she'd come down with a 24-hour flu or something stupid like that. Unfortunately, Cody and Walden had recognized her despite the full makeup, and Walden had gotten pretty pissed, but it was nothing compared to how she felt getting called a "spoiled princess" at work.

Once she joined the boys, they taped a bunch of interviews and she took them on a tour of the grounds. She figured they probably would've stood around like lumps on a log if she hadn't taken charge. Jay was far too shy to start conversations with strangers—even if he thought he was above everyone else, he was still a scared little boy at heart—and Cody probably would've asked dumb questions. Walden would've just kept shooting it all like the creepy plastic bag kid from *American Beauty*, probably reveling in their ineptitude. He'd claim it was some kind of cinema-verité thing and get an A+ from Hildebrand.

Brittany threw on her coat and took them out to the barn, a

maze of narrow, dark hallways—fully lit as they did the tour—which led to rooms made to look like a stereotypical serial killer family's house, with a small lab, and a dungeon where Cindy and two older women from the theater played zombie prisoners. She was one of several who roamed the halls, following people around, whispering whatever creepy things came into her head and screaming at them. They marveled at the mirror maze leading to the exit before she led them to the silo—which wasn't much to look at without the sounds and lights— where she described how things would look when the sun went down and customers arrived.

"Where's Cassandra?" she asked as they left the silo, heading for the corn maze next.

"Nobody knows," Cody said, the boom pole leaned against his shoulder as they trudged across the squelching lawn that acted as a graveyard. Jay practically tiptoed, sneering and grunting in disgust every couple of steps. The four of them weaved between graves where rotting hands sprung up from the dirt like macabre flowers, and coffins that would be shrouded in mist and spooky green lighting at night. When it rained this was the worst place to be working, aside from in the corn maze and the parking lot, where a few of them roamed waiting for people to scare when they left their cars. They were expecting another light dusting of snow in a few hours, which would suck even harder, absolute hell on the people out here. Brittany typically wished she had the freedom to roam the grounds like them, but she was glad she'd be working in the barn tonight.

"Be nice if she called one of us to let us know," she said, even though she'd prepared to leave them in the lurch herself.

"True dat," Cody said.

Walden chuckled derisively and pointed his camera at Cody, who kept on walking, oblivious or just not caring. Sometimes Brittany envied him. He seemed oblivious to a lot of his flaws and generally just easygoing and care-free, where Brittany pretty much had to rehearse all the things she wanted to say to people throughout the day, and sometimes even practice smiling in the mirror to make sure it reached her eyes, like her former therapist suggested.

"Shit!" Jay said, stepping out of a small puddle and shaking his wet shoe. "Got a fucking soaker. There's a path right over there, you guys."

"It's faster this way," Brittany said. She was wearing the boots for her costume and didn't care about the muck. After a few more grumbles from Jay they reached the entrance to the corn field.

"I never understood why corn mazes are supposed to be scary," Cody said, looking up at the stalks with a big smile. Brittany recalled he was a corn picker for the Thompsons in the summer. Most farms used big combine harvesters these days, but the Thompsons needed their stalks intact for the maze, so they hired local boys and girls to pick them under the hot sun.

"Okay, Cornholio," Walden said.

Brittany ignored the comment. "Do you want me to take you into the maze? There's this big pole in the middle where Bill, one of the scarecrows, waits for people and scares the crap out of them. It's not much otherwise."

Jay shrugged. "Nah. It'll be better at night."

"Yeah, let's come back when it's dark," Walden agreed, pointing his camera toward the entrance and trudging slowly toward it while tilting his head and the camera for what Mr. Hildebrand called a "Dutch angle"—which had caused one of the burnouts in class to say *Dutch rudder*, causing kids who knew what it meant to laugh. "Actually, if you three walk into the maze like you're going in there to shoot, that'd be cool."

"'And they were never seen again,'" Cody said, getting it. "Good idea."

"It better not be mucky," Jay grumbled.

Cody looked back. "It's gonna be mucky, just get over it."

Brittany shrugged and led Cody and a reluctant Jay into the maze. "This is the corn maze," she said, improvising as they walked down the first stretch toward a fork in the maze. Corn stalks swayed in a brisk breeze on either side of them. "Two of our actors chase guests in here with a chainsaw and an axe. You have to get to the middle and solve the riddle if you want to be entered into the nightly draw. It's a new riddle every night." She turned toward the exit, calling out, "*Was that good?*" But Walden wasn't there. "Where'd Walden go?"

The corn began to rustle a few rows to their left. Brittany startled as the laughter of children arose from the same spot.

"Let's get out of here," she said, turning to go.

Cody gave her a shrewd look, standing in her way. "Come on. You planned this."

"The Thompsons didn't hire any child actors. Get out of my—"

"Then it's a recording," Jay said, looking a little on edge.

"There's no scares *out here*, Jay. It's just the clown and the cannibal and the scarecrow running around chasing people. Walden?" she called out again, pushing Cody out of the way.

"What?" Walden shouted from up ahead, stepping into the maze entrance as Brittany trudged toward it.

"Was that you?" Cody asked, following behind her.

Walden gave them a confused look. "Was *what* me?"

"Just now." Brittany had gotten just about enough of Walden with his Burt Reynolds mustache and stupid trucker cap. "Shaking the stalks and laughing," she said.

"It couldn't have been him laughing," Jay said from a little ways behind her. "It sounded like kids. *Plural*."

"I was getting some more shots of the graveyard. You heard *kids*?"

Cody nodded, stepping out of the corn behind her. "That's what it sounded like."

"You know there's an urban legend about the woods just behind the cornfield," Walden said, peering past them at the entrance.

"*Rural* legend," Cody corrected him.

"Whatever, bozo. Anyway, back in the '60s, two kids went out there to play one morning. I think it was off the Hamburg farm, actually, but near here. They were twins, a little boy and girl. The two of them went out one day and never came back. People searched for weeks. Apparently, an escaped mental patient from the old psychiatric hospital in Concord was found in the woods a little while later, but still no sign of the kids. He was living out there in some cave, I heard. They took him back to the asylum but he never said a word about the kids."

"That never happened," Brittany snapped.

"Look it up. Ask Jeeves or something."

"Nobody uses Ask Jeeves anymore," Jay said matter-of-factly. "Google's the most used search engine now."

Walden stroked his mustache aggravatedly. "Maybe we

should start calling you Google since you know *everything*." He turned back to Brittany. "Seriously, though, it's a real thing. They never found their bodies or anything."

"How come none of us ever heard of it?" Cody said.

"Maybe people from that time didn't talk about it. How would I know?"

Brittany watched the three of them cautiously. Mention of the cave had gotten her hackles up, making the spirals swirls in her mind.

The Snake was asleep but talk of the cave would rouse him soon. She had to think of something quick, before he woke and took over entirely, made her do something bad. Made her do something she couldn't take back.

The wind rustled the corn behind her again in the nick of time, causing a chill to run up her spine. "Whatever," she said decisively. "Let's just get back to the house. It's frickin' freezing out here."

"Mr. Bigglesworth," Cody added cryptically.

Walden laughed as she trudged off down the path with her arms across her chest. She didn't even care if the others followed her, she just wanted to get out of there as quickly and quietly as possible.

Soon, The Snake would come out whether she wanted it to or not.

There was work to be done tonight, under the cover of darkness. Work she didn't want to do, but had to be done. No matter how terrible it would be, and no matter the repercussions.

She didn't exactly know how she'd pull it off, or why The Snake needed it to happen, but when he wanted something done, it was easier for her to just go along with it. Fighting him only made him angry.

And making him angry led to worse.

Much worse.

3

JUST MY LUCK, Cassandra thought miserably.

She'd planned to get a ride to Halloween Village with her friend Mariska, but Mariska didn't show up to school this morning, and when Cassandra called her house once she'd gotten home herself, Mariska's mom said she was too sick to go anywhere tonight.

Meaning Cassandra didn't have a ride to Halloween Village.

Also meaning the rest of the group would kill her tomorrow if she didn't call the Thompsons and tell them to pass on the message that she couldn't make it out there unless someone— meaning Walden, since he was the only one with a car now that Brittany apparently didn't drive anymore—would have to pick her up. Unfortunately, no one she knew had a cell phone or a beeper, aside from Paul Preston, and he only had it to deal weed.

It was clear she couldn't just back out. They were counting on her. But how else was she supposed to get there without a ride? It was like ten minutes outside of town. A walk that far would probably take her at least an hour. Maybe Grammy would give her some money for a cab there and she could bum a ride off someone else to get home. Hell, she'd sit in one of the boys' laps if she had to, or ride in the trunk like a dead hooker.

Cassandra was still standing in the kitchen by the phone she'd just hung up when Taylor snapped a picture, nearly blinding her. She moaned, covering her eyes. "Quit it, Taylor, I'm not in the mood." Wandering into the living room, she blinked away the dark spots in her vision.

"We haven't played Humphrey yet," Taylor said.

"Not today, shrimp," Cassandra said, walking past her sister, who was already dressed like a little ghost girl. "I've got bigger fish to fry."

"Shrimps aren't fish."

Cassandra ignored her and thumped up the stairs. Grammy was watching *Passions*. In today's episode Tabitha and her doll-turned-real-boy Timmy had arrived uninvited to a wedding. The silver-haired man—she could never remember the names of the other characters despite having watched it with Grammy a bunch of times—told his daughter that wherever Timmy went, trouble seemed to follow. Cassandra grinned, thinking she could say the same about Humphrey.

"Hi, Grammy," she said, deliberately sounding glum.

"Oh, hello, Cassandra, dear," Grammy said, glancing away from her soap. She patted the bed beside her, cushy with her flowery duvet and pillows. "Come sit. We can talk during the commercials."

Cassandra trudged over and slumped down on the bed with a heavy sigh, leaning into her grandmother's heavy bosom. She watched the show not really paying attention until a commercial for laundry detergent came on, and Grammy muted the TV. "What's on your mind, sweetie? Why so glum?"

Cassandra told her about her predicament. Grammy listened patiently until she was done, stroking Cassandra's hair. "Well, it just so happens your sister and her little friend need a chaperone for trick-or-treats tonight. Tommy's mother had to take a shift at the clinic."

Cassandra groaned. "*Mingus the Dingus?*" Tommy Mingus was Taylor's most annoying friend. Cassandra loathed every minute he spent at the house, and even when she locked herself in her room with her music blasting he'd find a way to annoy her.

Grammy clucked her tongue. "That's not nice."

"He's *so annoying*, Grammy."

"Maybe he thinks the same about you."

Cassandra sputtered. "I'm not the one constantly following people around making farts with my armpits and telling dirty jokes."

"Boys will be boys."

"But I *can't* be the babysitter," Cassandra moaned.

"Why not?"

"Because the babysitter always dies first, Grammy. It's like one of the first rules of horror movies."

"Well, lucky for you, this isn't a horror movie."

"It sure feels like it right now," she grumbled.

Grammy sighed. "Cassandra, dear, sometimes in life we have to do things we don't want to do for other people. It's part of growing up."

"I do things I don't wanna do all the time."

"Oh really? Like what?"

"Go to school, talk to people, breathe."

Grammy clucked her tongue. "Oh, my dramatic little pumpkin. Mary Beth will be here to pick you up in an hour, you'd better get your costume ready."

Standing in the doorway, Taylor said *"Yesss!"* and pumped a fist, apparently having been listening the whole time.

"That's not fair, Grammy! I have to do that group project!"

"I'm sure they'll be perfect little angels. Won't you, Taylor?"

"Tommy said he's gonna pull your hair."

"That's it!" Cassandra leaped out of her grandmother's bed.

"Just kidding!" Taylor said hastily, scurrying down the hall as Cassandra chased her to her room, where her door slammed in Cassandra's face.

"This is gonna be a nightmare," Cassandra muttered to herself, leaning against her sister's door. With no other option, she went to her own room to figure out a costume.

4

BY THE TIME the sun went down and the haunt began letting people in, the documentary crew had already gotten at least a brief interview with most of the actors, the tech crew and makeup artists, as well as the Thompsons. Jay was surprised as any of them when Mrs. Thompson—who said to call her "Row, short for Rowena"—confirmed Walden's made-up-sounding story about the two kids who disappeared in the forest back in the 1960s.

"Ayuh, 1969, to be exact," Row Thompson told them with her thick Maine accent, looking directly at the camera like they'd asked her not to do when they started. "Summah of Love. Not in Crooks Corner, though, no suh. Not after them kids went missin. 'Scaped convict, it was, not a mental patient, like ya friend said. I was just a li'l girl then myself. Don't rememba much 'bout the search parties and whatnot 'side from lotsa big picnics in Wyndham Park, but I do 'memba the curfew for us kids. Used to be you'd hurry on home when the dinner bell rang, then be out playin til suppahtime. Not that summah, no suh. Home before the sun went down, and for darn sure no playin in them woods. Friend of mine's brotha went out with a coupla other boys messin 'round, that's who found the lean-to. Had to fess up to bein out in them woods and prob'ly got their hides tanned, but eventually ol' Sheriff Sikes—that's Deputy Sikes's pops, God rest him—he staked out with a coupla his boys and nabbed that sonuvabitch at that li'l teepee he'd been hidin out in, pahdon my

French. Fella said the devil made him do it or some crap, you b'lieve that?"

This stuff was perfect for the movie, and Jay was glad he'd thought to ask her about it. He still thought *Helloween* was kind of a dumb title, but it really did look badass in those opening credits.

Oh shit! he thought suddenly, his heart dropping into this stomach. *I left my Zip drive at school!*

He'd done the graphics for this morning's news broadcast and left the damn thing attached to the computer in the control room. Now he worried Hildebrand or the janitor might unplug it for some reason without dismounting it first, and something might happen to all of his hard work. It was unlikely, but optimism wasn't his strong suit.

If I lose those titles, I'm gonna kill somebody, I swear.

While Cody helped Mrs. Thompson remove her lapel mic after they finished the interview, Walden gave him and Brittany a smug grin.

"Told ya."

Brittany frowned, adding her usual dismissive: "Whatever."

As the sun went down and dark clouds rolled in, bringing a chill with it, Jay and the other boys all headed out to the gate to get quotes from people waiting to get in. Brittany had already begged off to get prepped for the haunt, but she'd promised she would help them out with a kill or two when she got a break.

There had to be a hundred people lined up when they got to the entrance, and more piling out of their cars and trucks in the gravel lot. Many of them were wearing costumes or masks at the very least, adults and children alike, to get a discount on admission and be entered into the draw. The little kids were excited. Jay didn't like kids much, and he'd always considered the major holidays to be for kids, especially Halloween, but as they made their way down the line, Cody asking questions, he began to share their enthusiasm. Maybe this would be fun, after all.

"Well, well, look who it is," Walden said.

A few groups of people down the line, Cassandra stood with a little girl dressed as a ghost he guessed was her sister, since Jay had seen them together a few times in town, and they looked kind of similar aside from the kid not being a goth. That little fart-smeller Tommy Mingus stood with them, holding a plastic trident. His chubby cheeks were rosy from the chill, and he wore a shiny red cape and a forked tail that stuck up in the air, with devil's horns sticking out of his messy hair.

"Yeah, the captain of the dork squad," Tommy replied, pointing at Walden, then made a fart noise.

Cody laughed. "That's pretty good."

"What's with the kids?" Jay asked Cassandra in annoyance.

Cassandra let out an exasperated groan, crossing her arms over her chest. She didn't look much different from any other day aside from two trails of blood from the corners of her lips and possibly a little heavier on the white makeup and black around her eyes. Jay guessed she was supposed to be a half-transformed vampire or something. "I got stuck taking them trick-or-treating for like two hours," she said.

"You loved it," Tommy said.

Cassandra made a throttling gesture, and Tommy hid behind her sister. "So anyways, my grandma made me bring them along." She shrugged. "Sorry."

"Wait," Jay said, getting a focus on Cassandra's eyes and zooming out to a wide shot. "Say all that again for the camera."

Cassandra rolled her eyes and stepped out of the line. The kids followed her.

"The more the merrier," Cody said, a sentiment Jay couldn't say he agreed with. "Mr. Thompson said you could come right in when you got here but he didn't say anything about guests. I'm sure they'll be okay with it but I'll ask if the kids have to pay."

Tommy jabbed at Cody's thigh with his trident. "I'm not a kid, doofus. I'm a tween."

Cody's smile faded. "Jab me again and you won't live to see thirteen."

"*Oooh!* I'm *shaking* in my *booties!*" Tommy said, but he didn't dare poke Cody again, which made Jay think he probably was scared.

The six of them returned to the house to find the Thompsons. While they did, Cody asked Cassandra's sister—who said her name was Taylor—what grade she was in and what her favorite class was and what kind of animal she'd want to be if she could. All the common things you ask to pretend you don't hate kids. The answers were sixth grade, art class and mother lion.

"Lions are pretty cool," Cody agreed, "but I'd rather be a cheetah. They run the fastest."

"I wanna be a narwhal," Tommy said, hurrying to catch up to Cody and Taylor up front. "Because they have cool *horns*!" On the word *horn*, he turned and jabbed Cassandra in the thigh with his trident.

"I swear to God, Dingus, if you poke me with that thing again, I will end your life right here."

"You wish!"

Jay turned to Walden, the two of them taking up the rear, taping things that caught their eye. "If we drown the little rats, you think their parents will give us medals?"

Walden raised an eyebrow at him. "Cassie's an orphan."

Jay bristled. He'd forgotten that, but wasn't about to apologize to Walden and even though he felt bad about the comment. "Yeah, well, wish in one hand, shit in the other," he said.

Walden clenched his jaw like he was about to punch him, but a giant monster with a flaming crow skull's face approached them, sparing Jay his wrath. Wearing a shredded black cloak and walking on stilts, the crow monster leaned down to peer closely at Taylor and Tommy. Without warning, Tommy poked the guy in the shin with his trident. It probably just hit one of the stilts, but whatever it had hit, the beak clacked angrily and the actor broke character to say, "You better take that thing away from him 'fore he gets in trouble."

"Gimme that," Cody said, snatching the trident away.

"Hey, give it back!"

Tommy leaped for it. Cody held it high as they continued to the farmhouse. "You'll get it back at the end of the night."

"Give it *back*, you dick!"

"Tommy, just leave it," Taylor pleaded.

"Calm *down*, Dingus." Cassandra said.

Jay turned to Walden again. "Who knew tonight would turn into a babysitting gig?"

Walden shrugged. "I'm just shooting the movie, man."

"Who pissed in your cornflakes?"

Walden turned to him with narrowed eyes. "I don't like you, Jay. You irritate me. Your nerdy little voice is grating. I'm here to do a job, that's all. So unless it's about the movie, just leave me the fuck alone, okay?"

Jay laughed. "Why don't you tell me how you really feel?"

"If I told you how I really feel, Jay, you'd cry. And I don't wanna deal with that right now. So let's just shoot the fuckin movie, huh?"

"Fine, jeez," Jay said. After what happened in Mr. Combs's garage yesterday with that weird black smoke—which he'd later decided was probably just a hallucination brought on by stress—he didn't think anything could scare him like that again, but the adrenaline coursing through his veins said different. He wanted to punch the asshole in the face, but he knew Walden would probably just take the punch like he did that time with Brunt and rain hell back down on him.

He's not worth it, Jay assured himself, hoping something awful would befall Walden before the night was over, and hopefully while Jay was there to point the camera and laugh.

Wish in one hand, shit in the other.

CHAPTER 7

1

8:37 P.M.
The Cave

What time is it?

Darla Knight awoke with cotton in her brain, a feeling of being half dreaming and half awake. It was pitch black, her arms and legs stiff. She remembered waking up at the hotel on her first night for the shoot in Crooks Corner and feeling somewhat similar. Her room was on the backside of the building, facing the parking lot and a creek that ran parallel to the main drag. It'd been so dark she'd thought she must've been wearing her sleep mask, though she hadn't felt it on her face. Then she'd rolled over and seen the blurry red numbers on the digital alarm clock, which with her contacts taken out she couldn't read at night.

I'm not in my room. Where am I?

Her body tensed, her mind crying out in sudden terror. It was one of those horrible nightmares again where she couldn't move a muscle and her whole body went painfully stiff like a charley horse. She'd only had them a few times before, and like the previous times, she reacted with pure, unmitigated terror. Her head swung and her body jerked from side to side as she moaned behind the fabric pushed up against her bone-dry tongue.

Can't be a nightmare, she thought, realizing she was actually able to move. She tried calming herself down to assess her situation. Focused on her breathing for a moment, counting with each inward breath. *No,* she thought finally. *This is different. I'm sitting up.*

Everything came back to her then, like playing back the beginning of a film in fast-forward: the stroll across the street to the restaurant, catching snow on her tongue, the kidnapping, the drive to wherever they were now. They'd dumped her in a chair, which felt similar to the canvas ones they had on set, and tied her to it roughly. She hadn't seen a wink of daylight since they'd grabbed her up off the street on her way to dinner and drove off with her, tied, gagged and blindfolded. Same as when she'd first awakened—she could only assume she'd passed out from pure exhaustion—she had no clue whether it was night or day. What she did know was that they'd taken her to a cave, judging by the smell (cold, wet stone and a sharp, animal stench, probably guano), the sounds (dripping water, the echo of voices and shoes scuffing against rock), and the general feeling of being underground. In the interim, she'd listened to these wingnuts go on and on about the "Cult of the Smiley Face" and how they were going to summon an ancient demon by sacrificing her for "the Stones," and making a snuff film starring "Darla Fucking Knight," which was a middle name she'd never bestowed upon herself when she took up the stage name for her first audition in 1976.

Not psycho fans, she thought, remembering what she'd assumed when they first started talking to her. *Just all-around psychos.*

Their acting reminded her of the handful of cheesy '80s softcore porn films she'd been in before her big break in *Psycho Kitties.* Poorly acted, silly plot, weak characterization. They flubbed lines and the director called cut and started them over multiple times. Was the cult real? Who knew. She wasn't even sure if their planned sacrifice was real, but everything else was obviously bullshit.

Before these idiots kidnapped her, she hadn't thought a director could get any more incompetent than the one shooting *House of Doors.* And she'd worked with some big egos in Hollywood, but this guy made them all look like Sally Field's Oscar speech. When the two of them were left alone overnight—they all had to work in the morning except for him—he kept going on and on about the importance of their "movie," and how the others didn't understand his vision, didn't respect his integrity or his work ethic and *blah, blah, blah*.

Once they'd gotten her in the chair, they'd changed her clothes, fed her and given her water. Providing her with light seemed to be out of the question. Darla assumed it was because they didn't want to have to wear their ski masks the whole time. They'd shouted abuse at her, called her every name in the book, told her that her movies were trash, that *she* was trash. Alone with the director, he seemed more sympathetic. She'd tried to convince him to take off her blindfold, telling him that she understood his "plight as an artist," and that she knew how hard it was to be a creative in a room full of idiots, but he wouldn't budge. The blindfold stayed on.

After a while, he'd fallen silent, and for a few minutes there Darla had thought he'd fallen asleep. Then she'd heard a soft, rhythmic clicking sound, followed by a short chuff of breath and a metallic clink. It happened a few more times before Darla realized what it was. She'd been slowly working the gag out of her mouth, and with a burst of anger fueled by disgust she finally managed to spit it out.

"Are you fucking jerking off?"

His reply was instant. "Huh? No!" This was followed by several louder metallic clinks, which she recognized as a belt being buckled. "How'd you get your gag out?"

"You dirty motherfucker. You *were* tugging it!"

"I wasn't jerking off, goddammit!"

"Bullshit," she said. "You were fucking rubbing one out to me, you think just because I've got a blindfold on I can't tell?"

It took a moment for him to reply. Finally, he said, "So what if I was?"

Her initial reaction was revulsion. Slowly, her thoughts began to move in a different direction. In the late-'70s a rape-revenge flick called *I Spit on Your Grave* was released. It was violent and ugly and banned for "glorifying rape," which in Darla's mind it hadn't done. In the movie, a woman is violently assaulted several times in the woods and followed home for further abuse. Later in the film, the victim—in a fearless performance by Camille Keaton, for which she won a Best Actress award at the

Sitges Film Festival—hunted down her rapists and murdered them one by one, which she did by seducing them.

I could do it, Darla thought. *It's acting. What would Jean-Claude say? He'd say, "Do it for the camera, snookum."*

"Do you want to fuck me, Mr. Director Man?"

"Huh?" he said. He sounded astounded.

"Do *you*... want to *fuck*... *me*?"

She heard him shiver, as if he couldn't control himself and had just cum in his pants. He swallowed audibly. "Darla Fucking Knight," he said. "You dirty girl."

"That's right," she said, gritting her teeth. "I'm a *very* dirty girl. You wanna know how I got the gag out of my mouth? *With my tongue*, Mr. Director Man. Imagine... what that tongue could do to *you*."

Another audible swallow. "You'd bite it off," he said cautiously.

"I wouldn't. I *respect* you. I respect what you're doing. I know that kidnapping me was the only way you could make this film. I would've said no to you before. I *might've* laughed in your face. I wouldn't've *understood*. But I do now. The rest of them, they don't get it. You and me? We're different from them. We're in *show business*."

"Yeah," he said thoughtfully. "*Yeah*."

"You and me, we know making something important takes *guts*. You have to take *risks*. You have to do things normal people would think are *crazy*. That dedication to craft, the things you have to *sacrifice* to create *true art*."

He was trembling now. She could hear it in the hissed breath through his teeth. "Jesus Christ, it's like we share the same brain," he said.

Holy shit, she thought. *This is award-worthy stuff, Darla. My performance of a lifetime.*

It truly did seem like she was breaking through, that this might actually work. "I didn't understand before," she went on, "but I do now. And I want to *perform* for you. I want to *please* you. Let me please you, Mr. Director Man. You wanted a Scream Queen? Why don't you let me be your *Cream* Queen?"

Again, he shuddered. "T-tell me..." He cleared his throat and tried again. "Tell me you wanna blast me into space," he said, almost in a moan.

Darla grinned slyly. It was her famous line from the *Ragers* sequel, the one that was playing tonight at the theater downtown. The one she was supposed to be doing a signing at, if she hadn't been kidnapped by this twisted motherfucker for this piece of trash movie. "'I'm gonna blast you into outer space, you piece of Earth trash,'" she said, using the exact same tough-motherfucker delivery she had in the movie.

"Fuck yeah," he said.

She heard his belt buckle coming undone as he shuffled toward her. And what would she do when he put it in her mouth? Bite down? Suck him dry? Convince him, like Camille Keaton's character in *I Spit on Your Grave*, that she'd make it even better if he untied her? That she'd let him fuck her? Darla wasn't sure which course of action was the wisest, nor the most unsavory. She only hoped she'd find some form of inspiration while sucking his dirty cock, if it came down to that.

"*Darryl!*" The young woman's voice, so loud and shrill it echoed off the walls of the cave, startled Darla.

Saved by the bell, she thought with an inward sigh.

"*What are you doing?*"

"Shit," Daryll muttered. His belt clinked. "What? I wasn't doing anything!"

"Bullshit," she said, echoing Darla from moments earlier. "You were gonna *fuck* her."

"We were shooting," he blurted out, apparently struck by divine inspiration. "It's a scene from the movie."

"What *scene*, Darryl? It's not in your *treatment*. The *camera's* not even on."

"We were rehearsing! Weren't we?"

Darla halfheartedly agreed they were rehearsing. The woman, Willa, didn't seem convinced. But she also seemed nervous to go at him too hard, as if she thought he might hurt her if she did.

"You should go home," she said calmly after a moment's deliberation. "Get some rest. For the shoot tonight."

Darla heard him sigh. "Yeah. Yeah, I probably should." The wheel of a lighter scratched against flint and a moment later she smelled the same pungent weed smoke she'd been ensconced in last night. He exhaled leisurely. "Okay. Hot Box said he'd be back after his shift."

They exchanged tense pleasantries and then his footfalls echoed through the cave as he exited stage right. For a long moment there was only silence. Then Darla heard Willa's footsteps approaching her. There was a rustle of fabric and the gag went back into Darla's mouth, tied so tightly behind her head this time she thought her skull might crack. The scuffle of footfalls again as Willa moved away. She let out a long, jittery exhale. Then she spoke.

"This is all bullshit, you know."

Darla made no reaction. She felt like the floodgates were about to open and Willa would spill it all, but only if she remained quiet and still. Not that she could speak with the gag in her mouth. This was an epiphany moment she was having, and Darla wasn't about to spoil it.

"Darryl and the others, they think this movie's gonna make them famous. I guess I kind of did too, but I wish I hadn't gone along with it. I made a mistake. I can't take it back now, but I promise you: we are going to let you go as soon as it's done. We're not planning to kill you, we never were. It's a... what d'you call it? A marketing stunt? The cult symbols all over town, the kidnapping, all of it. It's all bullshit. He's got this crazy idea you'll drop the charges once you see how awesome the movie is and how much publicity it gets from our arrest, but it sucks, doesn't it? Like, it's not good at all."

Darla considered whether or not Willa required a response. After a moment, she decided to nod.

"I thought so. I thought, I dunno... he was just so *invested* in this that maybe he'd turn himself around. Stop smoking so much. Stop dealing. Stop losing his shit and hitting me. But he's never gonna do that, is he? He's a loser. He'll always be a loser."

Darla couldn't help but nod again.

"Thank you for being honest," Willa said after another long pause. "I'm sorry. About all of this."

"Then let me go!" Darla shouted, but it came out muffled and unintelligible. She couldn't even express it with her eyes hidden behind the blindfold. All of her acting abilities were of no use to her. She could only sit there, entirely unexpressive, and hope that Willa would take enough pity on her to let her go.

Willa fell silent then, likely pondering her relationship to the man who'd just been ready to fuck Darla, if she hadn't come back when she had. Even if Willa didn't let her go, Darla was already grateful to her for that. A flint struck and the smell of a cigarette prickled her nostrils. She was just glad it wasn't marijuana again, thinking she'd probably gotten secondhand high from all of it last night. The verbal abuse and being constrained for hours hadn't helped, but she was pretty sure the real reason she'd passed out was the weed.

The silence stretched out, Willa's cigarette softly crackling and her exhales soporific, lulling Darla back to sleep. When she woke up again, she felt the presence of others in the space, even before she smelled the cloud of weed smoke. She startled and began pulling at her bonds again, to no avail. She couldn't tell how long she'd been asleep or how many of them were in here with her, but she suspected it was all of them, a suspicion that was confirmed when Darryl spoke.

"All right," he said, followed by the *beep* of the camera's Record button. "It's time for our Scream Queen's farewell performance."

Darla's blindfold came off, relieving some of the pressure on her skull. It was still dark, but this time it was at least penetrated by their flashlights, as well as candlelight from several ceramic skulls set around her on the floor. It *was* a cave, just like she'd guessed. She sat directly between what appeared in her peripherals to be two pillars—obviously the "stones" they'd been going on about. Moisture dripped from the slick cave ceiling.

Darla sighed as Willa untied the gag she'd tied so hard hours before, lessening the pressure on her skull, but she feared she'd have a bruise on the back of her head for weeks to come. She blinked hard, then looked at her captors for the first time since they'd blindfolded her.

They weren't wearing ski masks like last night. Now they wore thick black cloaks that covered them from head to toe, only their eyes lit by the flickering candles. She looked at the man who'd tried to fuck her earlier—probably sometime this morning—and held his gaze, trying to penetrate his soul just as he'd tried to penetrate her. Could she reach any of these people through their fog of marijuana smoke? Willa would likely be the easiest to sway, she thought, although she'd had her opportunity this morning to release Darla and hadn't, merely confessing and falling silent. Maybe she shouldn't risk provoking them. Maybe it was safer to just let them be done with their shitty movie and let her go, like Willa promised.

They might risk jail time for kidnapping, but not for murder. What good would all of this have been if they ended up on death row?

She sucked in a quick breath and opened her mouth to speak when her gaze fell upon the stone pillar to her right. It was decorated with spirals and circles and strange symbols that may or may not be letters carved into them. They were clearly too sophisticated and too realistic to be the work of these morons. Even Willa, clearly the smartest of the fivesome, didn't strike Darla as a budding artist. But if they weren't props, *what were they*? Who had put them here? How could they possibly be as ancient as they looked?

As her eyes followed the spirals her ears began to ring. At first, she thought the sudden light after so much darkness had frazzled her brain. After a moment, she began to wonder if these stones with their strange etchings weren't somehow *causing* the sound, like they'd plopped her down right between the prongs in a giant tuning fork some ancient cosmic being had just struck with a massive hammer.

"What's wrong with her?" Willa asked, looking at Darla with her brow furrowed in concern.

"Maybe she's gotta use the bathroom," the big guy they called Hot Box said in his Hugo the Abominable Snowman voice. "D'you gotta go pee, Ms. Knight?"

"*My ears,*" Darla groaned, wishing someone would plug them for her. "You don't *hear* that?"

Four of the idiots looked at each other with concern. Darryl moved the camera away from his right eye to look at her more clearly. "It's the Stones," he said. "They're calling to you. They spoke to me, too."

She could see by his expression that this statement wasn't an act. No way was he that good. "Nothing's *speaking* to me," she snapped.

He shook his head, making the camera move with it. "Not with words. With *visions.*"

"You're crazy," she said.

But then she *did* see something. It started out vague and indistinct, like images glimpsed before sleep. Then it became full-on visions, just like he said. She'd only ever seen images so clearly while painting, and what she saw now was violent, chaotic, *terrifying*: people screaming, throats slashed, body parts severed, heads parting from necks on bursts of blood like something out of a cranberry cocktail commercial, raging infernos, explosions, gnashing teeth, all of it flashed before her eyes like the film from the torture scene in *A Clockwork Orange*. The whine in her ears rose in a crescendo with the intensity of the visions, and diminished suddenly as the images faded away, leaving her staring dumbstruck at the man with the camera.

"*My God*," she said, burdened with the knowledge that everything she'd seen was real, that it would all happen, that these ignorant fucks were about to throw open the gate to some kind of world-ending cosmic entity, and that her death at the hands of these lunatics would be the start of it all.

"You see?" The director grinned at her. "I *knew* they would speak to you. Darla Knight, Darryl Knell. We're both D.K. Oh, I know, Darla Knight isn't your birth name, but it's the name *you* chose for yourself, and that's more important, isn't it? That has more *power*. You and me, we're kindred spirits."

She'd been blindsided by the vision, but she knew the only way to stop this, to prevent them from murdering her—*they're going to kill me, they're going to kill me and trigger the apocalypse, I can't let it happen, I CAN'T*—was to turn them against each other. Focus not on herself but on the other actors in the scene, like they'd taught in her Meisner classes. "W-why," she started shakily, then tried again, letting out a ragged breath as she tried to find her center. "Why don't you tell your friends how you beat off in front of me last night, Darryl?"

Darryl's mouth dropped open in shock. For the first time in possibly his entire life, it appeared he genuinely didn't know what to say. The others looked at him in surprise. The big meathead they called Hot Box pooched out his lower lip with a thoughtful nod, as if it didn't surprise him. One of the other men snorted a laugh.

"Are you fucking *kidding* me, Darryl?" Willa said. She smacked him hard on the chest. "I *knew* you were trying to fuck her!"

"Shut the fuck up, Willa! Goddammit!" The directionless director growled in frustration. Then he quickly got back to business, raising the camera to his eye again. "Fuck it, we'll cut that part out. Let's just get this shit done. Where's the knife?"

Hot Box handed him a kitchen knife whose blade glinted in the beams of their flashlights.

"Wait, you can't do this," Darla cried, struggling against the ropes. "You saw! You said you saw!"

Darryl grinned like a gameshow host, only his teeth were nicotine-yellow and a few of them crooked. "I saw. We're all gonna be famous after this. And *rich*."

Darla felt all of the hope deflate from her. He hadn't seen the same things she'd seen. He hadn't seen the truth. He'd only seen what the Stones—whatever they were—had wanted him to see to make what they'd showed her come to pass. He was nothing more than a puppet, and easy prey for whatever controlled the Stones. "That's not what—"

"*Scream* for us, Darla," he said. "*Scream!*"

"You can't do this! Don't you see what you're doing is—"

She flinched and her teeth came together audibly at the cold touch of the blade's edge against her throat. The tendons in her neck pulled taut as she reared away from him. She wouldn't scream, no matter how badly she might want to, no matter what he did to her. She wouldn't give him that. She wouldn't give *them* that. Neither these people nor the Stones, nor the entity or god or demon awaiting release from beyond them.

Darryl stepped over her, teeth gritted, pressing the knife harder but not quite hard enough to break the skin, as if he didn't have the guts to do it. "*Scream for me, goddammit!*"

In his anger, he'd foolishly left his legs wide open. Darla kicked straight up with her hogtied legs right into his crotch.

"*Aooooooooooooo!*" he cried, like he was auditioning to be one of the Werewolves of London. The blade fell from his hand with a metallic clatter and his hands went to his balls.

Darla felt gravity take over as the chair she sat in fell backwards. The back of her head conked hard on the cold stone floor, sending green and white stars shooting through her vision.

"You bitch!" Darryl groaned from somewhere above her.

"Let me out of here!" Darla screamed at the others, shaking back and forth in the chair, pulling at the ropes. The idiots stared at each other, too stunned or too high to do anything. "You don't understand what you're doing!"

"Maybe we *should* stop," Willa said cautiously.

Darryl raged at her, still clutching his groin. "No! Fuck that! We *have* to finish it! *We have to finish the fuckin movie, god-dammit!* We're gonna be *famous*! *I'm* gonna be *fuckin famous!*" Spittle flew from the cloak's opening as he shouted, his voice echoing in the dark depths of the cavern. He didn't seem concerned about the knife on the floor, closer to Darla than any of the others, yet with her hands tied behind her back she could do nothing about it. Instead, he reached into one of the deep pockets of his cloak to pull out a second knife. "Pick her up!"

Hot Box and the guy who'd driven the van moved around behind her. They grabbed her under her arms and hoisted her onto her feet, then set her down on the floor of the cave.

"You're gonna wish you never did that," Darryl seethed. He brought the video camera back to his right eye. "Get ready for your closeup, bitch. Better make it good 'cause it's the last chance you'll ever get."

Vaguely, Darla realized she was crying. She'd only ever been able to muster up real tears on camera once, and it had been in the weeks following the death of her old Bassett Hound, Angie. She'd loved that dog for twelve long years, and as a consequence the director of that film had gotten the most authentic expression of Darla's grief and despair that anyone had ever put to film. Still, she'd received no recognition for her performance, no awards or accolades, and only a few brief mentions in reviews about her "maudlin" and "melodramatic" portrayal.

"Hold 'er!" Darryl shouted.

Darla wrestled in their grip but it was no use. They held her firm. She couldn't even lift her legs to kick them, tied together at the ankles. All she could do was tremble and try not to cry out when the death blow finally came. She wouldn't give them maudlin or melodramatic. Her final performance would be dignified, even if it was in a snuff film.

Lost in her thoughts, she didn't notice the Stones when they began to hum.

In the next beat, Darryl thrust the knife blade between her ribs. The pain was shocking and overwhelming. She almost lost consciousness immediately, but the pain roused her and focused all of her sensation around the cold, hard steel. She shuddered against the blade, against the fist holding it there. Gradually her extremities became very cold, like leaping out of a sauna directly into an ice bath.

Darryl looked down at the knife, stunned. He let go and stepped back, looking at its hilt sticking out of her in absolute shock. His gaze fell to the ground, where the other knife lay, then back to the knife in her chest. Everything she'd seen and tried vainly to communicate had just hit him like a hammer.

"What the fuck?" he said, staring stupidly at the blood in the palm of his hand.

The others did the same: looked at the knife on the ground, then at the knife in her chest, then at the blood on his hand, their eyes and mouths contorted in confusion and shock.

"Cut!" the director said. "Fucking cut!"

But they'd already cut. They'd cut her wide open. Darla Knight, born Kimberly Jane Jankowski, felt the knife edge pressing against her lungs with every ragged breath. She felt her heartbeat grow sluggish, and her vision waned as the vibration in the Stones intensified.

They hadn't meant to kill her. It was *supposed* to be a prop knife. This sort of thing happened rarely on set, but it *did* happen. The dummy rounds accidentally swapped with real bullets, the fake knife for the real one, a special effect that went wrong, a car stunt that veered out of control. All tragic accidents, never to be repeated. Only they happened again and again. Just last year a stuntman was killed on the set of a sequel to *The Crow*, the film which, during shooting, Brandon Lee had been shot and killed by a .44 Magnum bullet.

The movie business could sometimes be an extremely dangerous profession, and not just for stunt actors. People got seriously injured and died all the time. Even Darla had broken all five of the toes on her right foot when it got run over by a Harley in *Bikers from Hell*, the sequel to *Psycho Kitties*.

She looked up frantically as the cavern began to rumble. The hum of the Stones was almost deafening now. The others noticed, looking around in growing terror. Hot Box and the skinny guy let go of her arms and she fell to her knees on the ground. The pain was distant, her entire nervous system focused on the sharp foreign object invading her body.

"*What's happening?*" Willa shrieked. Her voice seemed far

away, as if she were shouting from somewhere deeper in the dark cave, but she was standing five feet away.

In screenwriting they spoke of "inciting incidents," the moment which set the story in motion, and this was clearly it. Darla had never been the main character of this film: she was the death in the first reel. The kill that whets the audience's appetite for the carnage that was soon to follow.

Once again, Darla Knight found she was the girl running from the killer with her camera-worthy tits out, the one who inevitably gets murdered but nobody mourns, and she would die nothing more.

That was the last thought on her mind: *I'll die nothing more.*

And then she did.

2

8:47 P.M.
The Chamber

AS THE CAVERN trembled around them, Darryl and the others stared in stunned disbelief at Darla, lying dead on her side.

"What happened?" Willa cried, looking at him as if it was all his fault. "What the fuck *happened*, Darryl?"

"I don't know, Willa, I *don't know*!" He got to his knees beside Darla Knight and tried to pry the knife out from between her ribs. "It was the fake knife—it was the fucking *fake knife*!"

"Fake knifes don't do that," Max Strick said, his hood down as he scratched the short top of his blond mullet.

"Well, *someone* fucking switched it then! I don't fucking know!" He turned to Willa. "*You!* You were always jealous of the two of us!"

"*The two of you?*" She scoffed. "There *is* no two of you! There *never was* a two of you, you delusional fuckhead! She *hated* you! And now you fucking *killed* her! *You fucking killed her*, Darryl, you stupid misogynist motherfucker!"

Maybe I brought the wrong knife, Darryl thought dully, but he knew that he hadn't, at least not on purpose. *Maybe the Stones made me bring the wrong knife....*

But that wasn't true either. He'd tested it again after they'd entered the cave, pressing the springy plastic blade against his palm and watching it sink into the hilt. It wasn't even sharp plastic. Barely even made a dent in his skin. It *was* the fake knife, the same one he'd bought at the head shop downtown—yet somehow it had punctured Darla's perfect flesh right between her perfect fucking tits and ended her life right in front of his eyes.

I killed her. I fucking killed her. No more movie. We're all going to jail! I'm a kidnapper and a murderer!

The cavern shook overhead again, Darryl's phobia coming true. He stood abruptly, looking up in terror with eyes as wide as Darla's. *It's a cave-in*, he thought madly, the video camera forgotten at his hip.

The hum of the Stones had grown louder than he'd ever heard them, vibrating so hard it made the fillings in his teeth ache, and now he knew why. Darla's blood had *fed* them, and that was the point of all of this, *had* been the point this whole time. The Stones had *lied* to him, showing him what he wanted to see to get him and the others and Darla in just this place at just this time—just like with the van outside her hotel last night—so that he'd *murder* her, kill Darla Fucking Knight right between the Stones and unleash their *true power*.

But they weren't speaking to him at all now. He had a bad feeling the Stones were done with him entirely, that he'd meet the same sad fate Darla had, his muse, bleeding out on the damp floor of the cave.

A shriek arose from the cave floor. At first, he thought it was Darla, that she was still alive and calling out for help, but she was still dead, her eyes wide in shock and confusion and agony.

"Darryl!" Willa called from the entrance. "We have to go!"

Hot Box and Max Strick had already hightailed it. Dino stood with Willa, but it looked like even he was on the verge of abandoning them.

Then—like a magic trick, like something out of an old movie with cheesy special effects, probably something starring Vincent fucking Price—the first of the ceramic skull candle holders Willa had gotten from the DollarSave rose from the floor and shot directly at Darryl, eyes and jaws flaming, shrieking like one of those Mexican death rattle things they talked about on the news a while back, the ones the Aztecs used to terrify their enemies before they went into battle.

What the shit?

Darryl ducked as the flaming ceramic skull shot over his head, feeling the heat of it scorching his scalp. While the ground shook beneath him and he stumbled and fell, the four other skulls—one for each point of the pentagram—rose into the air and launched at him like heat-seeking missiles. He didn't stand a chance.

"DARRYL!" Willa screamed.

The first struck him in the right cheekbone, knocking him sideways. His cloak caught fire as the second skull slammed into his ribs—just about the same spot he'd stabbed Darla—and he fell back on his ass. The others hit him in the shoulder, the stomach, the knee, leaving a bright, blazing patch of fire in their wake which set him fully ablaze.

While the shrieking skulls which had been candle holders from the DollarSave only moments before hurtled off into the dark tunnel, Darryl rolled and screamed in agony. All of this was caught on his camera, which lay conveniently facing him, the footage turning white from overexposure at the flashpoint, twisting in and out of focus as he rolled and screamed, failing to put himself out.

He was dying. Darla Knight was dead. His friends had abandoned him. Even Willa had left him in the end, and after the way he'd treated her, the only person who hadn't just liked him because he sold them drugs, he couldn't even say he blamed her.

As the smoke from his own burning clothing, flesh and hair filled his lungs, Darryl finally lost consciousness, and his screams ceased.

The camera continued to record until its battery ran out nearly an hour later, videotaping as his body turned to a smoldering, blackened lump of fat, flesh and bone, and three short beeps of alarm signaled the end of the very short film career of Darryl Knell.

3

Tum Gob / The Watching Stones

Freedom.

At long, impossibly long last, *FREEDOM.*

Everything had worked exactly as planned. Better, even. They could not have hoped for a more positive result from Their many months of planning—a mere drop in the ocean of time They had spent languishing within the *Upask*, the Great Void beyond the *Tum Gob*, the Watching Stones which held Them captive, waiting, *seething*—and now, *now* the time had come round at last.

Their time.

They had been dreaming, drifting in that vast, endless Void for so long They could not even remember who or *what* had first imprisoned Them there, long before the big shaman of the ancient people had tricked Them. Or perhaps They had always been there, floating in the nothing between worlds, like gestating in a womb. Perhaps They had only seen this side of the *Tum Gob* once, when the dead shaman had accidentally summoned Them and for a brief period became Their *chuann*, Their vessel. Perhaps They were never meant to exist on this side of the Stones. Perhaps that was why They had never been given a body. Perhaps that was why They had been forced to give Themself a name. Was it possible everything They had told Themself had been a lie? That everything They knew was merely a legend fabricated in Their own mind? A fantasy of persecution and revenge? A dream of Godhood?

No.

"WE ARE DESTINED TO BE A GOD." Those words did not come from nothing. Someone had spoken those words to Us. Something. We were not birthed into existence with that knowledge. It is not delusion. It was bestowed upon us. We are Geth. We are a god, and We will be treated as such whether these frail beings wish to do so or not.

Already many of Their shadows—*inhak* in the language of Those Who Came Before—had fled the cave in excited numbers, bounding off its smooth rock walls and darting out into the night, while several remained behind to carry Geth's Multitude

—Geth the Many, or Their *aminhas*, in the tongue of the dead shaman—to a suitable host body.

The *inhak* were merciless killers, but they served Geth well. They had already murdered the actress and the drug addict and his friends, and now they craved more blood, more chaos, more carnage. Even if Geth did not entirely share their appetite, appeasing Their minions would provide Them the strength They required to possess a worthy vessel. One that would not betray Them as the shaman had, so many millennia ago.

In the beginning, there was always chaos.

But the chaos was necessary. It would weaken these people, soften their resolve, make them easy prey.

And then Geth the Many would reveal Themself, with Their new vessel and Their Holy Name chosen, and every single living soul in this town would kneel before Geth and *pray*.

PART TWO

HELLOWEEN

CHAPTER 8

1

7:36 P.M.
Halloween Village

When the sun finally went down and the overhead lights went out in the barn, Brittany got into character. Performing at the haunt was the opposite of theater, and in a way it was easier. She didn't have many lines to remember, only a handful of phrases she'd use to scare people as they wandered through the maze. A lot of them had come from The Snake's repertoire of creep and menace.

She'd already showed the boys where all the jump scares were throughout the maze: the blasts of air to startle people as they passed, the skeleton leaping from the shadows, the laughing severed head in a glass box, the black cat yowling in the window to a crack of lightning, the thrashing thing in the toilet. These were in addition to haunt actors like herself who could jump out and follow someone at any point, and the others populating various "scenes" throughout the house.

We got somethin special planned tonight though, don't we, honeypie?

Brittany ignored the voice in her ear. She didn't need another reminder about what she had to do, what The Snake would make her do if she didn't follow through herself. What the two of them had planned would put Crooks Corner and Halloween Village on the map. She just hoped, if she got caught, that her

117

dad would still love her. He'd always had her back, no matter what. Denise had wanted to throttle her creativity, to smother her ambition. Denise thought that being an actor-slash-singer should be enough for her.

Denise'll find out soon nuff, The Snake whispered to her, and his cackling laughter filled her head, making her nauseous. *'Sides, we ain't gon' get caught. Ain't no cameras back there, is there?*

No, there were no cameras where she'd planned to do it. That was why she'd picked the spot. She just needed to wait for the right moment to do what needed to be done. To quiet the persistent voice in her head.

Brittany and her constant companion slipped into the shadows and waited for the right opportunity, the spirals in her mind coiling and uncoiling to the rapid beat of her heart.

The Snake was wide awake now.

And he was *hungry*.

2

WALDEN TOOK out the first tape from his home video camera and popped in another, following along behind the others. Jay was wrong about the kids. As far as Walden was concerned, they'd add some much-needed comic relief to the movie. Tommy Mingus was annoying as hell, but he was also a wild card and sometimes actually funny. Taylor was the cute little kid you rooted for, with a bit of an edge. She was clever and sarcastic, and the Polaroid camera she carried around with her was just enough of a shtick to make her feel like a three-dimensional character. When the two of them died, the audience would *actually care*, as opposed to Cody, Jay and Brittany, whose deaths they'd probably be rooting for.

Cassandra was somewhere in the middle. Walden always thought she was kind of weird, even for an outsider like himself. The goth thing and the *I-hate-the-world* attitude were masks for something simmering beneath. She seemed to have a *get-them-before-they-get-you* mentality, which Walden understood, having been bullied quite a bit when he was younger. It was why he didn't let people push him around now, and why he'd stood up to Brunt that day to deflect the bully's attention from that poor sap who'd probably just end up getting beaten for it later. It was why he hated bullies in general, and always chose to intervene, whether it was his fight or not.

Jay was a bully. He was a weakling, but he lorded his specialized knowledge over people, using it as a weapon. Sure, he'd probably done it in self-defense when he was younger, falling back on an *I'm-better-than-everyone* attitude to protect his ego from whatever beatings he'd taken, verbal and physical, and from his own troubles about his dad being in the psych ward. By now it had graduated to first strikes. Walden didn't like it, and wouldn't stand for it when it happened again.

Just focus on the movie, he thought. *Fuck the rest of it.*

The outline they'd written in class had them heading into the barn first, where one of them—they hadn't yet decided who —would be lured into the shadows and murdered by Brittany, waiting somewhere inside. He hurried past Jay, who was following along with the camera held uselessly at his side, and caught up to Cody and the others. "Hey, Cassie."

Cassandra glanced at him, saw that he was pointing his camera at her and looked away with a huff. Her tolerance had clearly already reached its limit for the night, which didn't bode well. "Do you have to have that thing on all the time?"

"Yeah, so anyway, I was thinking it'd be smart for you die first, since you're not shooting any of it."

"*I knew it.* The babysitter *always* dies first!"

"Good point. But then you'll get to play the killer."

"I get to *kill* people?" She narrowed her eyes at Jay, who trudged along cluelessly behind them. "Can I start with him?"

"Nah, Jay has to live for a bit to keep shooting the fake doc. Also, it's better to keep at least one asshole alive. Gives the audience a death to root for."

"What about the Dingus?" she asked, eyeing Tommy.

"The kids need to live long enough for people to feel bad when one of em bites it. You know, for pathos."

She sighed in aggravation. "Well, how about you, then?"

Walden had already considered it. They'd established—in the main camera footage—that he was supposed to be shooting a behind-the-scenes about the doc for class. He supposed he could be the first of the crew members to die, escalating the stakes.

"That might work. As long as Cody takes my camera after. He can find it with my body."

"Okay, let's shoot some stand-ups here," Jay said, planting the camera down in front of the barn and spreading out the tripod legs.

The only legs he'll ever spread, Walden thought with a sly grin.

People were already inside, with more groups let in on a staggered basis. Screams and shouts and laughter, as well as all kinds of spooky sound effects, erupted from inside. Strobe lights flickered over the area, where murder clowns and dead hillbillies roamed, freaking out customers. A Halloween soundtrack and a steady heartbeat pounded from speakers set up outside.

"That's you, Cassandra," Cody said.

"Why me?"

"Because you're dying first."

"And because you brought the kids," Jay said.

Walden aimed his camera at Jay with a scowl. Jay frowned back and ducked behind the school camera to start shooting.

"Rolling," Jay said.

"*Okay*, gimme a second." Cassandra fixed her bangs and ran her tongue across her teeth. "Okay. The Thompsons' Halloween Village has been a stable event during spooky season in the small town of Crooks Corner, New Hampshire, for twenty years."

Jay called *Cut*.

"What? What's wrong?"

"You said *stable*. It's supposed to be *staple*."

"That's a dumb word. Can't we just say *popular*?"

"You were fine with it when we wrote it."

"That's because I thought Brittany was gonna say it."

"Say it however it works for you," Cody interrupted, lowering the boom. "Just not *stable*."

"This is *boring*!" Tommy whined. "I wanna go inside!"

"Give it a minute, Dingus."

"It's been like *five years* already!"

"Shut up, Tommy," Taylor said. "Let them finish or we'll never get to go."

Tommy threw his arms across his chest and sulked.

Jay called, "Three, two..." He pointed for one.

"The Thompsons' Halloween Village has been a popular

event during spooky season in the small town of Crooks Corner, New Hampshire, for twenty years," Cassandra said, using the professional voice they'd been taught to use for the news. "Ghouls, ghosts and goblins roam the grounds, but with a known serial killer prowling the area, this year's haunt *almost* didn't happen. Tonight, we'll be taking you inside the haunt for what some critics say might be the last time." She held her grim smile for a moment, then said, "Was that good?"

"That was great," Jay said, looking honestly impressed.

"*Nice job*, Cassie," Cody said.

"Yeah, good stuff," Walden agreed.

It looked like Cassandra was trying her best not to smile.

"There's a serial killer?" Taylor asked nervously.

"It's just for the movie, shrimp."

Cody looked around with a scowl. "Hey, did Tommy run off?"

Cassandra's scowl returned. "Dammit! That little shit disturber!"

Taylor turned toward the barn, where the screams and shouts of haunters and patrons continued. "He prob'ly went inside. All he kept talking about at school was how bad he wants to go inside the haunted barn."

Cassandra glanced anxiously toward the barn. Tommy Mingus was a troublemaker, but if he got hurt Walden knew she'd be the one to take the blame. "You think they'd let him in on his own?"

"He probably snuck in with a group," Walden told her.

Cody rested the boom pole against his shoulder. "Well, come on. I guess we should go find him."

Jay picked up the camera by the tripod and followed along behind them, probably hoping they'd managed to ditch the kid without trying, Walden figured. Either way, Tommy's little stunt just made the movie a lot more exciting.

3

Tommy Mingus loved a good scare.

Ever since he'd accidentally stumbled across a movie called *Dreamscape* while flipping through channels when he was six, he'd been obsessed with scary stuff. He'd read every single *Goose-bumps* and *Scary Stories to Tell in the Dark* he could get his hands on, watched reruns of *Scooby-Doo, Where are You?* and *Tales from the Cryptkeeper, Are You Afraid of the Dark?* and the *Goose-bumps* series. Now that he was twelve his parents allowed him to watch adult horror movies so long as they didn't have nudity, and *The X-Files* with them on Sunday nights. He wanted to be like Mulder when he grew up, only not such a doofus.

The scary sounds from inside the barn had become so enticing he couldn't wait around for the dumbos to finish their stupid movie anymore, so he slipped away while Cassie was talking to the camera. Hurrying over to the line, he found a big group near the front to squeeze in with, and entered the barn when the guy outside let them through.

Darkness closed in around them in the tight corridor. The people he'd snuck in with were slow and too tall for him to see around. He wished that big jock dummy hadn't taken away his pitchfork so he could poke them in the butts. That would've been hilarious, except Taylor wasn't around to laugh with him. This wasn't going to be as fun without her. She was pretty fun for a girl, even though she was a wet blanket sometimes, especially when her sister was around. He probably should've waited for them to finish their stupid movie.

"Screw em," he muttered.

Tommy ditched the group in the first open space, a room meant to look like a rip-off of the kitchen in *The Texas Chainsaw Massacre*. Some Leatherface wannabe with a blood-streaked apron was chopping up fresh meat from a pretty realistic-looking human calf on the counter in the middle. More body parts were sitting around all over the place: a severed head, a bloody torso, an arm, a bucket of hands which looked super gross. A human heart lay beating on the counter beside a bunch of kitchen tools —aside from the cleaver hitting the wooden cutting board, its steady *thump-thump, thump-thump* was the only sound in the room, not counting the screaming girls and the revving chainsaw coming from deeper inside the darkness of the barn.

"Cool!" Tommy said.

"Check out this little dude here," one of the teenagers from the group said, pointing at him. "He's *lovin* it!"

The other kids laughed and Tommy grinned proudly.

The cannibal cook snarled behind the sewn-up, latex human face mask. He grabbed a chunk of meat and threw it on a steaming grill with a hiss, raising a cloud of smoke.

"Hey, Latexface!" Tommy cried, hamming it up for the teens. "I take mine with mustard and lots of ketchup!"

The teens laughed and moved on to the next room. Latexface whipped back to the counter with an enraged growl and reached for something among the tools. "Where's my knife?" he muttered, his voice muffled by the mask.

Tommy laughed and left the kitchen as another group entered behind him. The heartbeat followed him into the next corridor. Strobe lights flashed intermittently, but otherwise it was pitch black. Tommy's own heart began to beat rapidly. He heard the teens scream a good distance ahead of him, but couldn't see them in the flashes. The hallway zigged and zagged. Tattered burlap and cobwebs tickled his face and hair. He expected a jump scare any minute.

On the next turn, the strobing became impossible to see, leaving him back in the dark. He shuffled forward a few nervous steps.

Laughter erupted to his left, making him jump. The severed head turned back and forth on a microwave plate behind glass, moving up and down on its working jaw, eyes rolling. It was obviously fake, but a pretty good scare, he had to admit.

"Haha, that's awesome!"

The clear plastic butcher curtains leading to the next room spread open to the roar of a chainsaw. A member of the cannibal family held the tool high over his head, lit from the room beyond.

"Nice try, butthole!" Tommy said after the initial shock. A closer look at the saw revealed it didn't have a chain. It'd probably sting from the vibration if it touched him but it wouldn't *actually* hurt him. While the Texas Chainless Maniac revved it closer to him, Tommy sidled past into the room, pushing through the blood-stained curtains.

He found himself in a disgusting bathroom, blood and cruddy brown smears everywhere. "*They drowned them in the tub!*" a lady dressed in a filthy nightgown shouted at him. She came at him with her arms outstretched, her gaunt face pleading. *"They drowned my babies!"*

Tommy moved past her and looked in the tub. It was filled with dank brown water, like that time the sewer had backed up in the apartment building where he lived and the toilet, sinks and tub filled up with gross water. Little baby dolls in little white dresses stained red floated within, several with their heads removed, bobbing amid their bodies.

"Weird," Tommy said.

"My babies, you have to save my babies!" the lady cried, running at him.

Tommy dodged her. "Get outta here, lady!"

She turned away from him before he had to defend himself and addressed the next group entering the room, repeating what she'd said to Tommy.

Something splashed in the toilet as he made his way to the exit. He peered down to see a little goblin-like creature trying to climb out of the bowl. It wore the same dress as the babies in the tub. Tommy figured it was supposed to be a mutant version of them. Maybe that was why they'd drowned the others.

"Awesome!"

He continued into the next hall. Pitch black. Horror music droning. Screams and laughter from ahead. He moved ahead, one step at a time, hands out in front of him. He jumped when a gust of air rustled his hair with a loud hiss. "Stupid," he muttered, moving on.

"Psst, hey kid," came a voice to his left. Tommy parted the thick black curtains there and peered into the space beyond, darkness tinged with a pulsing red light. All he could see was a dim face painted white in the dark, turning blood-red when the light flickered.

"You wanna see something *really* scary?" the face asked. It was a clown. Some *girl* clown, judging by the voice and from her soft face, probably not much older than himself. Tommy had seen *IT* on DVD, but Pennywise was a weird-looking old guy. Clowns didn't scare him much, anyway. Nothing did. That was why he loved horror so much. It was like a dare to himself. Laughing in the face of death made him feel invincible.

"Yeah," Tommy said, as if it was obvious.

The clown girl gestured him forward, beckoning with a white-gloved hand. "Follow me."

Tommy looked behind himself both ways, seeing nothing but darkness, then followed the girl into the throbbing red light.

4

6:44 P.M. - 8:47 P.M.
Grand Theater

RENNY HILDEBRAND and Elana Stabler stepped up to the box office window after the last group of teens headed into the theater gabbing and laughing. He just hoped there wouldn't be a lot of talking during the movie, although he and Elana had been to their *Rocky Horror* event last year and it had been a lot of fun, despite all the antics from the crowd. These old movies were great to watch in big groups, since he'd seen them before. *The Birds* was one of his favorite horror movies, and his favorite Hitchcock film overall, even though objectively Alfie had made better films. It was such an effective thriller, doing for birds what he'd done for showers with *Psycho*, and what *Jaws* did for sharks more than a decade later.

"Two for both shows, please," he said.

Stafford, the old fossil in the red usher uniform who usually ripped tickets inside and welcomed guests to the Grand, looked particularly ghoulish tonight. Renny hadn't been for a few weeks and wasn't sure if he'd actually aged that much or it was makeup for the event. In any case, he wore the top hat, cape and white gloves of a magician.

The old man smiled and said, "Two for the spooktacular double-bill. Of course."

Renny paid with a twenty. The old man printed off two tickets on the machine and handed them over, along with the change.

"Enjoy the show," he said.

"Thanks, you too," Renny said, and immediately cursed himself.

Elana ushered him along before he could correct his mistake. "You too?" she said with a grin, locking her arm with his.

Renny chuckled, shaking his head. "I always do that."

They got a large buttered popcorn—layered, the way Elana liked it—and two medium sodas, a Dr. Pepper for Elana and Renny's Coke. The girl behind the counter convinced them to make it a combo for an extra dollar, adding a box of Jujyfruits which Renny stuffed in his coat pocket.

The dimly lit theater was already bustling by the time they made their way inside, redolent of popcorn, old fabric, cheap cologne and sweat. Teenagers leaned over the backs of seats chatting with friends, others threw popcorn, whooping and hollering. Many wore costumes, and although masks weren't allowed, plenty had used makeup to make their faces into skeletons, devils, werewolves, cats, the Kiss Army, and all manner of imaginary creatures. The amount of imagination that went into his favorite holiday was something that never failed to make Renny—an excellent teacher who had only recently begun to consider himself failed as a writer, having only a single screenplay produced as an independent film that nobody had ever seen—smile exuberantly.

He put his arm around Elana, and she smiled down at him—Elana was the taller of the two by a couple of inches—easing her head into his shoulder as they walked down the aisle. Someday he hoped they could stop worrying about getting caught by Principal Elder and wouldn't have to slink around slyly, pretending to be just coworkers. Everyone probably already knew they'd been seeing each other for longer than some people in town who were *actually* married.

"There's two," she said, pointing. They made their way down to three available seats near the aisle, two rows back from the front. A couple about their age, dressed as the Cat in the Hat and a Who from Whoville, stood up to let them pass by. A teenager standing in the row ahead stretched, not noticing them behind him, and nudged Renny's right arm. Renny barely managed to save the soda from spilling but the top layer of popcorn fell out, crunching under his feet.

"Sorry," the kid in the jean jacket with a smiley face button on his left lapel said politely. Some kids had started making buttons based on the supposed cult symbol, probably because they thought it would be cool and counterculture to do so. The kid reacted in shock as he made eye contact with Renny. "Oh, hey, Mr. Hildebrand." He raised a hand awkwardly. "Hi, Miss Stabler."

"Hi—" Renny scoured his memory for the kid's name, who he vaguely recognized as a student from one or two years back.

"Hi, Franklin," Elana stepped in for him.

"Hi, Franklin," Renny repeated. "And no worries."

The kid let out a sigh of relief, then went back to lobbing one of the promotional monster balls for the *Ragers in Space* movie, which was playing after *The Birds*. It was an odd double bill, pairing peak Hitchcock with a middling Italian horror film, but the third *Ragers* film had become a cult classic after the director's macabre death, so Renny allowed it. Plus he'd heard something about some of the movie being filmed here, which he found odd considering it was a space movie. The toys were apparently facsimiles of the Ragers themselves. Renny hadn't seen the movie but it seemed like a rip-off of *Ghoulies*, which itself was a rip-off of the far superior *Gremlins*. Along with the promo toys, black birds hung from the lights on the ceiling and the underside of the balcony.

They took off their coats and got comfortable. He offered the popcorn to Elana, and she took a handful, nibbling in the way she did that always made him grin.

"What?" she asked.

"Nothin," he said. "Just feels nice to get out together."

She smiled. He knew she shared the same feelings as him—they'd talked about it often enough—but she just wasn't ready to be open about it yet. Coming here together tonight was actually a big step.

The lights dimmed and the first announcement came up, that old singing-dancing anthropomorphized theater snacks one from the Fifties urging people to go to the lobby and get a treat. It brought back warm feelings of nostalgia for Renny, who'd grown up with parents who loved the movies and had taken the whole troupe of them—three boys and his sister Adeline—to a film typically once a month. The first movie he remembered seeing, when he was probably three, was *Willy Wonka & the Chocolate Factory*. He remembered feeling both terrified and exhilarated when he left the theater with his parents and older sister. His father had told Renny when he was older that it probably wasn't a good movie for *very* little children, but in those days parents took their kids to everything. It wasn't until *Gremlins* and *Indiana Jones and the Temple of Doom* that the PG-13 rating made the distinction between child and "young adult." Too young for it or not, *Wonka* had sparked Renny's love of film and storytelling in general, and he'd watched it probably two dozen times since.

Elana wasn't as much of a movie lover, but she indulged him. He patted her thigh lovingly and she turned to him, whispering, "This isn't so bad, is it?"

He smiled. "Yeah. Maybe we could even neck a bit later."

She punched him lightly in his arm.

After the previews—the Grand played only repertory films, and had apparently managed to score *The Sixth Sense* and *Dark City*, both modern classics in Renny's opinion—they sat in comfortable silence, sipping their sodas and eating popcorn while the black and white film played. Kids gabbed and there was some laughter during what they probably considered "cheesy" effects but were innovative for the time—*How're you gonna shock them with practical effects after they've seen bullet-time?* Renny thought —but once the film got really tense, most of the chatter and laughter died down. There were even a few communal gasps, during the playground scene in particular, giving Renny hope for future generations of cinemagoers.

At the end of the bar scene, after the explosion at the gas station, and the shot cut to a bird's eye view when the soundtrack was near absolute silence but for the whisper of wind, the entire theater held their breath. When the first seagulls shrieked into the shot, Renny grinned at several audible gasps from the crowd. A shrill scream arose from the back of the theater. He figured someone had just goosed their date, but another cry from the seats to their right came in the moment after, then further cries from the back. Shadows flittered across the screen, shadows Renny knew from having seen this a dozen times shouldn't be there, as if the projectionist were making shadow puppets. Bird-shaped shadow puppets.

He craned his neck, thinking the theater had really done a wonder with practical effects—call it *Bird-O-Vision*—since the fake birds that remained attached to the ceiling appeared to be madly flapping their wings, flying in concentric circles against the nails or pins holding them in place.

As Tippi Hedren closed herself into the phone booth, Renny glanced back to the commotion. In the balcony, people were hurrying out of the closest two rows, pushing at each other. *Someone must've pissed themselves*, he thought. Then he saw the flapping thing in the dusty projector light.

And another.

And a third.

He looked directly above himself again just as one of the circling birds snapped free of its string and dove at the screen.

Impossible, he thought. Then his analytical brain took over: *They must've released trained crows... or something!*

"What's going on?" Elana whispered, gripping his hand tightly.

Renny didn't get a chance to answer. Someone in the rows ahead shrieked and threw their promotional goblin ball. It bounced off the stage and hurtled back toward the audience. It struck a teen boy, judging by the voice and build, as he screamed and stood up in the semi-dark theater.

Having taught kids for nearly a decade, Renny knew how bad something had to be for a boy his age to *actually scream* in a crowd.

Maybe he's a plant? An actor from the haunt or something?

As he thought this, one after another, like popping corn, the toys all started springing from the seats, and then almost the whole theater stood at once, screaming louder than any of the characters in the movie.

In the commotion, one of the crows flew down and struck Renny on the cheek, sharp and violently. He cried out in pain, pawing at it, shutting his eyes against the wings beating against his face. It let out an angry squawk as it fluttered away.

"What's happening?" Elana cried.

"That thing just divebombed me!" Renny shouted, grabbing his coat from behind him and draping it over himself and Elana. In the dim light from beneath it, he saw an emotion he'd never seen before in his typically calm and collected girlfriend's eyes: *unmitigated terror.*

"What the hell have you *done*?" she whispered in the dark shelter of his coat.

"Me? I didn't do anything."

"Not you," she said. "*Ernie Combs.*"

5

8:40 P.M.
Browning Street / Ernie Combs's garage

OBSERVABLE PHENOMENA, Ernie Combs scribbled into his journal, and underlined it twice.

The other day the boy, James, had *seen* something while the Machine had been running, Ernie was certain of it. Whatever it was had shaken him—*literally*, apparently, since he'd needed to void his bowels almost immediately after the phenomenon had been observed. The observers at Theta site, two of his former students and Elana Stabler's good friends, had apparently also seen a gauzy black wisp of smoke rise from the stones he'd discovered in the cave below Beta site, as if a candle had been snuffed out and the smoke had begun to swirl in a spherical motion before their eyes.

Like Ernie, Elana herself had seen nothing, though on the camera footage she'd later played for him, there was a visible smudge where his two ex-students had claimed to have seen something, hovering between the two stone pillars of the Duolith.

The time of this phenomena corresponded almost exactly to the Harmonic Wave Generator turning on and shorting out, which made sense, as the machine in his garage harmonized with the larger one at Beta, which in turn had been devised to "tune" with the Duolith Ernie had discovered in the cave system below.

For as far back as Ernie Combs could remember—which wasn't quite true, as he had vague memories of being in the womb—he'd considered himself an amateur spelunker. He'd spent plenty of time in the Boulder, Polar and Bears' Den caves in the White Mountains, and as an adult had driven to many other caves all across this great nation, seeking that immense sense of peace he'd first felt underground as a young boy, surrounded by the natural world, when his Boy Scouts troop had taken an expedition to Carlsbad Caverns. The feeling he'd had was immeasurable—if there were a way to measure peace, he'd try—as he'd contemplated the time it would have taken for sulfuric acid from the oil fields to erode the limestone from below in such a way that twelve-million years later humans would be able to walk through the empty space below. It had sparked his love of both science and nature, and eventually led to the discovery of the Duolith site deep within a cave in the woods beyond the Thompson farm, in a cold, dark chamber with strangely smooth walls. The pillars of the Duolith itself were perfectly rectangular and uniform, almost eerily so, carved with intricate symbols and phosphorescent spirals.

He'd found the cave by accident on a hike, literally stumbling upon it as he'd tripped over the rocks surrounding the entrance and nearly twisted his ankle. It had taken him weeks to map the cave system below, returning on his one free day every weekend—weather permitting—and he'd only found the Duolith chamber by accident on the seventh Sunday. He'd heard the sound of running water, a stream, through a crack in a small rockfall covering what was once another branch of the cave. It took him two days to clear the rockslide, and the week between had been agony, imagining what might lay beyond.

By the second Sunday, when he'd finally cleared enough to crawl through, he realized his imagination hadn't been capable of conceiving what he found. As a child, driven from one national park to the next by his nature-loving parents, he'd often dreamed of wandering off on his own in one cave or another and discovering something of value, something *noteworthy*, like Howard Carter discovering Tutankhamun's burial chamber. He'd been too young to fully understand at the time, but as he'd grown older, he understood this feeling for what it was: *ambition*.

His drive to be known for something important had never coalesced into anything real. After school he'd fallen into teaching, following in his parents' footsteps, which was a noble profession—or had been, at one point—but had never truly fulfilled Ernie Combs. He had *theories*, but none as groundbreaking or interesting as those that had come before, and no publishers were interested in his work aside from little-known science magazines, whose readers were quick to point out the flaws in harshly worded letters to the editors. He had *inventions*, and had patented quite a few of them, but nothing had taken off. When he found the rockslide, he'd been just about at his breaking point with his teaching career. He'd given himself two more years, at the most, to do something important with his life. If nothing came of it, he'd decided he would take what little savings he had and spend it traveling the world, following in the footsteps of the great explorers and adventurers. When the money finally ran out, he'd see if there was an opening for a science teacher in some small town or another and live out the rest of his days in quiet desperation.

When the Duolith had presented itself like a two-pronged wonder, he'd already been on his knees, and even if he hadn't, he supposed he might have dropped before it like a holy man before his deity and wept as he had then. The stone—unlike stalagmites, it was not made of calcium carbonate, as the scrapings he'd sent to have studied under an electron microscope later confirmed—had been silt-covered, and it wasn't until he'd wiped the tears from his eyes that he'd seen divots in its faces which proved to be etchings of an as-yet undetermined language. He'd sent out a few photos of the symbols themselves to a linguistic anthropologist who claimed it was unlike anything she'd ever seen before and was likely some kind of modern cipher, though without access to the rock she was unable to determine the age of the carvings. The geologist expressed a similar sentiment, as carbon dating was not possible for carvings, only the raw material itself.

The rock itself was likely around twenty-thousand years old, but the carvings were of an indeterminate age and the language unknown. For all Ernie knew it could have been carved fifty or a hundred years ago, although some of the rocks in the slide had been in place for so long that they'd fused together with calcium deposits, which made that hypothesis unlikely. It made Ernie think of the Lake Winnipesaukee "mystery stone," whose date of origin and purpose were still unknown, though it appeared strangely modern. Some people believed it to have been left there by an advanced alien race, though Ernie sincerely doubted that theory.

Two Sundays later, as he'd stood brushing off the remaining silt from the symbols, the alarm on his watch had begun to beep, signaling it was time to take his afternoon pill. But an odd thing happened, a very odd phenomenon that triggered his belief that this thing was not merely a religious relic of some kind but something perhaps—rudimentarily, at least—*scientific*, and instead of turning off the alarm and consuming his pill immediately, he'd let it continue to beep.

The twin stone pillars had begun to subtly vibrate.

Silt fell from their channels and divots in dusty clouds. It seemed like the stone itself was harmonizing with the little electronic beeps from the Casio Databank, almost like the metal in a tuning fork, the sound vibrations causing a like response in the Duolith itself.

Finally, he'd pressed the button to stop the alarm, only to discover the sound continued to resonate from the pillars. The vibratory hum trailed off eventually, but it had gone on long enough to make the assumption that it wasn't coincidental.

Whoever created these had likely used some kind of sound-making device—a flute, one of those recently discovered Aztec death whistles, perhaps even vocal harmonizing—to generate a sympathetic response from these stones. To what purpose, Ernie did not then know, but he was determined to find out.

The next time he returned to the cave, he'd brought with him a video camera from Hildebrand's classroom. He'd set a countdown on his watch and recorded the phenomenon when the alarm started to beep. The harmonizing resonance hummed after the final beep for the exact same duration each time. The slide whistle he'd kept in a box in his garage from childhood and a recorder from the music class wouldn't produce any reaction from the stones. Even his off-key singing at relatively the same pitch—or as close as he could manage—didn't elicit a single response.

And yet every time he'd let the alarm play out, the stones vibrated and hummed. Surely it wasn't possible these stones were only affected by sounds from electronic devices? In following visits he'd brought all kinds of electronic noise makers: a Casio keyboard, a Speak & Spell, even a tape recorder playing everything from light classical to Huey Lewis to the Nixon White House tapes. The result with each item was the same: the stones vibrated, emitting their eerie single-note hum.

It was then that he decided to bring in outside help.

Elana was the first person to come to mind, not solely because mathematics and scientific theory were intrinsically intertwined, but because she was the only one of his work colleagues whom he deemed to have the capacity not just to contemplate the things he had in mind for the Duolith but to extrapolate and theorize herself. It turned out he'd been correct in that assumption, and she'd become a fervent and valuable partner, unafraid to challenge his hypotheses and push the experiments well beyond where he may have taken them on its own. When it became unfeasible to continue their experiments from the Duolith chamber it was her idea to build the shed above it, although it was his idea to build the corresponding unit in his own garage that he could tinker with at his leisure.

The idea, she'd postulated, was not to keep replicating the same signal and response over and over, but to *change* the response. "Sound is about frequency, or hertz, but that alone doesn't seem to affect the vibration it produces," she'd said. "If that were true your slide whistle would have worked. It seems to be specifically tuned to electronically produced sound, at least as far as we've been able to observe. Perhaps whoever made this had some kind of instrument that's no longer used or even known of, or possibly they weren't even aware of what they'd created, that it had any significance beyond the religious. Nevertheless, what we need to do now is determine the correct combination of frequency and *type* of sound."

Ernie had agreed, and they'd spend the following year tinkering and observing, adding all kinds of electronic gadgetry to the Machine at Alpha Site—the garage—in order to produce a very specific sound and frequency which would stimulate the Duolith to do something different.

Otherwise, all of the work, all of the experimenting would have been for naught.

Yesterday, both James in the garage and the two former students observing the Duolith in the chamber, themselves under observation by Elana in the shed positioned approximately sixty feet above them, had finally *seen* something. According to the data and audio recording, the Duolith had produced a sound unlike any prior iteration, which had in turn appeared to coincide—and thus may have *caused*—the tremors felt throughout Crooks Corner.

Ernie had managed to find the short in the Machine—it was the pager's circuit board, not the Tamagotchi, as he'd earlier suspected—and he replaced it with another he'd bought at the used electronics store before returning to his garage after school. He was sure this time the experiment would replicate the results from yesterday, and that he'd be able to sustain the phenomenon for a long enough period to observe it firsthand.

And what exactly was the phenomena? What was the effect they'd been trying to reproduce all this time? Truthfully, Ernie had no idea, and if he'd voiced this to Elana he was sure she'd say the same. Neither of them had never broached the subject of *hypotheses*, likely because neither of them had wanted to admit to themselves they had no concept of what they were actually *studying* while attempting to alter the frequency of the Duolith's vibrations. If they did that, if they voiced these very valid concerns, it would call into question the very nature of the Duolith itself. The *who* had created it, and *for what*. They had simply needed to know if it was *possible*. And so he hadn't been entirely straightforward in his description of The Machine to James the other day. But it was as close as he could come to something *scientific*, and in his experience, laypeople were dazzled by pseudo-scientific mumbo-jumbo. He could have just as easily passed it off as something to do with the relatively unknown dimension of quantum mechanics, or told him it was a newfangled *frappuccino* maker. Anything rather than admit he didn't know *what* the Machines did, nor how they actually worked in conjunction with the Duolith. That they'd been merely tinkering in the vain—or *vainglorious*—hope that *something* they did would finally unlock the true purpose of those damned stones.

Something *had* to, surely.

And then what? he asked himself.

And then we'll observe, analyze and hypothesize, just as we've been doing all along. The scientific method, in other words. Except we'll finally know just what it is we've been studying. If the Duolith is metaphysical or—he almost didn't dare think it—cosmic in origin, we may someday be spoken of in the same way as Oppenheimer. The atom was just there, waiting for someone to split it. Just as the Duolith was there waiting for me to find it, and for Elana and I to crack its code.

Hegel, Ernie's bicolor cat of sixteen years, rubbed up against his pantleg as he turned the crank and punched in the same sequence of buttons he'd entered yesterday. She purred up at him sleepily. Hegel usually stayed out of the garage unless he'd forgotten her nighttime feeding, which he'd specifically made sure not to forget tonight.

"Go away, puss-puss," he said distractedly, pushing her away lightly with his shin. Her yellow-green eyes regarded him dismissively and she trotted away with a disgruntled meow, weaving under the legs of the workbench.

Satisfied Hegel wouldn't interrupt the experiment, Ernie lowered his goggles and turned on the Machine.

It took a few minutes to warm up, but when it finally started to hum and rattle, items in the garage began to tremble. A wrench wobbled until it fell off the worktable with a clang barely audible beneath the sound of the Machine. The "skinned" Furby fell on its side, staring blankly. The trash can spasmed like R2D2 pitching a fit. The heavy automatic garage door opener trembled above his head.

Still, nothing like what the two observers at the Duolith site had seen—nor what James had *likely* seen—appeared over the green X he'd taped on the floor. Not even a dark smudge like they'd seen on the videotape after Jay left last night.

The Machine remained on past the duration it had during the previous test. Five seconds. Ten. Until finally Ernie saw what he thought to be a small dark spot in the spot James had been staring into yesterday. He blinked several times, moved his head back and forth and even wiped the goggles with the handkerchief he kept in his back pocket. Still, the dark shape remained fixed in place, trembling slightly, barely perceptible but unmistakably there.

This is it! Observable phenomena! Proof!

Proof of what, exactly? he quizzed himself.

Well, now, that was the question, wasn't it? Now came the difficult part: the surmising, the hypotheses, the A to B, the ifs, ands and buts.

Then the smudge began to move.

At first it was small movements, side to side, up and down. He wasn't sure if he'd actually seen any movement until he held out a trembling finger to cover it in his vision and the smudge clearly moved an inch or more out of its range, in either direction. As if it were testing the water.

And then it *flew*.

It rocketed up toward the ceiling, bounded off toward the far wall, then shot diagonally toward the shelving on the wall opposite.

Turn it off, a small voice in his head told him.

After two years studying those damn stones, spending most

of his waking hours not spent at work digging and dusting and toiling away on these Machines, he deserved *some* sort of reaction. Didn't he? Well, this was it. *This* was a reaction. This was the Duolith finally fulfilling its intended purpose.

No, he told the voice—of what? Reason? His conscience? Cowardice? *Let's see where this goes.*

The smudge hovered in front of the tools, back and forth, as if observing them. As if it had *intelligence.*

Turn it off, the voice said again, louder this time.

But he wouldn't shut it off. This was what he'd been waiting for. He thought about how excited Elana would be to see footage of this tomorrow. She would have been here tonight if not for her movie date with the imbecile. Why she wasted her time on him, Ernie would never know. Not that he was interested in her himself. Science was his only mistress. Science and—

The smudge was gone. When he spotted it again, it had dropped down to the worktable, hovering over the electronic parts and tools laid out there, again as if studying them, and in a literal blink—his eyes were sore from keeping them open in a state of excitement—it vanished.

Where the devil could it be? he wondered.

The de-furred Furby stood up on its own and blinked. The plastic rods for its removed ears moved like twin metronomes.

Not on its own, he thought. *It's the Duolith entity! It's making it move somehow!*

"*Me hungry*," the Furby said, its beak opening and closing in response to the words.

Ernie jumped. The movement was one thing, but it *wasn't possible* for the robot to speak. He'd removed its synthesizer chip, another Texas Instruments TSP50C04, like the Speak & Spell, to use in the Machine. If the robot was talking—which, unless he was hallucinating, it clearly was—it was doing so not from its electronics, but some other force altogether.

Reason returned to him in a flash of anxiety and he turned off the Machine.

Or at least, he *flicked the switch* to turn it off. But the Machine kept running and the Furby flapped its skinned ears and rose off the table an inch, a foot...

My God! I can't stop it!

Ernie scurried over to the outlet, dropped to his knees—his

mind made the connection to his first sight of the Duolith, on his knees in the cave—and he pulled the plug. The Machine kept rattling and humming, with no power supplying it.

Hegel meowed beneath the workbench. The robot turned toward her, rotating in mid-air like an anthropomorphized helicopter.

"Hegel! Shoo!"

He spoke too late. The possessed Furby—for that was what it was now, clearly possessed by whatever force or entity The Machine had summoned via the Duolith—launched itself at the poor feline. She yowled in pain as the beak darted at her, pecking away like a real bird exacting revenge on its mortal enemy. Blood splashed against the legs of the workbench and Ernie's pantlegs as he hurried over to prevent her demise.

"No-no-*no!*" he cried.

Its black plastic shell glistening with gore, the Furby dropped to the cold concrete floor and blinked its blood-pinked eyes up at Ernie. He stopped in his tracks, feet from the thing. Hegel jittered, her insides ripped out like the mutilated and plundered shells of one of the many electronics scattered around the garage.

"*Me hungry,*" the demonic Furby said again. Then it blinked innocently and fluttered its ear sticks to lift itself off the floor.

Ernie ran. He dashed for the inner door, neglecting his poor dying friend, and scrabbled at the handle. He heard the buzz of the Furby's ear-wings nearing and twisted the handle just in time, yanking it open and slamming it behind himself as the thing thudded against it on the other side.

"What have I done?" he said aloud. His own voice startled him in the darkened hallway, but he repeated himself regardless.

"*What have I done?*"

6

8:40 P.M.
Hammer Road

The kids had really tired Jenny da Costa out tonight, having convinced her to take them "*just one more block, Mom*" the past three streets in a row. But these were the times she'd regret missing out on once they were old enough to trick-or-treat by themselves, she knew, and since they were eight and nine now, that could be as early as next year. Other kids their age were already going in small groups without their parents, some with their slightly older siblings. *Enjoy it while it lasts*, she told herself.

It'd been a long day slinging hash at the Eateria today, but she'd just have to suck it up a little longer, then get them back to their beds. Halloween falling on a school night was never ideal, especially after that snake Jacky Saovi left them behind to bang some stripper he'd met in Vegas when the kids were four and five.

She'd dated other guys since then, but it was always the same. Once they got wind of her kids, they'd skitter off like dead leaves in autumn. One guy stuck around for about six months and seemed to take a real shine to Justin, a teacher named Paul Bennington who'd turned out to be a pedophile. After he was murdered earlier this year, the state cops reported his computer had been filled with pictures of little boys in various states of undress. None of them were Justin, thank God, but he *had* taken lots of clothed photos of him, which conspicuously barely featured Rachel at all. Jenny was just glad she'd never asked him to babysit that one time she'd gotten called in to cover for Willa at the diner. She'd asked Jacky's mother instead, who she still talked to from time to time. God only knew what might have happened if she hadn't.

She'd just taken the kids through Janice and Simon Deacon's haunted house—which was actually just a haunted garage and a decorated front yard, despite what people called it—and both kids were hyped up on sugar and excitement. They really loved Halloween. Justin tore open a packet of Pop Rocks and poured some into his mouth as they carried on to the next house. He opened his mouth and turned to his sister with the purple candy crackling in the spit on his tongue.

"Gross," she said, swatting him away with her magic wand. She was Glinda the Good Witch this year. Justin was a cowboy with a silver plastic pistol he took out of its holster to pretend shoot just about every person who opened their doors tonight. *Click-click-click-click! You're dead!* It was exhausting, but Jenny supposed she wouldn't have it any other way.

"No more candy 'til we get home, Just," she instructed.

Justin crunched the mouthful of fizzy candy. "Aw, c'mon!"

"Mom's right," Rachel told him. "If you eat it all tonight you'll just get sick and barf like last Halloween, then you won't have any left for the rest of the week and try to sneak mine."

"Did not!"

"Did too!"

A ghost of a headache crept back in behind Jenny's eyeballs. They were getting worse the older she got—or the older the kids got, she supposed was closer to the truth. She rubbed the heels of her palms on her eyes. "Okay, two more houses and we're heading home, got it?"

Justin rolled his head dramatically. "Come *on*, just one more block!"

"Please, please, pleeeeease, Mommy?" Rachel said in her best sugar-and-spice voice.

"No buts. I've gotta get up early for work tomorrow and the two of you have school. It's already almost nine," she added, glancing at her watch.

Justin frowned, crunching the last of the Pop Rocks. "But you said we could stay up later tonight."

"You can stay up later when we get home."

They both moaned in disapproval, but once they turned onto the walkway of the Corman house, the grins returned to their faces and they raced each other to the porch steps.

Jenny caught up to them as the door opened. Mrs. Corman, a sweet elderly woman whose husband was chair-bound—not a wheelchair, but his La-Z-Boy, which he rarely left aside from bathroom breaks and bed—beamed a genuine smile at the sight of the kids, holding up a popcorn bowl filled with candy in red wrappers.

"Trick or treat!" the kids shouted.

"Oh, well don't you two look sweet! So nice to see children wearing respectable costumes. You know, I was Glinda the Good Witch when I was your age."

Jenny glanced at her watch. It was 8:46. If she could manage to get them home by just after nine, she might be able to get in a bath after the kids got ready for bed.

"I'm a cowboy," Justin said, as if that wasn't obvious, and as if he hadn't said it at every second door.

"I see that," Mrs. Corman said.

Justin pulled out his silver pistol to demonstrate it. He pulled the trigger. Jenny expected the same dry click it made every single time he'd pulled it tonight. The deafening *BANG!* shocked her. As did the sudden splash of warm liquid on her face.

Her gaze flicked up just in time to see a rainbow of loose Skittles flying every which way in a blood-red mist. A dime-sized hole had opened between Mrs. Corman's eyes, the back of her head blown out like an airbag burst from a steering wheel. The popcorn bowl split in half, and so did Mrs. Corman's glasses, both of which landed at her feet. She tumbled backwards into the foyer, the hem of her dress riding up above her tan hosiery, the carpet runner soaking up her blood like a sponge.

"Who's setting off dang firecrackers out there?" Mr. Corman called from his La-Z-Boy.

Rachel screamed. Jenny screamed. Justin looked at the tiny pistol in shock and let it fall to the porch boards with a distinctly plastic-sounding clatter, then screamed himself.

Elsewhere on Hammer Road, voices rose in panic and terror.

Jenny didn't think they'd make it home for nine any longer.

7

8:25 P.M.
76 Seltzer Street

"IT'S TOO late to carve the pumpkin."

Amelia Miller chuckled, sipping a glass of merlot at the far end of the kitchen island. Her long-time boyfriend, Zack Summerly, sat drinking a Smirnoff Ice on the far stool, looking at the sad pumpkin she'd picked up on discount from the grocery store, which sat squatly on the counter before him.

"It's Halloween," she said, already a little buzzed. "We've got scary movies, we've got popcorn. All we need is a jack-o'-lantern to make this perfect."

Zack grinned and sipped his cooler. "But we don't even have any candy."

"Not for the kids. For me." She leaned over the counter, reaching for his free hand. He took hers, small next to his own, and Amelia drew his hand toward her, his powerful, work-hardened hand, turned it to face her and kissed his knuckles tenderly. "It's a nostalgia thing. Come on, babe. We've had one every year..." She stopped just short of putting his index finger in her mouth. She knew it drove him wild, but just the thought of it got him grinning and moving closer to the counter and her sad, mutant pumpkin.

"All right. Pop the corn, I'll slay this ugly beast, fair wench."

Amelia grazed the tip of his calloused index finger with her lips, and Zack moaned, rolling his eyes in delight. "Your wish is my command," she said breathily.

As she got the Jiffy Pop out of the cupboard, turned on the burner and shook the package over the open flames, Zack took out the biggest knife from the drawer, the one he'd carved the pumpkins with in previous years, and used it to cut out the stem in a ragged circle. He removed it, pulled the slimy guts off the bottom, and started grabbing handfuls of its innards and tossing them into the trash bin beside the counter.

Amelia put on Cinemax (they were playing the Freddy movie where the kids could control their dreams), and fed Zack handfuls of popped corn, opened another bottle of Smirnoff Ice for him and topped off her wine glass. Zack had never been a wine drinker. It was one of the things she'd first liked about him. But she'd had to work at convincing him to switch from beer— when they met his brand had been Budweiser—to coolers. He'd started to get a beer gut in their second year of dating, despite working at the lumber yard, carrying and cutting heavy planks of wood day in day out. She'd finally convinced him to switch to Bud Light and then to coolers by reminding him he didn't want to be "one of those guys who can't even see his dick when he pees."

With the pumpkin's yellow-orange guts mostly in the trash (some seeds and lumps spattered the counter, which Amelia would clean before work tomorrow morning), Zack began carving out the rough shape of a face. He wasn't very artistic, which was another thing that had attracted her to him at first, seeing as she ran Crooks Corner's only art gallery and had to deal with people even more artsy-fartsy than herself all the time. She truly was a cliché, she often thought, especially after watching Carrie Bradshaw from *Sex and the City*, an intellectual, dating

Aidan, a guy who built furniture for a living. But to hell with it. Maybe Zack didn't make her *think* but he sure made her *moan*. And Amelia gave as good as she got.

It was like that old Pet Shop Boys song. She had the brains, he had the brawn, although to be fair both of them had the looks. Maybe they weren't making lots of money like the song said, but they were doing well enough to buy two bottles of the good merlot once a week—twice on a good week—and they *owned* this bungalow with the crappy linoleum kitchen floor she hated and popcorn ceiling in the bedroom. Whereas when she was still living in the city—*Carrie Bradshaw's city*—she was lucky enough to be able to afford one drink at the bar, even while sharing a rent-controlled one-bedroom apartment with her beatnik ex-roommate.

Zack stuck his tongue out the side of his mouth like Charlie Brown when he was concentrating, another thing she'd liked about him. He'd done it when he'd written his phone number down on a cocktail napkin at the Town Pump—a fun play on words, though she often wondered if the woman who owned the bar was in on the joke—and she'd just about died swooning.

"Wallah," he said, which always made Amelia wince, but she didn't have the heart to correct his pronunciation (which he called pro*noun*ciation). He turned the pumpkin around. It had Xs for eyes and a big crooked smile with wedges cut out to look like stitches, just like the graffiti she couldn't seem to avoid seeing all over town these days. Looking at it made her vaguely uncomfortable. Zack beamed at her like a proud toddler and she had to practically force a smile.

"What do you think?"

"Well, he's cute but he won't be replacing you any time soon. I'll get the candle."

She got a long candle out of the miscellaneous drawer—she loathed the term "junk drawer"—and cut the bottom third off with the kitchen shears. Zack took it from her and placed it into the groove he'd carved in the bottom. He put the lid back on, wedging it back into its proper place.

"You're not going to light it?"

"I was gonna wait until it's in the den."

In the living room—*not* the den—Freddy was using one of

the kids as a human marionette. She cocked her head to the side. "Light it here."

Zack shrugged and turned the jack-o'-lantern to face him. He got the green BIC lighter out of the fifth pocket in his perfectly snug-fitting jeans. He stuck his hand through the mouth—if she asked why he didn't remove the lid and light it that way he'd respond with his usual, "Work smarter not harder"—and flicked the wheel.

"*AHHHH!*" came a growl of pain. It sounded like it was coming from the pumpkin, and after all these years she'd never known Zack had any aptitude for ventriloquism. Zack's look of shock became a rictus of agony and he screamed, lifting the pumpkin into the air.

"That's not funny," Amelia said.

Fake blood began spattering the fridge, the counter, Zack's face and snug-fitting shirt.

"It's not *funny*, Zack. *Stop it.*"

But Zack wasn't laughing. And if he was fooling, it was better acting than he'd ever done in his life. He brought the hand and the pumpkin down hard on the counter, surely hard enough to shatter it. But the pumpkin didn't break, and it didn't let go of his hand. The bottle of Smirnoff Ice fell off the counter and shattered on the floor.

"Get—the mallet!" he cried, waving with his free hand.

Amelia felt woozy. This wasn't a gag. If it was, Zack wouldn't have been able to prevent himself from laughing, and he certainly would've stopped the second he broke the bottle, if only to say "Party foul" and start cleaning it up.

Amelia planted her wine glass on the counter and headed for the large utensil drawer. Halfway there, she fainted. She was unconscious before her head hit the awful caramel-colored linoleum.

Minutes or hours later, she couldn't tell until she looked at the clock on the stove—it was minutes, probably ten or fifteen since she'd gotten the candle out of the drawer—Amelia woke on the floor with a splitting headache. Her hair had stuck to the crummy linoleum in a small puddle of dried blood and she had to hold on to it close to the roots to pull herself free. Still, she ended up pulling at least five or ten hairs right out of her head, which stayed stuck to the floor, sticking up like an ugly mole.

As she rolled over, still holding her head, flashes of what had caused her to fall came back to her in blood-red Technicolor.

"Zack..." she said, in a panic.

The kitchen was bare. The guts of the pumpkin had been spread all over the counter and on the floor among splashes of blood, but Zack and the pumpkin—*which couldn't have come to life, that's just not possible, not in real life*—were nowhere to be found.

"Zack!" Her own shouting hurt her head. "Zach, are you all right?"

Her first thought was that whatever had happened, real or imagined, had caused a lot of blood to be spilled. He'd driven himself in a panic to the hospital, completely forgetting about her lying on the floor unconscious. Or maybe, just maybe, he'd gone upstairs to get bandages and passed out in the tub. It was bad, but at least it was better than the alternatives.

What are the alternatives?

She didn't even *want* to consider them. Not with how many horror movies she'd seen in her lifetime.

Amelia stood up quickly and swooned, grabbing the counter to keep from falling again. She thought she probably had a concussion, and wondered if she should go to the hospital as soon as she found Zack.

You're still buzzed. You had half a bottle of wine. That and the knock on the head, you have to take it easy.

When her vision cleared, she saw the knife Zack had used to carve the pumpkin was no longer on the counter. It didn't appear to be on the floor, amid the copious amounts of red she didn't dare hope was mostly merlot and pumpkin guts. Had he taken it with him? Where the hell was he? Why wasn't there an ambulance here? Or the police?

As she thought this, the sound of sirens zipped down the street, red and blue lights flashing through the kitchen window. The first was followed by a second, with the firetruck's airhorn blasting into the night.

Something's going on out there. Something bad.

In the silence that followed, sound erupted from the television as the channels changed again and again. She turned to see its blue light flashing over someone sitting in Zack's ugly recliner. Her shoe squelched in a large, dark stain on the rug, the sound and squishiness under the sole immediately detestable.

"Zack...?" she called out. He must've been wearing one of his hoodies because his head seemed very large. Or maybe he'd bandaged himself up and was wearing an ice pack on his head. Could his injury have been so bad he'd completely ignore her lying unconscious on the floor? Did she need to call the ambulance herself?

On the television, the occupants of the mall in the original *Dawn of the Dead* mused upon why the zombies were attacking the mall, and Ken Foree delivered the classic "no more room in Hell" line. The channel changed to some religious program with the televangelist urging his audience to put their hands on the TV screen. He looked strangely like Phil Collins. The channel flicked again.

Amelia stepped around the chair, catching sight of the deformed face of the thing sitting there. She leaped back in pure terror, before realizing what she was looking at, then got a better look at the figure. Zack had stuck the jack-o'-lantern over his head, resting comfortably on his shoulders. She couldn't see his face within the moving shadows of its shell, flickering in the blue light of the television, but it was definitely him, judging by the muscle-tight clothes and the hard-working hands she'd know anywhere.

"You scared me half to death!" she said with a relieved sigh. "I was hurt, why didn't you check on me?"

"Only half?" the pumpkin said, its carved mouth moving like a real mouth, not like a hand puppet's. She didn't know how Zack was able to make it move like that, but it was clearly his voice she heard from its pumpkin-flesh lips.

"Zack? What are you—"

"*Not* Zack. No, We are *much more* than just *Zack*. We are *Geth*," he said, though Amelia heard *We are Death*.

She took another hesitant step around the chair, and her heart dropped into the pit of her stomach.

Zack's head wasn't inside the jack-o'-lantern. It *couldn't* be inside the pumpkin because his head lay on the sofa, in her spot, propped up against the blood-streaked silk throw pillows in a dark stain on the suede they'd just had drycleaned last week.

"We are so pleased you finally joined us, Amelia Miller. Are we not, Zachary Summerly?"

On the sofa, Zack's mouth opened in what Amelia had once considered an endearingly goofy smile, black blood pouring from his lips onto the suede.

The pumpkin turned to Amelia. She made to run for the kitchen, but Zack's cold, dead hand shot out and grasped her wrist, holding her firmly in place.

"Oh no, you must not leave," the jack-o'-lantern said. "Not until We manage to scare your other half."

Both the pumpkin man and Zack's severed head erupted in cackles, and suddenly Amelia's headache was the least of her concerns.

CHAPTER 9

1

8:30 P.M.
Halloween Village

Cassandra had never babysat anyone besides her sister before, and now she'd lost the kid at the haunt. If she'd been paying attention instead of doing the stand-up for the fake documentary, Tommy would never have had a chance to run off. Then again, if Mariska hadn't flaked and Tommy's mother hadn't had to take a late shift, she wouldn't have had to babysit Mingus the Dingus in the first place.

The five of them hurried to the front of the line for the barn haunt, Cody in the lead. "Hey, Brett," Cody said to the older kid letting people inside. "I think the kid who was with us snuck in here when we weren't looking. Is it all right we cut the line?"

Brett looked down the long line of anxious customers. He seemed hesitant, then nodded. "You're next."

Cody clapped him on the shoulder. "Thanks, homie." He smiled back at the others. "We'll find him."

"I guess it pays to know people," Cassandra forced herself to say. She didn't like having to be beholden to a jock, but credit where credit was due.

He chuckled. "Friends in low places."

Cassandra laughed like a hyena. She covered her mouth quickly, realizing how crazy she looked. "Sorry. I'm just worried."

"He'll be fine. The worst that can happen is he gets scared out of his wits. Probably do him good, the little turd."

"He is a little turd," Taylor said. "He's a turd burger!"

"You mean *burglar*," Jay said behind them.

Taylor shook her head. "That's dumb. Who would steal turds?"

"You'd be surprised."

Cody's friend let them into the barn. People behind them expressed their aggravation at the unfairness, but the guy explained they'd lost a little kid "and wouldn't you expect the same if it was your kid that was lost?"

Cody led the way into the dark tunnel, with Cassandra behind him and Taylor at her feet. Cassandra liked scary movies but she didn't enjoy being scared in real life. She knew it was all just plastic skeletons and rubber rats, but it made her nervous just the same.

Cody looked back at her. "You scared?"

"*No*," she said indignantly, her cheeks burning.

"She's scared," Taylor said.

"Shut it, shrimp."

She noticed Cody's sly grin as he turned to face the front and continued forward. She followed a few steps behind him, checking out his butt in his jeans. *Gross, Cassandra*, she scolded herself. *Does he have to be so fucking cute, though?*

They entered a really disgusting kitchen. Sausage links hung from the ceiling, which she assumed were meant to have been made from the human body parts strewn all over. The cannibal chopped up meat on the grimy counter, his face hidden behind another face. *Chop-chop-chop!* Fake smoke rose from a grill behind him.

The cannibal leaned over the counter and roared, waving his knife at them, and Cassandra just about peed her pants. The sound of the heart beating over the speakers could have been her own for how fast it thrummed in her chest.

Taylor snapped a photo of her, the flash blindingly bright. "That's going on the fridge."

"No flash photography, please!" Jay barked. "You're gonna mess up my CCD."

Cassandra rolled her eyes. He was probably right, but why did he have to be so annoying about it?

"What's a CCD?" Taylor asked her.

"It's like a light sensor," she said. "He's right, you shouldn't use the flash when we're taping, at least inside in the dark."

"Okay," Taylor moaned.

They continued through another dark, twisting hall and stepped into a disgusting bathroom. It looked so gross she could practically smell it. "*They drowned my babies!*" a girl from school shouted at them. Cassandra recognized her as Heather something, a sophomore who smoked cigarettes with Cindy Jansen in the parking lot at lunch.

"Hey, Heather," Cody said. "Did a chubby little kid come through here a few minutes ago? Maybe on his own?"

"We're not supposed to break character," Heather muttered through the side of her mouth. "But yeah. He was just here." Her eyes widened and she peered around wildly, swinging her head back and forth. "*My babies, you have to save my babies!*"

"Thanks," Cody said. "You're real scary, by the way. Great job."

Heather sputtered, then ran at Jay's camera, waving her arms dramatically. "*They drowned my little ones in the tub!*" she screamed.

Jay reared back but held the camera steady. Walden taped both of them.

"Come on," Cody said. "He's gotta be close."

Cassandra and the others followed him into the hall.

2

Brittany found the perfect gift: a smartass little kid, all on his own. Even better, he thought he couldn't be scared.

He's bout to find out just how wrong he is, yes sir, said The Snake.

She knew where all the cameras were in the main halls, and where best to avoid the other actors, but she'd been smart, and left a black cloak from the drama class costume closet tucked into a darkened corner. The narrow crossover corridors running alongside the maze where actors could sneak past customers without being seen were only used by her, Jason—who played the chainsaw murderer, despite sharing a name with the killer from *Friday the 13th*—and the techs. Jason never came this far into her territory, and once the haunt opened for the night the techs only came through if there was a problem with one of their toys, which was rare.

She led the kid onward, through the red-lit tunnel. He was impatient, too, pressing her for details and when they'd get there, like a kid in the backseat on a long drive. Little did he know, he was hurrying her toward his own demise.

"Come on, what's taking so long? What's so scary, huh?"

"This," she said finally, turning to him with the knife she'd stolen from the cannibal kitchen as she'd toured the boys through the maze. The kid's eyes went wide, and for a moment Brittany wasn't sure she could do it. It was easier with Mr. Bennington. Everyone in Crooks High knew the retired math teacher had been inappropriate with young boys. Some people even said he'd deserved it.

Tommy Mingus didn't *deserve* to die. But that was *why* she needed to do it. Like John F. Kennedy said about having to put a man on the moon, not because it was easy but because it was hard. Anyone could kill a pedo. It took a real sick mind to murder an innocent kid, no matter how annoying he might be. Denise might not understand, but her dad would.

That was how The Snake had put it, anyhow.

Not like she could argue. Put up too much of a fight and she'd black out and wake up an hour or two later having done what she'd been struggling not to do. It was better to give in. Easier. And with herself in control, she was less likely to get caught. The Snake liked to make a mess. If not for her meticulous cleaning after she'd woken up from his control, Bennington's house would've been loaded with DNA evidence.

Tommy put on a brave face, barking a laugh. "That's not real." He was a pretty brave kid. Too brave.

"Oh, it's real," Brittany said.

"Bull plop."

Brittany stuck the end of the blade into the wall beside him with a *thock* audible over the horror music and screams in the main halls and scare rooms. The kid looked frightened now.

Last chance, Brittany, she told herself.

Coward, The Snake said. *Do it. Kill the li'l piggy 'fore it's too late.*

The kid made to break away but she caught him by the collar

and pushed him against the plywood wall. The devil horns on their plastic hairband fell off of his head and his whole body began to shiver, his jowls jiggling. *"Hel—!"*

Her sweaty gloved palm muted his cry, much as The Snake wanted to hear the little piggy squeal. No one would believe it was real, like that scene in the theater in *Scream 2*, where Jada Pinkett died right in front of the audience and everyone just thought her death was part of the show. But the less chance of getting caught, the better. The boy was doomed the moment he'd followed her into the crossover passage. No reason to doom herself to prison, or worse.

Zip-zip-zip went a fly over their heads, sending out the lunging skeleton to jump scare people in the maze behind the boy's trembling head. The group screamed, less than an inch of plywood between them and true horror. The little piggy kicked out at her, but Brittany had years of dance and gymnastics under her belt. She'd even taken a few self-defense classes under the guise of being worried about her own safety. She deftly dodged his wild kicks and used a shin to hold his weak little legs against the wall. His struggles shook the plywood but did nothing to free him. He stuck out weakly with his small fists but she twisted out of the way and they struck nothing but air.

Now or never.

"Didn't your parents tell you never to follow strangers?" she asked. He tried to shake his head but her hand wouldn't allow for the movement. Before she could change her mind, she plunged the knife between his ribs. The boy's eyes opened so wide she could see the whites all the way around. Blood poured out of the hole in his winter jacket like crimson syrup. He gasped, his breath whistling. Brittany realized from her study of anatomy that she'd punctured one of his lungs. She pulled out the blade and plunged it in again and again, not quickly but me-thodically. Less chance of blood splatter on her costume that way. She watched the hope and the life drain from the little pig-gy's eyes, just as she had with Mr. Bennington. When she was sure he was dead, she removed her hand from his lips. His lifeless body slid down the wall.

It didn't elude her that she'd crossed a boundary just now, a moral line in the sand behind which she couldn't ever return. It felt different than it had with Mr. Bennington. He'd deserved what she gave him, and while the brat was maybe just too stupid to live, he hadn't done anything *bad* to justify losing his life. He'd just been in the right place at the right time. Strangely, she didn't *feel* any different, as if that boundary, that line she'd crossed, was only an illusion. Maybe it was. Maybe the only reason people were told *thou shalt not kill* was because it was so easy, because life itself had no deeper meaning. It was all just a series of events and choices leading inevitably to our own deaths.

Brittany uttered a single, surprised laugh.

Without wasting another moment, she hoisted the boy up under his armpits, turning him around so she'd be less likely to get his blood on her. He was chunky but couldn't weigh more than ninety pounds. She waddled him to the place she'd decided to leave the body during her weeks of planning, the toes of the boy's sneakers dragging along the floor in front of her.

The discovery of his corpse would be the best jump scare in the haunt, and the biggest news in Crooks Corner by tomorrow morning's comm class.

Why report on the news when you can make it yourself? The Snake asked with a hysterical cackle.

Smiling her actor's smile, Brittany dutifully agreed.

3

THE BARN SMELLED like motor oil, straw and stale animal dung as Cody led the others through it, wishing he could just ask Chet or Row to turn on the lights and call off the haunt until they found Tommy. It was a familiar smell, seeing as he'd spent a lot of time here over the past two summers picking corn for the Thompsons.

He was pretty sure they'd find Tommy unharmed once they reached the other end of the barn maze, probably laughing in delight at all the awesome, gory things he'd witnessed. He could just about hear the little brat saying, *What took you guys so long?* It might have been smart to suggest Walden or Jay meet them there, "cut him off at the pass" like they used to say in those black-and-white Westerns his dad sometimes watched. But he hadn't been thinking ahead. It was easy for him to think ahead during a game. He could see his opponents' plays before they made them, like a chess master saw upcoming moves. He'd duck and dive and weave like Neo in *The Matrix*, driving the ball toward the goalposts.

Coach said it was almost supernatural the connection he had with the ball, with the game. But it was just analytical. A lot of the guys on the other teams were meatheads. Heck, most of them on his own team were, skating through school on their athletic abilities, hoping for a scholarship, only caring about the cars, the fans, the girls. Cody had never much cared about that stuff. He cared about it, but it wasn't *life* to him like it was to some of the other guys, like Chimney and Brunt.

Cody cared about his parents and his friends and getting good enough grades to make his parents proud. He didn't know Cassandra very well, but as a fellow human and a classmate, he cared for her well-being. And even though he thought Tommy Mingus was a little jerk, Cassandra was responsible for him. Her sister actually seemed to like the kid, so Tommy couldn't be that bad once you got to know him.

After the bathroom where Heather Platz had been whining about the baby dolls drowned in the tub, a big guy in greasy coveralls lumbered down the short hall toward them, holding a growling chainsaw. Cassandra screamed and grabbed Cody's arm. He looked down at it, then at her. She caught his eye and let go immediately.

"Shut up," she said.

Cody grinned and sidled past the homicidal maniac. The others followed him, moving against the wall as the actor revved the motor.

The screams and shouts from elsewhere rose in intensity, an almost solid wall of voices singing a sustained note of terror. In the same instant, the chainsaw maniac slumped against the wall. A splash of fake blood struck Cody, Cassandra and her sister as the bladeless saw seemed to attack the actor's throat. The hockey mask fell off, revealing a pale, terror-stricken face.

Why is it warm? Cody wondered, wiping the sticky mess from his face.

Jay shielded the camera from the blood, and wiped the lens with a tissue. "Watch the camera, jackass!" he shouted.

"Help me!" the chainsaw maniac shrieked, letting go of the handle. The motor kept running, suspended below his Adam's

apple, lodged several inches into his throat. Cody figured he must've had some kind of catch and harness to keep it hanging like that. A chainsaw without a blade wouldn't do anything but maybe give him a bad cut, which would explain a *bit* of the blood but not the rest, and especially not the bits of fake flesh and blood flying every which way. The guy was a great actor. No wonder Brittany had wanted to work here for the season.

"Let's go," Cassandra said, pulling her sister along.

Cody agreed and carried on, if only to prevent himself from getting more of the warm fake blood on his clothes. They really should've mentioned the stunt before they entered, or at least given out ponchos.

"What the fuck?" Walden cried.

The actor's body had slid down the wall when Cody looked back, the chainsaw buried into the plywood behind him. The severed head bobbled for a moment on the surface of the blood-soaked steel bar, then slid off and fell to the floor. It rolled toward him, the eyes and mouth in a wide expression of terror. It looked so realistic Cody instinctively kicked it away from him in disgust.

Taylor shrieked, covering her eyes.

Pounding footsteps and screams entered the space as a big group of people came pushing and shoving through the doorway behind Walden. The young guy in the lead dressed up to look like Shaggy from *Scooby-Doo* waved his hands frantically, shouting "*Go! Go! Go!*"

Jay wasn't even using the camera anymore. He held it from the top handle, hanging useless at his side. "What's happening?" he moaned, clearly freaked out.

"Just move!" a woman in the group shouted.

The anxiety in her voice was contagious, kicking Cody into action as more people rushed into the narrow corridor behind them. He wasn't sure if it was smarter to keep moving forward or go back. He just had to hope they'd already past the center of the maze. He'd been in this old barn a bunch of times, hanging out with fellow corn-pickers on their smoke breaks, and he knew even though it had probably been standing for at least fifty years it was unlikely to hold up during a stampede.

The recorded wails of the babies from back in the bathroom grew suddenly louder, as if the sound was following them.

An older man shouted, "*They're coming!*"

"What's coming?" a boy their age replied.

"Is this real? Is this part of it?" Cody asked anxiously, hurrying forward with Cassandra and Taylor right behind him.

"I don't know," she said, "just keep going!"

He did. Still, the wailing seemed to be catching up to them, their high-pitched tone buzzing like a swarm of bees.

"*OHMYGOD!*" another woman cried.

Pushing through a mess of cobwebs that felt decidedly more real than the ones clearly made of cotton batting, Cody risked a glance back at the crowd following him, in time to see a pale pink thing about the size of a watermelon leaped onto Heather Platz's head. She screamed and clawed at the frantic movement of the thing tangled in her hair.

Cody stumbled into the next room, a stone-walled Chamber of Evil with a book opened on a lectern and an old organ decorated with heavy silver candelabras. The organ keys depressed and rose on their own, playing sinister music from the pipes. In the far corner, a werewolf in jeans and a letterman jacket shook the bars of the tall cage it stood in. It took him a moment to realize it was animatronic, not a person in a costume. Regardless, it was surprisingly realistic, with wild yellow eyes and foam spraying from its peeled-back lips.

Taylor let out a shrill scream. Cody turned to see little black spiders crawling all over her hair and shoulders.

Cassandra just stared at Taylor as her sister danced and shook, trying to rid herself of the crawling menace. "Stop it, Taylor," she said. "Taylor, *stop it.*"

"It's not me!" the little girl cried.

Cody didn't care what Cassandra thought Taylor had to stop. He leaped into action, helping Taylor swipe off the spiders —which felt strangely artificial, almost like plastic. Walden and Jay stomped the things skittering all over the floor. A small army of them scurried toward Cody's feet, and he stepped on them before they could reach him. They crunched underfoot like the army men he used to play with when he was a kid, leaving brittle bits on the floor instead of the goopy guts he'd expected.

They are plastic, he thought. *But how—?*

His thoughts were cut short as the people behind them piled into the room, voices raised in fright. The guy dressed as Shaggy appeared to be fighting something off of his chest. A closer look revealed it was one of the baby dolls from the bathroom. Cody blinked to be sure what he was seeing was real. The little fingers had grabbed fistfuls of the guy's goatee. Its little legs kicked madly, the rage in its cherubic features shockingly realistic. Another baby doll clung to Heather Platz's thigh, kicking and biting like just the one on her head. A dozen more crawled into the room on their hands and knees, their cries rising in an ear-splitting crescendo.

Cassandra had grabbed her sister by the shoulders and started shaking her. "I said *STOP IT!*"

Tears spilled down Taylor's cheeks. "It's not me, I *swear!*"

Cody had no idea what was going on between Cassandra and her little sister, but he couldn't watch her hurt Taylor, and there were more important things to worry about. They couldn't stand around arguing with the room getting more and more crowded. He grabbed her by the shoulder. "You're hurting her, Cassie. Let her go."

Cassandra seemed to snap out of it and let her arms fall to her sides, scowling down at her weeping sister. A baby doll scurried into their tight circle and reached for Taylor's left boot. He kicked the thing away, regretting it immediately as it struck the wall and its cries intensified, even if it had felt distinctly hollow and rubbery.

What the heck's going on here?

More screams arose from the new people. The doll clinging to Shaggy's goatee bit into his cheek, causing a gout of blood. A third and fourth doll had climbed onto Heather and she dropped to the floor. They crawled all over her prone body, grabbing with their little rubbery hands and biting wherever they found flesh.

Cody stood immobile. There was nothing he could do to help these people, not with Taylor in his arms. He'd have to put her down and run the risk of these things eating her alive. He had to protect her. He'd let Tommy slip away and hopefully the kid had made it to safety—not likely, but *hopefully*—but he wouldn't let anything happen to Taylor.

What did she mean, 'stop it'? he wondered suddenly. *She thinks* Taylor's *doing all this?*

A familiar voice shook him from his thoughts. "*HEY!*"

He turned and found Brittany beckoning to them from a

secret doorway within the fake stone wall, a red glow emanating from within. Cody didn't waste any time. He dashed for it, and the others followed, dodging attacks. Brittany stepped aside and held the door, then pushed it shut behind them.

"What's happening, Brit? This is part of it, right?"

"Follow me," Brittany said urgently, heading down the narrow passage. Cody did. The others kept pace behind them.

"It just started happening all at once," Brittany said as they moved. "All over the barn."

"*What's* happening?" Cassandra snapped.

Brittany stopped suddenly and looked back at them, her dead serious expression bathed in red emergency lighting from the floor, making her face look sinister, like the climax of a campfire horror story. "The scares are coming to life," she said.

"*Come on,*" Walden said as they resumed their trek through the back halls. "This can't be real—*can it?*"

"Listen to those screams. You think we convinced everyone in the haunt to play a prank on just you guys?"

"It's real," Jay said.

Cody glanced back, noting the fear in Jay's eyes. His face was pale and waxy like cheese.

"Those spiders were plastic but now they're alive," Jay said.

Brittany kept forging forward, leading them through the winding red maze. "I don't know how or why this is happening, but we have to get out of here."

"What about the others?"

"What *others?*"

Cody nodded toward the black plywood wall separating them from the screams and cries in the main maze. "Out there."

"You can't save *everyone*, Cody. We have to think about ourselves right now."

Cody wasn't sure he agreed, but with Taylor shivering in his arms, it was clear he couldn't go back and try to help any of those people, if they even needed saving. He still couldn't wrap his mind around any of it. Could everything they'd seen just be really realistic animatronics? Was that even *possible*?

Squeaks and squeals rose above the screams and shouts of terror from behind the inch of plywood. Brittany began lifting her legs awkwardly as she moved. "Look out!" she called back.

Cody looked down just as the floor became covered with

wriggling black bodies. *Rats*. He danced out of their way on his tiptoes, hugging Taylor's face against his chest. "Don't look down," he said to her.

His right foot came down hard on one of them, but it didn't crunch or squelch like he'd expected it to. It felt rubbery under his shoe, like stepping on a dog's chew toy, and he almost lost his balance. He accidentally stepped on several more as they continued ahead, until the mini stampede dwindled, leaving only a few stragglers scurrying between their feet. They were running in the opposite direction, away from the exit.

"Are these...?" Walden began.

"Rubber," Jay finished for him. "Rubber rats. Rubber rats running. Rubber rats running with rabies." He let out a wild, high-pitched laugh.

Cody didn't like the sound of Jay's voice. It sounded like he was on the verge of losing his marbles.

The red maze ended at the old wooden side door of the barn. Brittany reached it first and struggled to push it open. Cody put Taylor down to help her.

"*Why* are they running, though?" Walden asked.

"Isn't that what rats do?" Cassandra said. "They're always being gross and scurrying around!"

"I *mean*, what are they running *from*?"

The door swung open with a rusty screech and fresh, chilly air blew into the narrow tunnel. Cody had a moment to catch his breath before a giant, clawed hand swung down at him. He ducked, shielding Brittany against the outer wall of the barn. She pushed him away with a sneer.

"I can handle my—" she started angrily. The protest died in her throat as she caught sight of the massive creature standing to the right of the exit, towering over them.

It was the giant crow demon they'd seen earlier, the one Tommy had jabbed with his trident. Only now the crow skull's smile grew impossibly wide, and real flames burst from the carved holes in its face with a crackling roar.

"James?" Brittany asked warily.

"What?" Jay snapped.

Before Brittany could respond, a terrified voice from behind the crow mask cried, "*I can't stop it!*" The monster's other arm swung at them. Cody and Brittany stepped out of the way a split second before its razor-sharp claws swiped the air where they'd stood. *"It's not me!"*

Maybe it's Taylor, Cody thought. He had to hold back the urge to laugh. He would've looked like a crazy person.

The crow monster cackled, spitting flames.

"Oh, God, please help me!" the man behind the living mask cried. Before the monster could take another swing at them, involuntarily or not, Cody grabbed Taylor up in his arms again and sprinted toward the graveyard. It wasn't safe, enshrouded in a loose green mist and just as teeming with moving obstacles, but it appeared to be the only way back to the parking lot.

He dashed between caskets and gravestones. Brittany followed until she caught up, running alongside him. The others weren't quite as fast, hurrying along awkwardly behind them as if it was their first time running. Jay didn't make a single complaint this time as their shoes and boots squelched in the wet grass. The corpse hands they'd seen sticking up from the unsettled earth on their tour grabbed at their legs as they sprinted and weaved through the fake/real cemetery like a tire drill to the other end.

Bats flitted down to attack them from above, and Jay crouched as he ran, using the camera to protect his head, shouting at the top of his lungs. Cody struck a bat out of the sky and felt that same distinctly rubbery sensation as with the rats, making him wonder how they could actually hurt people if they were actually just rubber.

What the heck is happening here? he wondered again. A thought arose, or a memory actually, from yesterday. When they were deciding what kind of movie to make, Walden had said *Cheap effects won't kill you*, or something like that. *But they're trying now*, he thought. *They're really trying hard to kill us, Walden.*

A coffin sprung open beside him, startling Taylor in his arms and causing him to careen into her sister. The vampire that emerged moved like a marionette with its knobby joints, its clothes packed with some sort of stuffing. It bore fangs at them, its rubbery face fully animated.

"Sorry," Cody said, grabbing Cassandra's shoulder, holding on to her sister with his other arm. He just barely prevented her from falling in the muck.

"Thanks," she said, then reached into the black lace throat of her dress to flash her crucifix at the creature. "Go to hell!"

The rubber-masked vampire hissed and shielded its face with the hem of its cape.

Taylor screamed against Cody's chest as he leaped over one final skeletal hand in the dirt, coming to a skidding stop in the gravel at the edge of the lot.

"We can't all fit in my car!" Walden announced as they all met at the foot of the gravel.

"We can if we dump the gear!" Cassandra said.

"Hildebrand'll kill us!"

Cody chuckled ruefully. "I say we take our chances."

"Agreed," Brittany said. "Let's—"

Again she stopped mid-sentence, her eyes going wide.

Cody looked in the direction she was facing and saw nothing out of the ordinary—or at least, no more than what they'd already faced so far. Weaving between cars and trucks, terrified people swatted away bats and other flying objects he couldn't identify from the distance. Ignitions started and headlights winked on. Vehicles began pulling out of the lot, grinding gravel.

"Anyone who wants a lift outta this crazy fucking place, follow me." Walden gave Taylor an apologetic look. "Excuse my French."

Cassandra turned to Cody with an inquisitive look. "I'm going with them. Taylor can sit on my lap."

"What about Tommy?" Taylor moaned.

Cody didn't want to tell her Tommy was probably already dead. By the looks on the faces of the others, they knew it was true. Fortunately, no one was cruel enough to voice their fear.

"Tell you what," he said, setting her down on the ground. "I'll stay behind and see if I can find him. Okay?"

Taylor pouted up at him. "I want you to come with us!"

Brittany grabbed his arm. He instinctively flexed, and she let go immediately, like she'd touched a live wire. "What does Tommy look like?"

"A little turd," Cassandra said.

Taylor kicked her sister in the shin. "Don't be mean."

"He's about yay high," Cody said, demonstrating. "Messy brown hair, chubby kid, rosy cheeks. Basically, if Eric Cartman was a real kid, that's Tommy. He was wearing a devil costume."

"Oh..." Brittany said.

"Did you see him?" Taylor asked excitedly.

Brittany's expression changed. It seemed to Cody like she was trying to hide something. "He sounds familiar..." was all she said.

Whether she'd seen him get hurt or worse, there was still a chance Tommy was alive out there, maybe hiding in the barn. Or in the farmhouse, safe and sound with Chet and Row.

Cody crouched to speak to Taylor face to face. "Someone has to look out for the kid," he said, as much as he didn't want to stay behind with the all horror going on here. "If he gets hurt or..." He stopped himself short of adding *or worse*. "We'll all be in big trouble for letting him run away."

"*Fine*," Brittany said. "I'll help you look."

"No. You should go with them."

"You know the farm but I know the haunt." She nodded with finality, as if she was trying to convince herself. "I can help find him."

Taylor looked back and forth between them. "Okay. But be careful."

"We will," they both said.

The girl wiped her nose with her sleeve, then raised her Polaroid to her eye and snapped a photo of Cody and Brittany.

"Ride's leaving!" Walden called. He and Jay already stood on either side of the car, Jay looking down at his own shoes, Walden behind the opened driver door.

Cassandra held Cody's gaze for a moment, then looked off. "Don't get yourself killed or anything, scrub."

Cody surprised himself with a normal-sounding laugh. "You too, Cassandra."

She smiled, putting an arm around Taylor's shoulders. "Let's go, shrimp," she said, ushering her sister toward the car.

As they headed off, Taylor pulled the photo out of the camera and shook it. "This one's going on the fridge," she said.

Cassandra hooked an arm around Taylor's head and gave her a light noogie. Watching them all pile into the car, Cody got a sick feeling in his gut it would be the last time he saw the four of them alive.

"Guess it's just you and me, cowboy," Brittany said, shivering and tucking her hands under her armpits.

Cody took off his letterman jacket and offered it to her. She pushed it away with an aggrieved look.

"You're gonna catch a cold," he said.

"I think that's the least of our worries."

"Just take it until you get yours back. I've got a big sweater."

"*Fine*," she groaned again, slipping her arms into the sleeves. Even though she was tall for a girl, it was still several sizes too big for her. She turned to face the chaos at the farm.

"You think we'll find him?" he asked, hoping to learn a little more about that look she'd tried to hide now that Taylor wasn't around.

Brittany shrugged nonchalantly, the shoulders of his jacket bunching. "If we don't get killed in the process."

Cody nodded, and the two of them started back toward the barn.

CHAPTER 10

1

7:45 P.M. – 8:57 P.M.
The Streets of Crooks Corner

Adam Brunt and the boys prowled the residential streets in his Mustang, looking for trick-or-treaters to harass. Fitz and Chimney sat in the back with a pillowcase between them full of stolen candy, chips and soda, and they still had a shit-ton of eggs left over from last night to chuck at kids, resting at their feet. Riding shotgun with an arm hanging out the window, Dave MacNamara spat a wad of brown saliva into his empty Surge can and stuck it back in the cup holder. From the speakers, Aaron Lewis screamed *fuck you*s to everyone, a sentiment Brunt fully agreed with. He turned up the Staind CD to counter the racket of the guys whooping it up in the back, high on sugar and ass-kicking. *Fuck them, too.*

"We gotta pick some bigger targets, boys," he said, eager to unleash his anger on someone new. "This is too fuckin easy."

"Like taking candy from a baby," Chimney said, laughing with his teeth stained brown from chocolate.

The other guys joined in, but Brunt didn't think it was funny. He didn't find much funny, at least not anything he didn't say himself.

"Hand me one of them Milky Ways," he said, reaching over the back of his seat and clutching his fingers like a greedy claw machine.

Fitz slapped a mini candy bar into Brunt's palm. Brunt closed his fingers around it and brought it to the light from the dash. "That's a fuckin Snickers, asshole." He threw it back. Fitz ducked and the mini chocolate bar hit the back window.

"They're the same thing," Fitz whined, his mouth full of bits of crunched-up plain potato chips.

"Snickers has nuts!"

"So does Milky Way!"

"That's Mars, you fuckhead! Now gimme a goddamn Milky Way before I drive us into a telephone pole."

"All right, I'll find one. *Sheesh.*" Wrappers crinkled as Fitz dug through the pillowcase between them. The dome light came on blindingly bright, making the road ahead hard to see.

"What the fuck?" Brunt bellowed. He reached up and flicked the light off.

"I can't see to find your Milky Way, fuck's sake!"

"Use a goddamn lighter!"

"Yo, chill, Adamsky," Chimney said, cracking his window to light one of his shitty-smelling cigarettes. "You're being very un-Dude." He held his thumb on the BIC's button, keeping the small yellow flame going to assist in Fitz's search, the lit smoke hanging from his lips.

Brunt scoffed. *Un-Dude.* All he wanted was a fucking candy bar, didn't seem too much to ask. He was driving these clowns around, after all. Drove them around all the time, and did any of these ungrateful fucks even ask if he wanted them to chip in for gas? Not a fucking once. As self-righteous as Cockmeyer was, at least the guy had the fucking courtesy to slip him a fiver every once in a while, even if every time he did Brunt thanked him for the head and laughed his motherfucking ass off.

Brunt turned onto High Street. Dead leaves from the maples on every other lawn covered the street and choked the gutters, and the sidewalks were filled with all kinds of little shits in costumes, moving from house to house in search of candy. Brunt growled in aggravation. Way too many adults on this street. It seemed like there were a lot more parents taking their kids out these days, which probably put a damper on the adults' fun almost as much as Brunt's own. The little kids, he understood. All that *stranger danger* bullshit. Definitely made it harder and harder to find kids walking alone.

He needed to scare the shit out of some brats and lay down some beatings before he lost his goddamn mind. That shit last night still had him stewing. Hildebrand coming out of Miss Stabler's house with his shirt untucked and unbuttoned. He hated that smug fuck Hildebrand and he hated Stabler even more for fucking that scrawny-ass dweeb. Sure, teaching math made her a nerd too, but she was still way too hot to be getting plowed by that loser.

"Here's your fuckin Milky Way, your majesty."

Brunt grabbed the candy bar, pushed it from the bottom and popped the whole thing into his mouth. He crumpled the wrapper and tossed it on the floor at MacNamara's feet with all the rest of the garbage.

"The fuck, man?" Big Mac said.

"What? Not my fault you're standin in the trash."

The acoustic version of "It's Been Awhile" started up and Brunt ejected the disc. It was too slow and whiny. He needed some sick tunes to get him pumped up for a good beatdown.

"Hey, grab me that CD," he said, reaching back.

"What CD?" Fitz said, already sifting through the CD binder.

"See deez nuts," Chimney added with a laugh.

"You're 'bout to see deez fists if you don't gimme that CD—oh shit, hold up," Brunt said, spotting something up ahead.

The headlights had picked out a hulking giant in a home-made Fred Flintstone costume trudging across Paoli Avenue at an angle. Only that retard Philbert Piper would be dumb enough to go trick-or-treating at his size and age, and only Philbert Piper would wear a shitbird costume like that.

Bet you anything his mom made it for him, Brunt thought. *That ugly old cow treats him just like a baby.*

He slowed the car to a crawl. The big dumb ape was kicking through dead leaves with his arms swinging and his head bowed like a goddamn caveman. He had one of those plastic buckets that looked like a jack-o'-lantern in one big meaty fist.

"There's Philbert Piper. That dumb fuckin retard. I'm gonna roll up on him. You better pelt him good, bud." Brunt rolled down his window as he crept up on the dummy. "Hey, Philbert! Why'd the chicken cross the road?"

"Huh?" The big dummy turned with a big stupid grin on his

face just in time to catch the egg Fitz chucked out the back window right in the center of his stupid mongoloid forehead. It cracked in two and spilled its yellow guts down his nose and face. Philbert began wiping it off frantically, moaning like he'd fallen into a pit of snakes.

"Booya!" Brunt shouted triumphantly, stamping on the gas. "Got that retard!"

"Drive-by egging!" Fitz shouted, laughing like a fucking hyena.

Chimney ran a hand over his short, bleached hair. "Man, that's *trés* not cool."

"Shut up. You don't like it, get the fuck out and walk."

"Fine, pull the fuck over," Chimney said, calling Brunt's bluff.

Only Brunt wasn't bluffing. If Stuckey Fucky wanted out, he'd let him out. The tires peeled as he slammed both feet on the brakes. "Get out," he said when the car stopped at an angle.

"Dude, I'm not walking home—"

"You said fuckin pull over, here we are. Get the fuck out of my car, bud."

"Dude, I was *joking*."

"Yeah, dude, chill out," MacNamara said.

Brunt turned, grabbing the back of his seat with both hands. "You guys wanna be butt buddies, fuckin *both* of you get the fuck out!"

Both Chimney and Big Mac just sat there blinking at him as if they *wanted* to try him.

"*GET OUT!*"

"Fine," Chimney moaned. "Jesus Christ." He got out of the back and slammed the door.

"You slam that fuckin door one more time, I ain't drivin you fuckin anywhere no more! Got it?"

Chimney stuffed his hands in his pockets and nodded glumly, like a little twerp getting lectured by his mother.

"You too, Big Mac, get the fuck out."

"Serious?"

"Do I look like I'm fucking joking?"

MacNamara huffed a laugh. He shook his head, the door creaked as he opened it, and he got out. Brunt noted how delicately Mac closed the door behind him. *Fuckin better*, he thought. But he was still mad.

"Take your fuckin spit can with you," he said, grabbing the Surge can and chucking it out the open window. He never saw Big Mac move so fast, not even on the field, as he did to get out of the can's path. A streak of thick brown saliva landed on the window frame and the can hit the mailbox behind Mac. Brunt had a mind to tell him to clean it up but figured fuck it, it wasn't worth the trouble or the time.

"Later, bitches," he said, then floored it out of there, leaving those two asshats in a cloud of black smoke. *Let em play hide the weenie with Philbert fuckin Piper, a coupla homos and a retard.*

He frowned at Fitz in the rearview, who'd remained silent throughout the whole ordeal. "You got something to say?"

"Nah, man. I'm cool."

"Sure you are, bud. You're fuckin cool, huh? Get your ass up front then, cool guy. I'm not your fuckin chauffer."

Brunt grinned as Fitz dutifully climbed between the seats and planted his ass in the shotgun seat. He'd reestablished dominance in the hierarchy and all was right in the world again.

Fitz held out a shiny silver disc. "Hey, I found that CD."

"Fuck those guys," Brunt said, snatching the new Creed album from Fitz and popping it in the deck. He skipped ahead to track six, and cranked up the volume. "Let's go find some kids to thrash."

2

LAST HALLOWEEN those high school jerks had stolen Matt Dukas's entire pillowcase full of candy. He and his pals, Kyle and Craig O'Donnelly, had planned their route down to the house during a sleepover weekend, then spent the night itself zig-zagging across rain-dampened streets from neighborhood to neighborhood, hitting just the houses they knew from previous years gave out the best goodies—the full-sized chocolate bars, not those little baby ones, the regular-sized bags of chips, the pops, sometimes even little bags of coins—only to run into those dicks on their way back to the O'Donnelly house and lose every last bit of it.

Well, not this year. Tonight, Matt had a big surprise for Adam Brunt and his goons. He met Kyle and Craig at their house and showed them what he'd planned while standing in the doorway.

Kyle startled, peering down at the shadowy shapes within the pillowcase. Then he giggled. "What's all that for?"

Matt told him.

"Oh yeah, screw those guys. Bunch of dicks."

"Yeah, screw those dicks," Craig said. He was a year younger and constantly trying to impress his older brother and his friends, which often meant just repeating what Kyle said with a few minor variations. Matt liked him well enough. Even if the kid was a little dim, he meant well.

Matt distributed the objects from his pillowcase so the three of them each had an equal amount, and they headed off, following a revised plan from last year which took into account who had moved away or died or just didn't seem to care about Halloween this year, judging by their lack of pumpkins and decorations. The plan was meticulous. They would only deviate from it to stop briefly at Matt's to offload candy and take a whiz, and to hit the haunted house on Hammer Road, just about the best decorated house in Crooks Corner aside from Halloween Village, which Matt's mom had taken them to last night. The plan could only be foiled by those high school football dicks, but this year the plan had a failsafe, all of which Matt had borrowed from his dad's collection from when he was Matt's age.

As badly as he didn't want to run into Brunt and His Grunts, he couldn't wait to see the looks on their faces when they opened these pillowcases up. It'd be a laugh and a half, for sure. He giggled just thinking about it as they headed off on their bikes toward the first house with their pillowcases billowing behind them like capes, strapped over their shoulders. Later on they would weigh heavily on them, but it would be worth it for the speed advantage their bikes would give them, going from street to street. Drop them on the first lawn, head up one side and down the other, then pick up their bikes and pedal to the next street over. Everything had gone according to plan.

They dropped their bikes on the Haigs's withered front lawn at the corner of Gordon Road and began their trek up the sidewalk to the first house with a light on. A sad-looking pumpkin that had obviously been carved by a child or possibly an adult with very poor motor skills sat heavily beside the door, a fat candle flickering inside. Kyle rapped on the door.

"Trick or treat," they shouted in unison at the smiling elderly woman holding a bowl full of Nerds and Sour Patch Kids.

"Oh, don't you look darling?" she said, instantly souring Matt's mood. He hadn't supposed he'd looked *scary*, as he'd glanced at himself in the full-length mirror on his way out the door tonight, but *darling* was the last thing he'd wanted to hear, especially when Kyle and Craig's parents had the kind of money to afford *real* costumes. "And what are you supposed to be, dear?"

"Freddy Kreuger," Kyle replied. It should've been obvious from the crappy foam hat and ugly red and green sweater to the metal—well, plastic made to *look* like metal—clawed glove on his right hand, but this lady clearly didn't know anything about the kind of movies Matt and his friends spent their weekend sleepovers watching. Craig was dressed as Indiana Jones, wearing the same crummy hat as his brother. Matt had decided to go as a skeleton—although his first choice, Patrick Bateman from *American Psycho*, had been nixed by his mother—with bones his mom had cut out of white fabric and sewn onto a black shirt and pants, partly hidden under his big coat, makeup on his face, and floppy rubber skeleton hands.

They each took their candy, thanked the woman and hurried down the steps. "Don't you look *darling*?" Kyle mocked. They all laughed as they crossed the lawn to the next house.

They stuck their hands in bowls of spaghetti noodles and peeled grapes for rolls of Smarties and Halloween Kisses. They took candy out of a bowl sitting in the lap of a stuffed dummy at one house, then got tricked by a guy pretending to be a stuffed dummy at the next, who leaped up from his chair and actually made Craig scream. They got Barq's root beer from another house, and Doritos from the next, where they paused briefly to share a single bag and can, chugging and wolfing them down. They hit every single viable house on Gordon, and returned for their bikes with their already heavier pillowcases slung over their shoulders.

Paoli Avenue was next. They dumped their BMXs in the grass beside Mr. Granger's fence and headed up the sidewalk on the east side. They'd only gotten as far as four houses when Craig spotted Philbert Piper, sitting on the curb with his head in his hands.

"Oh shit, what happened to the retard?"

"Takes one to know one, *Timothy.*"

"Don't call me Timothy, *Mansard.*"

Still bickering, Kyle and Craig—whose hated middle names they'd just hurled at each other—began to head up the street toward Philbert, ignoring the next two houses on the list.

"Guys, we don't have time to stop," Matt called after them. "Not if we wanna get to the Muldoonses before they run out of Pop Rocks!"

Kyle and Craig ignored him.

"Guys, you love Pop Rocks! Pop Rocks and soda, 'member? Guys, come on...!" Defeated, Matt sighed heavily and hurried over to them.

Sure enough, the big moose Philbert Piper was moaning into his hands. He had a hand-sewn Fred Flintstone loincloth over top of his normal clothes.

"What the heck happened, Philbert?" Craig asked.

Philbert ignored them, crying and sniffling. Craig reached out and touched his shoulder, causing Philbert to straighten up like he'd been touched by a ghost. "Huh?" he said, whipping his head around in terror. His mouth hung open and a runner of whitish snot dangled from his right nostril until he sniffed again, sucking it back up. His face and the front of his loincloth were caked with yellow stuff Matt at first thought was more mucus before realizing it was egg yolk.

"Somebody egged him," Kyle said, taking the words out of Matt's mouth.

"*Somebody?*" Matt said. "You know who it was."

"That means they musta hit this street already," Craig said excitedly, his cheeks rosy from the chill. "We should be safe for a while. Maybe we could even make it back to your place to dump our first haul before they even spot us!"

"Don't count on it," Kyle grumbled. "Those guys are like dogs, they can smell our fear."

"They can smell my farts," Matt said. "They're *not* getting our candy again. Not this year." He took out a bunch of folded Kleenexes from his pocket. He always kept a bunch in colder weather just in case his nose ran, ever since he'd gotten razzed for wiping his nose on his sleeve in class when he was little. He unfolded them and showed them to Philbert, like holding out his palms to a strange dog. "Want me to wipe that egg off your face, Philbert?"

Pouting, Philbert nodded his head exaggeratedly. "Uh-h-huh." He sniffled and his chest hitched as if he might burst into tears again.

Matt used the tissues to wipe thick, runny gobs of yolk and the clear stuff he knew from science in the first or second grade was called *albumen*, almost gagging as he considered that some of it could have mixed with Philbert's snot. Once he'd gotten most of it off, he tossed the last soggy tissue into the sewer grate.

"All right, big guy, you're all clean."

"Thank you," Philbert said with a big goofy smile.

"Don't mention it. Head on home and tell your mom Adam Brunt sucks farts."

The O'Donnelly brothers laughed at that.

"Let's get going, you guys. We got five minutes to make up."

As Philbert lumbered off back home, the boys headed to the next house on the list. It was another half hour before they bumped into Adam Brunt, and by then their pillowcases were full enough to be dumped off at Matt's house to start fresh.

3

8:38 P.M.
Stephano Road

"HO-LEEEEE SHIT," Brunt said, the Mustang's engine purring like a jungle cat as he and Fitz prowled the streets. "It's those three little crybaby bitches from last year."

The three losers were peddling around the corner on their bikes with pillowcases full of Halloween candy slung over their backs. They dropped their bikes at the corner and hurried off on foot.

The back of the car was already filled with the spoils of their plunder. All that junk food was a much better use of the backseats than Big Mac's fat ass and Chimney's boney one. What'd they need those guys for? It's not like it took *all four of them* to shake down all these little squirts. Usually at least two of the group ended up just laughing and cheering Brunt on from the sidelines. Might as well bring in the cheerleading squad, for all those two were worth.

"Oh, man, those little turds are *holding*," Fitz said. "Let's get out here and sneak up, get the drop on em."

"'The drop'? What're you, a nineteen-forties greaseball?"

"People say 'drop.' Don't be a dickhole."

Brunt pulled up to the curb and put the car in park. He left the keys in the ignition and didn't even bother locking the door when he got out. Anyone who was stupid enough to take Adam Brunt's Mustang for a joyride deserved the thrashing they'd get. He *almost* wished it'd happen.

Brunt caught up with Fitz at the sidewalk and they hurried to the street corner side by side. Fitz suggested creeping, but Adam Brunt didn't creep. Like Gramma Brunt once said, "Adam thunders into every room like a bull in a china shop." He'd been eleven or twelve when she'd said that, a tall, ungainly child, and he liked the idea so much he often envisioned himself as a bull when he "thundered" into unfamiliar situations. Horns forward, nostrils steaming. Sometimes he went as far as to kick like a bull's hind legs to psych himself up during a big game. It became his signature, like spiking the ball or the touchdown dances some of his teammates did, and some of his fans called him "Brahma Brunt." He didn't much like the name (he thought it made him sound like a Paki, whom he hated as much as kikes, chinks, beaners, gypsies, faggots, Guidos, dagos, frogs, retards, and the Paki's raghead cousins who'd perpetrated 9/11), but he liked the thought of it.

Brunt strode around the corner and peered down Clarker Road. The street was crawling with kids—by now most of the ones young enough to be accompanied by parents or older siblings were at home, counting their stash—but he spotted the trio of twerps right away, cutting across the lawns between the houses. Probably had some sort of a system like Brunt and his older brother had when they were kids, to reach the maximum number of houses in the shortest span of time. Their pillowcases looked heavy with loot.

Lumbering down the sidewalk toward them, Brunt rubbed

his hands together in anticipation—not for the candy but the beating he'd soon be handing down. Fitz's little scurrying footsteps as he hurried to catch up grated on him. Fitz had no stride. He carried himself like a little guy, and Brunt *hated* little guys.

The three little shitbirds were laughing now, heading up the porch steps to the next house. Between them and where Brunt and Fitz waited stood a tall hedge, a perfect place for an ambush. The kids couldn't cross the lawn to reach their next target without having to jump over a small fenced-in garden.

Oh, man, this is gonna be fuckin fun.

Brunt absolutely *lived* for this shit. The rush he got from laying down a good beating was better than getting drunk or stoned, and even better than busting a nut. Nerves tingling with anticipation, he rushed past the house and leaned back against the thick, bristly bush. Small thorns pricked his neck and he swatted them away, muttering, "Stupid fucking tree."

"Trick or treat!" he heard the kids say from a distance.

"Trick," Brunt said, grinning to himself.

Fitz snickered. "Yeah. Trick for them, treat for us. Right, Brunt?"

"*Shaddap.* You want those fuckwads to hear us?"

Fitz quieted.

They waited, breath pluming out in the mid-fall chill. It made Brunt think of the commercials for Cockmeyer's Dentyne gum fetish, and he wondered what that assclown was *really* up to tonight. He'd begged off for a "school project," he'd said, but what kind of dumbfuck did schoolwork on Halloween night? Maybe he was getting his dicky sticky. At least that would've been a decent excuse.

The kids were giggling up the sidewalk. "Two more houses and we can drop this off at my place," one of them said.

"Sweet, I gotta piss like a racehorse," said another, with a higher-pitched voice.

"More like My Little Pony," said a third.

Two of them laughed. The second one said, "Shut up, Kyle."

The three of them came around the corner, the taller one out front, dressed in a skeleton costume his mommy probably made for him, and the two shorter kids walking behind him. They all wore stupid grins. The taller kid's was the first to wipe off his face. He stopped in his tracks as Brunt and Fitz stepped away from the hedge, into their path. The mini-Freddy Kreuger stopped next, his eyes going wide. The one in the Indiana Jones costume walked right into the first kid.

"Oh... shit," Baby Freddy said.

Fitz laughed. He snatched the pillowcase out of the kid's clawed hand and reached a chocolate-streaked hand into it, crinkling plastic. The kid grabbed for it, but the skeleton kid held him back. Something about the look that passed between them struck Brunt as off. Last year these kids had pissed and moaned and the tall kid, if he remembered right, had even swung a punch at Big Mac. Now, they weren't just not fighting back, they were *preventing* each other from trying.

"Gimme that," Brunt snapped, tearing the pillowcase out of Fitz's hands. He opened it and peered inside, brightly colored wrappers standing out among the shadows.

Fitz grabbed the stash from the tall kid. The little one snorted laughter.

"Don't—" Brunt started, about to warn Fitz not to stick his hand inside. There was *something* in there, something these kids had hidden inside like those dye-packs the cops stuck in bundles of cash in heist movies. Mousetraps maybe? Thumbtacks?

Fitz screamed before Brunt could finish warning him. He danced around in terror and pain, up to his elbow inside the bag.

The three dipshits started smiling slyly. The one who'd snorted couldn't hold it back anymore and brayed laughter.

"You little shits," Brunt growled, opening his pillowcase and looking inside again, searching for the trap. Fitz yelped and danced. "Quit fuckin around, Fitz!"

Something moved inside the pillowcase in Brunt's hands, shifting the wrappers, making them crackle and pop like breakfast cereal, but there was another sound beneath it—it sounded like a *hiss*, like maybe they shook up the sodas and one of them had opened. But that wouldn't explain why Fitz was crying and dancing around like a pussy.

A dark shape darted out from the shadowy contents before Brunt had a chance to react. It latched onto his throat with a hot poker of pain, and he couldn't help but join Fitz in screaming.

4

MATT COULDN'T BELIEVE what he was seeing.

The trick had worked way better than he'd planned. Just a handful of rubber snakes and plastic spiders from his dad's old collection, distributed into each pillowcase. He thought he might get a scare out of them, enough to drop the pillowcases if he was lucky and give him and the O'Donnellys a chance to grab them and high-tail it back to their bikes. He had no idea he'd get such a crazy reaction as he did from the tall, skinny guy in the football jacket Adam Brunt had called "Fitz." The guy was screaming and dancing around like he just got his dick caught in his zipper, his arm still in the pillowcase up to his shoulder.

Then the thing flew out of the pillowcase in Brunt's hands and attached itself to his neck, and Matt knew something was very wrong. It was one of the snakes, somehow one of the snakes had launched itself at Brunt, like the ones from those fake cans of peanuts. Matt would've thought it was a joke, like Brunt had grabbed it and planted on himself, but the bloodcurdling *scream* he let out, just like his buddy's—no way would he do that, even for a laugh.

Brunt dropped the pillowcase and gripped the wriggling thing hanging from his throat in both hands. The sack of treats hit the ground with a heavy thump and crackle of plastic. The cords in Brunt's neck stood out. He was pulling on that thing for his life.

This was no joke.

Kyle immediately bent to grab his loot, reaching out with his claw hand.

"*Don't*," Matt warned, just like Brunt had tried and failed to warn his buddy. Kyle stopped.

"You hear that?" Craig asked.

Matt did. *Hissing*.

Craig dropped his pillowcase with a terrified yelp. Both his and Kyle's sacks squirmed on the sidewalk, like sacks full of real snakes instead of rubber.

What the heck? Matt thought.

Further up the street, a girl screamed. Then a boy. Then it became an entire chorus of shouting and screams, coming from both sides of the street, up and down.

Brunt was gagging, tearing at the rubber snake attached to

him. He coughed, and Matt figured he must've bitten down on one of those fake blood pellets because a spray of liquid spewed from his purple lips and oozed down his peach-fuzzy chin, bright crimson under the streetlamp.

That can't be real. Can it?

Fitz finally tore his arm free from Matt's pillowcase and it was covered in the four or five furry plastic spiders he'd planted inside. Only they weren't just stuck to him. They were *crawling* up his arm toward his face and chest.

Matt turned to his friends, who looked about as gobsmacked as he felt himself. They were staring across the street, and he followed their dumbstruck gazes. Flaming objects shot through the darkness. At first, he was sure someone was tossing lit jack-o'-lanterns, like kids sometimes did to rotting pumpkins in the days after Halloween. Then he saw one of their blazing faces turn in midair and hurtle across the street toward them, orange firelight flickering over the wet asphalt below it, and the carved face began to cackle madly.

Kyle's Freddy glove flicked open with a sound like knives scraping together, rather than the soft clatter of plastic. He reacted with shock as his arm swung out seemingly on its own, making him lurch forward and grab himself by the wrist.

"Guys?" He gripped the gloved hand tightly as it turned and swung at his face. "Help!"

"Take it off!" Matt cried, and then his own hands—wearing *real bones* now, not floppy rubber gloves—took on a life of their own and grabbed him by the throat. He choked out Craig's name.

Craig stood there in a daze, his gaze flicking between the both of them and the bigger boys writhing on the asphalt. "Y-you guys are f-foolin, right?"

"*No, Craig!*" Kyle gasped, the Freddy glove clawing inches from his face. "*Help me get this thing off! Quick!*"

Craig took a single step toward his brother. Kyle's hand twisted in his direction, the blades making sharp *snicks*, and Craig leaped back anxiously.

"Craig," Matt grunted, pulling against the powerful grip of the living skeleton gloves. "Craig, they're possessed! If you don't get it off, we're both—" He was going to say *dead meat* but the gloves cut off his voice and his breath.

Craig took another cautious step toward his brother. He reached out, hands quivering. The blades slashed at him and he retracted his hands quickly. Tears streamed down Kyle's face as he pulled the gloved hand back, struggling against it.

Matt felt tears running down his own face. If the big kids weren't dying, they would've called him a sissy.

Craig reached out again and grabbed the strap on the back of the glove. The knives slashed at him, but he managed to tear it open before the index finger slashed an angry red line across his right palm. The wound wept blood immediately, and Craig wailed in pain, already crying, leaping back from his brother and the monster glove.

Matt was beginning to see stars, his vision dimming. He didn't know what to do. If it was just one hand, like Kyle's, at least he'd have a chance to fight it. Now that Craig was out of commission, holding his palm and weeping for his mother, there was no one to save him. He considered running into a telephone pole or dropping to the ground, but he'd just as likely smash his own face in as harm the murder hands.

Suddenly there were large hands over his own, helping him pull. He looked up to see the concerned brown eyes of Philbert Piper in the pinpricks of vision he had left. Philbert tore the murder hands free from Matt's throat and Matt sucked in a big gasp of air, his vision clearing, the stars fading.

"Stop hurting yourself!" Philbert shouted at him, squeezing the hands so tight it hurt Matt's bones.

"It's not me," Matt rasped. "Help me get them off! Quick!"

Philbert seemed to clue in with a furrowed brow and tore the gloves off with a quick pull. They landed on the ground with a clatter and began rolling around on their back like big white bugs, unable to flip themselves over.

"You too, huh?" Philbert said, turning to Kyle.

Kyle nodded miserably, barely holding back the hand from his face.

Philbert snatched out with surprising dexterity, grabbing the glove and tearing it off before it could strike either of them. He held it for a moment, the blades slicing and dicing the air in front of him, then chucked it as far as he could.

They all looked around in silence at the chaos elsewhere on

the street, then down at the dying bullies rolling around in agony on the wet asphalt closer by.

"You saved us," Kyle said, awestruck.

Philbert shrugged. "I don't wanna play no more, okay?"

This surprised a laugh out of Matt. The big guy didn't even understand what he'd done, although Matt supposed he didn't really understand what was happening here himself. All the Halloween stuff had come alive, that was obvious. It just didn't make any *sense*.

"Come on, we gotta go," he said.

"W-where?" Craig asked, sniffling. Blood dripped down from his clasped hands.

"To my house. You too, Philbert. We gotta get out of the street."

"Sleepover?" Philbert asked, beaming. "Oh, boy. I'll have to ask."

"You can call your mom from my house!" Matt called back, already dashing up the sidewalk toward home, the four of them leaving their spilled candy and the screaming bullies in his dust.

5

As HIS BLOOD puddled on the concrete and his life ebbed away, Brunt's struggle against the reptile clamped to his throat grew weak. It wasn't exactly peace that overcame him then, more a sense of clarified rage.

Snakes, he thought. *Fuckin bag fulla snakes. Trick or fuckin treat, right? Trick's on me. Ha-fuckin-ha.*

Twisting to his side with a pained grunt, he saw Fitz rolling on the sidewalk nearby, covered in angry spiders, giant two-pronged red welts on his face and neck and hands. More snakes and spiders crawled and slithered out from the discarded pillowcases and scattered treats.

I'll kill those fuckin shitbird kids AND that retard, Brunt thought. *I'll kill every last fuckin one of em.*

It was the last thought in his mind before he died.

CHAPTER 11

1

8:59 P.M.
Halloween Village

"We need to be careful," Brittany said.

Though all manner of madness was happening all over the farm, the barn still appeared to be the epicenter of chaos, judging by the cries and strange sounds from inside.

This can't be happening, she thought for probably the tenth time since the whole world went crazy, which according to her turquoise Daytona "Beach" Rolex had only been about ten minutes ago.

A part of her wondered if what she'd done had somehow set off this horrific chain of events, if The Snake hadn't tricked her into performing some ancient ritual, but there was no way to know for sure. She'd killed the piggy—Tommy—and laid him against the altar in what the Thompsons called the "Sacrifice Room" near the exit. Almost the second she did, things started to come to life around her. The plastic spiders came first, crawling out of every fake cobweb in every dark corner of the room, skittering over Tommy's face, down his arms and legs, into his hair and open mouth. Next came the bats, flying down from a crevasse in the plywood ceiling and swirling around her head like a black rubber cyclone. She'd barely managed to escape and hurried back to the crossover corridors. When she'd heard Cody and the others in the Laboratory, Brittany decided against her better judgment—and against vehement opposition from The Snake—to help them get out.

Still, she thought they could make it to where she'd left the remains and get out alive if they played it safe. She planned to take Cody around the back of the barn and through the exit, directly to where she'd left Tommy's body. There were thick, bristly blankets for the actors in a trunk outside the barn. They'd throw the blankets over themselves and duck, the way they said to survive a house fire.

But first they needed to navigate the graveyard, and its animated army of the undead that had seemingly grown since they'd rushed through in the opposite direction. James Dooley still lingered outside the barn exit, involuntarily slashing at fleeing people with the Crow Demon's claws and setting them ablaze with its fiery breath, but she thought he would be easy enough to avoid.

"Through here," she said, leading Cody toward the cemetery.

"Really?"

"Would you rather go back through the barn?"

"Good point."

She continued on, back over the squelching grass, spirals twisting in her mind. *This was all my fault*, she thought. *If I hadn't killed Tommy, none of this would be happening.*

Bull-pucky, The Snake countered. *Life is messy. This ain't no more yer fault than that li'l piggy presentin hisself on a silver got-dang platter was yer fault. It was a gift, honeypie. A gift from the cosmos.*

Why him, though? You think it was a coincidence?

Course it was. Thinkin it's anything but is stupid, and you need to be smart now, Brittany Garner, ya hear me? You can sign that on the dotted line.

He was right. She needed to be focused and logical. Keep her head in the game, as Cody's coach probably said to the team.

She stopped near the edge of the cemetery, studying the skeleton hands clawing out from the ground, the Dracula leering from its coffin, the gnashing and slashing zombie torsos dragging themselves across the muddy grass, the rats skittering and squeaking over the hardpacked muck. If Mr. Thompson hadn't made it stretch all the way to the edge of the corn maze, they could've at least gone around it. If Jay was still here, he could probably figure out a way to get through using patterns, like his video games.

But seven years of gymnastics and dance had to count as some sort of advantage here. Not to mention Cody's athleticism.

Cody turned to her with a look of anxiety. "You sure we can't go around?" he asked.

Brittany shook her head. "It's the only way. Come on. You did this with a hundred-pound kid in your arms. Easy as pie."

His lips curled up in a slight smile. "*Yeah*," he said. "We got this." He patted her on the shoulder, then quickly retracted his hand as if she might bite him. Brittany had no intention of biting him, but she sensed The Snake tensing inside her, uncoiling in rage, eager to lash out.

"On the count of three then," she said.

Cody agreed with a nod. They both counted.

On three, they sprinted forward. Cody dashed ahead, faking out bony hands and rotting bodies and hopping over rats. Brittany leapt and danced out of their way. The vampire nearly grabbed her by Cody's jacket but she gracefully pirouetted, narrowly avoiding its sharp claws. By the time they reached the other side her boots and Cody's shoes and the cuffs of his pants were covered in mud splatters, but they made it through alive, and that was all that mattered.

Cody laughed, planting his hands on his knees. "We did it."

Brittany didn't share his enthusiasm. Screams of terror and agony only proved there was worse in store for them ahead.

That said, she knew this place better than them. She'd been working here for almost a month. She knew all the secret corridors and hidden rooms. She could run the corn maze by memory.

The Crow Demon roared outside the barn, breathing fire and swiping at stragglers. Several bodies lay haphazardly on the gravel, each of them hacked and slashed, two still on fire. Either James was no longer conscious or he was in such a state of shock he could no longer communicate his terror. The costume had entirely subsumed him.

"How are we gonna get past him?" Cody asked.

"Fake him out. That's a football thing, right?"

"Yeah."

"We'll do that, then. Head one way, go the other."

Cody nodded. "Which way?"

"Fake right, head left. Take the fastest route."

"Smart play, Coach."

Brittany grinned. "On three again."

She counted down and they sprang into action. As they reached perimeter, leaping over the dead, the Crow Demon turned to them with flames already stoked within its boney beak. As they neared, a fireball hurled toward them. She felt its heat on her face and arms as they faked heading around the creature. They both made a snap about-face as the demon kept going in the other direction, leaving the path to the exit wide open. They ran toward it.

In moments, they were back in the stench and darkness before the creature roared its displeasure.

"This way," Brittany said, leading him through the final stretch of tunnel toward the last room in the barn haunt, where she'd left Tommy's body.

The creepy mellotron music, witchy cackles and sound of thunder still played over the soundtrack, along with the steady beat of a heart and random real-life screams from elsewhere inside the barn. They pushed through the thick, black curtains into the Sacrifice Room a moment later.

The smell of blood was sharp in here, and though there were a couple of dead bodies—a man face-down on the ground, his arms and legs splayed, his face smashed into the floor like a pumpkin on asphalt the day after Halloween, and a woman sitting against the fake stone sacrifice table, her eyes glazed, her face covered in red welts—there was no sign of Tommy. Spiders skittered across the floor, which was painted to look like stone like the walls and ceiling.

"Jeez," Cody said solemnly.

Here, piggy, piggy, piggy, The Snake whispered in Brittany's head. He was just as surprised as she was, but rarely displayed such emotions. Had someone *removed* Tommy's body during the chaos? Why would anyone *do* that? He had to be in here somewhere. Maybe he wasn't actually dead? Maybe he'd... crawled away to safety. Maybe he'd told Thompsons what she'd done to him and they were calling the Sheriff's office *right now*.

Maybe some freak got peckish for baby-back ribs, The Snake said.

That's not funny, Brittany replied—though obviously just in her head, as she wasn't about to speak aloud to The Snake in front of Cody.

Well, it ain't like he done crawled away, The Snake said.

How do you know?

No blood streaks, dummy, he said, as if it should've been obvious. And now that Brittany had a moment to think clearly, she realized it should've been. If he'd crawled away there would have been handprints at the very least on the floor where he'd been. Definitely streaks where he'd dragged himself along the floor. And there was no way he'd have been able to walk away on his own, not with how many times she'd stabbed him.

"Well, he's obviously not here," Cody said. "I guess we keep going."

"Through the crossover," she said, leading him toward the curtains painted to blend in with the rest of the fake stone wall. "We can see each of the rooms through there without having to go in."

"Cool," Cody said, stepping into the red-lit corridor behind her.

They followed the tunnel to the next area, Uncle Pappy's TV Room. Brittany peered through the hole in the wall beside the curtained entrance. Uncle Pappy's ratty recliner was empty. Pappy himself—played by one of the older men from the theater troupe whose name she couldn't recall but he had bad dandruff and usually smelled like beer—was nowhere to be found. The tube TV set played clips from old horror movies on an extended-play VHS cassette. Right now the hippie guy with the glasses from *Texas Chainsaw Massacre* just found Pam's dead body in the chest freezer, but Brittany still didn't see a single sign of the one body she was actually looking for among the corpses lying surrounded by a bunch of crushed beer cans and very realistic-looking human bones.

"Jeez, where could he have gotten to?"

"I don't know," she said angrily.

Guess the chubby li'l fellar wasn't as dead as we thought, The Snake said.

He was dead. You saw me check his pulse.

But I didn't feel nothin.

Of course you didn't. You can't.

The Snake couldn't feel *anything* she felt, which was fortunate for her. It was bad enough having to share her mind with a long-dead serial killer. It'd be much worse if she had to worry about him feeling it when she went to the bathroom or—*eucchhhh*—on the off time she masturbated. He was respectful of her wishes to stay out of her conscious mind during these periods, as far as she could tell. Because if he didn't, she'd sworn she would never give him what he *truly* wanted: murder, and lots of it, willingly.

Brittany figured there was plenty enough death here to last him for a while, even if he preferred to be a part of it as it happened.

They checked the Laboratory and the Trophy Room, avoiding rats and spiders along the way. If she wasn't hearing screams from outside and catching glimpses of the occasional rat, spider and crying baby doll, she might have been able to believe it was all over, that whatever had happened here was like a freak rainstorm: one big dump and that was that.

"Maybe he got out," Cody said. "Should we check the house?"

"Maybe." She doubted it, but a part of her still worried he'd somehow survived and was telling on her right this second.

Squealin like the li'l piggy he is, The Snake said.

They continued to the Incantation Room, where the mechanical pipe organ still played Bach's "Toccata and Fugue in D Minor." Several more bodies lay on the floor here, among them a guy who looked sort of like Shaggy from *Scooby-Doo* and Heather Platz, both of whom looked like they'd been ravaged by wolves.

Poor Heather, she thought. She didn't like the girl all that much but whatever had killed her, it looked like a bad way to go. Her eyes and mouth remained wide in abject terror.

"Is everyone...?" Cody asked, unable or unwilling to finish the question.

Brittany nodded, still peering through the hole. "Looks like it."

And not a dang sign of Little Lord Fauntleroy, The Snake said.

"You think he could've gotten past us in the other direction?"

"It's possible, I guess. We might as well check."

Without waiting for approval, Brittany pushed through the heavy curtain and entered the room. Cody followed her.

"Poor Heather," he said, then turned toward the far corner. "Hey, wasn't there a—"

A low growl from behind the lectern cut Cody short. The large shape huddled in its shadow swept the thing aside, book and all, and pounced on Cody, knocking him to the floor.

Brittany leaped back in fright, realizing her error moments too late. In her haste to find Tommy, she hadn't even realized the cage was empty. The animatronic Teen Wolf—no longer just mask, clothes and stuffing over a crude mechanical body, meant only to shake its cage and twist its head violently back and forth —snarled and snapped its very real fangs in Cody's face.

Cody shut his eyes and turned his head, holding the monster back with his muscular forearms, as a runner of drool oozed off its long tongue onto his temple. But the beast had the clear advantage of being possessed by a supernatural entity.

Yeah, well, so am I, she thought.

I ain't quite supernatural, The Snake said. *But I 'preciate the sentiment.*

"Brit—" Cody grunted. "Help me!"

"Kick it in the nuts!" she suggested, the first move they taught in her self-defense classes. Cody complied, raising his knee swiftly with a grunt. It struck the wolfman dead-on but the thing didn't even flinch. Instead, it planted its paws—which Brittany was pretty sure hadn't even existed prior to its possession— on either side of Cody, giving itself an even bigger advantage, pressing its weight down on him. Cody growled against the strain, pushing back.

Meanwhile, Brittany scoured the room, searching for something to hit it with. Something heavy enough to do serious damage.

Or let the dang thing kill him, The Snake said. *Could be fun to watch.*

And then it comes for me next. No thanks.

The Snake sighed in defeat.

She spotted a set of candelabras on the pipe organ, cobwebbed and flickering with real fire. She was pretty sure they'd been fake plastic candles before, but she supposed since everything else had come to life it made sense they would, too. The candelabras themselves didn't look heavy but she remembered

Row saying she hoped no one would notice they were *real* silver, since they'd been in her family for generations.

Silver kills werewolves, just like in them stories, The Snake purred.

Brittany didn't bother to agree. She ran straight for the organ, tripping over Shaggy's legs and blasting out a series of discordant notes as she fell over the keys. She grabbed one of the candelabras, blew out the candles and whipped around to face the monster, feeling very Buffy the Vampire Slayer. Covering her hand with the cuff of Cody's jacket, she snapped off the cups from each stem, leaving her with what was essentially a somewhat sharp trident.

Teen Wolf was too intent on taking a bite out of Cody to notice her creeping toward it in a semicircle from around the overturned lectern. Cody had managed to get a hand out from under it and grabbed it by the lower jaw. It slobbered and snapped its sharp, yellow teeth at him, claws sunk at least an inch into Cody's chest, drawing blood.

"Hey, Biscuit Breath!" Brittany shouted.

The werewolf turned to her with a snarl but it was too late. She brought the silver trident down in a swift arc, all three somewhat sharpened ends tearing through the leather of its jacket. She felt it pierce the creature's flesh and ribs, and the beast reared back, howling in agony, its yellow eyes rolling wildly.

Cody gave the monster a solid kick, knocking it off of him. It fell on its side with a muted thud, its body rigid. The life left its eyes, the paws shriveled into the legs of its jeans, and the mask and clawed fingers changed from fur and bone and keratin back into floppy painted rubber. Tufts of cotton batting poked out from holes in its jacket where the candelabra hung limply.

"You saved my life," Cody said, sitting up and panting. "How'd you know that'd work?"

She shrugged. "I didn't *know,* but I had a hunch. It's silver."

"Wait, like *silver bullet* silver?"

"What other kind of silver is there?"

Cody shrugged. He winced as he tried to stand, holding his chest where the claws had torn through his shirt and skin. Blood had already soaked through in eight small patches across his pecs and collarbones. "It got me pretty bad."

"Could've been a lot worse." Brittany held out a hand.

Cody took it, and she helped him to his feet. Standing, he looked at her with a hopeful expression. "Hey, if silver killed that thing, that's good, right?"

"In what way is that *good*?"

"Well, Cassandra used a crucifix on the Dracula in the grave-yard and that worked, too. So like... maybe they're following horror rules?"

She shrugged again. "Maybe? Or maybe we just got lucky."

Cody hummed thoughtfully.

"Anyway, how do you kill a jack-o'-lantern?" she said. "Or a giant crow demon? Or killer baby dolls?"

Cody shrugged. "Wire coat hangers?"

Brittany burst out laughing before she could stop herself. "So offensive," she said, covering poorly.

He gave her a dopey look of apology. "Yeah, sorry. We should get going, huh?"

Brittany agreed, and led him back to the crossover. Halfway to Crazy Mama's bathroom scene she stopped in her tracks, a short, stocky figure blocking their path. His down-filled jacket was torn to shreds and covered in blood. His face, even bathed in red light, was as pale as Cassandra's.

"*YOU!*" the very *not*-dead Tommy cried in a voice much bigger than his body could possibly allow, pointing directly at her like something out of a nightmare. "*YOU DID THIS!*"

Brittany's heart raced. She turned to Cody to confirm what she was seeing was real and not a hallucination. He looked down at her with deep concern creasing his brow.

Now this... The Snake said, a smile evident in his tone. *...this is what they call an interestin development.*

2

9:01 P.M.
Old Route 14

JAY WAS IN SHOCK, that was the only way to describe it. As Walden drove them back to town he sat shotgun, wondering if what he'd seen yesterday had anything to do with what was hap-pening now, and if all of this had been caused by the work he'd been doing with Mr. Combs for the past little while. If it had been caused by Combs's bizarre "dark energy" experiment, that meant he was at least partly responsible.

Fortunately for Jay, stress seemed to amplify both his focus and his intelligence, rather than dull it. It was one of the reasons he usually waited until the night before a project was due to get started on it, or to study for an exam, and then spent all night hammering it out, usually listening to the *Quake* soundtrack or some other heavy shit while chugging cans of Rockstar.

What else could it be, dumbass? You know anyone else trying to open doors to realms that maybe weren't meant to be opened? That thing you saw yesterday wasn't just a hairball, and you know it. It was something *we weren't meant to see. Not with the naked eye, anyway. Maybe on some yet-to-be-invented microscope or some kind of specialized goggles. Not right in front of my goddamn face.*

Well, so now what? Go to Mr. Combs's house and get him to shut off the machine—the Dark Energy Convertor, or whatever he'd called it? What if it's already off? What if it's already done what it was made to do, and there's no way to put the genie back in the bottle? What if this was happening all over town, not just at Halloween Village? What if it's happening all over the world?

But that didn't make sense. All over Crooks Corner, maybe. The DEC was too small to affect the entire planet, even if its effects had reached five miles out to the Thompson farm. Whatever it had done, it couldn't be *unstoppable*. There had to be a way to fix this, or at least a way to *fight* it.

"What's that sound?" the kid piped up behind him.

"What sound?" Walden asked, focused on the dark road ahead.

"There's something in this box," the girl replied.

He heard the sound of cardboard sliding against each other, the same sound it made when he'd closed the box of toys earlier. His mind was still in overdrive but his body was still as lame as always. If he'd been more athletic, like Cody, or graceful like Brittany, he might have been able to twist swiftly and reach over the back of his seat to prevent the kid from opening the box. Even his mouth was still mush. He managed to get out something that sounded like, "*Nodo—!*" Then squeaky laughter filled the car, and those little monsters shaped like rubber ball chew toys sprang from the opened box and started bouncing all over the place. Hitting the ceiling, hitting the windshield, hitting the back of Jay's seat.

Both the kid and Cassandra started shrieking.

One of the things landed on Walden's right hand with a munching sound—*Num-num-num-num-num!* Walden cried out and the car swerved violently. Jay's head slammed against the window, hard enough for stars to shoot across his vision, almost hard enough to crack the glass. Another monster ball bounced off the ceiling and landed on his thigh. It chewed through the denim and a sharp pain erupted there, like he'd walked into a patch of thorns. His scream rose almost to the pitch of the little girl's behind him.

"Stop the car!" Cassandra shouted.

More and more of the little round monsters launched out of the box like popping corn with yelps and cries of "*Woohoo!*" Their voices reminded Jay of those *Worms* games he used to play.

Walden swung his hand around wildly. The monster—a little green, pimpled thing with big gold pirate earrings—held on for dear life. Jay slammed a fist down on the purple creature attached to his thigh. It squealed in pain with a wet crunch, and its tiny, razor-sharp teeth released his flesh and it rolled off of his leg, into the footwell.

Jay looked up in time to see a telephone pole caught in the headlights.

"*Loogout!*" he cried.

The car crashed and Jay was thrown forward, his head striking the dashboard.

He must've blacked out because when he opened his eyes again the car was on fire about twenty feet ahead of him and he was lying with his back against something hard. His head hurt worse than the worst brain freeze and his neck was sore. "He's awake," Cassandra said. He couldn't turn his head to see her but she was somewhere nearby.

"Good." Walden's voice came from a higher elevation than hers. Jay guessed he was standing and Cassandra was on the ground beside him.

"Wwwhat happened?" he groaned, his voice slightly slurred.

"We got in an accident. Those promotional toys for the movie," Walden said. "They got out of the box."

Jay hurt his head turning it too fast, looking for the creatures. "Where are they?"

"It all stopped after we all got out of the car," Cassandra said, crouching beside him. She had a cut on her forehead, a trickle of blood spilling down the white makeup on her forehead. Tears had streaked her mascara. She'd been crying.

"Maybe it's over?" Walden said, squinting in the direction of town.

"Does it *feel* like it's over to you?" Cassandra asked.

Walden shook his head and turned back to them. "No. And if my fucking car wasn't on fire, I bet we could still hear screams from the farm." He kicked a bent hubcap angrily into the ditch. "Fuck, that hurt!"

"Is everyone... okay?" Jay asked hesitantly.

"We're alive," Walden said, hobbling over on his injured foot. "Unlike my fucking car. We need to get back to town, make sure people are safe, see if we can figure out what the hell is going on."

"I know—" Jay tried to push himself up, then swooned and fell immediately back on his ass.

"You should relax a bit longer," Cassandra said. "You might have a concussion."

"I know what's happening," he groaned, holding his head. "We need to go to Mr. Combs's house."

Walden scoffed. "The science teacher? I doubt he knows more about this than we do. We were at Ground Zero."

Jay pinched the bridge of his nose, a wave of pain crashing through his skull. "He will. I think... maybe... he might've caused this."

Cassandra frowned. "Why would he *do* that?" Her little sister came over to join them and she held her hand.

"I don't think it was on purpose. He's working on an experiment. You remember yesterday when we all felt that tremor?"

"Sure," Walden said. "Almost knocked the whole movie theater down."

"That was because of the machine he's been working on."

Walden gave him a skeptical look, and Jay's initial instinct was to react angrily, until he realized he would've been just as skeptical if he hadn't seen it himself.

"What kind of machine causes earthquakes? And why would that have *anything* to do with what happened at—?"

"Just let him finish," Cassandra snapped.

Walden threw up his hands and took a step back.

"Thank you," Jay said. He swallowed hard. So much for his stress-induced superpowers. His brain felt full of paste. "I've been helping Mr. Combs for a while now, mostly just running around town getting stuff he needs for that machine. Weird stuff, usually. Last week he had me find a motherboard from an old Commodore 64. Yesterday it was a pre-hatched Tamagotchi."

"I used to have a Tamagotchi," the kid said, her eyes lighting up. She still had her Polaroid camera hanging around her neck and her right eye was already starting to turn purple. "She liked cake. I didn't like scolding her. Or cleaning up her poop."

"That's great, kid."

Cassandra's scowl deepened. "You don't have to be a dick."

Jay pinched his nose again. He took a deep breath in and out. "You're right. I'm sorry. My head is just really killing me and this is important information."

She nodded appreciatively. "Go ahead."

"So yesterday while I was at his house, he turned on the machine for the first time while I was there. The whole garage started shaking and eventually it popped a fuse or something. But before it did, I saw this weird black smoke or cloud or... *something*. It was all gathered in one spot and kind of just *swirling* around in front of me. I nearly got sick," he said, refraining from telling them he'd nearly shit himself. That was just a little bit TMI.

Walden turned back from watching his car burn. "What was it?"

"I dunno. But the machine he made, he called it a Dark Energy Convertor. He said it was supposed to make dark matter visible to the naked eye."

"Eye's don't wear clothes," the kid said.

"*Shhh*," Cassandra replied, without taking her eyes off of Jay's. "And yes, they do. It's called an eyepatch."

Walden approached him cautiously, as if Jay might be infected with something. "So you think that's what this is? Somehow he—what? Not only just made it *visible* but made it interact with things it shouldn't be able to affect?"

"I don't know, honestly. Dark matter is theoretical. Most experts still call it pseudoscience."

"Pseudo—what?" Cassandra said.

"Fake. Junk science. Bunkum."

"Well, clearly it's not fake," Walden said. "And if that machine *almost* worked the other day, it's *really* working now. Whatever he's done, it's like that line Jeff Goldblum says in *Jurassic Park*. Once you open Pandora's box..." He shrugged.

"Jar," Jay said.

"Huh?"

"It's Pandora's *jar*, not box."

"Jar, box—who cares?" Cassandra said, scowling at the two of them. "What are we gonna *do* about it?"

"Wait," Jay said, finally able to get to his feet. He swayed again and Cassandra reached out to grab his arm. "I'm fine." He held up a hand to stop her, then leaned against the splintery telephone pole. "You told the kid to 'stop it' back at the barn. What did you mean? Why did you tell her to stop?"

Before Cassandra could reply, the kid said, "My *name* is Taylor."

Jay pinched his nose, closing his eyes, willing himself to have patience. *We've all been through a lot and these people don't have the same capacity to brainstorm I do. I really need a Rockstar.*

"You wouldn't believe me if I told you," Cassandra said with a sigh.

"Half an hour ago we wouldn't've believed a box full of promo toys could come to life and crash my car into a telephone pole," Walden said. "Why don't you try us?"

Cassandra glanced back at her sister, who nodded. "Taylor has... I guess you'd call it a gift."

"I can make stuff move by thinking about it really hard," the kid said.

"*Make stuff move?*" Jay said, incredulous despite everything he'd seen tonight. Dark energy affecting the material world was one thing. Little girl psychokinetics was another altogether.

"Uh-huh," she said. "Ever since I was really little."

"It's true," Cassandra said.

"When did you find out about it?" Jay asked Cassandra.

"A few years ago, I walked in on the shrimp making her Furby fly around the room. The second she saw me it dropped to the floor. Like it just remembered about gravity. She pretended she wasn't doing anything, but I told her I wouldn't tell anyone, that it'd be our secret. Now we just use it to play little pranks on our gramma."

"Oh no," Taylor said, a hand going to her mouth.

Cassandra seemed to clue in to whatever her sister was thinking.

Great, so now they're telepathic, too? Jay thought sarcastically.

"Grammy Lauren," they said together.

"Maybe she'll be all right," Walden said. "Maybe it's only messing around with stuff that was at the haunt."

"Maybe," Cassandra said somberly, putting an arm around her sister's shoulders. Neither of them appeared to be hopeful.

Jay couldn't say he blamed them. Because if Mr. Combs's machine could affect inanimate objects all the way out at the Thompson farm, it would likely be hitting things within a certain radius of the machine, wouldn't it? Could be what happened—was probably still happening—at Halloween Village was way worse in town. It could be they were about to walk right into the belly of the beast without any way to fight these things off and without even a plan.

They had to be cautious. They'd been ambushed at the haunt. At least now they sort of knew what they were up against.

Who would've thought the proof of dark matter would happen in boring old Crooks Corner?

"Guys, look!" the kid said suddenly, staring down at a Polaroid picture she'd been holding.

Cassandra stood and studied it a moment. Her dark-mascaraed eyes went wide. She took it from the kid and held it out to Walden. "You're gonna want to see this."

Walden approached them and looked at it himself. "Oh," he said.

"What?" Jay said. "What is it?"

Cassandra came over and showed him the photo. It looked like a bunch of black blurry shapes in front of the burning car, almost as if the photo hadn't fully developed in random fuzzy spots.

"Is that them?"

"That's the toys, right before it happened," Cassandra said. "Taylor fell on her butt when we all jumped out of the car and accidentally took a picture. When she did the toys all just... they all fell on the ground exactly like her Furby did when I walked into her room that time."

"You think—what?" Walden said, stroking his mustache. "You think the *flash* did that to them? The *light*?"

"There were lights at Halloween Village," Jay said, shaking his head. "It can't just be the light."

"Well, what then?"

Jay considered it, the headache making his thought process muddy, the kernel of a hypothesis just beyond his reach. "Walden..." He swallowed hard, his throat dry. "...where are the cameras?"

Walden turned to the car.

"Shit," Jay said.

"Exactly. If these *things* don't kill us, Hildebrand will."

"All right, I'm gonna need some Tylenol and a can of Rockstar pronto. Then we need to find Mr. Combs. I think I have an idea but we need to talk to him first."

"If he's still alive," Cassandra said.

Jay nodded solemnly. "If he's still alive."

They gave each other fearful looks in the flickering firelight.

3

8:30 P.M.
Crook Street / Our Lady of Mercy Catholic Church

REVEREND CHARLES ANDERSON EARL was having what could only be considered a crisis of faith.

He'd lit a candle and knelt to pray before the statue of Christ, clasping his hands together as tightly as always... but when he made to address his Lord and Savior, he'd found himself at a loss for words, his mind as desolate as the desert Moses had led the Israelites through on their way to the Promised Land. He was as constipated verbally as he'd been physically for the past several days, despite the many remedies he'd tried.

Lately, he'd been feeling... not quite a lack of faith, more that something in his life as the spiritual leader of Crooks Corner's only Catholic church was amiss. While quite a few more sheep had joined his flock since the horrific attack on liberty, his sermons had taken a turn away from the light of the Lord and toward the infernal darkness of eternal hellfire and damnation. Its burden had taken a toll on him, mentally, spiritually and physically. That toll had a name, and it wasn't Satan.

Dr. Plummer had called it *bowel cancer*.

Its symptoms were the delightful combination of both frequent, explosive visits to the toilet and constipation. Rectal bleeding, lethargy, excruciating abdominal pain, and losing weight were among the others. His face, somewhat pudgy and tanned as late as this past summer, had gone gaunt and almost gray in the following month or so. While he still made sure his attire was immaculate and his body freshly scrubbed—more now than he ever had before, considering his ailment—many of his parishioners had noticed the changes, both in his demeanor and appearance.

Why? he'd asked God. *Why did You choose to afflict me with this horrible disease when my flock needs me now more than ever? Why, when this town—*this world—*is so very clearly losing its way?*

Of course, it was hubris to ask these things, to dare question God's Plan. *Blasphemy*, even. Jesus might have asked His Heavenly Father why He'd appeared to have forsaken Him, but Jesus was the *Son of God*, and even He'd been punished for His hubris.

Father Charles had accepted his punishment, for whatever sin he'd committed, but it didn't mean he had to like it. The Lord worked in mysterious ways, and this was certainly that. Was it for the sin of Pride he'd been stricken with cancer? It couldn't be anger, for his rage toward the cowards who'd perpetrated the vile act against America was surely *righteous*. His sermons reflected that fury. He was an instrument of God, and God was Wrath. Of course, God was also divine forgiveness, but neither Charles nor his flock were quite ready to forgive those monsters. If God forgave them, that was His business. In Charles' opinion, the terrorists and each of their seventy-two virgins could roast in eternal hellfire for some time yet.

Further bad news arrived early this afternoon, when Deputy Aaron Sikes had informed him that the previous morning a slaughtered lamb had been left at the Thompson farm (the site of that godless yearly event which vexed Charles and his parishioners the entire month of October). The deputy had informed him that Sheriff Nance had spoken to an expert from Florida who'd assured Nance there was a cult out there in the woods behind the Thompson farm, or what the deputy called the "back nine."

If there truly was a cult at work out there in the woods, it was far more than pagan blasphemy they'd be dealing with this year. Halloween—or *Hell*oween, as the reverend called it on pamphlets and signs his parishioners had put up all over town in letters blazing with hellfire—was the least of his worries. There were *wolves* living amongst them, dressed in sheep's clothing. *Anyone* could be a part of the cult's Satanic assembly: the town council, the mayor, the Better Business Bureau... It certainly wouldn't surprise Charles to discover Sheriff Nance himself was involved.

When he'd suggested this to Deputy Sikes—not the last part, since Sikes and Nance were close—the man had wavered. "Nance doesn't think it's *Satanic*," he'd said. "He said most cults are Bible —" Charles flinched, aware the deputy was about to use the term Nance himself had once invoked to describe Charles and his flock right to his God-fearing face: *Bible-thumper*. Instead, Sikes diplomatically nodded toward Jesus on His cross hung above the apse and said, "Misguided followers of the Big Man Upstairs."

Charles had huffed angrily. "Satan wears many *guises*, Deputy Sikes. Many, *many* guises. Who are these false profits, if not imps of Belial himself?"

"Belial? You mean Beelzebub?"

"I mean the Devil, Deputy!" Charles told him, wagging a finger. "*The Devil!*"

The conversation had stuck with Charles all day long, to the point that he'd considered leaving in the middle of the day, forgoing the upcoming Al-Anon group and men's discipleship meetings, to drive out to the farm and confront the Thompsons themselves, give them a piece of his and his parishioners' minds. Perhaps he'd even enter the woods and search for evidence of this elusive cult. Like everyone else, he'd seen the crude graffitied symbol on the backs of downtown shops and sidewalks and elsewhere. Like everyone else he'd *hoped* it was just aimless kids with nothing more constructive to do than vandalize city property.

To discover they'd been made by an *actual cult*, after everything these people had been through in the weeks following the cowardly attack on freedom, after everything Charles himself was dealing with... it felt like God was testing him, as He'd tested Job, and Abraham before him. Charles had knelt in front of Jesus, candlelight dancing in his moist eyes, and thought he might be failing the test God had given him.

He'd stood abruptly, remembering why he'd been called to lead his flock. God had chosen him at a very young age, while his friends had still been pulling pigtails and making mudpies in the playground sandbox. He'd stood up in the dirt in the middle of the grimy yellow vertical climbing tube he'd tumbled into and conked his head, and felt God's Holy Finger touch his heart as the sun shone down on him from above, as he'd breathed in the foul stench of stale urine.

Twenty-three years later he'd moved to Crooks Corner to lead a flock of nearly two-hundred mostly-pious souls, a number that was steadily growing every day. He had to remember *why* he'd been chosen, out of everyone he knew. He had to remember God's love for him was divine, despite what had recently seemed like evidence to the contrary.

I'll confront them, he thought. *Chet and Rowena Thompson. The Devil's imps. I'll confront them in the very midst of their heathenistic revelry. The pamphlets and proselytizing didn't work, so I'll go straight to the source. This is what God has asked of me.*

Ten minutes later he was in his Subaru, driving across town toward Helloween Village, the serpent's den itself. He expected a fair amount of opposition, probably even to be escorted off the property by Sheriff Nance or one of his deputies. But it was imperative that he try. He wore his Reconciliation stole over his cassock, and brought the wooden crucifix from his office wall with him, as well as his trusty brown-leather Good News Bible. He had to *attempt* to save the souls of those poor lost sheep, even if the town might hate him for it. God willing, some of them might even listen to his words, and heed them.

He'd just about reached downtown when a flaming jack-o'-lantern hurled passed the windshield, causing him to startle and jerk the wheel. The car swerved, tires squealing, his heart skipping a beat. Glancing from side to side and in the rearview mirror, he saw no one in the street aside from a few trick-or-treaters, surely too young and small to cause such mischief. The pumpkin itself had splattered on the sidewalk in a chunky mess.

"'Yea, though I walk through the valley of the shadow of death,'" he muttered, gripping the wheel a bit tighter.

Another cult symbol—the smiley face with Xs for eyes—came up on his left as he reached downtown, flagrantly spray-painted on the east side of Town Hall. Charles shook his head in disappointment and a fair bit of disgust.

Cultist philistines. They'll face His judgement, soon enough. We all will, praise be. But them first... if He wills it.

Main Street was nearly devoid of pedestrians, aside from a handful of teenagers likely out causing mischief, as they had last night all throughout town. Devil's Night usually saw the worst of the damage, but often Helloween was just as bad. Everyone else down here this late in the evening would likely be inside one of the last shops to close, the diner or the theater, which was showing terror films to more godless revelers tonight, further evidence the sleepy little town of Crooks Corner had fallen under the Devil's sway.

With sudden force the steering wheel jerked in his hands, all but wrenching out of his grip. His heart leapt as the car swerved into the next lane. Fortunately, there was no oncoming traffic, just cars parked along the sidewalk. He struggled with the wheel and managed to get it under control without damaging a single vehicle, his or anyone else's.

Power steering, Charles thought with disdain. *If idle hands are the Devil's workshop, power steering surely must be one of his tools.*

He drove on, passing the antique store and the DollarSave. The mural of the town founders planting their flag in the earth beside Mallow Creek, which ran behind the buildings on the other side of the street, had been defaced with another godforsaken smiley face. While Charles chewed on it bitterly—the history of this peaceful town shamelessly besmirched by vandals—a sudden onrush of pedestrians spilled out of the theater into the street. He slammed on the brakes, but the brakes didn't respond. In fact, the Subaru *accelerated*, and this time the wheel wrenched out of his hands, hurtling the car and himself toward the advancing crowd.

"Look out!" he cried at them, tapping on the brake and trying madly to regain control of the vehicle. *Too little, too late*, as he was fond of saying in his sermons. The front bumper struck a pedestrian with a sickening crunch that made Father Charles wince. The woman sprawled over the hood, rolling off to the side as the car continued forward at speed, engine revving, plowing down another person, and another, and a fourth, before slamming into the wall of the theater and stopping dead.

The reverend's head struck the Judas-playing steering wheel as men and women and teenagers screamed and fled all around him. But it wasn't over. Whatever had happened here, whatever was still happening, it wouldn't end with a simple car crash. The world had lost sight of God. In a godless world, anything could conceivably happen. In the moment before he blacked out, Father Charles heard the sound of the Subaru's wheels spinning and saw, with blood blurring his vision, the stick shift throwing itself into reverse, and he knew beyond a shadow of a doubt the Fourth Seal had been broken.

Lord forgive us, he thought.

And then he was claimed by the darkness.

4

8:37 P.M.
Outside the Dollarsave

SHERIFF NANCE DIDN'T LIKE a *ruckus*, and he liked a *commotion* even less, but that was exactly what he'd found himself in the midst of tonight as he surveyed the chaos up and down Main Street from the doorway of the pharmacy. *A ruckus*, he thought. *A commotion*, he thought with even more aggravation. *One big, ugly goddamned heck of a mess is what it is.*

Nance liked a good mystery, but a *commotion*, a *ruckus*, had always been something he could live without. He didn't especially like having to raise his voice, and he liked exerting force even less. They were often necessary parts of the job, but like a teacher who'd rather not discipline his students, he merely put up with them. It was why he let Deputy Sikes handle domestic disputes, bar fights and the like. Sikes was old school, like his daddy had been as sheriff before Nance. He was a good kid but he knew how to put on the pressure when it was needed. Nance was all about deescalation, a value he tried to impress upon his deputies.

Deescalation. Reasonable, rational arguments. Nance considered himself a sensible man, more than anything. Reserved. He stood back and observed a situation before jumping in, more often than not. Looked before he leaped. That ability to calmly and coolly assess in the midst of chaos had kept him out of trouble plenty of times, and had, he liked to think, prevented others from being harmed more times than he could count. Nance had only ever had to fire his service pistol three times in his twenty-two-year career. He prided himself on that. There had been times when any other officer of the law would have drawn down, but Nance had been able to calmly offer peaceable solutions to unpeaceful people.

As an elected peace officer, it was his sworn duty to make sure everyone in his jurisdiction followed the law of the land, and to keep the peace, as the name stated.

Assess and reason. It was his mantra in dangerous and potentially deadly situations, something he'd learned from his father, who'd also been a lawman, whose own father—a U.S. Marshal in New Mexico—had passed it down to him.

He'd even stood back and observed as his marriage fell apart after the girls left for college five years back. Rather than done a damn thing to stop it, he'd calmly and rationally assessed the situation when that walking dildo Marcus Beams, a spinning instructor from Boston, had swept in and taken his wife, Janine. She'd already been lost to him was how he'd rationalized it, long before the dildo had taken his place.

Nance chugged from the bottle of Pepto Bismol on his way to the Eateria from the DollarSave, hoping to grab a cup of joe and a late-night bite, when he saw what could only be defined as a commotion, a ruckus, and thus a thing that could not be assessed calmly or rationally, and could not be reasoned with. It was, from the look, a *mob*. Not an *angry* mob, but a mob nonetheless. They spilled out from the theater in a chaotic, panicked mass, unwary of potential traffic, and seemingly unaware of anything but their own blind terror.

But terror of what, exactly? Nance thought, eyeing the madding crowd. *Active shooter? Bomb scare? Or worse?*

Nance screwed the cap on the pink bismuth and picked up

his pace toward his cruiser, parked a few stores up. It had been a long day already. He'd first gone out to the Thompson Farm to double-check on the goat slaying from yesterday, which he'd followed with a brisk tromp through the woods to see about that cult. Aside from a few of those faces made of sticks and a fair amount of scratches on his forearms from errant branches, neither expedition had produced a damn thing, and if not for the fact that Ms. Knight had been reported missing by the film folk early this morning (meaning she hadn't just accidentally dropped her purse near what had appeared to be a scuffle, but could just as easily have been several someones loading a heavy and awkward piece of furniture into a van, for instance), he might've passed the whole thing off as a hoax. For all he knew the man he'd spoken to last night from Jacksonville passing himself off as a "cult expert" was part of it.

Nance was halfway to his cruiser when the purple Subaru station wagon he recognized as Reverend Earl's—what he called the Purple Piousmobile to much laughter back at the station—careened toward the crowd. He followed its progress, hoping Earl or whoever was behind the wheel would turn before it was too late. He winced as the car hit the first pedestrian, and then three more before crashing into the wall of the theater.

"Jesus H.—" he muttered, and stepped off the sidewalk, picking up his pace as he crossed the road, weaving through the oncoming rush of panicked bodies.

"Sheriff!" a familiar voice called from the crowd.

He sought her out. It was Debbie Green, the parttime dispatcher. A man jostled her with an elbow as he pushed past her. She flinched and shut her eyes, hunching her shoulders against further disruptions. Nance reached out to her, grabbing her gently by both her shoulders, enough to make her look at him in the eye. "You all right, Debbie?"

"I'm fine," she said, and nodded as if to confirm to herself it was the case.

"What's going on in there, Deb? Active shooter?"

She shook her head firmly, eyes closed. "It... you won't believe me if I tell you."

Nance looked over the panicked faces as the crowd began to clear around them, heading off in various directions.

"Okay. Get yourself to safety. I need to check on those folks," he said, nodding toward the four people laid out in the street and sidewalk.

Debbie nodded again, then wandered off toward the diner. Nance watched for a moment as she moved in a dazed, wavering path toward the other side of the street, then turned his attention toward the victims of the vehicular rampage. Debbie would be okay. These people might not be so lucky.

He bent to check on the mangled woman he suspected had been first to be hit. Her right arm was broken, bone peaking out, bleeding badly. Her jaw appeared to be dislocated. A flock of crows burst from the doors of the theater, drawing his attention away from the woman for a moment. They cawed and beat their wings madly, circled overhead a couple of times, then flew away into the night, heading west toward Hooper Street. He considered it a moment—*Bit odd for old Roy Stafford to use live birds for a show*—then returned his attention to the woman before him. He checked her pulse, finding it slow but steady. She'd likely need immediate medical attention, but she was alive.

The other victims were significantly less injured—he suspected the car had slowed upon the first impact, whether intentionally or by physics—and conscious, groaning and moving sluggishly in pain. Nance grabbed his radio off his chest and thumbed the transmit button. "Madge, this is Nance, come on back."

"Go ahead, Bert."

"We are dipped in all manner of shit down at the Grand. We need emergency services ASAP, I've got several people down—"

"What's going on?"

"You would not believe me if I told you." A shopfront window in the antique store shattered outward, preventing him from elaborating. Dozens of small things—*Too big to be bugs*, he thought, *but what else could they be?*—fell out of the newly created exit and began skittering along in the broken glass on the sidewalk.

Nance blinked. He was close enough to see what they *appeared* to be, but he *had* to be imagining it. *Tin soldiers*, he thought. The little tin soldiers scurried along on the ground like the most normal thing in the world. Eight-year-old Hubie Nance might have delighted in the sight. Fifty-two-year-old Bert Nance was far from delighted. In fact, he was just about as far from delighted, or calm or rational, as he'd ever been in his life. "Christ on a cracker—" he muttered.

A shotgun blast caused him to duck. He heard Madge call his name over the two-way but he ignored it, running in a crouch toward the safety of the opposite side of Reverend Earl's station wagon, just as another gunshot pierced the night.

What in the hell is happening? Nance thought, heart racing as he drew his sidearm from its holster. At least ducked behind the crashed Subaru he couldn't see the toy soldiers march toward whatever imaginary mission lay ahead. Not having to bear witness to *that* impossible sight made it a fair bit easier to calm himself and to think.

Got to check on the driver, he thought. Whether it was the reverend or some drunk joyrider, they hadn't left the vehicle, which meant they'd likely been struck unconscious by the collision. If they'd been wearing their safety belt like a good citizen, emergency services might not have to scrape their remains off the theater wall.

Nance turned on his haunches, the heels of his boots grinding on the concrete, and reached for the door handle. The driver slid partway out when he opened the door, and would have fallen into Nance's arms if he hadn't been safely buckled in. Nance thanked God for the small mercy. Hugging Reverend Earl —with his cassock and confessional stole adorned—was the last thing he wanted to do this evening, whether the man was deceased or not.

Gently, he pushed the man upright. He genuinely hadn't expected it to be Reverend Earl behind the wheel, certain it had been a spillover from Gate Night, some drunk teen taking the reverend's car out for a spin. *Thing musta lost control,* he thought. He unlatched the seatbelt, then—more viciously than he would have to anyone else—roused Earl with a few slaps to his cheek.

The reverend's eyes came open wearily. "Wh'appuned?"

"You've been in an accident, Charles."

The bleary gray eyes opened wider, the shock of the memory clearly coming back to him. "*My Lord,*" he said, smacking his lips like a man rousing from sleep. "Are they all right?"

"They're hurt but they'll be okay. Are *you* all right?"

The reverend nodded, wincing at the slight movement. "My

head hurts, but I'll be fine." He started to get up and woozily slumped back down. Nance put a hand on his shoulder, feeling considerably more genial toward the holy man than he had a moment ago. It was an accident, after all. He hadn't gone nuts and thought he'd run down a bunch of potential terrorists or anything.

"You're not going anywhere 'til the paramedics show up." Nance glanced around, surprised he hadn't heard any sirens yet. "Just relax. I'll find—"

The distinctive sound of the pump-action shotgun being racheted came from right behind him. He turned to see Angus McLean from the butcher shop down the street, dressed in his blood-smeared apron and pointing a stubby shotgun right at him. Without a moment's thought, Nance threw himself over the reverend, sprawling them both over the front seats and the Bible and large wooden crucifix lying there, just hoping Charles didn't have a concussion and that he hadn't just rattled his brain into a coma. The explosive blast came a moment later, buckshot smashing through the window and making little metallic pings on the roof of the car.

Nance rolled off of the reverend, simultaneously falling on his butt in the footwell and aiming his revolver at Angus McLean.

"*Waitwaitwait!*" the beefy butcher cried, raising both hands into the air.

Nance kept his sidearm trained on the man, not about to let him get the upper hand if this was a trick, though not exactly eager to fire on the man if he had to. "What in the damn hell were you doing firing that thing at me for, huh?"

"Wasn't you I was shootin at, Sheriff," the big man said. He pointed with his free hand over Nance's head. "It's *them*!"

"Them what?"

"The antique shop toys," the butcher said. "Goddamn pig I been splittin up went nuts on the table, an' I come out here to see all this horseshit. You're lucky I shot when I did!"

"Went nuts how?"

The man's bristly jowls shuddered as he shook his head, as if he couldn't believe it any more than Nance could. "Just started floppin around and squealin. Knocked me right on my ass and damn near trampled my balls, even though it ain't got no eyes in its head. I shot the sucker but it got away, run off down the back alley," he said, bobbing his head behind him.

Nance tried to process this, tried to reconcile what he was seeing and hearing with reality. He tried, but found himself unable. Nothing about this made any sort of sense. Reason had been abandoned.

"The wheel," the reverend moaned beside Nance.

"What about the wheel?"

"It drove itself into those poor people. The wheel turned and the car accelerated right into them, *all by itself.*"

Nance stopped himself from telling the reverend what he was saying sounded crazy. Hadn't he just seen an army of toys marching out of the antique store? Hadn't he watched a bunch of clearly fake crows fly out of the movie theater? Hadn't he just seen an entire theater full of patrons rush out of the same doors as if something had been chasing them, and seen the Catholic priest's car run down several of them like dogs in the street? Charles Earl was a lot of things, but he wasn't a damn *murderer.*

There was nothing *sane* about any of this.

And yet, he thought. *And yet...*

"The Fourth Seal," Reverend Earl said.

Nance scoffed. "Charles, you don't—"

"The Fourth Seal has been broken—isn't that obvious? Revelation 6:8. 'I looked, and there was a pale-colored horse. Its rider was named Death, and Hades followed close behind.' *Hell* followed close behind, Sheriff Nance. On Helloween, no less!"

Nance frowned, getting up from the wheel well and sliding out of the crashed car to stand. "You're talking about the apocalypse," he said, looking down at the prone religious man with blood trickling down his forehead. "The end of the world."

"Precisely," Reverend Earl said, sitting up and holding his head. "How else would you explain what's happening here?"

Nance looked off, squinting. The sound of sirens erupted in the night. One of the volunteer fire department's trucks by the sound. The butcher shrugged, letting the hand holding the shotgun fall to his girthy hip.

"I don't know, Charles," Nance said. "What I do know is that whatever's happening, people are gonna need shelter and words of comfort. I think it's time you and I started working together instead of at odds."

"I sincerely agree," the reverend said, and he held out a hand. His irises looked strangely dark in the shadow of the streetlight, Nance thought. He'd never really taken notice of the man's eye color before, although he'd once heard Sykes say he was so full of shit his eyes were brown. Nance thought now they were as black as a full-blood Indian's. Maybe he had some Winnipesaukee in him somewhere down the family line.

Nance regarded Reverend Earl's outstretched hand a moment, feeling for some reason like he was about to make a deal with the Devil. Then he took it, and helped the man of the cloth to his feet.

CHAPTER 12

1

9:11 P.M.
Halloween Village

"Tommy!" Cody said excitedly. "You're alive!"

Tommy Mingus ignored him, oddly dark eyes staring out from his pudgy, pallid face directly at Brittany. But it wasn't her fault he'd gotten lost and covered in someone else's blood. She hadn't even been with them when he'd run off.

"*YOU DID THIS!*" Tommy shouted again, raising a hand to point at her.

Brittany wore that same glazed-over look Cody had seen on her face many times in class, staring off to the right, usually while she doodled spirals in one of her notebooks. Spaced out. Sometimes Cody wondered if she had ADD or something, if maybe she was on a heavy dose of Ritalin. Tommy was accusing her of —what was he accusing her of? Causing all of this somehow? Whatever it was, it didn't make sense. The poor kid was probably shell-shocked. Like Taylor, he'd likely seen much more tonight than a child his age should ever have to witness. Like Cody himself—and Brittany too, he assumed—the kid was probably shitting bricks.

Cody held up his hands placatingly. "Hey, Tommy, buddy, it's okay. We're all scared. Let's just get you out of he—"

"*YOU DID THIS!*" Tommy shouted again, like it was the

only thing he knew how to say. Then he ran straight at Brittany with his head bowed like a charging bull.

He struck her head-on in the stomach before Cody could even react to what was happening. *What IS happening?* he wondered, rushing in to break them up.

Tommy slashed at her face with surprisingly sharp nails on his stubby little fingers. He got her a good one on the cheek, four streaks of blood rising to the surface, and another on her neck, before Cody lifted him off of her. Brittany just lay there against the wall, taking it, that blank look still on her face.

Tommy Mingus kicked and grabbed at Cody. He had the strength and ferocity of a wolverine, managing to get his fingers up into Cody's nose and pull. Cody growled in pain—his nose had been previously broken during a game against the Brewster Academy Bobcats last year—and he dropped the kid before realizing he could have hurt Tommy pretty badly, and the kid was just dealing with some serious PTSD.

Tommy landed on his feet and didn't waste a second. He charged at Brittany again, who'd just managed to sit up, leaning back on her hands. She raised her hands in front of her face, but Cody grabbed Tommy by the shoulders of his coat and held him in place. The smaller boy kicked and grabbed at Brittany, who skittered back against the wall on her hands and feet.

"Stop it, Tommy! Calm down!" Cody said.

Tommy turned and started at Cody again, kicking, punching and clawing, uttering little high-pitched grunts that might be kind of funny if the kid wasn't actively trying to kill him. Cody grabbed him around the neck and swung him around, putting him in a sleeper hold. "Stop it, Tommy, stop!"

Cody fell back against the wall and slid to the floor, cradling Tommy in his lap. The smaller boy kicked and wriggled, trying to break free, screaming and gnashing his teeth. He just wouldn't calm down, even when Cody wrapped his legs around him.

"Let him go," Brittany said.

She was standing over them, the fog in her expression cleared.

"He'll kill you," Cody said.

"Then let him. He's right, this is all my fault."

Cody struggled. The kid almost got free and he had to change his angle, harkening back to moves he'd used in wrestling before he'd gotten tapped for the football team. "Come on, Brit..." he said, almost pleadingly.

She blinked. "It's Brittany. Now let him go."

Cody didn't want to do it but the kid was ferocious, and outside of actually putting him to sleep—which he'd never done before—he couldn't think of a way to get him to stop struggling.

Cody let go all at once. The kid sprang to his feet with a scream of rage and ran straight at Brittany. She stood there, awaiting his wrath, and then simply stepped out of the way. The kid kept running and smashed his head against the wall behind her. He made a small pained grunt, stumbled back several steps, then ran at it again. Cody heard the plywood splinter against Tommy's forehead.

"Tommy, stop!"

Brittany shook her head, watching the boy smash his head again and again against the wall and claw at the black paint, the wood splintering, revealing the plywood underneath.

"It's not Tommy," she said. "Tommy's dead."

"What? He's *alive*, Brittany. He's gonna kill himself!"

"He's *not*. Look at the way he's mindlessly attacking whatever's in front of him. It's just like those *things*, Cody."

Cody couldn't believe it—*wouldn't* believe it. How could whatever was possessing the things on the other side of these walls possess a *kid*, dead or not? It was impossible.

So is everything else, he thought. It all made sense. It explained the holes in his jacket, the blood all over him, his pale skin. He was *dead*—but something was making him move with a killer instinct.

"We can't just let him do that," he said finally.

"He needs to run out of steam."

Tommy staggered back from the wall. His head was covered in blood, and still he attacked again.

"What if he doesn't?"

Brittany shrugged. "Then I don't know. But we need to go."

"We can't just leave him..."

"What are you gonna do, Cody? You tried to stop him before. You think he's just gonna relax and do what we tell him now? He's possessed by whatever those things are. And if it can possess him, it can possess *them*," she said firmly, pointing toward the haunt.

Cody clued in. There were ten, maybe twenty dead people on the farm he'd seen *so far*. If they all came back to life like Tommy had, no one still alive would stand a chance. He nodded. "Okay. I need to check on the Thompsons first."

Brittany shrugged. "Fine. Then we're out of here, before this gets a lot worse."

She held out a hand again. This time Cody didn't take it. The cold, calculated way in which she'd stepped aside to let Tommy run himself into the wall didn't sit well with him, whether the kid was possessed or not. While Brittany went on ahead, he looked back at Tommy once more, then followed her.

The plywood crunches and moans and grunts, smaller and smaller as the steam left Tommy's sails, followed them until they turned at the next corner.

2

9:21 P.M.
Old Route 14

MORE THAN ANYTHING, Walden merely wished he hadn't begged off work tonight to make their fucking movie.

Everything had been going pretty well until all hell broke loose—possibly *literally*—and all of the things at the haunt started attacking them, acting like they were literally haunted. Which would've been fine on its own—they'd survived, after all—if he'd at least gone in to work first and dropped off the box of *Ragers in Space* promotional toys. Then he'd still have his car, which was now a burning hulk on the side of the road a mile or so back, and he'd still have his video camera, which he'd left in the car when they'd leapt out in a rush to escape the Ragers, and was probably a melted hunk of plastic and electronics fused into the floor behind the front seat.

Helloween, he thought again, walking down the long, desolate stretch of road toward town. If he believed in the supernatural, he might have wondered if Cody was psychic himself. Then again, he'd thought telekinesis was something out of a Stephen King movie, but little Taylor Flynn had clearly demonstrated those powers, holding the Ragers at bay long enough for them to flee the crashed car before the fuel tank exploded. He'd also thought demonic possession—or whatever was happening here—was something out of a movie, but he'd changed his mind pretty quick on that front, too.

So maybe Cody was psychic. Maybe he'd known someone would open the gates to Hell at Halloween Village.

That's stupid. Why would he come with us if he knew that was gonna happen? It's just a coincidence.

"What's a coincidence?" Cassandra asked, walking a little way behind him, holding her sister's hand.

"Huh? Oh, nothing." He'd been walking ahead of them for so long, the whole group in a quiet funk—even motormouth Taylor had stopped talking—that he'd almost forgotten he wasn't alone, and he sure as hell didn't think he was talking aloud. That was something he usually only did at home, or in the projector booth, when no one else was around. He'd often found speaking his thoughts and ideas aloud solidified them, made them more tangible, easier to follow. Especially while writing a screenplay, when the characters and settings seemed to gain a life of their own.

Okay, so what would happen in a movie right now?

Lay it out like scene cards for a script, he told himself. *One after another.* He outlined everything in his mind.

1) They knew about Mr. Combs's Machine, the Dark Matter Convertor, or whatever Jay had called it, which—potentially—if turned off could stop all of this from happening. It had caused the earthquake yesterday, after all, and Brittany had felt that all the way out at the farm. Judging by what Jay had allegedly experienced in Combs's garage and what they'd seen in the photo, it was the likely catalyst—or what screenplay gurus would call "inciting incident"—which set all of this horror into motion.

2) They had Taylor, who could apparently deflect these entities—call them Possessors for lack of a better word—though her demonstration had proven she couldn't hold them off for too long without it being too much pressure on her still-forming brain. Also, larger objects may be more difficult for her to control. This was still to be determined, as she was still, like the rest of them, in shock.

3) Something about the Polaroid caused the Possessors to flee the Rager toys en masse *when Taylor accidentally snapped a pic-*

ture. Since it couldn't be the flash—proven by them being unaffected by lights at the farm—was there something about the act of taking a photograph that disrupted them? If so, what?

In a movie, the heroes would return to town armed with the limited knowledge they'd gained and stop the Possessors from taking over their town before it was too late.

But what if none of us is the hero? What if we're all just side characters? Comic relief, or worse: red shirts?

Collaboration was the key. Jay had dropped a bombshell back at the car, as had Cassandra. They needed to work together if they were going to survive this. He couldn't do this on his own. He was no longer in the driver's seat—neither literally nor figuratively—but still, someone needed to get the plot moving forward.

"We need to figure out a plan," he said. "Jay was right, we should probably talk to Mr. Combs, but first we should check on your gramma, Cassandra."

"She's mine, too," Taylor said.

"Right, she's yours, too," Walden said patiently. "Your place is the closest—"

Frowning, Cassandra said, "How do you know where we live?"

"I've seen you going there a bunch of times at lunch. You're right behind the parking lot."

"Right, where you and the grungies hang out."

Walden stroked his mustache. "Some of the goths do, too. Besides, I'm not really a grunger, or a skater, or whatever, I just kind of fell in with them because they smoke."

"That's a dirty habit," Taylor said.

"*Dirty Habit*, that's a good movie title. Inner-city nuns start growing weed to save their church. I need to write this down."

Cassandra sighed. "Can we focus, please?"

"Right. Sorry. So we check on your gramma first, make sure she's okay because you're first on the way to Combs's place. But I think we should also go to the school."

Jay piped up then, finally. He hadn't spoken since they'd left the wreck, just been staring at his feet and kicking the occasional piece of gravel, bottle top and whatever else happened to be in his path. "Why the school?"

"Because I wanna test a theory. If there's more of those things in town—I'm gonna start calling them Possessors, by the way, so we don't have to call them *things* or *creatures* or *entities* or whatever else we've been calling them—"

"They remind me of the *Sluagh*," Cassandra said, pronouncing it *sloo-ah*.

"What's that?"

"They're the spirits of the damned in Irish folklore. They come out on Halloween, or Samhain"—she pronounced this *Sow-win*—"to kidnap people and carry them away."

"Figures you would know that," Jay said. "How 'bout graboids?"

"Good reference," Walden said, "but nah. And I like where you're head's at, Cassandra, but I haven't seen them flying off with anyone. Whatever you guys wanna call em, I'm calling them Possessors. If they're in town, too—and judging by the sirens we heard a little while ago, it's probably a safe bet they are—we need to test out our options for getting rid of them. One of them is the cameras."

Cassandra nodded. "Because of the Polaroid."

"Right. And there's more cameras at school, for the photography class. But there's also a couple more video cameras. I didn't really get a chance to test it out because I was too busy shitting my pants—and by the way, *The Blair Witch* was bullshit. Nobody's gonna be running for their life and still bothering to point the camera."

Jay huffed a semi-interested laugh.

"But if cameras work *against* them somehow... even if we don't know exactly *why*, that's something. That's an organic reason to keep shooting, anyway."

"Why are we still talking about the movie like it's a thing?"

"Because it's the only thing I've got—*okay*, Cassandra? I know movies. I know how they work and *why* they work, and if I treat this like a movie maybe I'll have a good chance of surviving this thing, and maybe I can help the three of you survive, too."

"Fair," Cassandra said, looking down at her boots scuffing the asphalt. "Sorry, I'm just... this is a lot."

Jay huffed another laugh. "That's an understatement."

They came over the final rise in the road then, and the whole town lay spread out before them in the low valley, the lights in houses and the buildings downtown glimmering against the night sky. Walden thought it was pretty, and couldn't remember the last time he'd thought about Crooks Corner that way. Maybe when he was little, coming back late from visiting his grandparents in Portland. For so much of his teenage life he'd wanted to get out of this stupid little town, to get in his car and drive, put it in his rearview mirror, but now all he wanted to do was go back, to keep it safe.

After that, he wasn't so sure where he'd want to be anymore. Tonight had already fundamentally changed him. He'd witnessed death and almost died himself. He'd lost the car he'd spent over a year working and saving to be able to afford from the auto wreckers (he could just make out the ring of lights surrounding the lot's fence on the far side of town). This was the part in Joseph Campbell's hero's journey when the hero crosses the threshold from the known into the unknown. What lay before them was no longer the Crooks Corner they'd grown up in. It had changed—twice in as many months, if he counted the noticeable difference in people's attitudes and behavior, especially the adults, after what happened last month just a five hours' drive to the southwest, and what some still thought could happen again anywhere at any time—and it would possibly never be the same again.

Am I the hero, though?

His mind circled around to it again, and it was a question he'd asked himself often. In screenwriting, they said every character thought they were the hero in their own story. The villain, the sidekick, the love interest, the comic relief—each was the main character in their own narrative. He'd always wondered, for instance, what he might do if someone "went Columbine"—Jay had always been the most likely candidate, but now he wasn't so sure—at Crooks Corner High. Would he stand up to them, as a hero might do? He'd stood up to Brunt, when Brunt had started ripping on that minor niner, and Brunt had beaten the shit out of him until Mr. Hildebrand had come out of school and broken it up.

But what if Brunt had pointed a gun at him? Would he have been so quick to talk back? What if he'd been on one of the flights that struck the World Trade Center? Would he have done anything, *tried* anything, or sat back and let the inevitable happen? Would he be the hero of his own story, or just an extra? A background artist?

It was questions like these that kept him up late at night, dreaming up scenarios for his screenplays—which he considered Tarantino-esque—for movies which would only happen if he fucked off and left this little pissant town behind.

So yes, he wanted to keep Crooks Corner safe—its people, its institutions and much of its way of life—but only so it would be preserved like a time capsule for when he returned, the famous film writer-director. And when he told stories about where he'd come from, they would show footage of the sleepy little town and people would understand how difficult it must have been for the tortured artist to live in a place he'd considered mostly devoid of creativity.

"So we get the cameras, and then what?" Cassandra said, rousing him from his thoughts.

"Then..." Walden swallowed a hard lump in his throat. "... then whenever we encounter a Possessor—"

"*Sluagh*," she added.

Walden steamed for a moment at the interruption, then allowed himself to grin back. Every movie needed moments of levity, and after what they'd just been through comic relief was needed more than ever. "We'll keep the video cameras running nonstop and when we see one, we'll point them at it, and take their picture for good measure."

"Double-tap," Jay said. "Pown em."

Cassandra looked at Jay askance. "Do *what* to them?"

He shrugged. "Powning noobs. It means beating someone. Like owning, but with a P. It started from a typo, because the P is right beside the O."

"Why didn't you just say that then?"

"Hey, I don't rag on you for using goth slang."

"There's no such thing as *goth slang*."

Walden grinned again. "You know, Brittany said we'd probably end up killing each other tonight. I bet she never thought something would try to *kill us*."

"I hope they're okay," Taylor said glumly.

Cassandra squeezed her shoulder. "I'm sure they're fine, shrimp." She gave Walden and Jay a stern glare so they wouldn't say anything to the contrary. Walden hadn't planned to—it was hard enough for the kid already—and even Jay seemed to be in a better mood.

"Yeah. Cody's pretty tough," Walden said. "And Brittany..."

"Brittany's a spark plug," Jay said, grinning.

Walden laughed, recalling the comment Chet Thompson had made about her before all of this started happening. "That's as good a way to describe her as any. If anyone's got a good chance of surviving, it's those two."

"And they'll find Tommy, and make him safe," Taylor said, hope in her eyes.

Walden wasn't sure about that, but sometimes the hero had to lie to keep up morale, so he said, "Yup. They'll make sure he's safe. By this time tomorrow he'll be back and annoying your sister just like always."

"Can't wait," Cassandra moaned.

In the silence that followed, while the soles of their shoes and boots scuffed on the asphalt toward the lights of town, a thunderous boom arose from somewhere up ahead. He almost didn't see it at first, but then the enormous explosion engulfed a portion of the western edge where he'd just been looking a few minutes ago: the junkyard. First his car exploded, now the place he'd bought it did.

"Oh my God," Cassandra said.

Taylor clutched her sister's hand. "What's happening?"

They all watched in terrified awe as the fireball diminished, leaving an inferno in its wake.

Walden hoped however the explosion happened, and whatever had caused it, that it had done some damage to the Possessors and left as few casualties as possible. Having seen the footage of the Twin Towers collapsing and its aftermath, he didn't hold out much hope. Still, if anyone had died, he hoped they'd died as heroes.

"Come on," he said. And although every instinct in him screamed at him to turn around and run in the opposite direction, get as far away as he could from Crooks Corner and the haunt and just keep running until all of this was far behind him, he added, "We have to get moving. Before it's too late to stop this."

3

9:27 P.M.
Geromero Street Bridge

MIKE "CHIMNEY" Stuckey and Dave "Big Mac" MacNamara had been chain-smoking under the bridge when they heard the distinct rumble and pop of Brunt's Mustang on the street above. After all the shit that went down up there, the two of them had huddled under the bridge listening for things to die down. The last thing they'd heard before sirens wailed over the bridge was a massive explosion from the far side of town.

Mike was pretty scared, though he wouldn't admit it to Mac, even though he was pretty sure Mac was just as scared as him. Last night's shenanigans had gone just as well as could be expected, aside from getting spotted by Hildebrand at Miss Stabler's house. Tonight hadn't gone anything like they'd planned, especially after Brunt kicked them out of the car. After that it'd been complete fucking chaos, like out of a horror movie. They'd gotten divebombed by flying pumpkins and a three-foot-tall witch on a broomstick on their way to shelter. They'd only narrowly escaped a bunch of plastic skeletons literally chasing them through backyards and down back alleys.

Now here they were, hiding out like a couple of cowards under the bridge, unable to get home, all because that asshole Brunt kicked them out of his fucking car. He'd taken it too far picking on Philbert, though. Mike had a retarded cousin, although his aunt preferred people to call Bobby "differently abled." The kid was training for the Special Olympics for shotput, and considering he was built like an ox and had an arm like a catapult, Mike figured he had a pretty good chance of making it. That made Bobby cool in his books, Down Syndrome or not.

So Mike had stood up for Philbert, knowing he'd probably be outnumbered. He was glad Mac had stuck with him, even though it had slowed them down. Mac was *big-boned*, as he liked to say, which made him a perfect nose tackle but not a great runner. Still, he may have slowed them down but he'd stepped in front of Mike with his head bowed and arms crossed and the witch had crashed into him instead of Mike, knocking it off kilter and giving them a chance to get away.

The Mustang's rumble neared as Brunt turned into the parking lot. It drove in a wide circle until the headlights were pointed directly at them, shining into the tunnel like spotlights. It was the most light they'd seen since they'd hid down here, and Mike shielded his eyes as the engine grumbled like a hungry animal.

Mac took a step toward the car. Mike grabbed his shoulder. If Mac wasn't already nervous there would've been no way Mike could stop him from continuing. But he stopped and gave Mike an anxious look.

"Something's wrong," Mike said.

"What?"

"I dunno, it just feels... *off*. Ya know?"

Mac thought about it for a minute. He was a slow thinker, which most people mistook for stupidity. But in Mike's experience, he landed on the right answer more often than not. It just took him longer to get there than most people. After what seemed like forever, the two of them watching the Mustang as its engine growled, he nodded.

"Yeah," Mike agreed. "You ever see that movie with the killer car?"

"Uh-huh."

"You see anyone behind the wheel?"

Mac squinted. He shook his head slowly.

The engine revved, spewing black smoke into the air.

The thing about the Geromero bridge, one side was open and the other side had been closed off by an unfinished construction project for the past two or three years. If they wanted to run, they'd have to leave the tunnel racing toward the car and split off to either side.

"You wanna run for it?"

Mac nodded without a moment's thought.

"Okay, on three we—"

The tires spun before Mike had a chance to finish instructing Mac. Smoke rose from the asphalt and the car sped toward them. Mac turned and lumbered toward the chainlink fencing and plywood barrier. Mike stayed put a moment, caught in the headlights, trying to decide whether following Mac or bolting for the exit was likelier to save his ass.

As it turned out, the car made the decision for him, slamming on its brakes and peeling to a stop a few feet from where he stood in stunned silence, mouth agape.

Under the tunnel, he was able to see two pale shapes in the front seats. Brunt and Fitz, staring out at him with vacant expressions. The engine rumbled, louder in the closed space.

Mike hesitantly stepped toward Brunt's open window.

"Hop in, faggots," Brunt said, not turning from looking through the windshield at Mac. He looked like death under the dome light, his skin as white as soap where it wasn't angry red and oozing pus. He'd always had bad acne but this was the worst case Chimney had ever seen. Even Fitz looked like he'd gotten it in sympathy.

"You guys been, like, rolling in poison oak or something?"

"Get in the car, Stuckey, before I run you both the fuck over." Brunt finally turned then, looking up at Mike with a dead-eyed smile.

Mike didn't waste a second. He opened the door and climbed in before Brunt could change his mind and decide he'd rather just run them over. The way Brunt and Fitz were looking at him now, both of them smiling with black eyes, he wouldn't put it past them.

"It's okay, Mac," Mike called, though he didn't think it was okay at all. Mac swayed nervously back and forth before lumbering over to the other side of the car. He looked in, frowned when Brunt and Fitz grinned up at him, then got in beside Mike. The two of them shared an anxious look.

Whatever had happened to Brunt and Fitz, they didn't look right. They looked like fucking zombies. But Mike figured it was better to go along with them than go against them. They'd had a bad enough night since they left the car already. It couldn't possibly get any worse.

As Brunt reversed out from under the bridge, tires squealing and engine screaming, Mike hoped like hell he was right.

4

9:35 P.M.
Mr. and Mrs. Thompsons's Farmhouse

BRITTANY WAS first through the door. Mrs. Thompson closed it behind Cody, locked it and threw the latch.

"Oh my Lahd, I'm glad you two're safe."

"Is there any haunt stuff in the house, Row?" Brittany asked.

"No ma'am. Everything we got's out there in the bahn."

"Good." She looked over the small group gathered in the living room, several she didn't know, and a few from the haunt, who'd wisely removed any props or costume items they'd been wearing, probably at Row's behest. She was a shrewd woman, and even though none of this made any sense she likely would've noticed the pattern Brittany and Cody had already: that everything to do with the haunt had become possessed by some thing or *things*. But she doubted any of them had seen what she and Cody had just witnessed in the crossover corridors in the barn.

"Where's Chet?" she asked.

"Upstairs with a few others, boardin up the winduhs. They went up there after Chet turned off the gennies."

That 'splains the power goin out, The Snake said in Brittany's mind. They'd just about escaped the barn when everything, from the lights to the music and horror soundtrack, had abruptly shut off. With nothing but cracks of moonlight to carry them along and Brittany's knowledge of the corridors, they wound their way to the exit. But every sound from inside the haunt redoubled, making the two of them walk so closely together they may as well have been holding hands.

"That's good," Cody said. "You should do that down here, too."

Brittany exhaled sharply through her nostrils, annoyed that he was trying to take over. He could boss the guys working the corn field if he wanted to, this was her crowd.

Jealousy don't become you, honeypie, The Snake said. *Let him have his moment. He won't be round much longer, anyhow. You can sign that on the dotted line.*

Brittany didn't want to know what The Snake meant by that, if he assumed Cody wouldn't survive or if he intended to make it happen himself using her as the instrument. She might have been momentarily angry at Cody but she didn't want him dead. He was the one person here who could help get her back home. Aside from Row and Chet, these others were sheep. A bunch of community theater actors and horror fans. She was surprised they'd lasted this long, and by the looks of some of them, they only had by the skin of their teeth. They were scared, huddled together or sitting alone hugging themselves, praying silently. Hell, one lady had to be about seventy years old and the cigarette she puffed away on wasn't doing anything to calm the jitter in her fingers.

"These folks are just about too scared to do anythin but sit still and wait this shitstorm out," Row said. "But you two look like you could put in some hahd work. There's mah wood down cellar."

Cody nodded and hurried off toward the basement door. Brittany gestured Row aside.

"What's up, girl? You look a right mess."

"It got bad out there. How many of you are missing?"

"Twenty, maybe. This and the four upstairs are the last of us. Counted just over a hundred heads come through the gate tonight. These six are th'only ones made it up the house."

Brittany nodded. It didn't mean everyone else was dead, but it was a harrowing reminder of the hellscape they'd left behind. Likely there were others hiding in the corn field, the parking lot, in the barn where they hadn't looked, on the road and out in the woods. Some had fled in their cars like Walden and the others. But there were a lot of dead people out there, and that was what concerned her now.

"One of the dead ones," she whispered, "we saw it come back to life."

"*Zombies?*" Row said too loud. The two of them glanced around to see if anyone had heard. When no one reacted—they were all practically zombies themselves, only from PTSD not actual death—Row lowered her voice and spoke again. "Christ sake, that's all we need, ain't it?"

Brittany shrugged. "Whatever it is possessing this stuff, I guess it can possess people, too. Dead people, at least. Hopefully not the living," she added, and the spirals twisted in her mind, reminding her—as if she needed a reminder—of her own possession.

"Possession? Like *demonic*?"

"I don't know, Row. Whatever it is, it doesn't seem to have a purpose aside from mindless destruction, attacking anything in its path. We just saw a dead kid smash his own head to paste against a wall trying to attack us."

Row winced. "Jeez, I didn't need to hear that."

"I'm just telling you, we need to be ready for anything. We need weapons. Guns, knives, anything sharp or heavy that's easy to swing."

"Good thinkin. I'll get to lookin. You go on an' help Cody put up them barricades on the winduhs. Folks," Row said, addressing the others, "I know you're scared, but we're gonna need those of ya who can to staht movin furniture up against the doors and winduhs. More of yas the bettah. We need to proof this house 'gainst whatever's out there tryna get in. Ya got it?"

Nods from several of them, who stood up hesitantly.

"Good. We're gonna make it through this, folks, so long as we all stick togethuh and stay strong." She clapped her hands together. A few people startled at this, as if they were in a trance. "All right?"

Mutters of agreement met this, and while Row headed for the kitchen, people started getting busy, pushing sofas and chairs toward the walls, and moving the bookcase toward the door. Cody emerged from the basement stairs a moment later lugging a huge piece of plywood. Brittany took the bottom of the board and helped him haul it toward the front windows.

These sheep might have themselves a chance yet, The Snake said.

5

9:48 P.M.
Old Route 14 / Cunningham Road

THEY WERE ALMOST BACK at town, just about to head down into the valley, when Cassandra heard the sound of a vehicle approaching from behind.

At first she almost didn't hear it, smothered by the sirens in the town below, the sudden bursts of gunfire—she'd thought they were fireworks at first, but Walden informed them otherwise—the shouts and screams. When the distant headlights shone through the dark trees, they were spread out across the road, trudging steadily forward.

"Guys," she said. "Car."

They all looked back at once—fearful, not hopeful. Considering what had happened in Walden's Nova, it was a practical fear, at least in Cassandra's mind.

"We should flag them down," Walden said.

"You don't think we should hide?" This was Jay.

"They could be driving right into *that*—" Walden pointed toward town. "—with no idea what they're getting into."

"Good point." Cassandra nodded. "Let's flag them down. Maybe if they're not complete psychos we can get a ride back ourselves."

They all moved over to the right side of the road, up against the steep asphalt ditch leading to a hay field. The headlights washed over them, closer now, and they all began waving their arms.

As the vehicle neared, Cassandra was sure the driver would floor the gas and speed right past them. Who would pick up a bunch of teenagers on a dark, desolate road this late? And indeed, it appeared that almost happened. The engine roared and the—*Van*, she thought, *it's a black van*—picked up speed. Then, just as she thought it would blast by them, their voices rising in distress, shouting for the driver to stop, the van's brakes kicked in and the tires peeled, the van swerving to a stop about ten feet ahead of them. If it had gone any further, they wouldn't have been able to see it over the crest of the hill.

Walden ran ahead. "Come on!"

Jay followed, then Cassandra, pulling Taylor along, who looked up at her nervously.

"It'll be fine," Cassandra said, though she wasn't sure she believed it herself. If they were creeps—*Who else drives a black van?*—then they just wouldn't accept a ride.

"Hi," Walden said, looking into the passenger window. Then his mouth opened wide and he staggered back a step. "Are you okay?"

Jay stopped at his side, followed his gaze and said, "Jesus..."

Cassandra approached the window with Taylor, and finally saw what the boys had noticed. The woman in the driver's seat was drenched in blood from her long, currently straggly hair to her hands and clothing, the interior light making it the brightest red it could possibly be. She turned to them, her eyes wide white circles with dark, shining jewels of fear.

"Huh?" she said.

"Are you..." Walden started uncertainly. "Is that your blood?"

"No," the woman said.

Cassandra hadn't recognized her under all the gore, but now she did. She had a W name, like Willow or Winnie. "Hey, you work at the diner, don't you?"

"Uh-huh," the woman said sleepily.

Cassandra looked at the others. Walden shrugged. Jay looked clueless. No one seemed to want to be the one to ask.

"Hey, uh, can we get a ride into town?" she asked.

The woman stared at her, open-mouthed, for a long moment. Cassandra watched a runner of blood ooze from her top lip to the bottom. The woman closed her mouth instinctively and licked her lips. Cassandra almost gagged at the sight, which she realized was odd, considering all of the awful stuff she'd already seen tonight.

"Yeah... I guess so," the driver said indecisively. She leaned over the passenger seat and opened the door. Walden let her sit back behind the wheel before reaching in and opening the sliding side door.

Taylor gave Cassandra a look that said, *Are you sure?*

Cassandra nodded. She wasn't *sure*, but her feet were tired—the Demonia chunky platform boots she'd worn tonight were doing her no favors—and she needed to sit down. Plus, though the woman was covered in blood she seemed pretty docile. For all Cassandra knew, the blood was fake and the woman, Willow or Winnie, was high on E and on her way to a Halloween party in town.

"Go on, shrimp."

Taylor climbed in. Cassandra got in behind her, sighing as she sat, and Jay followed. Walden sat in the front. They closed the doors at the same time.

"Buckle up," the woman said dully.

Cassandra put on her seatbelt and made sure Taylor had done hers. The van pulled away from the ditch and continued toward town.

"You, uh, you okay?" Walden asked.

"No," the driver said. "I'm really fucking far from okay. My name's Willa, by the way."

"Sorry," Walden said, and told Willa his name.

"What happened to you?" Taylor asked innocently, after Jay had introduced himself, and Cassandra introduced the two of them.

Cassandra scowled at her and apologized to Willa.

"No, it's okay," Willa said. She caught Cassandra's eye in the rearview mirror and gave her a flat smile. "You look like you've been through a lot yourselves."

Jay huffed a laugh.

"Yeah," Cassandra said. "We were at the Halloween haunt when everything went crazy."

"Really? Good you got out of there when you did. That place is Deadsville. I don't think anyone's alive there at all."

Taylor clutched her hand. "Tommy and Cody," she said.

Cassandra hugged her and smoothed her hair. She told Willa what had happened, from deciding to make the movie all the way to the car crash. Jay and Walden remained silent for the most part, only nodding and adding *Mm-hmm*s here and there, while the woman nodded and listened, driving past the old mill and the fire hall, the shee-shee art gallery, the library and the smattering of houses in between.

Once Cassandra had filled her in on just about everything, their destination and the possible danger they might face ahead included, Willa said, "My boyfriend—well, we never really made it official even though we've been living together for like a year—he wanted to make a movie." She took a deep breath. "We went to the caves in the woods, out behind the Ellison farm."

"The weed farm?" Walden asked.

She shook her head softly. "I don't know anything about that. We... we kidnapped that actress, Darla Knight—"

"Wait, you *kidnapped* her?"

"It was just for tonight—it was *supposed* to be just for tonight. We were gonna let her go as soon as we were done with the movie. But Darryl took us to this cave and there were these, like, weird rock statues with hieroglyphs on them, and we were just supposed to *pretend* to kill her for the movie. A sacrifice. But Darryl used a *real knife*. It was supposed to be the fake one, but he really stabbed her and I think she's dead—I think they're both dead." A tear spilled down her cheek. "I just, I just ran and ran, and we were just about at the exit when Hot Box just blew up, he like *exploded*—"

"*Exploded?*" Walden said.

Willa kept talking, ranting at this point. "—and I got his blood and stuff all over me, I picked most of it off but I think there's still some in my hair, I-I think there's some in my hair still, and I just... I just *snapped*. My mind just went completely blank until I saw you in the road just then. I almost didn't stop."

"Well, we're glad you did," Cassandra said. "Sorry about your friends."

"And Darla," Walden said glumly.

"And your sort-of boyfriend," Jay added.

Willa nodded softly, watching the road ahead. "And Darryl." She looked like she had mixed feelings about this. A moment later she flicked on the turning signal, then turned right onto Cunningham Road, Cassandra's street. The entire neighborhood seemed eerily dark and silent. *Did it all stop?* Cassandra wondered. She didn't dare hope that it had.

"It's just up there," she said, pointing at the row of narrow townhouses.

Willa pulled over in front of their house. Taylor had trouble unbuckling her seatbelt, so Cassandra helped her. Walden and Jay climbed out first, and Cassandra helped Taylor down.

"Do you want to come inside?" she asked Willa.

Willa shook her head. "I'm just gonna go home. Take a long, hot shower. Thank you, though."

Cassandra turned to Walden, who shook his head slightly. She knew what he meant, that she probably wouldn't survive out there alone, but they couldn't exactly *force* her to join them. Not to mention, if what Willa told them was true, she'd just been involved in a kidnapping and murder, unintentional or not. "Thanks for the ride," Cassandra said. "Stay safe."

"You guys, too."

The pop of gunfire made them all flinch. A man's shout carried from a distance.

"We should get inside," Jay said.

They all agreed.

Willa nodded again and drove off. Cassandra was pretty certain they would never see her again, or if they did it would be on the news.

"Do you believe any of that?" Walden asked. "You think Darla Knight's really dead?"

"Anything's possible at this point," Jay said caustically. "I wouldn't be surprised if Santa Claus was real."

"Santa isn't real?" Taylor asked.

Jay gave Cassandra an apologetic look. Cassandra just shook her head. Of course, Taylor knew Santa wasn't real. What eleven-year-old didn't?

"Just kidding," Taylor said, breaking the awkwardness.

Jay let out a sigh of relief.

"Well, at least we've got our sense of humor back," Walden said. "Let's see how your gramma is doing."

They headed up the walkway to the house, Cassandra hoped they'd find Grammy fast asleep in her bed with an old black-and-white movie playing on the TV and a cup of warm milk cooling on the tray beside her. She hoped they'd find her untouched by all of this, unaware that anything had been going on at all.

But she didn't dare believe it. They'd been through too much tonight for optimism.

She used her key on the door and the four of them entered quickly, glancing out into the dark street before she closed, locked and chained the door. According to Grammy Flynn, Crooks Corner used to be a town where you could leave your doors unlocked and feel fairly safe, but "stranger danger" began to make parents paranoid a little after Cassandra came into the world and locking the doors whether the occupants were home or not became pretty normal, just like in the big cities.

"Grammy?"

Walden shushed her loudly. When she scowled, he whispered, "I hear something."

"Me too," Taylor said, a bit louder than Walden. It made him wince and put a finger to his lips.

He pointed up the stairs, then gestured for them to stay here. He pointed at his chest, and up the stairs again.

Cassandra shook her head fiercely. She wasn't going to let him go up there alone, but she agreed the others should stay here.

"I'm staying down here," Taylor said quietly. She looked up at Jay. "You hungry? Want something to drink?"

Jay looked at Cassandra. She nodded. "Be careful," she whispered. He smiled slightly and nodded at Taylor. The two of them headed as quietly as Taylor was able for the kitchen.

Walden jutted his chin toward the steps with a questioning look. Cassandra headed up. He followed close behind. She hadn't heard anything to begin with, but all the whispering and gesturing had made her anxious. Just the creaks of the steps under her boots made her tense in fear.

She reached the top of the stairs and heard what Walden and Taylor must have been talking about: tiny little scuttling sounds like mice in the walls. Only these sounds were coming from the bedrooms. Except for Grammy's room all of the doors were open a crack, but the only light came from the television in her room, under the closed door. The light from downstairs was just bright enough to reveal two of Taylor's stuffed animals—Lala Lion and her schnauzer, Orville—torn to shreds, their stuffing scattered in clumps around them.

Cassandra frowned at the sight, glad that Grammy had managed to defend herself against the toys, which she assumed had come to life along with everything else. She crept toward Grammy Flynn's door with a wide gait to prevent the floorboards from creaking too loudly. Walden followed closely in her footsteps, both of them avoiding the fluffy shells of Taylor's stuffies.

The TV flickered silently, but Cassandra heard its hum as they approached the room. The little scuttles, almost like ceramics rattling in a cupboard, was louder behind Grammy Flynn's door. She reached out for the door, turned the handle slowly, intending to push it open as gently as possible, but the stereo in her bedroom suddenly came on full blast, making her startle and push the door wide.

"Jesus!" Walden stage whispered behind her.

In the blue light from the television—*Diagnosis Murder* on mute—Cassandra saw Grammy Flynn wasn't in her bed. The covers were pushed over to the opposite side of the room. Movement on the floor caught her eyes: dark shapes about the size of mice skittering back and forth in the shadows.

Nine Inch Nails's "Mr. Self Destruct" kept blasting from down the hall. She couldn't hear anything above it.

"Grammy?" she called out.

This time Walden didn't chastise her. He was squinting at the floor, trying to figure out what was moving back and forth in a puddle of water from the plastic tumbler that had apparently fallen off of Grammy's TV tray and her pills scattered there. Another two stuffed animals lay mangled in the mess, Starfish the horse and Ella the elephant.

A pained moan came from the other side of the bed.

Glad to hear her grandmother's voice but worried she'd fallen out of bed and hurt herself, Cassandra made to step into the room. Walden grabbed her shoulder, holding her back. He pointed at the floor. She looked again but still couldn't tell what was moving back and forth and under the bed, until she glanced up at the antique china hutch, with its doors swung wide.

The Hummels were missing.

A chill ran up her spine and she practically leaped back from the doorway.

The figurines weren't missing. They'd been *possessed*.

Cassandra flicked on the light. The Hummels scuttled out of sight like cockroaches, under the bed and the dresser and hutch. Others hid under the bedspread, sheet and pillows. The ones on the bedside table ducked behind the radio alarm clock and against the lampstand.

"They're not attacking us," Walden said.

"Maybe they're scared of us," Cassandra said. She didn't think it was likely, not with the way the other things had behaved, but it was possible. The Hummels were only a couple of inches tall and ceramic, easily crushed under their feet.

"You okay, Grammy?"

"I've been better," came her voice from the floor on the other side of the bed. "I pressed the button on my medical alarm bracelet but no one picked up the call."

"Sounds like they're pretty busy out there," Walden said.

Cassandra stepped around the bed, keeping an eye out for the Hummels. She found Grammy Flynn lying faceup beside the bed. She'd managed to put a pillow under her head but she didn't look comfortable, and there was already an angry bruise on her right arm where she must've caught herself when she'd fallen.

"What happened?"

"Humphrey's been a very bad boy tonight," Grammy Flynn said as Cassandra helped her up gently. Her face gravely serious, she clucked her tongue against the roof of her mouth for emphasis. "*Very* bad."

Walden gave them a curious look. "Humphrey?"

"It's a long story," Cassandra said. "Let's get her downstairs."

6

10:02 P.M.
Mr. and Mrs. Thompsons's Farmhouse

IN LESS THAN HALF AN HOUR, all of the windows and doors in the Thompson house were either boarded up or covered by furniture, and everyone held a weapon: kitchen knives and meat mallets, rifles and shotguns, table lamps and fire pokers. Even the blood-streaked old woman in the filthy nightgown had a candlestick in her lap as she smoked endlessly. Not a sound had come from outside since they'd set about fortifying the house: not a scream, not a howl, not a screech. It was as if everything had just stopped altogether the moment Chet turned off the generator that powered all of the electronic equipment in the haunt. It was so quiet inside Cody could hear the jitter of the rifle in Chet's hand as he stood quietly by the door, waiting.

In the following half hour, the Thompsons let those who needed to check in on their families quietly use the phone until the phone line went down. No one at Brittany's house had picked up, and Cody's parents had planned to work late and spend the night in a motel near the power plant, whose number he couldn't remember off-hand. They'd also called Cassandra's house but gotten no answer, and left a message. They'd turned out all the lights and acclimatized to the dark when the phone line went dead in the middle of a call. The tearful woman hung up, whispering about her children, she had to go protect her children.

"Been a while since that's happened," Rowena said, hugging the fearful mother. "Not since back when we was still on the pahty line."

Rowena convinced the mother to sit with her and the two of them talked it out quietly until the woman calmed down. With the phone and the lights out, the rest of them waited for whatever terrible thing might happen next.

The first sound came from the basement maybe fifteen minutes later: a loud crash of wood and a crunch of glass. Chet and Rowena looked toward the basement door, a combination of anxiety and understanding on their faces that Cody almost couldn't see in the dark.

"Must've busted through the cellar door," Chet whispered. "Cody, come on down with me, would ya?"

Cody nodded and followed the big man to the stairs. He held the 20-gauge pump-action shotgun he'd sometimes used to scare crows, rats and possums out of the cornfield, and it made him feel like a badass. He paused to nod at Brittany, who held one of the large kitchen knives with the blade pointed downward. Perfect for stabbing. Not so much for slashing. "Keep these folks safe," he said in a whisper.

"Don't get yourself killed," she replied.

Chet descended down bare wood stairs. They'd creaked as Cody had lugged plywood up from the basement earlier. He knew every step would signal their approach to whatever awaited them in the dark. Chet paused on the second stair at the crunch of glass on the concrete floor below. One of the preserves jars had likely been knocked off the shelves, and now the culprit was trudging through the mess.

Downstairs was a warren of shelving and work tables, the furnace and the water heater, an unfinished bathroom and all kinds of junk. Chet reached the concrete floor and stepped aside, allowing Cody to step down alongside him. The only light came from the cellar door, one side of which had been smashed inward, yet Cody couldn't see much aside from shadows. The sound of scuffling on grit alerted him to something about ten feet to their left.

"Hell with it," Chet whispered, and flicked on the Maglite he'd taped to the side of his rifle.

Cody stumbled back a step, his heart feeling like he'd taken the drop ride at the county fair. His shins hit the first step and he had to grab the wall to prevent himself from falling backward, leaving only one hand gripping the shotgun. Chet's flashlight had illuminated three mangled bodies, all standing upright with their mouths agape and their black eyes unblinking, just like Tommy in the haunt.

"Jesus jumped-up..." Chet muttered.

He swept the flashlight across the room, shining over three, four, five more of them. Adults and children, each of them as dead as the next. There had to be at least a dozen of them down here. Cody figured they must've broken in after he'd brought up the last of the plywood, while people had still been dragging furniture and hammering wood. The crash they'd heard must've been the smaller preserve shelf closer to the steps. They'd probably all shambled down the storm cellar stairs under all the noise from upstairs and one of them had just clumsily knocked it over. If it hadn't fallen, no one would've noticed them until they'd already gotten upstairs.

A dead hand reached out from the dark to Chet's left and grabbed his wrist. Chet fought it off, the flashlight swaying back and forth as he gritted his teeth against the strength of the dead man. The others—all of them at once—began shuffling forward. The Maglite tore off the rifle and fell to the floor, shining on their advancing legs and feet.

Cody stood with the shotgun held at his side, unable to move. *These were people*, he thought. The phrase kept playing in his mind like a skipping CD. *These were people, these were people...*

Chet stopped fighting and instead let the dead man pull his hands toward it. The muzzle blast brightened the room for an instant, long enough for Cody to see the faces of the dead people had gotten closer while he stood there in a stupor. The bang startled him into motion. He raised the shotgun and blasted in the direction of the woman right in front of him, whose legs were all he could see of her. He felt a splatter of hot liquid on his face and hands.

"Come on, kid!" Chet shouted, even though aside from the scuffle of their feet the dead were entirely silent. Chet turned and started thumping up the stairs as Cody pumped the shotgun.

Cody fired in the dark above a pair of grimy Nikes moving toward him. With another spray of liquid—*Blood*, he thought morbidly, *you know it's blood*—the body toppled back into the darkness.

He pumped and aimed and fired at one body after the next, forgetting they'd been human until little over an hour ago, treating them like vermin, like the rats and the crows he'd shot at in the corn. *Chick-chick—BOOM! Chick-chick—BOOM!* He saw them ambling forward in flashes, and the ones he'd blasted lying on the floor at their feet.

It was only when the dry click of the trigger pulled without the accompanying blast that he snapped out of it.

"Come on, goddammit!" Chet shouted from above.

Cody looked up, then turned to face the remaining zombies, at least eight or nine silhouettes still shuffling forward despite the five or six he and Chet had already gunned down. Then he turned and hurried up the steps as fast as he could. Chet slammed the door behind him and leaned against it.

"Someone get a goddamn kitchen chair," he said.

Brittany stood by the door, looking at Cody with wide, dark eyes. "You're crying," she said.

Cody hadn't even noticed it. His face had felt wet but he'd just assumed it was more blood. "They were people," he said, not meaning to repeat his mantra but unable to say anything else.

Brittany cocked her head with a look of curiosity, as if she couldn't possibly understand what he meant. It reminded him of how coldly she'd stepped aside to let Tommy Mingus—dead or not—run into the wall behind her over and over. There was something not quite right about Brittany Garner. He'd always thought she was a snob and arrogant and sometimes uncaring, but he wondered now if there wasn't more to it than that. If she wasn't missing something vital that made Cody and other people tick.

Burle Adams hurried over and stepped between them, shoving a chair from the kitchen under the door handle and plopping himself down in it. In the moment their eye contact severed Cody saw the light leave Brittany's pupils, her expression as dead as the people downstairs.

Then, just as quickly as it had happened, the life returned to them.

"You good?" she asked, again with that practiced quizzical look.

"Yeah," he said. "How 'bout you?"

"I'm fine. You want a washcloth or something? For the blood."

"That's a good idea."

Cody followed Brittany toward the kitchen. He didn't know what that momentary lapse in her expression meant. Maybe it was something as simple as a staring seizure, like Grandma Gunderson started to get after Grampa G. died. But something about it made him think he'd need to keep a closer eye on her from now on.

He worried it might not just be dead people and haunt stuff they'd need to watch out for tonight.

7

10:06 P.M.
76 Seltzer Street

THE ENTITY WEARING Zack Summerly's body and a jack-o'-lantern for a head sat with the raven-haired woman's corpse in its lap, stroking her blood-drenched hair while the story box displayed tales of their rituals. The last time Geth had managed to escape its imprisonment, the people of the physical world had been much more primitive, though their superstitious nature and attunement to their environment had made them surprisingly clever and admittedly even powerful foes. These people, with their fiery elixirs in almost invisible drinking containers—Geth had come to learn these were called *glasses* or *bottles*—their unnecessarily large dwellings and their story boxes—alternately called "television" and "*Tee-Vee*"—made them docile, complacent and weak, whereas Those Who Came Before, the ancient people who had trapped Geth within the *Upask*, had believed deeply in ritual. They had been strong and cautious, acutely aware that death awaited them at any moment. For the people who'd replaced them in this land, ritual and tradition seemed more to be a form of entertainment than a way of life. Judging by their costumes, decorations and celebrations, and the stories flickering on the Tee-Vee like sophisticated versions of the shadow figures made in firelight on the cave walls of the ancients, the current occupants of this land had become desensitized to death and violence. Which was fine and well for Geth, since violence was the sole dominion of Their *inhak*, and thus, Their lifeblood.

Geth turned the slitted Xs of Their pumpkin eyes to the severed head of Their current *chuann* on the sofa. Whatever consciousness remained within the brain—which was minimal—could not be able to meddle with Geth's plans. *Like a spoke in a wheel* was the closest translation of Their thought, although in Geth's language of pictures and glyphs it would be unintelligible to any human mind, no matter the native tongue. The head needed to be severed, as it was possible, despite the *smallness* of the human mind, that the *chuann* could manipulate its body to work against Geth's will, as the shaman of the ancients had done so many *sawat*—what these New People called *years*—ago. Geth had chosen the big shaman as its host believing his trinkets and totems and status within the community would make it easier for Geth to subjugate his people. But the shaman had used his own body against Geth, a treachery which had only become evident once he had led Geth and several of his tribesmen—each of them Blighted by one of Geth's many *inhak*—back into the cave.

Geth cast these thoughts aside angrily, like a strong wind blowing away the ashes of the ancients. It did not like to think of such things, although having been imprisoned for so many years it had often been impossible not to. Still, it comforted itself knowing the shaman and his people were long gone from this world, as soon—in contrast to Geth's very, very long life—the New People of this community would be. Geth would outlast them as it had the dull-brained, flat-skulled things which had come before the ancients, and the giant beasts before them.

In any regard, the gourd and the headless body it had affixed to it would suffice as a vessel for Their essence, the *aminhas*. Geth did not require eyes for sight, as They could see well enough with Their mind, and the senses of Their innumerable *inhak* which cavorted murderously throughout this town transmitted directly to Their *aminhas*, allowing Geth to see many images and hear many sounds and feel many feelings all at once, each overlapping the stories from the Tee-Vee. Even better, being the eve of their holy day—this *Halloween*—on this particular evening Geth could walk freely through the streets with a pumpkin for a head and no one would *bat an eye* or *shake a stick at* Them. Of course, Geth could annihilate anyone who dared shake a stick at Them—as it had done to many of Those Who Came Before—but They derived pleasure from the notion of walking concealed amongst these people, a *wolf in sheep's clothing*, as they might say. Particularly as Geth the Many's *inhak* slaughtered them, using the humans' own rituals, totems and ceremonial garments against them.

This time would be different than the last, of that Geth was certain. They had learned much from Their dealings with the ancient's shaman. Most of all, not to underestimate these people.

Geth ran Zack Summerly's fingers through Amelia Miller's blood-dampened hair, her scalp cool against Their *chuann's* fingertips, while on the Tee-Vee a giant rolling machine with the face of a green monster led several other rolling machines to circle a dwelling filled with humans. *Circling the wagons*, Geth thought, a term that floated into Their consciousness from the slowly decaying minds of the dead Their *inhak* had inhabited. Geth flicked the upward-pointing arrow on the numbered wand and the current story—the glyphs on the bottom of the screen identified it as *Maximum Overdrive 9:30 to 11:45*—was replaced by another.

"*We now return to The Legend of Sleepy Hollow,*" a disembodied voice said over more glyphs, which appeared and vanished too quickly for Geth to discern their meaning. On the screen, a figure in a long coat, riding a horse and carrying a jack-o'-lantern under its arm like the one affixed to Geth's current body, chased a second man on a horse. This story was different from the others Geth had witnessed, performed by moving cave drawings—although again much more sophisticated—rather than living people. The word that came to mind, not from Geth's own mind but from the minds of the dead, was *cartoon*.

What an interesting people, Geth thought. *It would be a shame if We were forced to annihilate them.*

It did not need to be that way. Geth's *inhak* enjoyed violence —*thrived* on it, even—but Geth the Many yearned to be *worshipped*. Those Who Came Before could not accept this, and Geth had been forced to slaughter many of their people before the ancients had managed to trick Them and imprison Them within the Void beyond this world, employing their totems and glyphs and the bone instrument attuned to the Stones of the *Tum Gob*. There, Geth had spent many, many years, a mere pittance to Geth the Many but an eternity for these mortal beings, long enough that the people living in the area beyond the cave had grown arguably smarter, yet certainly fatter and more complacent, no longer fearing the horrors that awaited them in the dark, no longer—

"Timar! Hounds of the moon!"

Geth pushed the dead woman from Their lap with a cry of disgust in the shaman's dead language and stood abruptly, feeling the ache and friction in Their new joints from *rigor mortis* beginning to set in. They had spent much too long sitting here already, absorbing these worthless stories, stewing on the failures of Their own past, while out in the darkened streets Their *inhak* had their fun. The multitudes of *inhak* which made up the entity known as Geth were a part of Geth, and Geth derived Their share of pleasure from the frivolity, but it was no match for the excitement They obtained from shedding blood with Their host body's fingertips. Of this, They wanted *more*. And there was no more blood to shed in this dwelling that had not already begun to coagulate.

Geth picked up the knife Their host body had discarded when it had carved the ritual symbol into the skin of the gourd, the graven image that had summoned Geth to this dwelling *like a moth to a flame*. The surface of its blade—so much sharper and easier to wield than the weapons and tools of the ancient people—was tacky with the blood of the woman and her former lover. Geth the Many longed to feel fresh blood on Their host's fingers, just as They longed to witness these mortals falling to their knees before Geth.

And so these New People would, and *soon*.

The Machine which had helped free Geth required protection from those who may wish to harm it, and the first of Geth's initiates awaited Them there: one of the mortals They had blessed with Their Blight. While unable to free Themself from Their prison, Geth had still been able to make psychic contact with those whose minds could be easily attuned to, due to the tiny crack the sacrifice of the children had made in the *Tub Gob* decades ago, by the murderer who called himself "The Snake."

The crack had allowed Geth to blight the mind of the scientist who fancied himself an amateur spelunker, filling his head with notions he had already been toying with but could not quite put the pieces of together. Following their initial contact at the dead shaman's Watching Stones, the science teacher had fashioned a Machine unlike anything he could possibly have created on his own. Its harmonics had tuned to the Stones, calling forth Geth the Many to the border between worlds, not merely its un-governed *inhak*. The plant smoker had been easier to blight, his mind already opened by the effects of the—*pot, marijuana, ganja, weed*—and thus easier to manipulate beyond the sphere of the stones. Geth had seen through Darryl Knell's eyes how much the mortal world had changed since They had last been above ground. They had assumed as much when blighting the scientist —there were no scientists in the ancients' day, nor was there *science* as it was thought of currently—but with a single *inhak* planted in Darryl's mind, Geth had *seen* and *smelled* and *felt*— though these sensations were all visual to Geth, *like pictures in a book*—how different this world was than the shaman's. They had watched many stories of the New People play out on the Tee-Vee while Darryl and his various companions smoked their *ganja*, and had influenced Darryl to create a *new* story from his obses-sion with this *movie star*, Darla Knight.

Geth the Many's remaining *inhak* had killed Knell and the others who had released it with the necessary blood sacrifice, though it was no matter. There were many more out there who would bend to Geth's will by the next revolution of this wretched space rock, when its nearest star warmed and bright-ened the earth. And there were many, many more worlds to conquer.

But first, before leaving the dwelling of Their host and re-uniting with Their Multitude, Geth needed to choose a name linked to the spirituality of the people They intended to subju-gate. The symbolism of the name Geth chose was vital to the ritual and ceremonies they would use to worship Geth the Many, and the stories Their new followers would tell of Their wrath and mercy, to spread Geth's message and wisdom throughout the world. To spread Their *Blight*.

In the ancients' day, the name They had chosen roughly translated to *Tree with Many Roots*. To the shaman and his people, this was as close to *god* as anything. This time, They would bear a name They had heard spoken of with great reverence by Darryl and his companions, and again in a cartoon They had witnessed tonight: *the Great Pumpkin*.

With Their Holy Name chosen, Geth the Great Pumpkin stepped out in Their fresh new body and blood-stained blade into the night.

PART THREE

THE GREAT PUMPKIN

CHAPTER 13

1

10:12 P.M.
Cassandra's House

Cassandra and Walden helped Grammy Flynn shuffle down to the basement, locked and latched the door, and stuffed boxes into the small window alcove to hopefully prevent anything from getting inside. Once it was as safe as they could hope for, they all sat on or around the old ovular braided rug. They'd lined up all of her Hummels on the stairs and in a semicircle of protection around them, and Taylor and Jay had brought down snacks and drinks: two 1-liter bottles of Sierra Mist and a couple of bags of chips they passed around while Grammy Flynn quietly spoke. The basement smelled musty but always held a nostalgic feeling for Cassandra. It was where her father's tools were kept, as well as boxes of photos and their old records and other stuff that wouldn't fit in the cabinets and drawers upstairs, much of which had belonged to her mom and dad.

"I've lived in Crooks Corner my entire life, you know," Grammy Flynn said, rocking gently in her old wooden rocker. "I was born here on January 28th, 1928, on the night of the big storm, and I'll die here."

"Don't say that, Grammy," Taylor said with a pout, her lips stained fake-cheese orange.

"Oh, I'll be around for some time yet, God willing. But when I go, it'll be right here in my own home. And when they lay me in the ground, it'll be in the same cemetery they buried your mom and dad in, and your Grampa Fred. Already got the plot picked out right beside them. This town is in my blood. It's in your blood, too," she said, looking back and forth between the two sisters. "The both of you. Now you may not live your whole lives here like I did. Even your mother went off to Durham for school and she even went to Paris for her honeymoon. When I was a girl, things were different. I married young and then I had your mother and your aunt, and I put down roots. I don't regret it. I love this town, warts and all."

Sitting in a folding chair in front of the chest freezer, Jay stuffed a handful of cheese Bugles into his mouth and passed the bag to Walden, who passed it along to Cassandra. She had a few —they had already warned Taylor not to use them as "witch fingers" like she usually did, just in case the *Sluagh* took it as a sign —and passed them back to Jay. She washed it down with a sip of soda.

"But you need to understand: there are things in Crooks Corner that defy explanation. Always have been, even before what's happened tonight. Our friend Humphrey, he's just the tip of the iceberg."

"Grammy, about that—"

Grammy Flynn gave her a shrewd look, her lips pursed. "Oh, don't think I don't know you were playing tricks on old Grammy Flynn. That's *why* I asked you all to stick around a little longer before running off to whatever it is you've got planned for these uninvited guests of ours."

Cassandra and Taylor shared a guilty look.

"You see, I've always had a bit of a sparkle myself. Your mother had it and she passed it on to you. When those stuffies of yours came to life, Taylor—"

Taylor's eyes lit up at the thought of it, as if she'd always wanted them to come alive, and maybe even be her best friends instead of Mingus the Dingus. Then her expression soured, either at the realization that her toys would probably just try to kill her, or the fact that they still didn't know if Tommy Mingus was alive or dead.

"—they went wild, and neither of you were home to act as Humphrey, nor could I imagine you doing with them what they tried to do to me." She smiled proudly. "But I had my Hummels to protect me. They tore the first ones to itty bitty bits and got the doors to your rooms shut before the rest of them could get out. Then I had them watch over me until you showed up. I made them do that. I thought I was too old for it to work, that I hadn't used that muscle in my brain for too long a time, but I was wrong. You might not be able to teach an old dog new tricks, but that doesn't mean an old dog can't still do the tricks they've learned, just because they haven't done them in a month of Sundays."

"So you knew all this time Humphrey wasn't real?" Cassandra asked. "Why didn't you say anything?"

Grammy smiled. "Well, I suppose I didn't want to discourage you from using your gift. And you've gotten so good at it."

"That was all Tay. I'm not good at anything, Grammy."

"Never say never, Cassandra. You just need to believe in yourself, the way I believe in you. And when you do, I'm certain you'll *shine.*"

"Thanks," Cassandra said glumly. It made her sad to think about how useless she felt sometimes, how dim her future looked, with nothing that interested her and nothing to look forward to. A lot of kids her age already knew what they wanted to do with their lives. Walden wanted to write movies. Jay was into computer programming and planned to work in video games. Brittany was probably going to end up in politics, and Cody would likely be a football hero. What did she have? She liked to listen to music and brood (her current favorite, Stabbing Westward's self-titled album, played on endless repeat). Sometimes she did Wiccan rituals with her friends that never actually worked. The rest of the time she watched reruns of *Buffy* and *X-Files* and sometimes did her homework when she absolutely couldn't put it off any longer. She was a below-average student with no scholarly interests. The only thing she did well was take care of Taylor, and even then she'd just let Taylor's best friend run off on his own and probably die. What place was there for her in the adult world?

"The point I'm trying to make is," Grammy Flynn went on, "there's more to this town than what you see. Your sister and I, we can move things around a bit with our minds. Make them dance the jig, if we want to. But we're not the only ones with a gift. I once knew a girl who could predict the weather without fail. 'Rain tomorrow,' she'd say, even if the weather reports all said sunshine. Lo and behold, come tomorrow it'd pour cats and dogs, and she'd be the only one in class with an umbrella. Her folks said it was probably something to do with her bones, but she'd predict it, rain, snow or sunshine. She predicted the tornado in '63 that took the roof right off the Catholic church in the middle of Sunday Mass—saved everyone that day shouting over the good reverend while he was reading his psalms to get to the basement. That's the God's honest truth."

Grammy looked over the faces of the kids gathered around her. Her own face looked a lot older in the harsh basement light. Soon she'd be gone and Cassandra and Taylor would be all alone, left to fend for themselves. She only hoped when Grammy did pass away, she was old enough to take care of her sister legally, that they wouldn't have to live with some aunt or uncle they didn't really know. Or worse: get sent to separate foster homes.

"Something about this place is special, you see. But with the light always comes dark. It seeps in through the cracks. Like back in the Sixties, when that escaped convict murdered those poor children out in the wheat field where the Hamburgs grow their corn these days. Or in the Thirties, during the worst years of the Dust Bowl, when hundreds of timber rattlers came slithering out from the woods into town all at once, like they'd been called by the Pied Piper, biting anyone in their path. All of this actually happened. You wouldn't have read about it in your history books at school, but it did. Things happen here that defy explanation, you see. Always have, always will. I used to have a pet theory that Crooks Corner was built on an old Injun burial ground, but the Injuns were smart enough to leave this place alone, or so the local history buffs say."

Cassandra glanced in embarrassment at Walden, lowering her eyes quickly. She knew his mother was Winnipesaukee, and that some of the assholes at school like Brunt had called him things like "dirty Injun" and "redskin" and even worse, up until after the big fight when they stopped interacting with him altogether. Walden didn't seem fazed by what Grammy said, whether because he'd heard worse so often or because the old terms didn't offend him, she supposed she might never know. Either way, he sat in rapt attention to Grammy Flynn's story.

"There are places, I think, where the veil between what's real and what's *unreal* is thinner, like when you stretch a good dough too much. I believe Crooks Corner is one of those places. The unreal bleeds through the cracks like light through newsprint—not all at once, not usually, just enough for you to know it's there. That's why there are more folks like Taylor and I, and peculiar events like the rattler invasion of '35. It makes things like that, and murder of those precious little children in the Sixties, happen here more often than other towns of our size."

"Like Derry," Walden said.

Grammy Flynn perked up at this. "Robert Frost lived there, don't you know."

"Derry, Maine, not New Hampshire. It's a fictional town from Stephen King's books. You know, *It*? Pennywise the Dancing Clown?"

Grammy gave him a sour look. "Never was one for the circus, nor for occult flights of fancy. The *real* Derry's nice enough, and nothing like our Crooks Corner, at least not in the manner I'm speaking of. All of this is to say that perhaps the dough has stretched too far this time. Something, some cosmic hand or twist of fate, must've pulled it to the breaking point and let everything on the other side come spilling out."

A chill ran up Cassandra's spine. "Grammy, what would a place like that look like? Where the veil is, like, thin?"

The old woman thought a moment, her thin lips pursed. "Could be anything, really. Could be the old house at the end of the street no one wants to look at when they can help it. Or a place where one too many bad things have happened: a hospital or a prison or an old asylum. It could equally be something as simple as an apartment or a motel or an office building where more people than normal come down with similar symptoms not related to a particular sickness."

"Could it be a cave?" Walden asked.

"A cave with stones that have symbols on them?" Cassandra added.

Grammy Flynn's brow rose in curiosity. "In Crooks Corner? Well, there was that man they found out in the woods back in the '60s, the one who killed those poor little cherubs. The news report said the policemen found him in a lean-to of sorts, but some people claimed it was a cave. If it's the latter, I suppose that could be the likeliest spot, depending on how old those stones you mention happen to be. If they're *very* old, it would sure explain what kept the Injun tribes from settling here. I suppose a place like that could be *very* thin. Perhaps the stones have acted like thumbs in a dyke"—Grammy Flynn ignored Jay's snort of laughter—"until *something* disrupted them."

The humor drained from Jay's face suddenly. He turned to Walden and Cassandra with a grave look. "Mr. Combs's Machine," he said.

Grammy Flynn frowned. "What sort of 'machine'?"

Jay seemed almost apologetic when he said, "This thing I've been helping him with for a while. He never told me what it was or what it did, until yesterday. He called it a 'dark matter convertor.'"

The old woman clucked her tongue. "I'd say it's an *extremely* dark matter, if that's what caused it. Science has rules for a reason. You can't go breaking the laws of the universe willy nilly. There are protocols one must follow, or run the risk of severe danger."

Jay looked sufficiently chastised. "Well, maybe if we turn off the Machine—"

"I don't presume that will do it," Grammy Flynn said, her tone sharp. "Supernatural forces must be dealt with using *supernatural means*. Why do these Possessors as you call them only appear to be manipulating Halloween decorations and toys? Symbology *must* be important to them, at least on some base level. That means they'll likely respond to rituals and superstition."

"But Taylor's camera made them disappear," Walden said.

"Some cultures believe cameras can steal the soul," Grammy Flynn said. "Perhaps that could explain it?"

Jay's frown deepened. "I think that's a myth."

"Even so," Grammy Flynn said, "myth and ritual go hand in hand, don't they? The same goes for my Hummels. Like responds to like. One side of a magnet attracts it to another. One side repels. Perhaps these stones you mentioned act like magnets, attracting and repelling this strange force simultaneously."

"So what do we do now?" Walden asked, turning to Cassandra first, then Jay, then Grammy Flynn.

Jay smacked his lips in thought. "Maybe Mrs. Flynn—"

"Grammy Flynn," she corrected him.

"Maybe Grammy Flynn is right," he said, "and supernatural means *will* stop all of this. A ritual or something. But we still don't *know* the ritual, do we? I still say we go talk to Mr. Combs first. Make him shut off the Machine."

"If he hasn't already," Walden added.

"If he has, maybe he'll have some idea how to reverse it. He's a pretty smart dude."

"Too smart for his own good, clearly."

"I think we should still get more cameras from the school, too," Cassandra said, looking at the Polaroid in her sister's lap. "It doesn't hurt to be overprepared, right?"

"Why not get guns while we're at it?" Jay said, shaking his head. "If we're already going all over hell's half acre, why not?"

"The school's right across the road," Cassandra said, annoyed by his insinuation.

"Sure, but we have to *break in*, don't we? It's not like the doors'll be open at—" He glanced at his watch. "—shit, I mean shoot," he said, glancing sheepishly at Grammy Flynn. He lifted his butt off the folding chair and reached into the right pocket of his pants, pulling out something and popping it in his mouth. He grabbed the bottle of Sierra Mist sitting at his feet and took a few healthy chugs.

Hope he's taking a chill pill, Cassandra thought.

Jay stood up abruptly then, smoothing down the pleats in his pants. "Well, we should probably get started, huh? Thanks for the hospitality, Grammy Flynn. The chips and whatnot."

"My pleasure, young man."

Cassandra and Walden stood up with him. Taylor pushed herself up to a kneeling position, about to stand, but there was no way Cassandra would let her go with them, not after almost getting her killed earlier, and her best friend likely already dead.

"Uh-uh. You stay here, shrimp. You'll be safe with Grammy."

Taylor moaned in disappointment.

"But the three of you won't be safe without Taylor," Grammy Flynn said, causing Taylor to smile proudly and jut out her chin at Cassandra.

"But—" Cassandra said. She didn't really have any argument other than that.

The old woman rocked gently in her chair. "If it were up to me, you'd all stay here. But it seems to me you're the only ones who know enough about all of this to put a stop to it. I'll be fine on my own. I have my Hummels to protect me. And a basement full of your father's tools, if I need them. I'm still a bit rusty, but so are the tools." She smiled at this, as if it was more sinister than just a metaphor.

"All right, Grammy," Cassandra said. "Let's go then, shrimp."

Her sister came to her side, and Cassadra put an arm around her shoulders.

"Wait." Taylor turned around and raised the camera to her eye. She snapped a photo of the old woman, sitting all by herself in her rocker, surrounded by workshop tools and heavy appliances. "That's gonna be a good one," she said. "Love you, Grammy!"

"Love you," Cassandra said.

Grammy Flynn blew them a kiss. "I love you both, and I'm proud of you both so much."

Cassandra started to get a little teary eyed as she turned and headed for the boys waiting at the base of the stairs. But somehow, she had a good feeling Grammy Flynn would be safe down here, with or without her Hummels. It'd been a long time since they'd heard anything from outside, even sirens. She didn't dare believe it, but maybe it had stopped, like a rain squall or a tornado of paranormal activity. Maybe the clouds had passed and all that was left was to deal with the damage, to try and move past it.

Or maybe it's the calm before the real *storm*, she thought, taking her first hesitant step up the stairs, away from safety, toward danger and death and who knew what else. Grammy Flynn spoke of gifts and curses in Crooks Corners. Cassandra had always thought it was the most boring, whitebread town in America, but now... she had a feeling this town wasn't done surprising her.

After closing the door behind them, they made their way quietly down the dark hall toward the front door. Passing the phone alcove, the blinking red number 2 on the answering machine grabbed her attention.

While they'd helped her down the stairs, Grammy had said she'd fallen out of bed reaching for the phone, assuming it was Cassandra calling to tell her they were safe. Playing the messages would be pretty loud from the machine, but she knew that if she called the house phone from home and punched in the code, it would play the messages over the phone instead.

"Guys," she whispered. "I'm gonna check the messages."

It was too dark to see their expressions when Walden turned to Jay, who shrugged, causing Walden to nod.

She grabbed the cordless phone off the receiver and punched in their number, wincing at every musical beep. Something thumped against the floor above their heads from Taylor's bedroom. Taylor gripped her arm in fright and Jay gasped, but the sound died and nothing followed.

After a few rings the automated voice answered. Taylor stood close, still holding her arm and looking up at her as she punched in the four-digit code. *You have two new messages,* the voice said. *"Message one—"*

"Uh yes, hi, Mrs. Flynn, it's Douglas at DollarSave Pharmacy. Just calling to tell you your prescription is ready for—"

She pressed two to skip to the next message. *"Message two—"*

The relief she felt at hearing Cody's voice was immeasurable, even though he sounded as rough as she felt. "Hey, Cassandra. Brit and I are okay, but Tommy..." He paused, taking a deep breath in and out. "...he didn't make it. Tell Taylor we're both..." He paused again, another deep breath. "...we're both just so sorry, okay? It sounds like things might've died down—bad choice of words. Anyway, stay safe, okay? Hopefully we'll see you at school tomorrow."

The machine beeped.

See you at school tomorrow? Cassandra scoffed at the thought. As if life could just go right back to normal after this. Still, she was glad Cody had called and that they were safe, even if she was going to be in big trouble tomorrow because Tommy was dead. Her eyes prickled with tears. *Tommy is dead.* She'd never liked the little twerp but she'd never wished death on him—not literally. *Little Tommy Mingus is dead,* she thought again. *What are we gonna do?*

Immediately, she dialed star-69 to return the last call, hoping she was wrong about what Cody had said. That maybe *he didn't make it* meant Tommy hadn't made it to the shelter with the others, and he still might be alive out there on the farm. But the phone went dead in her hand. She lowered it, regarding it in mystified hopelessness, then sat it back on the base.

Taylor looked up at her with hope in her eyes.

I can't tell her yet, Cassandra thought. *It'll crush her. She needs hope. We* all *need hope.*

"Who was it? Walden whispered.

"It was Cody. They're safe. But they haven't found Tommy yet," she added, giving Taylor an unwavering look to sell the lie.

"They'll find him," Taylor said resolutely. "He's real good at hiding."

"I bet you're right. Let's get going, huh?"

2

10:23 P.M.
Mr. and Mrs. Thompson's Farmhouse

IT'S TOO QUIET, The Snake said.

Brittany startled. It had been minutes since *anyone* had made a noise, and aside from the rustling of the wind against the old farmhouse walls and the occasional shuffle of feet against floorboards, it had been almost deadly silent.

She poked Cody's arm. He looked down at her from peering through a knot hole in the boarded window with a tight smile.

"What's going on out there?" she asked, keeping her voice low.

"Nothing," he whispered. "It's like it all just stopped all of the sudden."

"But the people downstairs. The zombies."

Cody winced at the word. "I guess they're just standing down there. Almost like they're waiting."

"Waiting for what?"

Cody shrugged. "I dunno." He gave her a serious look, exhaling sharply through his nose. "That's what I'm worried about."

"The calm before the storm?"

He nodded. "Could be. Or maybe..." He shrugged again.

"What?"

"Well, what if they're waiting for us to do something? Like maybe if they can't see us, they won't attack us."

Now it was Brittany's turn to shrug. She didn't think this

line of thought was correct or even helpful. In fact, she was starting to think it was time to leave this place. According to some of the others who'd managed to get a hold of their friends and family during their phone calls, what had happened here was also happening elsewhere in town. This was as safe a place to be as anywhere, but everyone she knew out there was in just as much danger.

Don't pretend like you care, The Snake said rebuked her.

"Why are they doing this?" Cody said suddenly.

"Why's who doing what?"

"Whatever's possessing all of this stuff—you don't wonder why?"

Brittany frowned. She hadn't considered the question, and now that she was she couldn't think of a definitive answer. "Maybe it's like a force of nature," she suggested. "Something we've never encountered before. You don't ask a wildfire why it destroys cities. It just does."

"Sure, but that's *caused* by something else. What caused *this*?"

She shrugged. "I don't know, Cody."

He hummed thoughtfully. After a long pause, he said, "I was thinking..."

She waited for him to continue. When he didn't, she decided a normal person would react by prodding him. "About what?"

"Like..." He exhaled sharply through his nostrils. "... do you ever feel like there's all these voices in your head telling you what to do and what not to do, pushing you in one direction or another, and you just can't get them to stop?"

Brittany turned to him, feeling suddenly very exposed, as if he'd peered right into her soul and seen everything. "Sometimes," she said cautiously.

"It made me think, you know? Those things out there... they're sort of like us. Not whatever's controlling them, but the stuff being controlled. They're just sitting there, doing their own thing, and something decides to turn them all against us. And there's nothing they can do about it. But *we* can. Our parents, our teachers, our coaches, all these random adults, even our *friends*, they always seem to wanna push us one way or another, to be what they want us to be. But we have to choose that for ourselves. We have to do what's good for *us*. We can't live our lives for *them*. We have to live for *ourselves*."

Brittany nodded. He may have spoken it inelegantly, and it might not have been entirely helpful in their current situation, but what he was saying was one of the most sincere and true things she'd heard come out of the mouth of any of her schoolmates. "You're right," she said. "Just about my whole life, I feel like nothing I've done has been because I wanted to do it. Especially lately," she added, and the spirals began to uncoil in the back of her mind.

If you tell him, he's a dead man, The Snake warned.

You wouldn't, she thought back.

You really wanna try me, honeypie?

Aware that if The Snake wanted to, he could *make* her hurt Cody, with or without her compliance, Brittany closed her mouth.

"If we make it through the night," Cody said after a moment, turning to her with a half-smile, "I think I'm gonna be making a lot of changes, starting with who I wanna be friends with."

She saw his hand resting on his thigh and patted it, because that was what she'd seen friends do in these situations. He turned his hand over and held hers, squeezing it. She let the clammy hand linger in hers for a few more moments, just long enough that it wouldn't seem to him like she was eager to slip free, then let it go.

"We can't stay here all night," she said decisively. "This whole time we've just been reacting. We need to start getting *pro*active."

Cody turned, getting down off his haunches and sitting beside her against the wall. "You're right. I'm really worried about Cassandra and Taylor. Walden and Jay, too, I guess."

"Same," Brittany said, and she was surprised to realize she even hoped her mom and brother were still okay, not just her dad. Even Renatta, their housekeeper. She'd never really cared about anyone but her dad, the horses and Bella, but she supposed being so acutely aware of her own mortality had made her realize who and what were truly important to her. "I think we need to try."

"To leave?" He glanced around at the people gathered in the farmhouse. Seventy-three-year-old Francine McGillis, who played Grandma Sassafras, the crazy old matriarch of the hillbilly

Sassafras family, had fallen asleep with the candlestick in her lap. The others looked less scared now than bored. Whatever trouble remained here, Chet and Row and the few stronger ones in the group could handle without them.

"Yeah. I really think we should. They don't need us here. Chet and Row have things under control. As under control as they can be," she added with a shrug. The Snake didn't need to tell her he agreed. The spirals swirled in her mind, answering for him.

Cody considered it a moment, then he nodded. "I think you're right. But how? All the exits are boarded up and blocked."

"Shoot. I didn't think about that."

"Except..." Cody turned to the basement door.

Brittany's blood chilled at the thought. "We *can't.*"

"Well otherwise, we'll have to take down the boards. We can't risk everyone else's lives just because we want out."

"But those people downstairs—"

"They didn't move until Chet shone the light. I don't know if that's what did it, but we weren't exactly quiet getting down those stairs. Plus, we haven't heard anything from down there in forever. We've been sitting here in the dark so long, I bet we could go down there and get out the cellar door without using a flashlight."

Brittany agreed with a thoughtful nod, even though she wasn't sure going down there at all was a good idea. Still, Cody was right. They couldn't take down the barricades without risking everyone else's lives, and the only other options were to climb up the chimney or attempt a three-story jump out of the small attic window.

"Okay," she said. "But we stick together, and if any one of them makes a move you have to promise we run right back up the stairs to safety."

Cody stuck out his right hand with the pinky finger held out toward her. Brittany regarded it for a moment before he said, "Pinky promise."

She huffed a laugh, then curled her right pinky around his and shook it.

Cody smiled and nodded. "Okay. Let's go tell the Thompsons."

. . .

3

_9:25 P.M. – 10:37 P.M._
Grand Theater

FEAR IS ONLY A DREAM, Renny Hildebrand thought. The quote from the song that opened the old Robert Mitchum film *The Night of the Hunter* had occurred to him suddenly as they'd hidden under his coat while the theater cleared of screaming people. The things they'd been through were so strange and terrifying they could only have come from a dream under normal circumstances there was no way to convince himself what had happened—what could *still* be happening—wasn't real, despite how impossible they were. So he and Elana had remained in their seats, listening for the caws of crows that had once been props, and the goblin-like voices of the terrorizing promotional toys to dissipate.

After a long while, a loud crash came from outside, and the inside of the theater finally fell silent. He and Elana spoke in frantic whispers then, their faces closer than they'd ever dared in public. She told him about the experiments she'd been conducting with Ernie Combs, which explained their strange behavior in the staff room this morning. He'd known they were working together on *something*, but she hadn't told him anything about it. He didn't quite understand how it connected to what was happening here, or what was clearly happening outside, but the fact that they'd been trying to create something and perform experiments that should only be conducted in safe laboratory conditions made him wonder if he knew anything at all about his long-time girlfriend, and how much she knew about her lab partner.

With so many questions he wanted to ask her, he could only stare at her and manage to say nothing. She gave him a querying look, and when he didn't respond she dropped her eyes to her shoes. The silence between them stretched out for several minutes, while Renny thought about dark energy and ancient stone pillars in a long-disused cave.

"Is it safe?" Elana asked sometime later. A little too loudly, in Renny's opinion.

As if in answer, the *sproing* of rubber struck a hard surface nearby. Seconds later a dark, spherical object rolled in between their feet. His eyes had long since adjusted to the dark beneath their coats, so that even before the creature began jabbering in garbled, pitched-up baby talk he saw its painted eyes scowl up at them and its jagged-toothed mouth open wide, the soft rubber tongue wriggling. Renny didn't give it a chance to lunge, stomping straight down as hard as he could on its squishy face. It splatted beneath his shoe with a squeal of pain, leaving a sticky, gooey mess on his sole.

"Guess not," he said.

"What are we going to do?" Elana said much more quietly.

Renny thought about it a moment. If they'd responded to sound, maybe he could use a decoy. "I've got an idea." He bent slightly and reached down to grab the soda cup he'd spotted when he stomped on the Rager ball, just hoping the ice had melted and wouldn't signal their presence by rattling before he was able to toss it. The only alternatives were his keys, his wallet, and his late mother's engagement ring—which had finally been ready for him to pick up after school today—still in its velvety box. He wasn't about to part with any of those.

Gingerly he picked up the cup, the lip pinched between his middle and index fingers. Cold liquid spilled out over his fingertips, but no ice rattled within. Renny breathed a sigh of relief.

Elana gave him another quizzical look as he raised the cup. He mimed what he planned to do: lift the coat, toss the cup. Elana nodded in agreement, and he followed through. The cup clattered somewhere near the screen. He waited for a reaction, counting *Mississippi*s like awaiting thunder after the lightning. By *five Mississippi*, he decided they must be safe, or at least safe enough to attempt an escape.

"Come on," he said.

Another quizzical look. "Are you sure?"

Renny shrugged. "As sure as we can be. Besides, much as I enjoy being this close to you in public, we can't stay here all night, can we?"

She smiled lightly. Even in the dark he could tell she was blushing.

Renny lifted the coats from their heads and surveyed their surroundings. It looked like the entire theater had emptied, coats and popcorn and trash left everywhere. They stood on weary legs and slipped out into the aisle, where Elana took his hand before the two of them moved quietly toward the closed doors. The credits had long since ended and the house lights hadn't come up, leaving the sconce lights dim and making it slightly difficult to see the floor where they stepped. Renny felt something squish under his shoe and hoped it wasn't dead, though the idea that it might be alive was even less palatable. He rushed Elana up the aisle, hoping whatever it was would remain where it lay.

The lobby was deathly silent when they stepped cautiously through the swinging doors. *Silent as a tomb*, they might have said in an old horror film. Normally making such a reference would've amused Renny. After what they'd been through, he couldn't even crack a smile.

"Eerie," Elana said, looking around the empty lobby. The smell of fresh popcorn hung sharply in the air. Trash littered the crimson carpet, a coat, a hat, a scarf and several single gloves. An old poster for *The Maltese Falcon* had fallen off the wall and its frame had shattered, large pieces of glass lying flat against it where it stood propped against the wall. One of the dummies Mr. Stafford decorated the lobby with—which were adorned with costumes from some movie set or another, this one a cowboy—lay face-down on the floor, like a fallen enemy from a Clint Eastwood spaghetti Western. The two that remained standing on either side of the front doors looked like Henry VIII and Jack the Ripper, respectively. One of the cowboy's two ivory-handled Colt .45s lay close to where the mannequin had landed.

Renny stopped as they crossed to the wide, carpeted stairs, the hairs prickling on the back of his neck. "Why do I feel like we're being watched?"

"I feel it, too. It's..." She paused, turning to him with an expression he recognized as her *I'm-not-sure-if-what-I'm-about-to-say-will-upset-you* face.

"It's what?"

She licked her lips and swallowed hard. "It's the same feeling I get around those stones. In the cave," she added, though she hadn't needed to. What other stones could she have been talking about? Stonehenge?

That's what they are, you know, Renny thought. *Standing stones. Artifacts of some long-dead religion. If this was a horror movie, what Elana and Combs did out there would've summoned some kind of entity. Ancient demon. Extraterrestrial. Maybe an* extra*dimensional being. Whatever it is, it's possessing these things or controlling them telekinetically, and if it can do that with a plastic bird or a rubber toy and make it act like something real, it could likely get into just about anything. The important question is, can it* see *through those things—not with eyes, maybe, but with some paranormal form of sight—and if so, is that what we're feeling watching us right now?*

He wanted to convey these thoughts to Elana, but he glanced around the lobby once more instead. Amid popcorn buckets, soda cups, nacho trays, ticket stubs and discarded clothing, he saw no Ragers or prop crows. But did it—whatever *IT* was— even need objects to see through? If it was telekinetic—which was evident—it was possible, even *probable*, that it had other supernatural powers, as well. That was supposing it was a single entity at all. For all he knew it was dozens or hundreds of individual *things*, the paranormal or alien equivalent of an insect swarm. It was just as possible they possessed some kind of *hive mind*. Renny wasn't sure which prospect was worse.

He was still mulling this over when the presence—or *presences*— made itself known, causing both of the costumed, faceless mannequins to step forward robotically. Jack the Ripper raised its surgical knife. Henry VIII hoisted its shield to a defense position and held what appeared to be some kind of mace over its head. Both weapon and shield looked like something a kid might make in metal shop if the teacher was being lax.

Elana gripped his arm with a sharp inward breath.

Fear is only a dream, Renny thought again.

Only this wasn't a dream. It was a *nightmare*, but it was also —*somehow*—all too real.

As the mannequins staggered toward them, Renny weighed their options. They could return to the theater and try the back doors. Or they could run up the nearby stairs, which probably led to the projection booth and the roof. A catwalk led down to the parking lot from up there—he'd noticed it while walking along the other side of the creek in Wyndham Park a few times. Though he couldn't be sure if the door to the roof was locked, and he supposed it likely would be.

Meanwhile, the historical mannequins grew nearer by the

second. At first they walked peglegged like foals emerging from the womb, then they found their footing and learned to bend their limbs. Saucy Jack—even under duress Renny couldn't help but think in movie-isms, this one from *Spinal Tap*—slashed back and forth with the surgical knife. Henry VIII pointed the end of the mace toward them, like Babe Ruth calling his shot. It made an explosive *KRA-POW!* like a small cannon, accompanied by a burst of flame and smoke from its tip, and something launched toward them.

Renny stood stunned in place until Elana shoved him out of the way. The projectile whizzed through the space he'd left with a whine and plunked into the men's room door, leaving a splintery two-inch hole. "It's a gun!" she shouted at him.

Another report came, though no smoke or flame emerged from the tip of the dead king's weapon. A chunk of carpet tore up from the floor in shreds a few feet ahead the mannequins. Renny looked back to where he'd heard the sound. The old man, Mr. Stafford, dressed in his red usher uniform, the top hat, gloves and cape discarded, cowered against the stairwell wall with the missing Colt .45 in his jittery hands. Stafford fired again, the barrel belching flame. This time Henry VIII raised the shield, and the bullet ricocheted with a tiny spark and a loud gong. It struck the ceiling, sending down a rain of plaster dust.

"Run!" the old man shouted, his voice wavering.

Elana turned to Renny. He sensed what she was thinking as he was him, waffling between heeding the old man's advice and a desire to help him, despite the danger. Renny's gaze fell on the second pistol, lying on the floor between them and the mannequins, both of which had turned to deal with Stafford, leaving the path to the front doors clear.

Stafford fired twice more. The first shot went wide, zipping between the mannequins and striking the *E.T.* poster on the far side of the lobby right in the finger. The glass shattered and E.T. dropped to the floor, glass splintering.

Renny's conscience wouldn't let him run. He bent quickly, wary of the third as yet unmoving mannequin on the floor very near him, and scooped up the other gun. It was clearly a plastic replica, neither cold to the touch nor heavy like its metal counterpart. "These work?" he shouted at Stafford.

"They do now!" Stafford called back. He squeezed his right

eye shut and fired again, proving it.

Three more shots, old man, Renny thought. *Better make em count.*

He eyed the cylinder and found it empty, but maybe it mattered as little as the fact that they were plastic seemed to. As a yearly biathlon participant at the Gunstock Mountain ski area since he'd moved to Crooks Corner, he'd fired plenty of rifles, though they were .22s. He suspected the one-handed Wild West Peacemaker would kick like a mule comparatively, real or not. Preparing himself for the potentially wicked recoil, he eyed down the barrel, lining it up with the back of Jack the Ripper's head.

Here goes nothing.

He squeezed the trigger, expecting exactly that: nothing.

CRACK!

The pistol jerked in his hand—less so than he'd been expecting—and the slug plowed through Jack's top hat, flinging it off of his head.

"Ace shot, young man!" Stafford said, firing once more at Henry VIII. This time he managed to hit the thing in the left shoulder. The arm fell off and the shield hit the floor with a resounding clang. Undeterred by its severed limb, the king aimed its mace-gun at Stafford.

Renny aimed again and fired. The bullet struck Henry VIII in the back and the mannequin staggered forward, spinning roughly. Stafford shot once more and managed to hit it again, this time close enough to obliterate its head.

"Nice one!" Renny said as the headless mannequin dropped to the floor.

"We're not out of the woods just yet!" Stafford shot back. He pulled the trigger again, close enough to do real damage no matter where he hit the thing. But the pistol merely clicked. He pulled it again and again as Jack the Ripper reached the stairwell.

Stafford tossed the useless pistol aside with a frightened yelp and began backing up the steps. He tripped almost immediately and fell on his skinny butt, as the Whitechapel Murderer ascended the first step, swinging out at him with the scalpel.

Renny aimed again, this time going for a sure shot at center mass.

"Renny!" Elana shouted behind him.

Plastic fingers encircled his ankle a split second before he squeezed the trigger, and the bullet struck the Employee's Only door several feet to the left of the mannequin.

He wheeled around as the High Plains Drifter grabbed his other leg and began pulling itself up with fistfuls of Renny's jeans. The thing in Henry VIII must have leaped to Clint after its other body had been rendered practically useless. Stafford was in significantly more trouble, since his attacker had a very sharp weapon, so Renny twisted back and fired the .45 at the Ripper.

With an ear-splitting *CRACK*, fire erupted in his hand, shooting all the way up his arm to the elbow. Plastic or not, the pistol had backfired, splintering into pieces and turning his hand to shredded meat. He dropped the last bits of scalding—*metal? plastic?*—and looked at his injury, the remaining flesh burned black, finger bones and tendons visible, just as the cowboy dragged him down to the floor with it.

"Renny!" Elana shouted again.

He held his mangled hand up, fighting off the mannequin with his uninjured hand. The featureless face made it somehow more menacing, with no idea what it was thinking beyond blind rage, if it thought at all.

Its plastic hands slapped his away and reached for his throat, his trachea compressing painfully under its grip. Stars flittered in front of his eyes. Vaguely, he heard Stafford cry out.

KRA-POW!

He heard the sound of the mace-gun firing very near him, but felt no impact on the mannequin on top of him. As his vision began to dim, he heard another sound—something like a T-ball bat striking the ball—and suddenly his sight returned, the fingers relaxing their grip. The mannequin wriggled around on top of him without a head. Elana stood behind it, holding Henry VIII's mace. The head, missing its hat, was stuck to one of its spikes.

The plastic hands scrabbled on his coat for a moment longer, until Renny kicked the thing aside. It rolled off him and began flailing like a cockroach on its back, trying to get itself back to its feet. Elana fired the mace-gun, and the mannequin stopped moving. Barely a moment later, a candy bucket shaped like a jack-o'-lantern about five feet from where he lay started flopping on the floor toward him, hopping like the Easter bunny. Elana swung the mace low, batting the pumpkin into the base of the refreshments counter, where it splintered into long orange strips and fell dead in a scattering of popcorn.

Heaving a sigh, Elana dropped the mace to the floor with a thud. Henry VIII's head rolled off and struck the counter near the pumpkin. She got down on one knee and pulled her silken scarf out of her bag. Renny winced as she began to wind it tightly around his ruined hand. "That'll have to do for now," she said. "Think you can move?"

Renny nodded, sitting up. "I'll be okay. How's Stafford?"

"Just fine, thank you," the old man said. "Can't say the same for my poor theater. The old girl's taken quite a beating tonight, I'm afraid."

Renny huffed a laugh. "Haven't we all."

"Where's your emergency kit?" she asked Stafford.

"In the staffroom." He descended the last two stairs, then stomped down hard on Jack the Ripper's head. It caved in with a crunch of plastic. "Give me a mo," he said, tugging on his lanyard keychain. "I'll retrieve it for you."

Renny chuckled, marveling at the once-again-lifeless mannequins. "How'd you manage to take him down, anyway?"

Stafford chuckled himself. "Your lovely companion gave me a head start firing Henry VIII's mace. The stairs did the rest. It seems they're rather ungainly when it comes to walking, fortunately for all of us." Stafford unlocked the staffroom door and entered. The door swung shut slowly behind him on its pneumatic hinge.

Renny winced again as a wave of pain shot up his arm.

"We've got to get you to the hospital," Elana said.

"Who's to say the hospital hasn't ended up just like this place?" Renny replied.

Elana gave him a dark look. "I hadn't thought of that."

"Yeah," he said. "What we need to do is get to Combs's house as soon as possible. Patch me up as good as we can, then head straight over."

"What if he's...?" She stopped herself, her eyes drifting toward the dark night beyond the doors.

"You know how to turn off the machine, don't you?"

She nodded.

"Then it doesn't matter, does it?"

Elena shut her mouth audibly. He hadn't meant it to sound

callous, but the pain was just too overwhelming at the moment to pretend he cared whether or not Ernie Combs had been murdered by a monster of his own creation.

The staffroom door opened and Stafford stepped out carrying the med kit. He handed it to Elana. She laid it on the floor. Renny sucked in a pained breath while she unwound the sopping scarf from his hand. The wound was much worse than he'd first thought, the remaining flesh both burnt and bruised, his entire thumbnail torn off, the raw nail bed exposed. She cast aside her scarf with a wet splat, opened the med kit on the floor beside him, removed the bottle of antiseptic and twisted off the cap. She held it up for him with a pitying look. "This is going to hurt a lot."

Renny nodded. The pain was almost blinding already, what would a little antiseptic do—

A white-hot explosion of agony tore through his entire body from head to toe as the liquid splashed over the wound, like sticking his whole hand in a blazing fire all the way up to the elbow. He struggled to remain conscious, then felt the world shift as he fell backwards.

Hands caught him around the ribs before he could hit the floor. "Whoopsie daisy," Stafford groaned. The pain dissipated to a throbbing, burning ache and his head cleared, and Renny sat up straight again, allowing Elana to wind the bandage around his wound until it was wrapped like an oven mitt. She closed it off with a metal clip and gently kissed the bare tips of his fingers, a surprisingly tender gesture from his typically reserved partner.

He smiled at Elana. "I'm sorry."

She gave him her trademark quizzical look.

"For being callous about Combs. I know you're close. I've never really understood that, and I guess I've been standoffish with him."

She took his uninjured hand in both of hers. "It's okay."

"I really do hope he's okay."

Tears glistened in her eyes. They trickled down her cheeks when she smiled. "Thank you."

"Well," Stafford said. "I don't know about the two of you, but I could certainly use a stiff drink." He cupped a hand behind one of his elongated ears. "The bottle of Laphroaig in my office is calling my name, it seems."

Renny chuckled. "With the blood loss, I probably shouldn't." He turned to Elana, who shrugged. "What the hell. Pour me two fingers."

"Me too," Elana said, as Stafford wandered toward the stairs.

Renny gave her a surprised grin. "I thought you hate hangovers?"

"Considering I might've opened a portal to another dimension and gotten everyone in town killed, I probably deserve to feel crummy tomorrow. If we make it through the night, that is."

CHAPTER 14

1

10:24 P.M.
Our Lady of Mercy Catholic Church

Not too far up Main Street from the theater, at the end of a short street named after the town founder, Daniel Crook, Our Lady of Mercy was more packed than it had ever been, even during Christmas masses. Even so, Revered Charles Earl was not a happy man. Voices were raised in fear and suspicion. The people were frightened. They had lost friends, relatives, family pets. They didn't know who they could trust. In just a few short hours they had been subjected to more horror and trauma than any modern citizen of a civilized country could ever expect to witness in their lifetime. In just a few short hours, Crooks Corner had experienced their very own 9/11—a full-scale spiritual attack by a very powerful and unknown supernatural force. *Unknown to man, perhaps*, Father Charles thought, *but not to God*.

Once again, he looked over the faces of those who'd gathered here for refuge, marveling at how many were not already a part of his flock.

Nothing like a good tragedy to pull people together. To bring them closer to God.

In addition to his parishioners, he saw the Garners (with their tiny dog instead of their teenage daughter), who owned several car lots in the area, and Will Crampton with several of the staff from the Eateria down the street where Charles sometimes took lunch, a few still in their work uniforms; the Ludlows, who ran the arena, and three town councilors, though Mayor Aldershot was conspicuously absent; Sonya Chen, head of the Better Business Bureau as well as Crooks Corner's most prestigious realtor, and Tony Ellison, whose middling soybean farm somehow enabled him to drive a Lexus and live in a luxurious ranch house. These were influential people, people whose opinions mattered, and who—if their current mindsets could be swayed toward Charles's favor—could truly change Crooks Corner for the better.

There were also many faces he'd never even seen before. The town had changed rapidly in the past few years, with the addition of the new subdivision that was an easy commute to a lovely, safe area to live for many workers at the power plant near Hampton and the Segway headquarters that had opened in Nashua a few years back, where housing costs were somewhat higher. Some changes were for the better, like the refurbishment of the old schoolhouse and the mill, but others Charles could do without, like the new yoga and fitness center, or the growing Halloween aisle at the pharmacy.

"We need to calm these people down," Sheriff Nance said, closing the door after another group arrived following the radio announcement he'd called in about the "freak weather phenomenon." Both Charles and Nance had agreed that telling outsiders what was really happening here would only get them scoffed at. Nance had called the governor himself after receiving no response from Madge at dispatch. Governor Shaheen had said she would call in the National Guard, but had informed Nance that even at the state level the quickest they could mobilize was four to six hours. Nance had placed those calls over an hour ago, and they'd heard nothing back from either. The DJ had done as promised though, sharing the announcement between insipid ads and tracks of insidious horror-themed rock and pop music. They filtered through on the small battery-powered radio Charles had brought in from his office, which he typically used to listen to WVNH, a relatively new gospel station broadcasting out of Concord, while writing his sermons.

In the time since Sheriff Nance had helped him out of his car, it seemed like what had been happening outside had either slowed or stopped for the time being. Charles didn't believe for a second it was over, whatever *it* was, but it was good to have time to regroup and recuperate. At the moment, a few of his most devoted congregants handed out bottles of water, coffee and tea, and packets of cookies left over from the church's last gathering, as well as blankets for the elderly and those with young children. It was something but it wasn't enough. Tensions had begun to rise again, despite the relief, however temporary it might happen to be. Eventually, whoever or *whatever* had caused these things to attack people—be it alien, demonic, or the Dark Prince himself—would come forward to name their price, and they would need to be ready for it, both physically and spiritually. It was a price they could not afford to pay, for the good of their very souls, and so Charles had been rehearsing in his head the homily he intended to deliver once these people had calmed down enough to heed his words.

There are interlopers in our midst, he thought, imagining himself gripping the pulpit tightly to hammer in his point. *Vile, murderous snakes using our own lust for consumerism against us. Attacking us when we are at our most vulnerable, when we as a town have strayed furthest from God—that is to say, the night of this Pagan celebration of the occult which I call Helloween. Ephesians 5:11 says we shall 'have no fellowship with the unfruitful works of darkness, but instead expose them.' Yet every year we allow this ritual to proceed throughout our community unchecked, our friends and neighbors communing with evil spirits—with Satan himself! We permit ourselves to turn a blind eye to the mischief and violence that comes part-and-parcel with this night, right in front of our very eyes. Well, this is the end result, my fellow Christians. Dance with the Devil and the Devil will take the lead—*

A resounding knock at the door pulled Charles from his thoughts, causing a sharp twinge of pain in his bowels just when he was getting to the best part of his speech.

"Open up, Padre!" came a grizzled voice, muffled enough that Charles didn't immediately recognize the man who'd knocked.

Nance returned to the door, opened the slide over the Judas hole and peered out before turning back to Charles. "It's Trudy Bell and Randy Jacobs."

Of course it is, Charles thought. *Our resident Tweedledum and Tweedledee. Just what these people need right now. A conspiracy theorist and a gun nut to whip them up into a frenzy.*

"Well," he said reluctantly, "I suppose it wouldn't be Christian of us to turn them away."

"No, I don't suppose it would be," Nance said, and returned to the small grated window. "Leave the guns at the door," he instructed them.

"Are you outta your mind?" Trudy snapped back. "This is the only damn protection we got against them things!"

"Leave them at the door or you don't come in," Nance stated. "Simple as that."

Father Charles heard muffled grumbles between the duo. After several irate back and forths, Randy Jacobs said, "Fine. But if any of em get stolen, I'm personally gonna sue the shit outta the county *and* the archdiocese."

Nance chuckled. "I wouldn't expect anything less from you, Randy Jacobs." He watched as the duo offloaded their weaponry, the clutter of metal parts and ammunition loud enough Charles could hear it from a distance of several feet, even through the door. When the sound died, Nance unlocked the big heavy latch and drew open the door. Trudy and Randy slumped in, Randy in his grease-stained coveralls and a heavy camouflaged jacket, Trudy in her grimy orange public works vest over her lumberjack jacket. They were both cut and scratched in places, with streaks of blood and what appeared to be soot.

"Thanks for the sanctuary, Father," Trudy Bell said.

"Yeah, thanks, Padre," Randy agreed, nodding curtly without looking at Charles. He swung his big head around, looking at all of the people gathered here. "So this is the what you got, huh? Coffee and cookies, and what? Nothin to protect these folks but the Holy Ghost? No guns? Not even a single barricaded window?"

Trudy nodded suspiciously toward the sheriff. "There is *one* gun."

Randy huffed a derisive laugh. "Lotta good that'll do against those fuckers out there."

Nance smirked. "You're welcome to take your chances."

"We *took* our chances," Randy said, sharing a look with Trudy. "Took out a whole ton of em. Lured a dozen or more into the gas shed an blew their asses to Kingdom Come."

"So that's what that was," Nance said, regarding the loud boom they'd discussed sometime after nine.

"You say you killed them?" a young man asked. He'd been sitting with his wife and daughter, who were wrapped up together in one of the gray church blankets, the cherubic little girl asleep with her thumb in her mouth. They'd arrived with the girl wearing a ladybug costume, but it had been discarded outside along with the rest of the Halloween paraphernalia from the others.

"That's right," Trudy said. "Seventeen in one blow-up. Give or take."

"But how do you know they're gone?" the man asked.

"Oh, they're gone," Randy said haughtily. "Jesus Himself couldn'ta survived that."

Charles gritted his teeth. He considered interrupting the man to lecture him about blaspheming in the House of the Lord, but was curious to see where the young father was going with it.

"I only ask because Paulette and I, we fought off a big one, a jack-o'-lantern the size you'd see at the fair. It tried to eat our little ladybug," he said, casting a misty-eyed gaze at his daughter. "But we smashed it up into little bits."

"Good on ya," Trudy said.

"Yeah, but then it jumped. Her big brother's wagon took off with him sitting in it, the Red Rider Santa brought him for Christmas last year. Drove him right off the bridge into the creek. By the time I—" The man's face crumpled as he regarded his wife and remaining child. "That's why I ask if you're sure you killed them. Because we thought we killed it too, but then it took —" He gulped, tears spilling down his bristly cheeks. "—it took our little boy from us!" His wife patted his knee, looking up at him with moist eyes. He put an arm around her and drew his family closer, the two of them weeping over their lost child.

Trudy and Randy hung their heads, their bravado and good cheer temporarily dashed.

Pleased to see the two troublemakers chastised, Charles laid a hand of consolation on the grieving man's shoulder. "What was his name? Your son?"

"J-Jonas," the father said, his lower lip quivering.

"Jonas." Charles nodded, half-lidding his eyes as he looked up toward the ceiling, toward God. "A good name. A *biblical* name. With God's grace may his soul rest in peace."

"Thank you," the man said. The wife mouthed *Thank you, Father*, clearly not wanting to speak aloud so as not to wake the baby.

"You see, Mr. Jacobs, Ms. Bell," Charles said, ushering them away from the grieving couple and toward the door with outstretched arms, "you may believe what you've done was helpful, but it may only have served to further provoke these *things*, whatever they are."

"Drove off with your goddamn vintage Bel Air and Cordoba, too," Trudy said. "Damn things just up an' left on their own."

Charles glanced at Nance, who returned the look apologetically. The sheriff had been skeptical that Charles's Subaru had taken on a life of its own earlier, running over those poor people at the theater.

"What—pardon my French—but what the hell else are we gonna do here, Padre?" Jacobs sniped. "Sit aroun' singin 'Kumbaya' all dang night while them evil sonsabitches brutalize our people and destroy the town we love? *Some* of us grew up here, ya know," he added like a scandalous accusation.

Charles Anderson Earl may not have grown up in Crooks Corner, but he'd been its spiritual leader long enough that it *felt* like home, even more so than the city he'd grown up in. For Randy Jacobs to pull *that* card, in their darkest hour... even Jesus might have trouble forgiving such a transgression.

"Our esteemed sheriff has called the governor, and the National Guard have been summoned. We merely need to wait—"

"*Wait?*" Trudy snapped. "What if this is a terrorist thing? You ever think of *that*? I heard they was putting *poison* in the candy down in Hackensack and a few other places, too."

Charles glanced around at the faces of those within earshot —with Trudy's voice raised, it was quite a lot of them—and many had perked up at her accusation. People were eager to blame *someone*. And why not the very perpetrators of that vile act against America, as bizarre as the idea might be? They'd hijacked planes using box cutters and the threat of a bomb that may or may not have even existed. Charles had read the texts of many religions when studying for the priesthood, and he knew that in the Sword Verse of the 9/11 terrorists' very own Holy

Quran it said, *But once the forbidden months have passed, kill the polytheists wherever you find them, capture them, besiege them, and lie in wait for them on every way.* Could they somehow have hijacked two of the very things they despised most about the so-called "infidels," America's consumerism and its freedom, employing some kind of ancient djinn magic?

Charles scoffed at the thought... but it was clear that *some* kind of evil magic was at work here, be it Satanic or some Nameless Other.

Nance stepped in between the two imbeciles and the others, raising a hand in that diplomatic way he had. "Now, what use is there putting those kind of nonsense ideas in people's heads?" he said calmly.

Trudy struck her thigh with a fist. "So they get *mad*, goddammit! Like they *should* be!"

"And what good would that do? Can you answer me that?"

Trudy gave her companion a look of supreme disbelief, jerking a thumb in the sheriff's direction. "You get a loada this guy? Mr. Calm and Collected." She huffed, then set a fiery gaze on Nance. "Looks just like Dubya did when his Chief of Staff whispered in his ear bout them hijacked planes hittin the Twin Towers, right in fronta all them kids. Like he wasn't the *least* bit surprised. *Almost* like he knew something," she said, narrowing her eyes at him.

Nance's jaw tightened. "If that's what you believe, Trudy, you've gone deeper down the rabbit hole than I thought. In fact, I think you may have found Br'er Rabbit's porcelain throne."

Randy stepped in front of his friend as she sputtered. "I don't b'lieve it's terrorists, Nance, if that helps," he said. "I just don't think we can sit around here waitin for that second shoe to drop on our dang heads!"

"Exactly my damn point," Trudy said, pushing him out of her way.

The mutters of agreement from those within earshot troubled Charles deeply. He needed to get this under control before these people all rose up, demanding justice for the dead with violence. With the Sword.

It was partly his own fault, he supposed. He'd been whipping up his parishioners—and himself—into a frenzy during the past fifty days. His cup of anger, righteous or not, had runneth over, pouring into his sermons. *Turn the other cheek* seemed a quaint philosophy, something easily preached and followed in times of personal strife, though not so readily adhered to during these dark days. But it was important to remember Jesus and His Disciples had been persecuted at the time He'd given his Sermon on the Mount, from which the pacificist doctrine was taken. They were Crucified. Thrown to the lions. Sacrificed in the names of the many Roman gods. In the words of Emperor Trajan to Pliny the Younger, *They must not be searched for, but if they are denounced and found guilty they must be punished...*

Jesus had preached against *an eye for an eye* even as the eyes of his own followers were being plucked from their heads. Thus, it was perhaps one of the most important lessons in His teachings.

"Ms. Bell, Mr. Jacobs," Charles said, projecting his voice as he would during Mass, "you are of course both more than welcome to stay with us." He then lowered his voice, so only those within earshot could hear. "However, I do please ask that you keep your revenge fantasies to yourselves. There are women and children here, the elderly, as well, and it would do none of them any good to bring the wrath of whomever has besieged our community down upon the heads of these innocent people while they are merely trying to heal."

"Amen to that," Nance said, not the least bit sarcastically.

As Charles regarded the faces of the gatherers, the light from the hanging lamps seemed to brighten, and in that sharp illumination he found himself in the presence of the Lord for the first time since the one-two punch of 9/11 and his diagnosis. The near-constant sharp pain in his bowels dissipated. He felt suddenly healthy and mobile, certain he'd be able to genuflect or even run a mile without agony. The rage he'd felt no longer mattered. Not the fear, nor the cancer, either. He felt himself filled with the Holy Spirit and God took over, the words flowing out of him in a way he himself hadn't been able to conjure them in months, suffering a constipation of the mind as well as the soul. They bubbled up from somewhere deep within him, a God-shaped hole now filled with His eternal love and wisdom.

Reverend Earl's parishioners and tonight's newcomers to his flock listened in what could only be considered rapture.

. . .

2

Sheriff Bert Nance had heard just about enough of Trudy Bell's idiotic ramblings, and he'd been about to tell her as much regardless of his commitment to calm and rational when Reverend Earl finally stepped up to the plate. He'd expected Earl's plea to be churchly, perhaps even pious. What he did not expect was the complete and utter brain mush that came spewing from the holy man's mouth like verbal diarrhea, things that made even Trudy Bell sound sane by comparison.

"My friends," he'd begun finely enough, "we have found ourselves at a crossroads. A powerful evil has been unleashed upon this sleepy little town of ours, a darkness that will not relent until we are entirely removed from this Earth. Vanquished. Laid flat. The hounds of the moon are howling at our very doorstep, hungry for blood!"

The faces of those listening looked as perplexed as Nance felt himself. *Hounds of the moon?* he thought.

"Only the love and wisdom of our new Lord and Savior can hold them at bay," the reverend said, holding up his maroon-colored Bible with its gold foil lettering.

Oh, hell, here comes Charles Earl's Holy Crusade, Nance thought.

But the reverend surprised him again, reaching up with his other hand and tearing the Good News Bible in half, to the shock of many in the crowd. He let the pieces fall to the floor with two sharp claps, loose pages scattering. "Only through believing in Geth will we be spared from their fury! Only through accepting Geth as our divine protector, will we live to see tomorrow!"

Randy Jacobs stepped up to Earl with his hands held palms out. "Pardon my French, Padre, but who in the hell is Geth?"

"Took the words right outta my mouth," Nance muttered.

"Geth is the Sleeper from the Void!" the reverend cried, throwing his arms into the air as if in supplication to this deity, this *Geth*. "Geth brings life to that which is without life! Geth is the Living Cloud whose rain brings pain and sorrow! Geth has spoken to me, *speaks through* me to you here, now. From eons' slumber within the *Upask*, They have *risen*! *REPENT AND RE-JOICE!*" Earl turned in a circle, smiling beatifically as he surveyed the dozens of bewildered faces in his church. "We *must* give ourselves completely to Them: mind, body and spirit, *especially* our spirits! That is the only way this ends, do you not see? We must pledge our allegiance to Geth and spread Their Holy Blight throughout the land!" he cried, sweeping his arms wide in a grand gesture. "The Blight is peace! The Blight is the Way and the Word!"

"The guy's gone mental," Trudy said. "Cuckoo for Krispies."

Nance thought that was the first rational thing Trudy Bell had said since she'd gotten here, but even then it was an understatement. Charles Earl seemed to be having some sort of psychotic break, schizophrenic delusions of a kind Nance had never encountered, nor read about in his abnormal psych class at the academy.

"Charles," Nance said, cautiously approaching the reverend, whose back was turned. When he laid his hand on Earl's shoulder, the man flinched as if he'd been hit with a stun-gun. He wheeled around and stared at Nance, his wild eyes as dark as they'd been outside, moments after the accident.

"*You*," the reverend cried, pointing at him accusatorily. "You dare speak against Geth?"

"Charles, I think we ought to get that head wound of yours taken a look at."

The reverend shirked Nance's hand. "Get your filthy hand off me, unbeliever! Infidel! How is it you still do not believe, after everything Geth has shown us? Shall They prove Themself again? Would you like that, unbeliever? Would you like for Them to prove Their might and mercy?"

"I don't think that's nec—"

Nance didn't get a chance to finish. The sound of gunfire erupted outside, bullets plunking—*thock-thock-thock!*—into the doors and walls and shattering the stained-glass windows. It sounded like an army was out there, firing at the church from all sides.

"*GET DOWN!*" he shouted, dropping to his knees himself as cries of horror and shrieks of terror arose from those gathered in the nave of Our Lady of Mercy. Colored glass rained down on the people sitting and lying among pews, covering their heads. Even the formerly cocky Bell and Jacobs dove for cover behind the baptismal font.

Reverend Earl, meanwhile, stood perfectly still, both his arms and his smile spread wide as bullets whizzed by him. The rifle, pistol and shotgun fire continued for several more seconds before Earl reacted at all.

"GETH THE MANY COMMANDS YOU TO CEASE!" the priest bellowed, in a voice much louder than the one he reserved for his sermons.

And just like that, the firing stopped.

In the silence, Nance heard gasps and turned to watch as a camo AR-15—currently outlawed for sale and possession under the Federal Assault Weapons Ban, though Nance supposed Randy could've bought the weapon prior to the Act—and a sawed-off shotgun—also illegal—hovered through the window where some patron saint or another had just been, reduced to slivers of colored glass on the floor. Through another came six or seven handguns, from a .38 Police Special revolver to a gold-plated Desert Eagle, which Nance had forced their owners to get rid of earlier in the night. He'd done so to prevent someone from accidentally shooting themselves, or shooting someone else in the heat of an argument. He hadn't even considered the possibility they might—like everything else in this damn town—become suddenly sentient and turn against their makers. Whatever had been possessing toys and Halloween props tonight had found far more dangerous toys to play with, and just about a hundred and twenty ducks in a barrel to shoot at.

Is this Geth? Whatever it is controlling these things? Or is Geth what kept them away?

His query was answered momentarily, when the weapons floated over the ducked heads of mystified survivors, turning languidly as they neared the reverend. The sheriff's nostrils prickled at the acrid stench of propellant and spicy-sweet smell of splintered wood. Onlookers gasped and trembled. Several made the sign of the cross. Soon they all hovered around the holy man with his arms still outstretched, more than a dozen rifles, pistols and shotguns surrounding him in the shape of a ragged cross, every single one of their barrels pointed at the trio by the doors.

"Leapin Jesus!" Randy Jacobs rasped, peeling off his trapper hat and holding it to his chest in both hands, exposing the sparse strands of oily black hair stuck across his shiny scalp. Trudy Bell lay flat on her stomach with her hands clasped behind her head as if she were being detained.

The reverend's dark gaze turned in religious fervor toward Nance, his broad smile stretching somehow wider. "Do you still doubt Their strength now, unbelievers?"

Rising cautiously to his knees, Sheriff Nance began to wonder how in the hell he'd talk his way calmly and rationally out of this mess, when not a single thing about it was either calm or rational. Crazy as an outhouse fly or not, the reverend seemed to be tapped into the power of this Geth, and whoever or whatever that happened to be, it appeared to want them to worship it by the edge of a knife.

On the upside, Nance thought, *he can't ask me to kneel when I'm already kneeling.*

3

10:30 P.M.
Matt Dukas's House

PHILBERT PIPER and the boys sat cross-legged in front of the old wooden TV set in Matt's basement, eating the candy Philbert had collected in his coat and pants pockets after the pumpkin bucket had come to life and attacked him. None of them quite understood what was happening in town, but listening to Philbert try to explain his plastic jack-o-lantern bucket coming to life and attempting to eat him had given them all a good case of the giggles. It had been a welcome bit of relief, and Philbert had joined them until they all had tears in their eyes.

Matt's mom and dad hadn't been home when they arrived at the house, and he figured they'd probably gone to check on Uncle Tim and the cousins a few blocks over. He didn't much like his cousins—they were spoiled and bratty and ganged up on him whenever they could—but he didn't wish any ill will toward them. Uncle Tim was great. He was a tall beanpole of a man, who used to grab Matt by his hands and spin him around the yard in a helicopter until the both of them got dizzy. Matt really hoped they were all okay.

"I like Whoppers the best," Philbert said, squeezing a package of the chocolate malt balls into his mouth. He grinned, his teeth stained brown from chocolate, and speckled with bits of candy. Kyle and Craig chuckled, holding crackling Pop Rocks on their tongues. Philbert laughed along with them. After the initial fit once they'd gotten down here, Matt didn't feel much like laughing. He wasn't very hungry anymore, either.

"We should watch a horror movie," Kyle said.

Philbert's eyes went wide with fright. "Uh-uh!" he said, shaking his head so rapidly Matt could hear his jowls shake. "I can't watch no horror movies. Mom says they'll scare me real bad, then I might have nightmayors an' piss in the bed! I don't wanna piss the bed! Wake up all itchy an' wet? Huh-uh, no way!"

Matt and Craig snickered.

"Well, fine, let's just watch TV then."

"Mom says I'm not asposed to watch TV, neither."

Kyle moaned. "Well, heck, then, what are we gonna do all night? I'm getting bored, big time."

That's a lot better than being dead, Matt thought.

"I got an idea!" Philbert said excitedly. "We could tell stories."

Craig groaned. "Stories? That's re—" Craig quickly corrected himself, about to say the word Matt's parents had told him never to use, especially around people like Philbert or his cousin Jamie in Boston, who had Multiple Sclerosis. "That's gay," the other boy said instead.

"Yeah, big-time gay," his brother agreed.

Matt shook his head at his tragically insensitive friends.

"Nuh-uh," Philbert said. "Mom says stories are better'n TV 'cause we get to use our 'magination."

"Ugh," Craig said.

"Since Philbert *saved our lives*, maybe we oughta do what he wants, huh, guys?" Matt said, deliberately enunciating so they'd take the hint.

The O'Donelly brothers looked at each other and shrugged. "I guess that's fair," Craig said.

"Let's put on the radio, at least," Kyle said, rolling his eyes. "Jeez."

Matt agreed. He stood up and flicked on the radio to his favorite station, the hard rock channel out of Wolfeboro, in the middle of playing "Monster Mash," which he'd never liked very much despite it being a "graveyard smash." He turned the volume down so they could listen to each other's stories, and sat cross-legged on the other side of the dwindling heap of candy, grabbing a mini-Coffee Crisp someone must've gotten from across the border.

"Who wants to go first?" he asked.

Philbert shot up a hand. "I do," he said with his goofy chocolate-stained grin.

Kyle puffed out an exasperated breath. Matt shot him a glare and the kid mouthed *Fine*.

"Mom told me this one when I was yay high," Philbert said, holding up a hand to his shoulder, which even sitting on the floor was probably still taller than Kyle. "Out there in the woods behind the Thompson farm there was this—oh, I forgot to say 'A long time ago,' so just pretend I already said it, okay?—so there was a magic man who made the stars and the earth, and he also founded this town, and he was the bestest and strongest man in the whole wide world."

"You mean God?" Craig said smugly.

"Not God, huh-uh. His name was Danny Crook."

"Daniel Crook was just the guy who founded this crummy town," Kyle said, which was true. They'd learned about it in the local history unit a few years ago. "You said he made the stars and the earth. That's God, not some random butthead."

Philbert sighed heavily. "It's *my* story."

"Let him finish," Matt said, if only to move it along.

"Yeah, lemme finish," Philbert said, his voice lacking animosity. "So anyways the Magic Man built the first church here in Crooks Corner, right on the same corner where the Our Lady of Marcy is now, where the creek goes acrost downtown. Danny Crook was the first minister and also the mayor, and there was only a coupla houses and farms here way back then but he did magic for the people who lived in em, and lickety-split they all joined his church and told everyone around who would listen about the Magic Man and his special church."

"This isn't real," Craig said, shaking his head derisively. "Mr. Hamilton said Daniel Crook was a banker, not no minister."

Philbert sulked, his shoulders sagging.

"Well, the Pied Piper of Crooks Corner didn't happen either but it's still a good story," Matt said. "Come on and let 'im finish, okay? Go ahead, Philbert."

Philbert sighed again, his shoulders rising and falling dramatically. "I don't wanna."

"You see that? You guys ruined it."

Kyle tossed a Smarties wrapper into the small pile of trash. "This is dumb, anyway. We should be watching movies."

"Philbert's not allowed to watch em."

Craig sneered. "Well, his mom's *not here*, is she? How's she gonna know?"

"God'll know," Philbert said matter-of-factly. "And He talks to Mom, He'll tell her for sure."

Kyle and Craig shook their heads in unison. They both belonged to the Catholic church, part of Reverend Earl's congregation, but they weren't super religious as far as Matt could tell. Matt thought the priest was kind of creepy, but would never say as much to the O'Donnelly brothers. In fact, he kind of thought religion was weird, all of it, from the Hindus to the Mormons, and when those religious nuts blew up the Twin Towers, it also made him *fear* it. If some guy could convince a bunch of other guys to hijack planes and fly them into buildings full of people, what could someone like Pope John Paul convince people to do if he suddenly decided to turn evil? Sure, there were all kinds of cardinals and archbishops and stuff who'd maybe stand in his way—*maybe*—but if he was doing one of his speeches and said *We need to go and kill so and so*, on live TV broadcasted all over the world, he'd have a lot more influence over a lot more people than the president of a single country, even one as big and powerful as America. Although Matt supposed the pope didn't have access to the nuclear launch codes, so that was something at least.

Neither of Matt's parents believed in God. They were self-described "staunch atheists," and Matt himself wavered between atheist and agnostic, depending on the subject and how he felt about his life on any given day. They'd taught him to respect other people's beliefs even if he didn't believe them himself—"so long as they don't harm others," they'd always been quick to add. Still, Matt couldn't help that it concerned him how confident people seemed to be in their faith. How could they be so certain God exists, when there was so much that contradicted it? And if you could convince someone that an old man in the sky exists who saw all and heard all and judged whether or not you'd spend eternity in everlasting peace or eternal hellfire, it seemed to Matt you might be able to convince them of just about anything. Like blowing up buildings full of people for a harem of seventy-two virgins, for instance.

The four of them had fallen silent, and Matt's ears perked up as the DJ interrupted the commercial break for an "urgent announcement." They told people in Crooks Corner to "take shelter in their storm cellars or basements", and if they didn't have a basement they should go to the church with Reverend Earl.

That's weird, Matt thought, a shiver of anxiety crawling up his spine. Of all the people he could've been thinking about in that moment, it had been Reverend Earl, and then the radio announcer went and said his name, almost as if someone—*God*, Matt thought but tried not to acknowledge—had read his mind. The announcement repeated, then cut back to music. Matt recognized Metallica's "Until It Sleeps" from the opening drums and bassline. He'd listened to it a whole bunch when his Dad got the CD from Columbia House.

"We gotta go!" Philbert said suddenly, standing up with his eyes wide and his mouth hanging open, his arms hung loose at his sides.

"But we're already in the basement," Matt said. The timing of the announcement made him nervous, but it was something more than that. Something he couldn't pinpoint.

"Yeah, but your parents aren't home," Kyle said. "We could be in real big trouble."

Matt pointed to the high window they'd blocked with the cooler Matt and his parents used for camping. "Bigger trouble than going back *out there*?"

Craig shrugged. "We haven't heard anything out there for like an hour. Maybe it's all over?"

"If it's over, why'd they make the announcement, huh? That doesn't make any sense."

Craig couldn't answer this. He turned to his brother and the two of them shrugged.

"We gotta go," Philbert said again. "*Come on*, you guys."

Mike looked at the others. They shrugged again. Philbert looked down at him with an emphatic nod.

"Fine," Matt sighed. All three boys stood up together. "If you guys get me killed, I swear to G—" He stopped, looking at

Philbert. "If we take our bikes we'll get there in two minutes. You know how to ride, Philbert?"

Philbert looked excited. "Yup!" he said cheerily. "My dad taught me how when I was real little, smaller than you even."

Matt tried not to feel annoyed by the comment. He'd always been the smallest in their class, and Philbert pointing it out made him self-conscious.

"You got one big enough for me?"

Matt nodded. His dad's mountain bike was in the garage beside Matt's own. "Come on," he said reluctantly. "Let's get going, I guess."

Chapter 15

1

10:35 P.M.
Crooks Corner Secondary School

Walden found a chunk of cinderblock in the parking lot and used it to smash through the window in one of the backdoors and clear away the glass. Then he reached inside, unlocked and opened it, then waved for the others to enter. "Ladies first."

Cassandra shook her head. "Uh-uh, I'm not going in first. Why don't one of you go?"

"You two have the camera," Jay said, shouldering the baseball bat he'd snagged from Cassandra's neighbor's front yard. "What've we got? A bat isn't gonna do much if there's a bunch of Possessors in there."

"Especially since you can't bat for shit," Walden said.

Jay frowned at him. "How would you know?"

Walden grinned. "Educated guess."

Jay continued sneering at him for a long moment, then shrugged. "Fine, but I still get to keep it."

"Whatever makes you feel comfortable."

"I'll go first," Taylor said, bravely staring into the darkened school.

"No way, shrimp."

"But I've got the camera *and* Humphrey."

"Yeah, but it's *my* job to take care of you."

Walden sighed. "I'll go. Cassandra, you and Taylor follow right behind me, and Jay can watch our six."

"Wait, I don't want to be in the back."

"Then give me the bat," Cassandra said.

"Fine," he huffed. "I'll watch your sixes."

Walden stepped in cautiously, wishing he'd thought to bring a weapon like Jay and Taylor had. Once out of the streetlamp's light, enough of it flooded in to see down the stretch of hall, lined with closed classroom doors and dozens of lockers. The Communications class stood right before the T-junction at the end of the hall, leading off to the cafeteria on the right and the front foyer to the left. This afternoon when he'd left school there'd still been some decorations set up by the student council and dance committee for the Halloween dance last Saturday. Aside from the signage, there didn't appear to be anything left in this hall, which meant it had either been cleaned up or was out there roaming the halls and classrooms, looking for victims. Naturally, Walden hoped for the former.

Cassandra and Taylor entered behind him, hand in hand. Taylor held her Polaroid in front of her—her sister had made sure she had a couple of extra packets of film—the strap hanging from her neck, ready to shoot. Jay stepped in cautiously behind them, pointing the bat back and forth in a paranoid fashion. Walden was pretty sure he'd take a swing at whatever made a sound, be it Possessor or anything else. Whether he'd manage to hit them or not was anyone's guess.

The school looked different at night. Sinister. Creeping down the hall in the semi-dark with the only sound the light scuffle and slap of their footwear felt like something out of a nightmare. Even if they hadn't already dealt with things coming to life and attacking them, Walden felt like he still might've expected some kind of monster to jump out from a classroom door or any of the lockers, a werewolf or mummy.

As they passed by the auto shop, the sudden buzz-and-click sound of an impact wrench made Walden leap back from the door with his heart in his throat.

"What was that?" Cassandra whispered anxiously.

"Just a power tool."

"Who's at school this late at night?" Jay said, suspicion in his tone and expression.

Walden didn't think he wanted to know, but curiosity got the better of him and he crept up to the small window in the door to peer through. What he saw made him blink and shield his eyes to get a better look inside. The human skeleton from Mr. Abel's biology class was holding the impact wrench, depressing the trigger and grinding it across the surface of the shop teacher's desk.

Opposable thumbs, he thought with a shudder. *First tools, then weapons.*

"They're getting smarter," he said to the others, stepping back from the window.

Cassandra's dark eyes went wide. "What was it?"

"You don't wanna know. Let's get the cameras and get out of here."

The buzz and grind continued as they moved on to their comm class. Walden tried the door handle. It wasn't locked, opening easily.

They crept forward to the cabinet where Mr. Hildebrand kept the classroom equipment. It was padlocked, but Walden knew Hildebrand kept the key in the top drawer of his desk. So long as he hadn't locked the desk, they should be able to get all the cameras they needed and be on their way in a few minutes.

"Of course, it's not that easy," Walden said with a heavy sigh.

"What's wrong?" Jay asked.

"Desk is locked. We're gonna need something to jimmy it." He checked his pockets but his Swiss Army knife must've fallen out at some point, maybe when they'd fled his car before it caught fire. "Look around," he said. "Maybe there's a screwdriver set or something."

"What about this?" Jay said, holding up the bat.

"On the desk?"

"No, the padlock."

Walden shook his head. "That'll make too much noise. Believe me, you do not want what I saw in *there*"—he pointed at the wall between them and the shop class—"coming in *here.*"

Jay shrugged and began halfheartedly looking around by the edit computers. Cassandra and Taylor searched with a little more gusto.

"Never mind," Walden said, spotting the keyring on the desk beside the mug full of pens and pencils and the William

Goldman book he'd lent Hildebrand earlier in the week. He grabbed the keys and returned to the cabinet. After a moment, he found the right one and removed the padlock. Inside were several video cameras like the one that burned up in his car, along with stacks of batteries and tapes.

Walden grabbed one and held it out to Cassandra. She took it from him, then loaded one of the batteries he gave her. The camera came on with a beep when she flicked the power switch. "Sweet," she said.

"Come look at this," Jay called from the Edit 1 desk. The monitor was on and the bat stood against the desk. He clearly hadn't been looking at all, more focused on whatever it was he was doing at the computer.

"You already showed us the credits," Walden said dismissively. "Come get a camera."

"It's not *that*. It's footage from the haunt."

"Footage?" Walden came over, his interest piqued. "I thought we lost all the tapes."

"I put the last one I shot in my coat pocket when we got in the car," Jay explained, the light from the monitor flickering in his eyes as he stood over the computer. On the screen was a mostly dark shot of the room with stone walls where all the craziness had started. Cassandra and Taylor came over and stood behind Walden. "Check this out."

Jay played the tape frame by frame, the machine making little clicking sounds as the footage moved forward. Walden figured it'd be difficult to spot the things they'd seen on Taylor's Polaroid photo in the already dark footage. Then he saw Cody swatting one of the bats out of the air, slightly blurred in slow-motion. The second his hand struck the rubber creature, two things moved in opposite directions: the bat flew in a straight shot toward the floor, and a hazy black smudge flittered toward the camera in a way that reminded Walden of... *something* he couldn't quite place. In the next moment the footage broke up in scrambled blocks of pixelation.

"Oh wow," he said.

"That's not all." Jay rewound the tape and again played it forward frame by frame—*click-click-click-click-click*, as the camera spun in an errant circle and caught someone's foot coming down on a small army of spiders. This time, several black smudges jittered away from them, again toward the camera. This time he realized what their erratic flight reminded him of: *moths*. Moths made of shadow, each about the size and shape of a golf ball. Again, the tape pixelized.

Jay looked back at them with wide eyes. "It looks like they're going *into* the camera, doesn't it?"

"Weird," Cassandra said.

"Yeah, it—" Walden stopped as the tape heads made a low grinding noise, something between a dying motor and a mewling cat. The machine had begun to glow like molten lava from behind its hinged door. "What's going on with that thing?"

Jay reached past him hastily and poked the Eject button. He withdrew his hand and shook it out with a hiss of pain. "It's hot!"

The grinding sound grew louder as the tape door opened and an ooze of red-hot molten plastic belched out.

"My tape!"

Walden frowned, watching the superheated plastic cool into a congealed black lump. "Forget it. We gotta get out of here."

The others followed him back to the cabinet. He handed Jay a camera and a few batteries, threw a couple of batteries and a handful of MiniDV tapes into the pockets of his own army surplus jacket, then loaded one into the camera in his hand, and flicked it on.

"I can't hold this and the bat," Jay said sullenly.

"If we can figure out how the camera's work, you won't need the bat."

"Yeah? What if they *don't* work?"

Walden shrugged. He hadn't really considered the alternative. "If they don't, they're heavy enough to do some damage if you swing em."

Cassandra held hers by the top handle and swung it in an arc. Then she pooched out her lower lip. "Bitchin."

Walden chuckled at her use of ancient slang. He grabbed the single SLR camera from the bin, hung it around his neck by the strap, then said, "All right, let's get moving."

He opened the door as quietly as possible. Before he could take a single step out into the hall something grabbed him by the lapels of his coat and yanked through the doorway, slamming him up against the wall. The back of the camera made a good loud crack that echoed up and down the hall, which he supposed was slightly better than if his skull had done the same. He heard Cassandra and Taylor yelp and the shuffle of feet on the linoleum.

When he looked up from the gnarled, nicotine-stained hands gripping his jacket he found himself face-to-face with the skinny old janitor who looked like Harry Dean Stanton with a scruffy beard. His breath smelled like a whiskey-soaked ashtray. The name embroidered on his jumpsuit said ARLEN. The old man let go of Walden's left pocket and stuck a finger up to his own lips, silently shushing them.

"*What the hell, dude?*" Walden whispered harshly. "We *were* quiet until you slammed me up against the damn wall."

Arlen the janitor looked up and down the corridor with his wide, red-rimmed brown eyes. "They're roamin the halls," he said, keeping his voice low. Walden figured he must've been cleaning up in here when the shit went down. There were only two janitors that he knew of, and it was a pretty big school.

"We *know*," Cassandra said. "That's why we got *these*."

The janitor looked down at the cameras in their hands. "That's school property."

"No doy."

"Come on, old-timer," Walden said. A cloud of dust or chalk rose as he patted the guy on the shoulder. "Stick with us, but be quiet."

Arlen stroked his beard and nodded. "I just seen em back that way." He jerked his orange-stained thumb toward the cafeteria and front foyer.

Back out the way they came in, then.

They headed in that direction, Walden and the janitor in the lead. The old man didn't lift his feet, and the soles of his boots scuffed with every step. Cassandra, Taylor and Jay fell in behind them.

"Oh no," Arlen said suddenly, with a vigorous shake of his head.

Walden looked ahead. He could vaguely see several round, dark shapes close to the floor. All of their faces lit up with flames at once, brightening the far end of the hall: a small jack-o'-lantern army, lined up in front of the doors. Normally they would be smashed by the time everyone returned to school the day after Halloween. Tonight, all the pranksters were apparently too busy.

"Oh, no-no-no-no...." The janitor kept mumbling to himself, tugging a flask out from one of his deep jumpsuit pockets as he backed up, until he hit the shop room door and startled.

"Oh *shit*," Jay said from behind them.

Walden glanced back over his shoulder. Blocking their way at the other end of the corridor were two strange shapes he couldn't quite discern until he remembered seeing them several times this week. It was the quartet of monsters (witch, mummy, vampire and werewolf) someone had made out of construction paper and taped up to the wall outside Principal Elder's office.

The jack-o'-lanterns advanced, slumping forward on the floor, their sharp-toothed grins growing wider. The paper monsters closed the distance, their flimsy limbs wobbling like the tube man out front of Brittany's dad's car dealership, their feet bent against the floor.

"Cameras on?" Walden said.

Jay and Cassandra nodded.

"The ones at the doors first." Off their decisive nods, he said, "And... *action!*"

They all pressed Record and aimed their cameras at the jack-o'-lanterns blocking their way out the back. The living pumpkins continued their lurch forward unabated with hollow thumps. Behind Walden and the others, the monster squad moved closer with slithering swishes of construction paper.

"Nothing's happening," Jay said.

"Taylor, take a picture."

Taylor looked up at him, fiddling with the Polaroid. "I have to load a new pack!"

"Why didn't you think of that before, shrimp?"

"I forgot about the one I took on accident!"

The sound of shattered glass turned their attention to the janitor. A bony hand reached through the window pane and grabbed Arlen by the throat. The old man wailed in half-drunk horror. Another hand shot out with the impact wrench making its menacing *rat-a-tat-whir*.

Taylor screamed and dropped the film cartridge. It skittered a few feet away from her on the waxed floor.

"Aim at the skeleton!" Walden said, turning his camera toward the shop class door. Cassandra and Jay did the same, making him think of the Ghostbusters, and how horridly unprepared they all were for any of this.

The janitor whimpered as the wrench clicked and whirred just above his right ear.

"It's not working!" Jay said, glancing over his shoulder toward Walden. "What do we do?"

Walden didn't know why the cameras weren't working, but he figured what had worked before was liable to work again. He bent to grab the fresh Polaroid cartridge from the floor. "Taylor!" When she finally looked away from the janitor's terrified face, he lobbed it at her.

The jack-o'-lanterns continued their thumping advance. The paper monsters swished closer.

Taylor finally loaded the film, but it was moments too late. The air wrench wheezed and whined, gouging a bloody hole into Arlen's temple. The old man yowled and dropped his flask. Amber liquid glurped out onto the floor as gore poured down the front of his uniform.

"Oh my god!" Cassandra cried.

Taylor raised the camera and snapped a photo. The flash lit the corridor and the skeleton hands let go of Arlen, retreating through the window pane along with the air wrench. The janitor slid jerkily down the door, leaving a streak of blood, and slumped onto his butt on the floor. Already dead, he fell sideways, his glassy red eyes staring straight ahead, blood pouring from his lips.

The door handle rattled, turning back and forth, but not far enough to open. The air wrench clacked and whined inside. Sooner or later, the skeleton would figure out it needed something more tactile than bone to turn the handle—a rag, a shirt sleeve—and it would come clattering out to kill them all. Fortunately, the air hose wouldn't reach much further than a few more feet out the door, but Walden figured it could do damage to them with or without the wrench.

Taylor yanked the photo out of the camera, tossed it aside and turned to face the pumpkins blocking their way out. Their faces blazed in grotesque parodies of rage, making Walden wonder if the Possessors actually understood human emotions or if they were just aping what they saw on the faces of the people they'd attacked and killed. Either way, it was disturbingly lifelike.

"*StopitstopitSTOPIT!*" Cassandra shrieked, her eyes squeezed shut and her hands on her temples.

In the same moment, Taylor snapped another photo. In mid-jump, the pumpkins all slumped to the floor another few inches closer to them, their blazing candles all winking out at once.

"It worked!" Taylor said.

Cassandra opened her eyes and blinked at the silent, motionless pumpkins. She grabbed her sister and kissed her on the top of her head. "You did it!"

Walden smiled at her. "Way to go, Taylor!"

"Guys, monster squad at six o'clock!" Jay said.

Behind them, the paper monsters rushed forward. They were close enough now for Walden to see their faces, each wearing different yet similar expressions of fury, whereas this morning they'd looked docile and almost goofy, like monsters on a cereal box.

"Get em, kid!" Jay said with a hopeful grin.

Taylor turned to face them, raising the camera. She pushed on the button but it didn't click. With a shaken look, she turned the camera around. "The pitcher's jammed!"

"What does that mean?" her sister asked.

"It means it won't work!"

Walden looked back at the uneven row of darkened jack-o'-lanterns. He didn't know what happened to the Possessors when Taylor took their picture. He didn't even know why it worked. If the pumpkins reanimated while he and the others ran at them, they'd be close enough for a deadly attack they probably wouldn't survive. But with no other option, he figured it was worth the risk.

"Screw it," he said. "Jump the pumpkins!"

He grabbed a stunned Jay by the shoulder and tugged him into motion. The four of them ran at the silent, unmoving jack-o'-lanterns.

"Please don't wake up, please don't wake up," Cassandra chanted as they ran.

Walden leaped, followed by the others, each of them landing on the far side of the pumpkin army with a squeak of their soles. The jack-o'-lanterns remained unmoving and unlit.

Jay turned back to give the sad-faced hobo pumpkin closest to him a swift stomp. His shoe went right through the shell into the hollow guts, splitting it in two, and he laughed triumphantly. "Let that be a lesson to the rest of you!" he cried.

"Let's go, man!" Walden shouted from the doorway.

The remaining pumpkins lit up all at once and rose from the floor, hovering a few feet in the air, turning toward them and shrieking as they preparing to strike.

"Oh shit," Jay said, dashing to catch up with the others at the door.

The jack-o'-lanterns shot toward them like flaming cannonballs. Jay slipped through the door and Walden slammed it behind them, holding them shut. Hollow thuds struck the inside of the doors a moment later.

"That was close," Walden said.

"And pointless," Cassandra snapped. "What a waste of time!"

"Not entirely," Jay said. "We don't know why the cameras didn't work, but now we know for sure the Polaroid *does*."

"Maybe." The others turned to Walden. He peered into the school through the shattered window. The skeleton managed to get the door open and met the paper monsters in the hall. It looked like they were conferring with each other. Walden frowned and added, "I'll explain on the way."

Jay turned to him as they headed across the parking lot. "Well? What's your big theory, Einstein?"

"Okay. This is gonna sound crazy, but what if it's not *just* the camera? What if it's combination of the camera *and* Taylor's powers?"

"What do you mean?" Cassandra asked.

"Like your grandma said. Like responds to like. What if it wasn't just Mr. Combs's machine that caused this? If it was science *and* ritual, the machine *and* the ritual sacrifice of Darla Knight, then maybe it takes science *and* the supernatural—or whatever the hell your Humphrey thing is—to stop the Possessors. Maybe the video cameras would've worked, too, if Taylor used them instead of us. Or if she did whatever it is she was doing when she took the picture, if that makes sense."

As the older kids pondered this, Taylor fished the exposed film out of her camera and tossed it into the trash bin. "This one's spoiled."

"How many more packets do you have, kid?" Jay asked.

She shrugged. "A couple."

Walden nodded. "Okay. Next time we see one of these things on its own, we need to test my theory."

"Huh?" Taylor said, looking up from her camera.

Cassandra gave her a light noogie. "We'll fill you in, shrimp."

2

ALMOST EXACTLY TWO hours after Their release from the *Upask*, Geth the Many arrived at Ernie Combs's house on Browning Street, drawn by the persistent hum of the tuning device. Their journey had been uneventful from the cheery bungalow on Hammer Road with its intoxicating aromas of blood and death to the drab, two-story Victorian home Combs had lived in since he was born. The few souls who had witnessed Geth the Many in all Their glory had not paid Them a moment's attention. Ordinarily, this would have irked Geth. Above all else, Geth the Many wished to be feared and worshipped, and Their machinations in the church through the Blight in the reverend's mind would soon make that a reality. But Their immediate goal was to protect the device from potential harm. They had seen through the shadow tucked deep within Combs's cerebral cortex that he had first tried shutting his machine off, and had then cut the power entirely, leaving the house dark, as it was now. But when Combs had tried to strike it with a hammer, hoping to damage its inner workings, Geth had commanded the mechanical owl to attack him, still streaked with the feline's blood. Since then, Combs had cowered, pitying himself for the predicament he himself had put his pathetic town in.

Geth's pumpkin lips rose in a grin. With a renewed sense of optimism, They set off toward the house.

The sound grew louder as Geth approached Combs's garage. To Combs, the sound was nearly excruciating. He felt it in his fillings and crowns and it had even caused him to expel the contents of his stomach, though fortunately through the mouth rather than the rectum. Much as Geth enjoyed the various scents of death, They *loathed* the pungent stench of processed human waste. The body They occupied had voided its bowels sometime during the walk, and the smell was nauseating. Geth decided, once They had secured the premises surrounding the machine, They would clean Their human body and change into new *clothing* from Combs's wardrobe. The clothing likely wouldn't fit—Combs was tall and lean, while Zack Summerly was slightly shorter and muscular—but feeling a little discomfort around the biceps and shoulders would be favorable to reeking of filth.

Geth could, if They wanted, transpose Their essence into Combs himself, but two very important factors prevented the Many from doing so. One, it was preferrable that once Geth had chosen a Holy Name for Themself that They remained within the vessel in which the name had been chosen. Legends would soon be written about Them, and conflicts over Their appearance would not be beneficial to building a following. More importantly, They required the science teacher's consciousness to remain whole. Geth may have seeded the idea to him through Their Blight as to what the scientist should build—as the God of the Torah and the Bible and the Qur'an had instructed Noah to build his Ark—but it had been Combs himself who had planned how to build it and made it reality. With his head removed, very little of that information would remain of the man to be useful. And since his head would need to be severed—Geth would not repeat the mistake They had made occupying the shaman's body, leaving the head intact—transposing into him was not advisable.

At great last, Geth the Many stood at the foot of the driveway leading to Combs's garage. The mechanical door rattled audibly, the entire structure vibrating to the earth-rumbling sound of the machine.

They saw through the eyes of the toy which had killed the mewling animal that Combs had returned to the garage, weeping and sniffling and hugging his knees, the hammer held loose in one hand. If They spoke to Combs with Summerly's vocal cords, he would not hear Geth over the sound of the machine, which hummed to the tune of the voices of Those Who Came Before. Instead, They reached out to the *inhak* burrowed deep in his brain.

Open the door, Geth commanded, not with words but an image of Combs doing just that: wiping his snot-slicked nostrils, standing up with a pop of his knees, and walking to the mechanism to push the button. Geth had controlled the objects under the sway of its *inhak* similarly—aside from the complexities of their consciousness, humans and objects were not that different. But the shadow within Combs was weak from having spent too much time away from the Many. Geth could not summon it to move the man's body unbidden of Combs himself.

Regardless, Ernie Combs did as Geth made him see within his mind. He wiped his nose on the sleeve of his blazer, stood with a *pop-pop* of his knees—it was small added details like these that made Geth's will difficult for blighted mortals to reject, seeing them almost as they would instructions from their own cerebrum—and walked on shaky legs toward the garage door.

Combs paused there with his left arm outstretched toward the button on the—*door opener*—the index finger extended. He seemed to sense that something was not right, that he hadn't *intended* to get up and open the garage door, more that something had *compelled* him to do so. This feeling that he was being manipulated was something he'd experienced many times over the course of building the machine whose purpose he'd never known. There was a vague sense of *wrongness* to it all, of *alienness*. But it also felt as though what he was doing could not be ignored. He connected that feeling with God, even though he did not *truly* believe, or at the very least being attuned to what he thought of vaguely as The Universe. It made him feel as though what he was doing was not only right but *predestined*.

Shaking himself from his stupor, he pressed the button, and the door began making its ratcheting, jittery ascent.

The man's shoes were revealed as the door rose: brown leather, pointed and polished. Darryl Knell would have called them *corporate shoes*. His checkered pantlegs next, scuffed and dirty from the garage floor. He wore a blazer over his torso, and tugged at the sleeves one by one, brandishing the hammer as a weapon. He did not know what he expected to see once the door was fully opened. He certainly did not expect to see the body of a dead man adorned with the living head of a jack-o'-lantern. When the door opened far enough for Geth and the blighted scientist to look each other in the eye, Ernie Combs glanced to either side of Geth, as if he had expected someone else to be standing in his driveway.

"You're a little old for trick-or-treating, aren't you?" he asked.

Geth's grin widened, the Xs of its eyes narrowing.

Ernie Combs startled, but his thoughts were only that the costume the man before him wore was more realistic than he had expected, and that he smelled *like shit*.

"We require neither tricks nor treats, Ernie Combs," Geth said, stepping under the still-ascending door and into the garage.

"Excuse me!" Combs said irritably.

Geth the Many wheeled around, reaching out with Summerly's right hand and slapping it against the science teacher's forehead. Combs was stunned still, his mouth hanging open and his arms lax at his sides, unable to move as Geth fed the *inhak* nestled in his brain a portion of the *aminhas*, a small taste of Geth the Many. Soon, Ernie Combs would be a docile and manipulable Blighted, ever faithful, never disobeying: the very first initiate of Geth's One True Religion.

There were others, of course: *inhak* buried deep within the slowly atrophying brains of dead humans spread about town, doing Geth's bidding. But these were lesser beings. Without the *inhak*, they were as useless as the many totems and artifacts had been before Geth had used them as weapons in Their first strike against the people of this town, who would soon become Their future worshippers.

Satisfied They had completed the first step in Their holy mission, Geth the Many turned and pressed the button on the door opener, causing it to rattle and clang back down toward the asphalt, and with a single image projected over a radius of at least twenty miles, Geth summoned all of Their *inhak* home.

3

11:01 P.M.
Mr. and Mrs. Thompson's Farmhouse

Cody was first down the basement stairs, wincing with every step. No matter how softly he lowered his foot, the wood beneath it creaked and groaned under his weight. Each step made him more and more aware this was an incredibly stupid plan. But what choice did they have? Brittany was right, they couldn't stay here all night. They had their own people to take care of. The others would fare just as well without them.

"Don't lose your cool down there," Chet had told them, holding his rifle at the darkness through the doorway before they began their descent. But halfway down the stairs, after Chet had locked them in with whatever remained down there, that was exactly how Cody felt. Like Austin Powers in the lesser but still pretty funny sequel, Cody had lost his mojo the moment the first of the dead had grabbed Chet by the wrist a little over half an hour ago. Every instinct since then had been on autopilot. Like Brittany said, they were just reacting to what was happening to them. They'd run from the barn because the things attacked them. They'd crept back in because Tommy was missing, then fled again when they discovered he was dead. They'd hidden in the house because the adults were all here. Like he'd told Brittany, they needed to start living for themselves, and to do that they had to be brave once more and get out through that cellar door.

His eyes had yet to adjust to the deeper dark of the cellar, but aside from the creak of their footfalls he heard no other sound, and saw no movement. But the dead could easily be standing as still as statues, unmoving, waiting in the dark. They didn't need to breathe, after all.

"I don't see anything," Brittany whispered. She was a single stair behind Cody, and he felt her breath on the back of his neck, sending a shiver down his spine.

He didn't respond, aware that Brittany's voice had signaled their approach if the creaking stairs already hadn't. Finally, his right foot came down on hard, blessedly silent concrete. He planted his left foot beside it and, with the light from the open cellar door shining in, he was finally able to see his surroundings a little better, albeit in muted grays and silhouettes. Scanning the floor for the bodies of the ones he'd blasted with the shotgun, Cody saw nothing resembling a corpse.

Of course they're not there. They were already dead when I shot them. They musta just got right back up and left.

No one stood within ten or fifteen feet of him, either, at least not that he could see. There were shelves, open on both sides, and he could see objects placed on them, mostly jars and cans. This was the Thompsons's pantry and workshop, as well as another junk space in addition to the attic. He saw a cluttered workbench butted up against the wall to his left, littered with unused and likely broken Halloween items. Nothing else he could distinguish in the dim light.

Brittany stepped down beside him, and the two of them began to creep forward.

After two or three steps, Cody's foot came down on the shattered glass he'd heard earlier, squelching in something he'd at first imagined to be a pig fetus or some other disgusting thing in formaldehyde, like the jars in Mr. Combs's science class, but he quickly realized was likely some kind of preserve. A pickle, maybe. He let out a small sigh and kept moving, able to see enough moonlight shining on the bits of glass to avoid them. He pointed out the mess to Brittany, and she stepped around it, moving along quietly behind him.

They passed the first shelf. Cody peered around it and saw nothing but more shelves, small heaps of boxes and what looked like a trunk. A groan of wood from directly above them got his heart racing and he looked up, expecting to see a zombie clinging to the rafters, but realized it was likely someone moving around upstairs. Still staring into the shadows above him, his hip struck something hard and sharp, and he spun around in sudden terrified panic.

Brittany blinked at him. "You okay?" she asked quietly.

Cody nodded, feeling stupid and embarrassed. He stepped around the table—which was covered in various tools, small scraps of wood and a wooden gravestone that had split down the middle—and continued toward the short stairs leading out the back of the farmhouse.

"Where'd they all go?" he wondered aloud. As he spoke, his shoe caught in some sort of fabric and he stumbled forward. The fabric came with it, falling to the cement floor in a clump. Turning to see what he'd done, Cody came face to face with a dead man. Instinctually he shot a punch directly at the dead man's face. It struck a cold, flat surface, which split against his hand.

"Shit!" he hissed, drawing back his hand from the mirror. His own reflection, his face pallid and shadowy in the moonlight, reflected back at him in the cracked mirror.

"There's nothing down here," Brittany said.

"Don't jinx it."

She continued on ahead as Cody shook out his fist,

frowning at the mirror. Brittany was right, though. It did seem like there was nothing down here. Why had they all just been standing down here in the first place, and why did they suddenly up and leave? It was creepy, sure, but even more than that it was *strange*. They could have come up the stairs and tried to break down the door. They'd clearly broken into the cellar through the bulkhead, the split boards scattered on the floor and stairs beneath it proved that. Why hadn't they come any further? Why didn't they try to kill everyone in the farmhouse like poor dead Tommy Mingus had tried to kill Brittany?

These were things Cody felt he would likely never understand, so he followed Brittany to the stairs leading outside. The remains of the door thumped against the frame in a strong breeze, and a light snowfall drifted through the opening, melting on the steps below.

Brittany began climbing up in a crouch to avoid striking her head on the splintered door boards.

"Be careful," Cody said.

"I will." She stuck her head out and looked both ways. "Nothing," she said finally.

Cody turned back to survey the cellar. "This is weird."

"This is normal. *Before* was weird."

"True," Cody said, climbing the steps to meet her outside. "I just mean, where'd they all go? And why?"

Brittany huddled up inside the coat he'd loaned her, shivering. "When I ask questions like that, my dad tells me not to look a gift horse in the mouth."

"That's a dumb expression. What if it's got tooth decay? Or a bunch of Greek soldiers inside it?"

Brittany gave him a shrewd look.

"What?"

"You're just cleverer than I expected, that's all."

"Gee, thanks. The dumb jock knows stuff. Somebody get him a cookie."

Grinning slightly, Brittany shoved her hands in the pockets of his coat and started off toward the field. "It's like you said before. People have preconceived notions about who we are just because of what they *think* we are. But we're more than just what people see on the surface."

"Yeah," Cody said sullenly, trudging along behind her in the squelching muck until they reached the corn maze.

Brittany gently pushed through the corn at an angle, spreading the stalks with her hands, parting it like curtains. It fell back against itself and Cody followed her in, holding a forearm up in front of his face and hitting the dried stalks like a battering ram. It reminded him of the signature move "Brahma Brunt" did on the field, and for a brief moment he wondered what had happened with his soon-to-be-former friends.

"Take Cassandra," Brittany called back. He couldn't see her until they broke through into one of the paths Chet had cut through it for the maze. She followed it to the left. "Everyone just sees this sulky Goth girl who's into witchcraft and smoking under the Geromero Street bridge. But she takes care of her little sister and her grandma."

"Does she?"

"Her parents died in that car crash, remember?"

"That was her?"

"You didn't hear the stories in school?"

Cody sighed. "I try not to pay attention to rumors and whatnot."

"Well, it's true." Brittany pushed through on another diagonal to the next pathway, and Cody followed. "She was nine years old," Brittany said. "Taylor was four or five. And Jay, kids at school joke he'll probably go Columbine someday, or at least end up in the same asylum as his dad. They say all he does is drink Rockstar and play video games, that is when he's not beating off. But you saw what he did with those credits for our movie. He did that in *one night*. I'd say he's a pretty talented animator, wouldn't you?"

Cody remembered seeing his title in flames, shooting toward the screen over the shot of the Thompson farm. "Yeah, that was pretty amazing."

"You wouldn't expect he'd be an artist, would you?"

"Nope. What about LeSabre?"

Brittany gave him a dark look over her shoulder. "You don't want to know what people say about Walden. But did you know he's been running the projector at the Grand the past few years? The manager there must trust him pretty well to give him that responsibility. Still, I'm pretty sure he'll leave Crooks Corner the first chance he gets."

"What makes you say that?"

Brittany shrugged. "I can just tell. He's been writing scripts and sending them out to people in Hollywood."

"How would you know?"

"I saw him reading a rejection letter in class one day. But he's not giving up on it, and I bet you ten years from now, you'll see his name in the opening credits of some low-budget horror movie or something."

Cody hummed thoughtfully. They stepped through another row of corn into a wider space, where a heavy cross made of railway ties stood. He remembered from last year this was what the guy playing the scarecrow would be hanging from until someone got close, then he'd jump down from the pedestal and chase them back into the maze. He wasn't here now, making Cody wonder if he'd been one of the dead people in the basement earlier.

"Do me now," he said.

Brittany chuckled as they crossed the makeshift courtyard. "You? Well, your parents are physicists. But you're a jock. I figure, you probably didn't necessarily want to be on the football team. You're good at it, obviously, but when I see you out on the field, you don't have the same enthusiasm as the other guys."

"You've been watching me play?"

"Sometimes. If I've got nothing better to do."

Cody laughed and mimed pulling a stake out of his heart. Brittany smirked and pushed through another row. He followed.

"So I figure," she said, "you feel like you're caught between two worlds. Science on your parents' side, sports on the other. But I don't really see you wanting to do either for the rest of your life."

"How do you figure that?"

"Well, I heard you were offered football scholarships to at least two schools but I don't think you've accepted any of them, otherwise we'd already know about it."

"We being who? Your whisper network?"

"I'm not into all that, I just listen when people talk. Also, you're not currently enrolled in any science classes. If you wanted to work at the power plant, you'd need to at least take advanced physics."

"Jeez," Cody said. "You should be a detective. Is that your

plan for when you get out there? You know, in the big wide world?"

She shrugged. "I'm a student of human nature, that's all. And everyone has their own story, don't they? It's just that the story we tell ourselves might not be the same one we tell others."

Brittany's words reminded him of Hildebrand's lecture in class the other day, about oral tradition and cavemen painting on cave walls and how stories made people who they are, the stories they told themselves and the stories they told each other. "What's that supposed to mean?" he asked her.

"Well, I don't know if you've noticed the spirals—" Brittany turned to look at him over her shoulder, but her face suddenly contorted in wicked pain, and she fell right into his arms.

Startled, Cody held her a moment, basking in her warmth against his chilly arms and chest.

"Sorry," she said, stepping out of his embrace and straightening herself, her cheeks rosier than they'd been from the chill. "I just got hit with a wicked migraine."

"Oof. My mom gets those. She thinks it's from working at the nuclear plant."

Brittany rubbed her temples. "Yeah, these probably aren't the same as your mom's."

Cody considered asking if she had some sort of condition that made her draw those spirals she mentioned, like ADHD or something worse, but he decided it wouldn't be nice to pry. If she'd wanted to tell him, she would.

"You think they're okay?" he asked. "Cassandra and them?"

"I don't know. I *want* them to be okay. I think what happened before, that's over now."

Cody nodded. "It does feel that way, doesn't it? Like blitzing."

"Blitzing?"

"You know, when the defense line rushes the quarterback before he can pass, trying to make him fumble."

"That sounds sort of like an opening salvo in debate class," Brittany said, letting her hands fall from her temples. "You fiercely attack your opponent's position, getting them off kilter before they can respond."

"Yeah, that sounds about right. That attack, it was fast and fierce, and then it just kind of ended, didn't it?" As he said it, they stepped out on the other side of the corn maze, between the field and the dark forest where the cult was supposed to be.

"You're right. That's exactly what happened." Brittany gestured toward the trees. "This way," she said.

Cody peered into the darkness. "You're kidding."

"Believe me, I wish I was. If there was an easier way, I'd suggest it. Going in there is the last thing I want to do."

Cody studied her face, and knew from the fear in her eyes as she looked into the dark woods that she was telling the truth. He peered into the darkness himself, the swish and sway of the cornfield behind them and the trees ahead the only sound.

Finally, he said, "I guess we're walking through the woods in the middle of the night with no flashlights, then, huh?"

CHAPTER 16

1

Renny swerved his big red truck nto Browning Street at just past eleven P.M. They'd sat a moment with Stafford, the theater owner, drinking his scotch and listening to him prattle on about how it was high time for him to step down and hand over the reins to one of his "protégés," as he called them. Renny knew that Walden LeSabre was likely the leading candidate for the job, since he'd been running the projector for some time now, as Renny usually swung by to see a movie at least once a week. They often showed older films on weekdays and newer stuff from Friday to Sunday. He'd seen *The 400 Blows* there, Bergman's *The Seventh Seal*, even a few Buñuel films. It'd be nice to know the theater was being placed into good hands, rather than sold off to some developer to turn into a gas station or one of those hip coffee shops that seemed to be popping up all over the place. Walden genuinely loved movies. They'd spoken about screenwriting on the handful of occasions they'd seen each other at the theater, and occasionally after class. They'd even commiserated over their lack of visual imagination, which made it difficult for them to picture things as they were writing, and had caused Renny to forgo screenwriting in school in favor of directing and producing, and eventually fall into teaching. Walden had continued writing despite his inability to imagine things visually, and apparently had several screenplays under his belt, at the age of seventeen. If anyone was a shoe-in to run the theater after Stafford retired, it was him.

If he survived, Renny thought darkly. Walden's group was meant to be shooting their project at Halloween Village tonight. If things out there had gone as badly as they had at the theater, it was highly likely *none* of them had survived, a thought that gave Renny a sinking feeling in the pit of his stomach.

He rarely got close to his students, and generally got the feeling that most of them only took his class because they thought it would be an easy A—*a bird course*, as they called it, which of course made Renny think of the birds that had attacked them in the theater. The kids this semester, though, especially the ones in Walden's group—he had a feeling they were going to do something big, not even necessarily in the movie business. Each of them was extremely bright and creative in different ways. If they survived, he hoped it would make them stronger and more resilient rather than fearful and cautious, better able to handle anything the adult world might throw in their path.

As for cautious, Elana's idea of driving carefully was definitely a lot more squirrelly than Renny's as she drove them from the theater to Ernie Combs's house. He would've driven himself if his right hand wasn't out of commission, though considering Elana hadn't driven stick before a few months ago, they were probably doing a decent job together as they swerved onto Browning.

"Well, that wasn't anxiety-inducing at all," he said, unbuckling his seatbelt.

"It could've been worse," Elana replied.

"True. We could've been chased by those *things*."

They'd seen plenty of people shambling in the road and sidewalks, but not a single inanimate object come to life as they drove the six blocks east and two blocks south to Browning Street. The majority of them were injured and bleeding, adults and children walking in a daze like the people he'd seen in news footage from 9/11, covered in blood rather than toxic dust, all apparently in the same direction Renny and Elana were heading. There must've been twenty or thirty of them moving at that odd, languid pace toward... *wherever*.

Elana had wanted to stop and help the first person, but Renny had insisted they keep driving to shut off that machine as soon as they could. After a few blocks further, seeing the extent to which these people were injured and how many of them there were, she agreed.

In addition to what he'd started to call the "ramblers," after the Allman Brothers song, there'd been plenty of junk in the street Elana had needed to swerve to avoid, as well as on sidewalks and lawns: from Halloween treats scattered around discarded buckets, bags and pillow cases, to dozens of smashed pumpkins and various costume pieces, like plastic pirate hooks and fake weapons and sheets with holes cut out for eyes. Strangely, there wasn't a single dead body anywhere.

"That's his house," Elana said, pointing down the street. "The one with all the lights out."

It was the only house on the street that wasn't lit, and even above the rumble of his truck Renny could hear the hum of the machine Combs and Elana had made together. Renny was struck with a sudden bad feeling and squeezed Elana's thigh as she attempted to step on the gas. She turned with that questioning look of hers, and he shook his head.

"Let's get out here," he said.

"What's wrong?"

A little girl wearing a red rain slicker shambled by his window on the sidewalk, her nose ruined and dripping blood. She reminded him of the dwarf at the end of *Don't Look Now*, a reveal that had always creeped him out. Up ahead, he saw two more ramblers, both adults, crossing Ernie Combs's lawn toward the garage.

"The poor girl," Elana said.

Renny pitied the girl, but he wasn't sure she felt anything. His idea that they looked like zombies had come to feel more accurate the more of them they'd passed. And if they *were* zombies, it would be wise to avoid them, whether they ate flesh or not. "Is there a back way in?" he asked.

Elana considered it, unbuckling herself. "We could climb get in from the alley, I suppose."

"Okay." Renny made to open his door, but he remembered the hand he'd usually use to open it was the injured one. He reached over with the left and awkwardly pulled at the handle.

"You okay?"

"I'll be fine." On the third try he managed to push it open. The door swung out and hit a man shambling by on the sidewalk, dressed in what looked like a homemade Austin Powers costume. "Sorry," Renny said instinctually, before realizing it was another rambler and immediately regretting the apology. He glanced at Elana, who cringed, freezing with a hand on her door handle.

The man's dislocated arm dangled limp at his side. When the door hit him, he'd veered slightly from his path and reeled around to face the door, revealing a portion of brain and skull that peeked through a hole caved into his forehead, blood and gore covering his face and lace cravat. His dazed eyes stared right past Renny as if he didn't see him. Renny remained in the truck, anxiously preparing for the man to attack. After a long moment the International Dead Man of Mystery righted himself, turned back to the house, and continued shuffling onward.

"They're gone, aren't they?" Elana asked.

"Dead? I think so. Whatever was controlling everything back at the theater must be doing the same to them. Leading them right to Ernie's house, for some reason."

"Like they're just another inanimate object."

Renny looked after the man, who'd reached the little girl on the lawn and headed up to meet with the others. "That's a really disturbing thought," he said with a shudder. Even after death there was no reprieve from whatever had infiltrated their sleepy little town. Now it seemed to be calling them to the machine, like a homing beacon. For what purpose, if there was any, Renny couldn't imagine.

He peered down the length of the truck to be sure the sidewalk was clear before stepping out and shutting the door quietly. Elana did the same on her side. They met around the back.

"This way," she said, heading off toward the intersection.

In moments they were hurrying as quietly as they could down the narrow alley, their shadows thrown long from the streetlamps above: ahead of them, behind them, ahead, behind. Finally, Elana stopped before a low chainlink fence with brambly bushes pressed densely against it on the opposite side. Twigs with dried leaves hung from a trellis near the gate, the plant itself long dead. Broken walkway stones led through shin-high grass to the white siding of the back porch extension. A rusty push mower with a grayed wood handle stood in the middle, forgotten for who knew how long.

"Not much of a gardener, huh?"

"I don't think it's high on his list of priorities." Elana reached over and unlatched the gate. It swung wide and squeaky into the yard on rusty hinges, and she stepped through. Renny followed her. She closed the gate behind them.

"What do we do if he's..." Renny stopped short of saying *dead*. "...you know?" he said instead.

"He gave me a spare key."

This was a revelation to Renny, although he supposed it shouldn't have been. Elana and Ernie had been work colleagues longer than she and Renny had known each other, whether or not this machine or theirs had been their first collaboration.

They ambled up the broken walkway to the back of the house, and Elana knocked on the painted-flecked wooden door. They waited ten, fifteen seconds before she knocked again, not much louder than the first time.

"We should give him a minute," she said.

Renny leaned past her and beat on the door with his left hand. "He probably can't hear us because of that damn machine."

Nearly a minute passed, and Renny was about to pound on the door again when they heard Ernie mutter gruffly from within. "Who is it?" he called behind the door.

"It's me," Elana said.

She's a "me," is she? Renny thought, vaguely jealous.

"Elana," she added, with a sidelong glance at Renny.

The latches and locks clicked and clattered. A moment later, the door opened partway and Ernie Combs peered out suspiciously above a chain lock. "What is it?"

"You're not supposed to turn on the Harmonizer without me being at Beta site. You know that. We have protocols for a reason, Ernie."

Ernie stared blankly at her for a moment. It seemed Renny could see the gears turning behind his eyes. "Yes, that's right. I'm sorry, I know I shouldn't have, but after last night with the electrical short, I just couldn't leave it for another night. And you had your plans," he said, with what could have been a slight sneer or facial tic in Renny's direction. "I'm sorry."

"There's no point to the experiments without the observers present at Theta."

"I'm sorry, but sorry's just not gonna cut it," Renny said over her. Elana shot him a glare, but he pressed on anyway. "Have you seen what's going on out there? People are *dying*, Combs. You've got a goddamn zombie hootenanny in your front yard!"

"He's right," Elana said, and Renny was glad for the backup. "You have to turn that machine off right now. Before more people get hurt. What it's doing is not what we designed it for."

"Isn't it? We wanted observable phenomena of a state of matter *beyond* what we can see. Is that not what we got?"

"What we got is *death*, Ernie! Lots and lots of *death*! We have to shut the machine off, *right now*."

He blinked behind his round glasses. "I can't."

"Why the hell not?" Renny snapped.

Ernie turned his dark eyes toward him. *Am I wrong or have they gotten darker?* Renny wondered. *Must be the lack of light.*

"*Because*," the man said, "I've tried. I even shut off the power to the house. But *it's still running*. Don't you see?" he said, turning back to Elana. "It's *autonomous* and *self-perpetuating*."

Elana huffed. "That's not possible."

Renny couldn't help but laugh. Everything they'd experienced tonight was impossible, but Elana quibbled about a machine that wouldn't allow itself to be turned off.

"Come inside and see for yourselves, if you don't believe me." Ernie unlatched the chain lock and opened the door wide, flashing a smile that made Renny nervous. Like the feeling he'd gotten when they first arrived on Browning Street, he knew something wasn't right here but couldn't put his finger on it.

Before he could say anything, Elana stepped through the doorway. He spoke her name, and she turned back to him in the darkened vestibule. *No, it's definitely not just the dark*, Renny thought, noting Elana's eyes remained the same color they always were. *Something's wrong with Combs. Maybe it's something to do with the Machine.*

As if to prove it, a dribble of blood spilled from Ernie's right nostril.

"You're bleeding," Renny said.

Ernie Combs blinked, as if the statement didn't quite compute. Elana reached into one of her coat pockets and brought out one of many folded tissues she kept in there, especially during the winter, and daubed away the blood on Ernie's philtrum.

"Thank you, Elana," Combs said, taking the soiled tissue from her and pressing it to the nostril. "Perhaps I've stood too long and too close to my Machine while it's been running. I have been feeling a bit of a headache. Would you like a cup of tea, Renny?"

"We really just want to shut off the machine. Right, Elana?"

Elana turned from giving Combs a concerned look and nodded. "Right, mm-hmm," she said.

"Well, I really wish I could help you. As I said, I tried turning it off and even went so far as to shut off the power entirely. Next thing you'll ask me to do is shut off the grid itself."

"Then we need to gut it," Renny said, holding the science teacher's gaze. "That, or smash it."

Ernie shook his head, blinking rapidly. "Oh, no-no-no-no, that just won't do. We mustn't *destroy* it. It could be the single most important innovation since nuclear fusion!"

"People are dying out there," Renny said.

"For a breakthrough of this significance, I'd consider that a very minor inconvenience."

Elana gave him a look of disappointment. "You don't mean that, Ernie. What's gotten into you?"

"What has *gotten in* to me? Nothing! It's *you* who doesn't seem to grasp the magnitude of what we've created, Elana. We've proven the existence of life beyond what anyone has ever imagined! Our Machine has *communed with God*!"

"God?" Renny said, incredulous. He'd always thought the man was a bit loopy, but now he really had lost his mind. "Look what God did to my hand! God doesn't make Halloween decorations kill people, Combs! God doesn't kill people and bring them back to life!"

"You doubt me," Combs snapped, literal spit flying from his lips. "Come! See for yourself, then!"

Combs grabbed him by the shoulders of his coat. Renny swatted the hands away angrily with his uninjured left.

"Renny..." Elana said, pleading.

"He's *insane*, Elana. Absolutely nutso!"

Combs's dark eyes widened, and his lips stretched into a wide, toothy smile. "Come and *seeeeee*..." he hissed.

. . .

2

GETH THE GREAT Pumpkin stood behind the inner door from the garage to the house, listening in on the conversation through the eyes and ears of the Blighted Ernie Combs.

Geth wanted to kill the intruders outright—They sensed the communications teacher meant to do the Machine harm, and possibly Ernie Combs himself—to send one of the shadowed dead to murder them, but it quickly became clear the woman was Combs's colleague, who knew almost as much about the Machine as Ernie himself. This would come in handy if Ernie Combs became compromised, if the Blight corrupted his mind, as it sometimes did. It would be good to keep Elana Stabler as a stand-in, close at hand. Conversely, Renny Hildebrand was of no use to Geth. His mind was empty, a void as black as the *Upask*. Unfortunately, They could not kill him without harming Elana. Neither could They blight her. The communications teacher was suspicious enough of Ernie Combs, whom he barely knew. If Geth seeded her mind with a blighted *inhak*, she could become unstable and erratic, as Ernie Combs appeared to be now. It was easy enough to control a Blighted's actions, but more difficult to direct their speech, particularly in conversation: a consequence, Geth suspected, of communicating in pictures rather than words. The languages of this people were far more expansive and nuanced than that of Those Who Came Before, and Geth still had much to learn than the Tee-Vee and Darryl Knell's limited vocabulary had taught it.

Regardless, it was evident Ernie Combs was losing control. Geth needed to steer him physically away from the altercation if They could not remove him from it verbally.

They made Combs reach out and begin to push the door closed. The communications teacher gave Combs a look of disbelief which quickly became anger. He stuck his foot in between the door and the jamb, preventing it from closing.

"Oh no you're not," Hildebrand said, pushing back on the door.

This was quickly becoming a disaster. The interactions of these modern humans were so needlessly complex and melodramatic, with their hidden agendas and emotions. Soon the communications teacher would be pushing Combs out of the way and stomping down the hall toward the garage, toward the Machine, toward Geth the Many. And then They would be forced to kill him in front of Elana Stabler, and she would need to be blighted, and that was not ideal.

Geth made Combs let go of the door, and it swung back swiftly, nearly striking Elana, who stepped out of the way. Then They spun Combs around on his heels, planting the image and sound of his teapot whistling on the stovetop. "I'll make us some tea then," Combs said, stepping into the darkened hall.

"We don't want *tea*, Combs."

"Please, let's have a civil discussion about this. I'm certain we can come to some sort of agreement about what must be done." Combs entered the dark kitchen. He poured water into the kettle, placed it on the burner and turned it on with a tick of the ignition and a hiss of gas.

"I *could* use some warming up," Elana said from the hall. Geth could no longer see them through Combs's eyes, but They could hear Elana and Hildebrand well enough through his ears.

"*Elana*," Hildebrand said in a tone of warning.

"I can *convince* him," Geth heard her whisper. "Just have some tea. Please?"

Combs stooped to retrieve the cleaning powder from under the sink (an image of children in army-green uniforms trudging through the woods and singing grotesquely arose in Combs's mind: *It makes your lips turn GREEN! It tastes like GAS-O-LEEN!*), and he poured a dash into one of three mugs he'd placed on the counter. He plopped a tea bag into each cup, covering the cleaning powder just as Elana and Hildebrand entered the kitchen.

"It won't be a moment," Geth said through Combs's vocal cords, turning to face them with what felt like an uncomfortably wide grin, which it quickly flattened. "Please, sit."

Elana sat at the small round table. Hildebrand remained standing. "*Renny,*" she said, in a similar tone to how he'd spoken her name earlier, though slightly more musically. Hildebrand pulled out a chair and plopped himself down in it with an aggrieved huff.

"So, tell me about this Machine of yours, Combs," he said, giving Elana a pointed look. "You say it can communicate with God? That's pretty impressive."

Combs chuckled softly. "Perhaps I was a little... *overzealous.* What I meant was *the God particle.* The Higgs boson," Geth said through Combs's lips, reaching back to an image of words in a book the man had read almost a decade earlier. "It's a particle physics term. Likely wouldn't interest a layman such as yourself."

"Hmm," Hildebrand said skeptically.

"We've never spoken about quantum excitation before," Elana said. "Our experiment was supposed to be replicating what we saw at the Stones, using the Harmonic Wave Generator and the Resonator."

None of this talk made any logical sense to Geth. They had merely implanted the ideas of resonation into Combs's mind— of tuning with the Watching Stones the way the shaman had with his magic dust and peculiar bone whistle, using the resonance of the Stones to seal Them within the *Upask*—and let Combs's imagination run wild with it.

The kettle started to whistle.

"Yes, well, it's... um, hypothesized that since the Higgs field exists throughout the universe it must interact with dark energy, and could perhaps even be responsible for its mass."

Geth did not know if any of this made literal sense. They had merely taken bits of scientific gobbledygook from Combs's cerebellum and mashed them together, hoping it would appease them. Hildebrand appeared to be absolutely baffled. Elana, however, seemed to be deep in thought.

Geth made Combs pour the tea. He crossed to the table with two steaming mugs, placing one in front of Elana and the tainted mug in front of Hildebrand. Elana picked hers up and blew on it. Combs returned to the counter, picked up his own mug and sipped from it. He hissed in pain. *"Sraki! Hounds of the moon!"* he shouted, placing the mug back on the Formica countertop.

"What was that?" Hildebrand asked, raising an eyebrow at Elana.

"What was what?" Combs said.

"'Hounds of the moon,'" the communications teacher repeated. "Never heard that one before."

"Oh!" In Geth's surprise at being scalded, They had blurted the first thing that had come to mind. "It's a, um... an ancient shamanic curse."

Renny raised an eyebrow. "Is that right?"

"Yes. Now, about the Machine. We can certainly discuss options of—you haven't had any of your tea, Hildebrand, I mean Renny."

Hildebrand stared him down. "I'm not thirsty."

"But I made if specifically—" Geth realized They wouldn't be able to convince him to drink it. It poured Combs's tea down the sink. "Very well. How's your tea, Elana?"

She sipped it. "It's good."

"Wonderful. Now, about the—"

The roar of an engine out in the street startled Geth. They reached out to the *inhak* converging around the house and saw that one of them had drawn a cherry-red car from the auto yard into the driveway. Geth compelled it to back up and park in the street.

"Someone else is alive out there," Elana said, giving Hildebrand a hopeful look.

Hildebrand stood suddenly, the chair legs squeaking on the floor. "Look, I appreciate your hospitality, Combs, but I'm gonna go see what I can do about that machine of yours—"

"*NO!*" Geth's frustration propelled both through Combs's mouth and that of Their *chuann*

Hildebrand turned to the garage door, behind which Geth stood, wearing the Summerly body.

"Who's in there?"

"Nobody," Combs said. "It was just an echo."

"An *echo*?" Hildbrand threw up his hands. "That's it," he said, and began stomping toward the back hall.

Geth made Combs run at him, head bowed.

"Honey!" Elana cried.

Hildebrand whipped around a moment before Combs could tackle him and threw an awkward punch with his left hand. Geth noticed too late to make the man move out of its way, and Combs's own instincts were slowed by the Blight. The fist struck him directly on the forehead and Geth's sight through Combs's eyes went black like when They had turned off the Tee-Vee in the Summerly vessel's living room.

3

"OH MY GOD, Renny! You *hit* him!"

Renny's heart thrummed in his chest. He hadn't hit a man since college, and even then he'd been given no other choice. He'd never started a fight in his life. Had never wanted to. He wasn't a violent man. "He was coming at me, Elana," he said, feeling embarrassed at his own anger. "What else could I do?"

They both stood looking down at Combs, unconscious on the floor between them.

"What are we going to do now?" Elana asked.

"I'm going to stop that goddamn machine is what I'm gonna do. You keep an eye on him. If he wakes up, hold him here."

"*Hold* him?"

"Just do it, Elana."

Once again, Elana closed her mouth audibly, shocked by his behavior. Renny didn't raise his voice at her, and Renny didn't hit people, and he realized he'd been acting very *un*-Renny tonight. But people reacted differently under stressful situations. And although he loved Elana more than anyone he'd ever loved in his life, she'd lied to him about what she'd been doing with Combs. If she'd told him the truth from the start, he might've been able to convince her to think twice about what they were doing. He might've prevented this from ever happening.

Could've, would've, should've. No use lamenting over things that might've been. Besides, it seems like Combs himself wasn't exactly being forthright with her about what they were doing together, either. Didn't even sound like Combs himself knew what he was doing, to be honest.

Renny gave Elana an apologetic look as she knelt beside Combs. "I'm sorry," he said. "I'll be right back. We'll make this right."

She nodded. "Okay, Renny."

It was only as he turned his back on her that he realized she'd called him "honey" just a moment ago when she was trying to warn him about Combs, right in front of their work colleague. Combs likely wouldn't remember it, not in his current mental state. Still, it would've been a milestone for their relationship, if he hadn't just blown it by punching out her closest friend.

Renny headed toward the garage, the hallway growing darker the further he treaded, the hum so loud he felt it begin to churn his guts. He reached for the door handle awkwardly with his left hand. Before he could grasp it, the door exploded inward. He quickly turned and hugged the wall, shouting for Elana to duck. Splintered wood and veneer battered him, slashing his face and neck. The door handle whizzed past him and hit the clock above Combs's rolltop desk with a resounding clang. The clock fell off the wall, slid down the rolltop with a sound like someone playing a washboard, and crashed to the floor a few feet behind where Elana crouched with Combs.

Scratched to hell and breathing heavily, Renny turned back to face the garage. What he saw caused his heart to leap into his throat, the way it felt plummeting down a steep drop in a roller-coaster.

In the garage doorway stood a man wearing a jack-o'-lantern over his head, the upper half of his clothing and hands covered in what looked like red deck stain or dried blood. The thrum of the machine throbbed behind him, making the pumpkin man and the walls around him seem to quiver and pulse to its strange beat.

The jack-o'-lantern's crooked stitched grin widened like a practical effect from an old horror movie, and fire blazed in the Xs of its eyes from the single candle planted in the bloody neck stump of what was clearly meant to be a cadaver. Even if it was just an incredible practical effect—*It has to be*, Renny thought— the face hidden behind the stump itself would've literally been on fire.

The thing with the pumpkin head flicked its red right hand toward Renny, and with that same rollercoaster feeling Renny's feet lifted off the floor. Then he was hurtling backward, and landed hard at Combs's feet with a heavy thud, jarring his injured hand and shooting a stab of pain up his spine.

It's real! he thought frantically, catching Elana's frightened gaze. *Whatever it is, that thing is not human, and it'll kill us if we don't get out of this house right now.*

As Renny got up on his hands and knees to face the intruder, the sound of shattered glass came from every direction at once, and deeper shadows began fluttering into the darkened house from outside.

CHAPTER 17

1

11:11 P.M.
The Woods

Brittany and Cody trudged through the forest, stepping over felled trees and pushing through low branches. The sky had cleared enough that the moon shone through mostly barren branches, making it easier to see than if it had been full dark.

Cody found the first of the cultist's stick faces by accident, literally walking into it, where it hung from a low branch. It scratched his face and he called out in surprise, pulling it down from the branch to examine it. The two of them studied it in the moonlight, a circle of intertwined twigs like a small wreath, with Xs for eyes and a stitched smile made of thicker twigs. It was just like the graffiti they'd seen all over town, and just like the one Brittany's brother Bradley had brought home from a hunt for her to see a little while back. Looking at it in the daylight in the comfort of her own home had been disturbing enough. Finding one in the woods in the dead of night was practically bone-chilling. Cody tossed it into a dark copse and they continued on their way.

After a while, they reached a place where the hum of electricity filled the air. Ahead of them stood what was apparently the source: a small, squat shadow, maybe fifteen feet square. Not a hunting blind or a cabin. It was a metal building with a flat roof, sitting in the middle of the woods.

"What is that?" Cody said, a few paces behind her.

"Some kind of electrical shed maybe?" Brittany suggested.

"Maybe," Cody agreed. "It's making my teeth hurt."

Brittany nodded. "Mine, too. Let's go."

Can you feel it? The Snake whispered as they continued onward. *We gettin close.*

Close? My house isn't anywhere near here.

Not your house. To where we met. You 'member that, don't ya?

Of course, Brittany remembered. How could she forget the single most traumatic and significant experience in her whole life before what happened tonight? Now that she thought of it, the entrance, or the place she'd fallen into it, was likely somewhere nearby.

The cave... she thought, and a sudden chill made her shudder as the familiar spirals uncoiled in her mind, her thoughts returning to what happened that day.

2

November 24th, 1998
The Woods

IT HAPPENED three falls ago but Brittany remembered it more clearly than anything else in her life. It hadn't been too cold for late November, around fifty-four degrees and cloudless. Leaves in browns, yellows and reds fell in the sunshine through the canopy, already a crunchy carpet on the ground. Her brother, Brad, had been stalking up ahead. This was the first and last time they'd gone hunting together. Dad had wanted him to teach her to shoot. He said it was important, living out in the country, to learn how to "protect the homestead," which sounded funny coming out of the mouth of Crooks Corner's richest car dealer. But they had horses and her toy poodle Bella, who'd been just a puppy at the time, so being able to keep the coyotes away was an actual necessity.

They'd been on their way to the blind Brad and her dad used for duck hunting, near a marshy pond where the three property lines were a little uncertain. The Garners' hundred acres bordered on the Thompson farm and Tony Ellison's, yet the only one of them with any sort of fence delineating their land from the others was Ellison. Out this far in the middle seemed to be neutral ground, fair game for any of them to use, although Brad and Gary Garner seemed to be the only ones who came out here with any regularity. Technically, this part of the woods was state land.

The shed—the dark, squat shadow with its eerie and ominous hum, growing louder by the second—hadn't been here the crisp, sunny day she and her brother traversed this part of the woods near the end of duck season. They hadn't yet reached the blind and Brittany had been looking up, watching the leaves fall in the sunshine, when the ground beneath her suddenly swallowed her whole.

She fell into a dark, cool cavern and twisted her right ankle upon impact with the ground, causing her to scream in pain.

Brad rushed to the edge of the hole she'd fallen through, about ten feet above her. "Brit?" he called. He squinted into the dark, a sliver of sun shining through his blond hair, falling through the opening along with a scattering of rocks and dirt that landed around her.

"Be careful!" she snapped. "You're kicking stuff down at me!"

"Sorry," he said, looking genuinely apologetic. "Shit, what the hell'd you fall into? Some kind of cave?"

Brittany had been more concerned with the pain in her ankle than where she'd landed until that moment. If she'd broken it, she'd be out of dance and gymnastics for a while. If it was bad, maybe forever. She glanced around herself anxiously. There could have been all kinds of creatures down there. Spiders. Bats. Snakes. It smelled funky, worse than the stables when one of the horses got sick. It was dark, and damp and her shout at her brother had echoed far off to her immediate right.

"No, it's an Easy-Bake Oven. Of course it's a *cave*, Bradley. You're gonna have to come down here and get me. I think maybe I broke my ankle."

Brad ran his hands through his hair. "Oh, jeez. Mom's gonna have a conniption. And Dad's gonna *kill* me."

"And if I die before you get me out of here, Sheriff Nance will throw you in jail."

Brad peered down over the edge again, causing a landslide of dirt and leaves to rain down around her. Brittany let go of her ankle to protect her head.

"Dammit, Brad!"

"*Sorry*, okay?"

"Just... I dunno... find a thick branch or something and haul me up. It's gross down here. It stinks."

"Shit, yeah." He left the hole and started looking around. For a short time she heard him trudging in the crunchy leaves. After a while she didn't hear anything, and began to worry he'd left her to die down here.

"*Bradley?*" she called.

"I'm here!" he shouted back, some distance away.

"Don't leave me down here!"

"I won't. I'm looking for a branch—*yes!* Found something! Gimme a sec."

A moment later she heard him trudge toward the hole, dragging a heavy branch behind him through the crackling leaves. His hopeful face appeared in the bright, jagged circle of light above her. "Can you move out of the way a bit?"

Brittany glanced back into the darkness of the cave. The walls were clearer to her now that her eyes had adjusted slightly to the dark. It looked like she'd be fine to move back a little, so she carefully dragged herself, holding up her injured foot, a few feet further from the opening.

"Okay, you can send it down now!" she said, trying not to sound as frightened as she felt.

Getting the branch through the hole caused a lot more rocks and dirt to tumble in, with how crooked it appeared to be and the angle at which it needed to be lowered. Finally, after a couple of minutes of wrangling, Brad managed to get the thing down to about two feet from the floor of the cave.

A howl of wind from the dark rustled Brittany's hair, sending a shiver down her spine, despite the air being strangely warm. She crab-walked as quickly as her injured foot allowed her, eager to get the hell out of there as soon as possible. Something about the wind from deeper with the cave made her think of dragon's breath. Or worse, something actually *real*, like a bear whose hibernation she'd disturbed.

Carefully, Brittany got to her feet, holding the wall to keep herself steady. With almost a decade of gymnastics and dance under her belt she had no trouble standing on one foot for a long period, but trying to balance on the bumpy cave floor and hug the tree branch at the same time, while being in constant throbbing pain, became a little taxing. Brad grunted as her weight on the branch pulled him down to his knees.

"Okay, I got it," she called up.

"Yeah, no shit. Gimme a second to figure this out."

At first Brad tried just lifting her. Then he tried leaning on the thicker end of the branch and lifting her like when they were little kids on the seesaw, only she was heavier now, the hole was too small and the cave too narrow. He pushed and pulled and did a lot of grunting, and Brittany lost her grip a handful of times, further hurting her ankle, until eventually the two of them decided it was impossible to get her out using the branch, and that Brad would have to leave her to go get some rope or a ladder or something.

"Wait!" Brittany said as he was about to head off. "How will you find me again? It's not like there's signs."

Brad grinned, seemingly prepared for this exact question. He reached into one of the pockets in his orange vest and held out a roll of bright yellow tape. "Like Dad says: always be prepared."

"Good." Glancing into the dark of the cave, another shiver passed through her. "Can you at least get me my gun? If there's bears down here, I don't want to get eaten."

"It's a rifle. And if there is a bear down there, you probably just wanna turtle up and play dead. Shooting it's just gonna piss it off."

"I'd still feel more comfortable if I had it."

Brad shrugged. "Fair." He left the hole for a moment, then returned with the rifle, holding it by the barrel and lowering it as far as he could reach. Brittany grabbed the stock and hugged it to her chest, hopping on her good foot.

"Don't be too long, okay? It's creepy down here."

"I won't. Might see what Renata's whipped up for lunch, though."

"You better not!"

Again, he grinned. "I'm kidding. We're gonna get you out of there, Brit," he said, then nodded, sealing the promise. In the next moment, he disappeared from sight.

Brittany laid the rifle down and sat beside it in the ragged circle of dirt lit by the sun, which was by now almost directly overhead aside from its low autumn angle. The air was much chillier down here than up on the surface. She worried if her brother didn't return soon she'd get so cold even a long hot bath wouldn't warm her up. Still, she had a few things to nibble on and a bottle of water in her pack. She also had her Discman and a mixed CD she'd made if she got too bored of sitting here worrying about whether or not Bradley would actually return, although she doubted it would be smart to put her headphones in this close to the dark cavern, from which another warm blast of air tickled her ears and rustled her hair. Brad had already told her she shouldn't be using it when they got to the blind, because it was important to always be aware of their surroundings. That included having her ears free to listen for danger.

She wished she'd thought to bring a flashlight, but it had been nine in the morning when they'd left the house and they hadn't planned to be out much past two or three, whether she managed to shoot a duck or not. Brad was very particular about not being out in the woods after dark. For one thing, he said Mr. Ellison grew pot somewhere on his property and the last thing they wanted was to get lost in one of his fields and mistaken for a thief. For another, the woods got pretty dense in some places, making it easy to get turned around. One or two false steps and someone could get lost out here and end up having to spend the night trying to build a campfire with twigs and stones, drinking rainwater from the few leaves that remained on the trees.

"'Always be prepared,'" she scoffed, mimicking her brother's words. Speaking aloud made her realize how alone she actually was down here. It would take at least half an hour for Brad to get back to the house, maybe longer to get back depending on what he brought with him—rope or ladder—and whether or not he could manage to follow his own trail markers.

Another howl of warm air made her hair stand on end. She grabbed the rifle and aimed it into the dark. "Is someone there?" Her echo was the only reply. "*HELLO?*"

It sounded like it went really far into the darkness. Hundreds of feet, maybe. How had it been here so long and they'd only just found it now, by accident?

Maybe it's an old mineshaft, she thought. The walls were pretty smooth, almost as if they'd been channeled underground, although there didn't appear to be any of the wooden braces to prevent the walls from caving in. Realizing this made her imagine giant ants or a massive snake, ten- or fifteen-feet tall, digging out this cave for its home. The thought made her shudder.

Yessssss, a voice hissed in her ear.

"What was that?" she yelped, whipping her head back and forth, the rifle clattering in her hands as she moved it with the motion of her head.

When no further sound arose for over a minute on her wristwatch, she allowed herself to calm, thinking the voice in her ear had probably just been her imagination, making the howl of the wind *sound* like it. She kept the gun in her lap, not aimed anywhere, just close at hand. Despite being alone, the feeling she was being watched was still pervasive.

You ARE bein watched, the voice said.

Brittany scrambled to her feet, momentarily forgetting her injured ankle until splinters of agony shot up her calf. She moaned in pain, whipping around on one foot, swinging the rifle wildly. "Who's there?"

Easy, girl, eeeeeasy, the voice said. It was deep and gravelly, yet oddly soothing. Like how a cowboy might speak when trying to tame a wild stallion. It had a slight accent, she couldn't tell what exactly, but somewhere to the south. A twinge of Appalachia, maybe.

We gotta get you outta here, toot sweet. It's gonna hurt like a bitch, but b'lieve me, you do not want to be out here once that sun goes down.

"Who are you?" she said, still hopping around on her good foot. "*Where* are you?"

That was the first time she saw the dark spiral uncoil, a shiny black snake slightly lit from a distance, so that only its shape and a smattering of scales could be seen. She screamed at the sudden invasion, at the sensation of slithering within her own mind, and fell back against the wall, dropping the rifle on the cave floor.

That's it. You c'n just call me The Snake, that's fine by me.

"*What...? What...?*" She repeated the word several times, unable to comprehend how the voice had come from inside of her own head, how it had infected her like a brain virus.

This'll be a lot easier if you jest calm yerself and play along. I c'n get you outta that hole. But like I said, it's gon hurt.

Okay, she thought, thinking over the voice. *Okay, get ahold of yourself, Brit. You're just scared, that's all. Or maybe a bit of broken bone got into your bloodstream and you're losing your mind. There's no snake, there's no voice. It's just me. I'm imagining it.*

If you wanna b'lieve that, that's fine, the voice said. *But you gotta get outta here one way or th'other. I c'n he'p you, like I said, an' you can go on pretendin I'm just you thinkin in another voice. But you got to listen to me or things are bout to get a lot worse for you, pronto.*

"Why are you doing this?" she shouted. Her own voice replied in an echo, startling her as it resounded off the walls, further and further into the dark cave, twisting like—

The Snake grunted in aggravation, and black, rough-scaled reptile coiled, its darkness filling her mind.

"Brit?"

Brad's voice. Startled. Confused. Closer than he'd been the last time she'd heard him. She remembered falling into the cave. Breaking her ankle. The excruciating pain. She remembered Brad trying to lift her up with the branch, herself struggling to hold on, to help him help her. She remembered him leaving, promising he'd be back soon and then... the rest was black.

She blinked. The low autumn sun shone right in her eyes. She was lying on her back, looking up at the mostly leafless trees with her brother staring down at her. She turned her head and her entire body ached, not just her foot. Somehow, she was lying on the forest floor. Had she passed out down in the cave, and Brad carried her up?

"How'd I get here?"

"That's what I was gonna ask you," her brother said. He stepped alongside her, peering down—*Into the cave*, she thought. *Where I just was a minute ago. Only the sun's much further west now. If Brad didn't lift me up, how did I get here?*

"I don't know, I—" She was about to say *blacked out* when The Snake uncoiled, and she remembered everything.

That's it. You 'member now, don'tcha? You an' me, we climbed outta that hole together. And now we gotta get outta these here woods, 'fore it gets too late.

Brittany pushed herself up to a sitting position, gripping above the injured ankle. The hole lay beside her, dark as The

Snake itself. It was clear from looking at it that she'd clawed her way out—but how?

She dragged herself over to the edge and peered into the hole.

A heap of large rocks had been piled up against the wall down below. They hadn't been there before. No wonder she felt so *sore*. She must've gone back and forth into the dark a dozen times or more, hopping on one foot, carrying rocks heavy enough to stack. Then she'd climbed up the precarious heap and pulled herself out of the hole by sheer force of will.

I never could've done that by myself, she thought.

That's right, The Snake said. *It's gon be you an' me for a while yet. We got work to do, and when it comes time to do it, you wanna remember what I can do fer you—and to you. You can sign that on the dotted line.*

"Guess we don't need this," Brad said, dropping the coiled rope that looked frighteningly like a snake at his feet.

Brittany peered into the hole, and another strong gust of wind belched up from below. Her whole exhausted body shuddered. "Let's get out of here," she said, eager to get home and get her ankle taken care of, aware it would take a while for them to hobble her back on one leg.

But also... *also*... she worried whatever The Snake was afraid of down there, whatever was causing those gusts of unnaturally warm wind, could do much worse to them than what she'd already suffered through.

She hobbled back home with an arm draped over her brother's shoulders, like the one-legged races they used to do at family gatherings. It took them over an hour to get back, but they arrived home long before the sun fell, and that was all that mattered.

3

11:20 P.M.
Brittany's House

BRITTANY COULD SEE her sprawling ranch house and stables in the moonlight, the indoor lights blazing as bright and warmly as ever. Dad always kept most of the lights on at night, at least until they went to bed. Even then the outdoor lights remained on until morning. It was precautionary, although he'd never said it outright. Ever since they'd moved out here to the country, he worried about home invasions more than he had when they'd lived in town. She wasn't sure if it was because they owned more stuff since they'd done well enough to open a second dealership in Wolfeboro and a third in Laconia, or because they were in the middle of nowhere, backed onto acres and acres of dark woods. Probably it was a bit of both. Whatever the reason, it made Brittany feel a lot safer knowing there was something—or some *thing*, The Snake had never specified—out there in the forest that was evil enough to terrify the disembodied voice in her head.

Things had gotten worse for Brittany after that day in the woods. For one thing, her recovery had taken some time and she'd been unable to dance or do much outside of school work. For another, she'd found it a lot harder to concentrate on anything, not just school and extracurricular activities, but even just holding everyday conversations had become a lot more taxing. There was always the other voice in her head, chiming in with inappropriate comments at inopportune moments, making her lose track of what she'd wanted to say and what the other person had just been saying. The constant daydreaming was another aggravation. She found herself doodling spirals in all of her notebooks and not remembering the last five or ten minutes, and had gotten caught by her teachers on several occasions without knowing what they'd been lecturing about. It was maddening.

Worse than any of this was the near constant urge to kill, itching at the back of her skull. Even poor Bella wasn't exempt from The Snake's evil desires. Britttany had been able to channel his rage, his needs, into murdering the pedophile teacher, but that hadn't satisfied him for long. Within a few months he was demanding her to kill again, someone younger this time. A kid. He needed a "blood sacrifice," and he wouldn't be satisfied with anything less. *An innocent*, was how he'd described his perfect victim. If he didn't get what he wanted, he promised to take over her mind like he had in the cave, this time long enough to murder her entire family while they slept. *And yer little dawg, too*, he'd said with a mirthful snicker.

So she'd promised she would find him a suitable victim. What else could she do? She couldn't let him murder everyone she cared about. The haunt had provided her with the perfect cover, and if all hell hadn't broken loose the moment she'd killed Tommy Mingus, she wondered how many more of these "blood sacrifices" he'd require of her.

How much wood could a woodchuck chuck? The Snake asked as they approached the stables.

The horses whinnied inside. They sounded fine, which meant they were one less thing she had to check on. Midnight, her five-year-old white Sabino, would be all right.

Shut up, she told The Snake.

You know, nobody knows you two're out here. You could slit this pig's throat toot sweet and drag 'im out to them woods.

Shut up, I said.

Aw, come on. Let me out to play, then. With ever'body who died tonight, what's one more body? You'd get away scot-free.

We're not killing Cody!

Okay, have it your way.

"You okay?" Cody asked, glancing back at her with a look of concern in the light from the house.

"I'm fine. Let's just get inside."

He nodded and followed her to the back door.

The house looked fine as they neared it. No shattered windows, nothing toppled or broken inside. Brittany took out her house key, unlocked the back door and opened it. She let Cody through first.

"Take off your shoes," she said on instinct. All things considered Denise probably wouldn't care if they kept their shoes on this one time. She unlaced her boots carefully, while Cody kicked off his. They left them on the doormat and stepped into the house in sock feet.

Cody gawped as he looked around at the wrought-iron chandelier over the kitchen table, the tasteful ceramic vases, the gold-veined marble surfaces and terra cotta tiles this year's home magazines were calling the Tuscan esthetic. "Your house is really nice, Brit," he said.

"Thanks," she said, ignoring the fact that he'd called her Brit. "Where is everybody? *Dad?*" she called out. "*Denise?*"

Cody turned his gawp toward her. "You call your mom Denise? That's so cool."

Brittany sputtered. "Bell-*aaaa*?" she called out.

Not a word or a bark in reply. She picked up her pace, heading into the bright hall. "Dad? Bradley?" She whistled for Bella. No yip or little click-clacks of her toy poodle's neatly manicured paws met her call. The house was deserted.

They're gone, The Snake said.

"No," she answered aloud. She wouldn't let herself believe it. They couldn't be dead. She'd do just about anything to see them again. Bella, Dad, Bradley, Denise, even Renata, though she knew their housekeeper would've left shortly after cleaning up from dinner, long before anything had happened. She lived in town, in a small bungalow with dirty white siding on the seedy side of the Geromero Street bridge. Brittany had followed her there once out of curiosity—more The Snake's curiosity than her own—and had just felt sad to see how she lived with her husband and two boys.

I mean they vamoosed, The Snake said. *Hit the road, Jack. Car ain't out front. They musta skedaddled when the shit hit the fan.*

The Snake was right. The keys to the Lexus and Bradley's truck weren't in the geode bowl on the accent table where they usually were when everyone was home.

"Stay here," she said to Cody, turning for the stairs.

"Uh-uh. Wherever you go, I go."

"Fine," she huffed, already trudging up the winding staircase. Cody thumped up behind her. When she got to her bedroom, she peered in and saw the "Royal Duchess" burgundy pillow with gold tassels on her bed where Bella normally slept was bare. Brittany's dolls lay scattered around the room as if a thief had been rifling through them looking for her vintage Barbies.

"My room gets pretty messy, too," Cody said.

Brittany fumed. "I didn't *leave* it this way."

"No, yeah, of course not," he added apologetically. "I was just saying."

Brittany pushed past him, headed for her parents' room. Voices drifted toward her as she approached, Cody in tow. At first she thought maybe her dad and Denise had locked themselves in the panic room with Bella—it should've been her first thought, but it had been so long since the last emergency when they'd had to use it—but the sound was different, more tinny than muffled. Music chimed in to accompany the voices, and she realized she was hearing a commercial. Her parents must've left their TV on.

She approached the door, opened a crack on the bright bedroom. "Dad? Denise?"

Nothing. She pushed the door open. The television remained blank but the clock radio beside the four-poster waterbed was on. The walk-in closet was open, and all of Denise's outfits were still nestled together on the hangers, meaning they couldn't be inside the panic room unless someone outside had moved them back.

I tolt you, they got outta Dodge, The Snake said. *Musta caught a bad smell in the wind an got the road on the show.*

Why are you talking like that?

It's that transistor radio, honeypie. All them hep cats talkin the talk brings me right back to the good ol' days.

"Whoa," Cody said behind her, his wide eyes falling over the furnishings and objects in the room.

The commercial gave way to the voice of the radio announcer she'd heard from the hall: *"Authorities in the Crooks Corner area are asking residents to take shelter in your storm cellars and basements as soon as possible. If you do not have a cellar, you're asked to join Father Earl at Our Lady of Mercy Catholic Church on Crook Street. Once again, authorities in the Crooks Corners area—"*

"So I guess they all musta gone to the church," Cody said with a shrug.

"I guess so."

"You think Cassandra and them would've gone there, too?"

"I dunno. I guess."

Cody nodded thoughtfully. "Guess we should probably go then. Make sure everyone's okay."

Brittany sighed heavily. "Yeah, that's a good idea, I guess."

"Yeah." He shrugged. "On the bright side, I saw plenty of coats to wear in the foyer."

"Yeah, you probably want your coat back."

He shrugged. "If you don't mind...."

Brittany turned off the radio and pulled off Cody's jacket as she returned to the hall. She'd been enveloped in the fresh, citrusy scent of his cologne for long enough now she kind of felt bad to let it go. Reluctantly, she handed it over.

"Thanks," he said, slipping his arms into it.

"Thank you," she said, a little too enthusiastically. "For-for letting me borrow it," she stammered. "I'm gonna go use the washroom, okay? I'll just be a minute."

"I'll be right outside."

She glared at him.

His already rosy cheeks burned redder. "Not close enough to hear you or anything. I'm not like that."

Brittany shook her head and chuckled as she headed for the en suite in her room. Cody stayed in the hall outside her bedroom door.

She locked the door behind herself and startled when she caught a glimpse of herself in the mirror. It'd been such a long night with so much going on she'd totally forgotten she was still wearing her psycho clown makeup. Sighing, she turned and sat on the toilet, humming while she relieved her aching bladder.

She wiped and flushed and went to the sink, where she washed her hands and splashed some cool water on her face. The makeup was waterproof and stayed on even in the rain, but she didn't have time to scrub it off. She just hoped she wouldn't die looking like a half-painted hobo clown.

When she looked up again, the mirror, the wall, the vanities and ceiling were covered in graffiti—a single word splashed in crimson everywhere she looked, dripping like blood. In the reflection she saw the heads of her family, Dad, Denise and Bradley, even poor little Bella with her little black dewdrop eyes, each of them severed and resting on the marble countertop. She blinked rapidly, horrified as she took in the horrible sight that hadn't been there moments earlier, turning herself around in a tight circle to see the blood-streaked word on the shower curtain, the clawfoot tub, the tiles at her feet.

She screamed.

"Brittany? Are you okay?"

She wanted to answer, but the word, the name, whatever it was written in the blood of her family—even though she knew what she was seeing in the reflection was a hallucination, that their heads weren't *actually* on the counter, that they were all still likely alive and well at the Catholic church—the word burned into her mind, whispered in her ears by a hundred voices, a thousand, like pitiful supplications to some ancient god.

Whoever or *what*ever this Geth was had infected her mind like The Snake had before, only Geth was far more powerful, she could sense that, and she watched helplessly in the mirror as she picked up the pair of shears from the drawer, opened them wide, and dragged them across her white-painted throat. She screamed and screamed while her blood poured down the front of her costume in a crimson river.

Stop screamin, The Snake said.

Cody burst through the door. He looked at her, and when she didn't stop screaming, he grabbed her by both shoulders and shouted into her face: "Brittany, what the heck's the matter with you?"

Brittany didn't listen. She *couldn't* listen. The image of her family, her Bella, beheaded and resting neatly on the counters under that one word that wasn't really a word but an incantation, a maniac's chant, it flashed over and over in her mind and she couldn't stop screaming, *wouldn't* stop screaming until she knew for sure it was gone.

STOP THAT HOLLERIN, GOTDAMMIT!

The Snake unfurled in her mind, smothering everything with the dark coil of his tail. Like getting hit with a bucket of cold water to the face, Brittany regained her self-control and opened her eyes to look at the mirror. She blinked hard to make certain what she was seeing was real.

Everything she'd seen had vanished: the severed heads, the blood-streaked word on every inch of space, the blood pouring from her gaping throat down the bib on her dress, all of it gone in the blink of an eye.

Her family was *alive*. She *felt* it. She hadn't tried to kill herself, either—she would never do that. But for some reason, it felt like prophecy. It felt like this Geth, whatever it was, had shown her not just what *might* happen but what *would*, if she didn't do what it wanted.

But what does it want?

Cody followed her gaze to the mirror and gave her a look of concern. "What got into you?"

"I'm okay," she said, though she wasn't sure she believed it. "I'm okay." And though she hadn't been *okay* since that day three years ago when she'd fallen into the cave, and she certainly wasn't any more okay now after having witnessed the death and dismemberment of her entire family including her little dog, she was at least able to convince herself to carry on.

"Brittany, we gotta get outta here."

He was still holding her by the shoulders. She shrugged his hands off of her and pushed past him into the hall. "Okay. I'm fine."

"Where are you going?"

Brittany entered her father's office, heading straight for the desk. Behind her, Cody said, "Wow," gawping at everything in this room, from the wood-paneled walls lined with animal heads to the framed antique maps. She jimmied the top drawer with her dad's letter opener, snatched the small key with its rabbit tail fob from within, and brought it to the gun cabinet, which she quickly unlocked.

Brittany laid aside the 12-gauge shotgun her dad used to shoot raccoons, porcupines and larger vermin, and a box of bird-shot, on the small table beside her father's mahogany leather chair. She did the same with the Winchester Rimfire .22 she'd had with her the day she'd fallen into the cave, as well as a box of .22 hollow-points.

That's the ticket, The Snake said eagerly. *Blow a hole through this li'l piggy the size of a hamburger. Cops'll think he broke in to rob the place an' your folks blew his ass to Kingdom Come.*

"Oh wow," Cody said. When she glanced up from loading the weapons, she noticed he was standing over the desk looking at her dad's stacks of research. He'd been collecting local newspapers and books from the area from decades past for several years, to eventually write a book about the strange and often macabre stuff that seemed to happen in and around Crooks Corner.

"What?" she asked, not really caring.

"That guy Row talked about at the haunt, the one who killed those little kids—he's a real guy. It's in the July 8th Crooks Corner *Gazette*, 1969. It pushed the July 4th parade to the second page. They had a curfew and everything, just like she said."

Her interest piqued, Brittany crossed the room to him, still holding the Remington.

"Whoa," Cody said, taking a nervous step back.

"The safety's on, dummy." She nodded toward the paper. "How'd you find that?"

Cody shrugged. "They're all chronological."

Of course it was. Her father was as meticulous in his home office as he was in his business. It was one of the reasons he still hadn't started writing his book yet. He said he needed to finish all of his research first before he could figure out the "right angle" to take on the subject.

"His name was Dandy McAmis, but he called himself The Snake."

It's Andy, not Dandy. Only my mama called me Dandy. Anyone else called me that, they learned real quick what callin me that gets.

"It doesn't say he blamed the Devil," Cody read on, "not like Row told us. Sheriff Sykes quoted him saying *'it* made me do it,' and when Sykes asked him what *it* was, he said 'the thing behind them stones, *Jeff* made me do it.'"

"Jeff?" Brittany asked, searching for the name on the page.

"That's what it says."

I didn't say Jeff, *dammit,* The Snake snapped. *I said* Geth. *Hard-G-E-T-gotdang-H, just like you seen on the mirror. That dumb son of a bitch Sykes didn't understand plain English, an' them papers sure was keen to make me out like a idjit. That's the dang thing I been worried for all this time. What I telt you bout when we was down in that hole. The ghost of that shay-men showed me what they done to lock it up tight behind them stones, an he said to me I got to do the same thing to stop Geth from gettin back out. It's like a gas leak, slowly seepin out into the air around it. Sooner or later, BOOM! And it's hungry, just like fire is. The shay-men, he tolt me killin those kids'd be like openin up all the winduhs in the house and clearin out the gas.*

Why didn't you tell me all this before? she asked, skeptical of her unwanted companion.

Would you've b'lieved me if I did? Hey, honeypie, there's this ancient bein, older than time itself, an' some shay-men an' his people from fifteen-thousand years ago done trapped it in a cave out there behin' a coupla big ole fancy rocks. Did it with a blood sacrifice an' a magic spell or some horse crap. That sound like a story you'da bought? I figgered convincin you to do what needed to be done'd make it so you never needed *to know.* She sensed his shrug. *I guess I was wrong, an' that's on me.*

I might've listened....

Bull pucky. Hell, if the shay-men didn't SHOW me exactly what'd happen if I didn't listen to 'im, I wouldn'ta b'lieved 'im myself. Anyways, the damned sacrifice didn't work, did it? Now we're up Shit Creek without a pole to fish with.

With Cody still absorbed in the old news article about her unwanted companion, Brittany returned glumly to the gun rack and sat for a moment with the loaded .22 in her lap, considering what little they knew about this Geth. Guns probably wouldn't do much good against it, but they could at least be used to protect them from the things it attacked them with. She could treat it like skeet shooting, which her dad had taught her well before she'd gone out with Brad to the woods on that crisp day in 1998.

"Come over here and take one of these," she said finally.

"Sweet," Cody said, stepping around the desk to meet her. He picked up the shotgun and hefted its weight. "I like the feel of this one better than Chet's."

"Good." She stood with her rifle. "Let's go."

"Go where?"

"The stables. We're gonna ride Midnight to town."

Chapter 18

1

11:20 P.M.
Browning Street

Jay knew they were screwed the second they rounded the corner onto Mr. Combs's street.

There was a hum in the air that only got louder as they neared, Walden, Cassandra and Taylor hurrying along a little ways behind him, and a whir and clatter like a thousand zippers in the world's largest laundry dryer. Over the rooftops on Hickox Boulevard, he'd caught glimpses of flying objects in the darksome sky and thought it was birds, maybe. Bats, potentially. Even his irrational fear of bats—though not quite so irrational tonight, after the haunt—couldn't prepare him for the sight that awaited on Browning Street.

As they'd crept through the neighborhood, the streets empty aside from shambling zombies who didn't appear to be interested in them at all, Jay had asked, "Where *is* everything? They were everywhere like twenty minutes ago and now it's all gone."

"Don't jinx it," Cassandra had said.

Walden replied, "I don't know."

Now we know, Jay thought, looking up at the massive cyclone swirling around Mr. Combs's house. It began about a foot or so above the lawn and driveway and climbed forty or fifty feet into the sky. Dozens of pumpkins, hundreds of random Halloween decorations, various neighborhood tricycles and bikes, rolls of toilet paper with long, fluttering white tails, treat buckets, masks —all of them spinning around the house like a supernatural cyclone. The sound of them crashing into each other as they circled was as loud as he imagined the ocean must be.

Standing on Combs's lawn were more zombies, at least twenty of them. Jay watched as two more joined the crowd from the sidewalk and street.

"What the fuck?" Walden said behind him.

Jay let out the breath he'd been holding. "They knew we'd be coming," he said.

"How could they know?"

Jay shook his head—but then he saw it: the cyclone parted and a lone figure stepped out onto the driveway. The figure, with its large, round head, appeared to be looking up at the Halloweenado. He stood between two cars, their headlights blazing toward the street and their engines revving, and raised his hands to the sky like a preacher rejoicing in the Word of the Lord. As he did, the zombies all dropped to their knees to worship him.

"That's not Mr. Combs," Jay said. He could tell not just because he'd never seen Combs wear a Halloween costume—let alone an *actual pumpkin* on his head, which this appeared to be —but also because the guy was dressed in jeans and a baggy sweater, and Combs was always well dressed, even on the weekends.

"Are those his cars?" Cassandra asked.

Walden sputtered. "You think Mr. Combs drives a cherry-red Bel Air and a mint-condition Chrysler Cordoba? No way is he that cool."

Jay shook his head distractedly. "Mr. Combs rides a bike. He's an environmentalist."

"No doy," Cassandra said.

Walden lit a cigarette and puffed on it anxiously. "So how are we gonna get in there? There's no way the cameras can do anything about *that*, with or without Humphrey. It's a fuckin guarded fortress!"

Cassandra shushed him. "Keep it down, are you *trying* to get them to hear us?"

"Maybe we could cause some kinda distraction?" Jay suggested. That would be his strategy in *Diablo II* or *Starcraft*. Distract the enemy and find another way through their defenses.

"*Distraction*," Walden said, turning away from the house with his hands on his hips to sneer at him. "This is *fucked*, Jay. We're absolutely fucking *fucked*."

"Language," Cassandra said, covering her sister's ears.

"Are you fucking kidding me? There's a *tornado of homicidal Possessors and literal fucking zombies* blocking the only thing that can stop them all, and you're worried the kid might learn to *curse*?"

"I already know all the swears," Taylor said proudly.

Walden gestured at her. "See? The kid knows all the swears."

"Cram it up your putz!" Taylor said.

Cassandra and Walden turned to each other with looks of surprise, then snorted laughter. It was the first of any sort of levity since they'd left her house, but Jay didn't much feel like laughing. They had to figure out what to do now that it wasn't possible to get inside the garage to turn off the Machine. This wasn't the time for fun and games.

"Could we all keep our voices down, *please*?" he snapped. "I'm trying to think."

Walden barked a laugh. "Oh, everyone keep your voices down. A Beautiful Mind over here is trying to *think*."

Cassandra joined in. "Ooh, the tortured genius needs silence, dontcha know."

Jay grumbled, his cheeks flushing a deep red. After all they'd been through tonight, how could they laugh and make jokes? They had to figure out who the man with the pumpkin head was, and why these things were worshiping him. They had to figure out a way to distract him and the cyclone and zombies he apparently commanded without getting themselves killed. There was no way Jay would volunteer to be to it. He was the only one with enough knowledge of the Machine—albeit limited—to even *attempt* to try and shut it off. But he couldn't try to rope Cassandra or Walden into it without looking like he was putting a target on their backs. That said, *something* needed to be done.

It turned out he didn't need to do either. The Pumpkin Man's head turned suddenly toward them, fire blazing in his carved-out eyes.

"See? You had to keep screwing around. Now he's seen us."

"We don't know he's seen us," Cassandra said.

As if to prove her wrong, the Pumpkin Man swung both

arms in their direction, one after the other. Objects shot out of the cyclone and hurtled through the air toward them. The blood-streaked Big Wheel struck the pavement near a werewolf mask some kid had tossed aside and it exploded before Jay could even raise his camera. The second object—a large orange trash bag with a goofy jack-o'-lantern face—hit the street a few feet from Walden and burst in a scattering of dead leaves he stepped back from cautiously.

"Those almost hit us!" Taylor said.

Cassandra turned to them. "So what now?"

"Whoever that guy is, he makes Taylor's powers look like a joke store magic trick," Walden said. "I don't think there's anything we can do against *that*."

Jay nodded. If they were lucky, and if Taylor's supposed powers really were real, they could maybe fend off a handful at a time. Any more and they'd be pushing it. And even that was a risk.

We have to get in there. We have to stop that Machine before it's too late. But how?

"We need to be ready for the next ones," Walden said. He turned to Cassandra with a quizzical look, and the both of them raised their cameras. "Remember to focus on them, Taylor."

Jay and Taylor raised theirs, awaiting the next barrage. Taylor looked surprisingly calm, as if she'd already been through it all. The only thing that betrayed her confidence was the tremble of the Polaroid in her hands.

The Pumpkin Man swung his arms again, directing his Possessors to attack, though this time it wasn't toys or Halloween junk. The car engines roared and their tires spun on asphalt and grass, raising clouds of black smoke and dirt.

"I don't like the look of this," Walden said.

In an instant, both cars leaped onto the road and turned sharply in their direction, peeling rubber, and before Jay could say *Oh shit*, they began chewing up the asphalt toward them.

He said it anyway.

Then they ran.

2

DODGING rubber bats and all manner of menacing decorations (*Is that a mummy*, Renny wondered, *a paper mummy?*), Renny and Elana carried Ernie Combs from where he'd collapsed on the floor to the kitchen door they'd entered through. Elana had convinced him they couldn't leave without Combs, otherwise they'd already be out the back door and on their way to the alley. Before rounding the corner into the living room, Renny glanced back to make sure the thing with the jack-o'-lantern face hadn't follow them. It stood a moment, perfectly still in the garage doorway, smiling wide with flames burning in its features, then did a swift about-face and headed back into the darkness of the garage.

Even with the doorway free and clear, there was no way to reach it through the mass of swirling objects in their way. They would have to forsake the Machine for now. They had to get Combs back to the truck and figure out a new plan once he'd regained consciousness.

Elana wrestled the man's legs into the crook of one arm and opened the door. A bat struck the top of her head, catching in her hair for a moment before flittering off again with a mousy squeak.

It could've killed her, he thought distractedly, hefting Combs from under the man's armpits through the back door, with his injured hand held close to Ernie's head. *It had the chance to kill her but it didn't even bite. Any one of those things could've killed us.*

Again, Renny glanced back over his shoulder as they lifted Combs down the steps to the shin-high grass, and his mind reeled at what he saw. Hundreds of those *things* had swarmed above the house. The racket of them was so loud he could only imagine he hadn't heard it from inside over the hum of the machine. Rather than warn Elana not to look, he urged her to hurry. She remained looking forward, moving quickly along the ragged stone walkway toward the fence, and Renny thanked a god he didn't believe in that Ernie's weight kept her focused on their goal.

Makes a good argument against consumerism, he thought, making a mental note to use it in his upcoming lesson on Marshall McLuhan. *The medium is the message, kids, and this one is a great big neon sign telling us to DIE.*

Halfway to the gate, the whir of the push mower he'd seen when they arrived caught his attention, closer than the din of the objects in the sky. He turned to see it rolling toward them, cutting a herky-jerky swath through the tall grass.

"Keep going!" he shouted.

This time, Elana did look. Her eyes went wide and she fumbled Ernie's legs, almost dropping him. She managed to right herself quickly and they pressed onward, the push mower slowed by the thickness of the grass.

The lawnmower leaped onto the walkway stones, its pace toward them quickening. Elana having trouble with the gate latch. It wouldn't open. Probably because it was so rusty.

"It's stuck," she cried.

With the mower bounding over the uneven stones toward them, the shed door flew open, and a pair of rusty hedge clippers hovered out, the blades aimed directly at Renny's head.

"Just yank it!" he shouted.

Elana hesitated to shift Ernie's weight, which was just long enough for the mower to close the gap. Renny felt it chewing the bottoms of his pantlegs and yelped in terror, leaping forward. Without that quarter inch of denim, the blades would have chewed through his Achilles tendons. Fortunately, they'd just torn the heavy fabric. He couldn't say the same about the hedge clippers, which had opened with a squeak of rusted metal and were ten feet from making a hack job of decapitating him.

Elana pulled as hard as she could and the gate swung open, bashing Combs's left ankle. The man wakened with a moan, looking around himself blearily. "Elana? What happened?"

They squeezed him on a diagonal through the gate as the mower backed up to take another run and the hedge clippers struck the trellis, causing them to spin away like an object in zero gravity.

"Not now, Combs," Renny snapped. "We can talk in the truck."

"But I'm perfectly fine to walk."

"We'll talk in the truck!"

The mower bounded into the alley as the gate swung shut behind them. They rushed along as it steamrolled toward them.

Renny glanced back again about ten feet from the street and saw that it had stopped suddenly, apparently no longer concerned with them now that they were a good distance away from the house.

"Let's put him down, see if he can walk on his own."

"I've told you I can."

"Well, we'll see."

Elana lowered Ernie's legs. Renny stood the man upright, only for the man to swoon immediately and fall back into his arms. He peered up at Renny apologetically and eventually got himself to his feet.

"Apologies, Hildebrand."

"Forget it. Let's just get to the truck, figure this out."

"Figure *what* out?"

Renny pointed to Combs's house. "*That,*" he said sharply.

Combs blinked rapidly at what now appeared to be a massive tornado of junk circling the house like the one that swept away Dorothy's farm. "Oh! Oh dear."

"Come on, Ernie," Elana said, holding out a hand to him.

Combs glanced at Renny for confirmation. On Renny's nod of approval, Ernie took Elana's hand and the three of them made their way to the truck, leaving the house and the cyclone behind.

3

GETH UNLEASHED Their *inhak* siblings upon the interlopers, making certain they would not harm Elana Stabler nor Ernie Combs. They still needed the two of them, unfortunately, even if Combs's mind had resisted the Blight and almost *thrown a wrench in the works* of Geth's plan. Besides, with the Blight still in the scientist's mind They could see and hear through his sense organs, which would allow Them to *keep tabs.* And so They allowed the humans to escape, forcing them to flee without actually meaning to cause them harm. Hildebrand, however, it would gleefully *slice and dice,* as the expression went.

While they fled, a new threat arrived in the form of four children. Under ordinary circumstances the young offspring of these New People would not cause Geth a moment's concern. This time, however, one among them was more powerful than the rest. She had already proven herself in earlier encounters she had faced with the *inhak*, and had even begun to remind Geth of the dead shaman, albeit this young thing was quite a bit less confident in her abilities than the shaman had been.

Geth turned Their eyes toward these new adversaries and stalked into the dark of the garage. They sensed fear and confusion in these children. The *inhak* permitted Geth passage through the configuration, and They stepped out between the two cars They had summoned from the auto yard, whose engines revved pleasingly. The story They had witnessed on the Tee-Vee with the green-monster truck had not been misleading. These machines truly were frightening. *Death on wheels*, was the common expression. They would soon put that expression to the test on these children.

Through the eyes of a werewolf mask discarded in the gutter, Geth watched them bicker a moment, searching for their weaknesses. They were frightened, weary. Their bodies would give out soon if they did not sleep. They did not send the *inhak* within the mask to attack them. The girl could easily dispatch one or two at a time. How exactly she was able to do so remained a mystery, as the mind of this child Geth the Many could not sense with its Blight. Despite her youth, she remained impenetrable, like a character on the Tee-Vee. Her magic—her *dwaska*, in the old tongue—was powerful. That made Geth nervous.

Geth was curious about the girl, this Taylor Flynn. Even the big shaman had been easy enough to possess, despite all of his totems and magic. They wanted to know why *she* was immune to the Blight, and that, Geth feared, would ultimately cost Them, if They were not able to do discover why.

Geth did not like this feeling: fear. Not in Themself. Fear *of* Geth was desirable. Their own fear was weakness, and a god could not afford to be weak.

Curious, They sent two weaker shadows from the configuration to test her. If she reacted in fear, They would send more, further weakening her resolve, and thus, that of her companions. If she did not, it would prove she was a far more powerful adversary than any Geth had ever faced before among these corporeal beings. If not, They would throw everything They could at the children, the entire configuration if it came to it. *Anything* to destroy this girl.

The *inhak* frightened them, but only seemed to make them more determined. Their fear motivated them, rather than caused them to cower. That in itself was enough to make Geth pay closer attention.

So be it, Geth thought. They could not let these children, or anyone, penetrate its configuration. If they were to destroy the Machine, Geth would once again be subject to the magnetic pull of the dead shaman's Watching Stones. The teachers had almost reached it, due to Ernie Combs's scattered mind reacting poorly to the Blight. Geth would not allow any further breaches of its inner sanctum.

And so, They sent machines to be rid of the meddling children.

They sent *Death on Wheels.*

4

MIKE "CHIMNEY" Stuckey had never been so terrified in his life, even in the moments he'd rolled his three-wheeler out in the back nine and ended up crushing two ribs and breaking his throwing arm. Even when an entire offensive line was running straight at him in a state championship game. Even when the Ferris wheel at the Crooks Corner County Fair got stuck with him and Kelsey Ratner in the second one from the top, and she started swinging it back and forth despite him telling her he was afraid of heights. None of these compared to how he felt sitting beside Mac in the backseat of Adam Brunt's Mustang. Mac's face was pale in the light of the streetlamps as they cruised the streets, and he shivered, huddled up in his jacket. If it was caused by fear or the cold air blowing in through the front windows, Mike wasn't sure. Probably a little of both, as Mike himself was shivering so badly his teeth chattered.

It had quickly become clear there was something very wrong with Brunt and Fitz. For one thing, they weren't playing Brunt's usual Creed or Staind CDs, or even any of Fitz's rap-rock bands on the stereo. The radio was tuned to the classic rock station from Wolfeboro, and Brunt had actually been *humming along* to that "Raise a Little Hell" song, which Mike was pretty sure Brunt had called "pussy rock" before. To make things worse, those blotches all over their faces, necks and hands weren't acne like Mike had tried to convince himself earlier. After a while they'd started to leak not just blood but a greenish-yellow fluid like sick snot, and he and Mac had seen the one oozing from the back of Fitz's neck like the runny egg they'd thrown at Philbert. Not to mention the *stench*: something like a mix of rotting cabbage, raw sewage, piss and period blood. Fitz and Brunt had been belching almost non-stop, and the pungent fumes that rose from their bellies put even the worst of MacNamara's taco farts to shame.

The way they talked was even creepier. Brunt and Fitz were on a mission, hunting the kids they'd lost after they'd egged Philbert Piper. They wanted "payback," and Brunt had mentioned several times how badly he wanted to "kill the little shitbirds and that fuckin retard." Ordinarily, Mike would have assumed he meant beat their asses, but the look in Brunt's eyes had made him sure he planned to literally kill them, and Mike wanted nothing to do with it. And their eyes were darker than normal. He was sure of that, too.

Somehow, he and Mac needed to get out of this car and get as far away from their former friends as possible. He wished they hadn't gotten in the car at all. He wished they'd made a run for it, up the embankment and onto Geromero Street. They might've been able to outrun the Mustang, lose Brunt in an alley or a backyard. He wished he had the guts to reach over Brunt's pustulating shoulder and turn the wheel, crash them into a telephone pole. If he thought that would stop them, he might've. But Brunt and Fitz were wearing seatbelts—another reason to think something was off, considering none of the boys wore seatbelts aside from Cody. Mike had clicked his into place as quietly as possible so as not to alarm them, and had convinced Mac to do the same with a few meaningful looks.

"Hey," Mike started, hoping he might be able to distract them from their mission. "Uh, we've been out here lookin for those little pricks for hours. Don't you think we should give it a rest?"

Brunt's dark eyes glared at him in the rearview mirror. Mike looked away quickly, unable to hold his former friend's gaze. "What's the matter, Mikey? You a pussy?" He glanced at Fitz, who looked back at him with a sadistic grin. "You know what we do to pussies, don'tcha, Mikey?"

"We f-fuck em?" Mike said.

"That's right." Brunt grinned. "We fuck em. Now me and Fitz've been real nice and obliging to all your bullshit tonight, Mikey. Even pulled over so Big Mac could drain the main vein, tiny as it is. But we *ain't* gonna stop lookin for those little motherfuckers until we find em, even if it takes the whole fuckin *night*, even if we have to wait for em at their fuckin *school* tomorrow, not that there's gonna *be* any school tomorrow or *ever*, not with my man Geth behind the wheel."

"You got that right," Fitz said, as if what Brunt said made all the sense in the world. And that was another thing. The two of them kept talking about some dude named "Geth." At first, he'd thought they'd been saying *Death*, which made sense considering how hellbent they seemed to be on killing those kids. After a couple of times though, it was clear they were saying *Geth* with a capital G. Mike had no idea who the hell this Geth could be, and if he'd had the gonads to go for a piss when Mac did, he might have had a chance to discuss it with him.

Strange things going on at the Circle K, he thought, misquoting Keanu Reeves from *Bill & Ted*.

The radio DJ broke in with an announcement: "*Authorities in the Crooks Corner area are asking residents to take shelter in your storm cellars and basements as soon as possible. If you do not have a cellar, you're asked to join Father Earl at Our Lady of Mercy Catholic Church on Crook Street. Once again—*"

No reason why, just that it was an emergency. It was a local station, but Mike figured what was happening here in Crooks Corner hadn't made it to the surrounding towns. At least not yet.

Brunt turned off the radio. "Bullshit," he said. "Ain't no church gonna protect you from Geth."

"You got that right," Fitz said again. "Geth rules."

Mike saw Brunt's blood-stained teeth in the rearview as his friend grinned. "Yeah," Brunt said, raising a hand for Fitz to high five. "Geth *rules*," he agreed.

Mac gave Mike a nervous look, clearly liking all of this about as little as Mike did himself. Mike decided to throw another Hail Mary pass at getting them out of the car. "Hey, guys, uh... you think those, uh, little shits..." Mac glared at him and kicked his foot, but Mike wouldn't let fear stop him from saying what he needed to. They had to get out, before their former friends did something they'd all regret. "...what if they heard what the DJ said and went to the church?"

Brunt and Fitz glanced at each other.

Without a word between them, Brunt slammed on the brakes and spun the steering wheel, sending Mike careening into Mac, whose head slammed against the window. Then they were peeling away in the other direction.

Brunt caught Mike's eye again in the rearview mirror, and a chill ran down Mike's spine. "You better be fuckin right, Mikey," Brunt said. "'Cause if you're not, or if you're fuckin with us, you're gonna see what Geth does to apostates. And trust me, bud, you *do not* wanna see that."

"You got that right," Fitz said, digging a finger into one of his scabs, causing thick, milky-green fluid like a Shamrock Shake to ooze down his cheek and splat onto the shoulder of his jean jacket.

Mike had no idea what the hell an "apostate" was. He sure as hell didn't believe Brunt and Fitz did, either. He *did* believe whoever this Geth guy was wouldn't like him screwing with their plan, and he hoped to Hell they'd find those kids at the church, where someone—Reverend Earl, the sheriff, even the church organ player, Mrs. Delacroix—could convince these two hotheads to chill the fuck out.

5

IF SHERIFF NANCE hadn't expected Reverend Earl to start in on the awesome power of his new god Geth and go on to demonstrate it with a barrage of semi-automatic gunfire, he certainly hadn't expected what the man would do next.

With Nance himself, Randy Jacobs and Trudy Bell held captive by Geth's sentient weapons, Reverend Earl instructed his parishioners to retrieve the arts and crafts supplies from the Sunday school room in the basement, which he then had them distribute to the remaining terrified and bewildered men, women and children to make, as Charles put it, "graven images" of their new lord and savior, whom he called "Geth the Great Pumpkin," just like the *Charlie Brown* Halloween special. In their agitated state, no one seemed eager to laugh or sputter at the reference, which was lucky for them, Nance figured. Between then and now, Earl had commanded two of the stronger male parishioners—the blond-haired Magnusson twins—to take down the rood cross from above the chancel. They'd had to get a ladder and it had taken them some serious maneuvering, but eventually Jesus and his cross were laid on the altar floor. Charles then covered his erstwhile savior with one of the gray church blankets.

"We must draw portraits, write poems and stories, and sing songs praising Geth's love and mercy, if we wish for Them to spare us!" the reverend preached from behind his pulpit, wearing a smile without a hint of the sour grimace Nance had caught him wearing the last few times they'd encountered each other. Madge had mentioned she'd heard the man had been diagnosed with the Big C. Nance didn't know where she'd heard it, but the reverend seemed quite nimble now, leaping up the chancel steps and striding up and down the aisle, leaning over people to praise and critique their art.

And so, like workers in a Chinese sweat shop, the frightened men, women and children spent the next hour or so using crayons and pencils to write about the things they'd each experienced earlier in the night, and to draw pictures of Geth, whom Earl had described reverently. "You know Their face," he'd said, always referring to Geth as *They* and not *him* or *it*. "You have seen it on the walls of our downtown establishments and in our streets, They of the Stitched Smile and Xs of Eye!" Kids and adults wept as they fashioned art upon threat of death, experiencing their losses afresh. It made Nance think of that art studio he'd heard about in North Korea, where painters and sculptors created monuments and propaganda about their supposedly peaceful and democratic country and its "Great Leader," Kim Jong Il.

So much for the Land of the Free, he thought with a bitter inward chuckle. *National Guard still won't be here for five or six hours at the earliest, no matter what Governor Shaheen said. What the hell are we gonna do until then? Can't sit and watch these poor people praise some psychotic charlatan.*

"My friends," the priest said, gone back to gripping the pulpit's smooth wooden edges. "I am being told that the Almighty will be visiting us *in person*. Soon you all will bask in Their glory and might, as I have! You will bear witness to Their wonderous miracles and splendid wrath! They will anoint you with Their purity and strength!"

"Speak of the Devil and he will appear," Nance muttered.

"Shut your piehole, Nance," Trudy Bell whispered.

Nance noted the two knuckleheads weren't so emboldened now that they were under the threat of their own weapons, but he gritted his teeth and said nothing. If the two of them had never shown up here, badly misquoting the old Brothers Grimm tale by bragging they'd taken out "seventeen in one blow-up," there'd only be three or four handguns pointed at them instead of a dozen, including some pretty heavy artillery, which he doubted was even legal. The sawed-off 12-guage and AK-47 were against state laws of possession, at the very least. Who knew if they'd purchased the others through the proper channels.

I have to do something, he thought, *before this Geth gets here and makes things worse. Can't let these people bow down to a monster. Bad enough we got to deal with that halfwit Dubya in the White House.*

But what could he do? The second any one of them stood up to the reverend, Geth's armada of weapons would blow them away. He'd thought they couldn't possibly be watching everyone in the church all at once, but the last time he'd shifted his weight to his other knee, the guns had all swung in his direction like they were on a pivot attached to him. He'd raised his hands in the air and dropped to both knees, anxious and in pain.

So what now? Anything I try'll get me hurt or worse: one of these folks.

Nance looked over the people, each of them fretting over their drawings and stories. He doubted it was possible to concentrate with all that was and had been going on tonight, but somehow they were working away. Maybe it helped to take their minds off the horror. A couple of kids up way past their bedtime were drawing happy stick men with pumpkin heads and bright moons.

Graven images, he thought again.

It gave him an idea.

The Crooks Corner's town council had invested in CCTV cameras to deter crime in the downtown core mid last year, on the street and inside several businesses. Since then the right to privacy outside of a person's home was no longer much of a right. Of all the members in the Better Business Bureau, the only holdout on the initiative had been Reverend Earl. He'd balked at the idea of a camera on the outside of "his" church, and had suffered even more vandalism as a result, with graffiti on the exterior walls, a fire started in his dumpster, and broken windows. He certainly would not have allowed surveillance under his own roof, which Nance proved with a quick scan of the church's high corners, seeing not a single camera bubble.

Maybe I could buy us some time.

Nance raised a hand. "Charles?" he called, trying to project his voice across the room. The weapons spun around to face him.

"Dang it, Nance, keep your trap shut!" Randy Jacobs whispered hoarsely.

Nance paid the man no mind. "Father Earl!" he said, louder. He almost stood up but eyed the weapons cautiously and reconsidered.

The reverend looked up from where he'd been trolling the pews, admiring his new flock's artwork with his hands clasped behind his back. "Sheriff Nance," he said, his newly darkened eyes shining from his beatifically smiling face. "Have you decided to repent?"

"Not precisely, no. But I do think I'd like to help out your friend. This Geth of yours."

Earl blinked. His smile faltered. "*Help?* In what regard could you presume to *help* Geth, Sheriff?"

"Well, it's about your graven images, as you call them," Nance began cautiously, trying to ignore the slight advance of the reverend's arsenal as he spoke. "Now, poems and drawings and whatnot are all well and good, but this is the new millennium. If you *really* want to get some dope's attention, if you really wanna sell folks on *gettin high on Geth*, or what have you, I figure you really should be using video."

"Video?"

"He's right," Gary Garner said, standing up with his notepad and pencil held to his chest. "When I started doing commercials for the dealership, the name recognition alone went up by a thousand percent, isn't that right, Denise?" Sitting at his feet, his gorgeous wife nodded in agreement. "Then you've got your bill-boards," he went on, "and bus stop signs, and newspaper adver-tisements..."

"Exactly my point," Nance said, interrupting before the man —who was well-known to have the gift of gab necessary to sell cars for a living—could do a whole seminar on the subject. "You get this Geth on TV, maybe in one of those half-hour infomer-cials or hell, on the eleven-o'clock news, and you've got yourself a good million eager converts just waitin to hear his Good Word. More, if you uplink to the closest satellite."

Reverend Earl eyed him suspiciously. "You could do that?"

"I could. I know the governor. I bet she could get Geth on channel 40 tonight, if he wanted it. It's a little late, but that in-somniac crowd is practically a captive audience. And those late-night shoppers spend a whole whack of dough on pure garbage. Shamwows and Ionic Breezes and Ron Popeil's Showtime Rotis-series. They'd buy into Geth's doctrine wholesale, I'd bet. Get right in there on the ground floor. You'd have your first converts within a couple of hours, these folks here not included."

Charles turned his suspicious dark eyes on Gary Garner, who nodded, then sat again with his wife and teenaged son, who held a white toy poodle shivering in his lap. Their daughter, a few years younger than the boy from what Nance recalled, didn't appear to be with them. It was possible she hadn't survived, though unlike many of these other folks, the family didn't look to be grieving.

"What would you need to make this happen?" Earl asked.

Nance pretended to consider it. He already had an inkling of a plan, he just had to hope this Geth was dim enough to fall for it. "Well, one or two of us would need to go to the city council office and get the cameras they use for their meetings. If that's not too much trouble, I'd like to be one of em."

The reverend looked off a moment, his lips moving as if he was talking under his breath. Or, more likely, talking to Geth. "Not you," he said. "Him." He pointed to Gary Garner.

"Me?" Gary said, looking surprised. "I don't know where the cameras are."

"Tell him," Charles directed Nance.

Well, that puts a damper on it, Nance thought. *But I can still make this work. Garner just needs the right person to go with him.*

"Someone needs to go with him," he said. "There's a lot of danger out there, in case you haven't noticed."

"Geth's *inhak* will protect them."

Sheriff Nance was about to mention that Geth's *inhak*, whatever the hell they were, had done a piss-poor job of protecting the people of Crooks Corner thus far, when a heavy thud near his feet caught his attention. It sounded like a ceramic jar striking the wood floor and rolling a few inches. His gaze dropped to Trudy Bell, whose eyes had widened in absolute horror. Sheriff Nance caught a look at what she'd evidently noticed and did his utmost not to let his reaction reach his face.

Jesus Christ, these two came armed to the tits, Nance thought.

Between Trudy and Randy Jacobs lay an Mk 2 pineapple grenade from WWII. A *fragmentation* grenade that'd kill anyone in a fifteen-foot radius and do a hell of a lot of damage to anyone within fifty feet, meaning just about everyone in this church.

Randy glanced at it, lying midway between their hips pressed flat to the floor, and his expression mirrored Trudy's. It must've fallen out of her jacket pocket. The pin, fortunately, was still intact, and equally fortunate, the sentient weapons hadn't seemed to notice it. Either that or they didn't know what the hell it was. Whichever the reason, one of them had to get it tucked away again before the reverend got a look at it, and he was already on his way down the aisle toward them.

"Well, Charles, I just don't think I can put my faith in your god quite yet," Nance said. "I'm happy you've found the way and the light and whatnot, but it just ain't in me to take orders from someone until I've looked him dead in the eye."

The reverend's eyes widened, almost as wide as Trudy's and Randy Jacobs's. "Still an unbeliever! Surely, the *inhak* have impressed upon you the true power of Geth's will!"

"If you mean the floating artillery," Nance said, glancing down to see Trudy reach out slowly for the grenade, her eyes on the shotgun she'd brought in with her, floating about their heads with the others, "it was a very impressive spectacle, I'll give him that. But I must admit I've seen better shows on the Fourth of July."

"Sheriff!" came a gasp from the pews. Judy Delacroix, the elderly woman who'd spent every Sunday morning hunched over the church organ for the past twenty-seven years, caught his eye and shook her head gravely.

"Ha!" Reverend Earl spat, sneering. Little white gobs of spittle had foamed in the corners of his mouth. "You *dare* to challenge Geth's power?"

"I do, Reverend." In three good strides, the final pew would be out of the holy man's line of sight and Trudy's not so subtle maneuvering would be on full display. "I surely do."

Reverend Earl took another step forward.

Two more steps and he'd see the grenade.

Two more steps and they'd be in a heck of a lot more trouble than they already were.

A goddamn ruckus, Nance thought again.

But if he could stall Earl just long enough, they might be able to use the grenade in favor of the good side. Maybe even do some real damage to this Geth sonofabitch when the man finally came around.

Sheriff Nance weighed each of his options, a lot quicker and more frantically than he ever had in his fifty-seven years on this planet.

CHAPTER 19

1

"I thought she'd be black!" Cody shouted over Brittany's shoulder as the white horse galloped toward town.

"Why?" Brittany called back, flicking the reins to get Midnight to run faster.

"Well, she's called Midnight!"

"And she's white, like the moon at midnight."

"Isn't the moon blue?"

Brittany eyed him skeptically. "Have you ever seen a blue horse?"

Cody had seen a horse so black it almost *looked* blue a few years ago at the county fair, but there seemed to be no point in arguing, and after a moment or two of silence, something more concerning caught his attention. The 10 Acre Truck Stop stood a little ways ahead of them, dark against the night sky despite being open twenty-four hours a day. It was a great place to get a cup of coffee after a bush party or an early breakfast after an all-nighter, and like the times he'd been there or driven past it with the boys, a bunch of cars, trucks and big rigs were parked out front, but tonight all of the interior lights and even the signs over the pumps had been shut off. He'd never seen the lights off there before, not once in his seventeen years in Crooks Corner. Even during the blackout a couple of summers back, they'd run the lights and kitchen on a big generator they had out back.

As they passed, he saw broken plate-glass windows—one of the cooks hung out from one, arms dangling, clearly dead—and the front-end of a K-Car had bent around one of the pillars holding up the fuel island canopy, its driver also dead, their head and shoulders punched through the windshield.

Seeing the place dark and full of death just like Halloween Village made him wonder if Crooks Corner would ever spring back from what happened tonight. All of that depended on if anyone survived, he supposed. It made him glad his parents were out of town, even if he hadn't been able to contact them to let him know he was okay himself.

For now, he thought.

Midnight whinnied and reared up suddenly on her hind legs. Cody held tight around Brittany's waist, Brittany herself gripping the saddle with both hands, shushing and whispering to her horse. Midnight got settled after a bit of this, getting back down on all four hoofs, allowing them to relax their grip. Brittany let out a breath, and Cody realized he'd practically been squeezing her in a bearhug the whole time.

"Sorry," he said.

"It's okay. What's wrong, girl? Hmm?"

Cody spotted what must've spooked the horse standing in the middle of the road. Between them and the Sheriff's station up ahead, a raggedy-looking man stood in silhouette just outside the sphere of illumination from the next highway light. Moths and other insects flittered in its pale-yellow glow.

"Who is that?"

"I don't know," Brittany replied. "But Midnight doesn't scare easily. Whoever that is... I think we should steer clear."

"Works for me," Cody agreed.

Brittany started Midnight in a trot across the wide road to the ditch on the other side. The raggedy man matched their movement, stepping briskly with a herky-jerky gait away from the bug-crammed lamplight, its limbs swishing with the sound of hay rustling in a stiff breeze. Midnight made a sputter and turned back toward the truck stop.

"Come on, girl," Brittany said, stroking her mane.

The raggedy man stopped, again attempting blocking their path. Tufts of straw fanned out from his sleeves and collar. He wore a potato sack over his head, and as he approached the lamplight Midnight stood under, Cody saw that he had the cult's symbol painted in black on his face. Something about it made

Cody think he wasn't a human under all of that hay and ragged clothing. The way it walked, maybe. Or the fact that there didn't seem to be any eyeholes cut into the burlap. He supposed it could be so frayed the guy could see through regardless, but Cody didn't think that was right.

If it could make zombies out of the dead, it could easily bring a scarecrow to life.

"I'm gonna lure him away," he said, close to Brittany's ear.

"We can make it if we gallop."

"Nah, she's too scared. I'm gonna lure him away so I don't spook Midnight when I blast his ass to grass."

"Or hay," Brittany said.

"Yeah, or hay," Cody agreed.

Brittany nodded, and said, "Okay."

Cody slipped off the horse and both feet slapped down on the pavement like gunshots in the silence. The raggedy man didn't react, just stood there quietly watching them.

"Easy, girl. Easy," Brittany said, stroking Midnight's neck.

As Cody crept away from them, the scarecrow's head turned to follow his progress. Slowly, Cody lowered the shotgun off his shoulder by the strap and gripped it in both hands. He was maybe twenty feet from the scarecrow but Brittany had assured him the birdshot had a decent range. He figured he was a good enough distance to blast a hole through the raggedy man and not frighten Midnight into bolting.

"Hey, dummy!" He waved. "Hey, strawbreath!"

The raggedy man turned to him, cocking its head.

"You got two seconds to get out of our way before I pump you full of lead!" Cody grinned at this. He'd always wanted to use that line.

The raggedy man made no move in any direction.

Cody gave the scarecrow another few seconds' reprieve. Then he said, "Suck on this!" and pulled the trigger.

He aimed low, and the scattering of birdshot made hundreds of little sparks on the asphalt. Midnight whinnied. The shotgun had more kick than Chet's and threw Cody back a couple of steps, almost putting him in the ditch. Gravel slid down the embankment under his heels. He was pretty sure he'd wake to a large bruise on his shoulder tomorrow—if he ever woke again.

"Next one's going in your chest," Cody bellowed, feeling like he may have finally gotten his mojo back. But the raggedy man didn't move, and so, with another moment's hesitation (it could still be a person under the clothes and straw, just trying to scare them—a really, *really* dumb person), Cody pulled the trigger.

This time the birdshot struck the raggedy man in the chest, causing one of the straps of his overalls to fall like it had dressed as the Fresh Prince for Halloween. It didn't cry out or fall backward. It just stood there a moment, looking down at its chest. When the scarecrow turned to face Cody, it was clear the blast had cut a hole right through it. The lights from downtown shimmered through the overall bib and lumberjack jacket. Cody had a moment to register this before it came for him, striding jerkily across the road.

"Oh, shit," he muttered. His shoes ground into the asphalt as he spun around, leaped over the ditch, catching his ankle sharply, and ran in a dash for the pump island. If he could just draw it away long enough for Brittany and Midnight to get to town, he'd hole up in the truck stop overnight, hoping daylight would put an end to this reign of terror.

He was halfway to the island when he heard hoofbeats pounding on concrete. "Grab my hand!" Brittany shouted.

Cody half-turned. Midnight had skirted around the scarecrow and ran in a full gallop toward him. Brittany stopped the horse a few feet away from where Cody stood, and reached out to him. Cody grabbed her hand as the raggedy man awkwardly closed the distance between them. He stuck his right foot in the stirrup and swung his left leg over Midnight's rump.

"Thanks," he said, wrapping his arms around her.

"What was I gonna do? Leave you to die?"

Brittany tugged on the reins and Midnight galloped away from the truck stop, down into the ditch and back up onto the road.

Cody glanced back over his shoulder as they headed toward town. The raggedy man stood in the dark against the moonlit scud of clouds, watching them. After a moment, it went limp and tumbled to the ground in a heap of straw and old clothes.

asked, glancing back at them in the rearview mirror as she continued driving.

"We were planning to stop his machine," Walden said, his hair whipping in the wind as he turned to the opened back window. "But that guy with the pumpkin mask—"

"*Geth*," Hildebrand said. "And it's not a mask."

"Guess what?" Taylor said, confused.

"*Geth*," the communications teacher repeated. "G-E-T-H, I think."

"What do you mean 'it's not a mask'?" Cassandra asked.

"It's an actual jack-o'-lantern come to life. Like everything else tonight. And what's worse, I'm pretty sure there's no head underneath it, just a bloody stump. It possessed Ernie—Mr. Combs—and then it attacked us with more of those things. Chased us out of the house. I don't think it wants us to turn off Ernie's machine."

"If it's protecting that machine, that's even more reason to turn it off," Walden said.

"I've got the next best thing," Ms. Stabler said, and flashed them a smile in the rearview.

"What's that supposed to mean?" Cassandra asked sharply.

"There's a second machine in the woods above the Stones," the math teacher said. "The Resonator. If we can shut that off, I think it will stop what's happening in the cave, whether or not the Harmonic Wave Generator is still running."

Mr. Hildebrand gave them what he probably thought was a hopeful smile, but looked more like he was smiling at a terminal patient in a hospice. Cassandra tried to comprehend everything she'd been told—*harmonizers* and *resonators* and a man walking around with a pumpkin for a head, controlling a bunch of Halloween junk like Carrie after prom—but none of it made any sense. All she knew for certain was that despite their recent victory they still weren't safe, and they wouldn't be safe until that machine was shut off, which she supposed would suck the man with the pumpkin head back to whatever world or dimension or Hellmouth he'd come from.

It was all very *Buffy the Vampire Slayer*, and despite having wished on a handful of occasions that she lived in a more interesting town like Sunnydale, all Cassandra wanted now was to have her old, boring Crooks Corner back.

. . .

3

Jay scurried down the walkway between the random bungalow whose lawn he'd crossed and the two-story house beside it. He stopped in front of a tall wooden gate with cutouts in the wood shaped like stars and the moon where he was able to see the backyards and the fences beyond.

He wasn't worried about being chased any longer. He'd watched the muscle cars follow the others in Mr. Hildebrand's truck—with Ms. Stabler driving for some reason—and he hoped they'd make it to safety. It hadn't been his intention to abandon them, but fear had made him leap before he looked. It was something he often did, let fear make up his mind for him, but he hoped this time it had been for good reason.

Someone still needed to shut off the Machine. Mr. Combs had been sitting in the truck between the other two teachers, and judging by the steady hum beneath the rattle and clatter of the cyclone, it meant he hadn't turned it off himself before the man with the pumpkin head brought an army of junk to attack them.

Jay didn't know how Ms. Stabler and Hildebrand fit in to all of this, but he was glad they'd gotten to Mr. Combs before the Pumpkin Man could hurt him. Jay didn't consider Mr. Combs his *friend*, per se. But he did care enough about his former teacher's well-being that he didn't wish him harm. Even if his Machine may or may not have caused all of this, it didn't mean he deserved to pay for it with his life.

Jay rolled up the right sleeve of his coat and squeezed his hand through the crescent moon hole, reaching for the latch. His wrist caught but he pushed harder, wincing against the wood biting into his skin, until the tip of his middle finger touched cold metal. He pushed and lifted at the same time, and after a moment of excruciating pain in the meat surrounding his radius and ulna, he managed to lift the latch and pull open the gate with a rusty squeal.

Cautiously, he peered around the backs of both houses. The two-story had a doghouse and a few chew toys scattered on the ankle-high grass and patio stones, but the dog was nowhere in sight. The bungalow yard was mostly garden, the dead stalks of veggies and flowers swayed in the light breeze, the remaining leaves rustling with a sound like dead insects.

Jay took two steps onto the property and stopped with his heart in his throat. The neighbor's dog, a Golden Retriever named Dean, lay in the crunchy grass with a chew toy that looked like a giant moth in its mouth, and blood in the fur around its muzzle. Its brown eyes stared vacantly at the back of the house. It wasn't breathing. The patio doors had been smashed open, but the house was dark. Jay figured its occupants must be as dead as the dog.

How many people died tonight? he wondered morosely. *A hundred? A thousand?*

The entire population of Crooks Corner wasn't much more than seven thousand, but he'd witnessed at least three or four people die personally, and that had been just in the first few minutes at the haunt. If this had happened all over town, all at once, they could easily have taken out half the town within a couple of hours.

But why?

I dunno, he answered himself. *Ask the guy with the pumpkin head.*

He laughed bitterly as he stepped around the dog and crossed the small lawn to the neighboring fence. *Yeah, I'll ask and he'll just tell me everything. Like the speeches the villain gives at the end of a movie. 'We're not so different, you and I....'*

Jay stepped into the hard soil between two bare stalks, and climbed over the low chainlink fence. From here he could see the towering tornado of Halloween junk the Pumpkin Man seemed to be using as a barrier surrounding Mr. Combs's house. If he had to bet money, he'd guess the Machine was either keeping the Pumpkin Man alive or holding it in this world, the same way it had seemed to make that small black cloud appear in front of his eyes yesterday. Jay doubted that was all the Pumpkin Man was, just another black smudge like the things they'd seen on the tape and in the kid's photo, another Possessor. It seemed to have a sort of control over the others, and maybe they were all doing its bidding, like the wolves, rats and—Jay shuddered—bats that Dracula could summon and command. The Possessors were the

Pumpkin Man's "children of the night." The music they made was murder.

How am I gonna get in there?

You can't, the voice of fear responded. *Run. Run back home before you end up as dead as that dog back there.*

It was tempting. Two, three hours ago, back at the haunt, he was ready to run all the way back home, lock his bedroom door and never come out again. There was no way in hell he'd have gone right back into the chaos of the barn like Cody and Brittany had, just to save the life of a kid he'd only just met.

But he couldn't keep running his whole life. He'd run from social activities, he'd run from potential friendships, he'd run from anything that might cause him embarrassment or pain and hid in his room, sucking down Rockstars and filling the emptiness inside by killing noobs and NPCs in various video games until he crashed from exhaustion every night. Maybe it was fear of abandonment because his dad was institutionalized when he was young. Maybe it was pure cowardice. Whatever it was, he was done with it. He didn't want to be an NPC for the rest of his life, repeating the same actions over and over like a poorly written script. The only way to break the pattern he'd made for himself was to act against his own programming. To actively fight against it.

Tonight, he'd actually gone out and done something with *real people*, outside of his computer. He could chat with people online just fine, on ICQ and MSN and while playing his games, but when it came to face-to-face encounters, he was always screwing up, always saying the wrong thing, making people angry, getting angry with them. And sure, he wouldn't exactly call the kids in his project group his *friends*—especially not Walden, who'd made it explicitly clear how much he disliked him—but they'd been concerned for his well-being at various points of the night, and other than his mother it was more than he could say about most people in his life. Cassandra was pretty all right, and her little sister wasn't the worst kid he'd ever met. And even though Cody was a jock and Brittany was a spoiled rich snob, he kind of had to admire their bravery, risking their lives for that jerk little kid none of them had even liked.

Jay often played the hero in video games, killing *glitchers* (the cheaters who used game bugs and hacks to beat their opponents), and sniping *spawn-killers* (the d-bags who stood where players entered the game, waiting to easily picking them off). Now it was time to play the hero for real. Somehow, some way, he'd sneak back into Combs's house and get that Machine turned off. He knew the things people said about him. He'd prove them all wrong. He'd save everyone in town and then they'd know he was better than what they thought of him. He would never have gone Columbine on his school—he didn't even *like* guns in real life, they were too loud, too heavy, too greasy—and he wouldn't end up in the mental hospital like his father had, either.

I'll save them all, even if they hate me. That's what a true hero would do, right? That's what Batman would do.

Sure, the voice of fear said. *And die in the process.*

"Maybe," he said out loud. "But at least I won't die a loser."

His mind made up, Jay looked all the way up once more to the very top of the cyclone, as high as the lowest scud of autumn clouds, then trudged across the broken, weed-choked patio stones into the next yard.

4

MATT PEDALED FAST ENOUGH to beat the Devil, which was exactly who he was speeding away from, at least in his admittedly narrow worldview, heart hammering, thighs cramping, shouting back at the others to keep up.

Somehow, after everything, Adam Brunt and his goons had found them. The Mustang roared up the street, spewing slate-gray smoke from its tailpipe as it barreled after them. Matt was certain Brunt and the tallest of them—Brunt had called him Fitz —had been dead or at least in the process of dying by the time Philbert saved the O'Donnelly brothers and Matt himself. The thought that he might have killed them with his prank, which he'd only meant to scare them, hadn't sat well with him, but with all the death and chaos they'd seen he'd been able to convince himself it wasn't his fault, that Brunt and Fitz might've died anyway, whether or not the two enemy factions had run into each other tonight. That was how he'd left it, believing he'd accidentally killed two of the town's worst high school bullies and not feeling too good about it, while also glad he and his friends had been the ones to survive.

Then he'd heard the glass-packed muffler rumbling, and Craig's cry of fear, and saw what was clearly Brunt's ugly mug behind the wheel of the Mustang, covered in the oozing red bumps the rubber snakes and plastic spiders had left on their faces. How they'd survived, Matt could only guess. He'd seen a few other people shuffling around like extras in a Romero zombie movie on their way to the church. He couldn't tell if they were dead or just shellshocked, but he supposed if whatever it was had been able to make all the Halloween stuff come to life, it might be able to reanimate the dead, too. Which put him and his friends, and their new friend Philbert, in very deep shit.

Somehow Brunt and his goons were still alive, and out of sheer bad luck they'd been riding past Town Hall at the exact same moment the Mustang came tearing onto Main Street.

"Fuck me!" Craig had shouted, and sped up.

Matt saw the car a moment later, followed by Kyle, and they'd pedaled harder to catch up with Kyle's older brother. Philbert trailed behind until Matt called back, warning him that the guys who'd egged him earlier were on their tail. That got the big guy moving quickly, pumping his long, thick legs until he was in the lead. He knew the way as well as the rest of them. He turned the big bike onto Crook Street and glanced back, looking exhausted. As he began to slow, Matt and Craig sped up and passed him. Kyle trailed a good ten feet behind all three of them. The Mustang was just about on his back tire.

"Get moving, Kyle!" the older sibling shouted back.

Kyle looked worse than Philbert, and the rapid rise and fall of his shorter legs might have looked comical under different circumstances. With his eyes in wide, white circles of terror and his big coat wide open, flapping in the wind, the green-and-red striped Freddy Kreuger sweater beneath, Matt only pitied him. The Mustang could run him over in an instant, and they were still almost fifty feet away from the church's wide steps.

"*Help!*" Craig called out.

"*HELP US!*" Matt shouted at the top of his lungs, which would have been louder if he wasn't running out of breath from avoiding the psychos on their tail. He didn't think anyone in the church would hear them over the roar of Brunt's car, but they had to try *something*.

Philbert joined them, his voice a lot deeper and louder.

Just twenty more feet. Maybe someone'll hear us.

A loud crash startled him, and then Philbert's bike—Matt's dad's bike—went flying ahead of them. Matt glanced back to see Philbert sprawling in the middle of the road, scraping up his hands and knees and rolling toward the sidewalk. Brunt had driven past Kyle, who stood with his bike perpendicular to the church, watching in terror—and, Matt couldn't blame him for the hint of relief he saw in the younger boy's eyes—as the muscle car roared past Philbert and kept coming.

We're dead, Matt thought.

The engine revved.

He didn't dare look back.

He didn't dare waste his breath shouting for help he knew they'd never get.

He pedaled like it was the last thing he'd ever do, because it was pretty likely that it was.

Then he felt it. The rust-flecked chrome bumper struck his back wheel and the bike skidded at an angle. Matt felt his feet leave the pedals first— he'd been pedaling standing up so his butt had already been off his seat—and then the handles tore out of his grip. He felt himself being lifted into the air, and for several moments he was reminded of those old dreams he used to have where he'd try jumping sidewalk blocks and find he was able to leap two or three or even more. Then he hit the road, asphalt tearing his knees and elbows with a burning sensation. He rolled and struck the road again, and a sharp, jolting pain ran up his left leg. He heard a thin metallic clatter like when they'd raced shopping carts down Holland Road, which he suspected was his bike crashing somewhere behind him, followed immediately by the screeching of Brunt's tires. He lay sprawled along the curb, and his gaze settled on a crumpled Pop Rocks package, sailing past him in the trickle of melted snow as it ran into the gutter.

Then he blacked out.

5

AFTER GETH HAD RUN the children off in a manic frenzy, the circling configuration parted, allowing Geth to reenter the house through the garage. They peeled the clothes off of Their *chuann* as They moved down the back hall. The stench of sweat and urine and *sraki* was overpowering. They headed directly to Combs's washroom and into the tub. Hot water poured down Their skin, which had already begun to turn a slight but distinct grayish color, similar to the old bar of soap Geth found in the corner of Combs's tub. They lathered the decaying flesh and let the water wash the suds away, which They had watched several women do in the stories on Tee-Vee. The New People seemed to have a fascination with the unclothed female body, and not quite as much the male. Geth found both forms somewhat repugnant, though if They had to choose again—and They might be forced to do so soon, depending on how long They could manage to stave off the putrefaction of this *chuann*—They decided They would probably choose a woman.

Believing the *inhak* within the vehicles were moments from dispatching the children and the interloping adults who'd swept in to rescue them, Geth took a moment to bask in the praise and adulation from the reverend's congregation, through Reverend Earl's sensory organs. They wrote stories and poems of Geth's terrifying might, and drew images of varying quality in many different poses and settings: standing in a cornfield with Geth's arms spread wide, watching a house burn to the ground with its occupants screaming in the windows, or hovering over the town with Summerly's decaying fingers splayed like a puppeteer's. Geth reached down to clean between Their host's legs and found the penis had stiffened, pointing at an upward angle like a dowsing rod toward the faucet handles.

As Geth marveled at this phenomenon—clearly brought upon by the exaltation of being treated as it should be, revered as a mighty and all-seeing god—the *inhak* failed once again. Geth let go of the hardened penis and turned Their attention toward the car chase, only to discover that both vehicles had driven off the road and crashed, unable to recover.

"*TIMAR!*" Geth shouted, slamming a fist into the ceramic tiles, cracking them and the wood behind them, tearing open the skin on the Summerly body's knuckles, an injury which would only worsen over time.

The girl was powerful indeed. Much more than They had first thought. Geth felt the erection *wither like a leaf on a vine* (a phrase They had gleaned from Reverend Earl's comprehensive knowledge of the Christian Bible), and cursed Their defeat. Blood spilled from the *chuann*'s knuckles, mingled with the running water and soap suds, running clear as it swirled into the drain.

The failed shadows leapt eagerly from their destroyed vehicles to the closest animatable objects to correct their *colossal cluster fuck* (a colorful phrase Geth had learned from Darryl Knell), but Geth filled their primitive consciousnesses with the emptiness of the *Upask*, and they immediately turned to swirling dust which eddied away into the ether. Geth did not relish killing Their siblings, but doing so would show the others failure was unacceptable. *Kill or be killed*—that was Geth's motto from here on out. In fact, it would become Their principle teaching, when the blighted reverend wrote its Holy Text.

With the host body clean—or as close to clean as a slowly rotting human body could get—Geth stepped out of the shower, dripping water and blood on the furry bathmat. The cramped room stank of feline urine and *sraki*, a testament to the pathetic human necessity for affection and companionship, caring for and cleaning up after lesser animals. If the *inhak* shat and stank, Geth the Many would have sent all of them back to the *Upask* without a moment's hesitation—or turned them to dust, as They had just done to two of Their strongest. At least in the dead shaman's time, animals served humans, protecting families and helping them hunt. The vast majority of domesticated animals Geth had witnessed here tonight had been quite useless in both regards, and the *inhak* had quickly dispatched the worthless creatures. Geth felt no remorse in doing so. Humans were beneath Them, not worth a moment's pity. Their pets were certainly no more deserving of Geth's mercy.

Geth escaped the smell of the feline's filth and entered Combs's bedroom, discovering yet another bothersome human necessity: clothing oneself. Life would be so much less complicated without modesty, although They supposed in frigid temperatures some sort of dress would be required. It had been so

much simpler in the shaman's time. Each human had only required one set of clothing from adulthood to death, which it was
merely repaired when it wore out. Cursing the era Geth had
found itself in, it opened drawer after drawer searching for the
right pairing of shirt, pants and socks which would become its
signature style, a phrase it had borrowed from Combs, who
thought of himself as *well-dressed*. The task would have been
easier with Combs still here, his memories available to reference,
but since he was not it took a fair amount of wasted time and
blood shed among his wardrobe before Geth found a suitable
outfit.

Fully dressed, Geth stood in front of Combs's full-length
mirror, admiring Their new look: brown penny loafers, striped
socks, a pair of pleated gray slacks and a light blue paisley dress
shirt, tucked neatly into the hem of the pants. Dark blue sus-
penders held up the pants, rather than a belt, and Geth tucked
Their creaking thumbs under them and pulled them outward
slightly, as They had seen a man do on the Tee-Vee to indicate
casualness and confidence. A blood red bow tie completed the
look. The pumpkin flesh curled upward in a crooked smile,
which quickly faltered when They noticed a small blotch of
blood on the shirt close to the hem of the pants.

"Timar! Sraki!" Geth shouted, wiping at the stain with the
thumb of Their uninjured hand.

Geth plucked one of Combs's silk pocket squares out of the
top drawer and wrapped it around the *chuann*'s injured hand,
using its free hand and pumpkin lips to secure it tightly. The
bloodstain was not large enough to be noticeable. In any case, if
someone dared point it out, Geth would make an example of
them by turning them into nothing but a wet stain.

"Townspeople of Crooks Corner," Geth said, using a tone of
voice They had seen a pastor use in one of the stories in the Summerly house, "we live in frightening times. Believeth in Us and
We shall restore order. We will keep the hounds of the moon
from the door. Kneel before Us and We will make your dreams
come true. Reject Us, and you will know only nightmares."

Geth threw on one of Combs's blazers on its way out the
front door. The configuration parted once again, and They
swaggered out onto Browning Street. Multiple *inhak* descended
from the swirling pillar in their chosen objects and formed a suit-

able chariot. Geth stepped into it and sat, feeling quite regal. The chariot then turned north toward Our Lady of Mercy, and whisked Geth toward the next step in Their holy mission, new and improved from the last time They had ventured beyond the *Upask.*

Tonight, Geth would make Their Tee-Vee debut.

CHAPTER 20

We don't have a chance in Hell, Walden thought as Hildebrand's truck rumbled through downtown, heading toward the woods.

When they'd managed to push those mint classic cars off the road, crashing them with nothing more than Taylor's power and their video cameras, he'd felt for a moment like the odds had finally turned a bit in their favor. Then he remembered the towering cyclone surrounding Mr. Combs's house, and the man with the pumpkin for a head apparently in charge of them all. There were likely a lot more Possessors than there were people left in Crooks Corner, and a whole lot more junk to attack them with, not even including the zombies. A few cameras and Humphrey weren't going to make a dent in that, no matter how hard they fought against it.

Worse, now there was one less of them to fight back. Jay was a coward, sure, but at least he'd been another pair of hands. He could hold a camera and keep it steady. He'd proved that at the haunt. Walden didn't wish him dead, but he couldn't help but hope the guy would at least get his ass kicked a little for abandoning them when they needed him the most.

Selfish asshole, he thought, gritting his teeth and holding on to the side of the truck while Ms. Stabler took the corner sharply onto Main Street.

He heard the familiar rumble and peered around the side of the truck seconds before the car came into view at the far end of downtown. A bunch of kids and an adult sped across the inter-section on bikes, with Brunt's shitty blue '90s Mustang hot on their trail. He was chasing them, that much was clear as he blew through the red light at the intersection, following the gang up Crook Street toward the church.

They'll be fine if they make it to the church. Sheriff Nance is there. The reverend, too.

Sure, that was a fine thought. Good even. He could *pretend* he hadn't seen them. Cassandra and the others didn't seem to be aware of anything going wrong, so no one would know different but him. He could maybe even convince himself he didn't need to intervene if he tried hard enough. But that just wasn't how he'd been raised. He was taught to stand up for himself, and for others. It was partly why he'd stepped in front of that kid whose name he didn't even remember when Brunt was about to beat him into a bloody pulp, and ended up taking the beating himself.

"Hey, Ms. Stabler!" he shouted through the sliding back window Mr. Hildebrand must have had installed in the cab of his 1952 Ford F-1 Pickup, which would've only had a single, un-openable pane of glass.

The math teacher caught his eye in the rearview.

"Could you let me off on Crook Street, please?"

Hildebrand regarded him over Combs's shoulder. "You sure we should split up?"

He'll kill me this time, Walden thought. Then he nodded. "I just saw Adam Brunt chase some kids on bikes toward the church."

"Ugh, I *hate* that guy," Cassandra said.

Walden saw the resolve solidify in Hildebrand's eyes at the sound of Brunt's name. He turned to Ms. Stabler. "Do we have time to stop?"

She shrugged. "It's your truck. The longer we spend there, the more that pumpkin-headed maniac has a chance to wreak havoc in our town."

"True."

They blew past the Grand, where Walden would've spent his night working if he hadn't blown it off for the class project. Hildebrand had said they'd been at the theater and helped Mr. Stafford take care of a handful of Possessors, and Walden hoped

Patrice and the others had also survived and weren't doing too poorly. From what Hildebrand had said and Ms. Stabler confirmed, it sounded like there'd been a bloodbath similar to the one at the haunt. *Would've been worse if I'd dropped off those last two boxes of Rager toys*, he'd thought. *But then I'd still have my car...*

Ms. Stabler made a wide country turn onto Crook Street, just about bounding over the curb on the left side of the road. Cassandra and Taylor held on for dear life, while Walden readied himself to jump out. Now he could see the damage that had occurred since Brunt had blown through the intersection. Philbert Piper—everybody's favorite Crooks Corner resident except Brunt's, apparently—lay rolling on his butt in the road, gripping his right knee in both hands. His mountain bike had been trashed, the frame and back wheel bent irreparably. Further up the road, just about at the church steps, Brunt's Mustang was park sideways at the end of a trail of black tire marks. A smaller kid's bike lay crashed against the church steps. The kid himself was dangling from Brunt's fists by his winter coat, feet kicking madly.

"Let him alone!" one of the other two kids shouted at Brunt, just barely audible over the pleasing rumble of Hildebrand's truck. The kids—one slightly taller than the other but otherwise nearly identical—were being held back by Sean Fitzgerald. Mike Stuckey and Dave MacNamara sat in the Mustang's backseats, doing nothing. As Elana drove them closer, Walden saw that Brunt and Fitz looked even worse than normal. Under the streetlights their skin looked like melting wax, oozing blood and pus. He could see the expressions of pure dread on Stuckey and Mac's faces now, too. Something was very wrong with Brunt and Fitz —more than usual. Their eyes looked *dead*.

That's because they are, he thought. *Like those zombies we saw before. They're dead, and they're gonna kill those poor kids, too.*

Elana stopped the truck jarringly, the breaks squealing.

"Hey!" Hildebrand shouted out his window. "Put that kid down, dammit!"

Brunt didn't even look. His snarl turned into a blood-pinked grin and he lifted the kid closer to his face in a bicep curl. The poor kid—dressed in black pants with white felt bones sewed onto them—shot a look of terror back at his friends.

Walden leaped out of the truck bed, landing hard and painfully on the asphalt. Cassandra called after him but he kept moving forward, letting the momentum of his legs carry him where his head didn't fully want to go. Stuckey and Mac got out from the backseat finally as he began a staggering jog toward their zombie friends. Mike Stuckey stepped right into his way and held up both hands.

"I wouldn't," he said. "There's something wrong with them."

"Get out of my way, Mike."

Stuckey did exactly that, stepping aside with a resigned look, as if he'd already watched Walden sign his own death warrant. "Your funeral," he said.

"B-be careful, man," MacNamara added. It was weird to see them concerned for his wellbeing, considering they'd been right there to cheer on Brunt during the fight last spring. They were clearly scared out of their minds, but someone had to stop Brunt and Fitz from killing those poor kids. So Walden blew past them, prepared to do just that.

How come nobody's coming out to help? he wondered. Then a dark thought occurred to him: no one was coming because everyone in the church was already dead. Slaughtered all in one go, like dropping a stick of dynamite in a barrel full of fish.

He stopped at the foot of the steps, looking up at the three younger kids and his supposed peers. "Let the kid go, Brunt!" he said, doing his best to sound tough despite being winded.

Brunt's head slowly turned to him as if on a creaky mechanism, the snarling smile never leaving his lips. "Fuck off, LeSaw-bruh. This don't concern you."

Walden glanced behind him. Hildebrand was closing the distance between him and the truck. Mike and Dave stayed where he'd left them. Elana had gotten out of the truck and was hunkered down beside Philbert, a hand on the big lad's shoulder. Combs remained in the front seat. Both Cassandra and Taylor had gotten out and stood beside it, watching with deep concern.

"Put the kid down and pick on someone your own size," Walden said. "Unless you're too much of a pussy."

Fitz turned his head so violently that little flecks of blood and pus flew from his skin. He was still holding back the other kids with his hands, but now his attention was fully on Walden, which was exactly what Walden wanted. Sort of.

"Ready for round two, huh?" Brunt asked, his purple lips curling in a sadistic smile. His gaze moved past Walden as scuffs on the asphalt signaled Hildebrand's approach. "I see you got your teacher pal with you, all ready to ring the bell."

"Let the kids go," Hildebrand said. "Haven't we seen enough violence already tonight?"

Brunt's smile grew even wider, curling upwards like the Cheshire cat's. "No, I don't think I will. These little *pillow-biters* tried to end me an' Fitz. Now it's our fuckin turn."

"If you don't let em go right now, you're suspended. Both of you."

Brunt sputtered. "Suspended from what? You think school's gonna mean a fuckin thing when Geth takes over? It's *you two's* gonna be suspended then, not us. Suspended from fuckin *telephone poles*."

Fitz snickered. "Yeah, nailed up there like the heretics you are. Geth *rules*."

Walden shared a look with Hildebrand, who seemed to have come to the same conclusion he had, sharing his disturbed scowl. Fitz didn't say things like *heretics*. Walden was pretty sure he didn't know the word. But what did that mean? Were they dead and possessed like all the other lifeless things that attacked people tonight? Just two more reanimated objects for Geth's minions to play with? Or were they Geth's henchmen, alive and imbued with more power than the classic cars, the pumpkin-faced trash bag and the kid's plastic trike?

It doesn't matter which, my camera's in the back of the truck and so's Cassandra's. They're too far away to signal, and if I shout, these pricks'll know something's up.

"That's right." Brunt waggled his eyebrows. Pus oozed into his left eye from one of his many wounds and he blinked it away angrily. "Geth's gonna string up all the losers like you two who can't get it through their fuckin heads it's time to let go of the way things used to be around here. All the old rules went bye-bye the second he got free from the *Upask*. Geth *rules* now, and that means all the brown-nosin little pieces of shit like you *lose*. Ain't that right, Fitzy?"

Fitz nodded enthusiastically.

"I think they're possessed," Hildebrand said conspiratorially. "Combs was acting like this earlier. I had to punch him out."

"But Mr. Combs is alive, isn't he?"

Hildebrand nodded. "He's not saying much, but he's alive."

Walden felt a sinking sensation in his chest at his teacher's reply. If Geth could possess the living as well as the dead, how could they fight back against that? They had to use the only real trump card they held. "You have to keep going," he said.

"What?" Hildebrand looked at him in surprise. "You can't handle these two on your own."

"If you don't keep going, it's not gonna matter what I do. Don't you see? Geth's in charge now, like he said. The good guys lost. *He can take over our minds.* If he can do that... we don't stand a chance against him. Not on our own."

"That's right," Brunt agreed. The poor little kid hanging from his balled-up fists wriggled frantically, like an ant caught by the leg at the end of a pair of tweezers. "Run along, Teach. Let LeSawbruh take his lumps like a man this time."

Hildebrand gave him an imploring look, then he nodded. He jabbed a finger toward Brunt. "Once this is all over, and your tin god falls flat on his ass, I'm gonna see to it you two never graduate."

Walden almost laughed. He had to respect his teacher's bravado, misplaced or not, but he seemed to have no idea how far gone these two were. Maybe they were just possessed like Mr. Combs seemed to be, but Walden was almost certain they were as dead as grunge music. There wouldn't be any school for them whether they sent Geth back to the *ooh-pask* or not.

Brunt grinned. "*Oooh*, we're shakin in our boots! Ain't we, Fitz?"

Fitz literally started quivering. "Oh yeah, we're scared all right. Please don't flunk us, Mr. Hildebrand!"

"Shut up," Brunt said, and Fitz did.

With one last imploring look at Walden, Hildebrand turned his back on them and headed for the truck. Ms. Stabler rose from attending to Philbert Piper and met him there.

"C'mon, Brunt," Walden said. "Put the kid down and let's settle this one on one."

"Yeah, put him down!" the smallest of the kids shouted bravely.

"*Shut up,*" Fitz said, and slapped the kid in the Freddy Kruger sweater so hard across the face the kid almost did a three-sixty spin on the spot. Mini Freddy held the injury and sniffed as tears began streaming down his rosy cheeks.

"Leave em alone, fuckhead!"

Fitz turned his dead-eyed glare on Walden. "You want a piece of this, dickfuck?"

"Shut the fuck up, Fitz!" Brunt snapped.

Fitz turned to him in surprise. Brunt's fanatical grin became a sneer. Then he nodded and straightened his arms, lowering the kid to the cement. He opened both hands simultaneously. The kid's coat fell from his fingers and the kid himself turned and bolted for the church doors. All the while, Brunt didn't take his eyes off of Walden.

"Let the little shitbirds go, Fitz. We're gonna settle this beef once and for all," Brunt said to Walden. "Ain't we, *bud*?"

Fitz let the other two kids go. Whatever Geth was to these pricks, it was clear Brunt was receiving the majority of the instructions. He was still the leader of their pack, despite taking orders from someone else. Some*thing* else.

The boys ran to meet their friend, and all three started pounding on the doors together, taking up a chorus: *"Let us in! Help! Please, let us in!"*

Brunt moved in on Walden, cracking his knuckles one by one.

Fitz did the same, jerking his head side to side, his neck popping.

It was only now, with the two dead football players possessed by some ancient demon or interdimensional being slowly descending the steps toward him, that Walden LeSabre allowed himself to consider how truly and honestly fucked he was.

2

Brittany raced Midnight down the hill toward Crooks Corner, Cody's arms wrapped around her waist and The Snake coiling and uncoiling tensely in her mind. Ever since she'd seen the name Geth written in blood all over her bathroom (which thankfully had turned out to be a hallucination, though hopefully not a *premonition*), The Snake had been on edge. She felt it even more so as they reached the first houses on the outskirts of town.

Geth is close, he whispered in her mind, causing a chill to run up her spine.

Speaking of close, the heat of Cody's minty-fresh breath on her neck and his muscular body pressed against hers caused a shiver of a different kind. She didn't want to acknowledge it, especially not now, under these circumstances, and it was easy enough to suppress, if she wanted to. She'd been dulling her sexual urges for years even before The Snake entered her life and her mind, ever since puberty hit her at the relatively young age of eight. It was necessary, to maintain her good grades and the high standard she expected of herself in both drama and dance. After The Snake's arrival, she'd done it to prevent him from "getting his jollies"—his words, not hers—from the involuntary reactions of her body. Even though he'd promised not to peek through her eyes while she undressed or used the toilet, there'd been times it was clear he was aware of what was happening outside of his hidey hole—like tonight, when he'd responded to Geth's name in the bathroom, where he wasn't supposed to be eavesdropping. Just knowing that had been enough to make her want to *never* experience those things, despite desperately wanting to experience them.

Like a debilitating childhood illness or impairment, The Snake was a thing Brittany had been forced to live with, and in many ways his presence had dictated how she lived her life. If she survived the night, she planned to change that. No more cutting out what she truly wanted in life. She'd live for herself for once, whether or not her unwanted companion approved or got his jollies.

These thoughts she hid below the surface, where she'd learned over time and testing The Snake couldn't hear. He only appeared to notice her conscious thoughts, which made it simple enough to keep unwanted or intrusive thoughts secret from him.

They hurtled past manicured lawns and large houses—though none quite so large as hers—and eventually past the lumber yard and the feed store, which gave way to downtown Crooks Corner. Soon they were racing past the Eateria, which was brightly lit and yet looked as deserted as the truck stop had been, then the Grand Theater, avoiding a familiar maroon station wagon that had crashed nearby, surrounded by what looked like bits and pieces of little green army men. As they crossed the intersection at Hooper Street, nearing the Belmont Hotel, Cody shouted very close to her ear to be heard above the thunder of Midnight's hooves.

"Did you see that?" He let go of her with his right arm briefly to point at the road up ahead.

Whatever he'd spotted, she'd missed it. "See what?"

"I think I saw Mr. Hildebrand's truck turn onto Crook Street!"

"I guess you were right!" she shouted, the wind in her ears. "They must all be going to the church!"

Brittany urged Midnight onward. As they neared Geromero Street, she began to hear what sounded like shouts. She couldn't tell who it was from the distance and Midnight's clomping, but it was clear from their timbre something bad was happening very near, probably out front of the church judging by the direction.

Are they back? Has it started again?

You think it ever stopped? The Snake sputtered. *C'mon. You're smarter'n that. Geth won't stop until everyone in town is deader than Kelsey's nuts. An' I ain't stupid enough to b'lieve that don't include yours truly. I'll prob'ly just up an' vanish like a fart in the wind.*

Brittany almost thought, *Good.* Then she realized she'd have to die to make it happen.

"What the heck is that?" Cody said, letting go of her waist to point ahead of them again.

Brittany scanned the road ahead as they passed the pharmacy, searching for what he'd seen. Aside from another crashed car outside the theater and all of the many signs of death and destruction, including multiple bodies in the street, she saw nothing.

Until she did.

Holy crow, The Snake hissed, coiling tensely.

A chariot of some kind seemed to be hovering several feet above the Geromero Street bridge, moving toward them down the center of the road. Sitting atop it was a man wearing what looked like a giant pumpkin mask.

That ain't a mask, an' it ain't a man, either, The Snake said. *That's Geth. An' what you seen in the bathroom mirror, that'll seem like a mercy compared to what he'll do to you and yours. You can sign that on the dotted line.*

Midnight whinnied and came to an abrupt stop, almost jarring the two of them right off of her back. Her eyes rolled around in her head, and she began trotting backwards.

"Is that thing *floating*?" Cody asked.

Brittany shook her head, patting Midnight's flank. "It's Geth," she said.

"What's a guess?"

"*Geth*. G-E-T-H. I don't have time to explain, we have to get to the church and warn everyone it's coming!"

Ain't no point warnin em. Geth's gonna bowl over that church like a twister in a trailer park. We gotta hit the bricks, honeypie. Scram, vamoose, twenty-three skiddoo on outta here.

"Would you shut up for a minute?" she unintentionally said aloud.

"I didn't say anything," Cody said.

"Not you. Sorry. I need to think."

Midnight kept trotting backwards, while Geth's chariot turned onto Main Street and moved swiftly across downtown, clearly floating. This close, she could see the chariot was made up of all kinds of Halloween junk and odds and ends they must have picked up from various yards and houses—the same sort of things that had attacked them at the farm and then some. Geth's feet, dressed in what appeared to be polished brown leather shoes with pointed toes, hung a foot above the asphalt.

"It looks like Mr. Combs," Cody remarked.

He was right. It did look like something the science teacher would wear, even possibly was something right out of the man's wardrobe, only the individual pieces didn't quite match. But that didn't matter. She had to convince Midnight to keep going, or they'd have to dismount and run on foot. Judging by the speed of the chariot, there was no way they'd make it to the church before Geth.

Brittany scanned the area as Midnight continued her backwards trot with another sharp whinny. "Easy," she said, stroking her neck. "Easy."

Then she spotted it. In less than a minute Geth's chariot would be turning onto Crook Street and floating toward the church. She had to warn them, and she knew just how to do it.

She just hoped they'd hear it in time to prepare.

3

"CHARLES, stop where you are and look up," Sheriff Nance said, a vague plan formulated in the three-point-two seconds it had been since the reverend had taken his previous step. The fragmentation grenade still lay at his feet between Randy and Trudy. She was still reaching for it, as slowly as her frantic mind would allow. "Tell me what you see."

The reverend's smile returned, crazed and full of old-time religious fervor. "Are you trying to fool me, Nance?"

"Just favor me a moment, then we can go back to playing wayward soul and shepherd."

Charles held his gaze a moment longer, then craned his neck ever so slowly to look up. "What precisely am I looking for?"

"The hounds of the moon," Nance said with a grin, unable to help himself. Reverend Earl's eyes bugged out, and Nance held up a hand palm out to pacify him. "Just joshin you, Charles. Relax. Now you see that black spot, up there on the top rafter? Looks like a bull's head?" He was pulling this out of his ass, but he had to hope the natural human preponderance to see significant things in random patterns and images hadn't been affected by the entity that had apparently taken control over the rest of the reverend's brain.

Earl squinted up at the rafter for a long enough time Nance had to wonder if he hadn't shot for the proverbial moon and missed, hounds or no hounds. Then the reverend's eyes alighted and he nodded proudly as if he'd solved a Magic Eye image. "I see it."

"Good. Have you ever heard the story about the man who had this church built? The *real* story, I mean. Not the one we tell to outsiders."

The reverend's smile faded. He blinked rapidly. "I know a timber baron named Daniel Crook founded the town, and this church was the first building in the town proper, built from the timber produced at his sawmill." He said this as if by rote, like a kid reciting facts in a middle-school presentation. It made Nance wonder how much of the real Reverend Charles Earl was still in there, or if this Geth was just using him as a human puppet, to be discarded once he'd served its purpose like the rest of the junk it had left in its wake all over this once-fair town.

"That's all true," Nance said. "Crook ran a few sawmills across our great state and up there in Vermont, too. Out in the woods beyond the Thompson farm was where you could find it back in those days. But that isn't the most interesting thing about our town's founder. Not by a stretch."

The reverend took two more strides toward them, his eyes never leaving the sheriff's. In Nance's peripherals—he didn't dare take his eyes off of Earl's—he saw Trudy draw her hand back and tuck the grenade safely into her pocket.

Charles took the two last steps, until he finally stood face to face with Nance, though Nance remained on his knees. People were blatantly watching them now, looking up from their pads and drawing implements. "Tell me, Sheriff. Tell me the real story of Daniel Crook."

Nance nodded toward the church ceiling. "That bull there is Dan Crook's brand. You can see it on the rafters in anything built in those days. It was his signature. And if Dan Crook was fond of anything, it was putting his signature on just about everything he could. Vanity was his weakness, Charles," he said, lowering his head and raising his eyebrows to impress this fact upon him. "It's a weakness shared by many rich and powerful men, I suspect. Maybe even most. Sure, they might act like they're above critique from us little people, like it doesn't matter to em, they might even *believe* it, but those words chip away at em a notch at a time, until it's about all they can think of. And men like that, they don't have a change of heart when that happens, at least not toward kindness. No, it's at that point they reveal their true nature. See, when a man of great stature suffers the indignities of the little people, salt of the earth types like you and me, their focus whittles away to a fine point. *Revenge* is what they want then. As cold and pure as a blizzard in February."

"Revenge," Earl said.

"That's right," Nance said. "Can we sit, Earl? Think that'd be okay with Geth?"

The reverend didn't seem to hear the sarcastic bite in Nance's query. "I suppose it would," he said.

Nance stepped over to the nearest pew and sat. Charles followed and sat down beside him. Nance leaned back a bit and stretched out an arm over the back of the pew, taking up more space than he needed. It was a power move he used with perps of various crimes and misdemeanors, unconsciously signaling to them that he was bigger, the dominant animal. Reverend Earl sat with his legs pressed together and his hands on his knees, his back rigid against the polished wood.

"That was the impetus of Daniel Crook's downfall," Nance said. "His vanity, but also a need for revenge. A long time ago there was a statue of him out there in Wyndham Park." He pointed in the direction of Town Hall. "Carved out of granite, our state rock, with fine little ribbons of smoky quartz, our state gemstone—though I imagine you'd be hard-pressed to find someone other than a geologist who'd call it a *gem*. When I say a long time ago, Father, I don't mean that in an exaggerated sense. That statue was toppled well before even the eldest of us here was a gleam in their father's eye. In fact, if you asked, I'd be willing to bet not many people here even know it ever existed."

"Why is that?"

"Because the people of Crooks Corner know how to keep secrets." Again, he lowered his head and raised his eyebrows. "Sure, we may hand down quirky little stories like these from time to time, but for the most part, we keep mum about our past. I don't suppose you heard about the Pied Piper, have you?"

Earl smirked. "Everyone knows the Pied Piper, don't they?"

"Of Crooks Corner, I mean." Nance leaned toward him. "One day, back in Nineteen Thirty-Five, during the height of the Dust Bowl, hundreds of timber rattlers came slithering through downtown. It was a Sunday, and church had just let out. Everyone in their Sunday best, which as you can imagine looked quite a bit finer than how most folks dress for church these days. Folks had started to walk home, or get into their cars, those who had em, when a river of brown and black shapes came winding up Main Street. Some say they came from the woods behind the Thompson farm, and I suppose I'd believe it. They bit just about everything that moved, or so they say. Folks panicked. Plenty locked themselves in this very church. Nobody died, to my knowledge, but a few people lost fingers or toes, and I'd bet dollars to donuts they ran through just about all the antivenom in the county that day. But there were no deaths, at least not from venom. Spared by the grace of God, some said."

Charles huffed a bitter laugh. Nance hadn't expected it, and hearing it almost threw him for a loop. The man was clearly further gone that he'd first suspected.

"Funny thing," he said. "According to legend, some city buster'd showed up a week or so earlier claiming he had in his possession what some said was a 'fanciful device' that could scare away vermin. Went door-to-door trying to sell em to housewives and old maids, like a vacuum salesman. Most folks swore he was a shyster. Others said he'd brought a rat with him, right into their homes, to demonstrate this so-called 'miracle' device. The ones who claimed it worked said the moment he plugged it in and turned it on the rat started gnawing at its cage, frantic to get away. The closer the device came to it, the crazier the rat got. Of course, even with the rat problem compounded by the Dust Bowl, most folks wouldn't have had the kind of money needed to throw away on a device with such a limited use. Then lo and behold, those snakes came winding through town biting everybody, and just about then that device started to look pretty darn keen. Buster had a truck bed full of em. He convinced the mayor to let him use the P.A. system they'd just had installed at the town hall, and within minutes those snakes were high-tailing their skinny little butts back where they'd come from."

"Surely that's not true," Earl said with a suspicious grin. "Is it?"

"Oh, it's true, all right. There's a patent, if you care to look, listed under the name of Russell P. Hedgewood, who has over a dozen other patents in the database. Not coincidentally, the salesman—who may or may not have been Russell P. Hedgewood himself—sold off every single unit in his truck that very day. You might even find one now and then at a yard sale or an antique shop. As for the man himself—the Pied Piper of Crooks Corner, as he was called—he wasn't seen by another soul in this town ever again. But Hedgewood, if that's indeed who he was, there's a record of his death in the Seattle papers, from a few months after this all went down. He died under rather tragic and mysterious circumstances in the home built by his grandfather. His body, you see, was found ensnared and practically mummified inside one of his very own contraptions, which just so happened to have been patented right after his so-called Vermin Disruptor."

"How odd," the reverend said.

"It is peculiar, isn't it? Although still not as odd as what happened to Dan Crook."

"What happened to him, Hubert?"

Again, Nance was thrown off. He and Reverend Earl had never been on speaking terms, when they could avoid it, and though Nance called the man by his first name in a professional manner, he'd certainly never been called "Hubert" by the reverend. It was *Sheriff*, most often. *Nance*, if Earl was feeling some kind of way about him. Anyone who called him by his first name called him *Bert*. Only his mother and Janine had called him *Hubert*.

"Well, Charles, he'd made a lot of promises, and he'd followed through on those promises by making a lot of folks wealthy in our once-burgeoning town of Crooks Corner, with the sawmill and the saloon and the bank and whatnot. But after the sawmill went under, and the teetotalers got their way in Washington, and the bank was forced to foreclose on so many homes the bank manager inevitably had to file for bankruptcy himself, those same folks didn't seem to care for or respect old Dan Crook any longer. People had lost their jobs and the town had fallen to disrepair. So one night, a bunch of men—most folks say it was his own ex-employees from the sawmill, though it could've been anyone in town, so sore were they for having put their trust in what they'd begun to think of as a swindler, a goldbricker, so no one can quite say for sure—they went out to Wyndham Park and pushed that statue right off its pedestal. Cracked and crumbled just about to dust when it hit the pavement, a consequence of all those filaments of smoky quartz, or so they say."

"Oh dear."

"Yes, sir. Oh dear, indeed. They say that was the final straw for Dan Crook. He'd been the mayor of Crooks Corner for three terms, but he was voted out of office only a week after the statue came down. *Ousted*, according to the papers, in a landslide victory for his opponent. His wife and children had died of diphtheria a decade or so earlier, shortly after the bidecennial celebration of the town he'd himself founded—who'd provided Crooks Corner in almost sixteen of those twenty years more wealth and prosperity than most towns in the Granite State had seen in those days. Dan Crook'd lost just about everything. A rich man whose wealth had been in decline for years, ungratefully scorned by the people of the town he'd built up from nothing. He was like a powder keg just waiting to explode. And explode he did.

"You see, Charles, it's *the lies we tell ourselves* that hurt the most. When those lies are exposed..." Nance clucked his tongue, shaking his head gravely. "Dan Crook told himself he was a great man, but in reality he was just a man like any other, who happened to be in the right place at the right time, using all the right patter to sway the right people's goals toward his own. We've had quite a few charlatans swing their dicks through these parts over the years, some of them claiming to be able to make people rich, a few of them even purporting to be the *Second Coming*, the new Messiah. But sooner or later, they come to realize they've messed with the wrong town. Live Free or Die, that's our state motto. It says so over the town council chamber, right there above where our disgraced former mayor and town founder Dan Crook sat for three terms."

Outside, something battered against the heavy doors, jolting just about everyone in the church, most of whom had been at least half-attentive to Nance's stories.

"Well, I guess the climax of my little story will have to wait. It sounds like His Nibs has arrived."

Reverend Earl had been sitting on the edge of the pew, listening intently. His brow furrowed, and he glanced anxiously over his shoulder at the doors. "What happened to Crook?"

"Another time," Nance said, dusting his hands with finality. "Shall I open the door, Charles, or would you like the dubious honor?"

"*Help!*" came a small voice from behind the doors just then. It wasn't what Nance expected to hear, and the hairs on the back of his neck stood on end. The pounding was joined by more, a hammering of fists against wood, as well as the voices of several boys. "*Let us in! Please, let us in!*"

Reverend Earl stood to answer the door. His scowl had vanished, replaced by the beatific smile he'd worn earlier. "Wonderful! More lost sheep for our Shepherd."

Nance stood to follow him, to prevent him from opening

the door, but the hovering weapons pinwheeled toward him, stopping him dead. He raised his hands, hoping to pacify them.

We can't open that door to more children, he thought. *Not with Geth on the way. But we can't just leave em out there, either...*

While the reverend approached the doors, Nance caught the eyes of Trudy Bell and Randy Jacobs, giving him ominous looks.

This is much worse than a ruckus, he thought. *It's a damned moral quandary.*

4

ADAM BRUNT FELT HIGHER than he ever had in his life, which was ironic, considering he'd been dead for several hours.

The pure *rush* he got off Geth, the *power* he felt surging through his body, through muscles which should have been atrophying, through a heart that shouldn't be pumping... it was unlike anything he'd ever experienced before. Better than alcohol, better than coke, better than the high he got from scoring a winning touchdown and the entire stadium cheering his nickname. Right then, Brahma Brunt could've bowled over the entire China shop and every other damn store in town, and he *would*, the second Geth let him out of his pen to play. He could've torn the little faggot Dukas kid's head right off his shoulders *with his bare fucking hands* if Walden Fucking LeSawbruh hadn't stepped up to him before he'd gotten the chance.

Brunt spat on the ground at Le Sawbruh's feet. His rage was so pure, so *righteous*, he was surprised the glob of spit and blood didn't hiss like acid on the pavement. "I'm gonna beat the red outta you now, you half-breed bush ni—"

Walden's kick came lightning fast, slamming directly into Brunt's solar plexus. It knocked the epithet out of his mouth and would've slammed the wind out of him if he'd had breath to exhale. But the sudden impact didn't rock him. Brunt stood stockstill. He had the power of Geth inside him, keeping him steady. And the shock that found its way onto LeSawbruh's secondsago-cocky face brought the smile back to Brunt's own.

"You're gonna wish you never did that, shitbird," he said, and grabbed Walden by the collar of his coat. He lifted the kid right off his feet as if he weighed nothing, even though they were roughly the same height and build. Not with Geth. Geth puri-fied and distilled his rage and poured it straight into his blood-stream. Geth made him stronger, able to withstand anything thrown at him and give it back tenfold. *A thousand*-fold. He was rock hard not just in his muscles but in his pants. In that mo-ment, with Walden Shitbird LeSawbruh dangling from his fists like the world's lightest and ugliest barbell, if given the chance to fuck someone right now, he wouldn't have been surprised to dis-cover that his load would blow a hole right through her.

Fuck yeah, he thought. *Geth fucking rules.*

And then he grabbed LeSawbruh by the crotch of his jeans and chucked him up against the kids screaming and whining at the door, knocking them over like bowling pins.

5

"WE HAVE TO HELP HIM!" Taylor cried.

Cassandra held her little sister's hand tightly, just in time to prevent her from running headlong toward the fight. Walden had bravely intervened to help those kids, but now all four of them were about to get killed.

"You're just gonna stand there and let him kill them?" she snapped at Mike Stuckey and Dave MacNamara, who stood by Brunt's shitty blue Mustang, gawping at the scene. The two of them glanced at her, then looked at each other. It was clear nei-ther of them had the guts to do anything.

"Real tough guys, huh? You're both cowards!"

"You don't know," Stuckey said. "There's something *wrong* with those two. Like wronger-than-normal wrong."

Cassandra shook her head in disgust.

Mr. Hildebrand and Ms. Stabler returned to the truck. Hildebrand opened the driver door for Ms. Stabler to slide in beside Mr. Combs.

"You're leaving?" Cassandra asked in disbelief. "They're gonna kill him, Mr. Hildebrand!"

He turned with his hand still on the door handle, wearing a look of disappointment. "I'm not leaving," he said, then leaned in to the cab. "I have to stay," he told Combs and Stabler. "But you have to keep going, Elana. You *have* to shut off that machine."

Through the opened back window, Cassandra saw the dismay in Ms. Stabler's eyes. After a moment, she nodded. "Okay," she said, her eyes suddenly shining with the beginning of tears. "I love you."

Hildebrand gave her a surprised smile, as if she'd never said it to him before. "I love you, too," he said. "And keep an eye on him, okay? He still might not be himself."

Suddenly it was like one of Grammy Flynn's soap operas, with revelations of a secret love and suspicions between them. Hildebrand took Stabler's hand briefly. They exchanged obviously loving smiles, then he let go, stepped out and closed the door behind him.

CLANG-CLANG!

The sound of the bell at town hall resounded through the street. The four of them looked at each other, unsure what was happening.

"A warning?" Hildebrand said.

The thought struck Cassandra like a thunderbolt. "The cameras!" She hurried for the back of the truck where they'd left them before Ms. Stabler and Mr. Combs could drive off with them. She reached in and grabbed both, then held one out to Hildebrand. He took it in both hands, gingerly holding it with the pinky and ring fingers of his injured right hand.

The bell rang again. *CLANG-CLANG! CLANG-CLANG!*

Ms. Stabler started the truck, looking over her shoulder to back up.

"I think those boys are dead," Hildebrand said to Cassandra, nodding toward the church steps, where Brunt bent to pick up Walden from the pile of freaked-out kids. "Adam and Sean. I think they're like the people we saw shuffling around in the streets, the ramblers, I called them, only Adam and Sean seem to be under the control of Geth."

"*Who is Geth?*" Cassandra said, frustrated beyond belief. She winced as Walden took another punch to the face

Hildebrand opened his mouth as if to answer her question, then his eyes suddenly widened. "Whaaaat the fuck..."

Taylor gasped. Cassandra nearly did herself. It was the first time she'd heard any of her teachers cuss, and probably one of the first times Taylor had heard an adult swear in front of her. But when she turned, she saw what caused him to curse, and she thought even Principal Elder would've forgiven him in that moment.

A ramshackle carriage made of the same Halloween crap and random stuff as the cyclone they'd seen swirling around Mr. Combs's house floated a good three feet above the road, just this side of the intersection. The thing with the pumpkin head sat in it like a king in its throne. Its hands were deathly pale under the streetlight, almost blue-gray. The carriage stopped, and the pumpkin thing rose to its feet. With each step, one of the possessed items detached itself from the chariot to cushion the descending feet—a lawn sprinkler, a plastic witch and cauldron, a TV/VCR with rabbit ears—until the creature reached the ground. There, it turned its jack-o'-lantern head to survey the scene, its stitched smile spreading wide in approval, blinking the Xs of its eyes. Seeing this caused a sick feeling in the pit of Cassandra's stomach and a crawling sensation on her skin.

"*That's* Geth," Hildebrand said, pointing.

Of course it was Geth. Who else could it be? It was the Pumpkin King. He was Halloween personified. It was the spirit of Samhain in flesh and blood and gourd. It was *Crom Cuach*, the Celtic demon also known as the Crouching Darkness, and the things that made up its carriage were the souls of the women, men and children whose lives it had taken: the *Sluagh*. Just looking at it chilled her to the marrow, and Taylor let out a little whimper Cassandra felt in her soul.

Ms. Stabler slammed on the breaks, stopping the truck just shy of crashing into the demon and its chariot.

"Ram it!" Mr. Hildebrand shouted.

Through the windshield, Ms. Stabler gave him a terrified look. She seemed to briefly considered it, then nodded determinedly and stepped so hard on the gas she rose from her seat. The truck responded eagerly, peeling away in reverse.

The demon Geth kept walking forward, undeterred by the half-ton of rust-speckled American steel rolling toward him. With about five feet from collision, Geth flicked a hand like it had when it launched the Big Wheel and trash bag at them back at Mr. Combs's house, and the truck jerked to a stop—only it didn't stop *running*, just moving. The wheels spun and spun, peeling rubber and raising a cloud of black smoke. Ms. Stabler leaned over the wheel in frustration, fighting with it. The truck skidded sideways until the wheels struck the curb, and Geth passed by it without a glance. The demon was thirty, maybe twenty feet away from Cassandra and Taylor but it was sauntering, taking its time.

Ms. Stabler finally stopped the truck with a look of defeat. In the silence, Cassandra heard meaty slaps, and remembered of Brunt's fists hammering Walden. She looked back to see Walden kicking up at Brunt from the ground. Brunt kicked the foot out of his way and swung a fist down like a piston, slamming into the top of his head.

Then the chariot of junk broke apart into its individual pieces and hovered there, blocking their exit like a giant moving net, ready to attack whoever decided to risk their lives in escaping. Geth's smile widened further. It ignored Philbert Piper, who was sitting on the curb weeping, and headed straight for Cassandra and the others. Cassandra drew Taylor in front of her and hugged her protectively, her camera level with Taylor's. She didn't dare try using them on Geth, with no way to signal to Hildebrand her intention before Geth did to them what it'd just done to the truck, or worse.

"*There* she is," Geth said as it neared them. Its voice was slightly gruff and deep yet surprisingly soothing, but the movement of its pumpkin lips didn't quite match what it was saying, and Mr. Hildebrand was right: there was no face under the jack-o'-lantern, just a hollow pit with a lit candle within. "Crooks Corner's very own little *inhak* slayer," Geth said, the flame flickering slightly when it spoke as if in response to breath it clearly couldn't be exhaling, from a body that was obviously as dead as Brunt and Fitz. "Turned them into dust as if by Our own hand. We are so pleased to finally meet you."

It smiled again, extending its gray and lifeless right hand.

Cassandra held her sister tightly, worried that if she didn't Taylor would shake the dead man's hand out of fear or politeness, but also aware that Taylor was anchoring her, that if she let go her own sanity might split apart and she'd faint like some Victorian lady in an old black-and-white movie. If she didn't hold on to some small piece of reality, some shred of love and goodness and hope and everything else this Geth stood against, she'd fall into a deep abyss and awaken to a world devoid of life, a world of nothing but death and pain and endless suffering, like the songs she loved to listen to, only real this time, not some depressive singer's fantasy.

Geth was The End. The end of Crooks Corner, the end of Taylor and Grammy Flynn and life as Cassandra knew it. And even though she'd never felt like she belonged, like she mattered, she knew that if she didn't stand against Geth, didn't keep Taylor safe from it, all of the pain that was sure to follow would be for nothing.

So she held on to Taylor, held her closer than she ever had in her life, even when they'd gotten the news about Mom and Dad, even at their funeral, standing beside their double grave, with the empty plots beside them reserved for Taylor and Grammy Flynn and herself.

She held her sister and looked the demon in its slitted eyes and whispered, "*No.*"

6

WALDEN LOOKED up through a sheen of blood and tears. His lower lip was split and his nose felt broken, streaming blood into his mustache and mouth. He tasted its salty, coppery tang and spat. His left eye had been beaten shut, and the right would have a shiner tomorrow—*If there is a tomorrow*, he thought, more out of practicality than morbidity. Because the truth was, these two goofs weren't just going to beat him to within an inch of death. They were going to kill him. Because Brunt and Fitz were dead themselves. He wasn't sure before but now he *knew*: Brunt's ice blue eyes had gone entirely black. They regarded him with the cold, dead glare of a shark as his fists—the left adorned with a championship ring that had already made several indents in Walden's face and upper body—rained down on him.

Walden had gone limp. The pain was immense, not just from Brunt's fists but from the intermittent kicks that Fitz bestowed upon his stomach, ribs and arms. Fitz, whose once-green eyes were also cold and black as oil in the ocean, staring at him from his pitted, blood and pus-streaked face.

Meanwhile, the kids Brunt had so casually tossed him into, knocking them all to the ground, had sat up and skittered out of the way, no longer banging for help on the church doors.

"Let him go!" little Freddy Kreuger said.

"Leave him alone!" said the slightly larger Indiana Jones.

Walden saw the glint of Brunt's championship ring, doused in his blood, as another fist came his way. He didn't even have the energy to move his head. As it collided with his skull it made the sound of a bell in his head.

As the next punch and kick struck him with a one-two blow, he heard the sound again and recognized it for what it was: the bell at Town Hall ringing out.

CLANG-CLANG! CLANG-CLANG!

Send not to know for whom the bell tolls, his grandfather used to say, a quote from some old book or poem, which he'd explained to mean that death comes for everyone sooner or later, young or old.

That had never been more valid than tonight, when Death had come indiscriminately for adults, children and pets alike. And right now, as he curled his fists to protect his mangled face and the bell pealed out twice more, it seemed like Death had finally set its sights on Walden Thoreau LeSabre.

7

Cody leaped off the horse right on Brittany's heels. While she headed back to Town Hall, pulling hard on Midnight's reins, Cody headed for the tall black fence that ran along the north sidewalk.

"Where are you going?" she called after him.

"I think I can beat him through the cemetery!"

It looked like Brittany was heading for the bell, Midnight fighting her every step of the way. A good enough plan, since the bell had been used to alert people of fires long before the P.A. system and the air raid siren became standard. It was big and heavy, made of brass now old and tarnished, and it was also pretty damn loud. They'd rung it during the bicentennial celebration a few years ago and people said they'd heard it clear across town. Cody himself had been on one of the parade floats downtown, just east of the theater, and had heard it well enough himself. They should be able to hear it at the church just fine. But he wasn't sure they'd understand the danger it meant.

"Be careful!" Brittany shouted. She was tying her horse to the bell rigging. Midnight whinnied and tried to pull away until she was secured.

"I will!"

Cody dashed across the street as quickly as he could while the chariot carried this Geth thing closer to Crook Street, trailing all kinds of floating junk behind it like exhaust. As he reached the cemetery gates, Cody realized he'd misjudged. Barring some sort of miracle, it wasn't likely he'd make it to the church before Geth did, whoever Geth was and however Brittany happened to know him. He just had to hope he'd be close enough once she got the bell ringing to add his voice to her warning.

The gates were wide open by some stroke of luck. He supposed in all the chaos the caretaker had neglected to lock them, and Cody couldn't say he blamed them. He turned swiftly, bolting up the brick roadway into the cemetery.

As he ran between the headstones and monuments, he couldn't help but remember the first time he'd had to run tonight, through the fake graveyard at Halloween Village. There'd been vampires in coffins and rotting hands reaching up from the ground to grab at him, harmless fun under normal circumstances, turned deadly—because of Geth, he supposed. Fortunately, St. Joseph's Cemetery appeared to be deserted. The last thing Cody wanted to run into while sprinting through a graveyard at night was a reenactment of *Michael Jackson's Thriller.*

Through the barren trees along the western edge of the fence, he saw Geth's chariot turn onto Crook Street. He couldn't see the church through a thick hedge, but the shouts from there grew louder. Whatever was happening, if they'd seen Geth or not, things seemed to be coming to a head.

Cody cut across the well-manicured grass, up a low hill, weaving between the tombstones there. With names like Booker and Clifton and Royce, this portion of the cemetery was the oldest, with stones that had crumbled and their names and dates worn to barely visible. The Crook mausoleum stood between him and the northwestern edge of the fence, and here was the only lighted area of the cemetery outside of the lamps illuminating the roadways. The accordion gate had been left open and the light appeared to be shining from the floor within: a discarded flashlight from its conical shape.

The bell began to ring out behind him, loud and true, as he passed the mausoleum. A shadow lurched into the light from within but didn't emerge before Cody blew past it, leaving who-ever or whatever it was in his dust. He was still a good twenty feet from the fence but quickly closing the distance, lungs burning and calf muscles aching. He was used to running short stints, except on the rare occasion Coach made him do laps. He'd just run about a quarter of a mile in two minutes.

Back at Town Hall, Brittany rang the bell again.

By the fourth clang, Cody pushed through the prickly hedge, then scrambled up the fence, planting his feet on the metal bars and vaulting over its spiked spires. He landed in the dead grass on the other side, the soles of his shoes skidding in bits of gravel from the ditch between the fence and Crook Street.

What Cody saw then shook him more than anything he'd seen yet.

"No," he breathed, shaking his head dumbly.

But it was already too late. *He* was too late.

Halfway up the street stood Geth himself—whatever he or it truly was—standing just a few feet away from Hildebrand, Cas-sandra and her little sister. It was holding out a hand to them. It was beckoning them near.

Cody thought he'd seen the worst of it, until little Taylor Flynn broke free of her big sister's embrace, and to Cassandra's and Cody's absolute horror, she took the monster's right hand.

8

"CHARLES, DON'T OPEN THAT DOOR," Nance said sharply.

The bell at Town Hall rang a fourth time, and the children banging and shouting to get in had fallen entirely silent since it started ringing. Whether it meant they'd given up or cut and run, Nance didn't know. He did know they were likely safer out there, at least for the time being, even if the boys themselves didn't know it. He also knew they couldn't further risk the lives of these people to save a few stragglers.

Everybody aside from Charles seemed to get that. Not a single soul pleaded for him to open the doors. They merely stared at the front of the church in solemn thought. With Geth on his way and the guns pointed at Nance and the dunderheads who'd brought the biggest of them, no one wanted to bring more children into this double bind.

"Mustn't turn them away," the reverend said, absently fingering his rosary. "Children in danger. Lost sheep, looking for a shepherd. Geth awaits them."

"They're gone, Charles. Listen."

Earl listened. In the silence, Nance thought he heard sharp voices and the slap of tenderizing meat, but it was probably his imagination, firing on all cylinders.

Finally, the reverend's eyes alighted. His beatific smile returned, spreading across his face. "They're here," he said excitedly, rushing up the aisle toward the altar. "Geth has come, my friends! Our Lord and Savior walks amongst us!"

9

"ONE... two... three... four—*jump!*

"One... two... three... four—*JUMP!*"

Jay kept trying to psyche himself up to do it, to leap through the intermittent space in the cyclone of toys, Halloween stuff and backyard junk just large enough—he was sure of it—for someone a little taller than himself to leap through, but every time he got to the "jump" part he chickened out again. It was one thing in a video game. It would have been so easy sitting behind a screen with a can of Rockstar at his side, using the W-A-S-D keys and spacebar to lunge forward and jump. And if not, if he timed his jump imperfectly—though he was relatively certain his count was correct—the worst he would suffer was a brutal digital death like the ones in the original *Tomb Raider.* Then he'd be right back on his feet to try again.

But this wasn't a video game, and he didn't need to remind himself of that fact. He'd just narrowly escaped getting sliced and diced by a rusty push mower the second he'd jumped over the busted fence into Mr. Combs's yard, only managing to stop it from steamrolling over him by jamming a pair of discarded hedge clippers between its blades at damn near the very last second. If he hadn't spotted them lying there in the ankle-deep grass just in time, he'd have been mincemeat.

Now he stood in front of the Junknado, even more menacing up close with its clang and clatter magnified by a million, the swirling junk crashing together like stones in a tumble dryer. He'd noticed the space in it quickly, since he'd been searching the yard for something to cause exactly that. He'd considered the push mower itself, but it was too heavy to chuck, and he worried it might come alive again even with the clippers stuck through the blades. The birdbath was also not an option. Too heavy, and filled with slimy, leaf-littered water he had no interest in touching without any hand sanitizer in sight.

He also didn't want to attract the attention of the Possessors —or what Cassandra had called *sloo-ah*—any more than he likely already had just by standing here. They seemed to be sentient, but whether or not it was sapience or they were responding to some sort of hive mind, like the Zerg and their Overmind from *Starcraft*, he didn't know. The Pumpkin Man seemed to be able to manipulate them, but that didn't necessarily make it their master. One thing he knew for certain was they were *vicious*, with or without the guy with the pumpkin head.

For now, they seemed to be more intent on protecting Combs's Machine than killing, and Jay aimed to keep it that way, at least until he was inside the house with the door locked tightly behind him.

When he'd noticed the space, making the backdoor visible at a five-second interval, jumping through it became not just the best option but the *only* option. Jay had an instinct about these things, and his instincts were rarely wrong.

He just had to work up the courage to actually *do it*.

"Okay, come on, Jay," he muttered, clenching his fists at his sides and punching his already sore thighs with each part of his mantra, the way he psyched himself up before a big battle with the game on pause. "You beat *Diablo II* on single player!" *Punch*. "You defeated hundreds of Zerg armies singlehandedly!" *Punch*. "You beat fucking *Max Payne* in DOA mode!" *Punch*. "You're a well-oiled *machine*!" *Punch!* "You trained *your entire life* for this one fucking *moment*." *PUNCH!* "You're the *only one* that can do this." *PUNCH-PUNCH!*

And now your thighs hurt right before you have to jump, he thought, angry at himself. He wasn't exactly well-oiled, either. Not without chugging a full can of Rockstar first.

"Forget it," he said aloud. "Energy drinks are a crutch. You don't *need* that shit. You're Jay Fucking Nielson. You're *Demon-Spawn84.*"

The empty space passed by the backdoor again, making it visible for maybe half a second, if he was lucky. There was a good two feet between the cyclone and the door itself. The door had even been left open, as if waiting for him to arrive and jump through it.

It was *perfect.*

Still, he couldn't help being terrified.

"One... two... three... four—*JUMP!*"

Again, he hesitated. It wasn't right. His timing was off by a split second. He would've gotten slammed by the cyclone and whipped backwards into the grass, broken and bloody. Maybe even *dead.*

"Okay," he told himself. He took a deep breath in through his nose, out through his mouth. "Okay.... One... two... three... four—"

On *JUMP*, he leaped into the air, launching himself forward, putting all of his trust and his life on his instincts. For a moment he was sure he'd mistimed it, that he'd feel the crushing blows of the cyclone pounding against his ribs and limbs, battering him to death.

Instead, he soared through the empty space and tumbled right through the doorway, landing on his side with a jarring crash that caused stars to shoot across his vision. He barrel-rolled onto his butt as quickly as he could and kicked the door shut just as the things making up the Halloweenado—the Zerglings or *sloo-ah* or Possessors or whatever they were *actually* called—seemed to realize the sanctity of their blockade had been breached.

BOOM! BOOM!

The entities pounded on the door, rattling its hinges, shaking the floor. Jay sat there staring at it, praying for it to hold. *It has to hold.* He was dead otherwise, and he hadn't just risked certain death jumping through just to get killed on the other goddamn side.

The hammering stopped abruptly. Jay breathed a sigh of relief in the moment of relative silence, believing himself safe, at least for now.

With an almighty crash the door tore off its hinges and launched directly at him. He'd been leaning forward slightly, sitting on the edge of his seat if there'd been one, and it struck him dead-on in the forehead. Even if its forward momentum hadn't continued pushing him backward, he would've fallen back anyway from the concussive blow. It pressed him down flat to the floor as a tide of Possessors flooded into the house.

The crooked grin of a poorly carved jack-o'-lantern was the last thing Jay Nielson saw.

PART FOUR

GRAVEN IMAGES

Chapter 21

1

"Come with Us, little one," said the thing with the pumpkin head, its lips moving like bad CGI, like the anthropomorphized snowman in that awful *Jack Frost* movie with Michael Keaton. Just looking at it caused Renny's guts to twist into knots. Any potential plea he might have formulated to free the three of them evaporated before it reached his own lips.

Speaking of lips, how is this thing able to talk? he wondered. *I guess the dead man's vocal cords must still be in its throat. Got to be at least a stump in there holding that pumpkin on its shoulders.*

Renny almost laughed aloud. Here he was quibbling with himself about how an entity that used telekinesis to make all manner of things murder people could possibly manage to speak, when all of their lives were on the line. He could only assume it was a warning sign for losing his mind.

The bell at Town Hall rang again, chiming out a warning they no longer required. The inscription on its brass plaque was quite apt at the moment: GIVE ME LIBERTY OR GIVE ME DEATH! A variation on New Hampshire's state motto—Live free or die—and possibly the phrase that inspired it, from that famous speech by some long-dead politician. Like him, that choice was no longer theirs to make. Death was already at their doorstep, liberty a privilege no longer granted. There was no way to prevent Geth from striding up those stairs and murdering every single living soul who'd taken shelter in the church, children and all, just as the things under its command had done all over town.

"No," Cassandra said again, shaking her head defiantly. Her voice was small and quavering, but she held her sister even tighter. "You can't have her."

Renny had to admire her bravery, but now was not the time to be impetuous. Everything they'd seen tonight had proven Geth as an entity of immense power, either supernatural or extraterrestrial. This thing saw no value in human life. It was not something to be trifled with. This was not something you just said *No way* to, and it would smile politely and say *Well, thank you anyway. Carry on.*

No, this was a thing that would *make* you go wherever it wanted. It could move people around like zombies—not the Romero kind, but the old Haitian voodoo zombies, slaves to their master, with no will of their own. And it could take their lives in an instant, if it wanted to.

So why hasn't it? Renny wondered.

Because it wants something from us. Or from Taylor, specifically.

Geth's pumpkin lips pressed together in an imitation of annoyance. "She will come with Us, or everyone will die," it said, its tone of almost bored aggravation, like a king who'd already sentenced several of his subjects to death, or a child pitting ants together in a dugout pit in his sandbox. "Do you not believe Us?" it asked. "Shall We demonstrate Our power once more?" Its right shoulder rose in a half-shrug. "Very well. Observe... and be humbled."

The three of them turned as Geth pointed toward the church.

"*No, don't—*" Renny began.

The pop and squelch of Adam Brunt's and Sean Fitzgerald's heads exploding silenced him. Bursts of bone, brain and blood, shimmering in the light from the church, fell in a torrential downpour over Walden and the horrified younger boys. The headless bodies stood upright a moment, swaying on their feet like boxers who'd been punched in the head one too many times, then fell with heavy thumps on the porch floor. Walden, surely close to unconscious, barely flinched when they landed in front of him.

"Holy fuck!" Mike Stuckey gasped. The two remaining boys in Brunt's crew still stood by the Mustang, far enough away to avoid being drenched in the blood of their dead friends.

Cassandra belatedly covered her sister's eyes.

"Now," Geth said, its tone more pressing, "We tell you again: the girl shall accompany Us, or We will extinguish your inconsequential lives, one by one."

"Okay!" her little sister cried.

"*No.*" Cassandra somehow sounded even smaller, like a mouse caught in a trap. "I won't let you."

"I *have* to," Taylor said. "You *saw.* If don't go with him, he'll make all our heads 'splode just like theirs."

Taylor broke free of her embrace before Cassandra could mount another protest. She took the monster's cold, dead hand.

Cassandra's right, Renny thought. *We can't let it take her.*

"Let me come with her," he said, unable to think of any other way out of this but a Faustian bargain. "A, uh... a chaperone!"

Geth ushered Taylor to his side. She stood looking up at Renny with tears shimmering in her eyes. "You are *all* welcome," the creature said. "This is to be Our church, after all. The Church of Geth, the Great Pumpkin."

Renny only managed to prevent himself from laughing by biting down hard on his tongue. He opened his mouth to say something smart, then thought better of it and merely stepped aside, allowing Geth and Taylor to pass, hand in hand. Cassandra gave him a pleading look. He couldn't ignore her, but the only thing he could do was follow Geth and Taylor, and suggest—with his eyes, not with words—that Cassandra come along with them.

Geth tapped Micheal Stuckey and David MacNamara on the foreheads as it passed them. Both boys shrank from its touch but were unable to avoid it, immediately taking on a dazed look that reminded Renny of kids doped up on too much Ritalin, their eyes vacant and mouths slack. Both boys fell into line behind the four of them, like the children of Hamelin following the Pied Piper to their doom.

My God, they're just like the others. Just one tap on their third eyes and they're completely enslaved. How can we stop that? How can we stop it from doing that to us?

Taylor glanced back with frightened, dark eyes as she ascended the stairs in silence alongside Geth. Renny hesitated at the foot of the steps, momentarily fazed by what just happened to David and Micheal. The two boys pushed him forward. He stumbled up the steps. The porch boards, slick with the blood and minced insides of Adam's and Sean's heads, made it difficult to regain his footing. When he finally righted himself, Geth and Taylor had reached the doors. He hurried to catch up with them.

Behind them, a familiar voice called Cassandra's name.

Only Cassandra, Taylor and Renny turned. Geth and the two boys seemed not to care at all.

Cody Brockmeyer dashed out into the middle of the road, stopping a short distance from the truck where Elana and Combs sat, waiting for the roadblock to clear. "Don't follow him!" he shouted, cupping his hands to make his voice carry. "He's evil!"

The doors swung open with a resounding boom against the outer walls. The younger boys and Walden, who was beaten so badly his right eye looked like a split peach and his face was barely recognizable, scurried out of Geth's path. Within the church, a hundred or more of Crooks Corner's residents sat in the pews and in the aisle, uttering gasps of horror and staring dumbfoundedly at the cause of their misery and suffering. Sheriff Nance and Reverend Earl were among them, along with many others Renny recognized. The three young boys in their blood-drenched costumes and winter coats scurried inside gratefully, eager to get to safety and away from Geth.

"Walden..." Cassandra said, her face knotted in sympathy.

The boy, who'd taken one too many beatings at the hands of sociopaths like Brunt and his pals, merely shook his head.

Without a word, without turning to dust or catching fire or being repelled from the church like a vampire from a cross, Geth crossed the threshold, ushering Taylor Flynn into its sanctuary, once Christian, but very soon to be the place of worship for a death cult raised in Geth's name.

And there's nothing I can do to stop it.

As if to prove this, Geth caused the doors to slam shut, sealing them all inside.

2

Sheriff Nance wasn't sure what he expected to see walk through the front doors of Our Lady of Mercy, but it surely wasn't what he got.

The thing holding the little girl's hand walked on two legs, wearing a human body and dressed in fancy human clothes, but it very clearly *wasn't* human. Like the drawings the reverend had displayed proudly to his newly initiated congregation, the creature had the head of a jack-o'-lantern, carved into the Smiley Face cult symbol, with the stitched smile and the Xs for eyes. All this time, he'd been sure it was a hoax. But damned if the demon that cult had apparently been worshiping wasn't standing right here before him, turning its slitted gaze this way and that.

Darla Knight, Nance thought, struck with a sudden sense of regret. With all that had gone on tonight he'd forgotten about her, but now the clues had finally fallen into place. He'd seen that same face drawn in the snow where Philbert Piper found her purse, and he was more certain now than ever that she'd been kidnapped.

The Satanic cult guy was right. Only it wasn't Satan they were communing with, it was Geth. The Cult of Geth. They must've called it here somehow. Summoned *it.*

You know how, he answered himself.

Of course he knew. How did people summon demons in movies? Blood rituals, or a human sacrifice. Meaning, Darla Knight was either gravely injured or dead somewhere right at this moment. Her blood had summoned this monster who considered itself a god. Whoever the Cult of Geth was, they obviously hadn't been prepared for what they'd unleashed, and most or all of them were likely dead themselves.

Three boys somewhere between nine and eleven years old scurried in before Geth, sticky with drying blood. Likely the boys they'd heard banging at the door earlier, before the ringing of the bell at Town Hall. He had hoped they would scurry off before Geth arrived, but it had been a vain hope. They'd been called here by the declaration of safety Nance himself had called in, inadvertently setting Geth's trap.

Two girls entered along with Geth, one around the same age as the young boys, the other in her late teens. Both had long, dark hair, pale skin and freckles: what some people used to call

"Black Irish." The elder girl's obvious concern for the little one meant she was either an older sister or close cousin. Who the younger girl with the Polaroid camera around her neck was to Geth, whether she was merely a hostage or something far more sinister, Nance wasn't sure he wanted to know. Whatever she meant to Geth, she was holding its dead left hand and scared out of her wits. Nance made it his number one priority to get her away from its clutches without calling too much attention to himself.

Two older boys and a man in his mid-thirties entered with them. Nance recognized the man with the bandaged hand as a teacher at Crooks Corner Secondary, a guy named Hildebrand. Something about him made Nance pause and hold his gaze longer than he normally would have, until the man grew uncomfortable and looked off. It wasn't anything physical, or at least he didn't think it was. Just a feeling, one of those deep-down gut feelings he'd get now and then, like last night outside the diner, holding Darla Knight's purse. Nance let his gaze fall on the two older boys who'd shuffled in behind them like a pair of teenaged zombies. The dead look in their black eyes reminded him of Reverend Earl. More of Geth's disciples.

The reverend himself was scuttling through the crowd, gathering up the poems and stories and drawings he'd forced them to do in the name of this affront to his erstwhile God. Once he got his hands full of them, he came bustling up the aisle toward Geth.

"Welcome, my Lord!" he cried jubilantly. "Welcome! I come bearing testaments to your—"

The smile widened on the ridged face of the pumpkin, but instead of acknowledging Father Earl's sycophancy, Geth turned to face Nance, who'd upon the sound of the Town Hall bell had returned closer to the doors, where Trudy Bell and Randy Jacobs lay staring up at the intruder in horror.

"Sheriff Nance!" Geth said happily, defying his expectation that it wouldn't—or *shouldn't*—be able to talk, let alone express emotions. "A pleasure to finally meet you! We are Geth." At this, it bowed slightly and scraped with its free right hand.

Nance almost sputtered. "*We?*"

Reverend Earl bowed his head, gathering the pages to his chest obsequiously.

"For We are Many," Geth said, and its right eye flattened in an approximation of a wink.

"Like Legion," Nance said. "I suppose you'll be pleased to know we're fresh out of pigs to cast you into, then."

Charles let out a gasped laugh, then quickly silenced himself, keeping his eyes on his shoes.

"Are you a Christian, Sheriff?" Geth asked.

"My ex-wife was Irish Catholic. To be honest, I'm a bit surprised you know the reference. I wouldn't expect a god to study the holy books of his competitors."

"We know a great many things, Sheriff. *Especially* who Our enemies are. Is that not so, Father Earl?"

The reverend nodded dumbly, clutching the pages dearly as if he'd produced them himself.

Nance took a moment to regard Hildebrand again, wondering what had gotten him thinking there was something important about the man. Hildebrand moved anxiously back and forth from one foot to the other like a child who had to use the potty, holding up his injured hand against his chest with the other. Was it the subject he taught that caused this gut feeling? Nance was sure it had something to do with the last time he'd seen him... but he still couldn't put his finger on it.

"No more dawdling, Father," Geth said in a pressing tone. "The time has come to introduce Us to Our flock."

"Oh, yes! Yes, of course!" The holy man laid the pages down carefully on a pew. "My friends," he said, trying to get the attention of the survivors, who—aside from several elderly folks or toddlers who'd fallen asleep under the rough church blankets—held their attention raptly on the visitor. "My friends—"

"*WE ARE GETH,*" the thing bellowed over the reverend, its voice rattling the remaining shards in the stained-glass windows, carrying all the way to the rafters and shaking the chandeliers.

Shocked gasps and murmurs ran through the crowd. An old man snored loudly as he awoke, bleary-eyed and confused. A baby began crying, swaddled in her mother's arms. The little toy poodle barked in Denise Garner's arms.

"*You will fall to your knees and worship Us, or be ground to dust at Our feet,*" Geth said, its voice steady and booming, simmering with barely contained rage as it walked casually up the aisle, all but dragging the girl along beside it. "*You will beg for*

Our forgiveness for your transgressions against Us, for the sin of being born of flesh into this cesspool of a world. Then, and only then, will you be spared. We will show you the Truth in the Darkness. We will anoint you with Our Blight. You will become one with Us, and We with you." Geth passed Reverend Earl without even so much as a look, regarding the terrified faces of the onlookers as they continued toward the altar. *"You will spread the Word of Geth far and wide, through the many lands of the Infidels. The Christian and the Muslim and the Hindu and the Buddhist, and every other religion which dares blaspheme against Us with false prophets and empty promises, shall be rendered little more than a memory, a fable. The Word of Geth shall murder all other gods. It shall reach up to Heaven and tear it down, plunge to the depths of Hell and freeze it, cause chaos in Nirvana and spread wide the gates of every netherworld to let the dead roam free. You, my first Acolytes, shall forever be held in high esteem. However long you may live, you shall have a seat at Our table. You shall be Knights in Our Holy Army. You will live long and live well, but only if you FALL TO YOUR KNEES BEFORE US and BEG!"*

With its sermon apparently complete, it turned at the foot of the altar to face the entire congregation, its pumpkin-lipped grin spreading wide across its inhuman face, reminding Nance of *The Grinch Who Stole Christmas*. He couldn't help but shake his head at the absurdity of it all. Did Geth really expect them to *worship* it? For what? Out of fear? And what would that worship entail? This "spreading the word" nonsense sounded suspiciously like an incitement to violence with its "Knights" and "Holy Army." And given that this thing's intrusion into their lives had begun with senseless murder and destruction, Nance didn't believe the odds were very high Geth would have them going door to door with nametags and pamphlets.

"Just like Mass, my friends," Reverend Earl said. Having returned to the front of the church, he began directing people toward the altar, starting with his reluctant congregation. "Line up single file to receive the Eucharist. There'll be no sacramental wine and wafers tonight. You'll simply receive a gentle tap on the forehead, and be filled with Geth's Love and Wisdom."

"Jesus, take the wheel," Randy Jacobs muttered, watching from the floor as Earl's congregation lined up hesitantly to receive the first of Geth's infernal blessings. "He's gonna turn em all into braindead cultists."

Nance didn't bother to mention Geth likely planned to brainwash Randy along with the rest of them, including Nance himself. He wasn't sure he liked the alternative much better, but the thought of becoming like the reverend made him wonder if a quick death wasn't the better of the two options.

What if there's no coming back from Geth's "blight," whatever it is? Doesn't seem like there's much of Reverend Earl left in him. The light's on, but nobody's home. Got to stop this somehow.

He glanced at Randy Jacobs, then Trudy Bell, and his gaze settled on the left pocket of her coat where she'd tucked away the grenade. So far, it hadn't taken on a life of its own, joining its fellow weaponry in holding them captive. The kill radius on it was quite wide, the maiming even wider. If he could somehow lure Geth away from these people, maybe he could use it.

Not likely to get him outside, he thought. *Means it'd have to be close. Earl's office or the toilets. Someone would have to sacrifice themselves for it.*

Someone, he thought. *You know damn well it has to be you.*

"Trudy," he whispered. When the hovering weapons made no move in his direction, he spoke a little louder. "Trudy—"

Both Trudy and Randy looked up, but a commotion up front drew their attention to the altar. At the head of the line, poor old Mrs. Delacroix, the church organist, struggled against the Magnusson twins.

"Sheriff Nance," the reverend called anxiously. "We could use your assistance up here, if you don't mind!"

"Don't do it, Nance," Trudy muttered. "You *can't*."

Randy agreed with a shake of his head.

Nance clenched his jaw, weighing his options. Clearly his opportunity to get the grenade without being noticed had passed. He felt like when he was a kid called up to the front of the class to work out a problem he'd never bothered to study for. If he said no, he'd not only be putting his own life at risk but those of the others, as well.

Whatever he decided, Judy Delacroix seemed to have a pretty mean case of buyer's remorse, and Nance couldn't say he blamed her. If he didn't step in soon, he was sure Geth would make an example of her. And it wouldn't be pretty.

"Be right there," he called reluctantly.

"*Dammit, Nance,*" Trudy said.

Nance ignored her, knowing she was at least partly right. Randy's illegal desert camo AR-15 followed as Nance moved up the aisle, sidestepping the growing line. Members of Earl's congregation moved up and down the pews, waking the young and old who'd fallen asleep and guiding others toward the crowd gathered in the aisle.

"Sheriff..." a young woman holding a sleeping baby whispered, terror in her wide brown eyes, bouncing gently on her heels.

Nance offered her a nod of sympathy but said nothing, not wanting to call Geth's attention to her and her baby. Gary and Denise Garner gave him grave looks as he passed, the toy poodle shivering in her arms. Nance cast his gaze downward in shame, continuing on to where the twins held Mrs. Delacroix by each of her frail arms. They made him think of Gestapo, despite not being German.

"Judy," Nance said as he approached. "How are you, dear?"

The old woman stopped struggling and allowed herself to smile slightly. Geth stood looking down at them from the altar with its carved lips twisted in an approximation of a sneer. The girl at his side stood stock still, shivering like dog, her moist eyes downcast.

"I'm tired, Bert," Judy said. He felt it in her voice, saw it in every line on her face. He sympathized and empathized. It had been one hell of a long day for all of them. "Please... just let me go."

Nance considered her words, and thought he understood their meaning. Not *let me go* as in *let me leave. Let me go* as in, *I don't have the fight left in me to struggle anymore. Let me die.*

He sympathized with that too, and a small part of him even empathized. It would be easier to just give up and eat a bullet. Let Geth's sentient weapons put a hole in his head. Probably a lot less painful than whatever Charles and the other of Geth's zombies were going through right now. Nance couldn't imagine, with all the monster had put them through tonight, that being one of its slaves could be any kind of mercy. He suspected somewhere in the back of the reverend's converted mind was a tortured soul crying out for freedom.

Suicide obviously wasn't an option, but he couldn't just let Geth turn all of these people into mindless cultists against their will, either. It reminded him of his own conversion performed by Reverend Earl's predecessor, at the behest of his ex, who'd insisted they have a Catholic wedding and raise their kids in the church. Standing here before the altar reminded him of the compromise he'd made to be with her, and the sad and downright pathetic end to their marriage. Outside of official duties, he hadn't set foot in this place since Janine had packed her bags and left. He was too embarrassed.

Now he was just downright mad.

The hard truth was, he'd always been suspicious of the devout. Of those who put their faith—their *god*—above all else, even family and friends. It was difficult to admit, even to himself, particularly in light of the events on 9/11. He'd tried to be open-minded and loving, but he worried about America's future, like Charles had himself before he'd had his own religious conversion. He envisioned a slow but steady erosion of their freedoms, and an uprise of Christian fundamentalism as a response—had seen it even from Charles and his followers, who were the furthest from Evangelical you could get, at least among Christians —and the thought terrified him.

And now here he was, about to turn these people over to Geth.

His own cowardice disgusted him.

But what else could he do? Let them all die as martyrs?

"I know, Judy," he said, trying to remain in the present, to stay focused and supportive. "And I wish it were that easy. But you've seen what this... this *thing* can do to us. There's a lot of people here who'll be hurt if you don't do what it says, not just you."

The pumpkin-headed freak nodded. "Do as your sheriff tells you. Come quietly, come of your own free will, and receive Our gift. We promise, it won't hurt. And then... no more pain. No more aches. No more tiredness or anxiety. No more fear of death, or leaving your loved ones behind. Doesn't that sound lovely?" Geth raised its voice so the others could hear. "All We want is ease your pains and suffering. Is that not what you all desire?"

Nance found it odd how the thing seemed to turn on a dime,

one moment Wrath and Fury, the next, soothing and reassuring. It reminded him of one of those scumbag televangelists like Jim Bakker and Billy Graham, or that old TV interview with Charlie Manson.

"It's the not being me that troubles me most," Judy said, her gray eyes jittering slightly as she gazed at Nance. "Ever since my Walter lost his struggle with Alzheimer's... I just can't stand the thought of it."

Nance remembered how close the two of them had been, with Walter performing the custodial duties for the church and Judy at the piano. His battle against dementia, the decline of his cognitive abilities and eventual withering away of his body, had been difficult on Judy, but she'd persevered. "I promise," he said softly, "I promise I'll do whatever I can to bring you back. Bring all of us back. I'll protect this town until the bitter end, I swear it."

Judy Delacroix nodded weakly. She let her entire body sag into the arms of her captors. After a moment, the tall Nordic men let her go, and Judy shuffled up the steps, stopping in front of Geth. "I can't kneel. It's not that I don't want to," she was quick to add. "Only... my joints won't allow it."

"Very well," Geth said. "We shall grant you special privilege, just this once. Soon, as promised, your joints will no longer trouble you."

Nance glanced back at the teacher, that gut feeling gnawing at him again—like a word caught on the tip of his tongue. "Geth," he said.

The creature faced him.

"Let the girl go, will you give me that?"

The young girl looked up at him as he spoke, a gleam of hope in her eyes.

"She's tired and she's scared," he said.

"We're all tired and scared!" a man shouted from somewhere down the line. Nance recognized Eugene Brunt, one of the mechanics who worked at Randy Jacobs's auto yard, from his gruff voice as much as his alcoholic slur.

Geth's pumpkin lips downturned. "This is not a negotiation, Sheriff Nance, and Taylor Flynn is not a hostage. She shall be Our most honored disciple. She is a very special little girl."

Taylor sniffled, her gaze back on the camera hanging from around her neck.

"I'm sure she is," Nance said. "But like I said—"

The flame from the candle inside Geth's head became a white-hot inferno, blazing through its eyes and mouth. *"DO NOT TEST US, LAWMAN! WE ONLY HAVE SO MUCH PATIENCE."*

Nance put up his hands. "All right. I give."

The candle's flame died down to a small flicker. "Judy Delacroix," Geth said softly, gesturing her near with its free hand. "If you please."

Tired, bleary eyes full of terror, Judy Delacroix hobbled up the steps to stand hunched before Geth.

"Thank you," the creature gently intoned.

"Please," she said. "Don't make it hurt."

Geth nodded slightly. It reached up with its free hand and, like the painting of God touching Adam's finger on the ceiling of that church somewhere in Italy, gently touched her forehead.

Their audience stared with apprehension, as Nance did, waiting for Judy to collapse or cry out in pain and terror or disintegrate into dust. But she merely stood there for a long moment, wavering slightly, as the dead man's finger left her forehead. Nance couldn't see her expression from where he stood at the foot of the steps, and he wished he'd thought to get closer before Judy went up. She could've been grimacing in pain or smiling from ear to ear for all he knew, though he sincerely doubted the latter.

After a long, tense moment, Judy Delacroix stretched to her full height with a veritable drumroll of pops and cracks, her bent spine straightened for the first time in the almost three decades she'd been hunched over the church piano.

"It's a miracle!" she gasped.

Nance winced as she leaped into the air, kicking up her heels. He was sure she'd bust her hip when she hit the floor, but Judy landed just fine, her leather shoes with their comfort insoles slap-slapping against the wooden boards of the altar.

But Judy Delacroix wasn't content to just dance. Her soles rose from the floor and she hovered several feet in the air, laughing giddily. The crowd gasped in wonder as the old woman beamed down at them, sprightlier than Nance could ever remember her, her once-tired eyes brimming with joyous tears.

"It's an honest to God miracle!" She shook her head in wonder, slowly descending to the altar floor. Grasping Geth's free hand in both of hers, she corrected herself. "No. An honest to *Geth* miracle."

The entity nodded, graciously accepting her praise. "You are quite welcome, Judy Delacroix."

The reverend's Danish flunkies tried to escort the smiling, newly agile old woman down the steps, but she shooed away their hands with a scoff, and descended the stairs easily on her own.

"Are you okay, Judy?" Nance asked as she approached him.

"It's *wonderful*, Bert. I can see *so much* now. *So much*. I haven't felt this alive in *ages*."

Her eyes were clearer than normal, Nance noted, but they were also darker. Infected with Geth's Blight, like the reverend and the others before her. She turned to the frightened, awestruck faces in the aisle. "There's no need to be afraid," she told them. "It truly is the *most wonderous* thing. The hounds of the moon will never sniff us out, if you accept Geth's Blight."

"What the hell are the hounds of the moon?" Eugene Brunt said.

Geth's forehead gnarled in a frown. Nance worried Eugene had just bought his ticket to the Great Beyond, or whatever lay in wait for them after this life. He was spared whatever fate Geth meant for him when the little toy poodle broke free from Denise Garner's arms and skittered down the aisle toward the doors, barking all the way.

A collective gasp ran through the crowd. Denise cried after it, "Bella!" Del Aimes, a beanpole of a man who ran the bulk food store, leaned down to try and grab it, his checkered shirt pulling out from the hem of his jeans. The little poodle leaped through the hoop he'd made with his large hands, reminding Nance of the jumps at the Westminster Dog Show Janine had made him and the girls watch back when the girls were still young. It was just the sort of dog he'd have expected to take Best in Show.

It wasn't a winner tonight, though.

The weapons up front swung on a pivot, targeting the yappy little thing as it ran toward them.

Bella scurried past Randy and Trudy and just about reached the doors—which wouldn't have provided it the freedom it desired, being closed, even if it had made it—when the guns began blasting. The sound was tremendous, echoing throughout the church, causing everyone but the deafest of the elderly to cover their ears. People screamed. The bullets obliterated the poor little thing. She burst in a spray of blood, bone and white fur. Her tags jingled as they landed in the sloppy mess she left on the floor.

Denise Garner moaned and attempted to run, but the Danish twins grabbed her by the arms and held her firm.

"Get your goddamn hands off my wife!" Gary Garner snapped. The awkward punch he landed on the scrawnier of the twins' jaw made the young man's hands drop from Denise Garner's arm. He reached up and touched the wound, apparently flabbergasted. His brother let go of Denise and grabbed Gary by his right wrist, wrenching it behind the car salesman's back.

"Let me go, you Nazi fuck! I'll sue you to Hell and back!"

The parishioners who'd been dutifully ushering people into the line hurried over to break up the fight, attempting to calm people down before chaos took over again. Gary and the twins struggled. Denise wept for her dog. Others in the crowd cried with her, horrified looks on their faces over another senseless death.

You almost had em there, buster, Nance thought with a satisfied grin, looking at the monster itself. *You just about had em sold on your line of bull. Then you had to go and kill the dog.*

Here it was again: a ruckus. But since Geth and the reverend were in charge and not Nance himself, it gave him a moment to think about what he planned to do next.

He wasn't about to let any more of these folks "become one" with Geth, if he could help it, let alone himself.

Scanning the crowd, which grew more agitated by the moment, his gaze fell upon the older girl who'd come in with Taylor and Geth. Her fear was palpable, and with good reason. Nance locked eyes with Hildebrand again, who still stood with her.

Suddenly, as if struck by a divine light, it clicked.

The last time he'd seen Hildebrand was a few weeks back. The teacher had been in Wyndham Park, showing the same girl and a class split into smaller groups how to use four or five professional-looking video cameras they had with them. Nance had jokingly asked if they had a permit to shoot there, to which the teacher had replied, "We don't need no steenking permits," with an accent like the Mexican guy from *The Treasure of the Sierra Madre*. Both of them had chuckled at the reference, and Nance had continued on his way to lunch.

It wasn't their exchange that mattered, although it certainly added to his hunch that him showing up just when he had, and with their nemesis itself, might indeed be a sort of divine intervention, despite the obvious fact that he'd never considered himself a believer. Especially not since Janine had left him for that dimwitted spinning instructor.

Because a communications teacher would have access to video cameras. And that meant his plan from earlier was not just still in play—with any luck on their side, it could actually goddamn *work*.

3

AS CODY RACED toward the church, the doors slammed behind his teacher and his friends, led by the creature that called itself Geth.

Stopping at the foot of the stairs, he looked over the mess on the porch, blood splattered over the doors and the walls, with pristine white shapes behind where the kids had been, like negatives of the shadows left at Hiroshima. Walden lay propped up on an elbow, the way the school photographer sometimes posed boys to make them look "cool" for photos. He looked like he'd been on the bad end of a brutal fistfight, likely at the hands of Brunt and Fitz. If he hadn't just seen their heads literally explode, he wouldn't have believed it was his former friends lying in front of him. Yet despite them having no heads, they were easily identifiable by their build and clothes, even drenched in blood. And the Adidas tearaways were unmistakably Brunt.

Ascending the stairs, Cody slipped in blood and hairy chunks of scalp. Walden shivered like a frightened animal as Cody approached him, staring open-mouthed with the only wide dark eye he could open at the headless bodies of Brunt and Fitz.

It didn't seem real, seeing them like that. Then again, not much of what had happened tonight seemed real, so much that he wouldn't be surprised to suddenly wake up sweaty and hot under the covers, only to realize all of this had been a very realistic, very bad dream.

"You okay, Walden?"

Walden huffed a laugh. "You should see the other guys." He reached into his damp coat pocket and pulled out a dark green pack of cigarettes, shook one out and stuck it between blood-reddened lips. "It blew up their heads like *Scanners*. How do you fight something like that? How do you even *try*?"

"I don't know. But we have to."

Walden's shoulders sagged. He leaned against the blood-splashed wall with a heavy sigh. "I know. We'll probably die either way, so we might as fucking well." He fired up his Zippo and lit the end of the smoke. Took a deep drag, and spoke on exhale. "You know, there was something fucked up about them: Brunt and Fitz. I noticed it even before they started wailing on me."

"What's that?"

He took another long drag, squinting in the direction of the moving wall of things floating above the road, blocking the vehicles in. "Their eyes were black. Entirely black," he said, the cigarette bobbing up and down. "Same as Mac and Stuckey, after that *thing* touched them. They looked like *zombies*. Nobody home, ya know?"

"I saw that before," Cody said. "Back at the Thompson farm. First with Tommy, then the people in the basement."

Walden blinked a ribbon of smoke out of his uninjured eye. "Was Tommy...?"

Cody didn't need him to finish. "Yeah. He tried to kill Brittany. I think this Geth thing must be using them against us just like it used the stuff at the haunt."

Walden nodded, then grimaced in pain as he pushed himself further up the wall to a better sitting position. "That makes sense. We figured they're like poltergeists, how they move stuff using telekinesis. You know, theoretically," he added with a shrug. "Help me up?"

Cody held out a hand. Walden grabbed it, groaning as Cody hauled him to his feet. "What are we gonna do now?" Cody asked.

Walden took another drag and looked off toward Mr. Hildebrand's old red pickup truck. "We were on our way to the woods when we saw Brunt and Fitz going after those kids. Mr. Combs and

Ms. Stabler built a machine out there. They think it's what brought Geth into our world. I dunno how, but turning it off's the only idea we've got to send it back to the Phantom Zone or whatever."

"Can't do that now though, can we? Road's blocked. We need a car to get out there. Or bikes."

Walden nodded toward the Mustang. "Doesn't look like Brunt's gonna be driving the Douchemobile any time soon. We could borrow it."

"Still have to get through the forcefield thing, though."

"Yeah." Walden dropped the half-finished smoke and ground it into the mess of gore with the toe of his right boot. "Guess we're pretty much fucked."

Cody nodded contemplatively. "Is Jay already inside?"

"Last I saw that little shit was back on Combs's street, running his ass away like Forrest Gump."

"We're all scared," Cody said.

"Sure, but we're all still here, aren't we?" Walden peered around. "Except Brittany. She skitter off, too?"

Cody shook his head. "She was the one ringing the bell to warn you guys. Saved my butt once or twice, too."

The brow above Walden's uninjured eye rose. "Oh yeah?"

"Yup. She's actually a really good person. You'd be surprised."

"Hmm. So then now what?"

Cody returned his attention to the church, mulling it over. When he thought deeply, his face settled into a deep scowl. His grandmother on his dad's side used to call it his "perplexed pooh" face. *Oh, lookit, it's Mr. Perplexed Pooh.* Whatever that meant, it always used to make him laugh. He didn't feel at all like laughing now. "I think we should do a bit of snooping," he said finally. "See what's going on in there. What we're up against. Maybe we can figure out some way to get them outta there."

"Sounds like a plan, Stan."

Cody didn't know whether or not it was a *good* plan, but he headed down the steps before he could convince himself otherwise. Walden limped down behind him, holding a hand against his ribs.

"You gonna be all right?"

"Are any of us?"

"Good point." Cody sidestepped the hedge below the shattered stained-glass window, hoping to find a way to get a good look inside. "Oh shoot..." he said, shoulders slumping at a sudden realization.

"What?"

"If we die, I'll never get to see *Goldmember*."

Walden snorted. "Yeah, man, I wanted to see that, too. I still haven't caught the new David Lynch yet, either. We're not getting it at the Grand 'til December."

"Bummer."

"Yeah. Guess we'll just have to survive then, huh?"

Cody grinned. "Guess so. Geth can kiss my butt."

"Yeah. Fuck Geth."

"Fuck him," Cody agreed. He didn't usually say the F-word, but it actually felt pretty good so he did it again. "Fuck Geth in his pumpkin ass."

Walden laughed, wagging a finger at him. "See, I knew you were cool. Wanna boost me up?"

They stood below a broken window. "Sure you're okay?"

Walden shrugged. "I'll live."

With a shrug, Cody bent and cupped his hands together. Walden put one foot into the cupped hands and grunted as Cody boosted him up to grasp the window ledge.

"Holy shit," he said.

"What?"

"Peter Pumpkinhead's up at the altar. Everyone's lined up to meet him like he's Bon Scott come back from the dead to save rock n' roll. Looks like he's blessing people, touching them on the forehead."

"Like at Lent?"

"I guess so." Walden gasped. "You know Old Lady Delacroix?"

"Yeah."

"She's literally floating right now."

Cody couldn't believe what he was hearing. "*Floating?*"

"Yeah. Geth touched her on the forehead and now she's five feet in the air, like Uncle Joe when he drinks the fizzy lifting drink in *Willy Wonka*."

"You think it's the poltergeists?"

"I was calling them Possessors, but sure, yeah. She's probably possessed, like Stuckey and Mac. I think—"

Whatever Walden was about to say was interrupted when a small dog started barking inside.

"Oh shit," Walden said.

"What's going on?"

"There's a bunch of guns floating around. *Big ones.*" A sudden blast of automatic gunfire made Walden jerk, and Cody almost lost his footing. Gasps and screams accompanied the gunfire, followed by the sound of chaos.

"They shot the dog, now people are going nuts."

"We need to get in there."

"You really wanna risk that?"

"Well, what else are we gonna do? Run away like Jay Nielson?"

Walden climbed down and a smile split his blood-streaked face, reminding Cody of Ash in *Evil Dead 2* after he goes completely nuts.

"Not run away," Walden said. "*Drive.*"

"And leave everyone in there to die?"

"We can't beat Geth. Not when it's in there creating a shit-ton more of those braindead cultists like Brunt and Fitz. They were *stronger* than normal, Cody. I couldn't fight em off. Shit, I could barely land a punch! What good could we do against a *church full* of things like that?" He nodded toward the end of the street. "But we *can* help *them*. If we could just break through the roadblock... get the Possessors to chase us instead of Ms. Stabler..."

Cody looked off toward the moving wall of junk. "Then they could get to the machine and shut it off!" he cried.

"Exactly!" Walden shrugged ambivalently. "Which may or may not suck Geth back to the dimension it came from, or whatever, but it's the best shot we have."

Cody started back toward the front of the church. "I'll see if I can find Brunt's keys."

Walden caught up, staggering along behind him. "I bet he left them in the ignition. Those two were on me like white on rice as soon as he slammed on the brakes."

"Good call. Saves me having to stick my hands in his pockets." Cody sneered toward the headless corpses. He definitely didn't want to touch either of them, let alone reach into the front of Brunt's pants, dead or alive.

Walden stooped with a pained groan and grabbed one of the video cameras Hildebrand and Cassandra had left on the porch.

"You're not seriously still making the movie, are you?"

"I'll explain in the car," Walden said.

At the Mustang, both of them peered through the open passenger window. Brunt's keyring with its fuzzy dice dangled from the ignition, like a pair of plush white testicles. He could almost hear Brunt's sadistic laughter ringing in his ears as he regarded them, and had to glance back to see if the heads of his former friends had spontaneously regrown, the two of them rushing toward him, ready to kill.

But their bodies lay still, exactly where they'd left them.

"Score one for the home team," he said with a sigh. "You want to drive?"

"You probably better," Walden said, squinting at him through his one good eye. "I've already crashed one car tonight. Besides, in case you haven't noticed, I'm half blind."

"Shit, I didn't even ask about the Green Machine."

Walden opened the passenger door and sat heavily. "That's another long story. I'll tell you on the road."

Cody went around the front and got in behind the wheel. "I've always wanted to drive this beast."

"She ain't pretty," Walden said, "but she's got some muscle under the hood. We're definitely gonna need it to outrun those fuckers."

Cody turned the key in the ignition. The engine roared, and the Mustang began to vibrate as it settled into a rumbling purr. He looked at Walden, who appeared even worse for wear in the shadows as he buckled in. "You ready?"

Walden squinted at Cody with his good eye. "Gonna have to be, aren't I?"

Cody nodded. He threw the transmission into reverse, made a three-point turn until they faced Mr. Hildebrand's truck and the endlessly moving wall of what Walden called Possessors at the far end of the road.

"Hold on to something," he said, and floored it.

CHAPTER 22

1

Cassandra was terrified, but she was also *mad*. Mad at herself for letting Geth take Taylor away from her. Mad at Hildebrand for trying to convince her there was no other way. She was even a little upset with Taylor for choosing to go with it, though she knew her little sister hadn't been given much of a choice.

She was mad at *Geth* most of all. For making her feel helpless. For making her feel *small*.

Cassandra *hated* feeling small, feeling hopeless and insignificant. She'd spent the greater part of her life harboring those sentiments: that she had no purpose, that no one cared about her, that she had no future to speak of and nothing she'd ever done in her life mattered at all. It was a big part of why she listened to angry and depressing music, why she wore all black from her socks to her mascara, so her outside matched her mood, and why she performed Wiccan rituals in the cemetery and under the Geromero Street bridge, to trick herself into believing she had a small measure of control over the uncontrollable.

With all they'd been through tonight, she'd wanted to change that more than anything—assuming she survived the night—to rise to the occasion and become the stronger person she'd always known was inside of her, struggling to break free. To kick back against everything and everyone in her life that had held her down. To do something *important* with her life.

Now, here she was letting this monster take her sister. Letting it destroy her town, kill innocent people and brainwash the survivors.

Cassandra had grown up Catholic. She'd been baptized in this very church by Reverend Earl and received her confirmation here. After her parents died, she and Taylor had stopped going. Grammy Flynn had already been too infirm to bring them each Sunday, and after the car crash, Cassandra had lost any of the little faith she'd possessed.

Yet she still remembered the Holy Communion, and the ritual on Ash Wednesday where Reverend Earl smeared ash on the foreheads of his parishioners in the shape of a cross, as an acknowledgement of original sin. Geth's ritual appeared to be something like that.

Cassandra wasn't fooled by the raving testimonials she'd witnessed so far, from Old Lady Delacroix and the few who'd gone after her. It was clear they were no longer themselves. They belonged to Geth now. They'd become its slaves.

Soon it would be her turn to approach Geth, to kneel before it and accept its "blight," and she knew she wouldn't have the courage to fight back. She'd cower before the thing like the rest of them had. Then, like the others, she'd be nothing, only *truly* nothing—a ghost in a hollow shell, not the nothing she'd already felt she was.

In the chaos after Geth killed the dog, the burly woman in the orange vest caught her attention, striding up on the right side of the pews. Cassandra had seen the woman lying on the floor when they entered the church, beside some guy in a green parka. Those floating guns had been holding them hostage.

Geth didn't appear to notice the woman's approach, as she reached into the pocket of her heavy coat, and when she removed her hand, it held something small, dark and round in a fist. She kept walking as the crowd continued to shout and fight around Tiffany's parents, then moved alongside the front of the altar toward Geth.

"Christ, Trudy, *no!*" Sheriff Nance shouted.

With her left hand, the woman reached for the thing held in her right and swiftly pulled something off the top. Cassandra thought it must be a soda, but if it hissed she didn't hear it—above all the noise, she hadn't really expected to—and the ring came off on her thumb like a tin of sardines. Cassandra still had no idea what was going on, why the sheriff had freaked out, nor why everyone closer to the altar where the two of them stood had suddenly fallen into a stunned silence.

"Say hello to bin Laden, you godless fuck!" the woman growled.

Geth's full attention fell on her now. Its pumpkin grin spread wide and it began to laugh.

The woman in the orange vest—Trudy, the sheriff said—took another step toward Geth and suddenly froze, like a kid playing Red Light, Green Light. Her left foot hovered a few inches above the first stair, and her eyes began to swing wildly back and forth. "Help!" she moaned, though her lips didn't move. It sounded more like, "*Hupp!*"

Standing there in confusion and mounting unease, the sudden realization of what the woman was holding hit Cassandra with full force, like the white cube van that had sideswiped her parents' Subaru Outback: *It's a grenade!*

Cassandra reared back in horror, but the people around her pushed back. She was stuck, barely five feet from the woman with the grenade. The pin had been pulled, and she'd obviously been intending to blow herself up along with Geth, likes one of those martyrs they talked about on the news, the ones who wore the suicide vests.

Which would be fine, except that Taylor was standing right beside him.

He knew, she thought. *He knew someone would try to hurt him. She's his fucking collateral!*

They had only a few seconds until the thing exploded the moment Trudy let go of the handle. She knew that from TV. Geth had obviously made her freeze in place, but how long could the poor woman hold the grenade like that? How long until she lost her balance and fell backwards? Would she still be able to hold it tight enough to prevent it from being "live"?

"*Do not move, any of you!*" Geth bellowed, surveying the crowd. "*Attempt to flee and we will cause Trudy Bell to drop the explosive! We have no use for her, nor any tolerance for apostates!*"

Cassandra stopped pushing against the crowd. Those who were in motion also froze, though not quite as stiffly as Trudy.

"Sheriff Nance knows the damage an Mk 2 fragmentation grenade can do to a crowd," Geth said, calmer now that the crowd had stopped pushing and shoving. "Is that not so, Sheriff?"

The sheriff nodded. "Unless you want to blow your friends and neighbors to bits, I'd suggest you do as Geth says, folks. Please."

Throw it, Cassandra thought as a desperate plea, hurling all of her mental energy toward the woman, wishing for her to throw it like she'd never wished for anything in her entire life, not even for God or fate or whoever controlled life and death to bring her parents back.

THROW IT.

And then, just like Cassandra had imagined it, Trudy's arm sprang like a mousetrap, chucking the grenade away from her as hard as she could with a startled grunt—"*Guh!*"

Everyone's eyes followed it, including Geth's, as it sailed toward Mrs. Delacroix's piano standing at the far corner of the altar. The top of the piano lay open, as if someone had been tuning it, and the grenade fell inside, hitting the wires with a discordant twang like a smashed electric guitar. For a split second there was no sound in the church but the ugly reverberated chord ringing out through the large open space.

Every single voice had hushed, awaiting the inevitable.

"*Everybody down!*" Nance cried, spoiling the perfect silence.

With a chorus of shrieks, everyone in the church did their best to duck from the explosion. Geth remained fixed in place, holding firm to Taylor's hand even as she dropped to one knee beside it.

In the next moment the piano erupted with a flat, unmusical *plonk*, and a smoky fireball sent shards of shellacked pine, black and white ivory and wire every which way. The stained-glass windows on the right side of the church blew outward, and the first two rows of pews toppled backwards, scattering glass and hymn books across the polished wood floor.

Screams of terror and pain arose from those closest to the blast as the barrage of splintered wood and piano keys and fragments of exploded grenade hit them, slashing throats, lacerating faces, stabbing through flesh and bone. A dozen or more lay on the floor, bleeding and moaning in agony.

Cassandra couldn't look. She'd seen too much horror already.

"God damn you!" Sheriff Nance shouted, lurching toward the altar where Geth stood. He got two feet before Geth used his powers to lift Nance right off the floor.

Weeping, Taylor remained crouched by Geth's side, still unable to escape.

Geth's gaze shifted from the sheriff to Cassandra's direction. She looked around herself in confusion.

Is he looking at me?

"*The sister,*" Geth hissed, its X eyes narrowing to slits.

Sheriff Nance dangled in the air, feet kicking slightly. Geth wasn't choking him like Darth Vader did to that guy, just holding him there, a few feet from the stage and several feet above the floor. Nance seemed to understand there was no point in struggling, that it would only make him look weak. He couldn't afford to look weak in front of everyone. Not now.

"We need to get these people to a hospital," he said through gritted teeth. "They need treatment."

"None shall leave this church, Sheriff Nance! If they wish to be healed, they merely need to ask."

"Let the girl go, at least, goddamn it!"

"Very well," Geth said, surprising both Cassandra and the sheriff. "Let us make a trade, shall we? The young Flynn... for the eldest."

Cassandra thought to ask, *Why me?* But her desire to save Taylor trumped her need for self-preservation. Besides, she thought she knew the reason Geth wanted to trade. She may have even known it her whole life, despite her lack of self-confidence or whatever it was that wouldn't allow her to believe it. She'd always been the one to instigate it, to push Taylor to use her powers, to play Humphrey. When all along it was her own power she was using *through* her sister.

I did it, Cassandra marveled. *I made her throw the grenade. Not Taylor. Me. Humphrey was always me! Did Grammy know?*

Geth jerked Taylor roughly to her feet. She cowered, still weeping. "Come to Us, Sister Flynn," it said. "A trade. Your hand for hers."

Cassandra felt her feet begin to propel her forward, not bidden by Geth's power but by her own—*Could it be courage? Is that what this is?*—getting the better of her. Suddenly she had reached the foot of the stairs a few feet from where Trudy still stood immobile, and Sheriff Nance dangled limply in the air.

As she'd done with the grenade, Cassandra focused all of her mental energy toward the sheriff. Slowly, he began to descend. Trudy was quivering now, as if she wouldn't be able to hold the pose much longer. So Cassandra focused her thoughts toward Trudy's foot, and it came down swiftly with a dull thud. Trudy gasped in relief.

"Yesssss," Geth said, its grin widening. "It was never Taylor. *Always you*. You'd shielded her mind from Us. Made her impenetrable, like a locked box. But *you*... you We see inside, to your very essence. We see the hurt you've tried in vain to bury. The pain. The shame. Come to Us, Cassandra. Be one with Us. Let Us take away your suffering. Let Us harness your anger for the good of your people."

Sheriff Nance landed softly on the floor. "If you need a sacrificial lamb, take me," he said, squaring up with Geth.

The pumpkin head whipped toward him. "We do not *need* you! You are *nothing*! You are an insignificant speck of sand in the ocean! A tic on the back of a cur with mange! This one..." The jack-o'-lantern eyes turned toward Cassandra. "*This* one is *special*."

"I'm not special," she said.

And even though she'd just freed Sheriff Nance and Trudy Bell from Geth's powers, she truly felt that. She wasn't special. She had a gift maybe, but that didn't make her better than anyone else. It was just a trick. Something to impress people with at parties. Or more likely, people would call her a *freak*. Just like Geth.

"Oh, but you are," it said. "The very fact that you do not recognize *how* special you are makes you *even more* unique. You are raw talent. Power untapped. You will be my most trusted disciple. You will stand at my side and together We will *unite the world* in peace and harmony."

It all sounded like a pop song to Cassandra, and without warning she snorted a laugh. She couldn't help herself.

Geth held out its free hand, undeterred by her judgment.

Cassandra focused on her sister. Tears streamed down the girl's face. She'd been through too much tonight, and worse was still in store for her even if they all escaped right now. Her best friend was dead. Accepting Geth's offer was the least Cassandra could do for her.

"Let Taylor go first," she said.

"Very well," Geth agreed, and opened its decaying fingers.

Taylor let go instantly, scurrying away, rushing straight to her big sister and wrapping her arms around her waist, burying her damp face against Cassandra's breasts.

"Don't go," she said. "Please don't go with him."

Cassandra felt her own tears fall, mascara running in itchy tracks down her cheeks. "I have to. I love you, shrimp."

"I love you, too! Ple-*hease* don't go with hi-him!"

Cassandra peeled her sister's arms from around her waist and held her firmly by the shoulders. "I won't leave you." Her gaze fell on the Polaroid as it swung from around Taylor's neck.

It couldn't. Could it...?

Frantically she grabbed the camera, swung it on the strap around Taylor's neck—hoping she didn't give the poor kid rope burns—and pointed it at Geth. With all of her will she pushed against the pumpkin resting atop the dead man's shoulders, and at the same time she snapped a photo. The flash went off, leaving a dark imprint of Geth on her retinas. Momentarily blinded, she dropped the camera. The automated grind and whir came as the photo ejected from its mouth.

Geth's laughter filled the silence. "Did you truly believe you could defeat Us with that toy? It may have gotten the better of Our *inhak*, but We are not so easily deceived. Come, Sister Flynn. Let us dispense with these childish games."

With her vision returned, Cassandra let her sister go and reluctantly ascended toward Geth. Sheriff Nance laid a consoling hand on Taylor's shoulder, and Taylor nestled into his side and wept.

As Cassandra approached, Geth held out its dead hand. She hesitated before taking it. It was cold, dry and somewhat stiff. She cringed at the feel of it. How many times had she wished to fall in love with someone like Edward Scissorhands or Gary Oldman's Dracula? Holding Geth's hand, the thought of standing at his side as he enslaved the world brought her nothing but horror and disgust.

I can't just let him brainwash everyone. How can I stop this?

She didn't know. But she feared she might be the only one

who could. Especially now, standing here, clutched by its awful hand.

At the back of the altar, where the church choir stood to sing during Mass and beneath where Jesus had hung on His cross until someone had taken Him down and placed Him under a gray woolen blanket, Father Earl held a hand up to his head. The hand dropped and he gazed at his palm, stunned. It was covered in his own blood. What looked like a black piano key had lodged in his temple. It stuck out above his right ear like one of Frankenstein's bolts.

Noticing this but unsure what to make of it, Cassandra turned her back on the priest and took her place at Geth's side.

With a loud snap, Trudy Bell's head twisted violently a hundred and eighty degrees, like the little girl from *The Exorcist*. Only Trudy Bell didn't puke pea soup or say anything slanderous about anyone's mother. She just crumpled to the floor like a puppet without its strings, sprawling over the altar steps. A man cried out her name from somewhere in the back of the church, behind the line of people waiting to be baptized by this insane monster, this demon who dreamed it was a god, but was nothing more than an extremely powerful bully.

Her powers were nothing compared to Geth's, but she had to keep fighting back with everything she had.

Bullies had beaten her down all her life. She wouldn't let the King of the Bullies win, no matter what it took.

2

THE MOMENT GETH held the little girl's hand in the hand of Their vessel, They had sensed something was not quite right.

This girl was no god. Geth felt no *dwaska* emanating from her fingertips, no supernatural power, human or otherwise. They felt no greatness nor omnipotence. It felt nothing but the same waxy flesh They had felt while stroking the Miller woman's dead scalp. Taylor Flynn may have been imbued with one of Geth's many powers, and her mind might still be impenetrable to Them, but in every other regard she was nothing but a normal female child of the human species. No more nor less significant than a humble louse, and surely nowhere near as powerful as the big shaman of the ancients.

Still, it would do to keep her close.

If forced to choose another *chuann*, an alternate vessel for Their *aminhas* should something drastic happen to the Summerly body, a human so short in years would be ideal. She would continue to grow and live longer than nearly everyone standing here. And though Geth was powerful, They were not impervious to harm. It was still possible the body They had chosen could be harmed beyond Their ability to regenerate its flesh. Soon it would begin to break down, no matter how much They attempted to keep the forces of time at bay. Already They could feel the flesh surrendering to rigor mortis and its insides beginning to bloat. And the pumpkin, suitable as a temporary vessel, would succumb to wither and rot. Human flesh was weak, but vegetable matter was even less robust.

If only We could trust the slippery minds of these New People, Geth thought. Even blighting one of them first would only make its mind more likely to scramble. Geth had tried it before with the ancients, and had quickly been forced to shift into the shaman, before Their *aminhas* could break apart and the *Upask* pull Them back into its dark, empty womb.

They would not make that mistake again.

And then, something wonderous occurred. The sister showed her true self to Them. Her *dwaska* was powerful, enough to temporarily counter Geth's own. It was the sister who had caused the cars to veer off course. Cassandra Flynn had been the one to blind and incapacitate Geth's *inhak* with her sister's toy.

Cassandra was the one, not Taylor.

She was not Their equal, by no means. But like the big shaman, she could prove to be Their nemesis. For Their own protection, for the protection of Their *chuann*, Geth would not let her out of Their sight.

She had been using her sister as a sort of conduit, like Geth used Ernie Combs and his Machine, and the drug addict, Darryl Knell. Cassandra Flynn had somehow shielded her sister's mind from Them, but had also veiled her own. She had hidden her powers so well she herself did not realize they were hers to wield.

The word *Humphrey* came to mind, flashing like a film title on a black screen. Geth did not know what the word meant, but it was the only thing Cassandra allowed Them to see. They had lied to her a moment ago, using the fear and confusion and self-defeat of the rest of these people to fool her into believing They knew her true self.

In truth, Geth could never enter her mind, even if she allowed Them access. She possessed even more *dwaska* than the big shaman had, and would likely tear Them apart the moment They attempted to penetrate her mind. Taylor Flynn was still a viable *chuann*. They would keep her close and easily accessible, should things go poorly. They would blight enough humans to protect Themselves so that any attempt to harm them, as Trudy Bell had with the explosive, would be swiftly stamped out and punished.

If she had managed to detonate it before the sheriff cried out....

Geth sneered. Their lapse in observation disgusted Them. In three seconds, the pumpkin flesh would have been entirely obliterated. Three seconds and They would have been left without a head to contain Their *aminhas*, and a body without a face with which to communicate Their message was useless. They may as well abandon their Union and scatter into Their millions of ungoverned *inhak*, content to kill and maim and destroy without motive, as they had in the time before Geth had united them. Made them strong. Gave them *meaning*. Outside of the *aminhas*, Their psychic union, the very essence of Geth, the *inhak* were anarchic, inconsequential beings, much like these humans.

Together They made a god.

Gods were anything but *small*.

As Geth had united the *inhak*, They would unite these disordered beings of fragile flesh, drawing together their collective consciousness into the *aminhas*, discarding the waste: their memories, ambition and individuality. They would tear down the societies of these diverse, endlessly clashing tribes and create a new world united once and for all in the name of Geth.

Then, once They were finished, They would rid Themselves of the witch, Cassandra Flynn.

Geth turned to look at the girl, a small, somewhat corpulent human female dressed from head to toe in black. With her warm, slender fingers—with nails painted black—entwined with the *chuann*'s slowly decaying hand, Geth smiled.

Unsurprisingly, she did not return it.

3

Grimly, Nance surveyed the carnage the grenade had caused. Roy Stafford, the old-timer who ran the theater, lay sprawled and groaning beside one of the overturned pews, surrounded by half a dozen hymn books, the foot of a piano leg lodged in his back. Alan Everson, a machine operator at the lumber yard, had been struck in the face by the metronome and knocked unconscious, his nose a red smear across his face. Yolanda Pressley and her elderly mother, both of them local musicians, lay huddled together, bleeding and crying, both suffering from multiple shrapnel lacerations. Sonya Chen, the realtor, was barely holding on to life, Leonard Gains from the road crew helping stem the blood from a slash across her throat with the jacket from her pantsuit. Marc Robitaille, an accountant who did a great deal of the personal taxes in town, had been struck in the head with the piano bench and lay facedown in a scattered stack of Bibles. He didn't appear to be breathing.

These were just a handful of the injured and dead caught in the carnage from Trudy's grenade. Nance berated himself for not throwing his own body over it when he'd had the chance. Just snatched it away from Trudy and dropped over it, sheltering the others from the blast. He'd seen it done, not in Vietnam but in basic training before his platoon had been shipped out. Some wiseass had been fooling around and dropped a live one, and their first lieutenant had honorably given his life to save at least six men by smothering it with his body. It'd been foolish of him —Nance, not his deceased CO—to believe he could've ever used the damned thing to their advantage. Like the other weapons those two chuckleheads had with them, it would only ever be used against them.

So he surveyed the carnage, tallying it up, hoping he'd get a chance to exact justice upon the demon who'd caused all of this, and soon.

It'd be a few hours yet until the National Guard could possibly mobilize and get their butts to Crooks Corner, and who knew if even they could take down Geth? They had the firepower, the skill and determination. But Geth could just as easily turn all of their weaponry against them. It could touch them all and make them into its disciples, *an entire army*—weekend warriors or not—with enough will and might and an entire arsenal of weaponry to murder scores of unarmed civilians in the name of Geth. Possibly even enough to take over local media and unseat the state government, at least until federal troops came in to stop them.

The damage and death toll would be *catastrophic.*

Got to stop thinking like that, he told himself. *Pessimism won't get you anywhere but dead.*

Cassandra Flynn—who was apparently imbued with a little bit of the same power as Geth, which made her either an extremely powerful adversary or a very dangerous potential partner —said her peace to her little sister, assuring her she wouldn't leave her. Despite everything Nance had seen tonight it still tugged at his heartstrings, the two of them weeping, terrified beyond anything kids their age should ever have to experience. Even with his own tough upbringing at the hands of an alcoholic father, Nance hadn't lived through anything quite so terrible until the Tet Offensive in Vietnam. It was something he'd hoped never to have to live through again, and certainly not on home soil.

What Cassandra did next surprised him: she grabbed her sister's Polaroid and took a snapshot of Geth. Blinking rapidly from the flash, Nance had no idea where she'd gotten the idea it would harm Geth, but it seemed by the way the monster reacted to it that it had harmed the smaller things, the ones taking over all the stuff and making them kill: the *inhak*, as Geth called them. And while Geth reveled in pride at foiling them again, it came to Nance all at once, in a moment of complete clarity amid all of the hopelessness and chaos.

"Hildebrand," he said, snapping to get the man's attention. "You and your kids broadcast that news program of your pretty wide, don't you?"

Renny Hildebrand stood just outside the radius of the blast. He appeared to be uninjured, aside from the bandaged hand. "Yes, sir, we do. Why?"

"Good. Because I have a proposal to make to our host," Nance said. He returned his attention to Geth. "You want disciples, Geth? You wanna spread your word? Well, maybe you heard on your little psychic radio connection what I told Father Earl before you showed up. I could get you on TV, and you could spread your gospel firsthand to the entire world. If that truly is your goal."

Geth's brow furrowed. "You would not be attempting to deceive Us, would you, lawman?"

"No, sir. You have my word."

Geth pursed its yellow lips. "We require more than just *your word*, Sheriff. Your word is meaningless to us. So, if you betray Us, if this is another *trick*, We will inflict swift retribution upon the people of this town *tenfold*. You *do not* wish to test Us, Sheriff."

Standing beside Geth, holding its cold, dead hand, the elder Flynn girl shook her head solemnly at Nance. He understood her fear, but this was the only way he could think to lure Geth out of this church, away from all of these innocent people.

Nance shook his head. "I wouldn't dare."

"Very well." Geth gestured with its free hand. "Renny Hildebrand, you may retrieve your cameras."

"Actually," Mr. Hildebrand said, "if you *really* want to get your message out, we ought to bring you to the school. I've got professional cameras and a studio where we broadcast our weekly news to the whole community on cable Channel 47. Not just to Crooks Corner but to just about every TV in the surrounding five counties."

Nance felt excitement tingle through his nerve endings. *We could really pull this off!* "You could go national in under an hour," he told Geth. "Soon as the local affiliates pick up the broadcast, they'll put you on the morning news. You'll go international by lunchtime. That's what you want, isn't it? To grab this world by the *cojones* and *squeeze*?"

Geth's pumpkin-flesh lips pressed together. Nance wasn't sure if it was deliberating or planning to vaporize the two of them on the spot for conspiring against it. Finally, it said: "Very well. Take Us to this... *studio*. But the wounded and the sick shall accompany Us. We shall heal them all, on your Tee-Vee, for all the world to witness and covet. We shall birth them anew in the Glory of Geth. Make them stronger. Make them One with Us. *Unite* them, once and for all."

The church doors swung wide with a sudden sharp creak,

slamming against the outer walls. Those among them Geth had already turned—the process had gone a lot faster after Judy Delacroix's testimonial, and a dozen or so had since knelt before Geth to receive its unholy communion—began approaching the wounded, drawing those still moaning and writhing in their agony slowly to their feet.

Ego, Nance thought. He was sworn to protect this town and its people. He'd done a pretty piss-poor job of it tonight, but there was still time. *Attack its ego. Make a fool of it. Show everyone what a cowardly charlatan it truly is. Take away its power.*

It could work. Or it could get him killed. Either way, he'd have done his best to protect the people who'd voted him into office. It was why he'd brought them all here. It was what he'd promised.

If nothing else, Bert Nance was a man who followed through on his promises.

4

WHEN THE PIECE of shrapnel struck Charles in the side of the head, it would be fair to say he'd had a religious awakening. With a thunderbolt crack through his skull, everything suddenly and blindingly crystalized with pure and absolute clarity.

This was a test. A test of my faith in God. I'd lost my way, lost sight of God's love, and in that absence I allowed Geth's Blight to worm its way into my heart. I have failed miserably, Lord. I repent, in Your name.

Charles vaguely remembered—like the memories of a dream upon waking, or what alcoholics experienced while "browning out," as he'd discovered during his weekly Al-Anon group sessions—that he'd sermonized about the interloper in his flock, this false god who walked amongst them. He recalled having told people, his own parishioners among them, to make graven images of this charlatan, and petulantly dismissed Sheriff Nance's stories of prior attempts by other poseurs to usurp the throne of the One True God in His very own place of worship.

He hadn't been able to help himself. It had been as if his soul had left his body—or rather, like his soul had been pushed down into a deep hidden recess within his mind, where he'd watched as Geth's words came from his lips.

He'd never truly *believed* the Word of Geth, even though his parishioners and the other survivors may have thought he'd undergone a sudden and drastic religious conversion, become a Geth-worshipping cultist. Geth was no more their savior than Simon the Sorcerer from the Book of Acts, who'd used levitation and other tricks to bewitch his fellow Samaritans into believing he was imbued with the power of God.

But Geth was no god. Geth was *Legion*. It had said so itself, had even joked with Nance about the Miracle of the Swine.

The National Guard couldn't help them. Only an exorcism would rid them of this demon, this plague of supernatural locusts. Only by calling upon God and His awesome, infinite power could Charles save this town from Geth and from itself.

I need to call the diocese. I don't have the expertise to perform the exorcism myself, certainly not on a demonic entity of such immense power.

It was clear that God had granted him another chance to prove his devotion. The explosion had been His hand at work— He had clearly blinded Geth's eyes to the Bell woman, and she might have carried out her holy duty, doing irreparable damage to the Beast itself, if Sheriff Nance hadn't called for her to stop. Instead, the blast had taken several of Charles's flock and injured many more, including himself, despite the injury's beneficial effect.

Yet it appeared the sheriff wasn't working at cross-purposes to him. While Charles contemplated his religious epiphany, Nance and the teacher managed to convince the abomination to film it at the high school's television studio. With reinvigorated religious conviction, Charles decided he'd been chosen to be God's instrument, tasked to carry out His wrath when and if the opportunity arose.

By Your will or by force, this false prophet will not be allowed to broadcast his blasphemy to the world. I swear it, Lord.

Until then, he'd have to keep pretending to be Geth's lickspittle and hope to God it didn't notice anything out of order.

5

THE ENGINE GROWLED. The Mustang lurched forward with a squeal of rubber on asphalt. Cody mouthed a silent prayer for the first time in as long as he could remember as the muscle car hurtled them toward the shuddering wall of Halloween stuff, toys and neighborhood junk.

Their only chance to beat Geth was for Ms. Stabler and Mr. Combs to get to that Machine and shut it off, before Geth turned the entire town into its minions.

They blew past the teachers sitting in Hildebrand's truck. It was so quick he barely caught the nervous look Ms. Stabler gave them.

Forty or fifty feet from the roadblock now, and closing the distance fast. With the speedometer climbing to 65, it'd barely take a few seconds to reach their destination.

Walden raised the video camera, hefting it onto his right shoulder with a pained grunt. Over the roar of the engine, Cody heard the small beep as Walden pressed Record.

The wall of junk seemed to shudder. Each individual object was already vibrating, bounding off of one another like living organisms, like the amoebas he'd seen under the microscopes in Combs's science class. But when Walden started recording it seemed like there was a tremor among them... although Cody supposed it could just have been his imagination.

Twenty feet to the blockade. It held steady.

The leather creaked as Cody squeezed the steering wheel, leaning forward as if the comparatively minimal addition of his weight might help the Mustang bust through.

Fifteen feet and still no break in the wall.

"Come on," Cody urged.

"Keep going!" Walden shouted.

The living objects bounded and swirled but still held.

Ten feet from it and Cody had to forcibly stop himself from jerking the wheel and slamming on the breaks.

Five feet and it was already too late.

Then, like magnets reacting to their polar opposite, the wall scattered outward. It reminded Cody of shrapnel from an explosion, and he winced, ducking slightly behind the wheel as the flying objects hurtled toward them, keeping the accelerator pressed to the mat and the wheel held straight, anxiously awaiting the first crash against the chassis and windshield.

Nothing came, but he still wouldn't allow himself to relax. Not until they'd blown through the intersection did he let out the breath he'd been holding. Glancing in the rearview, he saw the church doors had swung wide. The former blockade zipped right past Hildebrand's ancient truck and began to reassemble near the foot of the stairs into who knew what.

Walden laughed triumphantly, lowering the camera to his lap and turning to look out the back window. "We made it, man!"

Cody mashed the throttle and spun the wheel a hard left, then slammed on the brakes, peeling rubber. Behind them, the old truck lurched toward the intersection. He could see Ms. Stabler in the rearview mirror, a look of deep concern knitting her brow, her elbows horizontal as she leaned over the big red steering wheel. She clearly wanted to get this over with, and fast, and after a brief wave, she turned the truck toward the Thompson Farm and the woods from which he and Brittany had recently escaped, the engine chugging.

Through Walden's window, Cody spotted Brittany herself standing by the curb, holding Midnight by the reins.

"We're going back for the others, right?" he asked Walden.

"Yeah, absolutely. Combs and Stabler got this. And if they don't, it won't matter what we do."

Cody agreed with a solemn nod. They got out of the car, Walden grunting from the pain, still holding the video camera.

"Where's everyone going?" Brittany asked, walking Midnight along toward them.

"Stabler and Combs are heading to the woods," Walden told her. "Combs made a machine Ms. Stabler said might be able to put a stop to all of this."

Brittany stopped near the front of the Mustang. "In the cave," she said matter-of-factly.

"You know about the cave?" Walden asked. Before she could respond he added: "Never mind. We're gonna go back to the church to see if we can help. Wanna come with?"

Brittany's face went blank for a moment, the way it did when she drew those spirals in her notebook. Then she said, "I'm going to follow Ms. Stabler, make sure they're okay. I'll ride Midnight as close as I can to that cave. If she'll let me," she added darkly, stroking the horse's flank.

Walden nodded. "All right, stay safe."

"You too." She made eye contact with Cody, long enough that he gave her a tight, anxious smile. "Be careful," she said. "That *thing* in there... it's a lot more dangerous than you think."

Cody wondered how she knew, when they'd both experienced the same things tonight. "We will," he said.

She nodded, then leaped up onto the Midnight's back. With a double click of her tongue and a flick of the reins, she got the horse moving in a gallop back the way they'd come in a matter of seconds.

They left Brunt's piece of crap Mustang in the middle of the intersection, not worried about whether or not anyone might steal it. If someone was desperate enough to, they probably needed it more than he and Walden did. And Brunt sure wouldn't be driving it again.

"How do you think she knew about the cave?" Walden asked as they headed back to Our Lady of Mercy.

Cody shrugged. "She's pretty observant. Maybe she overheard something between Mr. Combs and Ms. Stabler at school."

"Maybe," Walden said, though he didn't sound convinced.

Philbert Piper sat on the curb, nursing a skinned knee. Cody had forgotten all about him in his haste to get to the church, and later to break through the barricade.

"You guys sure did peel rubber, huh?" he said as they neared him. "Mom says guys who drive like that got tiny ding-dongs, only I'm not s'posed to say that word. It's a bad one."

"Your mom's probably right," Walden agreed. He turned to Cody. "But you tell her this guy right here's got balls of steel."

Cody laughed.

Philbert shook his head vigorously. "I can't say that! Not to Mom! No way, no how!"

Cody turned back to the church, where Geth ushered what looked like Cassandra onto a chariot made from the living objects. Everyone else, including Taylor, Hildebrand, Sheriff Nance and the reverend, followed them out of the church.

Walden blinked hard with his good eye. "Is that *Cassandra* holding its fucking hand?"

"Looks like it."

"Huh. So where the hell you think they're going?"

Cody shrugged. "Wherever it is, we should probably stick with em, huh?"

The chariot led the way, hovering a few feet above the road toward them. The others followed on foot. What first came to mind was a royal wedding, because of how Geth helped Cassandra into the seat beside it, but what it really reminded Cody of was a funeral procession.

Whose funeral? he wondered.

A shiver passed through him then, because he knew the answer:

Everyone's.

CHAPTER 23

1

Renny Hildebrand was first through the school doors. Their procession had quadrupled as they walked the twelve blocks from Our Lady of Mercy to the high school. Renny, Nance and Taylor Flynn led the way, followed closely by Geth's floating armada of weapons. Behind them, Cassandra and Geth sat side-by-side like king and queen, in its chariot made of practically anything it could scrounge from yards and front porches, hovering a foot or two above the damp, leaf-littered streets. The wounded and their blighted shepherds came next, limping along or carried on stretchers from the church basement. Driving slowly behind the rest of the survivors, Cody, Walden and Philbert Piper followed in Adam Brunt's Mustang. During the rest of their journey, many more of the rambling zombies they'd seen earlier in the night joined the parade, trailing mindlessly after them in a conga line of the dead.

Sheriff Nance entered the school directly behind Renny, leading Cassandra's sister along by the shoulder. Geth and Cassandra herself came next, stepping down from the floating chariot hand in hand. The chariot itself again broke apart to serve as a barrier, enclosing them within the building. The crowd remained mostly silent aside from a few groans of pain and snapped directions from the Blighted.

Six jack-o'-lanterns had been lined up just inside the school, although they hadn't been there when he'd left this afternoon. One of the pumpkins had been stomped into the linoleum. A little ways further up the hall, the wall decorations the student council had put up—hand-painted ghosts, vampires, mummies and the like—lay haphazardly across the floor tiles. Arlen Price, the janitor, lay just outside the auto shop in a pool of his own blood, a power tool at his side.

"Oh, jeez," Renny muttered. They'd all seen plenty of carnage tonight, but a part of him was glad he had yet to be desensitized to it. Arlen wasn't exactly a friend but he'd been one of the only school employees who hadn't treated Renny like an outsider when he'd first started teaching here. He was a bit slow, but a kind and generous man, with a wife and a dog at home, a Chesapeake Bay Retriever named Bo, whom he and his wife spoiled, according to the man.

Now he's dead, Renny thought sadly. *His wife and dog probably are, too. Wish I could remember her name.*

"This way," Renny said, stepping over the pumpkins and heading for his classroom. Poor Arlen Price's skull appeared to have been cored by the power tool. Bits of his brain had dribbled out of his temple, running down his ear and neck to coalesce on the shoulder of his jumpsuit like cold strawberry porridge. It was more than Renny had wanted to see, but it had burned into his memory in the split second he'd glanced down as they passed.

He opened the door to the communications lab and ushered Nance and Taylor inside. The hall behind them was filled with people, packed literally from wall to wall.

Geth's sermon was filmed in front of a live studio audience, he thought, paraphrasing the old intro from *Cheers*.

He shook his head, finding it difficult to focus, thoughts scattered. It was probably some kind of trauma response. PTSD, or something. He'd need to get his back in the game to get this broadcast going. Geth, who glared at him with its pumpkin eyes narrowed, wouldn't stand for dragging his ass.

"This is my classroom," Renny said. "Studio 1, as we call it."

"Studio 1," Geth repeated. It gestured for Cassandra to enter first, as though expecting a trap, then followed itself.

The studio was large for a classroom. Even so, there was no way all of these people would fit. Even stacking all of the desks up against the wall or out in the hall, it would leave maybe twenty-five hundred square feet of space total, not including the control room, hefty studio cameras and news set. There had to be at least a hundred and fifty, maybe two hundred people lined up in the hall waiting to enter, with likely more outside.

For all we know, this could be everyone left alive. He shuddered again at the thought of how swiftly Geth had eliminated much of the population, claiming complete dominion over the town and its people in only a few hours.

We were completely blindsided. No way anyone could've predicted this. And now I'm about to play a part in Geth taking over the whole world. From lowly school teacher to Joeseph Goebbels in one day. How'd I get so lucky?

No use blubbering. The best thing to do at the moment was to get everything ready for their broadcast, whether he wanted to do it or not. He just needed to focus on the work ahead and hope the situation resolved itself.

He crossed the large room swiftly and stopped in front the news set. Everyone followed, crowding around the cameras. "Okay, first of all, I'm going to need those of you who don't need to be here to take a few steps back. We need room to move these big cameras around."

People looked around at each other but no one appeared to want to be the first to move, as if they weren't comfortable with the shift in control. Like they were all waiting for Geth to okay it.

Renny clapped his hands. "Move back, people! Move back!"

"Do as he commands," Geth bellowed over him.

That got people moving, faster and more carelessly than Renny had hoped. Yelps of pain, grunts of annoyance and plenty of frustrated dialogue ensued.

"Watch it!"

"You just stepped on my toe!"

"Can't you people just *move*?"

Finally, the crowd moved back enough to roll the cameras back and forth, though they wouldn't be able to do much of a dolly to push in on Geth. Renny didn't suppose theatrics would be all that necessary, anyway. Best to stick with pans and zooms.

"Geth, I want you to stand here," he said, gesturing to an X taped on the floor in front of the desk, between where the anchors would sit.

"Do not presume to tell *Us* where to *stand*, Renny Hildebrand!"

Renny shrugged. "What do I know? I'm just the director, right?"

"Director...?" The pumpkin tilted slightly, like the head of a curious dog, and regarded the blank screens of the two playback monitors set up in front of the desk on either side. "Is this a movie? *Maximum Overdrive, 9:30 to 11:45. A Nightmare On Elm Street 3: Dream Warriors, 11:50 to 1:50 A.M. We now return to The Legend of Sleepy Hollow.*"

With Geth starting to sound like Mr. Moviefone, Renny shook his head in exasperation. "This is a live news broadcast. I'm gonna be directing you from up there," he said, pointing to the glassed-in control room above and behind the set.

"You? Directing Us?"

"That's right. Unless you have some prior TV experience you'd like to share, you're going to need a director."

"For the Tee-Vee."

"That was the intention, wasn't it?" Renny tried not to sound exasperated but Geth was getting to be about as annoying as some of his denser students. "Walden? Cody? Where are you guys?"

"Right here," Cody said, a hand shooting up from behind the crowd.

"I need one of you on camera, the other in the control room to handle the switcher. I'll need Cassandra up there, too," Renny said to Geth, in a cautious tone.

Geth jerked her closer by the hand. She winced at the movement. "Cassandra stays with Us. *The sister* may go," it said, with a sneer.

Renny had figured this would be an issue. He assumed Geth wanted to keep her close because of her powers. They likely made Geth fearful, possibly even jealous.

If Jay and Brittany or one of his other students were here, he would've been okay leaving Cassandra with Geth. Since they weren't, it left him little choice but to insist. "Taylor doesn't know how to use the equipment," he explained. "I need at least one person to work the cameras and another on the switcher. I can floor direct if I have to, but we'll need one more person in that control room. Usually we have four."

"*Cassandra stays,*" Geth insisted. "Sheriff Nance will work your camera."

"I think I could handle it," Sheriff Nance said with a shrug.

Renny eyed him skeptically. Most people thought it was easy, but truly skilled camera operators were rare. "You know how to use one?"

"Just roll it around and point it at the man of the hour—that about right?"

Renny considered it a moment, then shrugged. If Geth wouldn't allow Cassandra to leave its side, there wasn't much reason to be choosy. It wasn't like they were shooting an Orson Welles picture. This was TV, and TV news at that. As much as he didn't want his final broadcast—which would likely be shown around the world once they were all blighted, if he couldn't figure out a way to prevent it—to be amateur hour, he didn't have the time or the preparation to do anything better. As they said in the business when things inevitably went awry: *Close enough for cable*.

"Sure, why not?" he told the sheriff.

"I could help," came a small female voice. A pale hand shot up from the group. After a moment, a slender young woman stepped out from among them. Even covered in dried blood as she was, Renny recognized her as Willa Rafferty, who'd been in his class about four or five years back. She'd been a decent student, and even though she'd never make a great producer or director, he'd always thought she'd deserved better than slinging hash for tips at the diner the rest of her life.

"Thank you, Willa," he said. "We'd love your help. Will you be all right on camera?"

She gave him a half-nod, half-shake of her head.

"Okay, you take camera 2. Nance, get yourself settled behind this one over here," he said, directing the sheriff behind camera 1 as Willa refamiliarized herself with the other.

"Walden, Cody, you guys get set up in the control room, all right?"

"Which positions, Mr. Hildebrand?" Cody asked.

"You boys pick. You remember how to go live?"

"Press the green button," Cody said with a nod.

"No, the *red* one."

"But—" Cody said.

"The *red button*, Cody. Remember? I'll stay down here and direct from the floor. When I count us in, you press that button. Got it?"

"Got it," Cody said, although he seemed confused.

"Cool," Walden said, nodding as if he understood the plan. Walden would likely take control up there anyhow, as a natural leader. The two boys headed off for the door beside the green screen that led to the control room stairs.

Geth had remained silently standing on its X the entire time Renny directed people around, clearly growing impatient. "When will We spread our message to your people?"

"It takes as long as it takes," Renny said. "That's kind of our motto in the business: *hurry up and wait.*"

He turned his attention back to Nance. "It's like steering a bike," he said, showing him how to grip the handles and pull and push the camera back and forth and side to side on its wheeled base. "Pull this one to zoom in, this one to zoom out." Nance followed directions well. The image on the monitor—the school channel's news logo—zoomed in and out sloppily, but it would do.

"All right, I'll go grab headsets for you two."

"You're the boss," Nance said.

Renny rushed over to the box where all the headsets and Lavalier mics were kept for the news broadcasts. He grabbed three headsets and a single mic. He didn't expect anyone but Geth to be speaking.

He handed off the headsets to Sheriff Nance and Willa, connected them, then approached Geth.

"I need to clip this to your lapel," he said, nervous to be standing so near it. "Normally we'd run it up under your jacket, but…"

"Do as you must."

Cautiously, Renny clipped the mic to Geth's lapel, then ran the cord down the dead man's chest and clipped the transmitter to its belt. As he worked, he glanced at Cassandra. She gave him a very slight shake of her head.

He was pretty sure he knew what it meant. *Don't try anything.*

Renny had no intention of it, not with over a hundred rounds of ammunition aimed at him and the crowd. Geth could shoot them all dead in seconds if it felt they were getting out of line. Only a fool would try something like that.

The kind of fool who'd walk a live grenade toward a living god? he thought, although Trudy Bell was dead, her body left on the steps to the church altar, not blighted like the other zombies.

"All right," he said. "I guess we're good to go." He thumbed the button on his headset. "Walden? Cody? You guys ready up there?"

Up in the control room, Walden gave him a thumbs up, sitting in front of the switcher. Sitting to his right, Cody spoke into the mic. "We're all good up here."

"Ready to rock at the top of the clock," Walden agreed.

"Okay," Renny said. "Sheriff Nance? Willa? You all set?"

Willa and Nance nodded. "As I'll ever be," the sheriff said.

"Okay, just follow the directions from Walden and you'll be fine. Don't worry if you mess up. Like we say in the business, *Close enough for cable.*" He turned back to Geth. "I guess it's up to you now," he said. "Should we get started?"

"Indeed."

"Remember, the monitors here and here, they're your playback. That's what people will see on their television."

Geth looked from one to the other. On both, Geth stood in frame—though he had a bit too much of what they called "headroom" from Nance's camera, which Renny would help him adjust—a closeup on camera 1, a wide on camera 2.

"Okay. I'll give you a five count. I'll say five to three aloud, and give you a sign for two and one. When I point at you, you can start."

"Why not simply point at Us?"

"Because that's not how TV works. Are we good?"

"Very well. We are good, Renny Hildebrand."

"Good. All right, everyone! Quiet on set!"

He didn't need to say it. The crowd was so silent he could hear the asthmatic wheezes of an elderly man on a stretcher laid out over two of the desks at the far end of the classroom.

"And... five, four, three..."

2

WALDEN WAS IN HIS ELEMENT. He loved sitting behind the large Ross Video Synergy switcher with all of its bright, colored buttons and levers. Not as much as writing, but still, when it came to comm class, this was his happy place.

Hildebrand counted Geth in. Walden pressed the red button with the word ON AIR on it, set on the desk beside the switcher. Hildbrand had specified the red button, which put them live on monitors throughout the school—if they weren't turned off—but not beyond. It was used for run-throughs—practices, in other words—and turned on the corresponding ON AIR sign above the door outside the classroom. It was the green button, the one beside it that said BROADCAST, that sent their news via a small satellite on the roof to TVs all over Crooks Corner and the surrounding counties.

Geth said nothing, just stood there blinking, looking at something slightly downward and to its left. The ON AIR sign would've gone on in the studio as well, and Hildebrand had given it the sign that they were live. Its jack-o'-lantern face filled the screen on camera 1, the one going to air. Like it had stage-fright, or something.

Does it know? Can it tell we're not really broadcasting?

"What's it looking at?" Cody asked.

Walden shrugged. "Fucked if I know."

Cody cleared his throat. "You're live, Mr. Hildebrand."

"I know," Hildebrand said quietly over his mic.

Walden switched cameras. "Camera 2, can you pull back a bit?"

Eventually, camera 2 rolled back to a wider shot, but it wasn't giving him a better view of what Geth might be looking at.

"A bit further, please."

"That's as far back as I can go," said the woman who'd driven them to Cassandra's house earlier in the night. Walden couldn't remember her name, although he knew it started with a W like his own.

He turned to Cody. "Can you see? I won't be able to get a good look over the board."

Cody stood and peered down into the studio, a reverse view of what they saw on the large program monitor above them. "I think it's looking at one of the playback monitors."

"Looking at itself on the monitor?"

Cody shrugged. "I guess."

Walden considered it a moment. "Camera 1, can you give me

a little less headroom?" When camera 1, operated by Sheriff Nance, didn't respond vocally or follow direction, Walden said, "Camera 1?"

"The only *headroom* I know is Max," Nance said.

"You're leaving too much empty space above Geth's head. Tilt the camera down just a little, okay?"

"Will do."

The camera tilted jerkily, but eventually got the shot Walden wanted.

"Perfect." He switched camera 1 from preview to program, making it live. Geth's face filled the large monitor above the switcher. Its head tilted. It blinked.

"It's mesmerized by itself on the monitor," he said.

Cody huffed a laugh. "Talk about vain."

Geth looked up suddenly, blinking at the camera.

"You're on," Hildebrand said, loud enough to be heard at home, for anyone who's watching.

Finally, Geth spoke. "People of this land. We are Geth. We have liberated Ourselves from drifting for what you would call *millennia*, ensnared within the *Upask*, the Void beyond the *Tum Gob*, a womb of endless, boundless Nothing so pure and dark We could only dream. And dream We did. We dreamed that when We finally returned to this land, We would unite your warring factions, your clashing cultures and beliefs, under the only True Religion: The Word of Geth. You ask for God to hear your prayers, and wonder why God does not reply? We are here to tell you, God *did* listen. God merely could not respond, as God had been banished from this land by Those Who Came Before. God listened, and God waited. And now God has returned, to answer all of your prayers. For *We* are your God. We will cure your sick and feed your poor. We will end your conflicts. If you accept Our love, We will make you One with Us. If you *deny* Us, you will be destroyed."

Geth paused, allowing this to sink in for the viewers at home —or the people it seemed to believe were watching it speak. Then, it began its sermon: "This, then, is The Word..."

Walden had sat mesmerized, listening to the pumpkin-headed fuck spout off its wild, grandiose delusions... but then something caught his eye, something he'd noticed earlier in the day but had forgotten about. Something that could quite possibly give them an edge against this gourd-faced freak.

A Zip drive lay in front of the graphics computer. Walden had been P.A. this morning, and Jay had been on graphics. The drive had one of those red Brother P-Touch labels on its surface, with the words PROPERTY OF JAY NIELSON in raised white letters.

Jay had left his Zip drive, with the opening credits to *Helloween*, plugged into one of the computer ports.

"Fuck me," Walden muttered, then glanced at the P.A. system to make sure his mic wasn't hot.

Cody glanced in his direction, apparently as mesmerized by Geth's sermon as Walden had just been. "What?" he said.

"I think I have an idea how—" Walden stopped himself, not sure whether Geth could hear them all the way up here in the control room even with their mics off.

For all he knew, Geth could read their minds.

Terror filled his veins like ice water and he winced, waiting for his head to explode in a violent shower of brain and blood. But if Geth had read his mind, it would've known they weren't *really* live, at least not beyond the school. And it would've known Hildebrand had mentioned the red button deliberately.

Maybe Geth's psychic abilities were like a TV, tuned in to different channels. Maybe it had picture-in-picture, maybe even a whole lot of different visions at once, like that old commercial they spoofed in *Wayne's World*, where they told two friends, and then *they* told two friends. But it couldn't possibly see *every* channel all at once.

Still, it was best to be safe. When ten seconds passed and Walden's head remained firmly on his shoulders, painful and bruised but not exploded, he took the pad of paper he'd used this morning for timing the stories and scrawled five words in all caps. He slid the pad across the desk and turned it for Cody to read.

LET'S FINISH OUR FUCKING MOVIE!

Cody looked up at him from the words on the notepad, a shrewd grin spreading across his face.

3

NANCE FELT like he was doing pretty good on the camera for an amateur, though he would've preferred his television debut to be anything other than it was.

Geth had launched into its sermon, what it called "The Word," a whole laundry list of bullshit. Coming here to shoot this broadcast had been Nance's own plan, but beyond getting Geth out onto the airwaves, he didn't know what the hell else to do. All he had left at this point was the truth. Geth could go on and on about how it wanted to buy the world a goddamn Coke and make them live in perfect harmony, but it was all just a sham. Supernatural or not, *powerful* or not, Geth truly was just another in a long line of grifters. The *epitome* of grifters, even. And the best way to counter a grift was with the truth.

Where the hell did Revered Earl get to? Nance wondered.

Charles knew the truth, or at least part of it. Some of these people did, too. The stories Nance had told earlier, many of the older residents knew about them. Some of the kids maybe, too, though they probably assumed they were just urban legends, stories meant to scare them into walking a straight line. Nance's predecessor had several notebooks full of them, each verified by paperwork he and his deputies had filed over the decades. The story of hundreds of timber rattlers slithering down from the hills, biting everyone from here to Sunday. The one about the kid whose house burned down, killing everyone in his family but him, and how he'd somehow slept through it all in his bedroom, the only room in the house that remained untouched by the fire. The one about the girl who'd warned everybody at the church about a tornado no one had predicted, and how they'd all managed to get down to the basement in the nick of time before the damn thing tore the roof right off and sent pews and Bibles and even Jesus on His cross all over the neighborhood. The one about the escaped convict who'd murdered those innocent children out in the woods beyond the Thompson farm, claiming the Devil made him do it. And the one about Daniel Crook, the town's founder, after the entire house of cards he'd built had fallen down around him.

These were a handful of the many stories the people of this town whispered amongst each other, but kept hidden from outsiders. This was Crooks Corner, a place where the fabric separating the known world from the unknown just happened to be a little thinner than most, where the sinister and the weird seemed to happen a little more often.

Is it all because of Geth? Bits of this thing leaking out over the years, the decades—its inhaks, *or whatever it called them, reaching out to us from beyond this Toom Gobe, influencing us? Is that why Auntie Jean always had a knack for guessing what we all dreamed the night before? Is that how Cassandra Flynn was able to counter its powers back at the church? Is that where the snakes came from that day way back then, and what made Dan Crook do what the old legends say he did?*

Right... the story. That was what Nance had in his arsenal, the only thing left to him, really. Geth may control all the guns and the demonic Halloween crap, but Nance had the truth. Geth's Word could never counter that—particularly filled as it was with brain-numbing, pseudo-biblical word salad, even callbacks to those "hounds of the moon" Charles had spoken about earlier. He just had to waste Geth's time until the National Guard got here. Let *them* deal with this thing. They'd most likely be walking into a bloodbath, but at least it would take Geth's attention away from the people of this town.

Still hours away. Geth'll be halfway through blighting everyone in town and well on its way to the national news. This was my idea. I got us into this mess, I have to find a way to get us out.

"Reverend Earl," Geth said, apparently finished with its load of bull for the time being. "Come to Us, that We may begin to anoint Our newest followers into the fold."

Nance glanced over his shoulder, searching for the man in question.

The reverend's hand shot up in the crowd. "Right away, my Lord!" Charles called.

Why's he hiding back there? Shouldn't Geth's P.R. manager be up front and center?

An interesting question, one that made Nance wonder if maybe Geth didn't have all the cards in its hand it appeared to.

The reverend emerged from the audience a moment later, blood crusted on his right ear and cheek. Gone was the blissful smile from earlier, and Nance saw the reason right away. A black rectangle stuck out of the side of the reverend's head, making

Nance think of Phineas P. Gage, the railroad foreman who'd somehow survived for years with an iron rod driven through both his skull and the left half of his brain. As Charles drew nearer, Nance realized it was one of the keys from the exploded piano.

Christ, how is he still standing?

Charles turned and stood at Geth's left side, opposite Cassandra Flynn, whose expression was just as one might expect of a hostage. But Charles looked anxious. Not only that, he looked *different*. It wasn't just the lack of smile. The darkness in his eyes was gone.

That hit on the head must've jarred it loose! Like in those old cartoons—he's himself again! Jesus H. Mahogany Christ, he better not let Geth see it!

"Camera 2, pull back a little so we can see them both," one of the boys in the control room said over the headset. Willa moved the camera back a few steps until she no longer had room to push back against the wall of Blighted townspeople standing in the front line.

"Reverend Earl," Geth said, glancing sidelong at the man.

"Yes, my Lord."

"You may begin."

Charles cleared his throat. "With whom should I begin, my Lord?"

"With this boy," Geth said, gesturing with its free hand toward the audience.

Nance glanced back. A boy up front, about eleven or twelve years old, looked around at the much taller adults around him in fear. His face was painted like a skeleton and a few fabric bones poked out from under his winter coat. Nance recognized him as one of the three who'd come tumbling into the church right before Geth and the others. The ones who'd been knocking, eager to get inside.

"M-me?" the boy asked, his voice shaky.

"Yes, you," the demon said. "Come to Us, Matthew Dukas."

"W-why me?"

"Camera 1, can you turn to get the kid?"

Nance ignored the direction, watching as Geth's brow furrowed. "You wanted to see Us up close—is that not why you pushed your way to the front of the crowd? You wanted to see if

We were real. *Really real. Like the snakes and spiders I stuffed in my pillowcase.* Is that not what you wondered?"

The boy nodded dumbly, his black-painted lower lip hanging.

The stitched smile widened. "Our very own Doubting Thomas. Come then, Thomas. Touch Us. Feel the cold hand of Death. See that We are real, and We shall make you one with Us."

"I w-want my m-mom," the kid said.

"Camera 1," the boy in the control room said more sharply.

Shut the hell up, kid, Nance thought.

Geth's Cheshire cat grin spread further. "Your mother is dead, child. Mother and father both. Among the first to go, in fact. They are shadows on a wall, like the dead of Hiroshima."

The poor kid shook his head. "No, that's not—that's not true!"

"Oh, but it is." Geth gestured him forward. "Come to Us now, boy... *or join them in death*."

Nance couldn't let this slow torture go on any longer. "Charles," he said, taking his shot before it was too late. "You remember earlier I was telling you what happened to Dan Crook?"

Charles blinked. He licked his lips and said nothing.

"Our town founder," Nance reminded him.

"Yes, of course," Charles said. "Daniel Crook, founder of Crooks Corner."

The reverend was lying, Nance was sure of it, and the man couldn't remember because he hadn't been present. Geth's Blighted had taken his place. It solidified Nance's theory that nothing was left of the person beneath while they were under Geth's control, but it gave him hope that the living who'd received Geth's Blight, like Judy Delacroix, could be brought back if they were somehow able to send Geth back to the Hell it'd come from.

"We care not about this town nor its founder," Geth bellowed. *"Come to Us, child, or perish like your forebears!"*

Young Matthew Dukas stepped dutifully out of the crowd, tears streaming down his face. He'd wet himself, the stain spreading on the dark fabric and white bones.

"The townspeople toppled that statue of him in Wyndham Park," Nance reminded Charles, eager to turn Geth's attention away from the boy.

"SILENCE!" it bellowed, the candle burning brightly within its mouth. *"You will remain silent, Lawman, or We will kill this boy for everyone to witness!"*

Nance shut his mouth. The reverend perked up suddenly, a ghost of that blissful smile returning. "Oh, but the people really should hear this story, my Lord. It's quite... uplifting. Yes, I truly believe it will benefit the process immensely."

Scowling, Geth blinked its slitted eyes several times, still watching the boy, who'd stopped between the two cameras, sniffling and wiping his nose on the sleeve of his coat. He was close enough Nance could smell the sharp scent of his urine. He could almost reach out and grab the boy, if he dared.

Finally, the monster said, "Very well. You may proceed, Lawman. But heed this warning: if you attempt to sabotage Our ceremony, *We will destroy you.*"

"Oh," Nance said, "I think you'll find this story quite enlightening, Geth. I assume you heard the beginning of it through the good reverend's very own ears."

"We did," Geth said impatiently, glancing askance at Charles.

"So you know the townspeople were fed up with Dan Crook's load of bull by the time of the Financial Panic of 1873, and that Dan Crook's bank, Crook Savings and Loan—which most folks in town had sunk their life savings into despite the inauspicious name—collapsed along with about a hundred others all over the country. He'd gotten them all rich from railroad bonds, but when the market crashed in Europe, all of those European investors cashed in their chips. It was a mess, Geth, setting off one of the worst financial crises until the Great Depression in the '30s."

"Camera 1," the kid upstairs said, "if you're going to be in this, you need to get closer to the desk mic. We can't hear what you're saying down there."

Hildebrand gestured for him to approach the stage, but Nance had no intention of getting closer to Geth, at least not yet. He ignored the directions, continuing his story, hoping it would intrigue Geth long enough to distract it from the Dukas boy. "Turns out Dan Crook was one of your earliest followers, Geth. Now you should know this, because it was your Blight, according to legend, or at least what I've surmised from it, that gave Crook the knowledge to do what he did. Settling here and building this town from the ground up. Making himself and his friends rich beyond their wildest dreams."

"And then lose it all," the reverend said, his eyes gleaming.

"We have no concern for wealth," Geth said, scowling at Charles. "Money is a fiction. A lie you tell yourselves to create further divides amongst your people."

"*Camera 1*," the kid said insistently.

Nance tore off his headset and tossed it aside. Hildebrand watched it hit the floor with a stunned expression.

"Be that as it may," Nance said, "Dan Crook *was* a very wealthy man, and he attributed said wealth to his occult activities. Back then a lot of wealthy people were into the occult, particularly communing with spirits. But Dan Crook was an occultist of a different stripe. He attributed his power to persuade and to gauge the world of finance to none other than Satan himself. But according to those old records my predecessor kept, and his predecessors before him, Crook mentioned stones in a cave, with what he called 'the Tongue of the Ancients' written on them. The Sheriff back then, he never did find that cave, but I'm willing to bet those stones of Crook's are this Tum Gob you mentioned. And Dan Crook, when they finally spoke to him after it all went down, he told the sheriff what happened to his first wife. That he'd taken her life in that cave, Geth. A human sacrifice for his Dark Lord. Much like I believe your Cult of the Smiling Face sacrificed the actress Darla Knight earlier this evening."

Gasps ran through the crowd. Hushed voices expressed shock.

"We know nothing of your town founder nor this supposed cult."

"Maybe it wasn't you, then," Nance said, playing innocent, glancing back at the floating AR-15 that had advanced on him, just about pressing into the back of his head. "Maybe he was communing with someone else in that cave. Or maybe it really was Satan."

"Satan does not exist," Geth said calmly. "Only We exist."

"Uh, excuse me, Mr. Geth?"

Nance turned to see an uncharacteristically meek-looking Gary Garner emerge from the audience, holding up a hand, his head bowed.

"*What is it?*" Geth demanded.

"I'm a bit of an amateur historian," Gary said. "And most of what Sheriff Nance has told you lines up with my research. I can't speak on your involvement in it, of course. I'm just saying."

Gary Garner made to return to his wife and son, then turned back. "Oh, and if you're ever thinking about trading in that junker of yours, I've got the best prices in five counties. We're running a Halloween promotion—"

"*RETURN TO YOUR FAMILY.*"

Gary startled, the salesman in him giving way to his previous meek demeanor. "Yes, sir, Mr. Geth, sir," he said, and apologized and excused his way through the crowd.

"Your stories have grown tedious," Geth said. It turned to Charles, snapping its dead fingers. "Reverend Earl, bring Us the boy."

Charles made no move, instead giving Nance an imploring look.

"You haven't asked why Dan Crook was questioned by the law at all," Nance said. "He was arrested for murder. *Multiple* murders, actually, thirteen in all. You see, he gathered all of his biggest investors together, promising to pay them back—and pay them back, he did, just not with money. He locked them all in the empty bank vault, and he set his bank on fire. Then he drove his own coach to the sheriff's station, because his driver was one of the men who'd toppled his statue, and he turned himself in. Told them everything.

"They didn't believe a word of it, of course, aside from the murders, which by the time Dan Crook finished his story the local fire brigade had already confirmed. Who'd wanna believe the town they lived in was founded by a Satan worshipper—and worse, that he'd actually convinced them and just about everyone else they knew to follow what he believed to be Satan's gospel? It's tough enough for me to swallow, and I'm five or six generations removed.

"Then lo and behold, it turned out to be *you* he'd been worshipping, likely without knowing it. It was you who told him what to do to make himself and the people of this town rich. My guess is you even knew it would end in ruin for so many people right from the get-go. You had him build this town so you could *feed* off of us, for *generations*, like tics feeding off herds of cattle.

To keep you and your *inhak* alive, or whatever consists of living for things like you, until you could figure out a way to escape.

"And then you did." Nance shook his head. "I don't know how you escaped, but you did. Couldn't have been the sacrifice, because you'd been through that before, hadn't you? Back in '69, with those two precious little babes in the field out behind the Thompson farm. That escaped convict who called himself The Snake. *He* said the Devil made him do it, too, at least according to the sheriff's record.

"But there *is* no Devil," Nance added, feeling suddenly like a TV detective about to inform everyone why it was he'd gathered them all here tonight. "*There is only Geth*. You said it yourself. Which means, unless they were just getting this stuff from the ether, it was *all* you. The murders, the rampaging snakes, the cult, and the founding of this town right at your front door—all of it down to you."

Geth pursed its lips. It remained silent for a moment, seemingly thoughtful. Nance had witnessed this with all kinds of criminals over the years: a struggle between self-preservation and conscience—though he suspected Geth had no conscience. It was all about *ego* with Geth, and Geth wouldn't let him get the upper hand no matter how true everything he'd said had been.

"You are a shrewd policeman, Sheriff Nance," it said finally. "We will give you that. Yes, it was Us. Of course it was Us. We told Daniel Crook to carve a statue of the quartz-striped granite from the cave beyond which We had been imprisoned. We imbued the statue with our living *inhak*, which in turn granted Crook his power."

"I thought as much," Nance said. "So when the townsfolk toppled the statue and it crumbled to dust, they unknowingly released these *inhaks* of yours."

"Correct. And they returned to Us in the *Upask*. But surely, Sheriff Hubert Nance, you must see that this monologue of yours only further *proves* Our power. Our *omnipotence*."

Nance nodded, pretending to be beaten. "You do have plenty of power, I'll grant you that. Telepathy, telekinesis, maybe even a limited ability to predict the future. But there's one thing you don't have that humans do, buster."

Geth grinned slyly. "Oh? Do tell, Sheriff. What is it which We do not possess?"

"Human instinct," Nance wheeled around swiftly to grab Randy Jacobs's camo AR-15. "The hounds of the moon are barking at the door, you carpetbagger prick," he said, and squeezed the trigger.

4

"WHAT'S HE DOING DOWN THERE?" Walden asked Cody, who was standing at the window looking down into the studio.

Sheriff Nance had completely ignored all of Walden's directions, instead going off on some wild tangent story about Daniel Crook, the town founder. Walden had heard a lot of the rumors about the man but he'd never really believed in them. The history books had whitewashed the story, of course, but the fire at the bank was common knowledge. The old bank building—now a realtor's office—still bore some of the black stains on its foundation.

"I dunno," Cody said. "I think he's trying to distract him. *It.*"

Was that all this was? A last-ditch attempt to distract the thing? If so, it seemed to be working. Geth could've killed the sheriff at any point, but it seemed content to indulge him even though he'd clearly pissed it off.

Whatever the reason, it bode well for Walden's plan. The computer had taken its sweet time booting up, and Jay's damn Zip drive was slow to load the opening credits. He needed time, and hopefully no more than the sheriff could provide.

"Come on, you fucker," he muttered.

"Holy crap," Cody said.

"What?"

"Nance has got the—"

A massive *BANG* from the studio smothered Cody's words.

Screams arose from down below as Walden sprang up from his chair so fast it rolled backwards and toppled. His ears still rang from the beating he'd taken and the explosion—or whatever it was—and he didn't even hear the chair crash to the floor.

With every muscle screaming, he hurried over to Cody and peered down into the studio. Sheriff Nance was holding one of the machine guns in both hands, its barrel smoking. For a moment, Walden couldn't tell who he'd shot.

Was it Geth? Did he kill the fucking thing?

Then the reverend, standing on Geth's other side, grasped his chest in stunned silence and dropped to his knees.

"Holy crap," Cody said again, shaking his head in disbelief.

Walden rushed back to the desk. He had under a minute to try and distract Geth, to stop it from retaliating, from killing the sheriff or worse. His index finger hovered over the mouse button. The cursor hovered over the Take button. A white circle spun in front of the black video screen as it continued to load.

"Come on, you piece of shit computer—*COME ON!*"

5

REVEREND EARL LOOKED DOWN at the dark stain blooming on his chest, the hole in him still smoking from the entry of the single bullet Nance had fired, ostensibly meant for Geth. He gasped, and his lungs whistled, his lips opening and closing like a fish out of water.

Nance locked eyes with him. The sheriff shook his head with obvious remorse. They'd never gotten along before tonight. The sheriff found him troublesome and Charles had always thought Nance was an officious prig. But Charles had believed that the two of them joining forces, both men who'd sworn allegiance to the people of this town, would be able to conquer this threat together.

Geth's Blight had been too strong for him to fight. Against his will, he'd sold out his parishioners, their friends and families. He hadn't been able to help it, but judging by the cold, black eyes of the people in the front row, it was already far too late to turn it around. At least for him.

I did my best, Lord, he thought. *I just hope it was enough.*

And then the reverend's soul left his body, and his body collapsed on the floor.

6

STUPID, Nance scolded himself.

Practically a lifetime of calmly and rationally assessing

ruckuses and commotions he'd just annihilated in a single irrational, spur of the moment decision that ejected the bullet from a .223-caliber Remington cartridge and punched it straight through Charles Earl's chest at approximately 2000 miles per hour. It'd been meant for Geth—Nance had aimed dead center at the son-of-a-bitch's pumpkin head. It should have blown the thing to chunks of orange and yellow fruit flesh, splattering it all over the high school news set like a watermelon at a Gallagher concert.

But he'd made a mistake. He'd gotten cocky, counting on Geth being too hung up on protecting its ego and image on television to predict what he had coming for it. Instead, it had managed to tweak the angle of the rifle in the split-second he'd pulled the trigger and the bullet meant for Geth blew out the back of the reverend's cassock, causing his purple vestment with its gold tassels to sail languidly to the altar floor, stained with hot blood.

Nance held the reverend's gaze in the moment before the man fell, assuring him in his dying moments that he hadn't meant to shoot him, hoping it would make up for what had been a contentious relationship, let him know that despite what had happened with the Blight, what he'd done to help had been appreciated.

Then the life left Charles Earl's eyes and he crumpled in a dead heap at Geth's feet.

Nance startled, not at the sight of the dead reverend but at the unbidden movement of his own hands. With a twitch of Geth's head, Nance swung the rifle upward like a courtesy salute to a superior officer, only instead of holding it out in front of himself, his traitorous hands lowered it, tucking the barrel under his chin, cold steel scratching against his five-o'clock shadow.

His trigger finger twitched.

I guess this is it, he thought. Squeezing his eyes shut, he struggled against the opposing force pressing his index finger toward the trigger.

His instinct for survival was strong.

Geth's will was stronger.

In a moment, maybe less, his brains would splatter across the audience, over the stunned faces of the people he'd sworn to protect. He couldn't fight it much longer. Hell, he knew Geth could make the weapon itself pull its own trigger if the bastard wanted.

It would be more satisfying this way, making Nance shoot himself. Especially after he dared challenge Geth's omnipotence in front of the world it planned to conquer.

Kelly, Jody: I love you, girls.

A picture of the four of them sprang to mind, the one on his desk of their once-happy family at Carlsbad Caverns in '92. Deputy Sikes often asked why Nance kept it there, considering his ex-wife was front and center with Nance's arm draped over her, the four of them smiling to beat all. Back in the good old days, before the whole thing came crashing down around him.

Hell, I suppose I love you, too, Janine. Despite all the bull we've been through, you're still the girls' mother.

It was the last thought on his mind before Geth made his finger squeeze the trigger.

7

CASSANDRA STARED in absolute shock at the reverend's crumpled body spilling dark blood on the painted concrete floor. Sheriff Nance had surprised her when he'd grabbed the gun. She hadn't expected it, hadn't even had an instant to push back against Geth's influence. All Geth had to do was turn its barrel ever so slightly toward Reverend Earl, the man who'd baptized her, who'd performed her confirmation and spoken homilies at her parents' funeral. Now that same man lay dead on the floor in front of her. Shot on live TV. And she hadn't been able to do a thing to stop it.

But she *could* stop Geth from killing the sheriff.

With a jerk of Geth's head, Sheriff Nance flipped the gun toward himself and pushed the barrel up under his chin. Despite her stunned disbelief, despite the grief she felt for the man who'd said such kind words about her mother and father as they were lowered into the ground, Cassandra managed to throw every available ounce of mental energy toward the gun, willing it to move just enough that the bullet would fire into the air rather than through the sheriff's skull.

Nance pulled the trigger.

She winced against the blast she knew was coming despite all she'd done to prevent it, against the sight of his face exploding toward her like a horror movie in 3D, in bright Technicolor.

The rifle merely clicked.

The trigger finger on Nance's right hand squeezed again and again and the rifle merely clicked, over and over.

Click-click-click-click-click....

Out of bullets, she thought, and sighed in relief.

Nance opened his eyes and actually grinned.

"You got me, Geth," he said.

"We got you," Geth agreed.

A blast just about as loud as the shot that had killed Reverend Earl sounded behind him with a blinding muzzle flash. Sheriff Nance's look of shock exploded outward in what felt like slow-motion, his nose and eyes and lips disintegrating, shattered teeth and bursting eyeballs flying outward in a fountain spray of deep-red blood.

The glistening red bullet stopped about a foot from her, spinning like a top but frozen in its forward momentum.

Cassandra hadn't stopped it herself. She'd expected it likely as little as Sheriff Nance had himself.

The bullet fell, plinking on the floor.

She turned to Geth, who returned her gaze coldly.

Nance fell forward, slumping face-first—or what was left of his face—on the floor between them and the cameras, revealing the handgun that had shot him in the back of the head. The little kid in the skeleton costume finally drummed up the courage to turn and run, grabbing Mr. Hildebrand around the waist. Hildebrand hugged him tightly, though her teacher looked as shell-shocked as Cassandra felt herself.

Shock became rage, and she rounded on Geth, attempting to tear her hand free from its cold grip. "Why did you do that? You didn't have to kill them! You didn't have to kill *anybody*!"

Geth regarded her expressionlessly, its stitched lips flat. "One doesn't ask why a volcano erupts nor a tornado destroys. Why does one dare question why a God does what They do?"

"*You're not God!* God doesn't intervene. God's a deadbeat dad! He went out for smokes at the end of the Bible and never came back. But *you*... you're nothing but a delusional monster with too much power. And if there really is a God... well, then I guess I'll see you in Hell!"

The spent bullet shot up from the mess of blood and gore on the painted concrete, and launched itself at Geth's poorly carved smile. Geth's slitted-X eyes widened in surprise as the bullet shot toward Them.

Cassandra felt joy, true, pure joy for the first time since her parents died, in the split second before the bullet struck Geth's ugly pumpkin face. She imagined it plowing through it, making a nose hole the size of a silver dollar, extinguishing the candle within and erupting out the back of its head in a burst of flesh and skin and seeds.

Instead, the bullet hit Geth in the middle of its face with a hollow, unremarkable *thuck*. It left a small indent where a nose would be, and tumbled down the breast of Geth's suit to land with a clink on the floor.

The monster stared at her for a brief moment before bellowing with laughter. "Oh, Cassandra! You do so very much amuse Us!" It laughed uproariously. The dead-eyed zombies in the front row laughed along with it as if an APPLAUSE sign had lit up above the news set, their voices almost robotic.

The laughter died suddenly. Geth turned to her with its pumpkin brow furrowed. "No more games, Cassandra. Now you shall take the place of your deceased holy man. Bring Our first initiate to Us. Bring Us the boy."

She shook her head. "*I won't.*"

"Then you shall watch as the people in this studio murder one another. The floors shall be slick with their blood, the air pungent with the foul stench of their insides. You shall—"

Geth stopped suddenly, its attention drawn to something to her right. Its lips parted slightly and remained open, as if whatever it was seeing had mesmerized it.

Cassandra turned to look.

On the playback monitors, the credits for *Helloween* played, with their slowed-down, inversed footage from different prominent areas in town. She saw her name written in fire over the wheel from the old mill, along with Brittany's over ducks on the pond, Cody's over kids playing in Wyndham Park, Walden's over a shot out the windshield of a car driving down Main Street, and *Directed by Jay Nielson* over the stark white branches of pine trees swaying slowly and sinisterly against a black sky.

It really was good, Cassandra had to admit. If none of this

had happened, Jay's credits alone probably would've gotten an easy A for their assignment. Her heart sank, thinking it. She hadn't thought of Jay since he'd run off and hoped, despite him being so annoying and leaving them in the lurch the way he had, that he was still alive out there somewhere. Who knows—maybe he was sending out an SOS on the internet to any of the dweebs he played his video games with.

"Geth," Mr. Hildebrand said, still hugging the kid with one arm.

Geth remained focused on the television.

Hildebrand called its name again.

"*Yes*," Geth said irritably, not looking away from the monitor. Finally the credits ended, and the screen went to black briefly before returning to a wide shot of Geth and herself standing in front of the news desk. Cassandra hated how bleached-out her face looked on camera, and thought she'd maybe cut down on the white foundation if she survived the night. Just a little.

"What is this... *Helloween*?" Geth asked Hildebrand.

"That's what I've been trying to tell you. Cassandra and the boys up in the control room, they've been shooting a documentary tonight."

"A documentary?"

Hildebrand put a hand up against the headset's earpiece, listening to Walden or Cody—but probably Walden. Cody was smarter than she'd originally thought but Walden was still the brains of the two. "That's right," Hildebrand said. "They've been making a movie about you. They want to tell your story."

Geth turned to Cassandra. "A movie... about Us?"

She nodded, following along. "Yeah, uh-huh."

"Nobody watches the news these days," Hildebrand said. "It's *movies* that really get people excited. Even the Nazis knew that, with their propaganda films."

"They would be excited... about Us?"

"Exactly! They want to tell *your* story—your *origin story*. Like Superman." Hildebrand scratched his head. "Or Jesus, I guess."

"Jesus. And people would... want to watch this film?"

"Of course! Are you kidding? Who wouldn't want to watch a movie about the origin of their god?" Hildebrand was really pitching it, sounding like a Hollywood agent and talking with his hands. "How they came into the world. How they survived millennia in the Void beyond the, um, the *Toom Gobe*. To save humanity from its selfishness and greed."

"And tribalism," Geth added. It blinked several times, seemingly in thought. "*Maximum Overdrive, 9:30 to 11:45. A Nightmare On Elm Street 3: Dream Warriors, 11:50 to 1:50 A.M. We now return to Helloween*," Geth said.

"We'll go and finish their movie," Mr. Hildebrand said, "then come back here and show it to everyone tonight on live TV."

"*On live Tee-Vee*," Geth repeated, seemingly mystified. "Yes, this does sound appealing to Us. Wise, even." With a decisive nod, it said, "We would like to resume creating this *Helloween*. Where shall We begin?"

Hildebrand listened to Walden for a moment. Then he said, "We'll begin where you did: at the *Toom Gobe*. In the cave."

CHAPTER 24

1

The truck picked up speed ahead of Brittany, the black smoke pouring from its exhaust pipe illuminated by the taillights. If she couldn't get Midnight to race any faster, she'd lose Ms. Stabler and Mr. Combs in the darkness ahead.

Don't matter, The Snake said. *Geth's gonna make em wish they was never born, an' you'd be wise to shake a tail feather outta town 'fore he does the same to us.*

Brittany shook her head, trying her best to ignore the persistent voice. She knew where they were going. If she lost them, she could find the spot again, even in the dark.

They were going to the cave.

Because of course they were.

Somehow she'd known this night could only end by returning to the place where the most traumatic event in her life had occurred. Since she'd met The Snake, everything had been tainted by trauma.

You couldn't kill a man without experiencing some sort of emotional trauma yourself—not unless you were a psychopath, which she most assuredly wasn't. And killing a kid... well, that was a whole different kind of traumatic. It wasn't like she'd *wanted* to kill Tommy Mingus. He hadn't deserved to die, and if she could've thought of any other way to appease The Snake, she would have.

Faking bloodlust, acting like she was truly evil, like she enjoyed what she'd had to do, even that hadn't helped. She'd thought by playing the role of a serial killer in her mind she could lessen her fear, and the inevitable feelings of remorse. The Snake would've taken her over and made her do it anyway, after all. He probably would've made it a lot worse for Tommy Mingus. The things he'd had her do to Bennington made her shudder to remember, but at least that sick pervert *deserved* what he'd gotten.

Midnight huffed and snorted as they blew past her house. It was just as she'd left it, still lit brightly by the spotlights in the hedges under the windows. The Lexus hadn't been returned to the garage, which meant her parents were either dead or at the church with the others.

She hoped it was the latter, even though it meant they were with Geth. If she survived the night, it would be good to try and make things right with Denise. With Mom.

Shoulda put em all outta their misery yerself, The Snake said. *Not like you ain't had plenty o' goddamn chances.*

"Shut up!" she said aloud.

Surprisingly, The Snake didn't retort. Midnight's hoofs pounded a rhythmic beat on the pavement, filling in the relative silence.

About half a mile ahead of her now, the truck took the next left, veering off onto Strong Mountain Road, which led to the Ellis farm, on more of a hill than a mountain.

Once they reached the road, Brittany steered Midnight onto the rugged macadam. It was darker here, their way lit only by the moon through the stark black treetops now that the taillights on Mr. Hildebrand's truck were hidden behind a hill or the trees. But she knew the way. She could probably ride it blindfolded.

As they pounded down the mountain road, Brittany could feel them getting closer to it. Like the old game of Hot and Cold she used to play with Bradley when the two of them were little. She was getting warmer. Soon, she'd be on fire.

Whole goddamn world's gon' be on fire soon enough. You can sign that on the dotted line.

She didn't tell The Snake to shut up this time. Even if he'd listen, it didn't matter. He was right. The world was going to end tonight. Whether what she'd done to Tommy Mingus had set it in motion or not didn't matter. She already regretted it more than anything else she'd done wrong in her seventeen years on Earth, and if she didn't do something to stop Geth, she'd *die evil.*

She didn't believe in Hell, not really. But she did believe in karma.

The Snake had proven its existence, a murderer killed in the electric chair in the '60s, trapped in the body of a seventeen-year-old "brownnoser," as he often called her. He could take over her body, but never for very long. It wore him out, wearing her like a people suit. He could only stand it for two or three hours at the most, and it enraged him that she was in control of herself the rest of the time. It pissed him off that she was able to enforce even a little bit of autonomy over her own body, and *that* was karma. The electric chair had nothing on what he went through every day, watching from the back of her skull as Brittany lived her humdrum small-town life.

The road narrowed to one lane as it wound through the trees, and the dark boughs of pines obscured much of the moonlight. Midnight didn't falter. She was an exceptional saddle horse with excellent night vision. Brittany had ridden her under some of the worst conditions, and didn't expect to have any issue taking her through the dark woods.

Up ahead she saw red lights illuminating a small area of trees. Ms. Combs must have stopped the truck. It wasn't likely to be anyone else this late at night, especially not with what was happening elsewhere. She suspected Mr. Ellis would've been attacked just like everyone else. He probably had guns to protect his crops, but just because he had them didn't mean they'd do much against what Geth could throw at him.

The red lights winked out, returning the copse of pines and spruce to darkness. Brittany rode harder, eager to catch up with them before they entered the woods. She could follow their flashlights, but it would be easier if she caught up with them sooner.

Their flashlights flicked on, cutting through the darkness. She urged Midnight just a little bit faster, and Midnight complied, tired, she knew, but Brittany promised to give her a treat the second they got back home. "A nice salt lick," she said. "Or a banana. You love bananas, don't you, girl?"

Midnight snorted her approval. Brittany stroked her mane.

In less than a minute they were trotting to a stop at the end of the road, where Mr. Hildebrand's truck ticked as the engine cooled.

The flashlights swished through the dark to her left.

Brittany tied Midnight to the truck's back bumper, patted and stroked her flank lovingly. She was a good horse, and Brittany was sad to leave her, knowing this was likely the last time they'd see each other.

"I love you, girl." She kissed the horse's muzzle, looking into her dark brown eyes glinting with moonlight. "If I don't come back, you just pull real hard on this knot and you'll get free, okay?"

What a tearful goodbye, The Snake said caustically.

Brittany ignored him, stroked Midnight's coat one last time, then headed off into the dark forest, her only companion the ghost of a long-dead child murderer—which she herself was now, she realized—her only source of light the shaky beams of flashlights deeper into the trees and the glimpses of moonlight through their boughs.

2

RENNY HILDEBRAND SAT in the front passenger seat of Adam Brunt's Mustang, Cody Brockmeyer driving them through the deathly silent, darkened streets from the school to the woods, where Geth's magic stone gate to another dimension awaited them.

Sitting in the backseat with the equipment they couldn't fit in the trunk piled up between him and Taylor, Walden got shots of each of them with one of the school cameras. Geth and Cassandra hovered a few feet above the asphalt directly behind them, seated in the chariot, protected by two of the biggest guns and the Swedish twins, who floated on either side like a couple of street magicians. In her reflection in the side mirror, Cassandra looked even more anxious than she had on their way to the school. After what she'd done to try and protect Sheriff Nance, Renny couldn't say he blamed her. The accord between herself and Geth was tenuous. It still felt like Geth might kill any one of them at any moment.

He'd been surprised by how easily he and the boys had convinced Geth to go with them to the cave, leaving the other survivors to return to the church with the rest of the Blight zombies and the remains of the floating artillery to watch over them. Although, Sheriff Nance had loosened the jar for them, wearing Geth down with his wild tales of the town founder and the hucksters who'd come to Crooks Corners after him.

Funny how this all started with urban legends. And now we're actually in one. Hopefully we don't end up the examples people use to scare each other around campfires.

For now, Renny was content not to have to watch as more people were turned into mindless, dead-eyed zombies. The Blighted guarding the rest of the townspeople had practically danced them back toward the church, all too eager to push them onward. The dead ones were even worse, seemingly as eager to commit violent acts as Adam Brunt and Sean Fitzgerald, pushing and even punching those who fell out of step.

Renny worried for them all, and for the survivors he imagined remained hidden within the dark houses they'd passed, their lights off to deter return visits from Geth's marauders.

They *had* to keep Geth occupied long enough for Elana and Ernie to get that damned machine turned off. Everyone's lives depended on them.

For a long while, the rumble of the engine and the light *beep* of the record button were the only sounds aside from the howl of the wind in Cody's open window. Nobody spoke. Fear kept them quiet. Renny glanced over his shoulder at Taylor, who seemed to have lost all interest both in her Polaroid and speaking, around the time Geth turned the little poodle into a furry pinata. She returned his gaze with blank-faced curiosity—in shock, like the rest of them. Numbed.

Renny wanted to tell her everything was going to be okay. That her sister would be all right. But they were beyond such platitudes. He was certain Walden would scoff, and it would lessen any credibility such statements held.

"'Member when you said you didn't want us going into the woods tonight with the school cameras, Mr. Hildebrand?" Walden asked, breaking the silence.

The boy wore a sly grin on his badly beaten face, but Renny didn't find it very funny, and he let out a rueful chuckle. He was acutely aware they were driving toward their deaths just now, like a pilgrimage toward a killing field.

Still, it was better to accept the little time they'd been afforded and use it to their advantage.

We'll just keep shooting, let it tell its story.

And then what? he asked himself.

And then... if turning off the machine doesn't send it back... maybe we can "accidentally" wipe the tapes with the bulk eraser back at class. And if we can't do that... well, I guess we'll just have to put it to air after all.

"You're doing a good job, boys," he said, realizing no one had spoken since Walden had attempted humor several blocks back.

"Thanks, Mr. Hildebrand," Cody said with a heavy sigh.

Finally, the caravan reached the northeast edge of town on Old Route 14, nearing the truck stop and the sheriff's station beyond. The landscape was dark out here, all fields and lone trees before they reached the forests surrounding the outskirts.

"Watch out," Renny said, having spotted a corpse up ahead, lying in the middle of the road. He'd already seen countless dead bodies in their path—many of them were rambling their way back to the church right now, like hippies on their way to Shambala—but something about this one troubled him. It lay at a weird angle in the stark light of the high beams, its legs crossed at the calves, one arm slung behind its back, its head twisted flat against the asphalt.

"I see it," Cody said.

They were maybe ten feet away from the body when it abruptly stood up, startling Renny. It wasn't a person at all, he realized. It was a *scarecrow*, the face painted onto its burlap sack the same Xs-and-stitches as Geth's face. The uncanny-valleyness of the thing must have subconsciously tickled his lizard brain, as it had when he'd first seen Geth speak.

Cody expertly swerved to avoid it. The Mustang was traveling slow enough that the movement barely jarred them in their seats. "That thing tried to kill me and Brit before," he said.

Renny watched the scarecrow in his mirror. It waited until Geth's chariot reached it, then the *inhak* picked it up and carried it like a ragdoll in the hands of an invisible giant. Renny couldn't help but think of *The Wizard of Oz*. If only Geth and all of its tricks turned out to be orchestrated by some insecure little man hidden behind a large curtain.

If I only had a brain, Renny sang in his mind.

His eyes alighted in the side mirror. He had to struggle to keep his excitement from reaching his face.

Geth has a brain! he thought excitedly. *Or a hive mind of sorts, anyway, with Geth acting like the hive's queen. If we could convince it to leave its body, possess someone or something else... maybe we could trap it!*

It dawned on him with the sinking dread of an impending collision that Geth could be listening in on everything he'd just thought. As the Mustang drove them past the brightly lit but clearly deserted truck stop, Renny began listing classic horror films and their directors in his mind to see if Geth had been listening in. Considering it had seemed to be uniquely interested in movies, he figured if anything might get its attention, it might be that.

The Cabinet of Dr. Caligari *by Robert Wiene.* Nosferatu *by F.W. Murnau. Tod Browning's* Dracula *and* Freaks. *James Whale's* Frankenstein. *Uh...* White Zombie *by Victor Helperin. What comes after that?* Bride of Frankenstein? *Son* of Frankenstein?

He glanced back at Geth in the side mirror. The creature sat quietly, almost regal, beside Cassandra. His eyes and Geth's Xs met and Geth seemed to regard him shrewdly.

Maybe it didn't hear me because it thinks differently than people do. How would an entity without a body think? A thing of pure consciousness, without a language of its own? An entity obsessed not just with horror movies, for some reason, but TV in general.

An idea came to him: *Could it be the images?*

Is that why it's not reading my thoughts? Because I can't visualize? Because I don't see images in my head when I think?

He tested it again, this time thinking about how badly he wanted to strangle Geth. How he wanted to tear the jack-o'-lantern with its shit-eating grin right off its shoulders and stomp it like whoever had stomped the one in the school by the front doors. He thought about hitting it so hard his fist punched a hole right through it. And even though he couldn't exactly *see* it in his mind, he imagined it so vividly he could almost *feel* the cold, lumpy and stringy pumpkin guts squishing between his fingers.

The feeling reminded him of when he was a kid, carving pumpkins for Halloween with his mom and sister. Cancer had taken her from them eleven years ago, and without the photographs of her, he wouldn't have been able to remember what she looked like, not even her vibrant, loving smile. He could *feel* it on a conscious level, the thought of how it felt when she smiled at him, he just couldn't picture it. It had always made him sad, that he couldn't visualize her in his mind.

But maybe that problem could turn out to be an advantage.

The scarecrow, he thought. *We could trick it into leaving its body, trick it into possessing the scarecrow.*

It could work. It could really work…

And if Elana and Combs shut off their Machine in time, we could really beat this damn thing!

3

ERNIE HAD BEEN ACTING strange all night.

He'd been fine at school, and later, when they'd spoken on the phone before she left with Renny for the theater. At his house, after the world went cuckoo bananas, he'd started talking about communicating with God using their Machine. When he'd suddenly changed tack, talking about quantum excitation and ancient shamanic curses, she'd begun to grow concerned for his mental wellbeing.

Ernie had returned to a fraction of normalcy once he'd regained consciousness outside of his house, but it was clear he was still not quite himself. She supposed being knocked unconscious might do that to someone. But she suspected this entity they'd drawn into their world, whatever it was, had been using him like a puppet.

"The hounds of the moon," she said, gripping the steering wheel tightly as the truck bounded over potholes on the macadam mountain road that led to the testing site, what they called "Beta site."

"Beg pardon?" Ernie said, his voice slightly slurred. He glanced over with his head still pressed against the passenger window. The light from the high beams gave his face a pallid, sickly glow. His balding scalp shone beneath thinned hair, and his eyes looked entirely black.

I'll have to take him to see a doctor soon. Those dilated pupils could be a sign of a serious brain injury.

"You said that back at your house," she said. "An ancient shamanic curse, you called it."

She held his gaze, taking her eyes off the road ahead for a moment.

Ernie frowned. "I don't recall that."

Memory loss, Elana thought. *Another symptom of brain trauma? Or something worse? When we first got to the house he was acting so strangely, I wondered if he was himself. What if he actually wasn't? What if this entity possessed Ernie like it possessed the things it sent to kill us, and those dead people we saw in the street?*

Elana swallowed a hard lump as a horrifying prospect occurred to her: *What if he's* still *possessed?*

She eased off on the gas a little as the road narrowed ahead to one lane. It didn't lead to anywhere but the Ellis farm, making it unlikely that anyone would be coming the other way to cause her to pull to the side. Best to be cautious, especially at night. Renny had only taught her recently how to drive standard, and she was still a little iffy with the whole thing, more an intellectual exercise than muscle memory.

"Ernie, what happened tonight? With the Machine?"

She caught his frown in a glance. "Whatever do you mean?" he asked.

"There was something at your house. Do you remember that?"

"Some*thing*?"

"Yes," she said. "An entity. It had a jack-o'-lantern for a head, carved the same as the graffiti we've been seeing around town."

Ernie's frown deepened. "An *entity*? With a pumpkin for a head? Elana, are you feeling all right?"

"It wasn't a hallucination, Ernie. Renny saw it, too. It *attacked* us. I think—I *believe*—it was working *through* you somehow. I believe it was *using* you, something like a human puppet."

"Elana, this sounds..."

"I know how it *sounds*, Ernie. But even you can't explain what we saw outside your house. The vortex."

"Yes, the vortex. That was peculiar."

"*Peculiar?* Ernie, we've been trying to replicate this phenomenon we observed in the cave for over a year, with no results until yesterday evening. Now there's a vortex surrounding your house and you call it *peculiar*?"

"Well, what would you have me call it?"

"It's more than *peculiar*, Ernie. It's more than *an incident*. People have *died*. People *are* dying right now. All because of something we created, to meddle with things we don't understand."

"Well, sure. But that's science, isn't it? Someday they'll build a particle accelerator so large they'll be able to collide heavy ions at a high enough velocity to replicate the Big Bang."

"Possibly, but they'll have *safeguards*, Ernie. What safeguards did we have aside from human intervention? Which only works, by the way, when someone is at Beta site watching the Resonator."

Ernie sat up and rubbed the back of his head groggily. "You're right. I was reckless tonight. Once I realized something was happening beyond my control, once it murdered my poor Hegel, I tried to shut it down but—"

"But what, Ernie?"

He shook his head. "I don't remember after that."

Elana eyed him for a long moment, long enough that she nearly veered off the road and had to ease the truck out of the ditch. With an old vehicle like this, it was difficult. She nearly overcorrected and crashed them into a tree on the far side of the road, then straightened out and eventually got them to their destination.

"We're here," she said, because Ernie had zoned out again, staring out at the dark woods with his forehead against his window.

She got out and watched as Ernie raised his head and opened his door. He tried to get out but the seatbelt—which Elana herself had buckled while he'd been out of it—held him in place. He tried to get out again but the seatbelt stopped him once more.

"You're still buckled in," Elana said, and *tsk*ed as if speaking to a child. She reached over her seat to unlatch the belt. Once she did, Ernie got out and shut his door behind him as if he hadn't even noticed anything wrong or different about what had just happened.

What if he is *still being controlled by that entity?* she thought again.

She had to put those concerns aside, at least for the time being. Shutting off the Resonator was the only thing that mattered. Renny and the kids were counting on them. *The whole town* was counting on them, whether they knew it or not.

We owe it to them. This is our mess. We have to clean it up.

Elana reached back behind the seats for the flashlights Renny kept there for emergencies, trying to ignore the creeping sensation on the nape of her neck at the thought of Ernie trying to murder her out there in the dark woods.

She held out the smaller flashlight for Ernie. "Come on."

He shuffled around the front of the truck. Elana closed the door and gave him the flashlight. He seemed not to know how to turn it on. Which would have been weird for a normal person but was even more peculiar for a gadget-head like Ernie.

"The button's on the bottom."

Ernie turned it to face himself and pushed the button. The light blasted him in the eyes and he looked away with a pained moan, turning the beam away quickly. Its light stabbed through the dark swath of pine trees to their left, where the path lay.

"Let's hurry. Everyone's counting on us."

They entered the tree line, their footfalls crunching on dead leaves and underbrush, snapping the occasional twig. Refusing to fully lead the way—the worry that he'd harm her still lingered in the back of her mind—she ushered Ernie along as close to side by side as she could down the narrow path through the tall pines. The ground was still slightly slippery from last night's snowfall, and she had to grab Ernie's arm twice to prevent him from falling.

She'd walked this trail many times, often in the dark, sometimes by herself. She could probably walk it without the flashlights if she had to. Tonight, it felt different. She'd been mortally terrified for the first time since she'd grown out of having to keep a nightlight on when she was six years old, when she'd begun to understand there were no monsters waiting to jump out at her from the closet or under the bed.

Because monsters didn't exist, not the kind children believed in. It was a notion she'd grasped at an early age and accepted as fact until just a few hours ago, when a literal inhuman *thing* attacked them in Combs's living room.

The truth was far more complicated, and much more terrifying. What they'd experienced tonight had destroyed everything she had considered to be truth and fact. It had obliterated all rationally-held beliefs in an instant. *There were worlds beyond this one*. Not out in space but *right here*, overlapping our own. And if there was a single entity like this Geth out there, it stood to reason there might be more.

Thunder rumbled in the distance as they moved deeper into the woods, and a shiver ran up her spine. The thunder grew nearer, sounding almost like hoofbeats, until it slowed and eventually dissipated altogether. Was there a storm coming? That would be just her luck, stuck out here in the rain and the dark without an umbrella, accompanied by a man who might snap and kill her at any moment.

He wouldn't hurt me, she thought.

That was true. *Ernie* wouldn't hurt her, not of his own volition. But if this Geth still held any sway over him, the odds were high that she wouldn't leave these woods tonight.

If it wanted me dead it would have killed me already.

This made logical sense. Unless, of course, Geth needed her for some other purpose. What if Geth *wanted* them to turn off the Resonator? What if turning off the Resonator would close whatever portal the Stones had opened, preventing them from pulling Geth back inside?

Then it would have let us turn off the Harmonic Wave Generator, wouldn't it?

She didn't know the answer to that. She *wouldn't* know until they turned off the Resonator. It was Schrödinger's Cat. Shutting off the Resonator would ensure Geth remained on this side of the Stones *and* send it back, until they knew for certain either way.

It was a hell of a gamble, but really the only thing they could do.

Elana stopped and listened, her heart pounding. She'd heard a noise behind them in the dark. She swung the flashlight back there, searching.

"What is it?" Ernie asked.

"Shh! I thought I heard—"

Snap!

The sound of another twig snapping made her all but jump, grasping Ernie's arm. He glanced at it, then at her. She let go of him, aware of his distaste for human contact—which at the very least proved there was something of him left in that massive brain of his.

She listened.

The wind picked up, howling through the trees, chilling her cheeks and hands.

Then something large began trampling behind them. She turned off the flashlight.

A deer? A bear??

"Ernie?"

"Yes?"

"Turn off your flashlight."

"Whatever for?"

"Just do what I say, dammit!"

Ernie flicked off his light, plunging the two of them into nearly pure darkness. The animal kept coming, twigs snapping, branches swaying. Elana's heart leapt into her throat, thrumming, her muscles tight, her nerves jittering.

"Ms. Stabler? Mr. Combs?"

The girls' voice shook her, just when she'd been about to tell Ernie to run. She turned her flashlight back on and swung it toward the sound.

The cone of light illuminated a very pale blonde girl wearing a heavy jacket and white stockings. The flashlight exaggerated her features, made her look monstrous. After a moment, Elana realized she was wearing makeup to make her look like a clown. It was Halloween, after all. But out here in the dark, it was still possible she posed a threat.

"It's Brittany Garner," the girl said.

"Brittany!" Elana sighed and lowered the flashlight enough so she could see the girl but wasn't blinding her. "What are you doing out here in the woods?"

"I followed you. I want to help."

"I appreciate it, but we've got it handled."

The girl looked off to the right, her eyes glazed and seemingly unfocused. They returned to Elana with intensity, bright and blue. "Mr. Combs is sick. You can't trust him."

Ernie scoffed. "That's preposterous!"

Elana looked at her companion, his arms crossed defensively over his chest. The gesture *appeared* normal, but she knew Ernie

Combs. He didn't have a belligerent bone in his body. If he thought someone was wrong, he'd merely shake his head dismissively at their ignorance or arrogance.

He's not right and you know it.

"Are you alone?"

Brittany stuffed her hands in her pockets and nodded.

"Did anything follow you?"

That glazed look returned to her eyes. "I rode Midnight. She's my horse."

A horse, Elana thought. *That must be what I heard.* "Well, since you're out here, you may as well come with us."

Once the girl met up with them, Elana prodded Ernie into moving, and they shuffled along through the fallen leaves with their swinging lights leading the way, Brittany right behind them.

"Walden said you and Mr. Combs have to shut off some machine to send Geth back to Hell or something?"

Elana smiled. "Something like that, yes."

"So you're the ones who brought it here," Brittany said. It wasn't a question, and Elana glanced back, prepared for vitriol. She was surprised to see inquisitiveness rather than judgment in the girl's eyes.

"It would seem that way."

Brittany nodded. "That's good."

Elana frowned. "Why is that good?"

The girl shrugged. "It just is. If you brought it here, you can send it back."

"That's certainly the hope."

They trudged along silently a little while longer, until they finally reached Beta Site, the flat, fifteen by fifteen shed where the Resonator lay, where she and Ernie had been studying its effect in conjunction with the Harmonic Wave Generator and the Stones down below.

Bizarre to think that all this time we'd been studying supernatural phenomena, rather than scientific.

"What's that weird hum?" Brittany asked.

"That, Brittany, is the sound of the Harmonic Resonator," Ernie said, sounding almost like he was back to his normal self. "It tunes with the Harmonic Wave Generator in my garage and boosts the signal to the Stones below."

"In the cave," Brittany said.

Ernie gave her a quizzical look. "Why yes, in the cave. Have you seen them?"

"No. But I was in there. I fell in this hole when I was out here hunting with my brother three years ago, and realized I was in a cave."

"Oh dear."

Elana seemed to remember Brittany having been absent from math class for the last part of a semester back then. "Were you hurt?"

The corners of Brittany's lips twisted downward. "I broke my ankle. I couldn't dance for almost a year."

"I'm sorry to hear that."

Brittany thanked her glumly.

The shed loomed up ahead, a gray monolith against the blackness. As they neared, she saw that the door stood ajar by nearly a foot, with only darkness beyond. The padlock lay on the trampled earth before it, discarded. Cold dread filled her. She exhaled it in a visible plume.

Who would be here? Who else has the key?

"Did you come out here tonight, Ernie?"

Ernie looked blankly at the opened door, then at her. "Not to my knowledge, no."

"Then who—?"

She didn't need to finish the query. Opening the door wider, she saw the culprits: George and Sarah Dukas lay haphazardly on the floor of the shed, their bodies broken. She gasped, clutching her chest as if it could heal the sudden hurt in her heart for the loss of her dear friends just by holding it there.

Why were they out here? What happened to them?

"Oh my," Ernie said, sounding only slightly perturbed.

"Did you know them?" Brittany asked.

"Yes," Elana said. "They were friends." She took a moment to compose herself—more time than they could afford to waste— then she stepped through the doorway. "Well, I suppose we should—"

George Dukas's eyes sprang open, and he sucked in a huge, raspy breath. Elana staggered back out in terror, uncertain whether her friend was still alive or possessed like the dead they'd seen wandering the streets back in town.

"*You need...*" George rasped. He sucked in another whistling gasp. The sound of a sucking chest wound. The puddle of blood beneath his chest widened, supporting her concern. "...*to stop it*," he finished.

Elana quickly got down on a knee beside him, but the life left his eyes before she could do anything to help him and his head slumped to the floor. She checked his pulse. He was dead. Avoiding the blood, she sidestepped over to Sarah, checking her for vital signs. She didn't need to. Her friend's wrist and neck were both cold to the touch. They'd likely been out here for hours.

The urge to lay her jacket over them struck her, or one of the tarps. It was a strange instinct, she observed, as if the dead would somehow be comforted knowing their bodies had been covered. Still pondering this, a cold realization gripped her.

That thing could still possess them!

"We need to remove their bodies from the lab," she said, turning to Brittany. "Will you help me?"

The girl had zoned out again, staring at George's head, cracked like an egg with his blood pooling around it. She looked up sharply and nodded.

Together, they picked up Sarah first, laying her on her back facing the stars that had peeked out from among the clouds. Then they went back for George. He was heavier by at least fifty pounds, and it was a struggle to get him out the door, but she didn't want to ask for Ernie's help. She didn't trust that Geth's influence might not transfer somehow to George's dead body and animate it like the rest.

She couldn't handle that. Not on top of the grief she was already struggling to hold back. Knowing they'd likely died coming out here with the purpose of attempting to shut off the Resonator made it worse. Their tragic ending, losing their lives to save everyone, and the fear that she and Brittany and Combs might die doing the same thing, weighed heavily on her. But there was no time to worry, no time to grieve, no time to succumb to fear.

They hefted George's dead weight out the door while Ernie looked on and laid him beside Sarah, the two of them high school sweethearts with a boy just a little bit younger than the youngest students Elana taught. She couldn't bear to think of what might happen to Matthew, and didn't have time for it anyhow.

"We need to get started," she told Brittany, then headed back to the lab.

"Can I help?" Brittany asked.

Elana glanced at Ernie as they reentered. He stood under the cold white track lights, surveying the equipment they'd assembled with dull eyes, as if he no longer understood any of it.

"I hope so, Brittany," she replied.

Then she turned on her heels, locked the door and drew the large bolt, and turned back to the room. She cracked her knuckles and headed for the Resonator control station to finish this.

4

MATT DUKAS HAD NEVER BEEN SO scared in his life. He wanted his mommy and daddy. He was too old to think such things, but that was what he thought: *I want my mommy and daddy.*

Kyle and Craig had found their parents quickly. Mr. and Mrs. O'Donelly had been waiting with the others at the church, leaving him alone. They looked like they were too deep in shock to even suggest that he join them, so he'd stood with Philbert Piper, near the four of them, until his curiosity had overwhelmed him and he'd weaved his way up through the crowd to get a better look at the man with the pumpkin face.

Geth. Its name is Geth and it's not a man. It's not a god, either, no matter what it says. God wouldn't do what it did to that dog. It wouldn't make the sheriff shoot Reverend Earl and then kill himself.

Matt still felt the sheriff's blood itchy and flaky on his face. He'd tried to wipe it off with the sleeve of his jacket but hadn't been able to get all of it. It was in his ear and on his eyelids. He needed to find a mirror to clean off the rest, but he didn't suspect he'd get a chance to do that any time soon, not with Geth's zombies watching over them.

And they were *mean*, Geth's followers. The Smilers. They pushed people who'd fallen out of line on their way back to the church, or even got too slow to keep up. A few of them *punched* people.

Matt hated the Blighted as much as he'd hated Brunt and his goons, who were just about the worst people he'd ever met, and he'd urged Philbert to hurry, worried the childlike man didn't fully grasp what was happening here. He was liable to go off on some tangent, distracted by someone's Halloween decorations or a cool car, which seemed to be his main focus before tonight aside from his mom and whatever they happened to be having for dinner that night. If they weren't above hitting old people and kids, they probably wouldn't even bat an eye at punching someone who was mentally disabled. Matt didn't want to get hurt by Geth's zombies himself, but he also wanted to protect Philbert, since Philbert had risked his life to save them way back when their own costumes attacked them, which seemed like forever ago.

"Wish we had some Whoppers," Philbert moaned.

Matt elbowed him. "Shh," he hissed. "You're gonna get us in trouble."

The main Blighted were up front by the altar, but some of them roamed the crowd, glaring at people with their black eyes. That was what scared Matt the most, even more than dying. The thought of becoming one of them, of being under Geth's control and maybe even watching it all through his own eyes: it terrified him. He thought he'd kill himself before they could take him, but then he remembered that Brunt and Fitz had been dead and it hadn't stopped Geth from using them like human puppets.

Even death can't save us from Geth, Matt thought. The thought would've been kind of cool if it wasn't so chillingly accurate.

He imagined a thousand Geth-worshipping zombies marching out of Crooks Corner toward Wolfeboro and Alton and Ossipee, gathering more followers on their way, like a snowball rolling downhill. He pictured a hundred thousand Geth zombies marching on Washington and swarming the Pentagon. He saw a million crossing the borders into Canada and Mexico, boarding flights across the world, sharing Geth's gospel, spreading its terror and hate. He couldn't stand the thought of being alive to witness this terrible prophecy unfold. But he was too afraid of death and what might come after to walk up to one of them and provoke them into killing him.

Damned if you don't, damned if you do. That was what his dad sometimes said. *Catch-22. Damned if you don't and damned if you do.*

Considering neither of his parents believed in Hell, Matt assumed he'd meant it metaphorically rather than literally. But being doomed to be a Blighted was about as close to Hell as Matt could imagine.

But Geth's not here, even if his zombies are. It can't turn any of us into them from wherever the group of them went with it, to shoot their movie. We're safe here, for now. At least from that.

"All right, line up, everybody!" the man who ran the diner shouted, clapping his hands loudly to get their attention. "Line up!"

"What now?" Matt muttered to Philbert.

Philbert sighed heavily, his big shoulders rising and falling. "I wanna go home," he moaned.

Matt patted him on the back. "Me too, big guy. Soon, I hope."

The crowd began shuffling forward, mostly at the not-so-gentle urging of the Smilers. People grunted and moaned as Geth's minions pushed and prodded them into a line.

"What is this?" the tanned man with the silver hair who'd tried to sell Geth a car said. "Your god's getting what he wanted, what do you need with us? Why can't we just go home and do all this tomorrow?"

The Diner Man's dark eyes grew cloudy. "Well, Gary," he said in an irritated tone. "Geth wants us to keep spreading Their message, so that's just what we're going to do. Maybe we should start with you, since you seem to be so eager to get things over with."

"What the hell, Will? You know this isn't right! It killed Bella!"

"Who's Bella?" the Piano Lady asked.

"Our toy fucking poodle Bella! You're worshipping a sadist, don't you *see* that, Judy? Your god is *insane!*"

The diner owner scoffed. "Your god drowned every living person on earth but Noah and his family just for a mulligan. It impregnated a woman *without her consent* and then murdered their child. It turned Lot's wife into a pillar of salt because she dared to look back as tens of thousands of people were burned alive, women and children included. Geth killed your dog. Which is more insane?"

"It killed more than a dog!" a woman in the crowd shouted. "It killed our Jonah!"

"Yes, some people died tonight," the Diner Man said, sounding bored. "People die all the time. But when *your* god takes someone, you say *it's God's will*. Or *it's their time*. When Geth does it, it's somehow a crime."

"This wasn't a goddamn tornado, Will! It was mass murder!"

"What do you want to hear, Gary? What would make this more palatable for you? 'And lo, the people of Crooks Corners were punished for their crass commercialism, their greed, their avarice and lusting'? Geth doesn't give a damn about any of that. Geth killed your family and your friends so that when They came to you with Their word, you'd pay attention. Geth killed them for the good of *the people who survived*. The greater good for the greatest number of people."

"Fuck this," Gary said. "There's gotta be two or three hundred of us and only twenty or thirty of them and a couple of guns. I say we fight back!" He looked around. "Who's with me?"

The salesman's rallying cry was met with downcast eyes from the crowd.

He looked appalled. "Come on, people! They can't fight all of us!"

"Shut him up," the Diner Man said, snapping his fingers.

A Blighted man in military parka—who'd been lying on the floor when Matt had first run into the church, reeking of motor oil and cigarettes—grabbed a shotgun out of the air and tried to slam the stock into Gary's stomach. The salesman caught it and they struggled. Gary had almost gotten the upper hand when a zombified woman—the one in the bright orange vest who'd had her neck snapped after she'd tried to blow up Geth with a grenade—stepped up behind Gary and grabbed him, jerking his arms behind his back.

"Bring him up here," the Diner Man ordered.

The Blighted duo hauled Gary up to the altar by either arm. He fought them all the way to the front but when they pushed him down to his knees, he finally stopped fighting and looked up at the diner man defiantly.

"I'll never bend to your god," he said through gritted teeth.

"Shut yer pie hole, Garner," the smelly man said.

"Pie hole," the Orange Vest Lady said with a chuckle. "I like that. Maple pumpkin pie, huh, Crampton?"

"You will bend," the Diner Man said, ignoring their banter. "And you'll *pray*. And you'll be *happy*, Gary." He smiled at the Piano Lady and the two holding him and all of the other dark-eyed zombies, who returned the smile all at once and all with that exact same smile.

It made Matt shudder.

"You'll be happy just like the rest of us," the man they'd called Crampton said.

"Not a fucking chance in Hell," Gary said.

"There is no Hell, Gary. There's only Geth."

With nothing left to say, the Diner Man reached out and touched the salesman's forehead. The kneeling man stopped struggling almost immediately. His body began to quiver all over, then stopped suddenly, his head lolling forward. The Blighted duo let go of his arms.

When Gary stood and turned to face the crowd, he wore the same exact smile as the others, with the same dark eyes, and Matt knew there was no way out of this, that they had finally reached the end.

5

CODY WAS DRIVING CAUTIOUSLY on Old Route 14 when the steering wheel tore free from his hands and the car pulled over on its own. It rolled slowly into the ditch, gravel crunching under its tires, then braked, the red back lights brightening the dark swath of trees behind them. The keys with their fuzzy dice fob turned in the ignition, and the Mustang's engine grumbled to a stop. The headlights and brake lights dimmed and went out, leaving them in the dark.

"Well, I guess we're here," he said.

Mr. Hildebrand peered out his window. "Where *is* here?"

"A little bit past the Thompson farm, out near Mr. Ellis's wee—" Cody corrected himself. "Mr. Ellis's farm."

"Everyone knows old man Ellis grows dope, you don't have to dance around it," Walden said, opening his door.

Cody shrugged and got out. Hildebrand followed him. The three of them stood on either side of Brunt's car and looked around at the dark stands of pine and spruce on either side of them.

Cody opened Taylor's door. She looked up at him with dulled dark eyes. "Are we here?"

"We're here. I wish you could stay in the car, but I think you gotta come with us, Taylor."

She nodded and joined them. Cody shut her door behind her.

"Where the hell's Geth?" Walden said, the camera on his shoulder. "Drives us out to the middle of buttfuck nowhere—"

The chariot rounded the corner as if his words had summoned it, the illumination of several flashlights and pot lights lighting its way, gathered from garages and lawns like a blackbird building its nest.

"Speak of the devil," Hildebrand said.

"There is no Devil," Walden corrected him. "There's only Geth."

The chariot came to a stop a few car lengths away and the entire caravan, including the two weird Swedish dudes and the creepy scarecrow they'd picked up along the way, lowered gently to the rugged asphalt. Geth again took Cassandra by the hand and helped her down. The Swedish dudes grabbed the guns out of the air and immediately returned to either side of Geth to protect it.

Cassandra looked as worn-down as Taylor. Cody felt it himself. He was exhausted, and sick and tired of having to worry he could die at any moment. They'd done everything in their power to survive the night. Cassandra had even used *magic*. Why wasn't this over already?

"This is the way," Geth said, gesturing toward the black woods, to a place that looked no less unwelcoming than the rest of it. "Gather your materials and follow Us."

"It means the gear," Hildebrand said.

Walden raised his one moveable eyebrow. "Yeah, I figured that."

The three of them gathered up the gear and, with Taylor close at Cody's heels, joined Geth at the entrance to the woods, which was easier to see now with a ton of light shining on it.

"Little help?" Walden asked, lugging the lights, a battery belt and the tripod, in addition to carrying the camera on his shoulder.

Both Cody and Hildebrand had their arms and shoulders full of equipment. Cody shrugged. "Sorry, man."

"I was talking to Geth. Dude can make all kinds of shit levitate but we gotta carry all our own stuff."

"That's a good point," Cody said.

"Actually, I kind of like it," Hildebrand said, huffing and puffing a few feet ahead of them. "Reminds me of college."

Walden pointed the video camera at their teacher. "Oh yeah, I've been meaning to ask: how come you never went into the business?"

"I *am* in the business."

"Yeah, but not really."

Hildebrand frowned, then seemed to consider whether or not he wanted to respond. "The hours suck," he said finally, "and it's too much about who you know rather than *what* you know. I think it'll be easier with you kids now, though. You can shoot something cheap on video, edit on your home computer and upload it to the internet in a day. Well," he added, "if we survive the night, obviously."

"Hey, we survived Y2K, we can survive this," Walden said.

It surprised a laugh out of Cody. Even Hildebrand chuckled.

"Yeah, I suppose you're right." Hildebrand sighed. "Speaking of the business, are you still writing despite your condition?"

Walden gave him a sidelong glance with his one good eye. "This just happened tonight."

"I mean your inability to see images in your mind."

"Wait, is that actually a thing?" Cody asked. "I thought that was just me."

"You too, huh?" Walden asked, a grin spreading on his busted lips. "You know, I always heard you had an empty head."

Cody laughed and instinctively elbowed him in the ribs. Walden hissed in a pained breath.

"Sorry."

"No worries, man."

"So that's the three of us with the same thing," Hildebrand

said, sounding like he had some kind of theory. "I'd imagine it's pretty rare. I've never heard of anyone besides you two that have it. That can't just be a coincidence, can it?"

"What do you mean?" Walden said sharply. "You think it's divine intervention or something?"

"I don't know." Hildebrand frowned. "I just think it's odd the three of us ended up right where we needed to be at just the right time."

Walden shrugged. "I used to say the only religion I wanna be affiliated with is the Church of Tarantino. After tonight, I don't know what I believe anymore. It definitely ain't the Word of Geth."

"Careful," Hildebrand hissed.

Walden shrugged the shoulder not hefting a bag. "Ah, Geth can cramp it up his putz."

Taylor giggled behind them.

"Nice callback, huh, kid?" Walden asked.

"You all right back there?" Cody asked.

She looked up at him, eyes somber. "I'm okay," she said glumly.

He laid a hand on her shoulder, and she seemed comforted.

Geth didn't seem to hear their exchange, or maybe it just didn't care, so they kept following the lighted procession along the brambly path for a while in silence, the only sound the crunch of leaves and twigs under their feet.

"My parents never took me to church or anything," Cody said after a time. "I'm not religious, but I believe in God."

Walden shook out a smoke into his mouth. He reached into the front left pocket of his jeans and took out his Zippo. "You mind?" he asked, holding it out to Mr. Hildebrand.

Their teacher took the lighter and struck the wheel. He retracted the flame a few inches from the cigarette. "I should probably mention that I don't approve of this."

"I'll quit when I'm dead." Walden huffed a laugh, the smoke dangling from his lips. "Which might be sooner than I expected."

"Fair enough." Hildbrand lit the cigarette for him and returned the lighter.

Walden took a big drag and put the lighter back in his pocket. "But seriously, if you think about it... if God or whatever is working through us now," he said, "if that's what you're proposing, God *also* let Geth get out in the first place, you know? Like, people thank God when a tornado spares their house, but if God did that, didn't He also send the tornado?"

"That's a valid point."

"So I don't know what I believe. But I know that if we make it out of this alive, without the three of us getting Gethed, I'm gonna write about this."

"Nobody would believe it."

"Suspension of disbelief. And who knows, maybe God's a writer. He gathers up all the right people and puts them in life-threatening situations to see if they can work their way out of it."

"Okay, but who's watching?" Cody asked, intrigued by the idea.

Walden shrugged again. "Maybe there's a whole bunch of different deities up there, God, Buddha, Shiva—even the Great Spirit, like my mom believes in. Maybe they're all up there making up stories for each other, just like we do down here, to make them laugh or cry or scare them. A divine comedy. Or tragedy, depending."

Hildebrand hummed thoughtfully. "That's an interesting theory."

"I'd say this one's more of a horror story, though," Cody said.

"Yeah. But he ain't Stephen King, that's for sure."

Cody laughed.

"Anyway, I'm just spit-balling," Walden said. "Maybe Geth was even one of them at one point. A fallen angel, like Satan. Banished from Heaven or Nirvana or Valhalla or whatever. Doomed to live down here among the mortals."

"That's pretty cool," Cody said.

"I think Reverend Earl would call that blasphemy. *Would have*," Hildebrand corrected himself.

"And now he's dead. He played his part already. Exit stage left."

"Jeez," Cody muttered.

Walden pointed at him, the cigarette clutched between his fingers. "*Exactly*. Biblical stories have heroes and villains, just like all the rest. Jesus was one of them, the most devout believer, God's only begotten son, and look what happened to Him."

"Does that make us the Three Wise Men?" Hildebrand asked.

Cody laughed again.

"Nah," Walden said, the smoke held between his teeth. "I'm Judas. You two can be Thomas and Saul."

"I don't really know much about the Bible," Cody admitted. "All that *he begat him* and *she begat her* stuff put me to sleep."

"Saul was beheaded, Judas hung himself, and they say Thomas was martyred."

"That's not good."

"No, it's not. But they played their parts, because that's how it was written. 'So it is written, so it shall be done.' It even says at the start of the Book of John, 'In the beginning was the Word, and the Word was with God, and the Word *was* God.' That's from the final gospel. The *last word*, in other words. Right before Revelation."

"'And I looked and saw a pale horse,'" Hildebrand said ominously. "'And its rider's name was Death. And Hell came with it.'"

The quote made Cody's spine tingle. "Brittany's horse is white."

"Another coincidence?" Walden asked with a grin. "Anyways, I'm sure we can all pretty much agree Geth is Hell. Or at least *Geth's way* is Hell. Dead but not dead. A puppet on a string. Technically the Bible says *Hades*, not Hell, but potato potahto."

"I'd rather go down fighting than be a part of Geth's twisted religion," Hildebrand said quietly.

"And that's why we're all here. We're on the same page, so to speak. 'Cept for the kid," Walden said, glancing back at Taylor, who'd been shuffling along silently behind them the entire time.

"You okay, Taylor?" Cody asked again.

"I'm worried about Cassandra."

"We're gonna help your sister," Hildebrand told her.

"That's why we're doing this," Cody agreed. "To help everybody."

"*We have arrived*," Geth boomed from somewhere in the trees ahead. The four of them pushed through the trees and found Geth and the others in a wide clearing, their feet back down on the ground. The many lights hovered overhead, pointing down at a dark, ragged-edged hole about ten feet from side to side among the moss and rock and fallen leaves.

Even without counting her makeup, which she'd mostly

seemed to have wiped off on their trek through the woods, Cassandra looked like a zombie. Cody hoped Geth hadn't somehow turned her into one of its braindead cultists while the four of them had been yapping about God.

Walden dropped his extra gear and aimed the camera at the cave entrance. It beeped as he started recording. "So this is it, huh? Pretty anticlimactic."

"Maybe it's nicer on the inside," Cody suggested, lowering his gear to the forest floor.

Hildebrand did the same. "Looks like a real hole in the ground," he said, making all three of them chuckle.

"Definitely not a lot of curb appeal," Walden agreed. "So this is where you lived, huh, Geth?"

"Not here," Geth said, turning back to them with a scowl. "We were imprisoned within the Great Void beyond the *Tum Gob*."

"Can you tell the people watching at home what the *Tum Gob* is?"

"They are the Watching Stones. They protect the entrance to *Upask*, much like your Pearly Gates protect the entrance to Heaven."

"That's great," Walden said. "Only, do you mind saying that again, but incorporating the question in your answer this time? Like, 'The *Tub Gob* are the Standing Stones, yadda yadda yadda.'"

"*We will not repeat Ourselves. Do not press your luck, Walden LeSabre.*"

The Swedish twins goosestepped forward menacingly, raising the guns and pointing them at the four of them.

"Don't shoot them!" Cassandra said, her eyes finally coming alive.

Despite the imminent danger, Cody cracked a smile, relieved that she hadn't been turned.

"We will not harm them," Geth said, "so long as they do not continue to test Us. We do not like this... *mirth-making*."

"Okay, okay," Walden said, raising his free hand in surrender. "I'm just trying to make this documentary the best I can for the silver screen. If we're gonna get your Word out there, or whatever, we're gonna have to think bigger. We wanna hit movie theaters, not just TV."

"Theaters," Geth said quizzically.

"Like the one downtown," Hildebrand said. "Where your *inhak* attacked us with fake birds and promotional rubber balls."

"Ah, yes." Geth's jagged smile widened. "That was rather fitting, was it not? *The Birds* at 7 P.M. *Ragers in Space* at 9:20."

"Exactly," Hildebrand said. "Except we want *Helloween: The Rise of Geth* in both slots at every theater across the country. Across the *world*."

Walden pooched out his lower lip and stroked his mustache. "*The Rise of Geth*. Catchy."

"I like it," Cody said, even though he didn't really appreciate them messing with his title. This was all about getting Geth psyched about the movie, and if he had to make a few compromises, he was just happy they weren't life or death.

Geth repeated the title musingly.

"It's a really good title," Cassandra said.

The demon regarded her. Its expressions weren't perfect, like a psychopath mimicking a normal person, but Cody thought it might be surprised.

"Do you believe so?" Geth asked.

"Yeah. It projects a, um... a strong, masculine image," she said. "Very godlike."

Geth nodded. "Very well. We approve the amendment. Let us complete this... *documentary*. Proceed into the cave."

Cody shared a look with the others. It was clear the idea of lugging all of the gear down there didn't appeal to any of them, but if it had to be done, they would do it grudgingly. Cody lifted the generator.

Walden raised a hand. "One more request, Geth, if you don't mind."

"*Speak.*"

"Could you please get your *inhak* or whatever to carry this stuff down for us? We're pretty tired, and we're gonna need all of our energy to make this movie perfect for you."

Geth's scowl deepened, and for a second or two Cody thought it would just make Walden's head explode like it had to Brunt and Fitz. Finally, it said, "Very well. Begin your descent, and We shall convey your.... *stuff*... behind you."

"That's really cool of you, Geth," Walden said. "You know,

Sheriff Nance was wrong about you. You're actually a pretty chill dude."

"Jeez," Cody said. It didn't seem right to speak ill of the dead.

"He's right," Hildebrand added. "Maybe if Sheriff Nance had taken the chance to let you tell your side of the story, he'd be here with us now."

"It is unfortunate he decided to betray Us," Geth said. "He would have made an excellent disciple."

"Yeah." Walden shrugged. "Oh well, you can't help someone who won't help themselves. Let's get going, huh?"

He practically skipped toward the cave, and Hildebrand followed close behind.

"Come on, Taylor," Cody said, ushering her toward the cave entrance with a hand on her shoulder.

Walden climbed down first, and Cody gestured for Hildebrand to go next. Once he had, Cody held Taylor's hands as she swung her legs down through the entrance and rested her feet on the third rung down. Stones tumbled into the opening, clattering against the walls and on the floor not too far below.

"Hey, watch it with the rocks!" Walden shouted.

"Sorry!" Cody called down.

Taylor's eyes were wide and full of fear. She glanced down into the darkness.

"I'll be right behind you," he told her.

"Me too, shrimp," Cassandra said close behind them.

Relief swept over Cody at the sound of her voice. Tears had streaked what was left of her makeup, and when he smiled, she gave him a sad smile back.

Bolstered by a sudden, inexplicable sense of hope, Cody descended into the mouth of the cave.

6

BRITTANY STOOD BY THE DOOR, watching as Ms. Stabler poked button after button and flicked all kinds of switches. The machines had a bunch of screens whose purpose she could only imagine, reminding her of how she'd felt when she'd first stepped into the control room above the studio in Mr. Hildebrand's class and realized she'd have to learn how to use all of the equipment there. It seemed to her that what Ms. Stabler was doing seemed kind of overly complicated, even more than the switcher in the studio at school. Why build a machine that required so many buttons and toggles just to turn the damn thing off?

"Nothing's working," the math teacher said finally, turning with a hand on her hip and an exasperated look. "Ernie, could you *please* try to help me?"

Mr. Combs looked up from staring at the blood on the floor. He seemed to be even more gone than he was before. Geth was controlling him. The Snake had warned her. It was dormant when she'd first approached them but it didn't seem to be dormant now.

Brittany approached Ms. Stabler at the desk, hoping she'd be able to help. Two monitors stood in front of Elana, who was tapping with the index fingers of each hand on the keyboard. One of the monitors appeared to be for the computer, typing out all kinds of weird computer language as Ms. Stabler pecked away. The second was turned off.

"What's this screen for?" Brittany asked.

Ms. Stabler glanced up at it. "Oh, that's to monitor the Stones," she said absently.

"What stones?"

"The Duolith Stones. In the cave. The Resonator," Ms. Stabler said, waving vaguely behind them, "amplifies the tones sent from the Harmonic Wave Generator and projects them down to the cave below us, to attune with the Stones."

"Well, shouldn't we see what's going on with them?"

Ms. Stabler looked at her as if she hadn't even considered it, she was so focused on getting the machine turned off. She reached past Brittany and turned it on.

The screen brightened slowly, eventually showing what looked like black-and-white CCD camera footage of the inside of a brightly lit cavern. At its center were the two rectangular pillars Ms. Stabler had mentioned. They almost reminded Brittany of what a tuning fork might look like if it was sticking out of the ground.

It was what lay slightly behind the stones that caught Brittany's eye, and she gasped as The Snake said, *There she is! Our leading lady just made her final appearance.*

Even as small as she was in the camera's view, Brittany recognized Darla Knight lying on the floor with a knife in her chest. An overturned director's chair lay between the stones at her feet.

"Oh no," Ms. Stabler said. "Is she... dead?"

Who's the shish kebab in the corner? The Snake said.

With her focus on Darla, trying to see if the actor was breathing or legitimately dead, Brittany hadn't noticed the charred black lump at the bottom of the screen approximately the size and shape of an adult male.

I don't know, she answered in her head.

A clink from behind them caught her attention. Brittany turned to see Combs had picked up a tool from among the many on a rolling cart beside the main part of the machine, the one making the atonal hum. Earlier she'd tried to hum at the same pitch but couldn't manage it, despite all of her many years of vocal training. It was something like a chord but not exactly. She found she couldn't really pinpoint what it was when she tried.

Combs turned to face the machine, holding the wrench more like a weapon than like he was intending to fix anything. His dead, black eyes regarded the machinery for a long moment.

"Thank you, Ernie," Ms. Stabler said. "Although I don't know what you can do with that wrench."

What he did startled both of them. He struck the computer keyboard Ms. Stabler had been typing on with the head of the wrench. It pinged against the plastic, loud enough to be heard over the hum. Seemingly satisfied with what he'd done, he struck the computer tower, smashing several lighted diodes, and again, making a switch fly into the air.

"What are you doing?" Ms. Stabler cried. "Are you *insane*? We can't shut off the Resonator without that!"

Kill him, The Snake hissed.

Mr. Combs kept bashing away, making the telephone fly off its cradle and smashing a few keys loose from the keyboard. Ms. Stabler grabbed at his hands but he turned with fury in his black eyes and launched her all the way across the room. She hit the floor and her head slammed against what Brittany assumed was the Resonator. Her eyelids fluttered as if she might pass out.

You gotta kill him. It's the only way you gon' stop this.

I can't kill my science teacher!

You do it, gatdammit, or I'll take over an' do it for ya!

Brittany had foolishly left the .22 hanging from Midnight's saddle, and looked over the collection of small tools on the cart for a suitable weapon. She picked up an Exacto knife, extending the blade several clicks, then crept up behind Combs as he continued to smash the computer station.

"Stop it, Mr. Combs!" she shouted.

Combs either didn't hear her, or wouldn't listen. He struck the screen so hard it cracked and left a purple smear under the plastic.

"Mr. Combs, if you don't stop that I'm going to hurt you."

"What are you doing, Brittany?" Ms. Stabler said groggily.

"I have to," Brittany said. And when Mr. Combs broke the mouse with the wrench, she swung out with the knife, slashing through the back of his jacket and leaving a long red slice in his skin.

Combs stopped smashing. He whipped around on the heels of his brown leather shoes, covered in muck, and fixed his dead-eyed gaze on Brittany, wielding the wrench like a weapon.

You made him mad now, The Snake said. *Yer gon' have to finish this, honeypie, one way or th'other.*

Combs swung out with the wrench. Brittany backstepped, ducking out of the way. She held the Exacto knife out. "Don't make me do this, Mr. Combs."

Combs swung again. It swished through the space Brittany ducked away from as she took another step back, swerving to avoid the puddle of blood.

Mr. Combs stepped forward and swung again. Brittany met him in the air with the blade. It slashed the back of his wrist but he held the wrench firm as blood spilled from the wound.

"Ernie, please stop this!" Ms. Stabler cried.

Combs ignored her, taking another step toward Brittany. His left shoe slipped in the blood and he lost his footing. The right shoe slipped and he fell forward.

Brittany wasn't ready. Combs fell against her and the two of them toppled to the floor, landing in the blood of Ms. Stabler's friends. The breath exploded from her lungs as his full weight crushed her. She cried out and Mr. Combs howled, dropping the wrench. He rolled off of her, and she saw what she'd done.

The Exacto knife was stuck in his chest all the way to the hilt. A gout of blood poured out of the wound and Mr. Combs gaped at it, the darkness gone from his eyes. His head rolled toward Brittany and he blinked rapidly as if he didn't understand what had happened or what he'd done.

"Ernie!" Ms. Stabler called, remaining where she'd fallen.

"I'm... sorry," Mr. Combs gasped.

And then he was dead, just like that.

Brittany sat up, gasping for air.

You did what you had to, The Snake said.

Shut up! she shouted in her mind. She was so angry, so distraught, she'd almost spoken it aloud.

"You killed him," Ms. Stabler said.

"I didn't mean to."

Ms. Stabler pushed herself to her feet. She crossed to Brittany and held out a hand for her. Brittany took it and her former math teacher helped her up.

"Well, I suppose it was for the best. He wasn't himself anymore, was he? I think he was possessed by that *thing*."

"Yeah," Brittany said, looking down glumly at her former science teacher. She'd actually kind of liked him when she'd been in his class. He was dorky and a little stuffy but he'd always tried his best to make science fun. "I'm really sorry, Ms. Stabler."

"Call me Elana," the teacher said curtly. She gazed sadly at Mr. Combs for a long moment, then turned abruptly and returned to the computer station. "This equipment is damaged irreparably. I won't be able to use it to shut off the Resonator now."

"What are we gonna do now?"

"I don't know. We may have to return to Ernie's house. Try to turn off the Wave Generator at the source. Maybe it's unguarded now that everyone's at the church."

"But that'll take too long."

Time we ain't got, The Snake hissed.

Elana shrugged. "I'm afraid we've got no other choice. Without a keyboard this system can only be accessed by voice commands, but we've only ever used it for two-way communication with Alpha Site."

"Alpha Site?"

"Ernie's garage," Elana said, and her gaze drifted to his corpse on the floor. She shook her head despondently.

Boop.

Brittany turned toward the computer, where the small sound had come from.

Boop. The sound came again.

She approached the monitor. It was cracked badly but she could see there was text on it, and a flashing cursor thingy.

    HELLO?

    IS ANYONE THERE?

"Ms. Stabler—I mean Elana. I think you should come see this."

Elana came over. She squinted at the screen. "Oh. Oh my," she said, surprised. The keyboard was too badly smashed, missing multiple keys. Elana grabbed the mic, which was on a bendy adjustable arm like the one in the news control room. She brought the microphone to her lips, pressed a button and spoke clearly into it, like she was trying to get someone who only spoke a little English to understand her.

"Hello. This is Elana Stabler at Beta Site. Who is this?"

Her words printed on the screen, some kind of voice-to-type thing. A moment later, another message arrived:

    ITS JAY. JAY NELSN.

"*Jay?*" Brittany said, just about shouting his name in her ela-tion. He was the last person she'd expected to hear from tonight. Frankly, she'd thought he was a goner the moment things began to get crazy. He was a sheltered kid and computers were his life. But he was exactly the person they needed on the other end of this machine.

"Jason, are you alone?" Elana asked.

    YA. THY FOLLOWD ME INTO THE HOUSE BUT I
    LOCKED MYSELF IN THE GARAGE. HOW DO I
    SHUT THIS STUPID THNG OFF?

"Are you able to see the control panel? The green digital readout?"

After a moment the *boop* sounded with another message:

    ITS BROKN.

"Oh no," Elana said, without pressing the button.

WHT NOW?

"How much did Ernie tell you about the Wave Generator?"

NOT MUCH. ITS CRAZY IT DOS ANYTHNG. AND
NOW ITS SMASHED UP RL BAD.

"We don't have time for this," Elana muttered in exasperation, then depressed the talk button. "Jason, I want you to look for a six-sided panel. Like a stop sign. Can you find that for me?"

The pause was excruciating. Brittany shared an anxious look with Elana. Finally, another message arrived with a beep.

I SEE IT.

"Okay, Jason, you're going to have to remove the panel. Are you able to do that?"

READY TO RAISE SOME HELL.

"Great. Let me know when you have it opened."

Brittany turned back to look at the machine. Its hum sounded different, and now she realized it had been oscillating between at least two or three different sounds. That was why she couldn't pin it down.

You see that? The Snake hissed.

What? Brittany asked.

Turn your dang head! Lookit the cave.

She turned back to the monitor displaying the cave. It was badly cracked, but she could still see the walls and stones becoming brighter, as if glowing with some sort of paranormal power. After a moment, the lights themselves floated into the room like ghost orbs on those faked haunting videos she'd seen online.

She didn't know what was going on in there, but those didn't look like orbs or sprites or anything particularly supernatural. They *looked* like the lights from her communications class.

After a moment, a lone figure stepped into the cave, carrying something on his shoulder. Brittany would've recognized his hat and mustache anywhere. He pointed the camera at the charred body on the floor, then toward the stones.

"That's Walden," she said, pointing.

Fixated on the other monitor, Elana merely glanced over.

Another figure entered behind Walden, a taller boy with slightly longer hair, still wearing the coat she'd loaned him at her house. "And Cody!" Two more stepped in behind them. A man about Cody's height, and a young girl.

"It's Mr. Hildebrand and Taylor!" she cried.

"*What?*" Elana pulled herself away from the other monitor and joined her. "Oh! Renny!" She touched his image on the cracked screen briefly, then hurried back to the microphone, this time pressing another switch at its base. "Renny! Can you hear me?"

Several more figures entered the cave. Two tall blond men with large guns followed by Cassandra and the thing with the pumpkin head: *Geth.* None of them seemed to hear Elana on whatever communication device was set up inside the cave.

Elana repeated herself, watched the monitor, then reluctantly let go of the mic. "Ernie must have damaged the connection somehow." She stepped back with a somber shake of her head. "If Jason can't get the Resonator turned off, Geth won't let them come back up alive." Her voice quavered. "It'll turn them into automatons, like it did to Ernie." She turned to Brittany with a sickly look. "Won't it?"

Brittany considered lying. In the end, she nodded.

You need to get yer butt down there, The Snake said.

What? Why me?

I chose you 'cause there's a hole in you, girl. Jes like me. Always has been, an' you know that. You felt it, 'til I showed up in your life an' filled it. An' that's why Geth'll choose you, too.

Brittany studied the monitor again. They were all gathered around the stones now. Walden seemed to be interviewing Geth. Cody held the boom mic over Geth's head.

You want me to just go down there and basically kill myself?

Heck, you been lookin for a chance to redeem yerself since ya kilt that li'l piggy, ain't ya? Well, here it is, giftwrapped all nice fer ya. The shay-men showed me zactly what they done to trap Geth that first time. They cut off its head so it had to go into someone else. Then they sacrificed the fella it went to, an' used that

*bone whistle that sounds jes like that doohickey over there t' send its
spirit back beyon' them Magic Stones.*

The Snake was right. Britanny did want to redeem herself.
But the thought of dying, before she'd truly had a chance to live,
terrified her.

Why should I trust you?

*Because a world with Geth in it ain't a world where I c'n come
out to play any time I want, ya get it? Geth turns everyone into one
of his voodoo zombies and just where does that leave me, honeypie?*

But how? she asked. *I can't just walk in there. They'll see me.*

*Well guess what? Your good ol' pal The Snake knows of another
way in. A secret way through the back. You sneak up behind Geth
and bash that mother's brains in. You smashed a punkin 'fore,
ain't ya? Just take that wrench and make that fat head into a gat-
dang punkin pie. I'll take over from there.*

Brittany watched the screen, considering the inconceivable.

Boop.

Brittany and Elana returned their attention to the main
monitor.

Two words had appeared on the screen:

THEYRE INSIDE

7

JAY NIELSON HAD no idea how he'd survived after the
Halloweenado smashed down Mr. Combs's back door and
kayoed him, but he clearly had a pretty hard noggin to survive
two successive concussions within a few hours of each other.
That had to count for something.

When he came to, he'd found the house completely
trashed. Mr. Combs would've had a fit to see it like that. The
guy was so fastidious about everything aside from his garage,
where absolute chaos reigned. With his head swimmy, his guts
in a knot and just about every bone in his body screaming in
pain, Jay dragged himself from the doorway through the
kitchen to the dining room table. He sat there for a long time,
watching the shadows of the cyclone rattle and crackle past the
windows, like clothes in a tumble dryer. He might have passed

out again. He wasn't sure. Time had passed, but he wasn't sure how much.

Need to get to that machine, he reminded himself. *Need to turn it off before it's too late. If it's not already too late....*

He pushed himself up from the table, stumbled back several steps and caught his footing against the back of the couch. Woozy. Heart pounding. It felt a lot like one of his energy drink hangovers.

I'd kill for a Rockstar right now.

Wish in one hand, shit in the other, kid. His dad's words echoed in his mind. Usually, the phrase would make him solemn, make him hate his life. All Jay could think about now was how much he missed his dad. His mom hadn't taken Jay to visit him in... was it over a year already? But the man they visited was nothing like the father he remembered from before. Erratic, hyper-intelligent, often speaking in nonsense and riddles, quick to anger—but *loving*, he remembered that. The man in the hospital was slow and sluggish, his emotions flat. Something like how Jay felt now after the double concussion.

He'd often wondered if he'd had a father at home if he wouldn't have turned out to be such a social pariah. There were times when he'd sneer at himself for even caring, but deep down he did care what others thought of him. He wanted to be loved and appreciated just like everyone else. His reaction to these conflicting feelings was to lash out at everyone. Push them away before they could get close and inevitably abandon him, just like his father had. It would be tragic if it wasn't so cliché, so normie.

Quit stalling, he told himself. He pushed himself up from the sofa and staggered into the hallway, heading for the garage. The lamp and side table had been knocked over, and the old photos of Mr. Combs and his parents at various stages in their lives—from a sepia-toned pic of him in a snowsuit holding a sled to one from the '60s or '70s dressed in a convocation gown, holding his diploma—all tilted, some with their frames shattered, others lying on the floor, leaning against the wall. Jay wondered where Combs was now. He hoped to find the man holed up inside the garage, but if he was, why hadn't he shut off the Machine by now? The more likely scenario was that he'd been killed trying to turn it off. The thought depressed Jay more than he'd imagined. Mr. Combs was about as close to a friend as he'd ever had, even though the man was more than twice his age, and after all the time they'd spent together he still couldn't remember Jay's name.

Jay slumped against the door to the garage. The hum was so loud he could feel it resonating through his entire body. His first instinct was to head straight in, but that was a noob move. In a videogame they'd be waiting for him. This would be a jump scare moment, and the music would start pounding until he'd killed off whatever was in there. He decided on caution. His hand felt incredibly heavy when he raised it to thump against the door, and the beating on it rattled his head, making him swoon.

"Mr. Combs?"

No answer.

He knocked once more, waited for as long as he could stand with his head throbbing painfully, then reached for the handle. Expecting to find it locked, he was surprised when the handle twisted easily and the door pulled inward.

Staggering out of the way, he drew the door open just enough to peer inside and fell against the wall. The garage was fully lit. He saw no movement. There was a dark red stain on the concrete floor near the X where he'd seen the first Zergling materialize before his astounded eyes. He wished he'd told Mr. Combs what he'd seen then, rather than keep it to himself. If he hadn't been so concerned that Combs might think he was crazy like his dad, he would've told him. It might've prevented all of this from happening.

He stumbled in, holding the doorjamb and then holding the high shelves and finally the worktable as he shambled forward like some kind of zombie. The red stain on the floor was clearly blood. Chunks of pink flesh and white bone lay scattered around it, as well as what looked like matted black fur. Something had killed Hegel. Jay didn't like cats but he felt bad that Mr. Combs's friend had been turned into a splat on the floor.

"Mr. Combs?" he said again, and again heard nothing back.

He stumbled further into the garage. It looked like someone had been trying to smash the Machine. Likely Mr. Combs. The Zerg had probably attacked his cat and Combs had made a break for it. Maybe he'd escaped long before the Halloweenado got here to protect it. Maybe he was still alive, somewhere out there, along with Cody and Cassandra and the others.

It surprised Jay how much he wished he could see them again. Even Walden's face would have been a welcome sight at the moment.

Wish in one hand, kid...

Jay tripped over the foot of the rolling tool rack and his vision grayed. For a moment he was in freefall, then his flailing hands caught something cold and metal, a vibrating thing, and he preventing himself from landing on the hard concrete. When his vision returned, he was leaning against the Machine, right near the keypad and green monochrome screen he'd often seen Mr. Combs typing on.

A single message remained on the screen:

> GOODNIGHT, ERNIE.

"It's a chat!" Jay said excitedly, and immediately regretted raising his voice. He could still hear the cyclone of junk circling the house, even above the oscillating hum. If he could hear *them*, they might be able to hear *him*.

Carefully, trying his best not to misspell anything with his head still throbbing and his body feeling like he'd been thrown into a trash compacter, Jay began to type. He didn't expect anyone to respond. The message was probably from last night, and even if it did get sent tonight, the probability that the person on the other end was already dead was extremely high.

"*Hello,*" came a familiar woman's voice, surprising him. "*This is Elana Stabler at Beta Site. Who is this?*"

His tenth-grade math teacher? Was she the one Mr. Combs had been working with all this time?

Ms. Stabler's words had appeared on the screen beneath the previous message. Responding with the keypad felt like he was trying to move underwater. Finally, he sent the message. She quickly asked him questions about what she called the "Harmonic Wave Generator," which he figured must be what Combs had called a "Dark Energy Convertor" the other day, and Jay replied truthfully. He'd never understood how Mr. Combs had managed to take all of the electronic junk he'd hoarded and turned it into something that not only functioned but actually did what Mr. Combs had meant for it to do. It had always seemed more like magic than science.

It probably is magic, like Cassandra's gramma said. Half science, half supernatural.

Ms. Stabler asked him to remove the six-sided panel at the bottom of the Machine, and he fired back one of his favorite *Starcraft* unit quotes. Still slumped against the Machine, propping himself upright and barely conscious, Jay pushed himself off and stumbled toward the worktable.

Not even halfway there he slipped on a chunk of blood-slicked fur and flesh and went sprawling. If he hadn't instinctually thrown out his hands, he probably would've smashed his jaw on the concrete and knocked himself out a third time. He didn't think he would've come back from that, if he had.

Groggily, just about at the tail end of his energy, Jay pushed himself up to his knees. As he did, he caught sight of something white and gold and just about shouted, *"No way!"*

Mr. Combs may not have been able to remember Jay's name, but he'd remembered Jay's love of Rockstar Energy Drinks, and had left a twelve-pack of them under the worktable.

Jay laughed. He crawled over to the worktable, grabbed two cans out of the case and shoved them into his pockets. He would've grabbed more if he didn't have to also climb back up to his feet and bring a socket wrench or something similar back to the Machine.

He found the tool quickly, and opened the case to see an entire array of the different-sized bits. He grabbed a pair of wire-cutters and three different kinds of screwdrivers, shoving them in his pants along with the tall cans.

Walking back was nearly clumsier than getting there had been. With the added awkwardness of the objects stuffed into his pockets and the socket wrench case in his left hand, it made him walk with more caution. The last thing he wanted to do was fall over and crack open the cans in his pants. Have to deal with sticky underwear on top of everything else.

He made it back with no further issues, placed everything from his pockets on the floor in front of the hexagonal panel, and sat down slowly.

After finding the right bit, removing the panel was short work. The bolts weren't tightened too hard and the Machine itself was new, leaving very little risk of stripped threads. He'd gotten the third bolt off and began working on the fourth when the window above the work table smashed inward with a crash so loud it made his head pound.

Whatever it was landed on the floor with a thud and a jingle of broken glass. It rolled several feet and came to a stop.

"Fuck me," Jay said.

It was the Furby he'd brought Mr. Combs last week. It was skinned and slicked with blood, but definitely the same one.

"*Me hungry,*" the thing said in a weird electronic voice.

Jay startled. It'd only ever spoken gibberish before. It sounded more like the Speak & Spell he'd also found for Combs.

The Evil Furby hopped around like a bird to face him and stared at him with its weird, almost dopey owl eyes.

Jay pushed himself up and typed frantically on the keyboard. He whipped around at another tinkle of glass and saw a green monster mask and a dirty hand cultivator had joined the skinned Furby, standing on either side of it.

"*I'm going to eat your eyes first, Jay Nielson,*" it said in its strange Stephen Hawking voice. "*Then I'll gobble up the tender bits.*"

Jay slid down the Machine and slumped to the floor with his back against it. He had no fight left in him. His CPU was over-taxed and the peripherals were all shot.

Jay looked at the cans of Rockstar.

Time for one last pick-me-up?

As he thought this, the Evil Furby's little ear-wings fluttered with a mechanical whine and all three intruders flew into the air, darting directly at him.

Chapter 25

1

Walden was first to enter the chamber. The cave was strangely warm, and already he was sweating through his layers. They'd passed two dead men in various states of terror and injury, but even that hadn't prepared him for the stench of death, of burnt flesh and blood and shit in here, which struck him like a slap in the face.

He saw the charred body on the floor first. The stink was so putrid he tried to cover his nose with his sleeve, until he realized he wouldn't be able to use the camera with one hand. He removed his arm briefly to thumb the record button and tape the grisly sight, then returned it to plug his nose. He panned up to the overturned director's chair, between the two stone pillars. There was another body lying prone behind them, but from the angle Walden could only see the leg of a woman, her boots, thick wool socks and a smooth, slender calf.

Finally he took in the sight of the so-called Watching Stones Geth had been yapping about all night, and thoughts of who the dead bodies might belong to and their horrid smells quickly evaporated.

He'd expected to be unimpressed. To shoot Geth a pithy quip about how a couple of lame rocks had trapped him for thousands of years. Holding them in his gaze, he couldn't bring anything funny to mind. They were actually impressive, the etchings into their surfaces in various loose designs and patterns pleasing to the eye. They almost seemed to twinkle in places, especially in the indirect illumination from the camera light.

He thought to say *So this is where the magic happens*, but the sentiment suddenly felt disrespectful. Not to Geth. He didn't care at all about offending Geth, not anymore. To the people who'd hewn these Watching Stones from the stalagmites they must've been before. To the people who'd been wise enough and brave enough to trap this demon behind them.

Walden pointed the camera at them, but the image in the viewfinder went bright white, as if he was pointing it directly at the sun. He reared his head away from the sight and turned the camera quickly, hoping he hadn't fried the CCD. He cried out in surprise.

"What's the matter?" Hildebrand asked.

"Fuckin things nearly toasted my camera."

"I'm picking up a weird, kind-of humming noise from them," Cody said, holding the boom mic under his arm with one hand and pressing the headphones against his right ear to hear better. "It almost sounds like... *voices*?"

"The *Tum Gob* sings in the voice of Those Who Came Before," Geth said. "Them, their ancestors and their descendants. Only they can open the passage, and only they can seal it." The demon smiled. "But the ancients had no knowledge of your *science*."

Cody stepped around to the other side of them. "Oh jeez! You guys'll want to see this." He paused before adding, "Or not..."

Walden stepped cautiously around the Stones, giving them a respectful, almost reverential distance. When he saw who the woman on the floor of the cave was, it hit him like a knife in the chest, like the one protruding from hers. "Holy shit!" he gasped. "Holy shit." It seemed to be all he could say. He'd been so eager to meet Darla Knight ever since he'd first heard she was coming to town. He'd even sort of spied on her while she'd been eating one night at the diner with a bunch of the crew, and considered approaching her as they left to talk about his script. But they'd all gone back to the hotel together, and he'd chickened out, losing the opportunity. He'd hoped to meet her tonight at the haunt but things hadn't turned out that way.

He never could've imagined he'd see her like this. A legend, one of Hollywood's great Scream Queens, lying dead in a puddle of her own blood. He'd seen her die so many times it almost didn't feel real, and he had to watch her face through the viewfinder, waiting for her to blink, to make himself believe it.

Saddened and disgusted by her death, Walden returned to the other side of the Stones, where Cassandra and Geth stood with its twin blond *Gethstapo* and limp scarecrow security detail.

"I guess this is what our resident cult was up to," Hildebrand said. "A human sacrifice, to summon Geth from the Void."

"Indeed," Geth said. "Just as Those Who Came Before made their sacrifice to their nature deity, their sun god, to bring warmth to this land and their people, Daryll Knell and his friends made their sacrifice to the god of wealth and fame, this deity you call *Holly Wood*."

It looked like Hildebrand would've done a spit-take if he'd been drinking something. "That's one way to put it," he said.

But Walden was curious about something, still holding Geth in a closeup shot. "So Those Who Came Before... were they like the Winnipesaukee or...?"

"The ancients occupied the land long before tribes," Geth said. "They merely spoke of themselves as The People. We were named The Tree with Many Roots." Frowning, Geth continued, "It was not a name spoken with reverence. The ancients understood that We, Geth the Many, are composed of multitudes. What We said to the Sheriff was not what you call a *joke*. As many as there are of you, there are tenfold of Us. We are Geth the Many. It is useless to stand against Us."

"Resistance is futile," Walden muttered, but no one responded to the joke. *No Trekkies in the house, I guess*, he thought.

"But you don't have bodies, is that right?"

This was Hildebrand. Walden turned the camera toward him.

"We are without form, beings of pure consciousness. That is why We require a *chuann*, what you call a *vessel*, to contain Us."

"Otherwise, you'll—what? Break apart?"

"Our *inhak* were ungoverned until Geth united Us. As your people do now, We lived in chaos. Geth made Us One."

"But then who's Geth?"

Walden was impressed by Hildebrand's hardball questions. He wasn't pulling any punches. Dan Rather would be proud.

"*We* are Geth."

"Right, but before Geth the Many—there had to be Geth the One, didn't there? Separately, you're *inhak* in chaos. Together you're Geth the Many. But who was Geth *before*? Who was the Geth that united all of you?"

Geth scowled. "*We* are Geth. What Geth was before is of no consequence."

"Okay," Hildebrand said, clearly unimpressed by the response. "You think in pictures, is that right? That's why you like television so much?"

No wonder it can't see inside our minds! Walden thought. *That must've been what Hildebrand was getting at before....*

"What you call *images*, yes." It gazed at Hildebrand shrewdly. "We see nothing within your minds. We find that troubling. Do you not *think*, as your people call it?"

Walden shared a look with Cody and Hildebrand.

"We're not the brightest bulbs in the box," he said.

Hildebrand laughed. Cody shrugged.

"Yeah, we're pretty dumb, I guess," he said grudgingly.

Geth studied the three of them with its Xs narrowed for a long moment, then nodded. "Very well," it said. "So long as you are fit to complete your task, it does not matter how... *dim* you may be. There were many people such as yourselves among the ancients. They were still useful to the shaman. But they did not make suitable *chuann* for Geth the Many."

"*Dim*," Hildebrand said. "That's a good joke. It's fascinating to me how you seem to understand nuances of our language like wordplay without a language yourself."

Geth turned to him. "How do you understand this world without the ability to form images in your minds?"

Hildebrand considered it, then shrugged. "Well, I guess because we know what we've seen. I can imagine a mountain, I can describe what it looks like, because I've seen mountains. I don't need to visualize it. I guess it can be limiting, but I suppose it just makes my need to communicate with words stronger. That's why stories are so important to me, especially movies and documentaries. Although I mostly read nonfiction. I'm reading this one now—"

"*We do not care about books,*" Geth said dismissively. "Reveal more to Us more about *movies*. About your god, this Holly Wood."

"I like all kinds of movies," Walden said, eager to play along if it bought them more time. "You could say I'm kind of a film buff. That's why I work down at the theater."

"I like comedies," Cody said. "Especially *Austin Powers*. That's smashing, baby! Yeah!" he added in a passable impression.

"Smashing," Geth said quizzically.

"Yeah, it's like... one of his catchphrases." Cody shrugged. "It's British, I guess."

"I'm a Tim Burton fan," Cassandra said. "*Beetlejuice* and *Edward Scissorhands* have to be two of the best movies ever."

"*Ed Wood* is rad," Walden added.

"The movie or the director?" Hildebrand asked.

"The movie *and* the director. *Plan 9 from Outer Space* is one of the wildest movies ever made. You should see the audience when we show that one. Crazier than any screening of *Rocky Horror*."

"I like Disney movies," Taylor chimed in, standing close behind Hildebrand, her face brightening for the first time since they'd been at her grandmother's house. "Cinderella... and Sleeping Beauty... and the Little Mermaid... oh, and Snow White! I can't forget Snow White, she's the fairest of them all."

Hildebrand listened to her with a patient, fatherly smile. "See, Geth, this is why it's so important we make *your* movie," he said. "Books are great, but *movies* can connect with anyone. Even if you can't read, or you don't speak the same language, you can get a pretty good sense of what's going on. The danger. The emotions."

"Emotions," Geth repeated.

"Yeah, like happy or sad or scared," Cody said.

"Oh, yes. We very much like *scared*. Our *inhak* find that especially thrilling."

Hildebrand chuckled ruefully. "You know, most people don't *like* being scared. Not for-real scared. We like scary movies or books and things like the Halloween Village, but we know that those things aren't really going to hurt us. They're *safe*. It's probably difficult for you to understand, being a god and all. You're probably never scared."

Geth's brow furrowed for a moment. "No. I do not believe We have ever been scared. However, We do not experience emotions as you understand them. There are no *sensations* to what we feel. Perhaps what we feel is not truly *feeling* at all. Perhaps your language does not contain a word to precisely describe Our state of being."

"What about when the shaman tricked you?" Hildebrand asked. "I bet you felt pretty angry then."

"Anger is a fire in Our *aminhas*. Like water boiling, Geth the Many stirs and troubles."

"And when you realized you were getting sucked back into the *Upask*—you didn't feel scared at all then?"

Geth's Xs widened, its face contorting in rage. "*Do not provoke Us, Renny Hildebrand!*"

"Sorry," Hildebrand said, holding up his hands in surrender. He flashed a smile. "Got a little carried away, I guess. It's the investigative journalist in me."

Geth stepped toward him, and the two blond goons pointed their rifles. "You will question Us no further," it said. "We will tell you Our story, as We have promised. From the very beginning, or as far back as We can remember. You will listen and you will say no more until We have finished. Do you comprehend Us?"

Hildebrand nodded. Geth turned to Cody and then Walden, who agreed with a nod. Cassandra and Taylor nodded, too.

Apparently satisfied with their responses, Geth began its tale: "From the very beginning, We were destined to be a god. Those words breathed Us into being...."

2

"I HAVE TO GO."

Elana Stabler turned back from the monitor where Jay Nielson had just revealed he was in trouble. "*Now?*" she asked Brittany.

"It's important. I think I can help but not from up here."

"You're going to the cave? It'll take ages to get all the way to the chamber. You don't even know the way!"

Brittany nodded. "I know the way. And you'll know when to shut this thing off. Just watch the screen."

Elana turned to the cave monitor. "The screen? Why?"

"Just keep watching. You'll know when it's time."

"But..." She looked around, almost frantically. "...what if I can't shut it off? Ernie is dead, Jason is under attack, Renny and those boys are down there with that monster, who knows what it's planning to do with them..."

Elana flinched as the girl put a hand on her shoulder.

"You don't need to be scared," Brittany said. Her blue eyes were swimming. She looked terribly sad. "If anyone can do this, it's you and Jay Nielson."

Elana looked at the communications monitor. It had to have been minutes since Jason—whom Ernie had always called James—had last responded to her. The boy could be dead for all she knew. It was Schrödinger's Cat again. Jay was both alive *and* dead until proven otherwise.

Fat lot of good that does me, Elana thought.

Brittany gave her a lingering look. The hand remained on her shoulder. "Watch the monitor. Wait for my signal."

Elana repeated the words.

The girl's hand fell from her shoulder. "Good luck, Ms. Stabler."

"Luck is a mathematical improbability," she said. When the girl's expression clouded, she added, "But I believe we stand a good chance to beat this thing."

Brittany smiled.

Doing her best to avoid gazing at her dead friend lying behind the girl, Elana smiled back.

3

MATT DUKAS STOOD IN LINE, watching as the Diner Man, the one they'd called "Crampton," touched men, women, teens and babies on their foreheads like he was baptizing them, and one after one the victims of this macabre ritual turned to face the others, facing Matt, with the same dark eyes and the same eerie smile.

"I'm scared," Philbert moaned, too loudly.

"Me too," Matt admitted. Earlier tonight, before all of this, Kyle and Craig would've probably called him a pussy if they'd heard him say that. He didn't care about any of that anymore.

He just wanted to huddle in some corner and cry until his parents came to save him. Except he couldn't do that because he needed to be strong for Philbert.

Only ten people stood ahead of them in line now. The church had filled with the black-eyed people, the true Cult of the Smiley Face, the ones Crampton had turned and Geth had before him, and it was quickly becoming a more hostile place. The Smilers pushed and prodded and vaguely threatened the remaining seventy or eighty survivors. Matt heard snippets of it as they moved through the line.

"Soon you'll be One with Us, whether you like it or not."

"Don't worry about your cat. Your cat doesn't love you. Your cat *never* loved you. You don't need to rely on it being around anymore. Possessions are meaningless. All you need is Geth's Word and Geth's Love."

"We are so much happier living as One."

"We *love* Geth."

"We *worship* Geth and Geth alone."

"Geth the Many is the only god we need."

"The Great Pumpkin will make all of our petty disagreements just *drift awayyyy*," one woman said, ending in sing-song.

Listening to it all, Matt had balled his small hands into sweaty, painful fists. He was sick to death of Geth. He wanted Geth to die in a fire. He wanted Geth to get run over by a car. He wanted to stomp Geth's head and feel its pumpkin guts mushing under his boots.

But that wasn't going to happen.

What *would* happen, and very soon now, was that all of Matt's anger toward Geth, all of his fear, and his concern for Philbert, and the ache he felt in the pit of his stomach when he thought about how far he was from his parents, would simply end. He would be standing—or kneeling—at the altar, and Crampton the Diner Man would tap him on the forehead and he'd no longer be Matthew Andrew Dukas. He would be *One with Geth*. He'd be a black-eyed Smiler, just like the rest of them, threatening whoever was left with mean things about their cats and their children and their houses and all of their stuff.

Three more people to go. The anxiety twisted his guts into knots. His nerves were electric, making his whole body vibrate and his teeth rattle, like he'd been caught in a snowstorm without a coat.

The couple turned, smiling at him with black eyes.

The solitary man left ahead of him stepped up reluctantly. The man in the army jacket and the Orange Vest Lady pushed him to his knees, and the Diner Man reached out and touched his forehead.

Matt tensed. He grabbed Philbert's large, smooth hand. Philbert looked down at him in vague confusion.

The man ahead of them stood and turned. He smiled down at Matt with black eyes.

"You are so lucky, little boy," the Smiler said. "I would've loved to shake hands with God at your age."

Then the man stepped to the side and there was no one between Matt and Crampton. The Diner Man's smile widened. It didn't reach his black eyes. "Doubting Thomas," he said. "We've been looking for you. Thought you'd run off and hid in a corner somewhere, crying for your mommy and daddy. But here you are, and here We are. No more doubting, little Matthew Dukas. It's time to *believe*."

Matt shrank away from him. Army Jacket Man grabbed him by the left wrist. The Orange Vest Lady reached for his right, still clutched in Philbert's big sweaty fist.

"Now, Philbert," the woman said. She had bad teeth and wiry hair. "I know your mama would never want you to step in front of a boy with the opportunity to meet God."

"He's gonna meet God? Oh boy!" Philbert looked concerned. "Wait... I can meet Him, too, right?"

"You're next, big fella. But you gotta wait in line like everyone else. It's Matt's turn now. Ain't it, Matt?"

She winked at him. Her teeth were little brown things that looked like she'd never brushed them in her life. Matt cringed away from her.

Reluctantly, Philbert let go of Matt's hand. Orange Vest Lady snatched out and claimed it.

"No! No!" Matt cried, kicking and struggling, as they carried him painfully by his wrists to the smiling man at the altar.

"Relax, Matthew," Crampton said. "Just a little *tap* on the forehead and all of your fears and doubts will be gone."

But Matt *wanted* his fear. He *wanted* to doubt. He didn't

want to believe in Geth any more than he wanted to believe in the god Kyle and Craig believed in, or the god the men who blew up the Twin Towers believed in. It wasn't fair, and a god who had to force people to believe in them wasn't any kind of god at all, as far as Matt was concerned.

"My mom says you don't hurt kids!" Philbert blurted out behind him.

Matt turned to look as his friend lumbered up to them. The big guy threw a punch over Matt's head, a haymaker, they called it, and his fist caught Crampton in the face before he could react.

"Grab him!" Crampton shouted, holding his jaw. "Get him, you idiots!"

The Army Jacket Man and the Orange Vest Lady let go of Matt to focus their attention on his friend. Philbert threw the man aside easily. The woman grabbed him by the arm with both hands and two more Smilers—the one Crampton had called Gary and the thin, frail woman who'd been using one of the cameras at the studio—came in to fill the void while Matt stood by in a daze, too afraid to intervene. He turned to the people left in line, but they were all watching in stunned silence.

"My mom says I ain't s'posed to hit a lady," Philbert said, trying to pull his arm away from Orange Vest Lady's grip.

"You're mother's a wise woman. You just relax now. We ain't tryin to *hurt* you, Philbert Piper. You still wanna meet God, don't you?"

Philbert gave her a shocked look. "A course I do!"

"Well, then you gotta let us take you up to the man. He ain't gonna hurt you. He's just gonna tap you on the forehead.

"Then I'll meet God?"

Bad Teeth Lady smiled and nodded. "That's right."

Philbert stopped fighting. The three Smilers watched him for a moment, then let him go.

"Step up to him now, Philbert."

"Don't do it, Philbert!" Matt said. Hot tears spilled down his cheeks. "They're lying! They're bad people!"

Philbert looked back at him by the foot of the altar. "Bad people don't smile," he said with a laugh.

"You gotta kneel, Philbert," Orange Vest Lady said.

"Kneel," the camerawoman said softly.

Philbert looked at both of them, slightly confused. "Well, all right, but don't get scared when my knees go pop. It ain't some-body shootin off fireworks!" he said with a chuckle.

"We won't," Orange Vest Lady assured him.

With some effort, Philbert got down on his knees.

"No," was all Matt could say. He saw the O'Donnelly brothers off to their right, standing in front of their parents. All four of them smiled with their dark eyes watching as Philbert, the last of Matt's remaining friends, became one of them.

"Philbert Piper, now you are One with the Many," the Diner Man said. He reached out to Philbert's already smiling face. Of course he was smiling. The poor guy thought he was about to meet God.

Matt couldn't stand to watch this any longer. He turned his head, squeezing his tear-filled eyes shut.

"Good boy, Philbert," the Orange Vest Lady said soothingly. "Your mama would be proud."

"You don't gotta be afraid no more, Matt," Philbert said after a long moment. His voice sounded the same: deep and slightly slurred. But there was a wrongness to it Matt couldn't pinpoint, and he couldn't help but open his eyes to see what had become of his new friend.

Philbert Piper smiled down at him, his always slightly dopey brown eyes now fully black. "It's like a big warm Mom hug all the time," he said.

"It's your turn now, Matthew," the Diner Man said, glaring down at him with his perpetually smiling lips. "No more silly games. Geth is waiting."

4

JAY GRIPPED the can of Rockstar firmly in his right hand, intending to open it and chug it like some kind of videogame power-up to somehow get the advantage on the Furby and its pals that were hurtling toward him. He couldn't wait to get that instant rush as the effervescent, syrupy drink poured down his throat, cold or warm, even in the midst of mortal danger.

Wish in one hand...

"Shit in the other!" he cried, and swung out with the can in his fist.

It struck the skinned Furby dead-on, shooting pain from his knuckles all the way up his arm. The can punctured, spraying a fountain of sugary red fluid into the air, showering the possessed objects. The evil Furby spiraled back and to the left from Jay's direct hit, smashing into the hand cultivator, and the dirty garden tool shot to the right, slamming into the green monster mask in a perfect seven-ten split.

"How's that for a handful of shit, fuckers!" Jay said as all three of the evil fuckers fell to the floor.

He dropped the can and grabbed another, popped the top expertly and chugged until his eyes watered. The rush was instant, not from the sugar but from the fizziness. The sugar would hit him soon, but for right now, the fizz boosted him enough to get the final bolt off the hexagonal panel and return to the keyboard to update Ms. Stabler.

ITS OFF he typed.

He glanced over his shoulder. The things were still lying on the floor where they'd landed. Nothing came through the broken window. The inside of the garage remained silent.

Maybe that guy with the pumpkin head's gone on break. Away from keyboard. Be right back.

Whatever the silence meant, Jay wasn't about to take it for granted.

Boop.

Another message appeared on the screen.

> JUST US NOW. NEED YOU TO LOOK FOR A
> WHITE TOGGLE ON THE PANEL INTERFACE.
> THAT SHOULD RESET THE RESONATOR / WAVE
> GENERATOR LINK.

He almost crouched right back down to flick it when the monitor beeped again.

> DO NOT SWITCH IT YET!
>
> YOUR COMM MONITOR BEEPS, CORRECT?

Jay typed, YEP.

> OKAY. WAIT FOR MY SIGNAL, PLEASE.

OK, he replied, even though it seemed stupid and reckless to wait. Why not flick it right now? End this thing already.

Y'all need some good old-fashioned discipline, he told himself, quoting General Duke, his favorite *Starcraft* hero. *She obviously knows what she's doing, she's been working with Mr. Combs the whole time. Don't mess around.*

Jay hung by the monitor a moment, waiting to see if she'd provide further instructions. When nothing came, he slid back down to the floor and located the white switch among a bunch of diodes, capacitors, resistors and microchips on the circuit board.

His vision swam. The light dimming to the hammering of his heart in his pained temples made him worry. The Rockstar zoomies had hit him, and they didn't seem to be interacting well with his multiple concussions, like a symphony competing with a heavy metal concert.

Just gotta keep conscious long enough for Ms. Stabler's signal. Flick the switch, then you can pass out.

Just gotta...

His heart pounded like the thrum of the Halloweenado outside the garage.

...flick...

His eyelids fluttered.

... the swi—

5

RENNY KEPT Geth talking for as long as he could, quizzing him on the various aspects of being a so-called god, but he'd gotten cocky. He'd overplayed his hand, and eventually Geth had tired of his questions.

Fortunately, the only thing Geth seemed to be interested in more than murdering and torturing people was talking about itself. It went on and on about how it awakened in darkness, before there were people, before there was the Earth, when there were only tumbling rocks in an endless Void and balls of fire like sparks in the blackness. Renny didn't know if this was meant to be metaphor or literal, whether Geth had come to Earth on some rock from Outer Space or from a dimension outside of time and space. What was the *Upask*? How did the *Tum Gob* prevent Geth from crossing into this world? And who created them, since it seemed as though they'd stood here before the time of the "ancients"? If Geth knew the answers to these questions, it didn't bother to explain them in its rambling, self-serving monologue.

Walden shot the whole thing, peeking out over the viewfinder every so often to give Renny a pointed glance or raise his eyebrow in incredulity. Cody, meanwhile, followed Geth with the boom mic. Without questions to ask, Renny didn't have much to do himself other than to add the occasional *mm-hmm*, or *wow*, and nod thoughtfully. Rather than anger Geth, the brief interjections of interest seemed to embolden it—or Them, as it seemed to refer to itself in the plural: *Geth the Many, We, Our,* etc. It still didn't make sense to him, but none of this did, really. It required a human sacrifice to call it to the *Tum Gob —Did it smell the blood, like an animal? Could it sense the murder itself?*—and the sound from Combs's Machine was what had opened the gateway into this world. That was about the limit of Renny's understanding of the mechanics of Geth's summoning, and Geth seemed content to leave it at that. It seemed to be unduly concerned with making Renny and the others aware it had been born into the *Upask* a god and had bided its time to fulfill its destiny.

Now was that time.

All would fall to their knees before Them, or perish.

On and on this spiel went, in endless variations. Geth loved to talk. Loved the sound of its own voice. *And who does that voice belong to?* Renny wondered. Is it Geth's true voice? Or the vocal cords of the body it inhabited? If Geth the Many chose another to be its host, their *chuann*, would it sound the same, like Renny, like Walden or Cody or Taylor?

Again, questions he couldn't answer, since Geth wouldn't let him talk until it finished its endless sermon.

Meanwhile, the Stones sang along with their ghostly hum like a soundtrack to Geth's derangement. The chorus of the ancients' voices, sealed within the carvings on the rock like music stamped on a wax cylinder, ceaselessly vibrating. It was starting to set Renny's teeth on edge, although he had to respect whoever or *what*ever been clever enough or so in tune with the supernatural to have created them. Like all professional victims, Geth blamed Those Who Came Before for letting itself be sucked back into the Void, but it was its own failure. Would a true god be so easily manipulated? Was Geth so delusional it couldn't see that?

More questions, with no answers seemingly forthcoming.

Renny also wondered what Geth would do to them once the film was finished. Once they'd sent it out via satellite to every TV in the five surrounding counties, what then? Would Geth the Many turn them all into mindless, black-eyed zealots? Would it keep Renny and the others as pets, or would it kill all five of them, so that no one person possessed any more knowledge of Geth than it wanted?

Come on, Combs, he thought. *Turn off the goddamn Machine already.*

But maybe there was no one up there. Maybe Combs— who'd clearly been what Geth called *blighted*, prior to Renny knocking him out—maybe Geth had taken him over again, and he'd killed Elana in the woods. He'd left her body to rot among the pines and gone to the church to join the others.

Renny didn't believe it, not entirely. But as long as the Stones were still singing, he couldn't assume they were still up there, planning to turn it off.

All of this, everything they were doing right now, it was futile, just like Walden said.

Eventually, Geth would rule. Because modern humans might have the science, but they'd cast their rites and rituals aside in favor of Hollywood and videogames, internet piracy and iPods, 9/11 conspiracy theories and climate change. The priest was dead. The sheriff was dead. The scientists were all gone.

They had nothing left.

6

THE SNAKE LED Brittany through the dark woods. This time she'd been smart enough to grab one of the flashlights Combs and Elana had brought with them before setting off into the night. The trail was much easier without having to rely on the intermittent moonlight through the clouds and her own internal GPS.

It's close, The Snake whispered suddenly. *Can you hear it?*

"Duh, it's my ears," she said aloud, glad to be alone and allowed the freedom to respond with her voice. Replying in her mind didn't carry the same weight, the same aggravation. There was no emotion or inflection. "And I don't even need to hear it, I can *feel* it."

Must be just about right under us now. The hole's close.

"Good. It's cold and I'm getting sick of all this running around."

Won't have to worry 'bout that fer much longer, The Snake said, and although she couldn't hear his tone, she sensed the sinister nature of his comment. He couldn't have been clearer if he'd said *'Cause you'll be dead soon, anyways.*

Brittany didn't want to die. She hoped it wouldn't come to that. But The Snake would do what he wanted to with or without her—*Story of my life,* she thought miserably—so she decided she ought to make her sacrifice count by embracing it.

In the movies, the people who gave their lives for the greater good often had a terminal illness, or they were badly injured, or they were just ultimate badasses taking one for the team. They'd say things like *I'll only slow you down,* or *Take me instead,* or *Stay gold, Ponyboy,* and the music swelled and the audience left the theater inspired and maybe even a little teary-eyed.

Brittany wasn't any of those. She was the villain—or a side-villain, at least—who did an about-face at the end of the movie, sparing the hero or heroes by taking the bullet herself. It would make for a great redemption arc, but no one would cry for her departure from the movie.

Here we are, The Snake said.

She stopped and swept the beam of the flashlight around the small clearing. After a brief game of *is-it-or-isn't-it* with The Snake, she found the hole nestled within a thick patch of juniper.

"Oh, you gotta be kidding me! It's like three feet deep with thorns!"

You know what they say: the pricklier the bush, the prettier the prize.

"I've never heard that before."

Well, you just did. An' unless you brought a pair o' garden shears, best get those pretty little stems o' yers ready for some pain.

Brittany huffed angrily, then stepped into the junipers. The needles stabbed through the white stockings of her costume regardless of her caution, and she found herself wishing she'd bothered to grab a pair of jeans back when she and Cody were at her house.

Still say you coulda gotten away with killin him easy, The Snake said.

"You should be glad I didn't. He can help us."

Yeah, well, it still woulda been a helluva lotta fun.

A gnarled branch tore through her stockings, leaving a long rip down her calf. Blood bloomed on the stretchy white fabric in various places, but she made it through to the clearing in the middle with one last decisive jump, landing on the fallen leaves with a thud.

The mouth of the cave yawned before her, dark and warm, like a literal mouth. Aside from the hum, it reminded her of the day she'd met The Snake. The last thing she'd ever wanted to do was go into another cave, let alone the *same* cave. Yet here she was, about to climb into the hole. At least this time it was voluntarily. She wouldn't have to worry about falling and breaking any bones.

It's a bit of a jump, but you'll make it, The Snake assured her.

"What do you mean, *a jump?*"

Jest 'bout five, six feet down. Nothin a former gymnast like yerself got to worry about.

"I quit gymnastics for a reason, remember? I broke my ankle."

Quit bein a baby. Or maybe you'd like me to jump fer ya.

Considering she was just as likely to rebreak her ankle whether she jumped herself or The Snake did it for her, Brittany groaned, "*Fine,*" and stepped up to the hole. She shone the light down. Kicked a few pebbles and dirt inside. They hit the bottom with an echo.

"That's a lot more than five or six feet!"

Sure, maybe, but it's a tight fit. You'll be able to grab onto the sides 'fore you hit the bottom.

Brittany shook her head. "If we get out of this alive, I'm gonna get rid of you. I don't care what it takes. Electroshock. Heavy medication. Blasting 'Do You Believe in Life After Love' non-stop."

Sweet Jesus, anything but her! I promise I'll be good from now on, Miss Garner, I ain't foolin!

She didn't need to hear The Snake's derisive laughter to

know he was indeed fooling, despite his intense dislike of Cher and her latest hit. Still, playing it on repeat for an hour or two would teach him a hard lesson. Especially on top of whatever medication she could get.

She sat down at the edge of the hole and swung her legs into it. The warmth from below was surprisingly soothing against the bitter mid-autumn chill.

At least I won't die of hypothermia.

There's that can-do spirit! The Snake goaded her. *Come on, then. Time's a-wastin!*

She tucked the flashlight into a coat pocket and slid off the edge into the hole, spreading out her legs and gripping the side of the cave with the heels of her boots. Up to her hips, she held on tightly to a thick, twisty juniper root with one hand and an outcropping of granite with the other. The root suddenly tore free from the ground, and she lost her grip on the rock and fell until she was up to her neck. It held firm, like a prickly rope, and she reached out with her feet until she got another hold. With her free hand, she reached into her coat pocket and snapped on the flashlight. Its beam was blinding as she pulled it out and aimed it into the cave.

Ain't too far to drop now.

It was likely a good six- or seven-foot drop, but a foot or two beyond her footholds the roof of the cave disappeared into the dark. It was jump now or try to climb back up.

"It is if you want me to walk anywhere after this."

Can't hold on to that root ferever, honeypie. Prob'ly a metaphor in that somewheres.

He was right. She couldn't just hang here all night, not while Elana and Jay and the others were counting on her. She doubted the root would support her weight forever, anyway. She had to drop down into the darkness.

Consider it a leap of faith, The Snake said.

Brittany held her breath. She counted to three.

And let go.

Her elbow bashed against the cave wall, her feet skidded off the edge of the roof and suddenly she was in freefall. There was a brief moment of exhilaration before the panic set in. Fortunately, even that was short-lived as her feet hit the ground. Pain spiked up her calf and she tucked into a roll. She came to a stop sitting upright against the cave wall and gripped her left foot.

She moaned in pain. It didn't feel like a break, not like her right ankle had felt the last time she was down here, but it was bad enough to debilitate her for nearly a minute. She breathed through the pain and eventually was able to let go and try to move it around.

Her cry echoed through the cave.

Keep it down, dammit, The Snake said. *Ya want that sonuvabitch to hear ya?*

"This is your fault."

Blah, blah, blah. We can point fingers all night long, but you got a punkin to fuck up. Stand up and get movin or I'll take all the credit when you save the gatdamn day.

Brittany winced and pushed herself up, using the wall at her back. She put weight on her foot and the agony shot all the way up her leg. "I think it's twisted."

Well, hop on the good foot, honeypie! We ain't got all night!

With a few more agonizing pressure tests, she found she could walk without as much pain on her tiptoes. She hobbled over to the flashlight, which had skittered off on the floor of the cave, pointing its beam toward the dark interior cavern.

The hum was much louder down here. Almost a presence of its own. It came from where the flashlight had been pointing before she'd grabbed it.

Gonna wanna turn that thing off now. Stones ain't too far. Jes follow yer ears.

Grudgingly, Brittany flicked off the light. The darkness was pure and perfect, and if not for the hum and the warmth in the damp air she could have imagined she was in outer space.

She hobbled forward, holding out her arms.

After a few awkward, painful steps, she reached the entrance, feeling cool, wet stone on her fingertips. She felt along the rugged walls, taking one hopped step after another, feeling her way through the dark. The hum grew louder and the air grew warmer. For a while there was only pain, the breath in her lungs, and The Snake egging her on. After a whole lot of suffering, she started to see light ahead. It was dim at first, and she only noticed because the rock around her was slightly more visible, glistening with moisture. Eventually she could see her hands and legs again, and was grateful to be able to see where she was stepping.

In a little while, the cave opened to a wide, well-lit chamber. Standing in the shadows behind the rockface, she heard a voice above the hum within. A man, deep and gravelly. He sounded handsome.

Sure, if you like em tall, dark and homicidal. Hang on a minute, that sounds like me.

I was gonna say, Brittany replied in her mind. The last thing she wanted was to get caught now, after all the pain she'd gone through to get here. *Now what?*

Now, take that wrench an' creep up real slow. Gonna be hard with that busted foot, but if that ugly mother's facin away, the hum'll take care of the sound.

That's it? No inspirational pep talks? No final words?

Well... The Snake paused, considering his response. *How bout despite you bein a royal pain in my proverbial ass, yer head made a pretty decent flophouse these past few years, an' when all's said an' done I'll miss ya. You can sign that on the dotted line.*

Aw, that's sweet, she said sarcastically.

Listen, you know as well as I do, that's as close to emotional as I ever get. Now get yer butt in there, honeypie.

Brittany slipped her hand into her coat pocket and felt the cold steel of the wrench in her grip. Without warning, her mind returned to earlier that night, waiting in the dark with another weapon in her hand for some lone child to draw near. The sensation of the boy's blood on her hands, her cheeks and throat disgusted her. Part of her wished she'd just let Tommy Mingus kill her when Geth had taken over his body. But then, she supposed she wouldn't have had this chance to help everyone now, as slim a shot as it was.

Here goes nothing, she thought, and stepped into the chamber.

7

CASSANDRA HAD BEEN PRETTY MUCH BEEN in a daze since she'd failed to prevent the murders of Reverend Earl and Sheriff Nance, and as they'd traveled from the school studio to the cave in the woods, she'd just been glad for a reprieve from further violence.

Even the addition of the living scarecrow to their band of not-so-merry travelers hadn't seemed to faze her. Under normal circumstances its herky-jerky movements and subtle menace would've put her on edge. But it wasn't any more frightening than Geth, and even though Geth could be somewhat unpredictable, Cassandra was pretty sure it wouldn't kill them until *after* they'd finished making its movie. They were safe for now. All except for Taylor.

Fortunately, Mr. Hildebrand and Cody were protective enough of her little sister that Cassandra merely had to keep an eye on her. It was almost funny to think she'd started out the night supremely annoyed to have to take care of her little sister and poor Tommy Mingus, and now she was just glad to have the shrimp close, despite the danger they faced. She would've been safer with Grammy Flynn, of course, but Cassandra preferred to have her sister close.

It had always been the two of them against the world. Grammy Flynn loved them and cared for them, but she could never really protect them from the outside world, seeing as she rarely left the house herself.

Besides, Grammy Flynn would be fine on her own. At least until everyone in Crooks Corner was no longer fine.

Cassandra didn't have any illusions that Geth would even keep her alive much longer after they'd broadcast the movie. In fact, she didn't expect it would keep her around long enough to see that happen. If so, it would probably be for the best. She didn't particularly want to stand alongside Geth as it turned all of her friends and family into mindless zombies or splats of blood and gore on the walls and floors.

Geth had only been talking for maybe ten minutes but it felt like hours, when movement from the depths of the cave caught her eye. A pale shape, briefly appearing and returning to the darkness within, not from where they'd entered but the other side. For a long moment she thought it had been a trick of the light, then the pale shape emerged from the darkness again slowly, creeping out from the cave.

It's Brittany!

She was still in her scary clown costume from the haunt, but with a coat over top, and holding something in her right hand, some kind of small weapon which she raised slowly as she neared Geth. Cassandra was the only one facing her. The blond twins were focused on Cody and Mr. Hildebrand, with their backs turned. The scarecrow was focused on Cassandra, watching her closely with its hooded face and painted-on eyes. Geth itself paced back and forth in front of the camera, its back also to Brittany.

Walden raised his head from the viewfinder but as far as Cassandra could tell he made no indication he'd seen Brittany enter the chamber. Geth didn't react to Walden's slight movement, still riveted by its own self-absorbed origin story.

Cassandra couldn't wait for Combs and Stabler to shut off the machine or for the Stones to stop singing.

Brittany needed a distraction. The time to act was now.

But what?

The idea came to her suddenly, and again she was glad Geth wasn't able to read her mind or her sister's. What she'd tried back at the school hadn't worked exactly as she'd wanted, but with the new information uncovered by Mr. Hildebrand, she hoped this time it would. She focused on the guns in the hands of the tall blond twins, not trying to prevent them from firing like she had with Sheriff Nance, but to make them fire on their own. She wasn't so cocky as to think bullets would kill Geth, not after the last time. And instead of merely *thinking* about it, she imagined the twins turning the guns on each other and pulling the triggers. An explosion of gunfire brightening the cave, louder than the Stones, and their chests exploding in bursts of blood. She envisioned this, pictures in her head, like Geth and Mr. Hildebrand talked about earlier. She focused on these images until they were as clear as what was happening in front of her, Geth pacing, Brittany closing in, and the boys recording it all for posterity.

Their last stand, caught on video.

The twins wheeled away from the boys suddenly, and for a brief moment Cassandra was sure they'd heard Brittany approaching Geth, until what she'd pictured in her mind happened in reality. The guns erupted with brilliant flashes of white and dual thunderclaps, and both men were struck. Anger flashed in their dark eyes and they fired again. Cassandra hadn't imagined this part. This was *better* than she'd imagined. Geth had said its *inhak* were chaotic, violent beings. Bullet after bullet pounded into their bodies, turning them into shreds, until neither man could hold on any longer, and the guns fell clattering to the cave floor. The men stood wavering like drunks for several seconds, staring at each other, blood pouring from their arms and chests and faces, then they fell alongside their discarded weapons.

"You... little... BRAT!" Geth bellowed, turning its fury on her with its flame blazing within.

Brittany ran the last few steps and swung out with a stifled grunt. The weapon—it looked like a wrench—struck Geth on the back of the head with a hollow sound like a fist through cardboard. The flames burst outward through its eyes and jagged lips and Geth screamed in rage.

Brittany pulled her arm back. Bits of pumpkin guts and flesh flew from her hand. She swung it at Geth's head again.

This time Geth sidestepped swiftly, rounding on Brittany in the same movement and throwing out its arms toward her. Brittany rose several feet off the ground and flew backward until she hit the far wall. Her head bounced off the rock and she slid down to the cave floor on her butt. The wrench pinged and skittered across the cold stone.

Even though she was a good fifteen feet away, Cassandra made to step in to help, but the scarecrow caught her by the arms. She tried to pull free but its grip was surprisingly strong for a bunch of clothes stuffed with straw.

"Let her *go!*" she heard Cody shout. In the next moment something came swinging into her vision and struck the scarecrow's head. The stuffed sack burst open like a pinata, scattering straw and dust, and the sack fell between their feet. The hands of the headless scarecrow continued to fight her, but Cassandra pushed against it with her mind as well as her arms, and the scrawny thing went flying.

She turned to see Cody still holding the mic pole like an extended baseball bat. The mic hung loosely from the end of it, the cradle busted.

"Thanks!" she said, out of breath.

"Forget it!" Cody bent to drop the mic pole and picked up one of the discarded guns. "We gotta help Brit!"

The others were cautiously approaching Geth: Walden

holding his camera like a large blunt weapon, Mr. Hildebrand with a light stand. Only Taylor stayed where she was, her arms hung limp at her sides.

Cassandra went to her, laying a hand on her shoulder. "You okay, shrimp?"

Taylor looked up with big fearful eyes and nodded.

Cassandra kissed her on the top of her head. Her hair smelled like her strawberry smoothie kid's shampoo. "You stay put where I can see you. I'll be right back," she said, then realized it was exactly what people in horror movies said right before they died. Even the character who first pointed out the cliché, Randy Meeks from *Scream*, had died in the second one.

Reluctantly, aware that this might be the last time she hugged her sister, or anyone, Cassandra left Taylor behind to help her new friends slay the monster.

8

WHEN ELANA SAW the two blond men shoot each other on the cave monitor, she knew it must be the signal Brittany had spoken about. She returned to the comm station and pinged Alpha Site, expecting Jay to respond swiftly, and for the Resonator to cease emitting its signal.

Nothing happened. Not even a message back.

"Come on, Jason..." she muttered. She pinged the station again. And again. She waited, watching the Theta Site monitor in dread. Geth towered over Brittany, who'd been thrown to the ground like Renny back at Ernie's house. The scarecrow grabbed Cassandra by the arms. The larger boy in the football jacket—she knew most of them by name but not their numbers, and the picture wasn't clear enough to see his face—swung a large pole at the scarecrow's head, obliterating it.

Elana pinged Alpha Site again... a fourth time... a fifth... losing hope with each failed response.

Is he dead? The last thing he'd said was 'yep.' It was so curt. He could have been under attack.

Down in the cave chamber, Renny picked up a light stand and closed in on Geth with the boys. Elana's panicked heart thrummed in her ears, as loud as the hum from the Resonator.

She pinged Alpha again. No response.

If Jason really was dead, there was no way to save Renny and the kids down there in that cave.

9

TRICKED! Tricked again! Sraki! Wretched humans!

The movie had been a ruse, and Geth had been deceived by it just as They had when the big shaman of the ancients had fooled Them into returning to the Stones, convincing Geth that his people would freeze to death or starve if they did not, and Geth the Many would be left without a *chuann* to inhabit.

If They did not secure a new host for Their *aminhas*, and quick, the *inhak* would soon abandon Their Union, reverting to their chaotic nature. Geth would be left with nothing.

Plenty of dead lay nearby, but a corpse would not suffice. They required a living *chuann* to contain Their Multitude. And with the heads of those alive within Geth's reach still intact, any one of them could easily subsume the *aminhas*. They would have to be swift. Tear off the head with the host's bare hands if necessary and find a suitable replacement.

The girl's face swam before them. *Taylor Flynn.*

Geth attempted to face her, but another gunshot struck Their *chuann* in the back, wheeling it sharply to the right. Something not quite as hard but equally destructive struck the jack-o'-lantern—a pathetic substitute for a head, in retrospect—and tore another large chunk from it, including Their right eye. Though Geth the Many did not require eyes to see, disfiguring Their face harmed Their vanity, and would allow the *inhak* further chance and motive to abandon their siblings.

No time.

The girl on the floor—this Brittany Garner—grinned up at Them with blood staining her teeth, her clown makeup smeared.

"It's over, Geth," she said. Her voice sounded different, unlike it had the previous times They had encountered her. It was, as these modern humans called it, an *accent*. "'Less you jump ship, you're a goner. You can sign *that* on the dotted line."

Geth seethed, leering down at the girl with Their one-eyed smile. Not only was the voice wrong, but something in her mind seemed not quite human, as well—the image of a rattlesnake prepared to strike came to Geth when They probed her mind, coiling and loosening.

Geth tried again to turn toward Taylor, and was again thwarted with a second shot to Their *chuann*, in the right shoulder this time. They could not sustain much more damage. Its tissues were already breaking down.

"Try it again and I'll blow your head off," Cody Brockmeyer said, and though Geth suspected he had aimed for it the first two times, if he did manage to perfect his shot, the next one would obliterate the head of Their *chuann*, and the *inhak* would abandon Them.

This left Geth little choice. They would inhabit Brittany Garner and sever her head the moment They were able, replace it with another.

And if that didn't work, if Brittany Garner would not make a suitable host, there were four other warm bodies left to inhabit.

None would leave this cave alive.

Before these wretched New People could prevent Geth the Many from shifting, They reached out to the Blighted at the church, calling every *inhak* to Their aid. Then They commanded the Multitude to leave the Summerly body and flood Brittany Garner with Their *aminhas*.

10

JAY AWAKENED to the beep of his alarm clock.

Not the alarm, he thought. *My alarm doesn't sound like that. Ugh, my head hurts! And my back. And my legs. Did I fall asleep in my chair again?*

It was loud. Sounded like Mom was vacuuming right outside his bedroom door, and some kind of hum from something even closer made his whole body vibrate.

Jay's eyes sprang open with a single, penetrating thought as the beep sounded again: *The switch!*

The Machine was right there beside him, the switch about three feet from where he lay on the floor. It took everything he had in him to push himself up. He swayed, sitting cross-legged on the floor, and scooched his butt over to what Ms. Stabler had called the "Wave Generator," and Mr. Combs had called the "Dark Energy Convertor."

Another *beep* came from the computer.

Jay swooned and fell against the Machine, the pain juddering up his shoulder into his skull. Gray began to fill his peripheral vision.

Come on, wake up, Jay, he told himself. *WAKE UP!*

He slapped himself in the face. Hard.

Stars flooded his vision but the grayness retreated. He sucked in a deep breath, every part of his body punished, in agony, but especially his head. It thumped in time with the fluctuating hum of the Machine.

He turned, propping himself up by his shoulder.

Another *beep*.

His arm felt like it weighed a hundred pounds, the movement as slow as something from a nightmare. After what felt like minutes—though only a solitary beep sounded—his index finger reached the switch. It took every ounce of strength he had left in him to tug it down.

He collapsed exhausted against the Machine, exhaling sharply... and nothing happened.

The Machine continued to hum. The vacuum cleaner clatter and roar of the Halloweenado remained omnipresent, grating at Jay's every nerve.

Until it all stopped abruptly, leaving only silence.

Beep.

Another message. Jay barely had the strength to turn his head. When he finally managed it, he saw five words printed on the screen in blocky green text:

IT WORKED! THANK YOU, JASON.

Jay laughed, truly happy for the first time since his dad was sent to the institution. Even this small movement hurt him. He tried to turn around to reply, but his legs buckled beneath him and his arms felt like wet noodles against the cold metal. He slumped against the Machine, which began to tremble and sputter like a dying engine.

Jay felt a bit like that himself. A smile touched his lips. He was glad he'd done good, that by flicking the switch here the Machine in the other station had stopped working.

The morning sun has vanquished the horrible night, he thought, a phrase from the end of one of his favorite retro Nintendo games.

Then his eyelids fluttered closed, and he lost consciousness once more, this time for good.

11

Cody had missed his first two attempts to blow Geth's pumpkin head right off its shoulders, but he didn't plan to miss again. The rifle's aim had been off, and even though he was close enough to Geth it should've been an easy target, he had to make sure he wouldn't miss and wing Brittany. She'd been incredibly brave to sneak up on Geth and attack it—braver than any of them had been—and the last thing he wanted to do was reward her with a slug to the chest or head.

"Hey, Pumpkinhead!" Cody said.

Geth turned to him with a powerful roar. The holes in its face shone impossibly bright, but not from the candle inside. It looked like white light was pouring out from it, like neon streams, into Brittany's eyes and ears and mouth. The sustained roar seemed to be emanating from this stream of light.

Cody pulled the trigger again, half out of shock. The bullet went wide, blasting a chunk out of the wall. A rain of rock and rock dust fell around Geth and Brittany. The white light kept moving like headlights on the freeway between them.

"What's it doing to her?" Walden shouted over the competing sounds.

"It's switching bodies!" Cassandra yelled back. "We have to stop it!" She jerked her head forward and stared hard at Geth, obviously using her powers against it. The stream of light wavered. Several tiny bits of light flittered away from it like sparks, but the majority of it kept pouring into Brittany. It was working, but not enough.

Cody raised the rifle to his shoulder and took aim.

"Cram it up your putz, you big ugly jerk!" Taylor shouted behind them.

"Stay back, Tay!" Cassandra called over her shoulder.

The Polaroid flashed as Taylor snapped a photo.

In the same instant, Cody pulled the trigger.

He expected another wide shot, particularly with the distraction of the camera flash. But Geth's head exploded, bursting in cold, wet chunks that splattered Cody and the rest of them within range.

Without a head to contain it, the white light swirled up from the dead man's neck stump in a bright mass that hurled toward Brittany. Within seconds it had entered her body entirely.

They were too late. It had taken her.

Silence, aside from the hum of the Watching Stones.

"Brit?"

"Is she okay?" Mr. Hildebrand asked.

For a long moment she lay there, her eyes, nostrils and open mouth shining with Geth's terrible light. Then the shine dimmed, and she leaped to her feet like one of those French circus clowns.

"Shoot me!" she cried. "C'mon! You gotta shoot me!"

"Shoot you?" Her voice sounded weird. Like the one she'd used when she played the lead in *Cat on a Hot Tin Roof* last year.

"I got it inside me, Cody, but I cain't hold it back for long! Ya gotta shoot me now!"

"Brit—I can't!"

"Do it, Cody!" Walden said.

"Shoot her, Cody!" Cassandra agreed.

Cody's palms sweated, the rifle jittering in his hands. Listening to them was like a nightmare version of the chants from the bleachers when he had the ball and was running for the end line. But the others hadn't made friends with Brittany. They didn't know the warmth she was capable of, and the insight she'd offered into each of them.

He turned back to Brittany. Her eyes had gone entirely black now, just like the eyes of Tommy Mingus and the people in the basement. "Shoot me, you big, dumb ape!" she snapped.

Those aren't her words, he thought. *It's Geth. Or... something else. Something rotten.*

He raised the rifle and nestled it against his shoulder. His lower lip trembled. He didn't want to shoot her. But it was like those people in the basement. She wasn't herself anymore. She had Geth inside her, maybe even *all of Geth*. If he didn't shoot her now, it would kill them all for betraying it.

"Do it, Cody!" Mr. Hildebrand encouraged him.

His finger hesitated on the trigger.

Then Brittany snarled like an animal and lunged at him, her fingers curled into claws. Cody squeezed the trigger. The rifle fired and she pinwheeled in the air, landing with a solid thump back where she'd started, only now Geth's headless body lay beside her amid chunks of pumpkin.

Silence closed in around Cody as he hitched in a breath, devastated by what he'd just been forced to do. He let the rifle fall to the ground.

I killed Brittany. She was my friend and I killed her.

When his mind cleared, he thought the gunfire had deafened him. But his hearing was fine: the cave actually seemed to be filled with true silence. The others looked around as if they'd noticed, too.

Then he realized what it was. The singing from the Watching Stones had stopped. The voices of Those Who Came Before had finally fallen silent.

In the next moment, white light began pouring out of the wound in Brittany's chest, her eyes, her nose, her mouth and even her ears, with a sound something like TV static and a thousand screams, the light shooting toward the Watching Stones.

12

WHEN THE WATCHING Stones stopped singing, Geth the Many rapidly became Geth the Few as the *inhak* abandoned Their new *chuann* like fleas leaping from a dead dog, sucked dozens at a time into the endless abyss beyond the *Tum Gob*.

Timar... They thought. *Hounds of the moon...*

Even this thought was difficult. As Multitudes, Their thoughts were more vibrant, more sophisticated. Dwindling down to One, Geth began to lose Their sight, Their intuition, until at last it was just Geth itself, no longer a god, just a single *inhak* like the others.

Then even Geth itself was whisked away, back into the Void.

13

WALDEN WATCHED in astonishment as a hole opened in the air between the now-silent Watching Stones. A portal to the Void beyond, sucking the light right out of Brittany's body, gobbling up every speck that had once been an entity too big for its britches.

"It's getting sucked back in!" he cried. "It worked!"

"Elana must've shut off the Machine," Hildebrand said, a smile spreading across his face.

Cassandra laughed. "We did it!"

As the last of Geth's *inhak* disappeared into the *Upask*, Taylor snapped another photo. "This one's going on the fridge," she said. She pulled out the photo and shook it. Cassandra threw an arm over her shoulders and squeezed her tight.

"I thought we were fucking goners there, for a while!" Walden marveled. He was so relieved he didn't even realize he hadn't been recording any of it since Brittany attacked Geth. He'd missed the best parts of the movie.

Shit! he thought. Then: *Oh well. We'll just have to fix it in post.*

He heard a sob and turned back to find Cody with his shoulders slumped, looking down at Brittany's crumpled body on the floor of the cave. A tear spilled down the big guy's rosy cheek. He wiped it away absently with the back of a hand.

"Oh, shit, Brittany," Walden said, turning to her. Blood had turned her white clown dress red. Her glassy eyes stared vacantly beyond them, at the space where the hole between the Stones had been, as if she'd been watching Geth's light leave her body.

"She saved us," Cassandra said. "She's a hero."

Cody sniffled. He wiped another tear and started taking off his jacket. Walden figured he was planning to place it over her body.

Then Brittany sucked in a huge breath, her eyes springing wide.

"She's alive!" Cody said, and ran to her.

But Walden wasn't so sure. Geth could still be inside of her, lying in wait for one last jump scare.

He glanced down at his feet for the guns.

14

Brittany shot awake from a terrible nightmare. She'd been walking alone through an endless ocean of darkness. A Void. Pure nothingness. It seemed like ages she'd spent there. Centuries. *Millennia*. She was angry. Angry at those who had sent it here. Over time, the resentment grew and grew like a piece of grit in an oyster. The bitterness, the rage, became a pearl of light so bright it could no longer be ignored by its siblings, walking alone themselves. It drew them together. It made them One. They were Geth the Many, Geth the Multitude, The Tree with Many Roots, and together They were *strong*. They were *powerful*. They were *a god*.

"She saved us." Cassandra's voice came from somewhere beyond the darkness. "She's a hero."

"She's alive!" Cody sounded excited.

Who are they talking about? she wondered.

When the sights around her returned, Brittany blinked several times and looked up into the glistening eyes of Cody, who knelt beside her. He was crying, a hand pressed against her chest. It hurt much more than it should, and she meant to tell him to ease off on the pressure a little. Then she remembered everything The Snake had told her to do. He must've taken over in those last few minutes. She didn't remember anything after Geth had thrown her and she'd conked her head against the wall.

Walking alone, she thought, remembering her dream. She didn't dare hope what she thought was true, not without testing it. *Hello?* she called out in her mind.

"You're alive," Cody said, smiling through his tears.

The Snake didn't reply. No snide remark. No coiling and uncoiling of its long, scaly body, creeping in her head. Nothing.

"He's gone!" Brittany said.

"Geth?" Cody asked.

She coughed, and hot liquid spilled from her lips. *Blood. It's my blood.* "Did we end it? Is Geth gone?"

Cody nodded. He sniffled and wiped his nose on his shirt sleeve. For some reason he'd taken his jacket off.

He was going to lay it over me. I'm dying. The Snake is finally gone and I'm dying.

She blinked languidly, already feeling the pull of whatever it was that came after death. She hoped, wherever it was, it was nothing like the endless abyss that had trapped Geth and the *inhak*. "Can you... will you hear my confession?"

Cody looked shocked, as if she'd just asked him to pull down her pants and screw her brains out in front of everyone. Then he leaned forward. With the hand not pressing the rag of torn shirt between her breasts, he took her right hand. Her blood slicked their fingers. His warmth radiated through her rapidly chilling body, getting colder by the second.

"I'm not a good person, Cody," she told him.

"What?" He frowned and held her hand tighter. "That's not true."

"It is true." She sucked in a ragged breath. Her collapsed lung bubbled blood, making a sucking sound. "I've done things. Awful things. *Unimaginable* things."

"We've all done crummy things, Brit...."

It took a fair amount of strength to even shake her head. "Not like this," she said. The others had gathered around behind Cody now. She wasn't sure she could admit to what she'd done with Cassandra and Taylor watching her. But she *had* to confess. It was why she'd risked her life to save them, after all.

"I... it was me that killed Tommy Mingus," she said. "Mingus the Dingus. I did it."

"*What?*" Cody leaned in closer, as if he hadn't heard her correctly.

"*I killed Tommy*," she said again, loud enough for the others to hear.

Taylor moaned. Cassandra hugged her tighter. Walden and Mr. Hildebrand looked surprised.

"I deserve to die," she said. "I deserve to go to Hell for what I did. I think that's where Geth is. That Void. I think that's Hell. Just nothing but you all alone forever and ever."

Cody shook his head. "Well... maybe you had a good reason."

"I thought I did," she said. "But that doesn't excuse it. I don't think it does."

He seemed to consider it. "Maybe what you did just now cancels it all out. Maybe you can get a do-over."

"No," she said. "No do-overs, Cody. I'm... dying." As if to prove it, she coughed again, losing her breath. Blood spilled down her chin. She didn't have the strength to wipe it away.

"We'll get you an ambulance."

"My left lung is collapsed." She sucked in another ragged breath. "Ordinarily... that'd give me a few days... but in case you haven't noticed... that's... a lot of blood you're holding back."

Cody looked down at the rag. It'd already soaked through, painting his fingers dark red. "I'm sorry," he said.

She smiled. "Don't. You're a good person, Cody. Whatever it is... you're struggling with... I know... you'll do okay."

She felt her smile start to slip away, and the sights around her began to fade. Cody squeezed her hand tighter. "Stay with us, Brit," he said, but already his voice sounded like it was coming to her through several feet of water. The others crowded in around them, looking down at her with what seemed to her to be genuine sorrow.

They forgive me. Despite what I did... they forgive me.

The faces of her friends were the last things she saw as her world was swept away in a vast, warm light.

15

"SHE'S GONE, CODY," Renny said somberly, patting the young man on the back. "You did what you could."

Cody looked up at him with shiny eyes. "D'you think she's right?"

"Right about what?"

"About Hell. Do you think it's just you and your thoughts all alone forever? Like where Geth went?"

Renny considered it a moment, but it was too philosophical and he was too tired, and truthfully, he didn't know what he believed anymore. He'd always been agnostic, more inclined to believe in the inherent goodness of humanity than in any deity. But in a world where things like Geth could exist, it was possible a true god could exist, as well. Or many. "I don't know, Cody," he said. "I do know that if Hell is real, I don't think any rational God could've watched what happened just now and send Brittany to a place like that."

Cody wiped his tears and stood. "Yeah," he said, smiling lightly. "I think so, too."

The five of them were quiet for a long while—pondering life's deep questions, Renny suspected—as they each regarded

Brittany, covered by Cody's letterman jacket, and the remains of Geth's host body, and the silent Watching Stones, which held back Geth and any other entities that might lie within that endless abyss.

"So now what?" Walden asked finally. "Now that it's over, we're all gonna be famous, right?"

"Famous?" Cassandra asked, still holding her sister.

"Well, yeah. We've got the best fucking movie *ever made* sitting on these tapes we shot tonight," he explained, patting the video camera excitedly. "Fucking *Helloween*, you guys! We did it!"

Cody and Cassandra looked at each other, their eyes alighting with strained excitement. Renny wasn't all too eager to burst their bubble, but he also knew they shouldn't get their hopes up. "We can't ever show this footage, Walden," he said calmly. "Not to anyone. We have to erase it all. Every single tape."

"*What?*" Walden just about snapped. "Are you *crazy?*"

"No, Mr. Hildebrand's right," Cassandra said. "Geth wanted us to spread its 'word.' If we show this to people... how do we know they won't try to bring Geth back? Some kind of, like, crazy death cult. A *real* one this time."

"Or some new Machine," Renny added. "Built with government funding."

Walden looked them over like he couldn't believe what he was hearing. "Guys. Be reasonable...." He turned to Cody, desperate for backup.

"They're right, Walden," Cody said. "We have to get rid of it. All the stuff they made at the church, too."

"And this is gonna be a lot harder," Renny said, "but we have to promise each other we'll never talk about this. Not to anyone. Not ever. Not even each other."

Walden stood stroking his mustache in silence for several seconds. "Okay, we'll erase the tapes," he agreed finally. "But how the hell are we gonna make sure nobody talks about it? There's almost seven thousand people up there who saw just about all the stuff we did. They've got friends and relatives who *died*. Businesses destroyed. You expect them to just pretend like all that didn't happen?"

Renny shook his head. He didn't know what he expected, and he doubted they'd be able to make it work. A conspiracy like that... it was too complicated, with too many variables to pull off.

"We have to try," he said, as much to convince himself as the others. "And if people talk anyway, we just have to act like we don't know what they're talking about. Change the subject. Call them crazy, if we have to. Make it just another urban legend. Like bigfoot."

"Or UFOs," Cassandra said.

"Or Mothman," Cody added.

"Exactly. *Geth is not real*. Not anymore. We have to swear on it."

Renny stuck out his hand. One by one, the kids—three of them just about adults now, on the edge of seventeen, like the song—stuck their hands into the middle, one on top of the other, each of them swearing there was no such thing as Geth. Once Taylor and Cody and Cassandra had all put their hands in, they turned to Walden. He looked them over, disbelief still in his eyes, then reluctantly stepped into the circle, resting his hand on theirs.

"I swear," he said.

Renny gave him an appreciative nod. "Good. Because we're going to have to convince everyone up there to swear on it, too. And we'll need all the help we can get."

CHAPTER 26

1

Our Lady of Mercy hadn't been this bustling since the day of the tragedy, and Renny Hildebrand couldn't have been happier.

It was a beautiful day in late-August, two years following what came to be known as the Big Storm of '01. Renny and Elana stood at the altar in front of the new reverend, a man named Hollister, as he spoke about death and parting and the bonds of holy matrimony.

Neither Renny nor Elana believed in all of the religious trappings, but if Renny had learned anything from his encounter with Geth it was that ritual was important sometimes, and they'd both thought it fitting to have their ceremony here, to bring happiness back to a place that had meant only fear and despair for so many.

Reverend Hollister knew nothing about what had happened here. He was From Away, and the people of Crooks Corner knew how to keep secrets. All he knew of that Halloween night almost two years back was that the town had suffered the worst freak storm in over a century. By the time the National Guard had showed up on that first morning in November, there'd been over three-hundred dead, and plenty more people with critical injuries to look after. They'd set up emergency triage while charity groups worked several months to rebuild the town. By the spring of 2002, it almost felt like things had returned to normal.

The National Guard—and following them, the FBI—had found many inconsistencies in the stories from survivors about a freak storm that had swept through town, but without anyone but a handful of alleged "lunatics" to confirm their theories, they'd been forced to give up the investigation into what had truly caused so many deaths within the span of hours, all over town. There were one too many gunshot wounds, maimings, decapitations and the like, which could potentially be linked to some kind of "mass-psychosis event," but water testing and other factors had proven inconclusive, according to newly-appointed Sheriff Sykes's sources. The "freak storm" became the official story, and both the investigative bodies and the townspeople stuck with it.

As for the cave, as soon as the outsiders left for good, a town works crew sealed off the entrances with dynamite and buried the rockslides under several tons of hardpacked earth. With luck, another passage to the *Tum Gob* wouldn't be stumbled upon for generations, if ever. Both machines and the shed above were dismantled.

Elana had only spoken of it once in the time since, late at night, during a storm nearly as big as the one made up to explain the tragedy. She'd told Renny she only wished they'd found a way to destroy Geth, rather than just send it back to the *Upask*.

"If we keep it a secret, even from each other," she'd said, sitting up in bed as the wind howled outside their window, "the next people it encounters, they'll be just as blindsided as we were. *More*, maybe. Next time, we might not be so lucky. People, I mean. Humankind."

Renny had thought about it a while in the dark, rain pattering on rooftop. He knew that she was right, but he also knew they'd been right to keep it secret, to never speak of Geth or the things it had told them again. It was one of those moral quandaries that, if one was lucky, only came up once in a lifetime, if ever.

Finally, Renny had said, "I think it's a chance we'll have to take."

There wasn't a cloud in sight at the church today. Elana's side was filled with more people they knew than Renny's, but because of Ernie Combs's death as well as the passing of their colleagues, the Dukases, they'd filled the empty seats with

Philbert Piper and his mother, as well as the orphaned Matt Dukas, whose aunt and uncle had kindly taken him in. On Renny's side were Walden, Cody, Cassandra and Taylor, as well as the girls' sweet, matronly grandmother, who hadn't "set foot in this church in over a decade," according to her. The rest of the church was packed to the rafters, even more than it had been on the night of the Big Storm, the night they no longer spoke of. And when Reverend Hollister pronounced them husband and wife, and Renny lifted Elana's veil and kissed her publicly—not for the first time, that had happened a long while back, but for the first time in front of just about everyone in town—the entire church erupted in applause.

Renny's heart swelled. They turned and walked back down the aisle, cheered by friends and family.

"So..." Elana said, smiling sidelong at him as they left the church. "How does it feel to finally be one of us?"

Renny smiled back. He was a part of Crooks Corner now, no longer an outsider, woven neatly into the fabric of their common narrative. "Honestly? I wouldn't have it any other way."

2

AFTER THE CEREMONY, Walden held their reception at the Grand Theater. When Mr. Stafford passed, Walden learned the old man had left the theater to him in his will. At first, he'd been annoyed, seeing it as just another anchor holding him to this town. Then he'd remembered Tarantino had done some of his best work at a video store, and Andrew Kevin Walker, who wrote *Se7en* and *The Game*, had worked at a record store. He decided he'd stick around for a while, at least until he got his foot in the door in Hollywood. There was a burgeoning screenwriting community online on a website called Zoetrope, run by Francis Ford Coppola, and he was making a ton of connections there with his latest script, a horror feature about a small community under threat from a cosmic entity.

After last night's screening of *Creature from the Black Lagoon*, they'd removed all of the seating and brought in tables and chairs from the legion hall. Renny had been insistent about holding their event here, and Walden had found a way to make it work cheaply enough for a couple living on teachers' salaries. They'd have to skip a weekend of screenings, but the place looked great, he had to admit.

It was weird owning this place at first, with his former coworkers suddenly his employees, but he liked to think he was a fair and even boss, and he never once told any of them "if they had time to lean, they had time to clean."

Soon, the theater was filled with people. Renny and Elana's colleagues, friends and family, students and former students, laughing and chatting and eating and dancing. It'd taken months for people to return to something close to normal, and even though children had still laughed and played in Wyndham Park, and the crowds at the Legion and Eateria were still boisterous, it had always felt like a part of these people had died along with the others on Halloween two years back, with Jay Nielson, Brittany Garner, Sheriff Nance, Reverend Earl and countless others. The mass funeral had been cathartic, but it hadn't yet purged them of their sadness, their pain, their dread that Geth or something like it might return, and this time they would not be spared.

Today changed that.

Walden could see it in the faces of strangers as he passed on Main Street, as he carried folding chairs and card tables from one place to the other with the kids he worked alongside. Smiles, untainted by the secrets their faces held back. Friendly waves. Honking cheerily at strangers. It was as if Renny and Elana's wedding had brought life back to Crooks Corner. Which Walden supposed was fitting, considering he happened to know Elana was carrying a little Hildebrand, due sometime in the spring.

After performing hosting and MC duties, with the DJ playing all the wedding hits and a film he'd spliced together from reel ends playing on the screen behind the dancing couples and children, Walden slipped into an empty chair beside Cassandra and Cody. They were holding hands and talking with their heads close together. Taylor was on the dance floor making a goof of herself with a couple of her girlfriends and Matt Dukas. She'd grown a full foot since that night in the cave, just about as tall as her sister now, practically dwarfing the poor boy.

"Don't mind me," Walden said.

Cody and Cassandra looked away from each other and smiled.

"Heyyyy, Walden," Cody said, patting him on the shoulder. "How you doin, big guy?"

"I'm good, I'm good. How are you guys doing?"

They both said "Good," grinning slyly at each other.

"Cool party," Cassandra said, bopping her head to the music, some hip-hop song which was the exact opposite of anything Walden would expect her to enjoy. She wore a black dress but she looked a lot less "goth" these days, since she'd gone off to college for special effects makeup. Her naturally dark hair was pinned up, and the pimples on her forehead she'd once used heavy makeup to cover had cleared some time last year. Cody looked sharp in a slightly-too-small suit, but he still had a bit of a baby-face and his cheeks were as rosy as ever. Both of them were just back in town for the weekend. Cody was on scholarship at UNH, playing for the Wildcats with a major in psychology and a minor in criminology. He'd said his time with Brittany on the night of the Big Storm had inspired the choices.

"I had to scrub a smiley face off the back of the theater last night," Walden said.

Cody and Cassandra leaned in, shock on their faces. He expected them to tell him not to talk about it, that they don't remember anything, and if he persisted, that there was no Geth, just like they'd promised each other. Just like the entire town had promised in the few hours before the National Guard showed up.

But *someone* had broken that promise. Possibly more than one someone.

"I saw one on the billboard outside the Thompson's old farm on the way into town," Cody said softly.

"What do you think it means?" Cassandra asked, equally quiet.

"It means people are talking," Walden said. "And we have to stay vigilant."

The others shared an anxious look. "We're barely here anymore," Cody said. "But we'll help if we can," he added, clasping Cassandra's hand and giving her an imploring look.

She nodded. "Yeah. We'll help."

"Has Grammy Flynn said anything?" Walden asked, aware the old woman had powers, just like Cassandra.

Cassandra shook her head. "She hasn't said anything about it since that night. I don't even think she remembers anything, to be honest. I mentioned Humphrey last night and she just looked at me and laughed like I was crazy or something."

Walden frowned at this. Were people *actually* forgetting? Maybe Grammy Flynn was just losing her memory. She was around the same age Mr. Stafford had been, after all. "But your power... Humphrey...?"

Cassandra raised her right hand and twiddled her fingers, the nails painted black. "Still gone," she said. "That's probably a good sign, right?"

Cody let out an anxious breath. "God, I hope so."

The DJ put on a slow song, and the three of them looked off at Renny and Elana on the dance floor. Elana had slipped off her heels. Renny was surprisingly graceful for a big lug. Elana was, too, for a math teacher.

Cody stood abruptly, holding out a hand to Cassandra. "Wanna dance?" he asked.

Cassandra grinned. "With a scrub like you?"

Cody laughed. "Okay, pigeon."

She stuck out her tongue playfully and took his hand. The two of them nodded at Walden—the kind of nod that held secrets—and headed off for the dance floor.

On the big screen above everyone's heads, the single-frame splice from Jay Nielson's flaming *Helloween* title flashed between scenes from other movies. Renny and Walden had scrubbed all the tapes they'd shot the following morning using the bulk eraser at school, but Walden hadn't been able to get rid of Jay's credits. After they'd learned what Jay had done for them, sacrificing himself to shut off the Machines, it wouldn't have been right. Walden had exported them to tape, then transferred them to film, and snuck them into the wedding reel as a tribute.

He sat back, watching the clips from movies he loved flashing before his eyes, and he wondered: Could they ever truly count on Geth remaining in the Void beyond the Stones? Those Who Came Before likely hadn't been so naïve as to believe themselves safe from a return of their deadly nemesis. And storytelling was as important for primitive societies as it was for modern humans, possibly more. Had the ancients passed down legends of Geth and the *Tum Gob* then? Or had they done what the five of them had agreed to in the cave that night—what the whole town had eventually agreed? To never speak of it again?

Walden supposed he'd never know the answers to these questions.

But it wouldn't stop him from wondering.

553

Afterword

The concept for this novel is one of my oldest, one of several reasons I chose to set it in 2001. It was somewhere between then and 2003 when I came up with the idea of setting a novel at a Halloween haunt that "comes alive," while college students are making a documentary about the haunt.

I believe I was shooting a doc about a local "haunted walk" at the time, for the TV broadcasting program I was in. I didn't want to make the book *entirely* autobiographical, so I decided the main characters should be in high school rather than college. Doing so also gave it that "coming-of-age" vibe I love from the Halloween stories I read in my teens and early 20s.

Another factor: the year 2001 always seemed futuristic, at least since the Kubrick film. (Or that old Conan O'Brien sketch, "In the year 2000...") Now that the New Millennium is well over twenty years behind us, it's kind of charming to think how *un*-futuristic it really was. Not many people had cell phones, and certainly not kids. The internet was still in its infancy, and the only social media was ICQ or MSN Messenger. School shooter drills were a rarity, at least on the news. No "Netflix and chill"—most people still weren't even aware of their DVD mailing service—no eBooks, no "next-gen" gaming systems—the first Xbox wasn't due to come out until November. It was also the year of the last rock song ever to hit #1 on the Billboard Hot 100 chart (Nickelback's "How You Remind Me").

Meanwhile, a major political polarization had begun to fester, surrounding the 9/11 attacks. No bigger divide had occurred since the Vietnam War, and I'd argue 9/11 made the divide exponentially wider, particularly due to 24-hour news channels. The industry I chose to work in had (*and still has*) a lot to answer for in my opinion—and this book is, in part, my own reckoning with it. "If [this] then the terrorists win," was a phrase spoken so often in the news in those early days, it eventually came with a winking sense of irony. "If we succumb to our fear then the terrorists win," for example. This constantly widening divide is one of many ways in which they *did* win, others being: the endless War on Terror, the constant tightening of airport regulations, Homeland Security, steadily increasing oil prices, etc., etc.

But enough about all of that boring stuff. Before we get on with those acknowledgments, I have one more thing to say about the story itself. I think it's probably easy to see I was inspired by Stephen King's novel *Desperation* in part, at least in the character of Geth. The religious aspect of the novel came about halfway through, when I decided I needed to add a main antagonist, that the enemy shouldn't be entirely faceless (even *Maximum Overdrive*, another obvious inspiration, has the Happy Toyz "Green Goblin" truck). Unfortunately, by the time I'd figured out what Geth was all about, worked Them into the story, and came up with what I thought was a pretty clever ending, I'd finally gotten around to watching Dean Koontz's *Phantoms* for the first time. It was at this point I hit my first major roadblock. Do I keep writing knowing the similarities were more than just obvious, and I could easily be thought to be ripping it off?

I bought the novel and devoured it immediately. It's a highly entertaining book, my favorite of Koontz's by far. It almost felt Crichton-like, in some regards (which I suppose is fitting, since another inspiration for the novel you've just read was his incredible 1987 novel, *Sphere*). And while there are some major similarities in the motives of my evil entity and Koontz's—the Ancient Enemy in *Phantoms* and Geth in *Helloween* both want to be worshipped as gods—I think—*I hope*—I did enough to tweak that concept that the things that are the same feel more like homage than straight-up copying.

If not... *mea culpa*. Which, of course, is Latin for *my bad*.

First and foremost, I need to thank my dad, John Ralston. I've thanked him many times before but he passed away in June, and my love of Halloween is in great part due to his influence. He used to decorate the house(s) we lived in back then and play the old SFX cassettes, making a real spooky atmosphere for kids. When I got too old to trick-or-treat, I took over most of the decorating—adding all kinds of fun things like spiders and coffin lids on pullies—while my mom and dad handed out treats. All of that was very formative for me. I might not be a horror writer today if not for Halloween at the Ralston house.

One night a few years back, my dad and I got talking about how popular *Woom* had become, and he told me he'd always known it would be a hit. When I asked him why—because I had no idea myself it would ever become as popular as it has—he said it was because it was "so unique." His passing while I was writing this novel made it difficult to go on for some time, but I think getting back to it helped in the healing. I wish he was still around to read it. I wish he was still around. Alas, that's not how life works. And we can only hope there is peace in the end for those we outlive.

Thanks to my wife, Sherri, for your endless support and diligent First Reader duties, making sure I don't get away with silly plot contrivances and continuity errors. This book would be so much the less without your patience and ability to call me out on my bullshit.

Thanks to Mom, for your strength and resilience, for making my Halloween costumes and reading us those "scary" kids' books to us when I was little, yet another reason I write horror today.

Thanks to ARC readers, some of whom caught most if not all of the little mistakes editing missed: RJ Clark (author of the *Staycation* Series, Piper Whelan, Alexus Johnson, Kristi Hyams, Kimberly Kraft, Diane Lorentz Navratil. Special thanks to Andrew Adams—author of *Black Widow Blues*—who caught twenty or more mistakes *after* we thought all the mistakes had been caught. (Any errors which remain are my own fault.)

Danika Meyerson, you are an amazing person and a wonderful friend. Without you, I may not have pushed through writing the first few chapters. Shannon Marie, your courage and kindness is inspiring. I curse your name. Jae Mazer. You are an extraordinary writer and a good friend. Stay awesome. I curse your names (as promised).

Crys Evans, Alexus Johnson, Randy Romero: I curse your names.

Thanks to the developers of the video game *Far Cry Primal*, whose Wenja language inspired that of Those Who Came Before, as I was playing it at the time I introduced Geth to the story.

Thanks to Daemon Manx, whose *Ojanox* Series gave me the initiative I needed to expand this novel from just a bunch of kids fighting inanimate objects to *a whole town* struggling against a seemingly unstoppable evil.

And thanks to fellow author Sean McDonnough (*Not Another '80s Horror Novel*) for the great tagline: *Halloween comes once a year. Helloween lasts forever.*

Lastly, thank *you* for taking this nostalgic trip back to Halloween in the early 2000s with me. Until next time, and as always —keep it creepy.

DR
December, 2024

About the Author

Author of the cult smash-hit *Woom* and *Ghostland* and more than 15 other books that aren't the cult smash-hit *Woom* or *Ghostland*. His debut collection was blurbed positively by the legendary Jack Ketchum. His novel, *Pedo Island Bloodbath*, was nominated for a 2024 Splatterpunk Award for Best Novel.

For 7 *free* dark fiction short stories/novellas including the prequel to *GHOSTLAND*, "The Moving House," signed copies of Woom, bookplates and merch, please visit www.duncanral ston.com.

For more delicious dark fiction, please visit
www.duncanralston.com and
www.shadowworkpublishing.com.

www.ingramcontent.com/pod-product-compliance
Lightning Source LLC
Chambersburg PA
CBHW030657010826
48974CB00007B/349

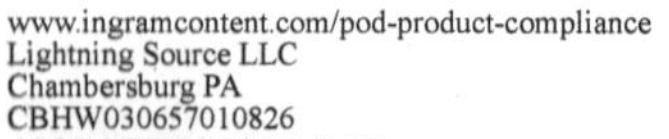